THE INLANDS I:

The Man with the Stone

RYAN CHRISTENSEN

authorHOUSE™

1663 LIBERTY DRIVE, SUITE 200
BLOOMINGTON, INDIANA 47403
(800) 839-8640
WWW.AUTHORHOUSE.COM

First published by AuthorHouse 12/27/05

ISBN: 1-4208-9543-5 (sc)

Library of Congress Control Number: 2005909845

Printed in the United States of America
Bloomington, Indiana

This book is printed on acid-free paper.

http://www.ryan-christensen.com.

Illustrations by Matt Low

For my family. And my beautiful girlfriend Deanna.
Thanks for the support and the patience.

PART I

THE MINES

"There are other worlds than these." –Jake, *The Gunslinger.*
Stephen King

CHAPTER 1

THE SURVEILLANCE ROBOT

1

Edwin Krollup was the richest man in town, perhaps in the country. He lived in a huge mansion on top of a hill over the old coalmines. Why he lived there was suspect, though most people agreed his house was purely for show, taunting the entire city below with his wealth.

His house was like a castle really, the towers of the Krollup dynasty he'd like to say, with large arches and a steepled gothic roof. It had three chimneys jutting from the slanted roof like bricked cigars, as if revealing to the very town below Mr. Krollup's constant appetite for Cubans.

There was a huge courtyard around the mansion, densely vegetated with gardens, trimmed trees and hedges, and a winding path that snaked around statues, each held atop carved pedestals like Doric columns. The yard was bordered by a stone wall, gated at either ends of the house, and monitored by the Krollup security team.

Money wasn't a problem for Edwin Krollup. In fact, he would never run out of money. Edwin Krollup desired power. Perhaps that explained his tall house, and the yard guarded by countless statues. And perhaps that explained why he created both local sports teams, the Blackbird baseball club, and the Pigskin football team, which itself had been involved in two Super Bowls. Unfortunately Mr. Krollup wears no tacky ring made of gold with the Pigskin logo splashed across it in diamonds, because his team managed to lose both championships; in fact, just last year Mr. Krollup himself became so angry in his President's Club box, that he ripped his cigar in half and wished the field would split in two so that the humiliation of his team could be stopped. During the half time show it was a coincidence that the field should cave in on the fifty-yard line, and the float that teen singing sensation Brittany Arrow stood upon broke in two as it collapsed down the chasm—needless to say, the game was delayed while the field was fixed, and poor Brittany was escorted to the infirmary. Edwin Krollup was delighted at the stoppage, but was ashamed to watch the remainder of the game. The Pigskins lost 43-14.

And here *he* sat, Edwin Krollup, looking out the curved windows from his bedroom with one of his coveted cigars held between two hairy fingers. He had the telephone to his ear. His legs were crossed, sticking out of the open flaps of his long robe, a robe he believed made him look like a king. He chugged on the long cigar and blew tendrils of smoke from his nose into the phone. Apparently he didn't like what he was hearing, because a man of Krollup's pedigree rarely stayed quiet. It was his voice that did all the talking, but his mind was on other things at the moment. This conversation was, at least for the time being, an effective method of patience.

"Listen, it isn't about wins; attendance is high because of atmosphere. You have to look at it from a business perspective if you want these negotiations to get anywhere." He wanted to add, *you nitwit*, but thought better of it. Perhaps it was the cigar that was calming him down, or the soothing notion of the sun against the panes of glass in his room, but he knew he wanted to sell his stupid baseball club; he hated losers, and the Blackbirds were a big bunch of them.

He took one last drag of his cigar and put the end out with his fingers, wincing slightly as the ashes fell between his knuckles. "So be it, but you're missing out Mr. Johnson. My club has potential, and if an ingrate like yourself can't reasonably see that, well, then you don't deserve the benefit of owning this team." He slammed the phone and muttered under his breath. He had gotten the last word, and that was good, but he hadn't sold the team, and that was bad. After offering big Barry "Five-Hundred Footer" Stocks a huge contract to come over to the Birds only to get downright rejected in a much ballyhooed press conference, well, his patience with the stupid team had diminished.

Edwin stood up, closed his robe and stuck his feet into golden slippers that had his initials embroidered in silver stitching. The little guy had to be done by now, there was no way around it. Edwin walked to the grand staircase, which curved downwards to the front hall. His robe fell behind him as he descended.

He walked across the marble, onto a lush carpet and past a fireplace that despite the comfortable weather outside, constantly housed a fire. He passed two maids, a cook, and a security guard doing his hourly rounds. He nodded to all of them, but never broke his forward stare. A man of his prestige rarely ever needed to converse with the common folk; he had people on the payroll that did such things for him.

Edwin turned into a corridor that led to two huge maple doors, both with sharp looking stones carved into them in a wooden avalanche that swung inwards when he pushed them. When they shut behind him he turned and locked the doors. While doing so his robe opened and a necklace popped out in front of him—a thick gold chain with a rock that hung near his hairy breastplate. When he clasped the stone for a second he seemed to levitate slightly, as if his feet hung suspended three inches from the plush red carpet. No, that couldn't be possible; it was probably some trick of the eye, but there was a slight fluff as his feet returned to the ground. Edwin tucked the stone back into his robe and closed it.

He was standing in an office—his office actually. There were huge bookcases against the far wall that touched the roof; they must have been filled with hundreds of books, and some shelves contained weird artifacts, like skulls that were chipped and arrows that were broken in half. On his wall he had mounted the head of an elephant, something he had flown in illegally from Africa, and in glass display cases he had mannequins dressed in armor, golden chest plates adorned in jewels, and weaponry that seemed to have dulled over the ages. He paid no attention to any of this. Edwin Krollup walked over to a wall with one simple picture in a simple silver frame; it was a picture of a mineshaft.

Edwin knocked on the wall under the picture. He waited a moment until there was a slight rumble from the other side, a sound like shifting stone. His brow furrowed and he pressed his hand firmly against the wall and pushed. Something funny happened next, for this wall he leaned against was actually a door. Edwin pushed himself right into the next room, and pulled his robe through the opening before the wall closed on it.

And there he stood, his slippers not on the plush red carpet in his office, but on rock that looked rather slick in places and dangerous in others. The wall he had pushed through was wood, and had silver hinges lined along the right hand side, but ten or so inches from the wooden door and plaster beyond, laid a bed of rock that crept into darkness. The smell in here was weird, like dank mud and old earth mixed with steel shavings and smoke.

There were extension cords snaking around the floor, connecting either to the drills atop a small table, or the television monitors secured to the wall across from Edwin. To his right there was a slight flickering light through sparse grout in brick, where he had patched up a wall himself between the fireplace and this little room. He could vaguely hear the logs splitting and wondered why he hadn't had the contractors build a better wall when they were finishing the house.

Because you weren't married then Eddie, and there weren't kids running around the house either...little spies they are.

That much was true. Edwin rather liked hearing the stories people came up with, how and why he built on top of the mines, and what specific purpose they served him. Ever since he purchased the property from the city, there were speculations that assumed he was a druid feeding the earth sacrificial bodies; that he was, he laughed at this one, building an underground shrine to the Auger mining crew which was lost in the mine explosions forty-six years ago.

Lying in the center of the rocky room, lit only by a few light bulbs hanging from the ceiling, was a crude looking machine: a square of metal with different cables leaking out like innards, two long arms with hydraulic pumps as elbows and stubby little steel legs that ended on blocks of aluminum with wheels at their base. Atop the abdomen of cables sat a small square of metal that had been hollowed and filled with what looked like the lens of a camera and the frame of a flashlight. From the lens exploded thick cables that lined into the back of the steel frame. Surrounding the mess of metal there stood three robots, two of which were alloy compositions of Edwin himself, only crudely different in that the robots domes were completely bald, and whose hands lacked the fingers necessary to hold a good cigar. All three were turned off.

Standing in front of Edwin—or *cowering*—was a short man in a white lab coat that unlike his oddly long hair, seemed rather clean. He stood with his shoulders stooped and his neck collapsed, staring up at Edwin with two puppy dog eyes that were attempting to elicit any sympathy they could. His wrinkled face was lined with silver shavings that looked like a tinsel beard; he was bald on top, but had long graying hair at either side of his ears, which hung down to his neck and curled up like greasy check marks. Both his hands were badly scarred, and were clasped together in front of him.

"Are you finished?"

The little man in the lab coat, who had a little cot set up in the corner of the rocky room, swallowed deeply until he could produce a sound in his throat. "It just won't stand up yet. The camera works fine, I tested it already but—"

"Step aside Leonardo." He pushed the little man as he walked to the mess of steel, which had been made from old box springs, sections of an old car frame and old VHS players. Edwin crouched beside the sitting robot and put his hands underneath each arm. He lifted it, only the wheels on the bottom of the robot's feet rolled along the ground and swooped its legs out from under it, sending both the robot and Edwin to the ground.

Edwin turned red, tilted to one side as he rubbed his rear. "Sometimes I don't understand your idiocy. You build robots with simple response devices… you built this robot from *scratch*, yet you don't understand why it doesn't balance?" Edwin got up and pointed at the stubby little legs on the machine. The wheels on the bottom of the robot were lined single file, like roller blades, obviously emphasizing the robot's tendency to lean and topple.

"Common sense Leo, common sense." He tapped his temple. "Every day it gets easier to understand how you got caught by the police."

Leo turned red. Thoughts of the outside world infuriated him because he was forced to leave that world, to leave it and enter this cave…this pathetic little operation. He squeezed his hands together very tightly until his knuckles turned white and the dirt that had been deeply stained was pushed further into his flesh.

Edwin bent down and tore every wheel from the robot with his bare hands. "Fix it, or I *will* tell the proper authorities where you are hiding. Sometimes I wonder why I saved you. Believe me Leo, there are people outside this wall that would be ecstatic to get the arrest." He smiled, and wished he hadn't put out the cigar in his room.

Leo swallowed again and waited to cool down a moment. "Y-you suhsuppose I should rearrange the wheels in a square pattern?"

Edwin crossed his arms and the rock necklace fell from out of his robe. When Leo saw this he shivered; he could feel the room vibrating under his feet, as if the rocks were calling out together in a terrible scream. Edwin was floating again. This time he could tell because he could see the rock wall under his feet…not around them, but actually under them. Edwin pushed the necklace back under his collar and with a light bump his feet fell back to the ground.

Instead of hesitating, Leo did just what he had said; he grabbed his socket and the wheels that had been scattered and started working with the terrible image of Edwin Krollup standing in midair as the rocks beneath praised him.

2

Little pieces of rock embedded in the ground started to crack from the surface and soar to the wall in pee lines. They stuck in places creating a thin dust, and Edwin Krollup sat watching as Leonardo bent over the robot's feet with the socket. One of the robots that had been standing was turned on; its eyes lit a luminescent yellow. It was holding the wheels in its palm.

Edwin's hand was inside a flap of robe, and he licked his lips as the pebbles splattered the wall in front of him; there was little sound, just the small cracks of dirt falling back to the ground. "Are you finished that poor excuse for a machine yet?"

Leo wavered at the sound of the voice behind him. The robot which held the wheels on its palm looked towards the master—as Edwin was deemed to be called during programming—and said in its rickety old robot voice, "in a moment sir."

That monotone voice…that *utterly* ridiculous drone. Edwin turned his attention from the pebbles for the time being and frowned at the robot. The ground underneath the robot split and rose a few inches and the machine teetered, losing the wheels on its tray hand, which fell onto Leo's head causing him to turn as he twisted the socket, missing the bolt and hitting his thumb. He muffled a curse word.

"None of that Leo, you don't want to teach these pitiless creatures that kind of rubbish."

"I'm sorry Mr. Krollup, it's just…"

"It's just nothing, you hurry and finish. You know what I can do to you." With anger in his voice, Edwin reached into his robe and grabbed the necklace, rising from the ground again, causing a big chunk of rock to rip from the wall and land on Leonardo's cot, shredding the mattress. Leo looked at his bed in horror—had he heard glass shatter? He looked under the bed quickly to see if his old aquarium had broken. "Look what you made me do Leo. And you won't be getting a new one till the end of the month. You should think first before you decide to talk back."

"Yes sir," Leo said, as he wiped the blood from his thumb onto his clean lab coat, which wasn't so clean anymore. He tried to duck his head down low enough to look under his box spring, but it was too dark to see anything.

Edwin returned his attention to the pebbles.

Five minutes later, Leo got up from his knees and dusted down his front. He didn't bother saying anything to Krollup—a name that seemed more monster than it did human. He just grabbed the remote he had built from an old VHS and blender and switched on the television monitors. A thick snow covered the screens and the room flickered a pale white. Leo bent down and turned on the camera inside the robot's head. Two monitors waved in and out between that irritating snow and a hazy image of two hobbled over robots, with the rocky wall behind a distant fuzz. There was no color; just navy blue and light blue almost, which most considered black and white.

Leo pulled the analog stick on the remote and both hydraulic pumps on the robot's arms revved to life. There was a grinding sound, and then both arms straightened as the robot lifted from the ground. The image on the monitors began to rise with the robot's head.

Edwin was fascinated by the procedure. The little guy was practically senile, but when it came to machinery, Leo couldn't be beat. When the robot was fully erect, standing balanced on its new wheels, Edwin clapped. He couldn't help it. This was a job well done. The camera even worked, which was the most important part if they were going to send this thing deep into the mines.

"Thank you sir," Leo said, until he caught sight of all the pebbles embedded in the wall beside Edwin. While he completed the robot, Mr. Krollup had legibly written on the wall with small rocks: **HURRY UP THEY KNOW ABOUT THE BOMB**. Leo lost his voice and had to swallow as his face flustered in a heat of anger. *Who knew about the bomb?* he wanted to scream, because he wanted those who knew to find him and take him away—a part of him did at least. It was funny. Leo had believed Krollup when he told him he would protect him from the police. He thought staying behind the chimney and in this mine was just temporary, but oh he was wrong. He had filled a permanent position, and Leo believed the possibility that Edwin Krollup had called for the set up with the police just so it would look like he saved poor Alvin. The idea wasn't so farfetched. Leo had gotten out of this stupid room once, through the door into Krollup's study. He had managed to shove a rock in the jamb when Edwin left one night, waited an hour and ran. He even managed to knock over a security guard, who had actually assumed a bum had broken into the house. But Krollup had stopped him. There was nothing surprising about it either because there was something special about Krollup. Something *terrible*. Edwin stood at the top of the grand stairs in the front room watching Leo run towards the doors with the anticipation of his freedom. He would have made it, maybe, but the statue that usually stood beside the door on the stand—Leo knew this because the stand beside the door was empty at this point—had somehow changed places. It stood in front of the doors with a menacing look on its stone face. As if it had been waiting for him. Edwin had been floating then too, and Leo just stopped dead in his tracks, waiting for the security guard to tackle him from behind. He was going to be escorted off the property but Edwin told the guard he wanted a couple of words with the little dirty man. This in turn led Edwin to thrust the little man back into his hole behind the chimney, and oddly enough, to magically block the wooden door with a sliver of rock from the wall. Leo even saw the rock extend from the wall in a thick arm that covered the door when Edwin left.

It wasn't normal. Not at all.

Oh yes, Leo was a prisoner. He knew this because the security guard that had happened to tackle him that night didn't recognize him. He was a dirty little secret. But that statue in front of the door. And its face, its *sneer*. Edwin was capable of doing things. The writing on the wall was proof. The pebbles Edwin had used were embedded so deep the legibility of the words was actually due to cracks in the rock rather than the actual stones.

So as flustered as the writing made the little man, there was no way he could really act upon such anger. He just practiced a simple breathing test...1-2-3 breathe out. It was as simple as that really. But he would have to get rid of that stupid little message. Maybe he could do so by proving a point to Krollup; the man did seem eager to view the robot's functions.

"You see sir," Leo said as he showed the remote control. "If I push the joystick forward the robot...err, well, I decided to call him Alvin2...he leans forward and the weight pushes the wheels in that general direction. With the gradual decline of the mines I thought this would be best suited, especially since my other idea with your Rolls Royce engine was so laughable."

Edwin smirked. "Indeed. I would never let those grubby little hands near my cars, no matter the business intended."

"Of course, of course." The robot leaned as Leo pushed the stick, and it started to roll forward slightly towards Edwin. Krollup watched this with delight, as he glanced from the monitors to the robot, back and forth, watching his face grow larger on the television screen.

"I have to tell you Leo, I prefer black and white to color. I've always thought black and white gave the picture a vintage crispness, you know what I mean, as if my kingship were timeless really." He posed for himself on the screen, opening his robe slightly and placing his hands on his hips like a superhero. "We've established two points here little man. Firstly, surveillance seems to work fine. And secondly, we know the hunk of junk can move, slower than tar that is, but hastiness in the mines would mean worse picture quality, isn't that right?"

Leo nodded.

"So we're left with its defensive capabilities. What if one of those *things* were to see it—I mean, would it be as easily dismantled as your last attempt?" Edwin walked towards Alvin2 the robot and knocked its steel abdomen; there was a hollow thud and an eerie metallic echo. "Truth be told little man, I'd like to see this thing take a couple of those werewolves down—or whatever *they* are—before getting knocked to pieces."

Leo grinned. Not on the outside where Edwin could see, but on the inside, where he knew this was his chance to rid of that blasted message on the rock. He had installed hydraulic arms on the robot, both to help the hunk of metal get back on its feet without Leo's help, and to pack one mean punch if anything out of the ordinary were to confront it. "You see sir," he said as he shifted the robot towards the message on the wall, "both of Alvin2's arms..."

"Don't call it that, it's so stupid. You don't have much respect for yourself if you can go ahead and give your name to such a piece of garbage. Show some pride little man."

"Yes sir...err both of this *thing's* arms have hydraulics, oiled quite well, and if I push these buttons here, both arms should come up and distend just like that, knocking whatever's in its path out for the count. Would you like to see?" Leo knew visual presentations were necessary with Krollup. Edwin nodded.

When the robot was a couple feet from the wall Leo let go of the joystick. The robot halted. Just looking at that stupid message prompted his anger to return, no matter his stupid breathing exercise. He pressed two buttons firmly and both of the robot's arms reached towards the wall, and just like that two smaller arms jutted out quickly and silently. Both collided roughly with the rock wall, chipping it terribly in one spot, and nearly exploding it where the other metallic fist hit. Needless to say, the message Krollup had spent ten minutes making turned to dust. Only the letters **HURR** and **MB** were still intact, and to Leo's broad knowledge, no such word as **HURRMB** existed...well, at least not in the English language.

"Bravo, bravo. You've both displayed your distaste with my sense of humor and partially destroyed a wall to the mines...if you ever attempt anything like this again I swear I will crush you. What if your stunt had caused a fall out in the mines, a blockage of some sort? We can't take those chances...we're lucky enough to have preserved the opening for this long...ridiculous. You're ridiculous. If my wife heard your display of heroic bravado, I'm telling you now, I'll strap you to this rustic piece of garbage and pray the werewolves chew you to pieces. It'll be better than what I have in store for you." Edwin's eyes were flaming. Leo was scared the man would float again, or worse yet even send the statue in *here*, in this little rocky room, staring at him with those blank eyes.

"I'm sorry sir...it won't happen..."

"Enough said Leo. Send your machine down the mine and turn off those other monitors. The snow on the screen is making me angrier than I have to be."

Leo did as he was told.

3

The mines sloped downwards at a 30-degree angle, and come the bottom of the hill upon which the Krollup mansion was built, the mines steeped to an almost unthinkable 45-degrees, until the slant met a flatbed surface of limestone and basalt. At this last half of the hill, the robot would roll down rather quickly and Leo would have to be very careful about how much weight he distributed to the forward momentum; in fact, he may just have to shift the metallic weight back to act as brakes.

Leo gave the machine—his Alvin2, though he would say nothing about it out loud—a final push into the entrance of the dark chasm and watched the disc of light from the mounted flashlight in the far distance. Then his attention shifted to the surveillance monitors. Everything on screen appeared dark, almost unnatural. The rock formations became pitch-black waves, illuminated slightly by a faint light that just looked a dim blue on screen. They could hear nothing. The monitors had no speakers, nor was the robot equipped with any audio enhancements of any sort. They just watched what appeared to be a boring fuzzy screen with a single circle of light in the center.

Edwin began to fidget. His patience was non-existent really, and despite the fact that he himself had been in the mines before, the thought of seeing things more clearly would have helped his apparent boredom ten-fold. "Why aren't they color little man?"

Leo, who was attentively watching the monitor and holding the remote, looked at Edwin for a moment. He was unsure where this was heading. He had remembered hearing Krollup's obvious glee with black and white imagery—it gave a timeless quality he had blurted—but nothing this man ever said seemed concrete.

"If they were color we wouldn't be in this predicament now would we? I can't see a bloody thing. Just black here, there and a little circle of white, which only makes the black more antagonizing. It's driving me mad just standing here in a trance by these dull boxes that should have been left back in the Fifties." He crossed his arms and looked as if this entire expedition was pointless. *It is*, Leo thought. The first robot they'd sent down was destroyed, entering wherever it was Krollup had discovered, wherever it was he was hiding from everybody else. They had sent many robots down. In fact, there had been six humanoid robots that lived with Leo, until Krollup had sent one to mount the surveillance cameras at the end of the mines, and after the first robot had never returned, he sent two more down after it. Neither came back, and this had driven Leo mad. These were his creations—his products.

Krollup sent them down just as an act of meanness, to prove there was no hope of escaping for this little man who had once built a bomb.

You are different now, are you not?

Leo watched the screen and nodded, he was different now, because he realized just what the consequences were, just what happened if you got caught, or, bribed to believe you were being saved from being caught.

"I'm sorry sir, you just said you believed surveillance monitors should be in black and white."

"No, that sounds like something a color blind bat might say. Am I color blind Leo?"

"No sir...but I just have to watch a moment, I have to make sure the robot gets down...I don't want to lead the robot into a wall or anything."

"That's right, you don't, because if you knock that hunk of junk into the backfill there's no telling what might happen to the mine. Though your fate is quite obvious."

In ways Leo wished he still had the bomb. Even if he went in the explosion too. He swallowed his fury back down in one big gulp. He remembered Krollup's anger when he sent the first surveillance robot down the mines, how he floated for a moment and how the rock split underneath Leo's feet...those terrible wolves that could stride on their hindquarters had gotten it. Hadn't only gotten it, but had ripped it into so many pieces that it looked as it did lying on Leo's cot before he got started on the blasted thing in the first place. Before the camera was disconnected, something had turned the lens towards the carnage and both Leo and Edwin watched those werewolves pounce on the machine and rip the cables in their snouts, snarling if they were shocked by wires. Leo saw something in Krollup's eyes then, something he never wanted to see again. His iris's looked as if they were made of flames, his pupils a vacuous hole from which the fire seemed to spew. No, he hoped that the robot's arms were quick enough to protect itself from those things.

"Why don't those things come up through the mines?" Leo said, without looking away from the monitor.

Edwin smiled. "The same reason why you haven't gathered the courage to escape through the mines yourself. Either they know about the 'black damp' or their curiosity of the mines unnerves them. You're afraid of them. I saw it in your eyes the first time you saw them on screen. Trust me, seeing them miniaturized is nothing compared to seeing them up close and personal. They tower over you, and you can actually smell the drool clinging to their fangs, as if their mouths are ovens and they're preheating for the main course."

"What is the 'black damp' sir?"

Edwin smiled. "Something the miners refer to in the hole as, well...a lack of oxygen, or too much carbon dioxide and nitrogen, I suppose; it's probably not so bad in these mines because there's openings on either side." Edwin looked at Leo. "That might not discourage them though. They probably breathe blood. If your stupid robots had installed the cameras in the mines the way I had intended, we could watch and learn. It would be nice to send these three," he pointed to the other three robots, "down with cameras and have them mount them to the exit of the caves. We are a security force for everybody outside this house, you know that right. To keep those things deep down *there* keeps us safe. In a way my secret should be safely kept because my secret involves a reasonable threat to our security, to our freedom. I've seen them Leo. I told you about that, when I was a kid I saw them, when I was dared to go into the mines. When I made my money I decided to become a taskforce against them too, not to let anyone have to confront them as I had, because I was lucky. I was lucky."

Leo pulled the joystick back as the robot hit the 45-degree slope. It helped a little, though he could tell the robot was still sliding down at a quickening speed. How fast he couldn't determine, but the black rock walls flew by in a dizzying fuzz.

"You should be proud Leo, you should be greatly proud in fact. You're my deputy you know that. Only you and I know of them, and only you and I can keep them secret."

Only you, though, right, because I'm a secret too, a dirty little secret, Leo thought. And the idea that they were protecting the world from werewolves was definitely the last thing on Krollup's mind. To say such things made him believe that it would drive Leo to work harder, because he was working towards a cause. Something else was down there though, something Krollup wanted badly, or he wouldn't have been troubling himself to search so thoroughly. *I bet it has something to do with his necklace, and the ugly rock hanging from it.*

"I think my going down there as a kid was fate really, what do you think?"

"I agree sir." Yeah right.

"I think I was meant to make money and to use it to keep the world safe from monsters. You're serving your purpose well Leo, people will remember that."

No, people will remember that I was a prisoner, a prisoner that had once built a bomb and was setup to get caught. People will remember their beliefs that I was a terrorist, a traitor, but this hero you speak of is just a lie. If such were true, then you wouldn't worry about destroying the mines; in fact, you would have done it already.

And then Leo saw the opening of the mines on the screen—a distant shape of bright light.

Edwin hushed Leo as if the short little man had been doing all of the talking.

Leo stopped the robot altogether about ten feet from the exit. He didn't want to make the same mistake he did last time, smashing the machine out into the open as fast as possible, bringing attention to itself and bringing the wolves up the bluff as a result. No, this time he would breathe. He would stare at the monitor for a moment and wait, perhaps for Krollup's insistence to move on. He could sense what was out there already. He could almost smell the wolves, and he didn't really want to lose his precious Alvin2 so quickly; he didn't want to roll it outside the exit only to have it mauled. Watching Alvin2 go down in shambles would almost be like looking back over his own life, looking at what he had become.

"What's the hold up, take it out already?" Edwin almost screamed.

Leo jumped at the sound of Krollup's voice. He jerked the joystick forward and they watched the exit move closer to them on the screen. They could see clouds. They didn't sway, nor did they move with the wind, they just hung still, over a part of the world that seemed darkest. Leo stopped the robot at the exit, turning off the flashlight as he did so. It was already light down there. Leo always wondered if the other end of the mines was just an opening outside the city, in the wild lands, and those lycanthropes were nothing but ordinary wolves, only the camera played tricks with their eyes.

"Take it out."

"What about those things?" Leo asked.

"What about them? If they come, punch them. That's what you built the stupid arms for isn't it?"

Leo shuddered, only he didn't make a sound that Edwin could hear. He was afraid to see the reaction if he had. Instead he looked at the monitors, at the black and white rocks that had crumbled on top of each other, creating this whorling haze that seemed to hang in the air. Seeing these rocks, these crumbled stones the sizes of buildings, lying in heaps proved his theory wrong. These mines couldn't lead to the wild lands outside the city, because the wild lands had gas stations littering the highway. And plus, wolves didn't come out of tents, nor did they have the capability to create such things, with pointed roofs and large flaps for doors. Leo was afraid of the possibility—the slight possibility—that there was another world deep inside our own, like yoke inside an egg, a world the Auger Mining Corporation accidentally opened while digging for coal. He shuddered again, watching the screen waver in front of his dizzying eyes; it was all real. He hadn't fallen asleep, he knew that much, because he could pinch his underarm and close his eyes, opening them to look at that screen and those ruined rocks, and the terrible lands beyond. He didn't want to send Alvin2 out into that wilderness; the sun blazed over the desolate grounds, and the flats were like parched lips. He wanted to bring the robot back up the mines, but realized, almost instantly—something he hadn't realized before—that he would never see Alvin2 again. Since the robot moved using momentum—it contained no transitory engine—there was no possible way the robot could get back up the mines. It was doomed before it had even descended, and Leo suddenly felt like he had killed his creation. He wanted to cry, but knew Krollup would have swatted him upside the head, maybe taken the remote control himself and hurried the robot into the werewolf settlement just to watch them devour it.

He inched it forward, watching the rocks pass by. Boy, it looked as if an entire mountain had fallen, had decided its time was up and collapsed upon itself. The lands beyond seemed flat. The robot came up to a cliff, a rocky plateau that overlooked the wastelands beneath. Leo shivered. He saw *them*, those things. They were just blurry forms on screen but he could sense them, he could sense what they'd do if they saw his robot. He watched them run around. Two of them were chasing a weird looking animal, running on all fours as the poor animal scurried back and forth trying to dodge them. Leo watched as one of the werewolves pounced fifteen feet in the air landing directly on the animal's back. Leo turned away; he didn't want to watch.

"Did you see that, the beast tore the head off that thing with one swipe of its arm!" Krollup was ecstatic. He probably saw a bit of himself in the werewolf. He slapped Leo on the back, nudging the control slightly. The robot urged forward an inch, close enough to waver at the edge of the cliff.

"Oh jeese," Leo muttered and he pulled the joystick back…but Alvin2 wouldn't budge. Krollup had caused the wheels to jam on a rock. He pulled back again, only to watch the robot's head waver on screen and the black and white go fuzzy as the camera was knocked from side to side.

"What are you doing? Quit playing around Leo, get the robot around them, get it around the bluff and down onto the path…get it over there, yes there, you see, that mountain pass, get it down there. I want to see those Towers." Krollup tapped the screen, pointing towards some terrible looking rock formations. They were huge daggers of stone that sliced deep into the sky. Leo couldn't bear to look at them; they were like teeth.

"The wolves though sir, they'll get him, they'll get my robot."

"He's got a weapon now, doesn't he? Why must you worry about everything? Get it down there, get it past the wolves, get it nearer the Towers."

Leo nudged the joystick back again. "I think it's stuck, it won't move." He moved the stick around in a circle, but the robot didn't budge.

"Gimme that," Krollup yelled, and he grabbed the control and roughly drove it forward and backward until Leo thought for sure the robot would dash forward in a mad spill down the side of the bluff, down *there*, where *those* werewolves lingered and tore the heads off animals.

It didn't.

Instead both men—who stood dumbfounded behind a fireplace in a room that led to mines—saw a sword in front of the lens. The one who carried it was far too fast to see, but they both swore the person wore a rag of some sort across his or her face.

"What was that?" Edwin said. Leo grabbed the remote from Krollup's fidgety hands and brought both of the robot's arms up. He slightly turned the abdomen of Alvin2, as much as it would allow that is, until the lens was pointing south—or at least south of the mine's exit (*or to the things there it would be an entrance*).

All they could see on the screen was the far off lands that were but a haze. The top of his baldhead shone the light from above him.

And then a head rose onto the screen from the ground. It stood and looked into the lens, the one eye that had not been concealed by the rag determining what to do. It was a man, Leo could make out that much. He had the eye of a man, curious, aged and sunken by war perhaps, and short-cropped hair stuck up rather messily where the rag was tied.

"Hit him, whatever he is." Krollup grunted. He had grabbed that ugly rock around his neck again.

Leo smashed the buttons down and both hydraulic arms pumped out. The man jumped, and three blades on either arm stuck out like feathers below the elbow. He fanned his arms and the blades sliced through the hydraulic cables as easily as a knife cuts through hot pie. Both arms fell dead at the robot's side, and the masked man crawled up the front of Alvin2 and stared deeply into the lens, as if he could sense something behind it.

The man's brow furrowed; he flipped off the robot and landed on the edge of the bluff. He brought his sword from behind him and held it in front of his concealed face. It was slightly curved, though it widened at the tip; there was smudged black on the blade and Leo didn't have to know the color of the stain to know what it was. Blood. Dried blood.

The man looked over the bluff and then he quickly jumped to the side.

Edwin cursed out loud. He grabbed the crude rock in his hand and looked as if he was thinking very hard.

Should I do it? he thought. *Should I wish for the stone on the bluff to crack and fall to the grounds below?* He massaged the rock along his palm. The stone underneath him moved slightly and he looked into the mines. There was something too risky about the thought, as if doing so, as if moving stone down there from up here could somehow tear apart the connection. *He looks familiar, doesn't he Eddie, like the man that handed you the necklace almost, the man that told you about the Towers when you were a kid?*

He watched the screen.

Suddenly werewolves jumped from behind the cliff, three of them, their snarling snouts dripping coats of saliva that took the tainted tinge of gravy on screen. They ran forward and knocked the robot down on its back. The lens snapped to the side and rolled. Leo exhaled deeply, sadly.

They watched the masked man chop the arm off one of the werewolves. He jumped and stuck the blade of his sword into the back of the monster. The werewolf fell on its face; it moved around for a moment and then lay still. The man was gone after that. Neither Leo nor Edwin saw where he went. The werewolves turned towards the robot; they yawned and exposed mouths of razor teeth.

"Plant the camera; we might as well have extended surveillance."

"I can't," Leo grumbled, "that thing severed the hydraulics."

Krollup let go of the rock around his neck. It wasn't worth it to destroy the mines. The mission was over. The robot was a sham.

The lens went black before they could see the werewolves any closer.

"Turn those monitors off. Due to this…this embarrassment, you get nothing but bread and water for the next week." Edwin turned and left the room through the hidden door. The rock arm extended from the rock face a second later and blocked the exit.

The funny thing was, Leo had eaten nothing but bread and water—when he wasn't catching stray mice—for three months. This wasn't a punishment; what Edwin had done to his mattress was far worse. He pushed the rock aside and overturned the ratty old bed. Under the disgusting box spring sat an old aquarium he had begged Krollup for; he said he wanted it to build a robot.

The pump was still in tact, and Leo felt relieved; in fact, he felt an entire load roll off his shoulders.

4

Edwin relied on the stone around his neck too much; he knew that. He shouldn't have even attempted to bring that bluff down, but he had this sudden urge to watch the incredible horror grow on the faces of all those terrible *things*. Watch them drown in a sea of rocks.

He was upset, but he wasn't cursing out loud anymore. When he opened his office door, his wife was standing in the light with her arms crossed. "What was all that noise?" Yes, some of the noises leaked out, but Edwin had a long list of excuses. He looked at his beautiful wife, who was eight years his junior—Edwin Krollup was 40 years old, and she was 32.

"I was talking to those investors about the Blackbirds…you remember, the out-of-towners who were interested in purchasing the team?"

Maggie Krollup, short for Margery, which itself was a rather tedious abbreviation of Margeret—a name Edwin loathed—uncrossed her arms and looked at her husband of two years rather curiously.

"It certainly didn't sound like your voice coming through the walls, that's for sure."

What right did she have spying on him anyway? She was like her two stupid sons, the spies. Edwin grabbed the stone again, but then relaxed; he was paranoid. His psychologist told him so, that was all. "That's because they declined any purchases…the nimrods, and I got so angry I started pushing things from the shelf. That was it, you heard the books falling and my feet stomping the floor…my hands bashing the desk." He clapped, startling her.

She relaxed. He studied her for a moment. When he first met her he was unaware of her extra baggage—those kids—but they seemed to help his image. He was a family man now, and the media planted him with the ideal adulation he had been lacking when he was still single. Being rich was all image, yet there were those desperate to tarnish his appeal, those who dug so deep in background investigations to question his rather poor upbringing. Information he would have rather ignored. "Mr. Krollup, you are a very successful man, yet you grew up in, some would say, a dysfunctional setting, with a father who drank too much. Drank himself to the grave actually. For starters, are you afraid in any way of fate, that you may follow in your father's footsteps and drive into the side of a mountain, burying yourself under loose rock?" Edwin had listened to that mug little reporter, pushing the microphone in his face, and Edwin wanted to hit him—

"Are you okay Edwin?" she asked. She had beautiful red hair.

"Yeah, I'm just nervous about my flight."

"Your flight?"

"I told you. I'm going to Italy to talk to the Ministry of Art about buying some Michelangelo for my collection. I shouldn't be long."

"Fine. Jimmy and Cole are having some friends over for pizza tonight. I guess we shouldn't be expecting you." She cocked her eyebrow.

"Keep them away from my office."

"They know."

"Just keep them away."

"It's locked for crying out loud. *I* haven't even been in there."

Edwin wanted a cigar. "You have no need to go in."

He turned and walked away when she said, "why do you keep secrets, secrets from your wife?"

Sometimes he just felt like yelling, "YOU'RE A MEDIA DIVERSION, TO KEEP THEM OFF MY BACK, SO WHY CAN'T YOU DO THE SAME?!" But she wasn't; it was just anger. Instead he slightly turned and muttered, "it doesn't concern you."

Maggie didn't like his tone. "I'm picking the boys up from school," she muttered and walked away herself.

5

Edwin didn't need to worry about tight security at the airport; he was a powerful man. He walked through the concourse with a team of budding professionals, all vowing their chance to wow Krollup in some way or other; he walked to his very own gate, which had a ramp secured to his very own jet.

He boarded his Concorde, which was aptly called KrollupAir—a name printed in gold letters by the tail—and lit a fat cigar. He could smoke if he wanted; it was *his* plane, the pilots worked for him, and his leather seat had already weathered grooves beneath his rear.

Edwin kicked his feet up on the Chestnut table, and twiddled his finger through the dark smoke exhaled from his mouth. The plane took off and Edwin smiled.

The plane was stripped of its back seats, and in their stead was an abundance of cargo space.

More than enough, Edwin thought. *More than enough.*

CHAPTER 2

JIMMY AND COLE

1

Neither Jimmy nor Cole knew about the mines behind their fireplace—well, that is, they didn't know about the "operational mines," some might say. Of course they knew the mines existed, though the legend was a little before their time. So the story of the mines was really a "heard it through the grapevine" type of gossip that school chums heard passed down by their own fathers, who frequently made childhood dares to see who had the guts to duck under the wood barricades and actually go into the mines. Many of these men held a grudge against Edwin Krollup, though they stifled their lips about it; most were actually employed under the Krollup name, whether they were in the coal mines, the preparation plants, the Oil Refineries, or the rigs. Some, regrettably enough, blabbed their tongues to their kids, who unfortunately went to the same private school as Krollup's stepsons. These were the men that as kids had dared Edwin to go into the mines, using their brutish qualities as incentives for this young boy to prove his manhood…well, his boyhood at least. They'd tell their kids how Edwin was once a skinny little wuss who couldn't hold eye contact; the very fact that their fathers had made Edwin Krollup do anything was incredible enough, some of Jimmy and Cole's school chums thought. This was exciting news indeed.

"He's not our real father, tell them Jimmy, he's not OUR REAL FATHER," Cole would scream as he crunched his package of chocolate peanuts.

"Can it fatso," the kids would taunt.

"All of you shut up," Jimmy would say, standing next to his brother. "It's true, our father was a soldier, fought in the Gulf War, now beat that."

"But he couldn't *beat* the habit," some voice would call out from the vicious mob. And they would all pretend to smoke and then cough. They were mean, but Cole and Jimmy learned to accept that. Sure their father may have fought in the war, but the kids were right, he did smoke and cough and that got the best of him. Smoking was what had really caused the divorce anyway, what had really brought them to this stupid school, into that stupid Krollup mansion.

At this point Jimmy usually dove into the crowd with clenched fists, driving them wherever he could, but suspension taught him that fighting wasn't worth it.

But that was a year ago. Things had changed.

2

Jimmy and Cole were twins, but they weren't identical. No, Jimmy was thin and Cole was fat. Neither looked alike; in fact, you wouldn't be able to tell they were brothers. It was their mutual support. When their mother divorced their father, Cole cried on Jimmy's shoulder; the same stayed true when their father found out about the cancer. They bounded off each other. It was funny how the two were so different: Jimmy was strong and charismatic, and Cole was smart (he pulled off straight A's last report card). They balanced each other off, as if completing the perfect brother between the two—a boy willing to fight for what he believes, while understanding the merits of that belief.

But things had changed.

3

Their school was just outside the city. It was behind a large brick fence with a sign stating Trespassers would be prosecuted, with the school symbol beneath in a deep red—Ivy Raurus Middle School. There was a nice playground in the southeast park, a ground that had slides and a monkey bar that went twenty feet from one stand to the next (it was in this playground that Jimmy kissed his first girl), and there was a tether ball court with basketball hoops at either end. The southeast park was widely referred to as the recess fields. Most of the older kids, usually the grade sixers, came to this park either to wreak havoc on the younger kids, to start a pick up soccer game in the field, or to hide underneath the slide and smoke. Neither Jimmy nor Cole was ever caught underneath the slides. As they watched their father grow sicker, listening to his coughs grow coarser, they swore off the chance of that habit many times.

"Why would dad smoke? He shot people and came back from the Middle East without a bruise, and yet a little cigarette killed him. Doesn't make sense." Jimmy would kick gravel as he walked by the slide and Cole would look at his brother.

"Mom says life is all about wars. I think that's why she won't let us keep his last name...she's afraid we'll lose that war too."

"What war, Cole?"

"Dad may have been in combat and survived, but he lost another war. Mom says that's the moral war—the reason why people go to church, I guess. She said he chose to smoke because he lost the moral war and made the wrong choice. Makes sense."

"I guess."

Cole would take a bite out of a chocolate bar, or shove a handful of M&M's into his mouth and suck the color off the candy coating before biting into them. "You see those two girls under the slide. They're smoking because they think it's cool, but do you know why they're hiding while they do it?"

"Because they're afraid Mr. Higgins will catch them?"

"Well yes and no. A part of it is that, but it's mostly because they're ashamed they lost out on the moral war. Mom was right; they may feel cool, a little, but how cool do you feel about yourself if you have to hide?"

And then some kid, usually another grade sixer would jump out and yell, "hey Cone, Ice Cream Cone, I can see you getting fatter, when you die, they cut you up, and only find cake batter." Then they'd all laugh and that was that. The big kids used the park to make fun of the fat kids. Even though Ivy Raurus cost an arm and a leg to get into, the overall scheme of things stayed the same. Despite harsher discipline, kids were still cruel, were still tempted by vice, and still made up stupid little rhymes in an unsettling melody about cake batter.

4

As soon as the last bell rang on Friday afternoon, Jimmy ran to the coatroom and waited for his friends. He grabbed his book bag, shoved his *History of Japan* text in as far as he could and undid the top button on his collar. Boy he hated these uniforms, with the black slacks and the red vest with that stupid oval school symbol. He almost wanted to rip the thing off and shove it deep down in his bag, but knew that if anyone saw this, he would be in deep trouble. School loyalty was important here at Gravy Pukus Middle School, as most kids called it under their breaths.

All in all though, Jimmy was happy. It was the weekend now; he didn't have to worry about reading Chapter 4 in his Japan textbook, about collectivism, and he didn't have to sit in class tomorrow and count the chin hairs on Mrs. Dierdre's unusually round face. Now he got to sleep in and play video games. That was a weekend, *his* weekend, not perusing over school notes like Cole. He was afraid to say so, but Cole was beginning to look like a bigger dork every day: the way he held his book bag over both shoulders, and the custom made black slacks that couldn't originally fit over his butt. Jimmy realized two things. After awhile you didn't always need a shoulder to cry on and an answer to everything. Yes, their father had died, and yes, they had to move on with life, but that wasn't always bad. Sure they didn't get along with old Edwin Krollup, but there were the upsides; they were rich now, for one thing. Last Christmas at the Krollup mansion Jimmy got twenty-six presents; he was sure of it because he had counted them. That sure beat the measly three he got after his dad—*real* dad—died, leaving his mom with debt after debt, and the realization that nobody had any sympathy when money was owed.

Jimmy was actually happy for his mom, because *she* seemed happier; after his dad died she seemed worn. The checks weren't coming in anymore and she had to work two jobs, while also volunteering as a judge at the Territorial Beauty Pageants—a competition she had won for four years straight before he and Cole were born, ruling her ineligible due to certain rules about mothers being contestants.

Being rich was great; he even saw himself in magazines. Jimmy was in *People* magazine once, but only a side of his face, which was mostly covered by a long toque; the picture was of Edwin Krollup skiing with *his* family, the caption had read. Cole didn't like the attention; he missed his *real* dad, which was normal, but he cried himself to sleep, which was a little strange. Jimmy bet kids at school would quit picking on him if he just stopped shoving food in his face and crying every time the other kids said something about him. Jimmy had almost been expelled for punching a kid after he recited a rude little nursery rhyme, and Jimmy began to wonder why he had to be punished for looking after his brother, when his brother was fully capable of doing it for himself. Thoughts like this made him angry, so as he waited he almost wished that his friends would get here before Cole so they could just hop onto the bus without him, maybe go to the mall, and then go back to the Krollup mansion. Cole could just get a ride home with mom.

He got fidgety. The bell had rung like five minutes ago, and he knew Cole was apt to believing he was part of the group. Jimmy felt terrible about ditching out on his brother, but image started making sense in Grade six, it really did. He started caring about how girls saw him; he started putting gel in his hair, even though it felt terrible in between his fingers; and even though he was ashamed to say so, he even liked smoking. He knew his dad would roll over in his grave if he saw him, but there was something electric about holding that cigarette in his hand, as if he became older and more sophisticated all at once. Edwin Krollup smoked huge cigars every day and he was rich; it couldn't be all that bad.

"Jimmy, mom's here," Cole said from behind Jimmy, and all of a sudden he felt faint. Cole had beaten his friends again, and now he had to watch their faces when they realized Cole would be following them around again. He turned around and Cole smiled, wearing his knapsack on both shoulders like all the geeks, that stupid top button on his collar done up so tight the fat on his neck seemed to bulge over like a beer belly.

"Oh, well, I'm waiting for Ricky and James. I think we're gonna go to the mall, so why don't you just go home with mom. We'll see you at supper. They're coming over to eat pizza."

"Does Mr. Krollup know?"

"I dunno."

"Well, why don't we all go to the mall then? I could get mom to drive us, and then pick us up an hour later. We could pick the pizza up on the way home."

Just the thought of walking around the biggest mall in the city, looking for girls and video games with his fat, dorky brother made him feel faint again. His friends were going to kill him. He shook his head. "No, I just *thought* we were going to the mall, but I think Ricky and James just wanna come over and play Nintendo."

"Cool, I'll go tell mom you'll be right out."

As Cole ran to the front doors, a couple of students snickered, watching his belly bounce in front of him like a pumpkin in a vest.

"I just saw your brother," Ricky Paulson said from beside Jimmy, a short kid with bushy black hair (which was also gelled), his shirt unbuttoned to his chest. "Don't tell me he thinks he's invited."

James shuddered.

"He'll tell my mom, and I just don't have the heart to say no. He's been through enough. I heard a couple of people gave him a monster wedgie today, so bad his underwear ripped."

James smiled. It was a couple of his friends that had done it.

"Don't give me the 'you don't have the heart' garbage Jimmy. It was you who told everybody that he still puts sugar on his thumb before bed, and sucks it till he falls asleep." James laughed.

"That was a mistake. I was mad at him. He made a fool of me."

"Like he does everyday."

"Yeah," James attested.

"Well, are we still catching the bus to the mall?"

Jimmy looked down. "No, we're not going to the mall. Cole would have to come with us if we did."

"But Christy Jenson's going to be on the bus Jimmy. Christy Jenson. She has eyes for you." Ricky nudged Jimmy and Jimmy blushed.

"Yeah, well, my mom's waiting in the car. For now we're going to my house for video games and pizza."

Both Ricky and James looked scared. Jimmy knew why too; they were afraid of Mr. Krollup. They'd met him before, and he had been uncertain with them the same way he was uncertain with Cole and Jimmy. He keeps limits on the house too. The main floor was off limits. Especially any room near his office. He was just that way; there were many expensive things lying around, and Jimmy knew one thing for sure: he didn't want to be the one to accidentally knock one of those expensive things over.

"I don't think Mr. Krollup will be there tonight," Jimmy lied. Of course he didn't know this was the truth, because he hadn't yet known Krollup was in Italy.

"Then there won't be those stupid rules in your house?" James asked.

"Not if he's gone," Jimmy said, unsure where this was going.

"And the security guards?"

"They don't bother me," Jimmy said.

"Then we're going on a hunt," Ricky said. James nodded his head in agreement. "I think we should look for the mines. I know Mr. Krollup has them hidden somewhere. You said so yourself you hear strange noises when everything else seems quiet. I think that's because of the hauntings. Krollup may be rich, but sorry to say Jimmy ole pal, he doesn't have much for brains if he builds a house like that on top of an old mine." James laughed. "That would be great if we saw the ghost of Kenneth Auger in your walls or something, holding a pick as he shrieked at us to take the house off the mines so he can keep digging." He made a scary whistle as he held his arms out like a zombie.

"Shut up you guys. We can't do that. Cole will be with us and he'll tell. He's heard the stupid stories, and sometimes he has nightmares. I don't think I could bear sleeping another night when he wakes me up to ask if I'll come get some water with him."

"He's done that?" Ricky asked. He went into hysterics. "Does he wet the bed too?"

Jimmy gave Ricky a Charlie Horse and they went out to the SUV, which had been patiently waiting outside the front doors, Cole sitting in the front seat bragging to his mother about how he was going to hang out with the cool guys for a night of pizza.

5

The boys had wanted Pepperoni pizza (Cole wanted a large concoction of meat on his pizza, which he was granted because he had requested his own medium order), and Maggie Krollup, who despite being a mother, and therefore ineligible for the Territorial Beauty Pageants, ordered a Vegetarian pizza with half the cheese; a woman had to watch her weight. They ate in the dining room, and the pizza was served on silver platters, brought in by two handmaidens.

When the group heard Mr. Krollup was out on business, they were ecstatic. Jimmy even belched at the dinner table, something so forbidden by Krollup that if *he* had been at the table, Jimmy would have been thrown out of the dining room with little hope of leaving his room for anything that night. Maggie wasn't pleased with the poor manners, but she did hear the handmaidens snicker behind the kitchen door; there was something funny about gas, she thought. Especially when the gas in question erupted from the backsides of beauty queens in the dressing room before a major pageant; it just seemed to take away their glory.

After dinner the boys went up to their room with the strict warning from Maggie that the main floor was still off limits, even if Mr. Krollup was away. And then she blurted the infamous wisdom of every parent in the known world: "Rules are rules."

This was followed by a long shudder. Cole brought the remainder of his Grand Slam Meat Jammed medium pizza to his bedroom, wrapped in tin foil to enjoy later. Didn't matter if it was cold, he had said, pizza was still pizza. Ricky and James had rolled their eyes after that one. In fact, whenever Cole said a word at dinner they rolled their eyes; it had become reflex with the two. Cole had given them a nervous tic.

The boy's room was the seventh on the right once you got all the way up the grand staircase. It wasn't odd to see Cole huffing and puffing before bed if he had scaled that entire distance. In this case nothing was different, he had been clutching the tin foil to his chest, wheezing out of his tightly squeezed lips, and sweating at his hairline, which was cut quite short and showed a fair amount of scalp. Once he pummeled through the doorway, he collapsed on the sofa in front of the big screen television, and threw his feet on the table, next to the Nintendo Gamecube. Then he opened the tin foil and took a huge bite out of a slice of pizza. James and Ricky rolled their eyes.

Jimmy was in the closet pulling out a rack of video games, when Ricky interrupted him. "No Jimmy, you remember, right?"

"Remember what, guys?" Cole asked through a mouthful of sausage and bacon.

"Nothing Cone."

"Come on guys, don't call him that," Jimmy said. It was getting dark outside."I was watching that useless guard you got roaming around. He's too busy staring at your mom to care about us any."

"Shut up Ricky," Jimmy said, and gave the short smart aleck another Charlie Horse.

"What are you guys talking about?" Cole asked.

Ricky looked at James, and James stared back; they both smiled, as if the two were thinking the exact same thing. "You know about the mines, right Cone…err, Cole?"

Cole set the pizza down on the table and set his elbows on his knees. "I've heard stories about them, so what?"

"Well, your house is right on top of them."

"Yeah, they were boarded up, closed off, you know, sealed. Mr. Krollup had the money, and he wanted to build here, so he did. They wouldn't have let him if the site was too dangerous."

"Listen Cole. You're smart. How much do you think Krollup is worth?"

"A lot."

"And don't you think there are architects and engineers who could get used to seeing that kind of money, even if it is for ignoring certain bylaws and zoning restrictions, or whatever? Those mines are dangerous, even haunted, and we came here to search for them, to help the ghosts." Ricky made a scary face, opening his eyes as wide as possible.

"There's no such thing as ghosts."

"Oh, then ask your brother Cole. He's heard them at night."

Cole shot Jimmy a worried glance, hoping the other two hadn't caught it. Of course they had though. "Stop it you guys." Jimmy stopped sifting through the games and turned completely around to face Ricky.

"If you want to hang with us Cole, you have to join our expedition. We're going downstairs…"

"But my mom…*and* Mr. Krollup said downstairs is off limits."

"Listen, building this house on a mine broke some rules, so to find the mine we're going to break some rules too."

"Jimmy, come on, you remember what mom said, about moral wars. This is stupid, let's just play video games. I bet they flattened the mines into a foundation pad anyway. You can't build a house on mines." Cole pleaded with his brother, both with words and with his eyes. And then he saw something in Jimmy's eyes, something he didn't like. For some reason Jimmy reminded him of their father; there was just something about it that gave him the creeps. It was as if Jimmy had already chosen the wrong moral road, as if Cole's pleading was all in vain. *That look says he's probably gonna start smoking*, a voice somewhere deep inside his head said. Cole tried to block it out, but for some reason he believed it.

"Come with us Cole. It'll be good for you," Jimmy responded dryly. "Let's prove them wrong then."

"What about mom?"

"We'll have to find out where she is. Trust me, this is gonna be fun."

6

Jimmy stood as far over the railing as he could at the top of the grand stairs. He could see the front door, and sitting next to it on the left was a white statue—a man with his arms at his hips, looking to the side with a blank stare—and even farther in that direction was a mirror, a rather large one in a golden frame. From this Jimmy could see down the corridor; he couldn't see his mother, nor could he see the guard, but he could hear some pots and pans. There was a slight chance his mother was helping the handmaidens in the kitchen, though that was unlikely, since Mr. Krollup preferred the professionals stuck to the jobs around here. She could have been writing in one of the libraries—or dens, if you'd rather—a hobby she had picked up when she realized the housework was officially out of her hands (though tending to a house of fifty rooms was a tad bit for just two hands). Or she could be watching television in the theater; it was almost eight, and that meant that she was either ready to watch an old "Friends" rerun or a reality TV program involving homes and renovations. Jimmy was unsure; he couldn't make out much with just the mirror and the sounds.

He could go down and check himself, but something about this idea (which was actually Cole's) took away the adrenaline, the thrill of it all. He waved Ricky, James and Cole over to the staircase. "I can't see her anywhere."

"You guys are amateurs," Ricky said, and he went back to the room. A second later a huge crash camefrom the room, and both Cole and Jimmy rushed in to see what had happened. Ricky had ripped a drawer from a desk and had thrown it against the floor. Paper was strewn everywhere. Unfortunately for Cole, it was his homework drawer, and he looked at the mess sadly. "Wait a minute," he finally said.

And just as he finished the sentence, Maggie Krollup barged up to the middle landing on the grand staircase and yelled up to the boys, "what is all that racket guys? If you can't play nicely then I'll have to take Ricky and James home. Try to be quieter. If you guys wanna make noise, make it on the Nintendo. If you need me for anything, I'll be in the library reading a book. Okay." She walked back downstairs and Jimmy and James gave Ricky a high five.

"That was great man."

"I know parents," he replied.

7

They all stood at the edge of the grand hall, which led towards the library, the kitchen, the Great room and Krollup's office, which was deemed off limits. Of course, the office was the first place Ricky thought they should look. "If he doesn't want the mines found, then don't you think he'd lock away the room where they'd most likely be. The office it is," he had said as they walked down the stairs. First they had waited for the elderly night guard to walk by the marble entry, check himself in the mirror, and then proceed down the hall. He didn't notice them.

They ran down the rest of the stairs, and used the mirror to check if they could still see the reflection of his back walking towards the end of the hall. He was there, and then he turned, opened a door and disappeared.

And this was where they stood now: the front entry of the house, which led to the grand stairs, the theater (which was off to the left and through the huge maple doors) and the laundry room.

Cole gave the statue to the left a resentful look. He didn't care for the statues around the house. In fact, they gave him the creeps.

Ricky had taken charge of the expedition. As soon as they saw the guard turn into the next room, he waved them forward into the Great room, which like most mansions, was fitted with a grand fireplace; the room flickered with the glow of the fire. There were statues standing upon pedestals, looking every which way with their blank stares. Cole had remembered hearing Mr. Krollup say something about how stupid the Romans were, and how they tried to copy the Greeks by giving their statues blank eyes on purpose, ignorant of the fact that the Greeks had originally used polychrome paint to fill in the vacant corneas; time had caused the paint to peel and ultimately fall away, but that didn't mean it wasn't there.

The stack, which led from the fireplace through the steepled roof up top, was thick, thicker than any Ricky or James had ever seen; it had to have been twenty feet wide, and for some reason the stack piled against the wall fifteen feet behind it. It must have been deep, Ricky thought, because there was some*thing* else behind it. He waved them towards the fireplace.

They stopped. Jimmy heard a noise, he was sure of it. He didn't know where the noise came from, but for some reason it sounded like a drill...the deep whir of a drill. It was probably just the vents or something...*something,* maybe cold air clashing with hot air, but not a drill. Ricky got to the chimney first and peered in. "Hey Cole," he said, pointing into the fire, "why don't you go in and check. I hear third-degree burns are good for weight loss." He chuckled.

"Shut up," Cole said, wanting badly to reach into his pocket to grab his chocolates, but knowing they'd all snicker if he did.

"What do you think?" James asked looking in.

"There's a wall, a brick wall. If there is something behind there, nobody really wants to get in." Ricky must have had bad eyes, because Cole noticed one thing. The bricks weren't grouted in some spots, and something showed through the cracks—a dim light, but a light nonetheless.

You don't suppose that has something to do with the closet in our room? Cole didn't know. Heck, his eyes may have been playing tricks on him. Ricky was probably right anyway.

"Where's his office?"

"That's not a good idea, Ricky, what if somebody finds out? If he knows we went anywhere near his office he'd have us. If he found out any of our friends were involved, he'd find out who and then fire your dads. That's the way he is." Jimmy looked at Cole, who was playing with his pocket.

"Oh come on, my dad hates his job. What's it gonna hurt, Jimmy boy? I don't see any surveillance cams, do you?" Ricky was sweating; it was hot standing by the fireplace, so they left, one by one, towards the office with the big doors, the ones with the rocks carved in them. "Hey Cole, did you know these mines are actually called the Mines of the Dead?"

Cole nodded. He did, or he had heard it sometime or other.

"Personally, I feel we're doing ole Kenneth Auger a favor, trying to find them so we can release his ghost. Jimmy's just not getting any sleep anymore, what with the sounds coming from the walls at night. Ain't that right Jimmy?"

"Shut up, you'll scare him," Jimmy said.

Cole looked at his brother; he didn't completely hear him, but he was sure he knew what he said.

"Anyway, my dad said Auger Corp was the big mining company, till these mines swallowed them up, never to be seen again. You think your dad…"

"Stepdad, no more than that," Cole added.

"Sorry, your stepdad, you think he covered up the mines to keep it that way? To trap ole Auger down there so he could trash his preparation plants and put up new ones in the Krollup name?"

"That's just stupid," Cole said.

Jimmy said nothing because he knew what Ricky was doing; he was trying to get rid of Cole, and while a part of him knew that was wrong, another knew that in any moment those grubby little fingers of his would reach into his pocket and palm a handful of candy. Jimmy hated seeing his brother do that to himself. Hated it.

"He's upset, ole Auger, I can tell you that much." Ricky walked up to the door and tried to turn the knob; it was a huge brass knob shaped like a rock. The door towered over the boys. It was locked. They could smell cigar smoke. "Cops say they couldn't find him because he blended with the rock. After a while they say miners can do that, they can blend in with their environments, like those lizard things, only Auger didn't just blend in, he became this rock monster, a rock zombie. They say he started killing the dogs they sent down, so they stopped the search and boarded the entrance shut, so, you know, Auger the Rock couldn't get free. He knocks all the time. Jimmy hears it, don't you?"

Jimmy nodded. Cole stuck his hand in his pocket.

"Until one day when the barricades come loose, and Auger jumps out on a rampage. Who do you think he'll kill first, the rich man or the fat boy?"

Cole pulled the chocolates out of his pocket; he couldn't stand it anymore. When he felt like this, he needed to eat. It didn't stop at school. Why couldn't it just stop at school? He cracked the box open and poured the candies into his hand. He shoved all of them into his mouth, until his cheeks puffed out. His lips were smeared.

Jimmy looked at his brother, his younger brother of three minutes, and he rolled his eyes. He rolled them back until he could almost see his optic nerves. "Why do you have to do that Cole? Why do you have to constantly shove your face with that crap? I mean, look at you. You're a pig…a…a…never ending pit."

"Keep your voice down," Ricky said. "I got a dad that needs a job here."

Cole dropped the box. He opened his smeared mouth and a couple of half-chewed balls fell from his tongue, dangling from his lip before they hit the floor. *Not only at home, but also from your own brother.* He felt like crying. In fact, he started to, but he ran before they could notice. At first he wanted to run to his mom, but thought better of it; he didn't want her to see him like this, the way kids at school did. He ran upstairs to his room, instead.

Both James and Ricky laughed. "See, we told you, you *do* have the power to set him straight."

"Shut up Ricky."

8

He didn't slam the door; he just jumped headfirst into bed and sobbed into his pillow. *Why did Jimmy say that? Has he felt like this the entire time?*

Does he look at me like the other kids at school? Unfortunately he didn't have the answers. He pulled his head away from the pillow and noticed the shape of his lips on the slip, formed by chocolate. So that was what he looked like at school—a canvas of food. He touched his stomach and cried again. He wasn't always fat. He and Jimmy used to play baseball with their *real* dad, and he could always run and catch just as well as Jimmy could. But not anymore. He couldn't walk to his next class without breaking a sweat. It was his curse really, ever since they stopped playing ball when his dad got sick. That was it. He wasn't going to blame it on his real dad entirely, but...*but, what Cole? You're depressed, that's it. You eat because you're unhappy, and I guess in a way, you're unhappy because you eat.*

But you don't look bad, a voice said in his head. *You don't look bad, and what do you care what other people think anyway? Look at Ricky, he's skinnier than a starving dog, and his hair is so messy that the cool gel he uses just makes it look greasy too. Is that how you wanna look: hungry with bad hair?*

"I just don't want them to laugh anymore," Cole whispered. "I want Jimmy to look at me the way he used to. We're different, can't he understand that?"

He can't because you're stronger than he is. You may not think so, but you are. What would you say if I told you he smoked?

Cole shook his head. "I'd say he didn't listen to dad."

Then you're a better listener too. He's tried it with Ricky; he coughed but he liked it. A part of him, the part that you hold so strongly, well, that part told him to rip the cigarette, but the other part of him, the one he listens to more and more each day, that part told him that what he was doing was cool, made him seem better. In a way cool means shallow, your mother taught you that.

And all of a sudden that voice was gone. Cole even felt lighter. He stopped crying; he wanted to find Jimmy's cigarettes and rip the pack to shreds. He felt that powerful. He wondered if that sudden burst of cognition was just his self-confidence veering its little head into the picture; he had been ignoring it for some time now. But how did *it* know that Jimmy smoked? Cole wasn't sure; in fact, the thought sort of scared him. Had he accidentally seen his brother one day with a smoke in his hand, or was he just making up stories to make himself feel better? He believed the latter.

It wouldn't hurt to check though. If he smoked, he'd hide them under the mattress; that's where everything ended up, because it wasn't their mother that did the cleaning, it was the *help*. He checked under Jimmy's mattress and found nothing. Then a terrible thought came into his head. Jimmy would try to frame Cole if he were caught. Cole lifted the edge of *his* mattress, and yes, there they were, a battered pack of cigarettes; there were two smokes missing.

Cole took them in his hand and crumpled them into a ball; tobacco fell onto the floor in piles. He chucked it against the wall and it made a dull sound.

He walked to the closet and looked up over the clothes rack near the ceiling; it was still there, the same as it had been the first day he'd seen it when he threw an old shirt up on top and watched it snag on the hinge. It was hard to see, but it was there, the little door that had been painted over. The first time he had opened it (it had taken a minute of prying; the dried paint had sealed it quite well) he saw tin sloping into darkness. He heard something, a drill perhaps, but he wasn't sure.

He stood and looked at it.

9

When Jimmy came back to the room—which wasn't but twenty minutes after he sent his brother crying—he wanted to apologize. The boys had been caught outside the office door by the security guard; he had seen them on the stairs and was waiting for the right time to strike. Indeed he had found it, and Ricky and James had to go home. Ricky was on the verge of tears when he thought that his dad's job was in jeopardy.

Jimmy just didn't tell him that the guard let them off with a warning; he loved to see the little guy whimper. "What will he do? He's been in the Preparation Plant for seventeen years," he kept saying, over and over.

Yes, Jimmy wanted to apologize, but that was before he saw the tobacco on the floor in front of the bunk beds, and the crumpled pack of cigarettes lying against the wall. His jaw dropped, and he wanted to rip Cole to shreds. Only Cole wasn't in the room. He wasn't sniveling in bed like a baby (though what he said *was* pretty harsh, he knew that much), and he wasn't sitting in front of the television eating. He ran over to the heap of tobacco and cleaned it before his mom got back from dropping off Ricky and James. Why did he ever come in to apologize anyway? He was certain Cole would do something like this; he must have known about the cigarettes. Ricky had a big mouth and word got around, but what right did Cole have? Did he know how long it took to find a kid old enough to buy the pack for him? "Cole," he screamed into the empty room. He wasn't expecting an answer.

"In here," Cole responded. He was in the closet.

Jimmy was surprised by the playfulness in his voice, as if nothing had happened. He walked into the closet and found Cole sitting on top of the clothes rack; he had used open drawers as a stepladder to get up. He had a bed sheet tied around his wrist, which was anchored to the clothes rack by several loops. It hung in a long droop from his wrist; he pulled it to see if it was taut. "I thought I'd go down the tin here and see where I ended up."

"I thought we agreed it was just a vent, Cole."

"No, Jimmy, cause the door was painted—to hide it."

"Hide it?"

"Yeah, you should know a lot about hiding," Cole added, before submersing himself into the door. He used his feet to pull him in as he held the sheets.

All Jimmy could hear was this thin whine from within the walls.

"Cole," he said. He climbed up the drawers. "Cole," he called into the open door with the sheet flapping out like a pallid tongue. He received no answer; he stuck his head in the miniaturized door. The sheet tickled his chin. He could smell the tin; he could smell other things too. He didn't know what exactly, but he thought he could smell smoke and grease—the same things he and Cole smelt the first time they found this door, when they had agreed it was just a functionless vent. "Cole, are you all right?"

There was no answer. The rope was firm. Jimmy grabbed it and pulled. Everything seemed fine. And then he felt a nudge in the line, as if a fish had been lured by bait; it was becoming less tense. The sheet quivered and Jimmy could hear faint thuds on the tin, followed by heavy breathing. And then he saw Cole's head peering through the darkness; he was climbing his way back up the vent, pulling himself with the sheet, and digging both feet at the vent's sides. Jimmy helped pull him up the rest of the way. Cole was sweating. Both of his eyes were completely lidless and he gasped for air. When he was out all he said was: "close the door, close the door." Jimmy moved aside and Cole slammed the little door shut; it looked like he was searching for a latch of some sort to lock it, but found nothing and covered the door with some books he had lying around instead.

"What is it Cole, it looks like you've seen a ghost or something?"

Cole looked up and tried to blink, but realized both lids were still stuck behind his protruding eyes. "I think I saw Auger, Jimmy. I think Ricky was right. As stupid as that may sound, I think I saw him…there was rock. I could tell because there was a dim light, and all I saw was rock. And Auger built some robots, I think; at least they looked like crude little robots…Auger was under a glass case, lying down with his feet kicking out."

"Why didn't you answer me, I could have pulled you back up?"

"I didn't want him to see me. If I answered he would have peered out and seen me, then I would have had to come down with him and try to finish the mines." Cole started heaving in and out, as if he was having an asthma attack. "I swear Jimmy, if I hear noises in the closet, I am going to freak."

"Come on Cole, grow up, your eyes are playing tricks on you. You were probably just at the end of the vents and you saw the guard or something. No big deal."

"No Jimmy, no." He took the sheet off his wrist and threw it to the ground. "I saw…some*thing*."

Jimmy shuddered. "You gotta grow up." Then he hit him squarely in the arm.

"Come on. What was that for?" Cole rubbed his shoulder.

"Because you wasted Ricky's smokes. I was holding them for him."

"I did him a favor." Cole stared at Jimmy skeptically—he wanted to believe his brother, but he couldn't.

"Well, you owe him eight bucks."

"I saved him on medical bills."

They both climbed down from the clothes rack. And after listening to mom ream out Jimmy, Cole fell asleep watching the closet door, which he had closed himself.

10

Leo hadn't heard Jimmy call out to Cole in the vents, because he didn't know the vents even existed; they were up too high above the light bulbs. The fact that he was under the aquarium didn't help either, but he did know one thing. The filter was almost complete. With the bowl on his head he could at least do one thing: he could breathe recycled air. Breathe the *black damp*.

He would meet the boys though. Yes he would.

11

While Jimmy was asleep, and Cole was nervously watching the closet door across the room, Edwin Krollup was in the KrollupAir Concorde above the Atlantic Ocean, smoking another Cuban cigar. This was a celebratory cigar; in fact, this was his second since the plane had taken off. He wasn't alone this time either. There were statues strapped to the side of the fuselage in the cargo space. Among these there was a particular piece by Michelangelo. Tomorrow morning's paper would dismiss the purchases as incredible negotiations on Krollup's behalf. The Ministry of Art wouldn't dare go beyond that, Krollup thought smugly.

"I am capable of doing many things," he had said as he made the arm of a statue pull its other arm right out of its marble socket. "What if I were to wish such things upon Moses on Pope Julius II's throne? What if I had the great statue pull the horns from its head and use them to carve up its own stomach like steak?" They had gasped at the thought, watching the statue move on its own, no doubt wondering why Krollup had his hand clenched around an ugly necklace. "It is possible you know." He made the statue walk forward and punch a hole through the wall; its hand shattered upon impact, and its arm cracked to the elbow. "How much will you take for him?"

"We can't, he belongs to Florence," one of them spoke up, scared of course, but willing enough to keep such an invaluable piece of Italian history.

Edwin made the ground before him wave forward and knock the man to his feet. "What if I were to decimate Florence then? I have the will to do so," he said. "So much history going to waste because you feel the preservation of one artifact binds this city...so juvenile."

"But he is what this city stands for; he is our guardian. We can't sell something like that. Florence would never recover; we'd be hexed by the past, I can tell you that much." The woman who had spoken fell to her knees in pleading.

"You don't have much time. I can make your history a mountain of dust in mere minutes. You shouldn't underestimate me."

He handed them a check for $50 Million dollars. That also covered the cost of damage. The Ministry watched the statues board the plane, walking on their own...statues *walking* onto a plane. The Ministry, bound by rational thought, would pass the experience off as incredible rigging and illusion—the statues were merely hooked up to gadgets Krollup had implanted previously to carry his ominous effect. Nothing more, nothing less.

Edwin watched the statues as he smoked; they seemed real to him now. *He* could make them move.

"The day shall come when you are needed," he said. He felt more powerful than ever before.

CHAPTER 3

THE ROBOT BOMBER

1

On Saturday morning Cole woke up with a start. He could virtually see everything from the top bunk: the television, the pool table by the door and the bay window that looked out over the statue infested courtyard, but his eyes were trained directly on the closet. He was sure he'd find the closet door open, he was just sure of it, for in his dream that was how it happened—but no, the door was shut, and Jimmy was wheezing out of his nostrils, the way he always did when he slept.

Something about this calmed Cole. He had been sweating, his palms were clammy and he could taste pizza on his breath. He wiped his lips and climbed down the ladder, as quietly as possible.

This is how you did it in your dream too, he thought to himself, *only in your dream the closet door was already open and he was standing inside waiting for you.*

Cole shivered and stopped dead in his tracks. Auger *had* been standing in the closet waiting for him in his dream, and he wasn't normal anymore either; he was shaped like a rock. Ricky had been right—miners did turn into rock after long tours.

Cole put his hand on the knob and then pulled it away. He remembered Auger's blood curdling voice from his dream; it sounded like the earth shifting: "If we finish the mines, I have a surprise for you. But that's only if you come down with me to keep me company. It's been so long Cole, since I've gotten to work with somebody. Not since they sent the dogs down really, but I ate them. What use are dogs with a pick anyway?" And he laughed; he laughed as if it was the punchline to end all jokes.

Cole looked at the door. *It wasn't what he said, it was what he had in his hand, right? That's what's got you so worked up.*

That's right. Auger was holding a big box; it was white and had little black writing all over it, like prescription medicine, the kind of stuff his dad constantly took when he was sick. At first Cole thought Auger was going to say that it was he who had given his father cancer, that he shoved arsenic in his lungs while he slept, but then he read the other side of the box, when Auger flipped his hand over.

Invisi-Fat.

The word was printed in big red letters. *Invisi-Fat.* Yes, he could just picture it, swallowing two pills with water, watching his stomach melt down and his pants fall around his ankles.

"You already know what these are, don't you?" Auger mumbled.

Cole had nodded his head in his dream.

"One of these will make the laughing stop young man. Two will make your sniveling brother look like the ugly duckling. The outcome is your choice, as long as you take a pick and come down with me." Auger cocked his rocky eyebrow, and Cole could have sworn pebbles fell from his eyelid.

He grabbed the pick. Why shouldn't he? This was his magic ticket, and all he had to do was chip away some rock.

As soon as he touched the handle of the pick they were in the mines; there was a quick transformation, the clothes racks turned into sleek rock, and the carpet underneath hardened. Auger lit a lamp and held the box of pills up. "You know what you have to do Cole. You can either go on living as a joke, or you can be the one making them; it's your choice." He grinned and his cheeks split. Cole had lifted the pick and started to bring it down onto a piece of limestone when the tool was taken from his hand completely.

"You don't have to do this."

Cole turned to find his father. He was in the same outfit he had once worn when the guys went to play ball, his gray T-shirt and his cut off sweat shorts. He was glowing white.

"Dad?"

"Remember what your mom talked about?"

"But the pills dad, I don't wanna be fat anymore."

"He owes me, his step father built on top of my mines; he collapsed the entire eastern shaft. I…need…my…COAL!" Auger screamed and fangs jutted out of his mouth like white divots in his brownish lips.

"Remember what your mother said about moral wars? You're strained, pulled in the middle by two choices. You're like Jimmy, Cole, only you believe these pills will make you thin, much like Jimmy thought smoking would take the pain away. Who are you going to believe? The monster with the quick fix, or reason? Don't be tempted."

Cole had stood in the mine, wanting desperately to be thin, to escape the jeers, but his father was right. Right as rain. Right as White—he didn't know what that meant, but it felt real. *Important.* Yes. That's when he woke up.

It was all just a coincidence Cole.

No, that wasn't it though. Cole looked at the closet door. Whatever it was he saw last night, that was the truth behind his dream, everything else was probably just sugar coating. He wasn't sure if he really saw Kenneth Auger, a man who was left buried in his own mines years ago, but he was certain he saw something. And it was this wretched nagging that persuaded he find out just what that something was.

Cole opened the door. He didn't come face to face with Auger, nor did he see his father wearing shorts. What he did see was his makeshift rope made of bed sheets, and that tiny painted door above the clothes rack.

He went into the closet.

2

Jimmy loved to sleep in. He was even prone to doing so on school days, despite his mothers constant nagging. There wasn't much for him to do on Saturday anyway. He might just wake up, watch television for a bit and then sneak over to Ricky's house or something, if Ricky wasn't in too much trouble for ignoring Krollup's rules. His father probably reminded the boy who actually put the food on their table; he was always that way though, telling Ricky to behave when he went over to the Krollup mansion. There was no telling what might happen if Ricky screwed up. Ricky's parents were especially nice to Jimmy, and he seemed to understand that manners ran both ways: whereas Ricky was supposed to be polite at the Krollup's, well, Ricky's parents extended the same gratuity towards Jimmy when he came over to their house. "Boy probably tells his parents how we've been, as if he's spying or something," Ricky's dad had said, when they thought Jimmy was completely out of earshot. Ricky's mother had nodded. "Probably checks the house for stuff I mighta taken from the plant. Wouldn't be too surprised if he had a camera on him, no sir, I would not."

Yes, Jimmy loved to sleep in, and in a way, he loved how parents feared him. He loved the power, even if it wasn't his own they feared.

But on this Saturday Jimmy did not sleep in. On this Saturday, Jimmy felt something on his nose, something that tapped and tapped, and for some reason, tickled the bridge of his nose like prickly feathers. At first he'd moaned.

He thought it was his mom, trying to get him up early for some stupid chore to make up for his misdemeanors last night. But there were no words spoken, and she was more likely to pull him by his hair if her anger permitted. So then he thought it was Cole.

He turned onto his back again and opened his eyes, certain he would be staring into Cole's. But he wasn't.

For a moment he froze. He always had a dream similar to this, waking up with a Black Widow on his face, feeling helpless, as if his limbs were all stapled to the mattress, leaving him a torso attempting to flail.

Jimmy was looking at a spider, which had unfortunately bunked with him over night, by the looks of it. It was brown and its pincers were quivering under its many eyes; it was staring back at him. Its little legs tapped his nose, as if *it* were sent in by his mother to wake him up. It would be a good punishment, because he hated spiders more than anything else in the world. But she wouldn't do something like this. To put a spider on his face would have meant she placed it on his nose, and his mom hated spiders just as much as he did. *It was Cole*, he thought, almost suddenly. *He's mad about last night. He's trying to prove a point.*

And with this thought his body relaxed. He could move again, and he quickly flicked the terrible thing off his nose. He tried to see where it landed, but it was too small. He hoped he hurt it bad though, that was for sure.

And just as soon as his jitters subsided, he heard something more horrible than the sound of those little legs scuttling on his face.

He heard a scream. A *terrified* scream.

When he saw the closet door was open, he knew where that scream had come from.

And when he would find the bed sheets tied to the clothes rack, he knew who was behind it as well.

3

Cole used his feet to steady his body in the vent; it was steep, but not steep enough for him to lose any control. If he lost traction with his feet, well, of course he had the bed sheet, but for now the sheet was only a means of balance and support. His legs were taking most of the punishment.

He wasn't really sure if he should be in here. He was sweating; it seemed dank, but that wasn't it at all. He had a box of chocolates in his pocket, and when he felt it knock his thigh there was a moment when he believed he had brought the Invisi-Fat pills from his dream, that he had somehow tricked them from Auger. "They'll shrink the inches around your waist," he said to himself. He smiled. If Auger knew he had gotten them, he would have crushed him—but Auger was only a phantom in his head…a phantom of his dream, really. In real life he was dead.

"That's right, dead. Dead like Stalin," Cole said. Something about this calmed him. Whatever it was he saw last night couldn't be Auger, because Auger died. Had disappeared in the mines years ago. For some reason he knew this mission was in vain, that when he got to the end of the vent he'd see the security room in the light of day or something.

But what about the robots Cole, you saw them just as clear as day, and you thought that maybe, just maybe there was a slight chance one of them saw you?

They were in the security room too. It's all beginning to make sense; they're some kind of surveillance mechanisms, that's all.

But the man under the glass didn't look like any guard you've ever seen.

Big deal, there are rooms in this house he'd never been in, which meant there were probably people he'd never met. What was the point of worrying anyway, this was just a harmless trip to make sure he was right.

That's just it buddy, you're not definite. Last night it was Auger you saw, and this morning you turned him into a guard—one you've never seen before, but a guard nonetheless.

Cole's foot swung into midair; he steadied himself with the sheets. He was at the end of the vents. He untied the sheet around his wrist and pulled as hard as he could. About two and half extra feet of bed linen bunched behind his back as the sheets tensed on the clothes racks; this was all of them, every set of extra sheets in the closet, all tied into some crude rope. He pulled his feet back and wrapped the sheet around his stomach in a double knot; he felt like Tom Cruise in *Mission: Impossible*.

He crept to the edge. It was dark, but the room before him smelt wet; he could hear faint drips of water. Perhaps there was a leaky faucet in this room, he didn't know. He wanted to find a light switch, because he didn't have a flashlight. But he could hear fire, that sound was unmistakable. Maybe this was Krollup's office. He was sure, judging by the layout of the mansion, that his office had to be near the grand fireplace, maybe even close enough to hear the crackles.

He leaned forward.

There was something on the wall that reflected even the dimmest lights; he couldn't tell what it was but for some reason he thought of a fly's eyes. He didn't remember seeing anything in the room except for the robots and the man under the glass, so he just couldn't recollect what those things might be.

Maybe they're the glass cases Auger was working on. Maybe he's making a giant fly to help him break out of the house.

The thought was so stupid that Cole felt like smacking himself. But the room *was* wall to wall rock, so how could the wall show such a glimmer?

He held the sheets and pushed himself farther outside the vent. He didn't realize it at the moment, but a section of the sheet tied in the middle of the vent snapped.

The air didn't just smell wet, it smelt electrical, industrial even. *Does Krollup have a mechanical room, or a room where he hires somebody to build him things?* He could smell grease, and he could smell the acrid resonance of steel shavings. If only somebody could turn on a light, he would know for sure...

It was with this thought that the bed sheet let go entirely, and before he could grab hold of the lip of the vent, Cole tumbled down the side of the wall, banging his knee on the rocky ground. Yet it wasn't this scream that brought Jimmy from his bed. The noise that ultimately escaped Cole's lips was nothing more than a whimper. No, his real scream came later.

4

Before the lights came on, Cole heard a snap, as if a pull string were whipped. He scrambled against the wall, rubbing his knee; he looked up towards the vent, hoping it wasn't too high to get back up. The sheets were useless now; he would never be able to pull himself up that way. When the lights came on he noticed the vent was far too high above him to climb back in. And he noticed that the ceiling wasn't rock; it was plaster, and bare light bulbs hung from it, splotched in spots by stains and dead insects.

He was sitting on some bones; they were stabbing into his rear. *This isn't a surveillance room*, he thought with a sudden chill. He pushed himself away from the rock wall. Using his legs, he braced himself against the wall and pushed himself onto his feet. He looked to his left and saw a wooden wall with hinges—it was a door—covered by a thick mass of rock that almost looked like an irregular arm. Whatever was in here wasn't supposed to leave.

"Who are you?" Somebody asked in a menacing tone.

Cole scrambled against the wall. He looked forward. He saw three robots; all staring at him with glowing eyes, and standing before them was a short man in a stained shirt with underwear on. His long hair was sticking up on the side, some of which had stuck to his baldpate and created the ugliest comb over ever attempted.

Cole didn't answer. He didn't know how to.

"Have you come to stake your claim? I wouldn't doubt it, boy. If you expect me to put up a fight, you've been deceived. I *want* to go." Leo smiled at Cole. His teeth were terribly malformed. He hadn't seen a dentist in some time.

Cole looked down at the ground and saw three mice scurrying around the rocky surface, dodging cables and metallic parts. *Look, that glimmer you saw Cole, that was just those television monitors; they look like they're set up for surveillance purposes.*

Leo noticed Cole's captivation with the mice. He bent down and quickly grabbed one in his fist. "I'm crazy, kid. They were all right about me, you know, so come and get me, take me outta this hell, take me to the police if you wish. Jail can't be much worse." He stroked the mouse's back and then gave it a queer look. Before Cole could look away, the short little man had the head of the mouse between his puckering lips. He bit down and there was a terrible crack. He'd eaten the head right off the mouse with a sickly smile, chucking the body onto the pile of bones when he was finished.

Cole couldn't hold it anymore.

He screamed.

5

Jimmy wasn't sure if it was the scream that scared him the most, or the fact that it was muffled.

He ran into the closet, his heart beating a mile a minute. The scream was loud, but it was thin too. Almost hollow. That stupid spider was far from his mind now. He jumped up the drawers and sat on the clothes rack. He looked at the hole in the wall with the little door. He wanted to scream Cole's name, but thought about what Cole had said when he came back up the vents last night—he didn't want whatever was down there to hear him.

But that scream though. That was the mark of *true* fear.

He gripped the bed sheet and pulled; it felt light. "Cole," he whispered into the vent. Were the sheets even attached to anything? He pulled again, and before he knew it, the end of the sheet spit out of the vent and onto his lap. It was frayed, as if it had been harshly pulled apart.

Oh no.

Jimmy crawled into the vent, braced his feet against either side, and started to climb down.

6

"No, no, you mustn't scream," Leo said. He ran over to the boy and covered his mouth. Cole tried to retreat, but his back was already against the wall; he could already feel his socked feet grinding the small bones.

His hands reeked of grease, and Cole could tell they were badly scarred. It even looked like his fingertips had worn down to the bone. He squirmed. He didn't want to open his mouth and taste them; he could only imagine what would happen to his tongue.

Leo bent closer towards Cole and studied his face. He could see genuine fear in the boy's eyes.

It's as if the boy didn't know you were even here.

"You're not here to take me away, are you?" he asked the boy, gripping his mouth firmly and licking the blood away from his own lips.

Cole closed his eyes. He didn't understand the question, so he didn't answer.

"Did Krollup send you in because my robot failed? He warned me of this, yes he did. He told me there were people outside these walls that wanted to get their hands on me. Just nod your head 'yes' or 'no'." Leo studied the boy. His robots whirred behind him. He was exhausted, and the thud of this boy falling from that vent above had woken him. For a second he thought it might have been Krollup—*hoped* it was Krollup, to finally punish him. Waiting was worse. He glanced at the vent and though about escape.

Escape? There was no way.

Cole was madly turning, trying to get Leo's disgusting hand away from his mouth.

"You're just a child, how could Krollup expect you to take me away anyway? He's not the peaceful type. If he's unhappy, he's violent. Look what he did to me last month when I suggested I use an engine of his to build a robot." He lifted his dirty shirt, exposing a pale stomach that clung to his ribs like a sickly blanket. There was a huge bruise near his belly button; it looked like the skin was terribly swollen.

Cole squirmed.

"I suspect if you were taking me to the police, you'd want to hurt me too."

"Perhaps, sir, the boy happened to stumble upon the room by chance. Everything is probable."

Cole looked behind the ghastly old man to see who had spoken. One of the robots had moved forward. Its voice was a grating whir.

"Is this true? Was it chance that you found my unfortunate quarters, or were you sent in here to apprehend me?"

"I'm sorry sir, but perhaps you should remove your hand from his mouth. In doing so he will be able to answer," the robot said.

Leo looked at the boy skeptically. He knew his hands probably smelt, and he knew they looked *infected* enough to draw vomit, but he couldn't dare let the boy scream; he knew the terrible things Krollup would do to him if anybody found out about the mines. "If I remove my hand, you have to promise me you won't scream again."

Cole didn't want to open his mouth, but he didn't want to inhale the stench of Leo's hand anymore either. He blurted, "I promise," as quickly as possible—perhaps too quickly.

"What was that young man? 'Hyprama'. What does that mean? Is that some kind of code? Are there others up there, waiting to come down to help you?" He looked up at the dark hole in the wall. Cole wasn't sure if the old man was joking or not, but he did feel the hand tighten on his lips; the feeling was horrible, as if he'd rubbed his lips over a scab.

"I," Cole enunciated more thoroughly, ignoring the tangy, bitter taste of the old man's palm, "promise...I...won't...scream."

Leo relaxed, cocked his bushy eyebrow at the boy and let his hand fall down.

Cole pursed his lips.

"That's good. Keep your lips tight. We don't want anybody getting worked up outside the walls." Leo walked over to his cot. The mattress was badly ripped. "What are you doing in here, boy?"

Cole was still in shock. He didn't know what to do. And more importantly, he didn't know who this was. He knew it was the same man he had seen under the glass last night, but—

"Are you Ken—?" He lost his breath. "Are you Kenneth Auger?"

Leo looked back at the boy. "Am I Kenneth Auger? Young man, may I assume you ask overweight men if they're Elvis Presley?" He kind of giggled and then sat down on his mattress, which sunk under his weight. "Does Krollup know you're in here? Or, better yet, does he even know who you are?"

"Yes, yes he knows who I am, but no...no, he doesn't know I'm in here."

"You've heard the stories of the mines I take it. Just curious are we? If Kenneth Auger is anywhere, he'd be down there." Leo pointed into the darkness, where Cole could hear the dripping water. "I've been in here for a good eleven months, and I have yet to see him myself, though I've heard the stories. Was rather scared to bunk in here all alone at first, but nothing's happened."

Eleven months? Bunking in this room? Cole was very confused. This was no place for a person to live.

"I can see your curiosity. I should know, I was once a kid too, though you couldn't tell to look at me. I guess I should do two things—an apology and an introduction. First off, I'm sorry for doing what I did to that mouse. I thought for certain you were here on Krollup's orders. I needed some way to prove a threat to you, you understand?" Leo smirked.

But I'm just a boy, Cole thought, *how could I possibly be a threat?*

"So with my apology covered, I suppose I should introduce myself as well." Leo stood up and walked past the robots. He held out his hand, and Cole noticed his palm was stained black, probably from the grease he'd smelt earlier. "I'm Alvin Leonardo, though I prefer to be called Leo, you know, like Da Vinci." He stood back when he realized Cole wasn't going to take his hand. "I haven't done this for so long, you see. I haven't been in the type of situation where I'd have to introduce myself to a stranger." He pushed both hands through his hair, and pulled the strings that had decided to nest on his baldpate. His hair sprung into greasy check marks under his ears. Leo searched the room for suitable pants. When he found an old pair of work pants, he jumped into them, and then he threw on his lab coat. He looked better, but not good. "Perhaps now I look more like a Leonardo." He put both hands behind the lapel of his lab coat and stood by his mattress smiling. So he was a scientist.

And Cole realized one thing about the man, something he couldn't believe he hadn't realized earlier. Before he could act upon any of his suggestive thoughts, Jimmy flew out of the vents and landed directly in front of the robots. He had both fists clenched.

"Okay old man, you're not so tough now, are you?"

Leo was shocked himself. He hadn't expected anybody else to be in the vents. To be quite honest, neither did Cole. "You can play nice all you want Auger, but neither of us are gonna help you finish these mines. Don't make me hurt you," he said, in his most menacing tone—one that might have worked at school, but not in the company of protective robots.

The robot that had done most of the speaking grabbed Jimmy by the shirt and lifted him two feet into the air. "You must not threaten Master Leo."

"I'm sorry, but who is this?" Leo asked. Cole didn't know what to say because he was still quite surprised to see that his brother had come down after him.

"Let go of me," Jimmy muttered, trying to pry the robot from his collar.

"You must not have been in the vents long enough to hear that I confessed my true identity...I am not Auger, I am Leo."

"Okay, Leo, tell this stupid thing to let go of me." Jimmy tried kicking but realized it wouldn't get him down.

"AL4, let him down please."

The robot did. Jimmy dropped to the ground, smacking the sloped wall and sifting through the cluttered bones.

"Maybe I was wrong. You were sent first to negotiate. He's the muscle." Leo smiled. Jimmy sat on the ground breathing hard.

"No, no, that's my brother. My twin actually."

"Twin? You don't look like twins."

"Fraternal. I'm Cole. He's Jimmy."

"So are you double teaming me, or has this entire incident unfolded by pure chance?"

Jimmy stood up, menacingly pumping his fists. His face was flustered. "I came because I heard my brother scream, and I don't let things happen to my younger brother."

"By three minutes," Cole added, and Leo smiled.

"I waited in the vent while you were strangling him…I didn't know what to do, so while I talked it over, I realized you had let him go and given me the chance to come down."

"Strangling, no, no, I was merely persuading the boy not to scream. I made the mistake of revealing my unlikely choice of diets."

"No matter, he still screamed like you were about to kill him." Jimmy stepped forward, but stopped when the robot lifted its arm again.

Cole watched this, looking from the robots to the scientist…he had this thought—no, it was more of an image. When he first heard the old man's name he saw a clear picture of a newspaper; he didn't know why, but as time passed he began to realize what the print had read in that quick flash: **City Hall was on the Brink, though Mayor Saved by Edwin Krollup's Security Team**.

This was followed by grainy television footage, led by a reporter holding a network microphone, with his fake hair up in a coif, standing in front of the City Hall steps while people dashed wildly behind him. He was talking about a left wing conspiracy, as burly guards escorted out the mayor. But Cole couldn't recollect anything from this; it was all just a coincidence, the footage and the headline. Yet the robots, there was something about them—

Cole watched Leo and Jimmy argue.

"You're hiding in here, aren't you?" Cole asked.

Leo turned to look at the boy; he may have realized something also.

"From the police, I mean. You're hiding from them. That's why you thought we were in here to take you. Didn't matter much if we were anyway, right, because you would have just triggered one of the robots to explode."

Leo turned and walked back to his cot, while Jimmy fell silent.

Cole had another image in his head—a robot, fitted with a bowler hat and a suit; the hat was pulled down low enough to cast a shadow over its metallic face. It was supposed to blend in with the City Hall patrons.

"What are you talking about, Cole?" Jimmy asked.

"Remember Jimmy, almost a year ago when there was that media blitz? We were locked in our rooms. Nothing good was on television but breaking news garbage, and you got so mad because you couldn't watch *The Simpsons*. There was that threat on City Hall; the police came across evidence that proposed terrorist operations, some letters or something, and Mr. Krollup's security force and the police caught that robot in City Hall, wearing the suit and hat. Before it was set to explode, they had a bomb team ready to dismantle it. When word was out, people went mad; the mayor didn't even know. Knowledge of the bomb was secret. Mr. Krollup was commended. We were locked in our rooms because he didn't want us to screw it up, you know, the cameras and all were here constantly."

"Sorta, I mean, I do remember being mad cause I couldn't watch *The Simpsons*."

And then the boys could hear a faint grumble. They looked over and Leo's face was hidden in his hands.

"It's true then, you are *the* Robot Bomber?" Cole asked.

Leo snorted.

"Why are you here?"

"Everybody only hears one side of the story," he muttered through his hands. He snorted again. "It's rather convenient that incriminating letters end up on the front step of a police station, isn't it?" He asked.

"What are you talking about?" Cole asked. Jimmy seemed confused; the only news he watched with any regularity was sport's scores.

"I am an inventor. You see these robots, I made them. They're mine, but what does anybody need them for? AL4 is only good at responding to simple voice commands, and it only acts upon certain programmed actions; it can become exacerbated if a person's pitch is changed. But who cares? Who needs such an invention? I've been turned down my entire life. At labs, at assembly lines. I had ideas that would help, inventions that would make things easier, *innovations*, but nobody took me serious. You see, I never got a University degree. I never even graduated from High School; my stupid Science teacher tried to explain to the class that it wasn't possible to construct a thinking machine from a toaster. He was clearly making fun of the report I had drawn up for him, because I *did* make a robot out of a toaster and old bicycle parts, and I had clearly stated how, but I was just a laughing stock; it is some people's mission to drive down others. I was bald then too, you see. Unfortunately I was granted a recessive gene that left men in the Leonardo family rather hairless by the age of sixteen. Kept me out of Vietnam. Recuiters thought I was ill. Sure they did.

"I tried to make the teacher understand that it was possible. I even brought my robot in, only it malfunctioned, or something, because it wheeled over to the teacher and bashed him on the head. Of course I'd muttered my desire to hurt the stupid professor before class, but it seemed unreasonable that a toaster could respond to human emotion. I was expelled.

"Nobody wants to buy a complex invention from somebody without a diploma. They like to laugh; they don't believe in uneducated capabilities— this is a society based on credentials. What was I supposed to do? I'm not going to resort to flipping burgers, especially when I designed a robot that would replace burger flippers in the future, and run on the grease cooking on the grill. I was desperate. I was living on Spam and Oatmeal. I was an outcast, and most people like me took a road meant for us. If everybody was going to laugh, then people like me were going to shut them up. When I look at you Cole, I'm reminded of myself at that age."

"I'm not like you."

"But kids laugh, bullies shove. You're a victim, right?"

Cole blushed. He took out his chocolates and shoved a handful into his mouth.

"I mean no offense, but people are cruel. I bet you get great grades too. We're victims, you and I, only I made a difference. I became a hired goon. Where machines could be designed to do good, they could also be made to do terrible things. I'm not proud, but I made a robot that could drill into a bank vault. I sold it to a crime family for three-hundred thousand dollars. You can live on that kind of money for a long time, you know, especially when you're pleased with simple things. I didn't need a big house, or great designer clothes—Izod was big then, the yuppie look. I just needed a lab to work on my inventions. When I ran low on cash, I went to people who would pay for my bad ideas; there was better money in that, it seemed. And then the computer age was born. I had ideas about computers years before they actually came about. I knew there were other uses for phone lines. But the computer gave people like me greater resources. Did you know that there are web sites for hired henchmen? Yes there are. Some of them are just hidden within other legitimate sites, like, uhhh…there's a link on the NRA homepage…it's hidden but it's there. It's true; I've seen it. All you have to do is leave your email address and mail comes pouring in.

"That was how I got the job to blow up City Hall. These e-letters are anonymous, you see, so I didn't know who I was working for. But that gets you thinking, you see. It could be anybody really. I was set up easily, and found even easier the day I was supposed to blow up the building. I told them I would be sitting in a car across the street, pretending to read a map or something; and they were supposed to drop off the cash when I pulled away into an alley. I had the robot dressed in a suit I bought from a street vendor, and put an old fedora on its head; it was set to explode at 3 O'clock. I sent it in at 1:30, still rather iffy about what I was doing, because you see, I never created a machine for murder. Never. But the idea seemed enticing because I went to school with the Mayor, I did. And he was a bully. Chuck was his name, and I hated him. I still do. Payback is always a dream, you see. I'm sure you feel the same, don't you Cole? Yes, but I had my doubts. I knew there were many other people in the building, and I did...*do* have a conscience, despite what you may've heard. You may not've seen it on the news, but the robot I sent in to the building was equipped with a working bomb, but it only disconnected the cables in its head; that's all. It did create a big noise, but that was just for show. In the end my conscience did get the best of me. I'd made two robots: one with the ability to blow away the entire building, and the one I sent in.

"None of that matters in the end. They say experts dismantled the robot, but I don't believe that. How is it possible? What was there to dismantle? Next thing I knew, there were armed men approaching my car. That was it, I was caught, and I was named the Robot Bomber by the folk with the microphones. Rather suspect how they'd know I was in my car though, isn't it? How they'd know where to find me."

Leo looked away from his hands.

"But, but they never brought you to trial...you, you disappeared. Everybody was worried for awhile. The mayor even had to live in a safehouse out of state till things cleared."

"Krollup came to me with an ultimatum, you see. Either I helped him here, while he provided protection from the police, or I went to jail for the rest of my years. He said he would make the proper authorities believe I was gone. What do you think sounded like the better deal?"

"That doesn't sound legal."

"It wasn't. But there were too many coincidences. Far too many." Leo leaned forward. "I think Krollup anonymously sent me the job to blow up City Hall. Not for any personal reasons or anything, but as a lure."

"How? I mean, he wouldn't have known who you are, or how to get hold of you."

"That's true, but I never told you that I had approached him before with an idea that would revolutionize mining. He turned me down. Trust me, he has better ways of doing such things. Better than any machine. I left him my email address, you know, in case he changed his mind. Months later I got the mail regarding the City Hall job. I think he set me up."

"You're a terrorist? And to think, I was gonna knock your block off." Jimmy cowered against the wall with Cole.

Leo looked down again, watching his dirty fingers tremble. "No, I'm no terrorist. I just thought you two were sent in here to free me, to take me to jail."

"Free you and *then* take you to jail, that doesn't make much sense." Cole said.

"I'm a slave in here. I showed you my stomach; he expects perfection, but he doesn't give me the equipment I need to achieve that. These robots are just crude designs adapted from my original concepts...but constructed with technological pass-me-downs. AL4 speaks using an old baby monitor; that isn't right."

"You're afraid of Mr. Krollup too?" Jimmy asked.

Leo looked away, his cheeks turning red.

"Why did Mr. Krollup build on top of the mines?"

Leo put his finger to his lip. "Shhh, be quiet for a moment." He listened. "Does Krollup know either of you are in here?"

"No," Cole said, irritated by the redundancy.

Leo crept over to a stack of bricks that had been laid against the wall. Cole could see a slight flicker of light through spots, and a thin trail of smoke. *That's the wall you were looking at last night behind the fire, the one where you noticed spots in the grout were missing.* Leo put his face against the bricks, pulled his head away a little and scratched his fingers along the grout. Little pieces of rock fell to the ground. *That's why his fingers look like that,* Cole thought, *so he can see out of the fireplace; he scratches little windows, and I'm sure there's blood on the bricks because of it. Jail* would *be better, if he's stuck in here. Look at his face; it's completely white. He hasn't seen the sun in almost a year.*

Leo crunched his nose against the brick. "Listen, everybody's hurrying. Does that happen often out there?"

Cole stopped dead in his tracks. "Only if Mr. Krollup is arriving from an extended stay away."

Leo watched figures move through the fire. He saw two maids walk by, carrying dusters, and he saw a guard jogging by; he was talking into a radio. "He'll come here first, if that's true. He always does."

Cole looked up at the vent in horror. "What are we going to do then? He'll kill us; he has so many rules. We'll go down the mines. Jimmy, come on, we have to hide."

"No, you can't go down there," Leo said. He was still looking through the sparse cracks he made in the grout.

"Why not, we have to hide, there's no other way out?"

"That's not a way out. Wait, hold on." He watched. He heard voices, but the fire was too loud to make any of them out. Leo could smell his breath on the brick; he could smell the months he'd been in this cubby hole, waiting, and he could smell his own failure as a human being. His was the stink of failure. "He just walked by," Leo said. There were thin tendrils of smoke seeping through the cracks in the brick.

"What?" Cole asked. He froze in place. Jimmy had done the same thing ten minutes ago when he realized he was in the presence of a madman.

"From left to right. Any time I've ever seen him through the fireplace, walking in that same direction, he's always ended up in here."

"What should we do?" Cole turned around and tried jumping, just to see if he could grab the lip of the vent. He didn't even come close. "Jimmy, what should we do?"

Jimmy shrugged. He looked pretty upset that he decided to come down the vents.

They all stood silent for a moment, straining to hear.

"He'll come through that door behind the rock." Leo ran over and put his ear to the wood. He could hear dull footsteps, but they had to have been at least fifty yards away. "How steep are the vents?"

"I don't know, I can't reach them…I can't reach them. We're dead, he'll have our heads…our heads."

"Do you think you can climb back up them?"

Cole thought about this. The bed sheets had snapped, so he wouldn't have anything to pull himself up with, but if he jammed his feet against either side and used his fingers, he just might be able to climb back up. "Maybe, but I'm not completely sure."

"Are you willing to try?" Leo asked. He listened to the door behind the rock again. Footsteps, closer this time. "He's coming."

"Yes, yes. But I can't get back up."

"You can with a lift," Leo said. He ran over to the robot called AL4. The robot whirred and then moved forward.

"Step on my arms, young sir," the robot said.

Cole stepped up.

"No, let me go first Cole. I can climb the vent and grab the remainder of the bed sheets. Then I can come back down, grab you, and then you can use the sheets to pull yourself up. You won't be able to climb the whole way without them, trust me."

Jimmy jumped up on the arm of the robot and it lifted him as high as it could. Jimmy had to hop an inch to grab the edge of the vent, and then he climbed in. His legs disappeared.

"Your turn, young sir," the robot said, and its arms descended.

Cole jumped on, balancing himself by grabbing the robot's head. The robot lifted Cole to the tin perch. He climbed into the vent, and just as his legs were swallowed by darkness, the rock arm in front of the door withered into the wall and the door opened.

It was Edwin Krollup, and he was smiling.

7

At dinnertime the boys sat across from each other. Mr. Krollup sat at the head of the table in a huge chair with carved armrests, and the boy's mother sat opposite him. She was smiling.

"Edwin, are you going to tell them?"

The handmaidens were just beginning to bring the food from the kitchen. They set trays on the table and placed a plate of steaming potatoes and steak in front of Krollup. He muttered his thanks. The boys looked at Edwin and he grew overly concerned. He made sure his necklace was concealed. "I brought David from Italy."

"You say that like it's an everyday thing. He went to Italy, as you both know, and he negotiated Michelangelo's most famed statue from Florence. It has found a new owner—news of this will be all over the world by tomorrow." Her smiling lips almost touched her ears. "Simply amazing. The only other way I thought this could happen was through some elaborate art heist, or something. You proved me wrong Edwin."

He stifled a grunt, as if she knew he had used his necklace to intimidate the Ministry.

"Yet such things seem trivial when rules are broken," Krollup said, as he chewed a piece of steak. Both Jimmy and Cole worriedly looked at each other. They had gotten back up the vents safely. Cole had watched Mr. Krollup come into the room with the Robot Bomber. When he heard Jimmy whisper at him, he turned and pulled himself to the dangling bed sheets. There was no way Krollup could have known they were in there...well, not unless the Bomber told him. He was a terrorist, and terrorists couldn't be trusted. "Did I not tell you Maggie, that even when I'm gone, certain areas of my house are off limits?"

Maggie nodded, unsure where this was going.

Jimmy swallowed hard, and Cole traced his finger over the box of chocolates in his pocket.

"I have ways of seeing what the guards don't, and some guards find it in their nature to let certain things slide. You two had friends over last night, is that right?"

Jimmy nodded.

"What were their names?" Krollup leaned forward. He was holding his steak knife out, as if he was deliberating its destination.

Jimmy didn't want to say, he didn't want to let his friends down. He put food in his mouth instead, and chewed slowly.

"Cole, who were they?" He demanded.

Cole gripped the chocolates. Jimmy gave him a desperate look that said, *don't tell him, whatever you do, don't tell him.* But there was something about the way Krollup stared, as if he'd hurt the boys if he had to. "Ricky Paulson and James Whittaker." Jimmy shuddered and dropped his fork.

"Ricky Paulson and James Whittaker. Okay. Good. Do their parents work under my name?" He pointed the knife at Cole; he must have known he would have to be patient with Jimmy and he just didn't have the time for that.

Cole nodded and looked down at his plate. The food didn't look so appealing anymore.

"Very well then. They'll be surprised come Monday. I'm quite aware that a certain aging security guard gave you a warning for attempting to enter my office, and in doing so, promised you he'd keep the confrontation secret from me; that was my idea boys, my scheme. My full intentions had been to give you hope that your pestering little secrets were safe from me. I hate secrets, they're like vile insects, multiplying on every whim."

"What are you doing, Edwin?"

"You know very well what I'm doing Maggie. Your two boys were seen outside my office with two friends. They even attempted to turn the knob on my door, despite the restrictions I set on such actions. Preposterous. Before long, Ned the guard came by and scolded the boys, and then he promised them the encounter would stay safe from me as long as it didn't happen again. I loathe secrets in my own house. The very fact that he promised them a warning but told me anyway seemed like he was bent between authorities, and I just can't have that in this house."

"You fired Ned? You told him to tell the boys it was only a warning. You told him."

"Because of their actions, three men, Maggie, are going to lose their jobs, and two of those men have nobody to blame but their own sons, for disregarding rules they should have been taught to keep."

"You're going to fire them too?" Jimmy asked.

Edwin glared at him. "Should I promote them? If their sons are such spies, shouldn't I wonder where they inherited such actions?"

"Mom," Jimmy pleaded.

She just looked at Edwin and turned red. There was nothing she could do now.

"Both of you go up to your room. You're not fit to sit at the table with us civilized adults." He snapped and two handmaidens ran into the dining room and snatched up the boys' plates.

Cole and Jimmy were ushered out of the dining room, and they scampered up the Grand stairs and ran to their room, seven doors down.

"Why did you have to do that?"

"Your boys are curious. There's no doubt about that, but all my life curiosity has been a curse; they want to stake their claim, that much is for sure. Perhaps this situation is completely Freudian...perhaps both boys feel a certain jealousy with every man you end up with. Haven't you ever wondered why your first husband smoked?"

"You jerk."

"Yes, because he was driven to the brink. A father collapses under the pressure of his offspring. His escape was cancer. Good for him, he found a loophole."

"What are you saying?"

"I never told you what happened to my father, did I?"

Maggie shook her head; she had actually read what happened somewhere awhile back, but didn't want him to know that.

"He escaped me too, only I encouraged it; he used to beat my mother."

"Did he have cancer, too?"

"If you can call drunken idiocy cancer."

"I'm sorry," she said.

"Why?"

She cocked her eyebrow.

"Just keep your boys away from my office." He wiped his chin and stood up. "The truck should be here with David soon. I have to wait up for it."

CHAPTER 4

THE GENERAL'S THRONE

1

Edwin stood in the courtyard, facing the electric autumn air; the sun was just descending over the tree line, branding an aura over the leaves which appeared dark brown through Krollup's cigar smoke. He felt no gratitude for such beauty; in fact, it wasn't the sun that he was really staring at. He was looking over the statues in his yard; there were dozens upon dozens of them, standing on their own pedestals, looking out over the stone wall, watching the house as if they were hired guards.

He stood beside a large granite bull, its head lowered as if in grazing. He blew his cigar smoke against the heft of its side, and the bull's head moved. Small wafts of dust fell to the ground. He massaged his necklace and grinned.

His was a nasty grin, for he wore the mask of sadism. You saw the swollen bruise on Leo's stomach. Unfortunately the little man felt it in his nature to inquire the use of a luxury car engine for one of his robots; Edwin saw this as attempted thievery...as a preposterous ploy to vandalize *his* property. In a fit of anger he let loose a stone from the wall pelting Leo in the gut, sending him to the ground in a messy clutter. Such acts of violence had become a Krollup trademark. Why else would a terrorist cower behind the dank walls of a fireplace?

Krollup was in dire need of something to go into those mines; he hadn't felt ready to send in statues, nor did he want to attempt to close off the mines by using the necklace. When little Leo had come by his office with a proposal—robot miners, who didn't work for money, but for fresh grease and oil changes—Krollup had refused only because he had better methods for doing such things. Leo left, obviously hurt, but the drawn up blueprints for those robot miners were not forgotten. Krollup had kept the little man's business card, as Leo had guessed, but where the little man insisted Krollup had mailed him, it was actually another of Krollup's goons, one that had such insight into those "secret web sites."

He fell into a trap. But in the end he did get to send his robots down the mines.

Edwin's train of thought was ceased by headlights. The truck had pulled up Hillside road and parked in front of the gate. Edwin gave the guard manning the post the thumbs up, and the gate pulled open. The truck resumed, and stopped at Edwin's side.

The driver rolled down the window and stuck his head out. He was smoking too, only the thing perched on his lip was only a cigarette. Edwin felt more masculine, despite the differing statures of the men. The trucker was 300 pounds. The big man took the cigarette off his lip and cocked his eye at Krollup. "Where da ya wannit?"

"Here is fine, gentlemen. I have my own forklift to come around and take the packages to the cargo bay, since you're both *so* narrow-minded you've come the front way—an entrance I reserve for V.I.Ps." He cocked his own eye. Of course his arrogance seemed shallow, since Edwin *was* standing out front waiting for the truck; in fact, he never intended the order to go around back anyway, he just always met attitude with a brand of his own. And Edwin Krollup was accredited a fierce mean streak.

"Gee, sorry mista, we just got the order in and it juss told us to come to the house. Didn' say nothin about no road to use." The big guy put out his smoke and shut his truck down. "Anyway, what you got in there? Heavy an' all you know. Big boxes. Felt 'em lurch on one corner, thought they'd bring the whole truck over."

"Were you driving like maniacs?"

"No sir, just gotta take rights wide, ya know, or we'll end up taking out a sidewalk, or a pedestrian or something." He giggled, but stifled immediately when he saw Krollup's face.

"If anything is broken inside, you'll understand what it feels like to be in a tipped truck." Edwin signed the release form and shoved it back to the driver, who was short and fat. The man had lit another cigarette. The passenger was already around back opening the trailer.

When the forklift engine fired up, the stout little driver waddled over to the rear of the truck, and checked if the ramp was secure. He was sweating; he had never been so afraid of another man before. Of course he knew who Krollup was, but while he drove the heavy order over, he had this feeling Edwin was just another snobbish rich man with too little appreciation of the mindless jobs people like him had to do. But he was wrong. Krollup was almost like a vampire. He had a weird look in his eye. He meant business was what that look said.

There were four huge crates in the semi trailer; each belted to the side of the truck. The passenger hopped out of the forklift as the fat driver climbed up the ramp, holding onto his pants for dear life. They both undid the belts around every crate. Nothing was knocked over.

The forklift slowly brought each of the four crates down the ramp, while the fat driver sweat it out; he was sure one of the crates would tip, but nothing happened.

"Pry the boxes off," Edwin said, as he crunched the cigar in his teeth.

"Well sir, wouldn't you like to keep them on till you get your driver to take them round back to the cargo bay? You know, so they don' git damaged or anything." The driver was rubbing his hands together roughly.

"I'll worry about that. Why would a mindless drone question my intentions?"

"Sorry sir, you're right. It's none of my business."

Walking into the back of the truck to grab his crowbar, the driver, or Freddy C to his friends, cursed himself for taking such abuse. He even went as far as smacking his arm as hard as he could; there would be a bruise above his elbow the next day.

Freddy hurried the bar down the ramp and stuck it in the crate and pried as hard as he could. When he thought he could go no longer, the nails separated and the box collapsed leaving three walls standing like a trifold with a roof on top. There were four columns of tarps, secured to the pallets beneath by rope and nails.

"What are they?" The passenger asked.

"Leave," Krollup demanded. He didn't need to say it twice. Both men were in the truck and out the gate before Krollup had loosened the ropes on the tallest of the four tarp towers.

He could see stretches of white marble when the tarp was tossed by wind. He unwound the rope and tossed it aside. The tarp lifted into a comical curve like an umbrella and Edwin slowly pulled the canvas until the heft of it had slid over David's head.

He didn't need a forklift to ship the statues. He didn't need one in Italy when he loaded them on his jet, and he certainly didn't need one now.

He looked around the courtyard. It was empty. Only the statues loomed around him. Most windows in the house were dark. The handmaidens had all left after dinner, and the guards were usually asleep at this time, using their swivel chairs as makeshift beds. He didn't feel any eyes on him, except—

"Curse them. The spies," Krollup sneered at the second story window with the drapes open and the lights turned on. It was the boys' room.

Edwin turned and walked back to the house, leaving the statues be for the moment.

2

It must have been midnight. Cole didn't know, but there were shadows dancing on the wall, as if an autumn breeze was blowing in from the east. He didn't wake from some dream about Auger, he had just laid down with his eyes open, watching the ceiling as if it were some captivating movie.

He didn't want to budge; he wanted to stay this way until morning, until he could see the sun through the window. But those noises. They hadn't just wakened Cole, they had jerked him up.

You weren't in a deep sleep though, Cole. You were hovering, you know, you were preoccupied; you were just using sleep as a method to ignore certainties, but that doesn't always work…sometimes sleep emphasizes things. That was true. He hadn't been dreaming at all; he had just heard the noises and then turned over.

You've been replaying it in your mind all night. In a way you're worried your dad—your real dad—is going to strike Jimmy. You're worried he's going to rise from the grave and strike him down for his rebellions, for making the same mistakes.

No, he wasn't afraid of that at all; he was afraid that Jimmy had forgotten their father and decided upon a new one, yes, that was it. Things weren't normal anymore, and that scared Cole the most. A month ago he would have punched himself for saying so, but normalcy was, at least in these terms, trying to live up to Krollup's standards and in the mean time remembering their father for what he was: a war hero who had decided his good deeds were an allowance to take up vice, as if the two would balance each other out. But for Jimmy at least, their father had become more and more invisible, to a point that he, Jimmy, had decided to take up the very vice that nailed their father's coffin shut. In a way, Jimmy reminded Cole of Edwin Krollup; they both desired this power, which seemed to derive from the need to overcome struggle. In Jimmy's case, it was the struggle of acceptance in a new school; he either hung with his brother, or he took up smoking and hung with the cool kids. Or he hid other kid's smokes. Yeah, right…

Cole heard another bash outside in the courtyard and he shivered. He pulled the blankets up around his eyes and peered at the ceiling. He could hear Jimmy breathing underneath him; he tried to imagine a wheeze in his brother's breath, as if he was fighting to take in clean air.

Just like your dad. You hated hearing him breathe. Before they stuck the hoses in him, he sounded like a shoddy car engine; in fact, you were determined the doctors would have to start feeding him oil, just so his breathing would stabilize.

No, no, no, he didn't want to think of his dad. Not now. He was too upset with Jimmy. Jimmy *should* have hurt him, he *should* have given him twenty Charlie Horses and rubbed his hair down to the scalp. But—

But Jimmy wasn't upset. Cole had ratted out Jimmy's friends, an act so utterly looked down upon it could score Cole with daily snake-bites and Indian burns till he was forty, but Jimmy wasn't upset. He didn't say a word when they strode up the stairs to their room after they were suspended from dinner, and he only sat down on the couch in front of the television and watched the blank screen. He was almost catatonic. at that moment Cole was ready for anything. He was ready to get pounced on, and he even had the escape route down the vents, only he wondered if it was any safer with the Robot Bomber? He forced that thought away from his head immediately.

But Jimmy said nothing; he thumbed his fingers around and watched the blank screen.

It wasn't until you approached him that he said anything…you were so eager to see, no, to feel what he was going to do to you that you just wanted to get it over with. In a way, his silent treatment was a worst punishment than his fists, because it took away any chance of predictability.

So Cole had approached him; he diverted his hunger for the moment and jumped from the bunk bed and walked over to the television. "So what's it going to be, are you going to hit me, or yell at me, or both?"

Jimmy said nothing; he only placed both hands on his lap.

"Come on, I know I'm an idiot Jimmy, I know, and I know James and Ricky are gonna kill me, but don't do this. You know I can't lie to Krollup, you know I can't. You know how scared I am of him."

"And you should be scared of him," Jimmy finally said. He turned his head and stared at Cole, only his eyes seemed different, almost maniacal. So Cole saw this and waited. He waited for the fists or the verbal lashing, or whatever his older brother of three minutes wanted to dish out, only nothing happened, no fists connected, and there were definitely no curse words thrown. "Have you ever noticed how many people are scared of Mr. Krollup?"

Cole shook his head. He didn't know where this was going (though he did believe Jimmy was referring to the man behind the fireplace—the Robot Bomber), and the fact that this was so out of the ordinary was *worse* than a slap in the face.

"He walks as if he's overcome with something…as if he's been, I don't know, lifted higher in the air by someone, or something. You ever notice that?"

"I've noticed that he's a jerk."

"Yeah, well that jerk's got an entire city under his heels. Remember in Social Studies, when we studied local business and infrastructure?"

"You were listening?"

"Kind of," Jimmy said absently. "This city was nothing thirty years ago. Cracker factory went out of business and left hundreds of people jobless. This place was on the verge Cole. Auger Mining was still around, but it was teetering, and they tended to hire cheap labor from out of town because minimum wage went down, and all those unions went bust. Auger Mining didn't do anything for the city like Krollup. Krollup brought professional sports into this town, and now we got tourists coming around just to catch games… well not *Blackbird* games. But that's beside the point, little brother. Krollup has made this city into an empire. Did dad have that kind of power?"

"What are you talking about?"

"To tell you the truth Cole, I'm sick of letting dad's shadow control our lives."

"You're not, or I wouldn't have found those smokes." Cole was hurt, so hurt that he had wanted to stuff his mouth with chocolate.

"But he controls yours. You try to live up to his standards, just like I used to, but why? Why try to please a dead man that didn't care enough about us to quit smoking? We both urged him to stop, and he said he did. Remember that, he looked us both in the eyes and he said he quit, he threw away all of the back-up packs he had kicking around, and we both believed him. We believed him, but guess what. We were young and dumb then. He knew that too, so he used that against us, so when we caught him smoking, it was such a surprise to us that we were hurt, no, we were *genuinely* hurt. Hurt to tears. But we let him get away with it because he was our father."

"Was?"

"Yes *was*. He's dead. He's dead because he lied to us. If he'd been honest, he may have been able to stop his cancer…maybe he wouldn't have had it period, but he lied, and we forgave him, and he went and ruined our lives."

Jimmy got up, patted Cole's shoulder and looked him squarely in the eyes. "It was his fault mom wanted a divorce; it was his fault we were poor; it was his fault we had to change schools and move here with Krollup; and it was his fault *I* took up smoking. I don't understand why we wasted so much time trying to make him happy, when nothing he did resulted in happiness."

"Because he's our dad, Jimmy."

"He was, Cole. He *was*. He can't be your dad when he's buried with lungs that look like oatmeal. We have a new dad, and you have to get used to it. I've been trying to make the adjustment, and guess what, I feel great."

"I can't believe you're saying this, Jimmy, and I don't wanna hear it anymore. I'll tell mom, I swear I will. I'll tell her you smoke, I swear."

"Go ahead, mom will be happy. To be honest bro, I believe she was getting sick because you were stuck. You can't hold onto the past, and she'll be relieved to hear that I've accepted Krollup for what he is."

"Yeah, and what's that, a jerk?"

"Our dad."

"A jerk."

Jimmy smiled. "You're looking in the wrong places for role models Cole. You can follow in dad's footsteps when you're dead, for now you should accept Krollup, and learn to appreciate him. Dad never did have any power."

"He was in the war, Jimmy. I'd like to see *your* dad go to war."

"Yeah, but nobody respected dad; he didn't have any power here, where it counts."

"Power, Jimmy, power? Dad survived the war, he came home with pictures of himself holding big rifles, and in the background you could see enemy fire."

"But it's like you always say Cole. When it came to the moral war, he lost. Mr. Krollup smokes, and he's alive and kicking. There are winners, and there are losers. Why choose to follow in the footsteps of a loser?"

"You jerk, you jerk!" Cole screamed and he hit Jimmy in the shoulder.

"You'll understand what I mean about *real* power when you see Ricky and James after they find out their daddy's are gonna be jobless." Jimmy had said this when he was halfway out the door. He left Cole, standing by the couch and the television with his fists balled and tears welling in his eyes. He had never felt such fury before.

Cole heard another bash outside the window, shaking him out of his hazy recollection. He didn't even know the guy sleeping underneath him anymore; it used to be the other way around. Cole used to dish the advice, and Jimmy would listen in dumbfounded silence.

So, let him turn his back; it isn't his life you're living, now is it?

There was a final crash outside the window; one that drove Cole to clench the bed sheets, his grip turning his knuckles white.

What was that?

It was so loud Jimmy had even turned in his sleep.

Maybe you should leave the mental notes for a bit, and check outside, you know, cause maybe somebody climbed the fence and decided to break the statues or something. Guards sleep when nobody's looking.

Cole shifted a bit. Should he?

He sat up on his pillow and looked out the window. The drapes were pulled away from the window in the middle, which had let some of the moon's light into the room. He saw the fence down the yard, a dark shadow against the trees, but he couldn't see anything beyond that.

He wasn't so courageous by nature, but that last crash was too loud to be a mere trespasser. He threw his covers off, and sat up, his stomach forming a mound under his shirt, which bunched up and showed his rolled up belly button.

He climbed down the ladder, trying to be quiet so he wouldn't wake up Jimmy (though he wouldn't have minded planting a foot in his brother's face).

Walking over to the window seemed the hardest. He drew little steps... *anything* could have made those noises, he thought. He curled his pudgy hands into the drapery and rolled his body into the fabric, until he was only a peering head wrapped in a décor cigarette. He looked out the window and didn't see anything; there was nothing that could have made those noises, and he was relieved. His hands loosened in the drapes and he let out a gasping breath.

What was that?

He pressed his face against the pane of glass and tried to see around the house. He was sweating. He hadn't realized it before, but the pallets in the driveway the delivery truck had dropped off were standing bare, with only four large tarps thrown aside on the grass.

He didn't want to believe it, but he had watched a stiff leg disappear around the side of the house, its movement rigid.

It could've been human, he thought.

No, because human legs weren't generally cast out of stone.

You're dreaming.

3

There were noises on the floor below. How could Jimmy sleep through that?

It was nothing, it was just a trick of your eyes, you know, like when you went into the vents and thought you saw Auger...just a trick.

No, but it wasn't trick of the eye in the vents, because the Robot Bomber *was* down there. If it had been a trick, then Cole would have found the other side of the vent empty.

Cole threw the drapes off him and crept to the bedroom door. What was he doing? He didn't know, but a sense of curiosity overcame him, just as it had when he climbed into the vents; he was simply weak that way, he supposed. He opened the door, and then stopped…he didn't want to go any further without bringing his box of chocolates.

He peered out into the hallway.

It was dark, but he could see the lights along the walls—he wasn't going to turn them on mind you, but knowing he could at least see them made him feel a little better. He heard more noises, dull footsteps, heavy thuds really, and he left the room. He walked the distance to the railing over the grand stairs, quite slowly, but he did make the trek, and that was commendable enough.

He looked down. It was so dark he couldn't see anything. Just dim reflections off the mirror. Whatever the noises were, he knew they must have been coming from the Great room. The real question now was whether or not he could go down the stairs to see for himself? This question didn't take much pondering at all. Cole wasn't stupid, nor did he want to fall into the same cliché situations he and Jimmy always mocked in those stupid horror flicks about burnt monsters with daggers for fingers. He didn't want to meet face to face with whatever it was that belonged to that leg.

There wasn't a leg, he persuaded himself.

But he had to know. That may sound stupid, but there were times in life when curiosity drowns you in utter contemplation, even when the answer seems easily accountable.

Cole wasn't dumb though, nor did he follow in the footsteps of those trashy films (which more than likely were able to give faces to the mysterious sounds he heard at night in this huge house); instead he walked back to his room and opened the closet door, unafraid of the chance a rock laden Kenneth Auger might be standing against the rack with a pick, because he understood such things were only imaginable.

He knew Krollup was behind the noises, in one way or another. And he remembered what the Robot Bomber said: *"He'll come here first. He always does."* So he jumped up the clothes rack and quietly opened the little door that was painted the same color as the wall.

4

Edwin Krollup was furious he had to wait; he hated those spying boys.

You should send them away to school, that's what you should do; you should tell Maggie there are great Military schools, maybe even dig something up on the boys that would make that kind of school seem more appealing. Get them in trouble, in other words.

Yes, that was a grand possibility; the fact they had spied the main floor (attempting to get into his office, the little maggots) didn't seem like enough evidence to send them away, but—

Just the thought of their little grubby hands on his doorknob made him shiver; they had been so close. And then what, they might have opened the door and seen his collection, played with his arrows, dented his Roman breastplate. Anything was possible. And if they had seen the framed photo of the mineshafts on the wall, might they have put one and one together and pushed the wall? Of course the door would have jammed against the rock behind it, but they would have known, and he couldn't let them have the slightest clue. Plus Leo was apt to talk. No amount of torture or intimidation was enough to deter a man when freedom was in the books. And with this thought he entered his office, unlocked the avalanche door and walked straight to the wall that was actually a door. He touched his necklace and he heard the rock rustle, and then he pushed the door open.

Leo was sitting on his bed. What Krollup didn't know was that little Leo had been standing atop AL4's extended arms, trying to reach for the lip of the vent. When the rock arm had slid back into the stone face, he jumped down from the robot and hurriedly sat upon his collapsed mattress, and tried to put on his most tired face. He was sweating, and his eyes told a tale that stemmed Edwin's curiosity.

"Little agitated, Leo?"

"No sir, I was just trying to catch a mouse is all." There were a few of them running about, but none of them seemed swift enough to dodge a hungry man.

Edwin scoffed at the little critters. "Shouldn't be eating them."

"I have no choice sir, you have me on a bread and water binge."

"Are you getting smart with me? I don't appreciate your wry sense of humor." He touched his necklace and a mouse was thrown from the rocky ground by a splinter of stone. It landed on Leo's lap. "There, eat your protein if you want to stay strong. You're no use to me dead."

The mouse was frozen with shock, and only stared up at Leo with its beady eyes; he wasn't hungry so he just let the poor thing off his lap.

"What's with your robot?" Edwin pointed out. AL4 was standing near the wall with both arms extended upwards; there wasn't enough time to set Leo on the ground when the rock moved, so he had to jump down. He forgot to tell AL4 to drop its arms.

"I was just checking its joints. I sometimes have to use mouse blood and crushed bone as grease, because I ran out of oil."

"Awww. Just wait till the end of October and you'll get more, plus your new mattress. You're lucky Leo, I spoil you."

Leo smiled. He wished AL4 *was* a bomb; he had a sudden flash of the robot wearing a fedora with a cheap suit on. He shrugged it away.

"Anyway, I just came by bearing great news."

"Oh."

"Yes, David just came; it's sitting outside. I'm so excited." Edwin did seem rather ecstatic. He was beaming.

"Can I see him?"

"Are you kidding me?" His smile was gone, replaced by a menacing frown. "And then what, you want to take a ride in my limousine?"

"It's just, I've always wanted to see it up close."

"I've always wanted to fly, but you don't see me jumping off any roofs, now do you? That's just like you Leo. I have something exciting to tell you, and you find a way to ruin it for me." He walked over to Leo and picked him up by the dirty collar. "I have no need for you right now anyway. Your robots have been complete failures, and if this robot here is any indication of the future, I shan't be using any of them later either." He looked at the wall by the monitors and a small hook formed in the rock; it jutted out of the wall just enough for Edwin to hang Leo up by his shirt.

5

After Krollup showed Maggie David, he retired to his office and snapped a key from an iron chest plate adorned in gold and jewels. The key seemed to fit in with the other fineries, so it was rather surprising when he snapped it off; it was almost as if he was desecrating his collection out of spite.

He looked at this key for a moment and twirled it in his palm; it was simple looking, like most keys, but the gold in which it was plated seemed fine, seemed rich. He walked over to his desk and sat down in his leather chair with the carved rock armrests, which he had made himself. He looked at the key a moment, almost ensnared by the luscious gold that twinkled the overhead light, and then he plunged it into a lock in a drawer in front of him. He opened the drawer and found another key inside. He took that key, which was also gold but had a single rock implanted on its face, and then stood and walked over to his bookshelf. There were drawers under his collection of Encyclopedias (Diderot's editions, of course), and he opened the drawer three levels down from the first shelf of books. Inside there was a box, and inside the box there were cigars. He drew two from the box, smelt them both and then locked the box back in the drawer, locked the key back in the desk, and stuck the first golden key back onto the chest plate.

He was a very impatient man, and waiting for the sun to completely immerse itself behind the mountains seemed to take years. It would probably seem longer when you put into account the fact that everybody needed to go to sleep, so it wouldn't be until midnight before he could put the statues into the house. He was disgusted with the thought.

He struck a match and lit his cigar. He puffed on it and watched the smoke dance around his feet, which were firmly planted on the desk in front of him.

He closed his eyes for a moment. He remembered years ago, when the rocky floor behind the fireplace was once covered by mattresses, and how he allowed his sister to test the slide, and to test the ground just to see if the mattresses were springy enough. That one slide was interconnected with the Master Bedroom, the boys' room (which used to be his sister's room) and the locked room at the end of the hall, eleven doors down and to the right, which was his mother's. She was sick, too sick to get into the vent, but you had to take those kinds of precautions in cases of emergency; he always used to say that. He protected them. He showed them his secret because they were united.

He had smoked half his cigar when he opened his eyes. How much time had passed? He didn't know. He decided to go into his bedroom where Maggie was getting ready for bed, peeling off her makeup and smearing her face in cucumber cream, or whatever it was women decided to mush their faces in pursuit of beauty.

The statues all quivered when he passed. He chugged his cigar and walked up the grand staircase; he chugged his cigar and walked down the corridor; and he chugged his cigar while he walked into his room, staring at the empty night through his bay window.

"Are you coming to bed?" Maggie asked. She was sprawled under the sheets, with a ghastly green cream scratched over her face; her hair was tucked into an ugly bun that brushed the wall, and in this dim light, looked almost like blood.

"I have to bring the statues inside," he said.

"I wish you wouldn't smoke in here," she said.

"A wish I will forever deny, I can assure you," he responded, and harrumphed, a guttural noise that escaped through his Cuban.

"I see. Those statues are really beautiful. You're going to be all over the news tomorrow." She yawned. That was good, she needed to sleep. "Only fifty million dollars. That's something. I wouldn't have thought they'd give them to you so easily?"

"Sometimes, dear, business is easily negotiable."

Ten minutes later she was asleep.

Edwin walked outside, tossing his finished cigar (he could finish a cigar in less than two hours) into a trash can, dousing the ashes with his fingers first. He traveled along the driveway and kicked aside all four tarps, which were still tangled to the pallets. Every window in the house was dark, every pair of eyes closed for the night.

Edwin cracked his knuckles, almost afraid of what might happen if he tried to move all of them at once; he had been able to do two rather easily, but not four, no way. He held the necklace in his palm a moment, juggled its weight, and closed his eyes. He would try one step first. He imagined a foot stepping, a leg moving forward, and he clenched the stone necklace until its jagged surface almost plunged into his flesh. He heard four heavy thuds, and he opened his eyes. The statues had moved. Even David had changed his pose slightly, bringing the hand usually rested upon his left shoulder down to his chest, as if he was ready to turn. Each of their left legs had left the pallets, and had touched the driveway.

He was sweating; this was too unnerving. He could feel the vibrations of the necklace ring up his arm; he was also floating, hung in the air by some unseen string. Levitating felt spiritual, as if he was in direct connection with another world, and every vein throbbed in agreement. He closed his eyes and thought of a right foot stepping; he saw a leg moving forward in his mind.

Should I try to move them all? Should I risk it? What if a statue loses its balance and falls to the ground in a shattering crash? He let go of the stone and fell back to the ground. The questions stirred an eerie sensation that this possibility was truly inevitable. And if such tragedy were to occur, it would surely happen to the only statue that really mattered.

David mattered.

The other three didn't; he brought them back as part of the final transaction, watching the fear arouse the usually timid Ministry executives. He closed his eyes and lifted into the air again. He imagined bodies walking, one foot and then the other, in a synchronized pattern of mobility; he could hear the stone crunching as the statues' joints moved and crumbled loose marble into a fine powder. He turned his body and directed the three statues, his body floating in the air with them, as if their magnetism brought him as a prize to whatever lay behind the cargo doors in the house. This part would prove the toughest; he had done it before, but each time he felt the strain so hard that he lost connection with the stone and tumbled.

He imagined the statue bending at the waist, twisting rock from its abdomen in dusty swirls. He imagined the statue's arm gripping the handle at the bottom of the door, and ripping it upwards smoothly, so the alignment wouldn't come off the tracking. He could hear the statue bending, and he could hear the protestation of the stone as it cracked and split; he could hear its hard fingers splaying and reaching under the door, holding it in a palm lined by the ages; he could hear the door wheeling along the track as the statue stood upright, lifting the door as it rose; he could hear and smell the crushed rock as the statue's joints rotated. Edwin opened his eyes and fell back to the ground again. His temples pulsated, and he could barely see straight. So much was taken out of him that it took a moment before he could get up on all fours.

And there stood the statue, its shoulders broadly fanned against the light of the cargo bay, the garage door rolling back along the tracks without a hitch; he had done it, he had moved the statue like a human. He could smell the acrid dust, almost like gunpowder.

He smiled. Each of the three statues moved inside and waited. He inhaled the powdered air, the smell of pride, of success.

What would you be doing if you didn't have this necklace?

He hated having that thought; he hated it, because he knew where he'd be all right. *He'd* be the guy behind the fireplace following the rules, instead of the one making them. He stumbled back to the General, who was standing in his new pose, with his sling bearing hand by his chest, his head turned so it wasn't looking off to the side, but directly at Edwin as he approached.

"I have to be extra careful with you," he said. The statue didn't move. "If I'm this worn out moving three at a time, how will I feel if I move thirty through the mines?" He looked at David absently. "It'd probably kill me. I'd probably have to take you all down in installments." Edwin leaned over and looked up at the statue: "There are so many possibilities down there, and I hold but one." He touched the stone and felt its powerful pulse. "Power is my alliance. What is a werewolf against David?" Edwin grinned.

He closed his eyes, and David proceeded, walking in huge strides that seemingly crushed the asphalt beneath him.

Cole, curled in drapes, saw David's last step before disappearing around the house.

You can guess what the noises he heard were.

6

Edwin loved to whittle, though he practiced a much different art. He preferred a challenge, a challenge most artists attacked using chisels and hammers. Instead, Edwin sat cross-legged in the Great room with four rocks before him; there was no trace of a chisel, nor did Edwin hold a hammer in his hands. His sense of carving wasn't a physical obstacle at all, for Edwin had the only tool he needed hanging around his neck: a simple rock that somehow called upon stone to heed its master's desires.

Three of the rocks sitting in the square pattern before him he brought from the garden, which had been part of a crude retaining wall—one which he had fixed simply by backfilling the void with smaller rocks, rocks which were flung so hard into the wall, they almost became bigger upon contact. These three rocks floated in midair, following Krollup as he brought them around the house; the three of them must have weighed two tons, but Krollup wasn't sure, for he felt no weight. Perhaps in his mind, yes, but it was an unconscious pull. They floated through the cargo door; when Krollup pointed his thin finger, the rocks spun a 90-degree angle and raced down the corridor towards the Great room. There he set them, in a triangle. These rocks were fine for the other three statues, but he needed something fit for a king to base the very feet of his general. Perhaps he could find something, anything, in precious metals. Gold maybe, though the marble and gold would mismatch like a poor man's wardrobe, and what kind of respect would he be paying his general if he did that?

Marble—marble, of course, he would use the very rock the statue was cast from. Michelangelo would be proud to have seen such a display of his masterpiece. There was a statue in the room, standing atop a small pedestal, with his head looking down and his arms tucked behind his back, as if portraying a certain shame. That was no look he wanted to present in this fine room. Where on earth did he receive that particular statue anyway? It was a monstrosity, really. Who would commission such a work, handing a fine piece of marble to an artist who obviously felt disdains with the world, and showed his or her apprehension through a shoddy sculpture?

No, no, no. This statue must go, Krollup thought. It was a wonder he hadn't realized this earlier. He clutched the stone around his neck, and the ugly statue before him, with the permanent frown chiseled with obvious frustration, floated above its pedestal; both of its arms came from around its back, dust falling from broken figments, and both limbs spread across its chest like a mummy. Then the arms disappeared into the marble, becoming a part of the chest, as the torso bulged with the added girth. The same happened to its legs; they were both crunched upwards, and were swallowed into the statue's pelvis, creating two large stumps that malformed the chiseled stomach of the sculpture, giving it a crude gut.

"You can't frown at me," Krollup said, as he watched the down turned head lose its chin entirely as it entered the collarbone of the statue; the curly cue hair spread into fine pieces of marble that collapsed, and further pushed the rest of the shameful statue's head into its shoulders, until the statue became one large mound of marble. It hung in the air twirling for a moment, like a twisting asteroid in a gravity belt.

He set it down to complete the square of stones before him, and then he had sat with his legs crossed.

When he whittled, he was in a mode of complete concentration, almost as if he was meditating. The three rocks he had brought from the garden were quick fixes, really. Edwin lifted them one by one, and the tops of all three were scraped flat, the rocks that were discarded falling in heaps on the floor. On each of the rocks he either collapsed the middle to form an obscured 'X', without the cross, or he formed little posts along the middle, almost to mimic the Greek Parthenon. When he was finished, he set the rock down, and decided which statue would go on which pedestal.

The hunk of marble that had been a statue minutes before, sat on the floor in front of Edwin. With this one he was confused. Should he actually build a throne, or should he just call it a throne, and build a pedestal like the others?

He sat, looking at the marble, surrounded by a pile of rubble, unaware that Leo had used AL4 to get him off the hook on the wall, and had been staring through the fire at the mysterious breaking stones, unsure what was really happening, but sure Krollup was behind it. He muttered few coughs from the thin streams of smoke leaking through the brick stack, but Edwin didn't seem to hear; it didn't matter much anyway, because Leo didn't watch long. He had climbed back onto AL4's outstretched arms, which weren't in need of oiling at all.

Edwin got it, he knew what he would do. He lifted the marble into the air and carved into the stone by will alone, closing his eyes, imagining a picture—a foresight, some might have said, which Edwin would have agreed heartily with.

When the throne was finished, Edwin set the newly formed marble on the ground; its top and bottom flat. Doric columns supported the sides of the throne, and both the bottom and top were vague sketches of cornice. This was supported all around David's throne, yet it was the middle that so enthralled Edwin. It was exactly how he had imagined it, as if his mind had extracted a pencil and traced figures along the marble.

The throne had a frieze—a term any art historian would probably agree with—drawn into the stone using the mind's eye; an eye that based its vision on reality and practicality. The image between the columns was a perfect representation of statues drawing toward a mine; David was even carved into the stone, his height towering over the others, which included equestrian sculptures, and both male and female figures cast in the nude.

He set the massive statue upon its throne, and commanded it return to its original position. The hand bearing the sling took solitude on its shoulder, and its head cocked to the side.

Edwin cleaned up. The rubble littering the floor was crammed into a spun stone, and shoved into the corner of the room, as if it were an expensive abstract sculpture; it actually looked neat, marble coiled into limestone and granite, until the irregular ball of stone was just a lopsided lump of rock yarn.

Edwin was exhausted. He retired, awaiting the news of the next day.

7

Just as Edwin Krollup had been putting the finishing touches on the General's Throne, Cole had climbed into the vent in his closet. He wasn't going in all the way; he just wanted to hear if Krollup went to talk to the Bomber.

He crawled in an inch; he could feel the coolness of the tin on his fingertips.

This is ridiculous, go back to bed, come on, what do you think, you think you're going to hear some diabolical conversation, and from that conversation you'll derive the source of those noises, and the owner of that leg?

Of course not, he just thought he'd have a look is all.

But then again, he was pretty certain there was no leg.

And then he heard a clink, as if something sharp had tapped the sheet metal. No, no, he must have been hearing things…but there it was again, a sharp clink, and then a grunt, yes, he was sure he heard the grunt, a short groan followed quickly by another clink.

Cole made sure he could find the opening of the vent, so he could pull himself out if something did happen.

It was dark. Too dark, and that made matters worse. The clink was getting closer. It was like looking into a well, unsure really what might pop up from the depths.

Clink.

Grunt.

Slowly, but surely, in a pattern; there was a sting behind that grunt too, genuine pain, Cole could hear it. He wanted to call down into the vents.

He let go of the opening of the vent and slid down a couple of feet, watching the darkness swallow his legs.

Clink.

Grunt.

Closer. He wasn't sure if he wanted his legs out of sight. Cole was sweating, and he was sure, he didn't know why, but he was sure something was coming up the vent. He was right.

Something grabbed his leg.

Cole stifled a scream.

A head appeared out of the darkness. The dim light from the opening of the vent shone off the top of the head, and the hair that did dip down the sides of the face seemed to glisten some of the light also.

"Oh, Cole, please, my fingers hurt, my fingers, help me out."

That voice, that terrible voice, and Cole kicked out, squeezing his foot out of the thing's squirmy grasp, connecting with the thing's forehead, blocking the reflection of light momentarily.

A muffled grunt followed the crack, and the Robot Bomber lost his grip on the tin; there was a screech as the tips of his bone scratched down the vent and his body careened down the slide. Leo, who had used AL4 to hoist him up to the lip of the vent, pulled his screaming hands and tucked them against his chest, as he turned his body and slid on his back, slowing himself with his feet. His fingers were bleeding; he *had* severed most of the flesh on his fingertips when he frequently dug at the grout in the fireplace. He landed with a thud on the mice bones, kicking AL4 firmly on the metallic chest, knocking it backwards a few inches. Both of his hands seemed useless. *Where would you have gone anyway, Leo? Statues guard the exits.* Leo shuddered, and stared at the aquarium he had been working on, and looked into the mine.

Cole had stumbled back up the vent, shut the little door, crammed board games and knick-knacks against it, and jimmied a chair under the closet doorknob.

He sat on his bunk and watched the door for a moment.

He fell asleep with one thought: *the Bomber's finally trying to escape.*

CHAPTER 5

THE MINISTRY'S CHECKMATE

1

On Sunday morning Cole woke up with a start. He couldn't believe he actually fell asleep; there was a moment in the night when he thought he'd never go to bed again. He'd always have to man the closet door and make sure the bomber never left the vents. But he was just a twelve-year old boy, and even when the term "sweat it out" applied to him, he just found a way to weasel out. He was almost ashamed of himself.

As soon as he did wake up, he realized the chair was still jammed under the doorknob. A moment of relief swept over him—but what if the bomber *had* left, finding some way around the contraption, placing the chair back under the doorknob before escaping?

Cole wasn't sure what to think of this. He would have heard it. If the knocks outside in the courtyard were any indication, he would have heard something in his room easily...unless he *did* hear it, and *did* wake up, but was fed some serum that knocked him back out and cleared his memory of the night.

Then you wouldn't have remembered blocking the door with the chair, dummy.

What was he getting so worked up about anyway? The chair was still under the knob; it was pretty sturdy, Cole made sure of that, and the Bomber was a little man. He had tiny arms like bending cables, and the squirm he uttered when Cole kicked him invited a few speculations about his pain threshold, or lack thereof.

But that's a hefty fall, he thought.

Perhaps he was unconscious at the base of the wall, with bones poking into his rear. Or perhaps—

No, you can't think of that…not until there's reason to, at least.

Cole wiped the image of a bloody body from his mind. He turned to get out of bed, and James and Ricky were standing there below him, looking up at him with fixed glares.

"James, Ricky, what are you doing here?" Cole asked, rubbing his eyes, unsure what to think of this. He saw Jimmy standing in the doorway; he had a look about him, almost an arrogant look, which arched his eyebrows and put a sneer on his lips.

And then he understood; he understood what Jimmy had meant last night when he said Cole would see the looks on James and Ricky's faces when they found out their dads would be unemployed, because Jimmy had phoned them and told them. That was it, he was looking down into the eyes of hurt boys who had found the source of their problems, and were deliberating some type of revenge. Jimmy nodded his head and left the room completely. Was this some type of lesson?

Cole swallowed. He didn't want to leave his bed now, no way. Ricky's eyes were twitching, and Cole could tell that his hands were clenched.

"You know what Cole, you know what my dad said when I told him Krollup was gonna fire him? He said we were gonna have to move, change schools, leave this city entirely. You know why? Cause Krollup Industries owns this town, and once you're blacklisted, you gotta leave if you ever want to work again."

Cole shivered. He looked at Ricky and realized his eye was bruised. Very bruised, and it was beginning to swell. Ricky's father must have hit him when he realized it was his son's fault that he was going to lose his job. Cole understood *his* own eye was going to be bruised momentarily, so he just held his chest out, breathed in, and when he felt it appropriate, let the air out of his closed lips; there was a wheeze, and Cole threw the covers off him. His bare legs were covered in goosebumps.

"I'm sorry," he said, but saw that it didn't matter. The boys were beyond upset. James seemed to be holding his arm oddly, and Cole wondered if his father had been a little rough also.

He climbed down the ladder, not exactly afraid of what *these* two were going to do to him, but afraid of the awful look Jimmy had given him when he leaned against the doorframe, watching. It was almost as if he had discarded their relationship, as if he had completely thrown away his sanity. "*You'll understand what I mean when you see Ricky and James after they find out their daddy's are gonna be jobless,*" Jimmy had said last night before he left the room, presumably to use the telephone. This was all a portrayal of power, it must have been. Jimmy hadn't just said that last night to hurt him; he had said it to prove something. He had acquired some deep-rooted sense of Krollup's power and used it through Ricky and James. They wouldn't have found out until Monday, when both fathers would find pink slips and receive their final checks, but here they were, Ricky and James, waiting at the bottom of his bunk bed with snarled lips and twitching fists. Jimmy wanted Cole to understand the magnitude of Krollup's power, to see how many people it affected—this was some little game to Jimmy, and he didn't mind using his friends as pawns if it proved a point.

When Cole reached the bottom of the ladder he turned, shut his eyes, and apologized again.

Both boys punched Cole in the gut, and before they left, Ricky turned and said: "This is far from over, Cole. This is far from over."

Cole fell back on Jimmy's mattress and clutched his stomach. He was crying.

2

"In an unprecedented transaction earlier yesterday, the Florentine Ministry of Art had released news that Billionaire tycoon, Edwin Krollup, of Krollup Industries, purchased four statues from the preservation group for an unbelievable 50 million dollars. These were just preliminary details of course, but as of this morning there was a violent uproar in the streets of Florence, Rome, Milan and Venice, as the news of David's departure hit the streets."

"You see," Edwin Krollup said from his perch, his feet sitting atop the table in front of him, a Cuban cigar clenched between his teeth. "They're upset, but it's not me they're upset at. The Ministry is going to get what it deserves. If it were my decision, the statue wouldn't have left Florence, but folks are greedy; that was established. So whose fault is it that people are angry? Whose fault?"

Maggie shook her head and looked back at the television set, which was broadcasting the morning news. The man on the set was a balding gentleman with a pasty forehead—one which foundation seemed to intensify. He was sitting in front of a mural of some darkened city with lighted windows.

"It's about time the Ministry catches flak," Edwin said, and he grinned.

"I find it terribly offensive that Michelangelo's greatest work has left Italy. The art world here has lost an ideal work, and I'm ashamed a price tag has been put on our history," some young woman said, as a road team traveled the tight streets of Rome to gather opinions on the matter.

"It's an evil thought to think David is American now," said another, a young man with spectacles and terrible acne on his forehead.

"I don't care how the negotiations went behind closed doors, I just don't see the decision resolving itself that quickly—especially considering the drastic measures. David was a part of this country's history, and I don't believe the Ministry would allow such a civic treasure to leave for a few million dollars. Pride is worth much more than money anyway, isn't it? I think the American made the negotiations at gunpoint, and pushed the Ministry back into a corner. I'm sure the Mediterranean Preservation Coalition is plotting a way to get the statue back, no matter the cost. I'm hurt that this situation wasn't brought about democratically, asking the Italian people how they felt about losing such a piece of our history."

"So you think this should have been a national vote?" The reporter asked the woman, who was smoking and carrying a book bag over her shoulder.

"I think the Ministry should have known the outcome if it had been a national vote. Something must have been going on beyond our attention for the decision to be made in a day. I am greatly unhappy with the choice, and hope they put a tight lock around the Sistine Chapel, or we may lose it too."

"I'm not the bad guy, you see that, I'm not the bad guy. I was sure they'd pin it all on the rich man, I was sure they would," Edwin said when a commercial came on.

"Yes, but she does have a point Edwin, she really does. No matter how much you paid, that Ministry should have brought the business to the people's attention."

"For what? So they can hamper an art collection. Let me tell you Maggie, the Mediterranean has hogged the most beautiful art this world has ever produced for thousands of years, and it's about time we spread it around."

"But what good is David in our Great room? He should be on public display."

"How do you know that wasn't my plan?"

"Because your collection has always been private. You get mad when the boys stare at one of your statues for too long," Maggie said.

"I could purchase velvet ropes and turn the Great room into a display case, I could do that. Will that get you off my back?"

"I'm sorry Edwin, I just agree with some of these people."

"Sure you do," Edwin said, and put his cigar out on the table. "Sure you do."

"Hi and good morning, this is Roy Olson of Global 3. There has been shocking news in the art world this weekend. The beloved David has left Florence, and has justly retired its civic duty as city protector—a duty the statue shared with the mythical Hercules. David, a marble statue constructed by Michelangelo using his fabled Subtracted Method in the 16th century, has finally found a new home, after nearly 500 years in Italy. American business tycoon, Edwin Krollup, had apparently flown to Florence on Friday, spent Saturday negotiating with the Ministry, leaving later that night with the statue aboard his private jet. The outcry in Italy has been especially maddening; there are reported protests outside the Accademia in Florence, and riots have persisted, many of them started by the Preservation Coalition, who had sworn Italy would keep tight grips on Renaissance art."

"Look, look, the Italians are turning themselves into Visigoths, rioting, destroying their own cities. Absolutely fantastic. The tides have turned. First the Romans thought they could ransack Greece…pompous, pompous…but now, look, they're doing it amongst themselves. What next, are they going to hang from the Pantheon screaming bloody hell as they rip to shreds the artwork of Caravaggio?" Edwin was laughing.

"It is rather sad to see this display of temperament," the reporter said, watching the monitor as the camera panned helicopter views of the rioters, smashing windows, trying to penetrate police perimeters. Suddenly he put his finger to his earpiece and stayed still for a moment. Both his eyes lit up and he looked at the camera. "We have just had some breaking news folks. Apparently the Ministry has spoken to Italian press due to the advent of the rioters. The David they sold to Edwin Krollup was a copy, repeat, the statue they sold to Krollup was a fake. We'll go to the press conference the Ministry is holding about the subject."

Maggie looked at her husband. Fear enveloped her eyes.

"Hogwash," he finally said after a moment. "Preposterous." He breathed in and out rather heavily, pumping his fingers up and down his palm until all of his knuckles cracked.

The scene was unprofessionally cut to a grainy television image of three people sitting at a table with microphones in front of their faces—one man and two women. Edwin watched this with rage…that was the woman who was nearly beheaded by a statue's arm during the supposed negotiations, he thought. She looked much better when she was in control.

"The statue was a copy?" One reporter asked.

One of the women spoke: "Yes, we were looking out for the general interest of the Florentine people, and we thought they'd know this. We didn't expect such violence as an outcome; we thought people would question every possibility before disregarding rationality and smashing windows instead. Mr. Edwin Krollup wanted to purchase David, though he didn't refer to the original Michelangelo, so we supposed the copy would have sufficed. The statue he purchased was the David we have on display outside the *Palazzo della Signoria*; fortunately we were giving it a thorough cleaning from the elements, a procedure we have done at the Accademia, so he must have assumed it was the real thing."

"Suppose he hears the news. Are you willing to exchange the real thing for the copy you sold him for fifty million dollars?"

"The money, he told us, was a charitable contribution to the preservation of Renaissance art. No way would we even discuss the sale of the original David for a mere 50 million dollars. I hope the Florentine people hear this and behave accordingly. There is no need to riot. I hope our solidarity with the Preservation Coalition hasn't been altered any," the fellow in the pinstriped suit had said, all the while with a subtle smirk lining his lips.

The press conference was then terminated, and Roy Olson of Global 3 was back on the screen, with his terrible skin and shiny scalp tucked underneath wiry hair. "And there you have it: the entire debacle could have been avoided had the Florentine Ministry of Art disclosed details prior to the purchase, rather than wait out several violent riots and then proceed to blame Italian people for their lack of reason in the situation. Poor Edwin Krollup has blown millions of dollars on a replica intended as a receptacle of pigeon poop. At least it's obvious enough to notice that most of his fortune is squandered on his forged art collection, rather than his baseball club, which lost its 23rd straight game last night to cap the season—"

And the television was turned off. Though it wasn't exactly turned off. Edwin had thrown the remote control right through the screen, which imploded as a hissing smoke carried out of the back of the monitor.

"Hogwash," Edwin said.

"Charitable donation?" Maggie asked.

"Absolute hogwash. They've turned me into the weasel; they managed to do it, can you believe that. A copy. Sure, they're just trying to take the flak away from themselves. They wouldn't have dared sell me a copy. Not for that kind of money."

Maggie swallowed hard. "They seemed sincere, Edwin."

"They seemed sincere? Good for them. They won't sound so sincere when they realize what it is they've done. If they did sell me a copy, they will never sound sincere again." With this he stood up and walked towards the kitchen, ignoring the stupid David standing upon his throne in the Great room—a throne Edwin had meticulously created from scratch, mind you.

3

Sunday morning breakfasts had become tradition in the Krollup household. While the cooks slaved away in the kitchen, the family would meet in the dining room, Edwin sitting in his master chair (which he had purchased himself from a French collector three years ago, since it was believed Louis XIV once owned and sat in it while feasting). Though breakfast had become tradition, the family around the table was anything but traditional. At least Edwin Krollup believed so.

Meeting Maggie was a circumstantial result of the media, which had termed Mr. Krollup an eligible bachelor, but selfish, hoarding his wealth from the public in a distasteful mock that left him a lone Employer among thousands of the working class that were very different from him, and hated him because of it. His money became a shield almost, and through its will designed a ploy the media used to turn the people against him, because Edwin Krollup was a greedy tycoon that didn't care about the average American worker.

He couldn't have any of that negative publicity, so Edwin decided meeting a woman was a fresh start. Maggie hadn't been the first choice of course, but she had been the smartest. He realized that now. The fact that she was barely scraping by, and had two sons to care for, hadn't been a topic of conversation either, because her interest entailed *him*, Edwin the person, not the Gazillionaire. One date turned into two, and each successive date was better than the last; it wasn't until she mentioned her two boys that Edwin had any doubts, but he had truly fallen for her. Edwin would confess, if he knew he were anonymous that is (for a man with such power didn't extend to others any of his weaknesses), that he truly loved Maggie, or Margery, or, though he hated the name, Margaret; that he loved her red hair, and the way she was always interested in his day; and most importantly, how she would ask about his mother. He would answer that her death was tragic, but her life was great, and that would be the end of it.

Yes, this family was anything but traditional, but he could sense something familiar about it. Ever since he met the two boys, he could sense something. He remembered watching his father and mother, when they were happy, and when his father was mad. Edwin's mother never really reacted, because she was always too afraid to reach that far. But if she ever did get mad, the things she said got her in big trouble with his father, and that was when a young Edwin had to shut his bedroom door and plug his ears, listen to his old records, or sing really loudly, despite what was happening on the other side of his door. When his little sister was born, he had to look after her too, and that became a task in and of itself. Thinking up lies to explain why they had to hide, why they had to plug their ears, or pretend the yelling they were hearing was coming from the little Zenith in the family room, and not from their mother as dad pushed her around.

And then he had gone down the mines, and everything changed.

He remembered wishing he could buy his mom a beautiful gold necklace with a diamond on it, like the one she had seen at the store, the one she had gawked over. He could never afford that for her, but standing there, and wishing as hard as he could had somehow brought forth the belief that, yes, there was the slight chance that he could get it for her. He didn't know where the thought came from, but he had rushed outside and had wished again, holding that oddly inviting stone around his neck, and the ground in front of him had split, secreting a nugget, a single gold nugget, which landed in his hand.

He knew he had something special, that didn't take a genius, but—

But his father had gone too far one night; he had hit his mother and broken her jaw, taking off in the old Ford, smoking his cigarettes, holding his swollen knuckles against his chest as he steered.

Did you want the stones to fall?

It was merely coincidence, he said to himself, just a coincidence.

Edwin was scared that Maggie's two boys might just have that same wish for him. He had married their mother, and in doing so, had taken their beloved father's place. It was a fear based on his childhood, just as much as it was based on impracticality.

Edwin held the same stone he believed aided his father's death, and hid it from both boys wishing neither would ever find out about it. If life was a chain built on coincidences, then he had lived afraid of the possibility that his end would be of another's doing.

For the first time in his life since he had received the stone, Edwin Krollup was paranoid.

4

On this Sunday though, breakfast was rather tense. Edwin sat in his Louis XIV chair contemplating what to do to the stupid Ministry if the statue was indeed a fake; he couldn't believe it, because *they* saw what he was capable of, and who's to say he wouldn't return for round two? That was their mistake.

Maggie ushered Jimmy into his seat, making sure he understood the mood Edwin was in, and in doing so, reminded Jimmy not to bother him. Jimmy nodded and sat down, playing with the fork in front of him. Ricky and James left after they had each punched Cole in the gut, escorted out by Jimmy, who hadn't scolded them in any way, but said goodbye in a way that implied he would never see them again. Jimmy didn't care in the least. He realized what this could muster for his reputation at school. Ricky and James would talk, and Jimmy could use their plight to acknowledge his potential power.

"Where's Cole?" Maggie asked, as they waited for breakfast to be served.

Edwin gave her an absent look.

Jimmy shrugged. "He was awake when I went in the room."

"Do you wanna get him? Food's almost ready. It's not like him to miss breakfast."

Jimmy hesitated. He didn't want to have to get him, pick him up from whatever fit he was throwing, because there were going to be questions. He knew that much, but these questions were going to be difficult to answer. He didn't want to say, "I'm making an example out of you Cole, so the other kids at school realize one thing about me. That I mean business, that I'm like the mob. If you make me mad, I don't just take you down, I take down your entire family. I got Ricky and James's daddy's fired, so don't think any of you are an exception." That wouldn't work, because Cole was still living under an old rule, one that should have died when their old man croaked. All of his talk of morality seemed lopsided anyway. Their dad smoked, he died, end of story. Talk of morality should have stopped there, but Cole hadn't let it; he let it go on and on and on, until he got fatter and lost his dignity. That was his fault, Jimmy couldn't do a thing about it anymore.

And just as Jimmy stood up to get his younger brother of three minutes, Cole walked through the door. His cheeks were red and his eyelids swollen. For a moment Jimmy felt terrible; this *was* all his fault. He had sent the thugs on his brother, *his* flesh and blood...but then the message behind this became clear. Nobody was safe from his wrath.

"Cole, are you okay, you look like you've been crying?" Maggie got up to rub his back.

Cole gave Jimmy an awful look, an accusing look that brought the pain back in Jimmy's chest. "I'll tell her about the cigarettes, I swear," that thought seemed to say, but Cole only sat down.

"Nothing mom, I just got some dust in my eyes, had to rub it out."

The food was served.

Edwin knew one thing. He was going to phone the stupid Ministry, and make sure the statue was a fake before he wished a load of stones fall on them.

5

"Is it true?" Edwin asked, after going through countless receptionists, who left him on hold with the sound of boring piano music. He stood in front of the David perched upon the throne he had whittled just last night, with the frieze carving of the statues invading the mines. He was studying the statue, looking for any imperfections; anything that may have indicated it was a fake.

"Who is this, please?" A woman asked, the one that had done most of the talking during the press conference.

"Who do you think? It's Edwin Krollup. Now I want a straight answer from you thugs, and I want it now. Were you telling the truth at your stupid little press conference, or were you just trying to calm the rioters? Be careful, your answer determines your future."

"I don't know how to answer that, Mr. Krollup. We usually don't comply with threats."

"Threats? Who said anything about threats? I want the truth. I want you to remember that no matter what, whatever you say right now isn't going to make you a hero."

"A hero, Mr. Krollup? We, and most notably I, don't really care what it is you think. Let me ask you a question. Didn't you find it entirely odd that we let go of such an invaluable statue after only a couple of hours of, what did they call it on the news, negotiating? The only negotiations involved in that building were between you and your rig team, on whether or not you should set up explosives on such and such statues. The very fact that you rigged the Accademia, and proceeded to destroy timeless pieces of art during your so-called negotiations should be answer enough, Mr. Krollup." She had a horribly sarcastic voice, one she didn't bother sharing with him when he had been standing before her. Rigged statues? Preposterous.

"Perhaps your precious statues weren't rigged Miss?"

"Mrs. Lorenzo."

"Perhaps your statues weren't rigged, Mrs. Lorenzo. Perhaps I moved them with magic. You ever thought of that? Did you ever begin to think that I am the world's greatest magician, and by waving my arm, I made a statue walk onto an airplane without the aid of forklift or crane?"

"Ridiculous."

"Is it? Or are you just making up excuses so you know that when this is over, nothing will happen to you."

"I never saw a statue walk."

"I watched you follow the statues as they boarded the truck to the airport. I saw your jaws drop. That wasn't merely a rigged trick. No, what you witnessed was pure magic, and don't think for a second that more damage can't be done to your precious art preservation, Mrs. Lorenzo."

"You are threatening us, are you not, Mr. Krollup?" She sounded afraid.

"All I want to know, Mrs. Lorenzo, is whether or not I returned home with the real thing."

There was a moment of silence. Edwin looked over the statue before him, looked at the perfect torso, the sculpted thighs, the milky complexion of the stone. Michelangelo hadn't signed it anywhere, or he would have known, yes he would. That would have made it easier. But nothing.

"There was a lot of damage done to the Accademia, Mr. Krollup."

"What does that have to do with my question?"

"Fifty million dollars is a lot of money, but fixing old architecture is a costly process in ensuring everything goes right. Fifty million dollars is too little to buy our history, Mr. Krollup. David has a civic responsibility in Florence, just as you have a responsibility at work. You're a financial representation of what your employees strive to work for; David is a representation of everything people want to become. He is a hero. He is our protector, and if you think I'm, we, the Ministry of Art, would just hand it over like that, well, you must have been mistaken. Do you understand? We took your money as, I guess you could call it a donation, and gave you those four statues as representation of the expenditure. Both sides go home with something, you understand, right?"

Edwin had hung up the phone and didn't hear this last part. He didn't care. Just as she had gone into that spiel about David being the protector, the Hero, well, he knew what she was leading up to, and he lost it, he literally lost it. He crushed the phone in his hand, its innards spilling on the carpet around his feet.

He had a fake, standing in front of him, looking off to the side as if it were the real thing. No, he could not have that, so he twisted the stupid statue's head until it looked right, not left, and he sculpted a sneer on David's face; he heard marble grind into dust as the brow of the mighty statue furrowed, and the upper lip snarled, exposing rough marble beneath.

You're only angry because they outsmarted you, he thought. *The fact that it's a fake doesn't hinder its mission any, does it?*

Edwin stood still for a moment, looking at the newly posed David, his David, a copy nonetheless, but *his* General. "It will always be my David against the wolves' Goliath, forgery or not," he simply said, trying hard not to scream.

When he felt the anger pass and was more or less clear headed, Edwin thought about the Ministry, and he thought about the woman he had talked to, how sure she looked during the press conference. He thought about the Accademia, and the statues, the artwork, the architecture around Florence; he thought about all of this and he massaged the stone around his neck. He thought about stones falling, tumbling from a hillside, and he thought about each member of the Ministry, picturing each face as he remembered them, behind windshields as they drove, or wincing as the sun got in their eyes. He thought about stones falling towards them, shattering the trees along their path, denting the earth.

You're too far away, you know that right?

But it worked when I was a kid, when I wanted daddy to get hurt for hitting mom.

That was just miles from your house, a short bike ride, this is thousands of miles away. A long plane trip. Plus, you don't know if dad was your fault. If you did, you wouldn't be getting help from the head doctor.

That was true. He didn't know. He let go of the stone.

6

Three days later, Mrs. Lorenzo of the Ministry of Art in Florence, got in a car accident. Apparently a boulder appeared out of nowhere in the middle of the road, splitting the asphalt—or so she had told authorities—and before she could swerve to miss it, the entire front end of her car wrapped itself around the rock's hulk like rigid embracing arms.

Nothing is a coincidence.

CHAPTER 6

Head Doctor's Spell

1

On the same Monday Cole's nickname would turn from *Cone* to Ratboy, Edwin Krollup had gone downtown to a very chic building with a glass foyer. He had gotten on the elevator and gone up twenty-five floors; those in the elevator with him heckled Edwin in their minds, because he, the giant Krollup of Krollup Industries, had been swindled for fifty million dollars. Edwin had ignored their eyes on his back, and jumped from one foot to the other, hoping for his stupid floor so he could get off. When the time came, he exited, and just as the doors closed behind him he heard them, all of them, either laughing or jokingly referring to him as the *Million-Dollar Clone*. Bottom feeders, he thought, nothing but bottom feeders. If he wanted to, he could buy this entire building complex and fire everybody from floors twenty-six and up, that was all it took, and then who would be laughing?

He walked towards a plate-glass door with the words, Innis Psychology, stenciled in a fine gold. There was lush foliage on either sides of the door. Edwin could smell dirt and dew and he loved it; he loved coming here. It was a load off his chest; he just felt lighter.

He walked into a nice lobby, which sat a receptionist, more foliage and a caged parrot.

The desk behind which the receptionist sat—a lovely blond with great big blue eyes—was made of glass also, and the name Innis was screwed boldly in the middle, using chrome lettering that glistened the overhead light. Edwin walked over to her.

"Mr. Krollup, so lovely to see you again. He'll be just a moment."

Edwin smiled, looking for anything behind her eyes, looking to see if she'd watched the news yesterday—and today, for David the clone was a popular topic to discuss—but she only looked down and searched through a sheaf of paper. He went and sat down in a plush chair in front of a large mahogany table with magazines on it. He opened his jacket and took out a cigar and lit it. He smoked it for a minute, and then he put it out in the ashtray and placed it back in his jacket.

Dr. Innis opened his door and peeked his head out. "Ahh, Edwin, I thought I heard you. Come right in. This is quite a surprise, you usually call."

Edwin stood and shook the doctor's hand.

When he closed the door he said, "I guess I shouldn't say a surprise, should I? With all the news I've been hearing, you're probably in distress. You should have your lawyers handle this, that's what I think. It doesn't seem particularly right for a people to rob anybody of such a significant amount of money and give them second class goods in return."

Edwin smiled. Dr. Innis was on his side, after all.

He sat down in the leather chair opposite Dr. Innis's huge desk, with all its psychological remnants littered about. The office was beautiful, to say the least. Its walls were just windows, murals of the skyline from twenty-five stories up, and there stood two large bookcases, just as Edwin had in his own office. "For now, Dr. Innis, we'll just assume the thugs said they sold me a fake to calm the rioters. It keeps me at ease."

"As it should. So what can I do for you?"

Edwin shifted, and for a moment he thought he was going to be sick. It was weird telling another grown man he was having fears and doubts about young boys, but possess them he did. "I didn't come here about the statue. For now the entire episode is a bad dream."

"Have you talked to your lawyers?"

"I don't want to. They've called me countless times, but I'd rather let it be, until everything boils down. That's the last thing I want, reporters coming down my throat even more. They started knocking on my gate yesterday, but most left for more exciting coverage. The ones that stayed are going to get mighty bored soon."

"They didn't follow you here? That's surprising."

"I can be quite sneaky."

"I see that," Dr. Innis said.

"I know this sounds weird, especially coming from me, but I suspect something from those two boys."

"Jimmy and Cole?"

"Yes. On Saturday my guard told me the two were trying to get into my office. You know how careful I am about privacy. Actually, this morning at breakfast Jimmy asked·me if he could try one of my cigars."

"This strikes you as odd?"

"Of course it does. One minute the boy detests me, and the next he wants to bond. Odd."

"Perhaps he's just looking to forget the past and move forward. Kids are like that you know. He may hold on to memories of his father, but what good do memories pose in the real world? Do they help him with schoolwork? Do they help him better understand the world? He wants his mother to be happy, sees that she is, and understands it's his turn."

Edwin cocked his eye.

"You still feel threatened, don't you?"

Edwin tensed, gripping both arms of the chair as if they helped to keep him from falling. "Why else would they want to get into my office? I'm not an idiot, I know they want to find the mines, but why?"

"Curiosity. Boy angst, boredom, who knows? There's nothing to feel threatened about."

"Isn't there? I'm new territory, or should I say, I'm a predator on *their* territory. I've thought about this, you know. What if their feelings for me mark an excuse that they're looking out for their mother's best interests? I am a stepparent, and I know the two were close to their father."

"I see," Dr. Innis said. "This paranoia all roots back to your initial problem. I believe we have yet to uncover certain truths here Edwin, and I'm sure you knew that. I've researched archived newspapers, and every article I've come across theorizing possibilities about your father's death have all ranged from freak rock slides to drunk driving. Nothing speculates your participation in any way, or the chance any second party could ever be involved."

"They're just speculations though. I wanted him to die, I wanted him to suffer after I saw what he had done to my mother."

"Yes, but that ranges into something paranormal, something we can't reach by merely talking about it. I've told you Edwin, if you want your minds full cooperation, you have to give me permission to hypnotize you."

Edwin stood up and blatantly blurted, "NO! What have I said about that? I don't trust the entire physics behind it. I don't want to know what you can, and can't open. End of discussion."

"Sit down Edwin. Please. I'm not asking just so I can make you a party favor. Do you think I'd actually trigger something in you that'll make you sing the national anthem every time you hear somebody cough, is that what you think? I'm a professional, not a carnival act. I wouldn't be where I am right now if I did such things."

Edwin sat down and crossed his legs. "No, there are other things I'd rather not tell."

"Such as?"

"That's none of your business Innis, end of discussion."

"Okay, okay, I get it. You've got your secrets, so do I, but just because I present hypnosis to your case, doesn't mean I want to pry at any of them for my own well being. Did you know that if I were to hypnotize you right now, I could mentally take you back to the exact minute when your father died in the crash?"

Edwin nodded.

"You wouldn't merely be discussing some past feelings you may or may not have had. This would be the real thing. For that one moment you'll be a little boy again, holding your mother as you wait for the paramedics, paramedics you called yourself, right? You could explain to me the coincidence of your wish and your father's death, not from your mind as it stands now, tainted by time, but through a mind that had yet to comprehend what was actually happening." Dr. Innis put his feet up on the desk in front of him and smiled. "Sounds cosmic, doesn't it?"

Edwin nodded. He was plagued by his own questions though, because this Head Doctor knew nothing of the stone round his neck. For now, his wish and his father's death had been nothing but coincidence, yet he had the necklace, and if he held it and wished his father was hit by stones, didn't that mean it would happen? Didn't it? If he could move statues, didn't that mean he could hope an avalanche of rock bury his father's old Ford pickup as the booze wore off and his knuckles ached? It did, but Edwin was scared Dr. Innis would find this out through hypnosis, and maybe even learn of its true powers, its true potentials and try to take it as his own while he was still zoned out.

But it would be nice to know for sure, wouldn't it? You've been living all these years with your father's death on your mind, on your hands—it's even made you paranoid of your spying stepsons. Wouldn't it be nice to know that it wasn't your fault, that it was some type of cosmic coincidence? Maybe you wouldn't be so edgy around the boys anymore, covering the necklace as if they've never seen the ugly thing before. Your rules have made them rebellious, not their desire to overthrow you in their mother's best interest.

Edwin smiled at this last thought, and Dr. Innis inched forward on his seat.

"You may have cracked me, Dr. Innis, and that's a feat not easily achieved with Edwin Krollup."

"Excellent. It's taken a long time, but you'll thank me in the end Edwin, trust me there, you'll thank me in the end." He stood up and started walking toward the tycoon.

"Hold on a moment there, doc. I want to get something straight with you before you dissect my brain. I want to know what you ask me."

"Of course."

"No, I want actual, physical proof of our conversation while I'm out."

Dr. Innis fell back in his seat, and the air let out of the cushion in a long growl. He had an odd look on his face.

"I want you to record the conversation. I know you types have voice recorders somewhere. You have to, I suppose. It's faster than taking notes. I want you to tape me speaking, and I want to hear it when you bring me back to. I know this sounds uptight doctor, but trust is hard to come by."

"There's no need to be untrustworthy Edwin. Believe me, some of the stuff you've told me over the years has become rather contrary to your PR image. I have information that could strip you of your demeaning authority. Stuff I could sell to the media to aid their ongoing crusade to bring you down. But have I? Have I once blabbed my mouth any? Personally, I'm hurt you would suggest trust issues between us, when I am clearly bound by confidentiality agreements.

"It's your choice now, Edwin, whether or not you want to be hypnotized, because you've certainly made me believe the entire method is a liability. I have many clients, Edwin, and many of them are very rich, and yet I've hypnotized *them*. You know what, maybe we can video this too, then. I could phone and order a camcorder, or call security to borrow a surveillance cam from the elevator, tell them my client has trust issues with me, will that work?"

Edwin could tell he hit a sour chord, and rather than drag this argument on any longer, he just agreed with the heated doctor, just as the heated doctor knew he would.

"Good. I'll show you my voice recorder." Dr. Innis was smiling in his head as he grabbed the Sony recorder, because he *knew* his rant would persuade Edwin that he was generally hurt. He knew Edwin wouldn't need to videotape the episode if he had to go through the trouble of actually ordering a camcorder. Because time was money.

He showed Edwin the recorder, and turned it in his hands as if proving to him it wasn't a fake in any way. Edwin didn't appreciate the sarcasm.

Dr. Innis stood and held his hand out; he was holding a gold necklace with a pendant on the end. "Follow this, Edwin, follow it as it sways from side to side. Follow it until you become it, see it until it blurs and becomes you; reach for it with your mind. Can you feel it in your temples? Good, good."

Edwin's head fell forward.

And Dr. Innis smiled.

2

Dr. Innis was a psychotherapist, but his intentions ranged far from helping his patients change some weird neuroses. He made a great living; he charged $450 an hour, but he was greedy, and had made terrible mistakes with women in his time. He had five ex-wives, all of whom hit him up very hard in their respective divorces. In the end he had given up three houses, four cars, and one kid, though he preferred to say he missed the Porsche the most. Regretfully he had to fork over five alimony payments until the five decide to remarry, but that doesn't seem hopeful. Out of spite, each of the five had formed a support group together that meant to rob him blind of every penny he ever made; and in doing so, they formed a pact that none of them would ever marry while he was still breathing. Dr. Robert Innis was in trouble.

He had to do something, anything to get more cash. And then he got it, this idea, out of the blue. He would get more money from clients without their ever knowing about it. Hypnosis became his ally, at least on the clients who allowed themselves to be hypnotized—there were some that couldn't, or didn't want to. He learned of safe combinations, security alarms, PIN numbers, credit card numbers, and he had his cousin, who became his second ally, disguise himself and reap the information he was given. Dr. Innis had a client who was a famous actress, and she agreed to a hypnosis session to uncover her brutal need for plastic surgery. Suffice it to say, the information he got from her paid for a three-week vacation in the Bahamas at a luxury resort.

Edwin Krollup was by far his most lucrative client. He was a billionaire, and he was willing to lay it on the line and spill his problems. That was good because it developed trust. Yet, he hadn't developed the *right* trust, for Edwin never let the good doctor bring out the necklace with the pendant. A client like Edwin meant patience, and Robert Innis knew that. He hadn't let Edwin's refusals get to him, because he had many other people to milk money from. But his baby, his main course was Krollup, and today was the happiest day of his life. He knew Edwin was smart, and he knew Edwin would have ultimatums, but Innis already had each of his requests countered. For instance, he had recorded many of their conversations over the last couple of years; he had kept the tapes, and he could use them easily, just by recording that one question Krollup expected him to ask: "what happened with your father?" Everything else was prerecorded. Dr. Innis had a more important question he'd wanted answered for a long time; he was sure the general public wouldn't mind hearing the answer either. "Why did you build on the mines? I mean, what's so special about some old, haunted mines?"

He had never gathered the courage to ask before, because he knew what a guy like Krollup would say: "None of your business." But now that he had the permission to put him under his spell, he could find out anything. About the mines, about his bank account…but now Innis only wanted to hear about the mines. He was fascinated by them, by the idea of building a mansion on top of them. "Tell me, Edwin, what happened to your father to make you believe you killed him?"

The voice recorder was rolling.

Edwin had just rolled his eyes under his lids and mumbled. "He hit my mom, he hit her, and I wanted him to get hit too. I did. I wished it, and then we got the call, we got the call from the police that they found his truck under the rocks, and I think I smiled."

3

Just as the surface of Edwin's mind thought about his father's death and answered Dr. Innis, another part, a much deeper part, thought of the mines, about the boarded up entrance with the "NO TRESPASSING" sign painted on; and the boys, the older boys huddled around him in a full circle, urging him to go in, forcing him because he was a baby if he didn't, a big baby—

—*and they looked down at me, I remember; they were staring at me with their big eyes, eyes I thought were intelligent because they were a couple of years older. They wanted me to go in, and I knew there was no way out of it, just as I knew they would hit me if I didn't squeeze between the planks. "Why don't you guys go in then?" I asked, I remember, and they just looked at me as if I'd said the stupidest thing in the world.*

"What do you mean?" One of them asked, an ugly one with a huge mole under his eye. "We already did. It's your turn, think of it as your initiation into our gang." *I remembered he winked at his friends, and then shoved me towards the planks over the entrance, a gaping hole with rocks that looked like teeth; it was like a mouth, that was it, and I was afraid. Afraid I would never see my mom or sister again; afraid that if I got holes in my pants, my dad would hit me and yell at me because pants weren't free, nothing was free, medical aid wasn't free, but he'd hit me anyway.*

"It's haunted," I screamed, but there was no letting up, their little circle, with their hands clasped kept me inside, kept me within so they could all just stare down at me, give me their evil eyes.

"No it ain't, it's just closed for renovations," another boy said, and I remember he had a snarled upper lip, and his hair was done up with mousse until his high bangs looked like a Hershey Kiss; he thought he was Elvis Presley,

*and I wanted to laugh, but knew he'd beat me if I did, he just had that look
about him.*

*I couldn't stop thinking about my dad. These boys didn't matter, they were
just bullies. I must have been walking the wrong way home, and they saw me and
thought they'd have a grand old time fishing me in the mines until dinner. But
it was dad, he was the one I was worried about, because I knew I wasn't going
to be home in time for dinner, and I remember he asked me to come home quick
to pick up some change to buy milk at the store, that was it, he needed milk, and
I was worried these bullies would never let me go. No milk meant dinner would
be late, and my dad wouldn't have that. He'd skin me alive, a punishment fifty
million times worse than anything these guys could ever hand out, but I wouldn't
let them know that because I didn't want a basis of comparison.*

*I remembered thinking, the sooner I get this over with, the sooner I get home,
and the sooner I get the milk—*

(— "Edwin, are you going to want to listen to this conversation on
tape?"—)

*I didn't care about ripping my pants anymore, because I could just hide them
in the closet, nobody would have to know, dad wouldn't bother with the twenty
questions because his mind would be on dinner, and the beer that went with it.
I told them I would, and they kind of gave me this weird look, like I agreed to
die for them or something; I didn't like that look. The Elvis guy gave me a snarl
of his upper lip and patted me on the back.* "Go then little guy, show us you're
worthy. If you're lying, we'll have to bloody your lip." *He laughed, and I
wanted to smash him one, him and his blue suede shoes, but he only pushed me
out of the huddle and I was standing before the planks. They looked ancient,
the outermost pieces of wood rotting as the teeth of rock hung over them; the
NO TRESPASSING sign had faded, and the red paint had chipped. There was
graffiti on a broken board that read **R.I.P AUGER**. I could have pulled the
wood and it would have broken away, it looked that weak, but I thought better
of it, I thought I'd leave it alone because something inside me told me not to touch
it, not to mess with it. I shouldn't have listened to that voice, because then I might
have had light, but I did listen, and I did squeeze between a moldy 2x4 and a
damp sheet of plywood, watching the thin line of sunlight turn into a laser that
quickly disappeared against a bed of rock—*

(— "Alright. Well I have really bad news."—)

*I was standing in the room that would soon be behind my fireplace, but I
didn't have that thought; I was just a twelve year old boy, trying to get this over
with so the Junior High kids wouldn't beat me up. That was all. This was just a
quick little task, for whatever reason those boys wanted me to come in for; that
was it, the end. I was just going to walk in a distance and then turn back, make
sure I never lost that small beam of light, because that was all the light I had. I*

kept turning back to find it, turning back to make sure I knew how to get out. I could still hear those bullies yelling at me from behind the planks, and for some reason I knew they had never been inside the Mines of the Dead, they were just trying to make some younger kid face the dark and the ghosts. They were wussies too, but were bigger, and therefore had all the power to do the pushing, but I was fed up. Soon I would grow up and I would take care of all of them. With that thought I heard something, and it wasn't the boys on the other side of the planks. It came from the darkness, deep within, and I remember the gooseflesh I had, the way my skin bubbled up. I didn't know what it was, but it sounded like a howl, a long deep howl. I wanted to turn around and run back to the entrance, break out of the rotten wood and pummel the bullies over as I sprinted home, forgetting that noise, forgetting the mines, thinking only about the milk.

But something about the howl drew me in further. I remember that. I didn't think about ghosts, nor did I think about Kenneth Auger, because I wasn't that type of kid; the real scary things in life happened inside the home, when you had to turn on your record player real loud and shut your door so you couldn't hear the bad things; scary wasn't a sheet with two holes cut in it for eyes, because that was fake, that was why I never got scared at Vincent Price movies. I was scared if I got home late from school when I was supposed to get milk.

And that howl reminded me of my mom, that was it, it was like mom's voice when she was scared, when I had to shut my door and pretend other things were happening. I started running towards the noise, for some reason I thought it was the best thing to do. I didn't think about anything else; the light behind me didn't matter at the moment, because I heard something that I was sure had to be my mom, and I thought she was getting hurt, badly this time, so badly that her voice was caught in these mines, and I had to get to her and save her.

And then I fell.

I was so stupid. A minute passed and nothing. I sat up, feeling dizzy, and I looked every which way, in front of me, behind me, to my sides, but nothing. Everything was black. I had left the rotten planks up because some part of me suggested I do so; I never thought that I may lose my light, that I may wander too far and forget which direction was which. That was why those kids picked on me: because I was an idiot.

I got up and felt around me. I felt rock to my sides. I realized my ankle sort of hurt. I must have fallen on it hard.

Which way should I go? Which way was the sunlight? I tried to hear the boys. I tried to hear their horrible voices, but nothing. Only the slight sound of water and the sound of darkness, which I knew didn't make sense, but does when you're lost in black, and you begin to think you hear things. I thought I heard my dad yelling at me in the distance, something about dirt, but I couldn't really tell.

I decided to pick a direction. I thought in a way luck would help me out. I turned and ran. It had to be the right way or I would have stammered, I would have second guessed myself and decided to turn around, but I didn't, I just ran hoping to see the small beam in front of me any second. I couldn't wait to see their faces, every one of those stupid Junior High boys, because I knew they had never crossed the planks. I knew that just as much as I knew—

I was running short of breath. This rarely happened when I ran, no way, because I wasn't an old man, I could run a long distance without puking, but it was true, I was gasping for air.

A voice inside me told me to cover my mouth, but I didn't understand it. The air tasted rancid though, as if it were sour, as if I was in the stomach of the mines and its acid was trying to break me apart from the insides. And all of a sudden I thought about the entrance, about the teeth around the lip of the rock, and for a moment I thought that maybe this entire tunnel was the monster's throat, that those bullies were ritualistically feeding me to this rock beast.

Run. Cover your mouth and run.

I ran.

I ran because I was out of air and it seemed like the right thing to do. I didn't care if I ran into the broadside of a rock face, as long as I didn't have to taste this place, feel it reaching down my throat to block my airway. I ran until my legs were strings. I didn't care. I couldn't stop. Days could have passed. Months even, but that didn't matter. Thoughts of milk didn't matter, because I knew, for some reason, that these mines were going to be the end of me.

Then I saw a small speck of light. I ran there, and I kept running, but that small speck seemed to float farther away. Even when I should have been closer, it seemed farther. I hated my eyes, and even when I left the mines and I was outside, all I could see was that small speck of light in front me.

4

Dr. Innis stood by the window, looking out at the streets below. A minute and a half had passed since Edwin had given him an answer about his dead father, but it wasn't enough. For a moment he was almost scared that he would have to wait for another time, that he might have lost his golden chance to find out the secrets of the mines, because he had too little on tape about the man's dead father, and if he used information from older tapes, it would seem rather redundant.

He looked at the hunkered billionaire. Did it really matter? That was the ultimate question. Would he really wake up and demand to hear the entire boring conversation? Or would he rush off like he did every other day? That was a gamble, and it was also a gamble to assume he could make Krollup believe he hadn't been hypnotized, because he had seen Krollup peer up at the clock and make sure what time it was before he was put under the spell. Of course he could change all the clocks back an hour or so when he was done, but that wouldn't account for the actual time on Edwin's wristwatch, or any other clock and watch in the natural world outside this office.

Innis grunted and looked at the voice recorder.

"I think I'll take a chance here. I can do one of two things. I can assume he'll only want to listen to a small portion of the tape before he leaves, because, well, he's rich, and time is money. Or I can take the tape out and pull the strip into tangles and rip it. That way I can blame it on the recorder, say it went haywire, lost everything. Maybe even give me a chance to hypnotize him again. But both deal with chances."

He thought about this for a moment, watching the traffic beneath him.

A sudden thought occurred to him. "I can ask him. He's under my spell. I can ask him, and even make him do the one I desire. It's brilliant."

He walked over to Edwin, who was still trapped in a huddle of Junior High boys outside the mines. "Edwin, are you going to want to listen to this conversation on tape?"

Edwin nodded and said "yes."

Good. "Alright. Well I have really bad news. My recorder is outdated; it ruined the tape at the end of our conversation, okay, so everything we talked about got erased. You have to remember to trust me Edwin, because I didn't mean for this to happen. It was just sort of bad luck."

Edwin nodded. "Bad luck."

Good, good. He sat on the edge of his desk and looked at Edwin's head, which had collapsed forward. He wanted very badly to reach into that coat and take the rich man's wallet, leaf through the sheaf of bills, but thought better of it; he wanted the man's trust. That way, he would never become a suspect if anything ever did go wrong.

"Edwin, I want you to agree with me about something here, okay?" The man under the spell nodded. "Good. I want you to agree about certain truths here. For one, pretend you're under oath. Pretend I'm a lawyer asking you questions. You can't lie, especially if this lawyer wants to know about your secrets. I know you have them, you said so yourself, but you have to believe that I'm doing good for you, getting these ugly secrets off your chest, letting you breathe a bit. Secondly, I want you to remember nothing of this conversation. Nothing at all. I know your mind is probably elsewhere right now anyway, but you have to remember this conversation was always about your father, even though it isn't. You understand?"

Edwin nodded and sort of mumbled. He had just squeezed through the planks and was standing inside the mine.

"Good. Tell me something Edwin. Tell me about the mines, when did you first go near them, or in them?"

Edwin shifted and his eyes moved underneath his closed lids. "When I was a kid there were rumors going around that those mines were deathtraps. That they were haunted by the missing expedition crews. I didn't believe them, ghosts are just make believe. I went inside the mines when I was a kid. I think I was twelve or so. Some bigger kids made me go in."

"I see," Innis said. "And you listened to them because?"

"Because they were bigger. I was a little runt back then, and those big kids made little runts do stupid things to amuse them. Kids for you."

"I see. What did you see in the mines?"

"Darkness. Complete darkness. I didn't know which way was which."

"Didn't you bring a flashlight?"

"No way. They made me go in unexpectedly. I was just walking home after school, and they grabbed me and took me up to the mines."

"Was going into the mines as a child the reason why you built your house on top of them?" Innis inched forward on the desk and looked at the man under his spell. He looked unsure about answering this, he really did, but Innis also noticed that the important part of this man's mind was elsewhere.

"Yes."

"Why?"

"Because I was given something at the end of the mines, that's why. I wanted to get my mom a gold necklace, and gold came out of the ground for me. I wished for it and it came. You're prying at locked secrets, and I don't like this."

"Oh, it's all part of the oath, Edwin. You see, you're kind of on trial, yes, just pretend; it makes it easier. Who gave you what at the end of the mines?"

"A Hunter. I don't want to say."

"Okay, let's go this route. What was at the end of the mines?"

"Desolation. Ruins. Werewolves and a Hunter. He told me of the Towers. He wondered where I came from, and wondered if the necklace would be much safer with me in my world. I didn't know what to think." Edwin shifted uneasily.

Innis was almost salivating. What was all this talk of Towers and Hunters at the end of closed up mine shafts? Either this man was a kook, or he had a great imagination. "Werewolves and Hunters, Edwin? I don't understand."

"The Wolves walk like men. They smell like blood and drool, and they have rows of teeth in their mouths, like sharks really. The Hunter gave me the necklace. I don't want to say more, please." Edwin shook his head and his lids moved ferociously, as if his eyeballs wanted to get out of their sockets.

Necklace? Innis got up from the desk and looked at Krollup. His head was slumped forward, but he was sure he'd always noticed a chain around the man's neck. A golden chain, but he'd never thought twice about it before. But there must have been something spectacular about that necklace. Perhaps it was worth millions, or it was made of some odd gold. Either way Innis had to know. He moved Edwin's chin and looked at the chain. Edwin was wearing a very expensive suit jacket, and Innis opened it; he undid the top button of Edwin's shirt and pulled the rest of the necklace out by the chain. On its end lay an ugly stone, about as big as the circle made by his thumb and forefinger. This couldn't have been expensive; it was ugly, yes, but expensive. No way. It probably had some sentimental value; it was probably the first stone dug from Krollup's first mine. It was a memento, no more than a sign of his success. He held the stone in his palm and he felt a terrible vibration ring up his arm. He let go of the stone right away, and noticed that he was sweating terribly; he felt his eyebrows puff up oddly and he could taste salt. For some reason, he had seen something when he touched that rock. He had seen the tops of mountains explode as liquid magma pushed its way out of the peaks in deadly fountains and sprays. The image had disappeared as soon as he had dropped the stone, but he remembered it; he also remembered the awful vibrations too. He tucked the chain back into the shirt, did the buttons back up and closed the jacket.

"Tell me about this necklace, Edwin."

"No."

"Why not?"

"I've locked that door."

"Why did I see those things when I touched the stone around your neck?"

"You're delusional, I suppose."

"What is that stone?"

"I don't know."

Innis looked at the man's face. "I see. Tell me then, about those Towers at the end of the mines."

"I haven't been there. I've only seen them. I don't like thinking about all of this—about the Wolf that tried to smile at me—about the smell."

The wolf that smiled? Well, that much didn't matter. "What is so special about these Towers?"

"There are other powers inside."

Innis smiled; he knew, of course he knew. "What kinds of powers, Edwin?"

"I don't know."

"Okay. Tell me more about the end of the mines."

"No. I can't. The door has closed there; it won't let me say more. It tells me you're lying."

"No, no. You're imagining things." Innis didn't know where that came from. Was there a part of his mind that was still awake, that was still under *his* control, rather than under Innis's spell? "Everything is fine, Edwin, remember that. You're making yourself worry about nothing. I can't lie, I'm under the same oath you are."

"Good," Edwin agreed.

"Tell me Edwin. Why did you build your house on the mines?"

"Because I want to get to the Towers. Because I know there's something inside. Something I want. If the werewolves allow. They block the way. I think they work with Auger."

"With Auger. You mean the miner? Why do you say that?"

"Because I've seen him; he tried to come back up the mines. I didn't let him."

"Is that so? Tell me Edwin, these Towers at the end of the mines, what do you want that's inside?"

"I don't know."

"I see. You've told me that your stepsons constantly search for the mines in your house. They must be hidden, is this right?"

"Yes."

"Where?"

"Behind the fireplace of course. I used it as an escape route, a panic room. I was looking out for my mother and sister. I put mattresses down so the landing would be soft for my mother; she had brittle bones. Arthritis. There were slides in the original plans, inside the walls…one in the Master bedroom, one in my mother's bedroom, and one in my sister's. If there was ever danger, they were told to go down the slides and hide in the mines until all was clear. I looked out for them."

"Good. Does your mother and sister know about the mines and the Wolves and the Towers?"

"No. They believed I was obsessed. My mom died though, years ago. I closed up her door to the slide, cause she'll never need an escape. My sister married a working class jerk. I looked out for her, but she wouldn't have it. The man she married worked for me. I told her he wasn't worth it, but she didn't listen, so I fired him; she left the mansion to be with him. I don't know where she went. She won't talk to me. I closed her door to the mines and painted it over; there was no need for it anymore."

Innis looked at Edwin and smiled. So there was much action in these mines, he thought. Much action indeed. He would have to see for himself, of course, but he took Edwin's word for it. He looked at the clock. Good, it had only been thirty minutes.

He picked up the phone and called his ally, his cousin Eddie.

"Listen, Edwin Krollup finally told me where the mines are…"

5

I tried to stand up, but my legs wouldn't let me; they just wobbled and tilted me to one side, then the other, and then I fell back on the ground. My ankle still hurt.

I could taste clean air. I felt the ground. I ran my fingers over the rocks and gravel and dirt, and I smelt them. Everything seemed different here. Everything was a sharp blur of lines. I felt like my vision was teasing me for the last time before entirely blanking out. I wanted to call out, call for my mom, maybe even my dad, but I found I had no voice to do so. It was just a little croak. The poison in the gut of the mines must have torn apart my vocal cords, or was maybe still working its way down, until it cloaked my heart in utter filth.

I closed my eyes and opened them again.

Just the lines against the light, though they seemed more defined; I could almost see three spires off in the distance, the jagged outlines of huge pillars. I rubbed my eyelids. So this was what old blind Mrs. Evans goes through, I had thought. She must wake up every morning and hope to see lines. What am I complaining for, it'll come back, I know it will, because I can see the lines. If I couldn't, well then I could throw a fit, but until the lines are swallowed by darkness again, I'm A-OK.

I waited a minute before opening my eyes again. I wasn't scared that I might go blind, I was scared what I might see when my vision decided to come back.

I opened my eyes.

The lines became solid, and colors filled out the pure white as if an artist had popped by with a pallet and a brush. The sky was long and blue. Everything was silent, the breeze, the animals (if there were any). Not a noise but my gasps, and I realized how loud they had been.

I thought about the bullies. I wondered what they might be thinking, because I had been gone awhile. I didn't know for sure, but it felt late. Maybe not here, the sun was still high and the sky was still blue, but back on the other side. Perhaps. I didn't worry about my dad, or the stupid milk I was supposed to get, because at that point I had forgotten those problems; they seemed worlds away, they seemed trivial.

I saw the spires in the distance, beyond the edge of the cliff. I was standing among strewn rock; something horrible must have happened here to silence the animals and ruin the land. I wanted to go home—

And I felt two hands grab my shoulders and lug me on top of the rock that had been behind me. I was shoved to the edge and told to duck, to cower. I saw a figure standing before the light, just a shadow at this point; his shoulders fanned out on either side, and I could see the hilts of two swords over his shoulders, criss-crossed.

Then I heard the first noise. A howl. A deafening screech. I pulled my knees up against my chin; I could hear my teeth chattering.

There were footsteps, many of them, though their speed alarmed me. They didn't seem normal.

The figure told me to stay put, and he pulled both swords from his shoulders and crossed the blades before him; he let both glide down the rock face, and I heard a terrible scream, and thought I saw blood squirt up the stone in a thick spray.

I heard a horrible voice, speaking in a tongue I wanted to forget, but knew I never would. Well, at least a part of me never would. "You have our prize Hunter. Give it here and be spared."

This Hunter only sliced down again and there was more blood. Much more.

I started crying. I didn't know what to do, so I got up and climbed the rock, digging my crappy shoes into footholds where I could find them. I felt wind pass by my ears, and thought whatever had made those howls found me and wanted me as its main course. I turned my head and the Hunter was gone; he must have jumped down to face—

To face those things…those terrible things. I saw an army of werewolves carrying swords and spears; and many wore iron breastplates and black helmets that squashed their pointed ears. Their muzzles were speckled with white and red, and they saw me climbing; they saw me trying to get up this rock face in my stupid shoes and I knew I was a goner. There were five lying on the ground without heads, and I knew this only made the surviving wolves angrier. I was ready to drop, hoping the fall would kill me before they did, but I was grabbed by my shoulders again. I looked up to see the Hunter pulling me to the top. How he got there so fast was anybody's guess.

"They will be here in a moment. Come with me and tuck your spine along this rock here. I will do the rest." Suddenly, a wolf jumped from the lower rock and landed beside the hunter.

"Give it up human maggot, or meet your end. The prize is ours, you promised so."

The Hunter fellow only sliced the wolf in two, and its gangly arms, which held a long sword, fell forward, while its bottom half went back down the rock and landed with a loud thud. "I don't make promises to my enemy," the Hunter said, and I realized that this man, this Hunter, was going to save me. I wasn't scared anymore. "Stay there, and don't worry." He took out the necklace with the stone on it, only this necklace was bound by string; there was no gold chain holding it yet, because I had added that later. He held it against his chest. "Forgive me Ae-Granum, for I promised I wouldn't be tempted," he whispered and then we were covered in a shroud of darkness, except for slight holes before our faces.

I went to speak but he hushed me, putting his dirty finger against my mouth. "Though they cannot see us, they can certainly hear, and I am in no strength to battle more of them. The necklace drains your soul," he whispered, and then removed his finger from my mouth; it tasted like salt and blood.

I could hear them, pounding the rock as they jumped and landed on the precipice, snarling, screaming in their guttural voices. They went right by us, without even looking. Some of them lifted their hideous noses, and sniffed the air, but they never found a scent; they just crashed the rocks and bashed their breastplates with their claws and howled at the sky.

"Wait a moment," the Hunter said when the last of them moved by. "Grak has yet to come. I can sense him; he knows much more, and he lusts us and this more than the others." The Hunter meant the necklace I assumed, but I couldn't tell if he was pointing at it or not. There was a huge thud as two clawed feet landed on the rock. I pushed my face against the holes and tried to look. I couldn't tell much, but thought I saw a figure standing in the sun, a figure which stood almost nine feet tall, and wore a crown of thorns and a black plate over its chest decorated with skulls, some with their scalps still on them. I thought about the old Indian stories I read in the library; this must have been the chief, this Grak. It stood still, sniffing; it could sense us, I was sure of it, but it didn't know where we were. It knew we hadn't gone further up because it and the rest of them would have gotten us by now.

"I smell you. A young boy is with you Hunter. Hand me the stone and I will let you live. The boy's scalp is mine, and I shall drink his brains like soup." It hissed after it spoke in that horrible mutter; it had a voice that could cut glass. I could see its teeth through the hole; there were hundreds of them, in fixed rows along its plump gums. If I was going to be scalped, and my brains pureed, I hoped those teeth weren't involved in any way.

The Hunter beside me exhaled loudly and I knew he had blown our cover. The rock that had encapsulated us blew outward in little pieces, some of which knocked into the huge wolf and forced it back down the rock face; there was a loud crack as it hit the stone beneath. I stayed against the rock, and the Hunter told me we had time, we had a few minutes before Grak would awake from his daze and come after us.

He grabbed me in his arms and jumped, skipping against the neighboring rock face with his feet and using his thighs to push us both over the rock the wolf was sprawled upon, blood leaking from its mouth in rivulets. We landed on the ground, and the Hunter let me roll with him. I had the wind knocked out of me, but was grabbed before I could try to get it back. He dragged me to the mines, a dark hole where huge boulders had smashed against each other and left a space.

"Who are you?" He panted. "What is your purpose coming here?"

I didn't know what to say. This man saved my life, but I was afraid of him all the same. "I'm Eddie. I came from the mines—some...some bigger guys made me come in."

"What is it you search for?"

"I just want to see my mom again."

"As do I, but these times are tough, young man. The civil wars wrought flames, and the Yilaks draw blood. These ruins are no place for you."

I started crying. "I don't know what you're talking about. I just need to get home and buy milk, that's all. That's all I want."

"Stifle your tears young man. I am David, and I don't stand for tears. Tears are for the weak, and the milk is sour." He looked back at the rocks, tried to see if Grak was moving. "Where is it this hole leads? Towards Lake Aena in Cassica, or does your path travel to the woods in the west?"

"No. Home. Back where the milk isn't sour, and where wolves live in the forest and walk on all fours and CAN'T TALK! It isn't this world. It isn't this world. This world is different. It's like Narnia...or...or Middle Earth. I shouldn't be here—I SHOULDN'T BE HERE!"

"Don't scream. You'll draw attention. There are more of them. They camp down there. They watch the Towers now, ever since the Wars. They want this." He showed me the stone bound in twine. "They know it was this that destroyed the Sordids, and they want revenge young man. This isn't safe here. Another wants it also, and as soon as he gets it, boy, life won't matter. Not this war, and not a victory. Nothing." He looked back and we both saw Grak rising from the rock face, rising with that blood spilling out of his muzzle, spackling his dirty fur. He howled, and the others above howled back and I knew they were jumping back down now; they were coming to get us. Grak turned to look at me and I knew he was trying to smile. He was trying to smile with that teeth ridden muzzle. I wanted to scream.

The Hunter unsheathed his swords. "Come boy," he screamed and he took me by the hand, leading me into the mines. The light got weird again, and I could tell it was the same for him; I could see his swords slashing the darkness, and I could feel his heart through his hand. We ran hand in hand for a few more minutes, and he stopped. He wasn't panting. He was contemplating something, breathing the way a man breathes when he deliberates a choice or substantiates his confusion.

Perhaps he was looking for an answer, or perhaps the answer he had found scared him. Scared the hell out of him. "Something's different. I feel different. Where does this lead, boy?"

I could tell he was looking at me; it didn't make me comfortable, especially in this dark. "To the entrance of the boarded mines. I'm not supposed to be in here."

He was breathing harder. "I don't feel right," he finally said, and he could feel the grip in his hand weakening. "There are other worlds than this," he said, but it was a mutter, some quip he was telling himself, so I didn't think to question him. Then he thrust the necklace into my hand; it was heavy. I could feel its burden, but it was my mistake to have taken it. Always my mistake. "Take this. To your world," these last words were cautious, almost disbelieving, but he handed the necklace over all the same. "It will be safe with you. The wizard will get it when it's needed, always remember that. You will find comfort in his company. Keep it safe. Keep it hidden. Keep it from you. It will poison you. The wizard spoke of guardians of old, boy, so you must become a guardian of new, Mystic's appointed bearer of the demon within. Go. Now. Run. There will be a war. The final war. RUN!"

And with that I did. I ran through the mines, holding this necklace in my hand, hoping the wolves wouldn't find me and tear my scalp from my head as their own little prize. I heard swords clash in the distance behind me, and I heard that deafening howl and I just wanted my mommy.

I wished I could find my way home. I wished with all my heart that I could find the sunlight and the planks (or this world's version of the closet into Narnia), and I felt this long tremor up the arm that held the necklace. I closed my eyes and saw the planks before me when I opened them again. There was no sunlight, but they were there, the rotten pieces of wood, and I thought I might hear swords clashing and more howling, but nothing.

When I turned I noticed the rock floor settling, as if it had become a wave of smooth stone. I turned and I ran through the wood. I ran home as quickly as possible. I wanted to see my mother again, in her youth, without those terrible spots, and the sagging flesh on her face that reminded me of a teepee strung up on only one post. I wanted to see her before she found out about the tumor, years before she would die, but I couldn't. The entire image left and I opened my real eyes. My surface mind took over and the deeper parts fell dormant.

6

Edwin sat before Dr. Innis, his eyes fluttering open. He had a smile on his face, but when he saw where he was the smile died immediately.

"Good, you're back. How was it? I saw you smiling like you were the king of the world. What happened?"

"I don't remember," Edwin said, rather sadly. He really didn't. He thought for a moment that it had something to do with his mother, but he wasn't sure.

Innis smiled himself. "Completely normal. You were probably just reliving your youth. Sometimes that happens. You zone out and another part of you takes over, your long-term memory I'll say, and it translates your life for you. For those brief moments time doesn't exist. The thirty-five minutes you were hypnotized became years of catching up. I bet you remembered lots of things."

Edwin looked down. "I don't remember. But I did have this feeling, as if somebody was trying to pry open locked doors, as if my temples were expanding."

"A nervous tic, I suppose."

"Perhaps," Edwin said. He gave the doctor a strange look.

Innis smiled. "I have bad news for you Edwin, and I'm sure you'll find this rather coincidental—"

"The tape broke while we talked, right?"

"Yes, but how did you?—"

"I had this feeling, I don't know what it was, but I just knew that I would wake up and see that your stupid little Japanese recorder broke."

"It was a shame, really."

"Did you find out what you wanted to know?"

"What do you mean?" Innis asked rather shakily.

"About my father, of course. Did I show any signs of guilt, or will I be able to remove these stupid mental shackles?"

"Honestly, you said you wanted him to die, Edwin. You wished for it, were your words. But you have to understand that the world runs on coincidences. It was just blind luck that you wished your father dead, only to find out your wish came true. Karma. I wish I could jump out this window here and land on my feet unhurt; it won't happen, but there is the slight chance that I might land on a trampoline, and make my final dismount in an open topped truck carrying pillows. If that were to happen it wouldn't be because I had it planned; it was just merely a coincidence that everything fell into place. You see?"

Edwin nodded. *Did I tell you about the necklace,* he thought? He was still wearing it, but the doctor wasn't being completely honest with him, that was for sure. He may have even touched it. "I can live with that doc, I really can, but I'm not sure I believe it."

"Really? Do you feel you need to be hypnotized again, Edwin?"

You'd like that, wouldn't you? "I don't know doc, maybe. But for now I have other things on my mind." He got up, shook Innis's hand and went for the door. He stopped before he went out and looked at Dr. Innis. "You know, I do remember something. Some bigger kids made me go into the mines when I was a kid. You ever go there before I built over top the stupid things?"

"Not that I can remember. Heard about them, though."

"Anyway, I remembered one of the bullies. He thought he was Elvis Presley. I didn't know then of course, but now, now I remember who that guy was. His last name's Paulson. Sid Paulson. I just fired him because his kid was spying my house with those two stepsons of mine. Now that's payback. He got his pink slip today when he opened his locker. I'm sure he remembered too. He remembered sending me down the shaft when I was supposed to go home. I hope he likes unemployment." Edwin turned and left, shutting the door behind him.

Innis sat down on his desk. He and his cousin Eddie would have to see those mines.

In time.

7

Edwin left the office and went out to the elevator trying to piece certain things together. His mind was a puzzle, there was no doubt about that, but for some reason he thought he could put this puzzle back together. When he had sent the robot down the mines on Friday, he had seen the wolves, yes, and he had always figured the wolves had won the war of which the Hunter spoke. Edwin knew this, because as a boy he feared those ugly things. He feared those blood speckled muzzles baring countless fangs; he thought one day they'd break through the rotten barricades blocking off the mines, tearing through the wood like paper, and they'd search for him and rip the necklace from his throat when they found him. Edwin lived with this fear until his father died when he was fifteen— then, incredibly enough, he realized he had enough power to take care of himself. He realized that this necklace wasn't but a bind with whatever that war torn place at the end of the mines had been, this necklace was a symbol of his impending manhood. This necklace would determine his future, and he knew that. His fear of the wolves had dwindled at that point, replaced by a brutal sense of responsibility for his father's death. Edwin knew he was responsible, because the necklace had that kind of power; it didn't respond to moral convictions—and perhaps this was why the Hunter had referred to it as poison. In other words, the necklace drew from the mind's desires; it was presumably designed to do so, Edwin knew that, but a part of him wanted so much not to believe it, and that part dragged him into a conflict with common sense. He hated his father, yet he didn't want to kill him; his decision to wish for the man's death was just a circumstantial result of his mother's broken jaw. He hadn't intended anything; he wouldn't have pulled the trigger of a gun, or physically pushed the stones into the path of the old Ford pickup, because Edwin Krollup wasn't a murderer. He was just a scared kid. That's all.

Edwin stood before the elevator doors thinking about this. He had thought the Hunters were gone, vaporized in the war with the Yilaks, but when he and Leo had sent that poor excuse of a surveillance robot down the mines, he saw somebody that reminded him so much of David that he believed the stranger must have been him. This stranger moved like an acrobat, and wielded a sword with unique precision. But it wasn't David. David would have been old, he would have been an elderly man if he had survived those wars.

He looked at the necklace and wondered why David had given it to him, and called him its new guardian. *It was either you or the wolves.*

But why hadn't the wolves come up the mines sooner? Why hadn't they found you when you were a child, and ripped the stone from your neck?

He thought about this for a moment. They hadn't come up because they were isolated from such options; they were terrified of the mines the same way David sensed the difference in them, or maybe the better word was *interchange*. Instead they were waiting for him to return; their power existed in their country, where the land was under their sordid authority. They only came up the mines when Kenneth Auger was with them, because only he would have known the truth—the mines were a door between worlds. The mystery of this reality drove those wolves to an incomprehensible patience. That was why they had come up the cliff so fast to attack the robot; because they wanted to believe whoever had the stone was returning from the mines.

When they finally swarmed up the mines, Edwin had halted their attempt; he had shoved them back down into the depths in very much the same way he had found his way back to the surface as a kid. The rock floor had become a tidal wave that shot the wolves back into the dark, and Auger stood before him, not watching the wolves scramble along the backfill as they were pushed by the stone, but looking at Edwin as he hung in the air. Auger was old now; his white wiry hair barely covered his scalp. He smiled and his teeth looked rotten.

"So this is what the Yilaks spoke of. The ruination of the Sordids, bound in this little stone hanging from your neck. This *talisman*. I see the very confidence it feeds you. I would very much like to have it, but I know it won't be that simple. Perhaps we could make a trade."

"You have nothing I want, old timer." Edwin had seen the man was carrying an old looking gas mask with dirty goggles, and he put them on his head, nodded and turned back to walk down the mines. He walked with a slight limp, and Edwin knew the man was dying. Or was already dead.

In a sense, Edwin was happy he was hypnotized, because it seemed to open up another part of him—a clearer part almost.

Edwin smiled when the elevator doors opened. In time he would find out just what power the other world held.

Edwin walked into the elevator. There were two other people inside and they snickered when they saw him. Edwin looked at them with a furrowing brow and simply said: "I'm worth billions, you termites. I could buy your house with what I'm holding in my wallet. If I'm not crying over fifty millions dollars, than it must be chump change."

They both shut up and stared forward.

8

On Monday Cole woke up, dressed, ate breakfast and went to school, sitting in the front seat of the SUV as his mother barreled down the road, curious why her little boy seemed so...well, she wanted to say upset, but she didn't know for sure.

Jimmy had gone to school earlier in the morning; he had gotten up early enough to catch Krollup at the breakfast table smoking his cigar, and he had asked for a puff. Edwin regarded the boy with a brief grunt, blew a thin line of smoke from his nostrils and put the monster Cuban out in his breakfast—three eggs, toast and six strips of bacon. *He'll break*, Jimmy thought. *He can't be all vengeful, because he was a kid once too, and he must know how kids think.* Jimmy took the bus, something he hadn't done since his mother married the richest man in the world. Jimmy even ignored the kids at school when they questioned Krollup's idiocy, spending millions of dollars on a fake statue, although he did ask if either or both of their parents worked under the Krollup name. Most kids shut up, because word spread, especially in a school like Ivy Raurus, where everybody else's business was your business.

Ricky came to school on Monday, but that was only because he craved attention, and he knew he'd get it. In a way Ricky came out of spite, but the consolation he'd receive was a grand addition; he even thought some of the girls would pay attention now that he was today's news, forced to leave the school he had tried so hard to get into because a little Ratboy decided to give names to the head honcho. And that was where the new nickname originated—in the foul mind of Ricky Jensen, whose father once thought he looked like Elvis Presley, and used that snarling lip to sneer at the very man who would fire him.

When Maggie stopped the SUV in front of the school's gates, she held Cole's arm and said, "what's wrong? Be honest."

"Nothing mom."

"No really, Cole. There's something wrong, and I want to know what it is."

Cole looked out his window at the schoolyard, which was obscured by the chain link fence; he watched the kids on the slides, pumping their legs on the swings, and he had the terrible thought that this was his childhood, *this*, sitting next to a mother that felt sorry for him when he moped because she knew, just knew, that he was the butt of all *their* jokes. He wondered what was going to happen to him when he crossed that fence; he wondered what the kids would say and he wondered if they'd hurt him. Ratting out your buds was the worst crime ever, at any age, Cole supposed, and yet he had done it because he couldn't take the heat from Krollup. He couldn't very well lie to those eyes. Because he was afraid of him. *Deathly* afraid.

Cole looked back at his mother, her red hair lying down her back in big swoops, and he wanted to cry into her shoulder. He wanted to cry into her shoulder yesterday morning also, when Ricky and James both punched him, but he realized one thing: he was his own man, and there was nobody there to look out for him anymore, not Jimmy, not dad, not anybody. "I'm fat, mom."

"No, you're just big-boned."

"That's not true and you know it. I was skinny before dad died, but then, then I just got fat. I carry these chocolates around with me all the time, and I eat them when I get nervous, or agitated, and people laugh. It's hard to face sometimes."

Maggie looked at her son for a moment, and thought she saw a lie. Well, not a lie, but not the whole truth either. She swept it away and wanted to burst into tears. "Your father always used to say, 'you are who you are'. That's a great philosophy Cole, no matter what kids say or do to you. Kids are cruel, they always have been. I should know, I have red hair. I used to want to dye it, when I was a young girl, because the kids teased me. I even bought bleach, try to get it blond or something, but I just couldn't do it, because I thought my hair suited me, you know. I liked the way I looked, and I know not many people can say that, but I could. I don't know why, but I could, and I know you have that same kind of power in you. The power that tells people to lay off, because you don't care." She breathed out and patted the steering wheel. "What does Jimmy do about this, Cole?"

Cole didn't know what to say. He hated to lie, especially to his mother, and just the fact that he couldn't lie to Krollup made it even worse. "I guess he tells people to back off." He closed his eyes for a moment and thought about what Jimmy had said on Saturday night. "He uses Mr. Krollup as a defense mechanism, because most of the kids' parents work for him."

"Good. Very good. You should do the same thing, say your stepdad isn't going to stand for this abuse. Look them in the eyes and tell them if they want to stay in this school, they better watch what they say to you. Does that sound good?" She smiled at him and Cole wanted to hug her.

"Yes, I mean, I guess." He looked back at the playground and gulped, because he was sure Ricky was out there somewhere, waiting for him, waiting to show him the meaning of this *more to come* business he had stated yesterday morning. "Thanks mom, for the ride and all." Cole leaned over, kissed her cheek and opened the door to leave. He tugged on his vest, pulled the waistband of his pants and patted the chocolates in his pocket.

Don't give them a reason to spit on you, a voice said in his mind. *Take away your targets Cole; get rid of them, because in the end you'll only remember being prey.*

It was his father's voice. Cole went through the gate and waited for his mother to drive away. She waved and Cole smiled. When she was completely gone, Cole backed against the fence and looked the playground over. Targets? His chocolates, for one thing. If they came around, they'd expect him to stuff his face full. Not today.

Cole walked towards the soccer field. He had a bottle of Aspirin in his backpack. And he had his fists clenched.

9

Ricky got to school at about the same time as Jimmy, because Ricky, unlike Cole, had the disadvantage of two working parents who were both out of the house by quarter after seven, which meant he had to stomach the city bus. His sole intention of the day was to receive sympathy, and if he was really lucky, to unload a fistful of trouble Cole's way. Cole did deserve it, because he *did* rat Ricky and James out, but in a way, Ricky had become questionably insane in his lust for revenge; he didn't just want Cole to feel the reverberations of his ratting for the one day, he wanted the tag Ratboy to stick with him until he had his own kids. Ruining Ricky's life wasn't a good thing to do, because a boy like Ricky wasn't dismissive; a boy like Ricky was vindictive.

He passed the name Ratboy around like it was a collection plate at church. Girls giggled, and guys were pretty upset that Ricky, the jokester, the all-around-good-guy, would no longer be with them—and why was that? Because Ratboy ratted him out like a rat.

When Cole pulled up to the school, Ricky had been lighting up his first cigarette of the day; he had been standing against the soccer post, the wind slightly moving his gelled hair to the side, while he told a bunch of kids standing around him about Ratboy. About how he was going to clobber him, and how they all should clobber the porker too once he was gone, was out of here, was no longer a member of this facility.

"What about Krollup though, man, Jimmy just been around and he bummed four smokes off me n' said he'd get Krollup to fire my dad too if I didn't? What if Cole goes and tells him what we're doing to him?"

Ricky laughed and his cigarette almost fell out of his mouth. "That's your problem. I don't care anymore cause my dad's already fired. Now, instead of punching Ratboy in the gut, I'm gonna feed it to him. You know, really feed it to him. I might even give him a cigarette burn, have one of you guys hold up his shirt while I do it."

Some of the boys nodded anxiously. The girls just giggled and said that was gross.

"All I know is that I want to make my last day worth it."

10

He wanted to grab the chocolates when he saw Ricky standing against the soccer post, holding that smoke, laughing it up with his friends. Cole couldn't see Jimmy anywhere, but he knew he must have been watching. He was probably smoking or something.

Cole even went as far as pulling the box halfway out of his pants before he felt his father nudge at him, reminding him that he would only make himself a bigger target. "You were a target for cancer," Cole said under his breath, "but that didn't seem to stop you from smoking." The voice never responded.

Then he heard the first of them. Somebody yelled out, "RATBOY FATBOY," and the crowd of heads turned, all of them, and he could feel their hate soaking in. There were some kids playing soccer. One was on a breakaway when he heard the crude rhyme, and instead of shooting the winning goal, he let the ball roll away from him as he turned around to watch what was happening. And Cole wondered what was going to happen. Were they all going to jump on him and make him pay for what he'd done to Ricky and James, or were they just merely an audience?

Cole swallowed a rock of saliva and he could feel his nerves reaching for that candy again. *No,* he told himself, *not now, now we have to be strong. We have to stand up to this because we can't make a target for them to jump on.*

"Hey fat boy, what did you have for breakfast, Wendy or Ronald Macdonald?" He laughed and his buddy laughed and they all laughed, and it all drove Cole to reach for the chocolates.

You can't do it Cole, leave the chococrap, say something back, give them a shocker.

A shocker, Cole thought? Of course, he would say something back; he wouldn't leave the ball in their court.

"No, I used your parents' entire Welfare check to buy crackers." That was fine, he thought. They both looked at him strangely because neither of them knew what a Welfare check was.

Good boy. Go over their heads; it makes them look like fools.

"Hey Ratboy, you're going to get a beating," some little jerk said.

Cole looked at him and spurted, "you should start going to sleep when your mom and dad fight, cause you're mixing your home life with your school life."

"Huh," the kid said, and he scratched his head.

The crowd separated as Cole walked up to Ricky, and Ricky, who hadn't expected this at all, just spit his cigarette on the ground and looked at Cole menacingly. He cocked his eyebrow and faked a punch, giggling as he did it. Cole flinched, and some kid in the crowd sucker punched him twice in the arm.

"Two for flinchin."

Don't cry Cole, in fact, laugh, and laugh hard. Do not give them the satisfaction; they want to see tears, so give them smiles, give them fury.

Cole didn't even rub his arm. "Look Ricky, I came over here to say one thing, and one thing only. I'm very sorry for what happened. I didn't intend on that happening, it's just, I can't lie to Krollup."

"Shut up Ratboy," Ricky said. "I don't care if you can't lie, because of you I have to move. My dad's looking for work in Montana. MONTANA, can you believe that? I'm not a rancher Ratboy, but now I have to be." He punched Cole in the arm. Cole went to rub his arm, but that voice stopped him. "Look at that everyone, the fat guy has guts." He laughed.

"I'm sorry Ricky. I feel horrible for what I did and for what's happened to you and your family, but you have to understand, I do *not* want to fight you."

Ricky looked at Cole for a moment and evaluated the sincerity in his eyes. The kid meant it, that much was true, and even if Ricky felt like giving the kid a break, that meant he'd be breaking his reputation. He told everybody he was going to work the fatso, so he meant to do it, no matter what. "SHUT UP," he screamed, and Cole really flinched this time. He even staggered back a couple of steps.

"Look Ricky, school starts in a couple of minutes. The teachers will see this, will see you and you'll just get into trouble."

"Doesn't matter fatty, I don't go here no more, but I'm sure if I did, you'd just *rat* on me anyway." He snickered.

"Hit him, Ricky," some guy yelled.

Cole turned his head to see who had blurted that last comment and when he did he felt a hard thud against the side of his face. His neck twitched and he heard something pop in his ear, something inside him that must have snapped, and he felt something warm trickle off his earlobe. His head felt heavy all of a sudden and he wanted to lay down and curl into a ball, just lie like a piece of garbage until somebody picked him up, but that voice inside him urged he stand his ground.

Cole wiped the blood from his ear and slapped it off his knuckles to the ground. "That was a cheapshot Ricky. What, are you afraid to face me man to man?" Cole talked with an odd stutter, but he got his message through. He wasn't going to back down. Cole held up his fists like a boxer, and Ricky noticed that if the fatty did hit him, he'd be doing more harm to himself, because his fingers were tucked against his palm. He'd most likely bust a couple of them if he landed.

Ricky, more out of surprise than anger, threw another punch, but Cole had anticipated it; he knew the guy was going for his stomach. Sometimes it cushioned the blow and gave that chance to counter with your own hit, usually against the jaw as the attacker's head was turned during the follow through.

Cole sidestepped, but still caught Ricky's fist in his kidney. He followed with his own connection, slapping Ricky's cheek. Tears suddenly welled up in Ricky's right eye. He pulled his head back in a quick snap and kicked Cole's leg, just as the bell rang for classes to start. Many of the spectators, including those who had formed a wall against the school so nothing could be seen from the windows, dispersed, afraid of detention.

Cole collapsed; there was a fine bruise on the other side of his thigh from landing on those mouse bones in the secret room, and Ricky's foot narrowly landed near the swelling. He wanted to get back up, but Ricky shoved his dirty shoe squarely on his stomach and turned it until the flesh underneath his vest compressed beneath Nike sole. He pressed harder and Cole thought his ribs were going to implode. This is the end, he thought.

Don't cry, Cole, don't give them the victory. He may have won the fight, but he did it to see you in pain. Without tears, he lost that battle.

Cole fought them; he fought those tears for the life of him, gritting his teeth until his jawbone ached. Ricky dug harder and harder, until his leg hurt from the exertion. He pulled it off and kicked Cole in the side. Cole rolled over; there were grass stains all over his uniform.

"Just like a rat to roll over and die," Ricky said, and he laughed, and so did the students that stuck around to witness the end.

This was how school went for a solid week.

CHAPTER 7

A Victim's Escape

1

Cole decided he was going to go back down the vents. He was going to confront the Robot Bomber again.

The decision wasn't automatic, and Cole had actually pondered the thought for some time. Would the Bomber welcome him with pent up fury (since Cole knocked the little man back down the vents), or would he greet him as a hermit greeted any company, with a sense of longing?

But there was another alternative, one Cole was very aware of but tried to ignore. Cole realized that any attempts to come back up the vents had stopped; he hadn't heard the clink and the grunt, and he realized that the games and the boxes he'd shoved in front of the miniature door hadn't budged. Cole had even gone as far as trying to stick his head through the fire to see if he could make anything out through the shoddy grout in the bricks. But he had seen nothing, and was only pulled out rather harshly by a handmaiden who thought the boy was falling in.

To be quite honest, Cole was afraid he had killed the man. In a way he *wanted* to hear the clink and grunt just to assure him that he wasn't a murderer. You could probably say he and Edwin Krollup were alike in that way: they both seemed plagued by a deep fear that somebody else's death was their fault. Cole had nightmares. In one he died. How, he didn't know, but he remembered the sky had separated letting through a radiant glow. It was through this that he saw his dad, and just as his dad held out his bright hand, Cole had felt something tug at his leg, and when he looked back he had seen the Bomber, two blood-rimmed horns jutting from his skull like broken splinters of bone. Cole realized his punishment would be the guilt, which would lead him to be haunted by that very image for the rest of his days. He woke up in a cold sweat and listened to Jimmy's breathing under him, muffled yet calm and peaceful, and Cole honestly thought he hated the boy, *his* brother.

But it wasn't a thought at all. Not anymore at least. It wasn't the fact that Jimmy had seen Ricky beat up Cole, and only stood and watched from a distance; it was the peculiar way he acted. He pushed people away. Ricky had gone to say goodbye to him, bless his heart, and Jimmy had only given him a glance as if to say, "we were chums, now we ain't, the world moves on, and I got more important things to do today." Ricky had read this, and he had a peculiar thought of his own, believing that maybe this *changed* Jimmy was in some way a part of the reason his father got fired. He didn't know why he had this thought, but as he drove in his parent's van a week later, watching the road to Montana wind by, he would feel infested by it, as if he had beat up Cole for something Jimmy may have suggested. He threw the thought away as quickly as it had come up, but it still made him feel uneasy.

Jimmy had changed, yet it was Cole their mother had been watching with intensified worry. At first she hadn't noticed her make-up clumped on his cheeks where his jawbone had begun bruising. At first she had dismissed it, but his injuries became more and more obvious. They weren't normal. And she'd remember their conversation in the SUV, how he had confessed that the kids called him fat. How they bullied him.

In the middle of the week Maggie had talked to Jimmy about it. Jimmy was chewing gum, trying to hide the stench of cigarette smoke.

"I would've done something if I'd seen it," he said, and he looked her square in the eyes, the same way he thought Krollup would under the same circumstances.

"Do you think maybe I should contact the school? If this is happening, I can't believe somebody in the faculty hasn't noticed."

Jimmy didn't know, and was getting bored of the conversation; he was proud of the little guy for standing up for himself, but for now he had other things on his mind. He had to hit up Ted and Marshall tomorrow for smokes, and Kyle owed him seven bucks plus interest because he loaned him money for lunch last week. His head had become names and numbers.

Maggie did call the school, and this mistake made it worse for Cole, so that by the weekend, he had finally decided what it was he was going to do.

2

On Thursday morning, just as Cole had unloaded his textbook from his backpack, the principal had come into the room and told him the counselor wanted to see him. Cole believed the man was up to something; it turned out he was, but Cole wouldn't find that out until lunch.

He wandered by doors, listening to teachers speak in muffled tones about wars and numbers and maps, and it all became a drone, one steady drone. The side of his head blared where Ricky had sucker punched him, and he stopped and grabbed an Aspirin from his pocket. He swallowed it with water from the fountain and felt it lug down his throat. His head didn't feel any better, but that monotonous drone disappeared.

He's up to something. Is it common for the principal to remove you from class to see a counselor?

Cole didn't know. It was a good question.

He walked down the halls littered with closed doors and muffled voices, and then he began to run, holding his hurt ribs with his arm, letting it dangle against his side. He felt like he owned the school. Without the other kids there to laugh at him, and push him around, he felt free; he felt as if he'd shed his handcuffs, as if the warden had gone to lunch.

But the feeling would change. When the bells rang, the warden would knock him over the head and shove those cuffs back on. Why? Because Cole provided a target. And when he denied them that target, they only punished him for playing hard to get. He was sure the counselor would ask him about this; she would ask him about his swollen jaw, and about his relationship with his stepfather, and Cole would take out his chocolates and eat handfuls and handfuls while he tried to answer, but none of that mattered, because Cole hadn't known that his mother made a mistake. She had called school administration, and she had cursed them; she had cursed them for her son's state, and she had cursed them for their inability to parent the students.

And what had this done? This had called to attention a faculty meeting about bullying. Cole's name was tossed around like a football because he was the prototypical victim; there were no astonished faces in the room. They knew he was *different*, and they'd made a mistake because they believed they could help. They made Cole a poster boy. Principal Heston made it his duty to go into Cole's class and feed these students, minus Cole of course, a harsh lesson on the brutal realities of violence, and the consequences down the road; he even went as far as stating a general fear. That the said person would snap one day, and take his or her aggression out on the school, seeing it as the root of his or her problems. The principal spoke for thirty-five minutes, using an anonymous name to play the victim of course, but due to Cole's coincidental departure around the same time the lecture began, the students pieced certain things together. And this resulted in what Cole feared the most. The kids thought Ratboy ratted again.

That lunch Cole was thrown against the school wall and punched seven times in the belly, and kicked three times in the shin; the kids didn't dare touch his precious face because they didn't want a moniker to advertise their bullying. They were just fine with concealed wounds.

And there were certainties drawn from the episode. Cole was certain that telling his mother about the kids at school had set off everything like dynamite plugged into a wedge of limestone. Cole was certain this would never end. Ricky had started a trend, and the name Ratboy would certainly follow him like a tail, no matter his age, his weight, his defense; it would always be there because kids were cruel and they never stopped picking. They would have probably continued picking until he was just a thin strand, a line of sanity with his madness already emerging.

On Friday night, some four days after his fistfight with Ricky, Cole made the worst decision of his life.

3

Jimmy had been sitting outside with a smoke clinging from his lips, his back nestled deeply into a large hedge, when he saw Cole through the bedroom window; he was pacing around frantically, from one end of the room to the other, and Jimmy wondered what the boy was doing.

Jimmy ashed the cigarette out on the wall and opened his jacket, pulling out a tin box that had the letter 'J' stenciled on it in weird lines. He opened it and placed the half smoked cigarette on top of the stack of cancer sticks he had hawked from other kids' collections as a sort of payment. As long as he didn't have to find an older kid to buy him smokes, the kids with parents who worked under the Krollup name were safe. It was a thriving business, and Jimmy had no less than fifty-six cigarettes crammed into that little box; he had hit up Charlie for seven today, because the kid had a daddy who worked in the Preparation Plant on the outskirts of town.

Jimmy popped three pieces of gum into his mouth, breathed into his cupped hand and smelt his palm. It didn't smell too bad, which was good, but he'd have to take his jacket off and douse it in Potpourri or something. That didn't matter right now. Right now, he had to go and see Cole; he was proud of the kid. Not once had he come screaming for help, and that impressed Jimmy. He knew Cole was upset at him for telling Ricky and James about everything, but he had to understand one thing: perhaps Jimmy was doing him a favor, giving him a chance to prove himself, prove his brawn. Even if he didn't understand it yet, Jimmy was sure he would after he talked to him. Jimmy had made Cole a man, giving him a vital chance to prove himself to the stupid students at Ivy Raurus.

Jimmy went inside and rolled his jacket into a ball. He ran up the grand staircase and jogged seven doors down to the right.

He opened the door and found Cole sitting on the couch in front of the television. The television was turned off. Jimmy could see Cole's reflection on the screen. He could see sweat in Cole's scalp, beaming through the short strands of hair, which was a slight auburn—half their mother's hair, and half their father's.

For a moment Jimmy felt all the time pass between them. He thought about playing ball with dad, tossing the red seams around the horn as Cole laughed; it was heaven, but Jimmy quickly erased the memory. That was just it: it *was* heaven. It was heaven now because their dad lied to them, and put the cancer sticks into his mouth when their backs were turned. It was memory.

"Cole."

Cole inhaled deeply, and then drew the air out.

"What do you want?"

Jimmy forgot what he wanted. He stood behind the couch and he stared at the back of Cole's head, with its short hair and its sweaty scalp, and he forgot what he wanted to say. He couldn't believe it. He could remember that Sally Watson owed him four cigarettes if her mommy wanted to keep working as an accountant at the Oil firm; and he could remember the way Charlie breathed a sigh of relief when he realized he was off the hook for the time being, but other than that, he couldn't remember.

"Leave me alone, Jimmy. If you want to prove some other point about your new crummy father, just stuff it."

What? Jimmy didn't understand. But he did see Cole's face, how swollen his jaw was. Some of the bruising was showing through make-up that had smeared away; he had let *this* happen to his younger brother? How could he have done that? He watched Ricky sucker punch him from a corner of the school—why hadn't he stopped the fight while there was still a chance? Thoughts loomed around his head, pushing aside names of cigarettes and names of people who owed them to him. Why would they do this to Cole if they knew he had the same bloody stepfather?

Why were they so afraid of *him*, and so unafraid of Cole?

Because you let it happen, some voice inside his head said. *You used him to your advantage so you could smoke; you used your brother as an example, and you know it too. So if you used him, why would people think you cared one bit about him? They don't, they think you loathe him. Maybe people take their anger with you out on him because he's more accessible. Little Charlie punched Cole in the gut three times today; he had a look of fear in his eyes as he did it, but he wasn't picturing Cole on the other side of his fist either. He was picturing you, and your smug look as you explained the power you had over his life, over his father's career.*

Jimmy closed his eyes and rubbed his temples. That voice had been so real, he was sure of it, but it was gone in a second, as if he had never heard it in the first place.

He looked at Cole and remembered what he wanted to say, almost as if that weird voice left it behind as proof that it had been there.

"I'm proud of you, Cole."

Cole turned around and Jimmy saw his entire face; his right jaw curved outwards until the lobe of his ear was slightly covered, and the bruising he had seen from the back was worse when it was fully revealed. His eye was surrounded by a purplish droop until small portions were covered by peach make-up. Stuff he had stolen from mom. He was breathing awkwardly, and Jimmy could see that he was holding one side of his stomach, almost caressing it.

"What did you say?"

"I said I'm proud of you. I've seen you lately. You don't take anybody's crap, and that's good. I saw you with Ricky, and you got a hit, and I was thinking, like, wow, this is Cole, the same Cole that cried when they sung the nasty nursery rhymes about him. This is Cole, and he *wants* to fight."

"You're proud of me?" Cole nearly stuttered.

"Yes I am."

"Shut up Jimmy. Don't say another word. I don't want to hear you say another word."

"What do you mean?"

"I MEAN I DON'T WANT TO HEAR YOUR VOICE!" Cole screamed, and Jimmy stumbled back a step.

"Calm down Cole. I don't know what's gotten into your skivvies but you don't got to take it out on me, okay? I just came to say you're making me proud, and all of a sudden that's a bad thing?"

Cole got up from the couch and walked around slowly, still clutching his side. "Do you remember what dad looks like?"

"What?"

"Do you remember what dad looks like?"

"Of course I do," Jimmy said. Cole approached him, his arm curled against his stomach, his hand hooked into a claw, pinching his sweater.

"What did he look like?"

Jimmy stopped and thought about this; the memory of his father had been wholly configured by anger, and every time he stopped to remember his face, it was clouded under cigarette smoke so heavy nothing could be made out. "He had brown hair."

"That's it?"

"What else do you want me to say, for crying out loud? What's your problem?"

Cole snatched the rolled up jacket from Jimmy's arm and felt it in his grip. He ran his hand along the seams until he came across the tin box in the inner breast pocket. He opened the jacket and removed it, staring at the simple 'J' pressed into its top. He looked at it in utter disgust and opened the box.

"Give those back, fatso."

Cole only looked at the smokes and shook his head.

"Don't make me hurt you, Cole."

"You can't hurt me, Jimmy, not anymore than your admirers have hurt me." Cole lifted his sweater up to his chin.

Jimmy's jaw dropped.

"These are from yesterday, and these ones are from today, and these two over there, well, I'm not sure, but they feel pretty fresh." Cole was standing before Jimmy with his pale stomach and chest revealed under the overhead lights, his sweater dangling from the pinched fingers by his nose. There were deep shadows underneath Cole's chest, but they weren't shadows and Jimmy knew it. They were terrible bruises, all of them, matching fists from students upset at Ratboy, and how he ratted out Ricky, and how he ratted out all of them to entitle a brief lecture from the principal. "Was all of this worth it for these, Jimmy?" He of course meant the cigarettes, and Jimmy knew it, but he couldn't take his eyes off the bruises; there must have been hundreds of horrible purplish red marks running all around the boy's fat stomach, and Jimmy understood why he had been holding his side. Because it hurt to let the flesh hang free, to let gravity pull on it.

Cole took out a cigarette and put it in his mouth; he sucked on it a moment and then took it out. He smacked his tongue against the roof of his mouth and made a disgusted sigh. He tore the smoke in half and dropped it back in the box, closing it with a firm click.

"I hope it was worth it, Jimmy." He dropped the tin box back in Jimmy's hand and left the room, left Jimmy standing with his smokes and the awful memory of those bruises. He didn't hear what Cole had said, but he knew all along.

All week long he had let *them* do this to his brother. He felt sick.

He turned to find Cole, but he was gone.

Cole had gone to the lawn technician's shed in the courtyard. He was getting rope.

4

Friday night went by at a snail's pace. Cole had to lie in bed and pretend to sleep as his stupid brother played a video game. The annoying beeps and rings and that ridiculous synthesized music grated his nerves, and though the wall partially covered the television set, the light from the blaring screen still illuminated the room like a nightlight.

Cole had the blanket up to his chin, and he was sweating; his scalp looked like it was made of wax. He had on a sweater, and a pair of jeans and running shoes; he could feel his back soaking up the cotton in his shirt, and he was sure any second the thing would expand like a fluffy balloon. But it didn't. It only dragged him further into the recesses of hot, until breathing made him thirstier. He needed to move, to get up. But he couldn't, he had to stay put and hope Jimmy turned that game off soon so he could go down the vents; he wanted to catch the Bomber before he knocked out for the night.

If he's still alive, that is.

But he ignored that thought, he had to, or he would have screamed. Cole felt like his feet were bleeding in his socks, but he had to ignore that too; he had to ignore his pesky conscience and his sweaty feet because soon, soon he would be out of this hot bed and into the vents, inching his way down to see the Bomber—

Cole wanted to fight back.

When Cole found the rope in the shed—two coils of it, one length rather thick, and the other a thin yellow strand that he could tie around his waist— he dangled both sets on his arm and left the dank room, the terrible stench of gasoline and grass and rusty iron following him as he shut the double doors that parked the John Deere tractor mower (it had been locked, but he knew Mario the lawn technician hid a spare key under a hedge). He paced uneasily through the courtyard, staring at the statues on their pedestals, hoping he wouldn't sense their eyes on him, but he did; he could feel all of them looking at him, so he rushed. He grabbed both coils of rope in his arms and ran, the loops of cord hitting his thigh as each leg pelted forward, and he stormed in the mansion through a back door.

He stopped and leaned against the closed door and peered through the plate windows above the knob; he looked at them—those statues—just to make sure they hadn't turned to follow him, to walk with him right into the house and twist his neck with their stone hands.

That leg you saw last week, that couldn't have been human, no way, no sir. Unless you were imagining things, I would guess it belonged to one of those statues.

He had lied to himself ever since he was curled in the curtains, looking out over the courtyard. It was possible. A statue couldn't move—but that leg, that enormous leg had strode right behind the wall; he had caught a quick glimpse of it before it was completely obscured by the house, and now, as he had run through the yard towards the house, he could feel them all staring at him, waiting for him to pass so they could turn and follow in a hunter's trail. He watched them outside, standing on their pedestals, capturing the dim glow of the setting sun off their grainy torsos and arms.

He shuddered and took one last look at the statues. The sun had almost dipped behind the mountains, and the shadows danced; there seemed to be movement on the statues' faces, arching their brows, moving their carved lips into the devil's grin.

He turned and headed through the Great room; the sound of the fire leapt out at him. David's clone stood to his left, and he wondered how Krollup could *ever* think that was the real thing; its pose was completely different. Even he, a twelve-year-old boy, knew that.

When he got to his room, Jimmy had already been into the video games, and Cole quickly tossed the rope onto the top bunk; he crawled into bed before Jimmy could turn around and say hello.

When he did, Cole only closed his eyes and pretended to sleep.

It must have been midnight, and the discomfort of lying in bed with clothes on was killing him. The television had turned off maybe twenty minutes ago, but it still didn't seem right. He could hear Jimmy beneath him, but the calmness wasn't in his breathing, as if he was faking it, as if he knew what Cole was up to. He was going to go mad in here; he felt trapped, like a lion in a cage with but a thumb bolt keeping it inside.

He gripped the covers and pushed them down a little, feeling the colder air caress his neck, and try to sneak into crevices formed by his sleeves. The rope was tucked against his side; it felt like a wicker basket poking into his jeans. He put his arm through both loops of cord and shifted a little. He strained to hear how Jimmy might respond to that. He heard nothing, so he shifted a little more, until he was completely on his side; he ignored the pain of the bruising. He heard nothing. He took a chance and kicked the rest of the blankets off his body.

Let's hope Jimmy's a deep sleeper tonight, Cole thought.

He brought his legs around and pivoted his body as he shifted; he felt the mattress slightly budge against the steel framing and he heard the joints creak. He stopped, waited to see if Jimmy would react, then put both soaked feet on the ladder. The carpet beneath compressed and the floor slightly groaned, but it was so subtle Cole knew nobody would hear it spare the bugs that made the sub-floor their home. He twisted the coils of rope around his shoulder and slowly descended the ladder.

There was a flashlight in the closet, sitting on the wire shelving beside Cole's old Cub Scout sash with the patches he had earned for lighting a 'natural' fire without matches, and tying a Nautical knot. When Cole opened the closet door, he turned the light on and quickly shut the door behind him. He flipped the light switch off and felt the flashlight in his hands; he clicked the on button and watched a disc of light form on the opposite side of the closet, illuminating a rack of shirts. It seemed okay. The last time he could remember using it was when he had gone camping, but that must have been years ago, because dad had still been alive; he remembered the way his dad would tell them about the war, about the gunfire and the explosions. And they would pass around a big bag of marshmallows, poking them through sticks, and their dad would tell them that he did this a couple of times during the war, sitting with the guys, remembering good times; and then he'd bring out a box of chocolates to make 'smores—

That reminded him, did he bring his chocolates? He was sure he'd need them. It would be a good idea to bring them. If he went down the vents only to come across a rotting body at the bottom, then he was sure his nerves would get the best of him, and it wouldn't only be his shoes that were filled with some discomforting liquid.

He set the coils of rope on the wire shelving and slowly opened the door. Where did he put them? He didn't have them when he had gone to get the rope because he went to his pocket when he felt the statues staring at him as he passed.

No, he didn't have them at school either because Aspirin had replaced the box, yes, how could he have been so stupid; he had to take Aspirin every day because of the swelling, and he hated the way the stupid pillbox felt in his pants. He knew the Aspirin was in his school pants, but where was his candy?

He left the closet and Jimmy moved; he rolled over and mumbled something under his breath. Cole didn't quite understand him, but he was sure he heard him say, "what was I doing the entire time?" Cole didn't know what that meant, and didn't care at the moment. As long as he was still asleep, everything was fine—but everything *wasn't* fine. A deep part of Cole urged him to find those chocolates, any chocolates; anything sweet that could fit in his pocket—

But he was at a loss. He couldn't remember where he put the candy because he couldn't remember eating chocolate for the last couple of days; he could just remember swallowing Aspirin at the water fountain.

You had them when you fought Ricky.

He did, and he replaced the chocolates in his pants with the Aspirin in his backpack. His backpack, yes, of course, he must have switched the box with the bottle of pills and just forgot about them—pain can do that to a person.

He grabbed his backpack and unzipped it...and there they were, a box of chocolate covered peanuts, sitting at the bottom of the canvas, the corner crunched where his text book had smashed into it. He grabbed the box and shoved it into his pocket.

Now go on and tie the rope to the wire shelving and let's find out if you killed the little guy or not.

Cole didn't know it then, but grabbing that box of chocolates was the best decision he ever made in his life.

5

The thin yellow strand of rope was just long enough to tie nicely around the clothes rack, and reach across the closet to the top shelf where Cole sat tying it into the bigger rope. He pulled on it and heard the clothes rack groan as the screws in the wall tried to give, but weren't allowed by the anchors in the studs. Cole had moved the boxes away from the miniature door and opened it, watching more of that paint chip and fall from the hinge as it turned.

He fed the thicker rope into the vent and listened to it as the frayed end brushed the tin. Cole wrapped a coil of the thick rope around his body, and carrying the flashlight in one hand, and the rope in the other, he thought he could manage going down the vent. Cole slid into the vent.

He clicked on the flashlight. The vent was at an incredibly stable slant, and he noticed something: this vent was large, too large even. If commonsense had kicked in previously, he would have noted how easily he fit into a conventional housing duct. He poured the light all around him and noticed one more thing about the vent; the bottom was smooth and almost seemed to divot in the middle. There were no lines signifying the end of one duct, connected with another unit. The bottom was just a continuous decline of shiny silver, almost like—

The slide at the playground, the one you're too old to use now, but used to love when you were younger.

Yes, of course, this was just like that slide; it sloped into an oblong 'V' in the middle to accommodate comfort. If these were conventional ducts, then sliding down would almost always mean your pants would rip, because they'd snag on the connection fittings.

He let himself go down the vent, using his feet ahead of him to guide his body, to keep him from going down too fast.

He got to a point where the vent turned slightly and he noticed a large hole in the side of the tin; he pulled himself up farther and shone the flashlight into the cut section. The vent sloped up inside, and the bottom was also smooth, bending in the middle. There was another hole up ahead and inside there was another smooth vent, as if they all connected into this duct and ran into the secret room from there.

When he saw the exit of the vent before him he let his body slide, clutching the rope when his feet kicked out in the air. He pulled his legs back inside and turned his body around, making sure the rope was steady. He shone the light on the ground and scanned it; there was nothing, only the snaking wires, old metallic parts and those mouse bones, all bunched against the wall in disgusting heaps. Where was the Bomber?

What are you worried about man, he's not lying in a pool of blood on the ground, that's a good thing. Maybe Krollup let him out, took him to the police or something. Probably got sick of his whining or something.

The flashlight multiplied in the screens of the dark television monitors on the wall. The robots were gone too; he hadn't noticed that before. He scoured the room.

Down the mines, check there.

There was nothing, only the fire outside the brick stack.

Cole pulled the rope; it still seemed sturdy. He unwound it from his body and let it fall to the ground below; he heard the end of the cord hit the rock. He was going to go down and check for himself, because he still had the sinking sensation that the little guy had wandered into the dark parts of the mine after he slid back down the vents with a foot print on his forehead. Maybe he had gone in utter delirium only to fall somewhere in the darkness to die. Cole hated the thought; he hated assumptions, period, but his nagging conscience pushed him down the rope, which swaggered with his weight. The mouse bones crushed underneath his sneakers and he shone the light everywhere again. He walked towards the mines, sweating heavily now, knowing something was going to happen, knowing he was going to find a little man on the rocky surface with blood spouting from his greasy hair in a pool around his head.

And then he heard something, a clink. Yes, he did, and not like the clink in the vent when the Bomber had been climbing up, but like a piece of metal striking rock.

"Leo?" Cole asked into the surrounding darkness of the mine.

And he was grabbed from behind, one dirty hand covering his open mouth, while the other helped drag him farther into the darkness. The flashlight dropped from his surprised hand and rolled on the floor, spilling light against the far rocky wall.

6

Edwin Krollup sat in his easy chair, which he set in front of David's clone. He was wearing his King's robe, and he was smoking a genuine hand rolled Cuban cigar, while slowly working on a glass of Brandy. It had been four days since his visit to Dr. Innis, and he was in a constant zone he couldn't very well escape.

Hypnosis had changed him, or altered him, he seemed to prefer to say, because he couldn't shake the image of those wolves—*or Yilaks, that's what the Hunter called them.* He even woke up in cold sweats, clutching for the necklace drooping over his collarbone. He held it in his hand and looked around him, waiting to see if a wolf would show itself beyond the shadows. In his dream they had come up the mines. *But that's not gonna happen, right, because time has proven you their absolute patience; they would have come much sooner if their desire was so great, and if they hadn't met Auger, it seems they wouldn't have come at all.* Edwin had wiped his forehead. *I'll surprise them,* he thought, touching the stone.

But tonight, though he denied it as much as his heart could suggest, he was afraid of sleep. Imagining the wolves in his house drew a cloak of dread over Edwin. This wasn't like him, and more and more he cursed Innis for hypnotizing him.

"What did you unlock?" He had asked as he puffed on his cigar. He was slowly remembering certain things: the Hunter and the cris-crossed swords he wore on his back; the way the wolves smelt, like blood and drool; and the way that Wolf had looked at him, wanting to smile, *trying* to smile, showing its devilish array of limitless fangs.

"Grak," he said aloud, startling himself.

Maybe the stone waited for you to remember the images you've been trying to repress—maybe the stone needs you to remember, is making you remember, because it wants to go home. You can feel it breathing in the night, hear its whispering sorrow. It longs just as you long, Eddie, and it's using the Towers as an incentive—

Edwin gulped the rest of the Brandy and looked at the statue in front of him, standing on its elaborate throne. He massaged the rock around his neck. "Are you ready?" He stared at David's blank eyes for a moment, then shook his head.

Edwin stood, and though a part of him heard Cole fall from the vent using the rope behind the fireplace, a stronger part insisted he go to bed and hope dreams stay away. Especially dreams of wolves.

7

Cole closed his eyes; he tasted grease on that hand. Grease and sweat, and he hated every moment of it, but he was relieved. Happy even.

"You mustn't say one word little boy, he's just outside the fireplace. One word and he may come in, and I can't afford to hurry right now, I have to conserve whatever energy I have left." He removed his hand from Cole's mouth. It was dark in the mines, though his flashlight was still turned on, and it had lit a portion of the mine which caught reflections off the glass the Bomber was wearing on his head.

All three robots were standing at Leo's side, and all of their eyes were lit like lamps. This also helped to cast light on that glass piece over his head. Leo was wearing an aquarium like a mask, with the pump still intact. Cole tried to keep himself from laughing, but he failed; it was the hardest thing he had ever tried to do.

Leo quickly covered the boy's mouth again and looked back into the main room behind the fireplace. "Be quiet."

Cole grunted and stopped immediately. Anything to get that hand away from his mouth.

"It's to help me breathe," he finally said, noticing the humor in it. Cole noticed the little guy had a fine bruise above his eyes; he felt bad of course, but he was also glad he didn't find the man dead, or dying. *Relieved*.

"What do you mean?"

"Look kid, I don't have to answer anything you say. I was on my way until you showed up, and you scared me out of my wits; I thought I was getting a surprise visit from you know *who*." He pointed out *there*, beyond the fireplace. Where the big guy lived. "I saw him outside the fireplace before I decided to make my way down. I was sure he was coming so I hid my breathing case under the bed. Ten minutes later and I looked out the fireplace stack again and I saw cigar smoke. So I left. And I'm not coming back. I'd appreciate it if you don't say anything until I'm totally gone, okay kid?"

Cole didn't know what to say. Just last weekend he was afraid this little guy was coming up the vents to terrorize his family, to take out all his aggression, but now he understood the little guy just wanted to get away. To live again, perhaps. To know freedom.

"I thought I might be able to get up the vents, you know. Before you decided to come down I never even knew they existed, but *other* factors were against me." Leo gave Cole an odd look, which intensified his round eyes through the glass bowl. "Namely, my fingers aren't what they used to be, and a foot in the head doesn't help your forward momentum." He grunted. "But I've been working on this for almost three weeks, and I'm not going to let this option slide because of fear, no way. Whatever's down there is down there; that's my sentiments. If they want to get me, let them. I'm not worth much alive anyway." His voice sounded drained coming from behind the glass, and Cole realized how white the man was. It reminded Cole how long he'd been trapped here.

"I'm sorry about that, but what was I supposed to do? I heard you coming up, but I didn't know what it was, and then you grabbed my foot...why the heck would you do that? Trust me, I react to stuff like that, I'm not gonna let something drag me down."

"I said your name."

"So, I know what you did at City Hall."

Leo exhaled slowly. "It was just a spectacle. The robot was a carnival act. That's all."

"All I'm trying to say is it's not everyday an accused bomber grabs your leg in a dark vent. And plus, I just wanted to apologize."

Leo took the glass bowl off his head and handed it to AL4. This way his voice didn't sound so muffled, and that thin sheet of shine was removed from his vision. In doing so he realized something on Cole's face, something he was surprised he hadn't noticed before. The right side of the boy's face was swollen, and there was runny make-up smeared around his cheekbone. "I see you feel my pain."

At first Cole was confused, but then he noticed the sincerity in Leo's eyes. He felt his cheek and slightly grimaced; he had been ignoring the discomfort for awhile now, but when people pointed the bruising out, the pain seemed to flare up again. He went to his pocket and only found the box of chocolates. He hadn't brought the Aspirin, which was a mistake. "Remember when you said you were picked on in school?"

Leo gave Cole an understanding look. "You have the same look Cole, I'm sorry to say. I noticed it when I first met you. That's why I was so surprised to find your foot an inch above my eyes. Because guys like you let the hand drag you down."

"I did. I mean I used to. But I got a clear message one day to hide my targets. Try not to give them anything to attack."

"That was a noble gesture, but of course there are difficulties with the theory. First of all, I found out that once you're a target, you're always a target. If the kids want it bad enough, they'll find a way around your defense." He pointed to his face. "I suppose that's why you've come down, isn't it Cole?"

Cole was on the verge of tears. He could hide his targets, keep his chocolates in his pants, but they'd find some other reason to make fun of him; it was human nature, or the nature of the bully, as it so stood. They had the knack for pointing out peculiarities. The lecture about bullying at school became Cole's fault because he left the room at the right time, and somebody noticed this, somebody made it a general point to make sure he got his beatings come lunch because they had to sit through an incredibly boring presentation. "I remember you'd said you finally fought back and got revenge, and I wanna know how you did it. I'm sick of them, and sometimes, sometimes I've thought about coming to school and paying them all back; it must have been what it felt like for you when you got your chance to pay back the mayor, you know, to shove a bomb into *his* building and watch the flames flicker. It's a sick thought, I know, but it's a nice thought. Kids younger than me hit me. Did that ever happen to you? They come up to me in groups and take turns hitting me in the stomach because they know the bruises won't show in class; and they know that if I rat, I'll just get it worse. I have to live with that, but I don't want to."

Before Leo could say anything, Cole pulled his sweater up. His flesh was irritated from the drying sweat, but all Leo noticed were the bruises. "Oh my goodness. This is all from the bullies?"

"That's the thing, they're not all bullies, some of them just take it out on me for the sake of finding a victim other than themselves, you know what I mean?"

"Nobody wants to be a victim," Leo agreed.

Cole dropped his sweater back over his gut. "I had this thought the other day, you know, because I was scared that I may have killed you when I kicked you down the vents, but I had this thought. A part of me wanted to ask you what to do about *them*, those bullies; that same part also made me find out if you were *actually* dead or not, too. I sat on it, because I was scared that a) I'd find you lying on the ground in a bloody heap; or b) you'd attack me for attacking you, a tit for a tat. But I came down. I risked the chance of finding you dead. That's how much this means to me, and I know you're on your way, I know you have your own bully, but please, from one victim to another, what should I do?"

Leo pondered this for a moment, and he scratched his baldhead. Flakes of scalp fell from his fingers, and floated to the ground. "You didn't happen to bring food with you?"

"No."

"Well, I could spare ten minutes. My guess is that it is almost one in the morning, and if that's the case, ten minutes is all I have. I believe it will be quite a journey down the mines, especially by foot, and I believe if I don't get a head start on the morning, Krollup will find me when he wakes up and I do not want that to happen. What I intend for you is actually quite simple. If you believe you can run to your kitchen, light-footedly of course, and fill a bag of some sort with food and water, and if you believe you can withstand loneliness for a day or two, then I have an answer for you."

Cole leaned in, waiting for the answer. "I left a rope dangling from the vent, so I can get back up, but I don't quite see the point in grabbing food."

"The point is actually quite simple, Cole. You have to make people feel bad about themselves, not about you."

Cole thought about this. He didn't quite understand it.

"Let me tell you one thing that I understand about your relationship with your brother. First of all, he is your age because you are twins, which secondly means he must be in the same school as you, unless he is of the privileged sort and gets to go to a special school, though upon meeting him I established one thing; he isn't incredibly gifted, except for perhaps his physical prowess, but that is something I know nothing of. But I do know one thing about physical prowess: it entitles its owner a sense of his or her own bullying. In your case, I thought for sure your brother would act as a security blanket *for* you; I mean, he did almost attack me for supposedly strangling you. The point is, he looked out for you *then*, but here you are *now*, with more bruises than I have ever seen in my natural life, and it poses an important question: where was he when all of this was happening? Either he goes to a different school than you, or he feels personal security is against his beliefs and decided to turn against his own brother. Rather disgusting if you ask me. So let me ask you this, Cole. Is your brother in any way responsible for this, this bullying?"

Cole wanted to cry. "He ignores me when it happens. And some of the kids that do hit me, or yell at me, are doing it because they're mad at Jimmy. He steals their cigarettes, and he uses Mr. Krollup as an incentive to do so; he tells them he can get their parents fired if they don't listen. There's a revolt against him, but they use me as the punching bag."

Leo thought Jimmy had a rather ingenious tactic there, but said nothing of it. Instead he was curious why Cole didn't use that same strategy. "Isn't Mr. Krollup your stepfather too?"

Cole nodded. "I don't understand why it's me, why it's always me. I really don't."

"Okay Cole, then my plan will work perfectly. If my mind is working correctly, then today is Friday, well actually this morning it's Saturday, but to anybody that cares it's still Friday night as they're busy sleeping in their beds. If you disappear all day Saturday, and even Sunday, you have the power to fill Jimmy with guilt, since he seems to be the main bully that matters here. Of course he'll worry about you, but the feelings ripping his insides will be the real deal, if you know what I mean. He may even confess to your parents that he feels it was his fault that you decided to skip town during the night; that he had treated you awfully for some time, and then guess what, Cole?

You win. When you return he'll have a deep appreciation for you again, well, not to say again, but he'll realize it much stronger."

"I did show him my stomach, and his jaw dropped. I think this might work."

"Yes it will. Go and get some food for yourself, and you can accompany me down the mines until the air gets bad, then you can hide. Bring some books or something, maybe even an extra battery for your flashlight, if you feel like it."

Cole turned and walked back to the hanging rope. When he pulled on it to climb back up he realized a terrible thing; he hadn't tied the thin rope to the thick rope strongly enough to hold his weight entirely. The knot separated, and the remainder of the rope slid down the vent and collected on his shoulders, drooping to the ground.

"Perhaps this won't work out. You won't have a way back up once I'm gone, especially if the rope happened to break again if you retied it. I need to take my robots for my own good. I can send AL4 to boost you up right now, if you'd like, and we can say our good-byes."

Cole stood on the mouse bones with the rope bunched on his shoulder and he had an incredible thought: his disappearance in the night might just be the final push to urge Jimmy to rip his cigarettes in half. "No Leo, I think tonight I'm going to try a delicacy. Is raw mouse in season?"

Leo laughed, something he probably hadn't done in some time; it even sounded outdated. He shrugged his shoulders. He couldn't tell if Cole was lying or not. Leo took the coil of rope from Cole and slid it under his cot.

And upstairs in the closet, the thin rope that had once been tied off dangled from the clothes rack, and its unsupported end drooped down off the top shelf and was finally pulled by gravity into a neat swing that steadied about ten minutes later.

8

They followed the path of the flashlight for what seemed like hours, but in the darkness, or in the belly of the beast as most would call it, time is swallowed like bait, and doesn't really exist. Time is only a measure between the sun and the moon, and where light is battery operated, time doesn't exist.

"I'd guess it is around two in the morning, though I've been known to make mistakes," Leo said, his hair bouncing with the uneven steps all five of them took, the robots lagging well behind as they struggled to get around the fissures. They'd already seen a dog's skull, cracked down the crown and busted at the bridge of the nose; it looked as if it were trying to speak in the path of the flashlight, the shadows turning its remaining teeth into a checkerboard.

There was a rat snaking its way out of the empty eye socket as they passed, and Cole shuddered; he hated rats, and he looked at the cracks in the backfill at either side to make sure there wasn't more of them struggling to get into the mine. There were more bones lying around, Cole was sure of that, but he kept them out of the path of the light, just as surely as AL4 cradled the aquarium against its steel abdomen. Cole stepped over polished stones that he thought might have been bones; either way, the smell got worse the deeper they went, and he started having second thoughts. Was this all worth it, having Jimmy feel guilty for something he'd tried to ignore? And that was assuming Jimmy even cared in the first place.

"What are you thinking about, Cole?"

Cole looked up. The light ahead of them danced into an unknown darkness; the silence ahead of them was both uncanny, and calming. "Nothing really. I just hope Jimmy appreciates this. I just hope he notices I'm gone. I might just stay down here until Monday, get my clothes all dirty, get everybody worried."

"Yes, guessing others reactions is always tempting." Leo snickered and looked at Cole meaningfully. "This is quite an adventure for me, you know. I've pondered doing this ever since I realized Krollup's intentions."

"What exactly are his intentions?" Cole kicked a small rock and it bounced feebly down the dark hole until knocking into a wall.

"He would want you to believe he was doing me a favor. He stressed to me that I owed him my allegiance because he saved me from prison. I remember sitting across the street from City Hall, waiting for the right time to blow the head off the robot, and they all attacked me, dozens of police and Krollup's security force; they found me as if I had been waving them over. I was torn, Cole. Torn. I told you I wasn't a murderer, and until that job, I had only built things that were able to crack bank vaults and and other odd jobs, but this time I was supposed to blow up a building filled with innocent people. Cole, have you ever heard of dualism?"

Cole shook his head.

"Well, suppose you split yourself into two different individuals. One of these said halves, we'll call them, has this deep-rooted desire to wreak havoc, to build a bomb and watch it go off; while the other half, well, it forms a chart stating the pros and the cons, emphasizing the cons over the pros. I was split like this."

"Do you mean you had an angel on one shoulder, and a devil on the other, like in cartoons?"

"In a way, I suppose, only I didn't have an angel. I had two devils on my shoulders all the time because I was a man bent on aggressions, Cole, and I don't recommend you do the same. Perhaps hiding out for a day is the best thing for you to do, because possessing two devils is awfully strenuous. I only wanted to make people feel as bad as I did. I made bad things because that was my state of mind, and when I realized I could make good money, that only triggered me to double my aggression. But one devil was always worse. *Persuasive.* He was the one that made me build a shed with a false wall at the back that slid away if you pulled at just the right angle. Behind that wall I hid my designs, some of them finished. I remember that shed the most, more than anything from my *old* house; it's hard to think of it that way."

"What kind of designs?" Cole asked.

"Robots like the one I had intended on sending into City Hall, had my *angelic* devil not interfered. When I was given that job, a part of me was ecstatic, because memory has many of its roots in evil. It's true, because you always remember those who'd punched you, more than you will remember those who didn't. Bullies are a disease Cole, I'm sure you know that, but there is a collective hatred for them, shared among you and I and many other boys and girls that either can't throw a ball or wear thick glasses because they were born of parents that gave them poor eyesight. Those with unfortunate attributes that make them targets—mine had always been my ability to build things. Bullies saw this as an oddity, I suppose, and it didn't help that I started losing my hair in my teens. My father had the same downfall, inherited by his father; the infamous Leonardo premature balding gene. You develop your hatred quickly. I was never beaten as you were, Cole, but they broke my things. Do you remember the toaster I told you about, the one I built in science class that could communicate and respond to human voice? The bullies took it upon themselves to prove a toaster couldn't respond to catcalls by bashing it with sticks while I was still holding it; they dented it and I could hear the programmed voice shrieking until it faded into a soft blip. Then they'd tackle me and rub my scalp until any hair I did have fell out.

"I tell you now Cole, it isn't fair. It isn't fair that they hit you, and it isn't fair they didn't appreciate my talent. Bullies are a disease, and I am living proof that you can never fully exceed their grasp. I think that's why I was torn in half by the prospect of eliminating at least one enemy. The Mayor, or Chuck as I'll always remember him, will always be the boy carrying the stick, bashing at my project while he laughed and called me a bald baby. It was hard not to agree with the devil in that aspect, Cole, and I suppose saying such would vouch for your former assumption that I was indeed a terrorist, but I assure you, I never thought about the other people in the building. For all I cared, they were just the Mayor's clones, laughing at little old me from their huge offices. This hatred drove me, split me into the halves of which I spoke. One half of me built a robot that would level the entire building, and my other half built a robot that would do nothing but lose its head. Yet there was still the conflict over which robot would enter the building and stand inside the lobby ticking silently. This was the climax of my dualism, when I realized whether or not I was a murderer. I thought of the moral implications, and I thought about how my scalp reddened when Chuck drove his knuckles into my skull. The devil had me in his grips, so to speak, but Cole, in the end you have to realize that no matter your aggression, you and you alone are going to have to live with the consequences, the guilt of that one image scarred on your memory, forgetting the bullies, forgetting your past. You will only see your mistake. That was what turned me away, urged me to send the shoddy robot and blame its misuse on malfunctions beyond my control."

Cole knew exactly what he was talking about, because he too had dreamt of living with the scarred image of his foot planted into Leo's skull, and the understanding in those two big eyes as his body started reeling back down the vents.

"But I've trailed off, and I see you're probably getting bored. Sometimes I rant, that much is obvious." He snickered again and then turned around. "AL4, you be careful with that glass, if it breaks, you break."

"Yes sir," it said in its oddly disturbing voice.

"What do you think Krollup will do once he finds out you're gone?"

"I see him flailing his arms like a monkey, and screaming at the top of his lungs, but then I remember, I'm his dirty little secret. So I don't know. He wasn't through with me yet."

"What is it he needed you for, exactly?"

Leo breathed out sharply and ran his hand over his baldhead. "To build him things, I suppose."

"He stole you from the police and guaranteed you safety just to build him things. I don't mean to be rude, but he has all the money in the world. You'd think he could just afford people to build him whatever it is he needed built."

"Yes, but this is a secret. Edwin's biggest concern is public knowledge. The fact that he built over old mines seemed peculiar to everybody, I know, because I heard about it all those years ago. People guessed why he did it, but nobody knew, and I think Krollup wanted the guarded secrecy with somebody else he could tell. Somebody else he could confide in. Unfortunately for me, I followed the devil on my shoulder, and accepted the City Hall job because my memory was tainted with revenge."

"What did he want you to build for him, Leo?"

"Robots. Crude robots, made from scrap materials he could find. Anything really. I was supposed to send these robots down the mines with cameras, and they were supposed to plant them as surveillance measures, but it never worked out. As if it wasn't supposed to happen, you know."

The air started getting denser. "It is almost that time, Cole. I'm afraid to say, I believe we may have to part ways soon."

Cole ignored him. "What did he want to see? I mean, down there," he pointed into the darkness, broken only by the disc of light bouncing off shelves of rock.

Leo shook his head. "I don't know, Cole. I'm sure I'll find out soon enough."

Cole could hear the lie in Leo's voice; it was as if he wanted Cole to hear it.

"Leo?"

"Yes Cole."

"Why do you do as Krollup says? I can understand if you're afraid of prison, but it seems to me that you'd be happy to exchange this place for jail any day." For some reason Cole had been thinking of the giant leg he had seen disappear around the side of the house.

Leo walked silently for a moment, looking straight ahead, perhaps imagining his impending freedom. They could hear the chirps of rodents, and the pitter-patter of their tiny feet as they strolled around them, no doubt sucking dry whatever rotten flesh still clung to bones scattered about. "It's hard to say," he finally said. "I suppose it would be easy if I believed I owed him favors for saving me from the police, from prison. I don't remember how he did so, because his security team was so rough when they reached my car at City Hall. Everything thereafter was just a haze, you see, but I didn't owe him anything. Have you ever watched your face in the mirror in the pitch black of night?"

Cole nodded.

"Then you've seen a different person stare back at you. Shadows play tricks, they do. For that one moment, you are looking into the glazed eyes of a ghoul, until you want your eyes to focus, to realize that it is just your reflection, but there's that one moment, that split second that you believe you're looking at something else. The same thing happens often with Krollup. I have seen in his eyes the very fires of a volcano, swirling in tantrums, and I believe for that moment I'm staring into the Devil's eyes. He can become a different person altogether, and in doing so, odd things happen."

Cole stopped and looked at Leo; he even pointed the flashlight into his eyes. "Like what?"

Leo grimaced and pushed the light off to the side. "I don't mean to scare you, he just has that effect on me."

Cole cocked his eye. "You're an easy person to see through, Leo. What odd things have you seen?"

"I've never seen a man suck down a cigar faster than him, I can vouch for that much."

Cole swallowed hard, unsure if he wanted to tell Leo of the giant leg, cast in white stone like bone, but a sense of the truth was hard to come by, and when an answer popped on by, you grabbed it by the lips and made it talk. "Have you seen things moving about on their own?"

Leo looked at Cole. A sudden understanding blossomed. "What are you talking about?"

"You know what I'm talking about, you do, I can see it in your eyes. You grew afraid when I mentioned it. Tell me Leo, what have you seen? It would only help what I saw make sense."

Leo's eyes grew cold, and the color (whatever color there was) drained from his face in quick gulps. He put his finger to his lips and pursed them, saying *shhhhh*, until the only clear sound was his heart beating frantically. But there was another sound also, a muffled beat almost, and Cole could feel it in his feet. A slight thump thump thump that kept growing.

"What is that?" Cole asked. The aquarium in AL4's arm shook until the glass knocked against its abdomen in shrill clinks.

"It's coming from that way," Leo said, pointing his shaking finger towards the darkness. "Can you smell that in the air? Everything's changed. The calm is gone." He tilted his head and flared his nostrils. The thumps grew louder, and with them came this intolerable sense that something was racing up, something fast. Something large enough to shake the mines.

Cole felt the hairs on his neck stand on end; he could smell the difference also, as if a storm was coming, filling the air with electricity. He looked at Leo under the brightness of his flashlight, watching the man's eyes dance in his head as he stood still, listening.

There were other noises.

A low howl. That was unmistakable.

A shuffle of thumps. Breathing.

Echoes of these noises.

Leo's heart.

There came this sense of an oncoming locomotive from the darkness, and the sound grew louder, clearer.

Cole turned his flashlight toward the gaping throat of the mine, into the growling gut; the path moved across the backfill and found the empty air. But the air wasn't empty.

Not at all.

Cole dropped the flashlight.

It spun on the ground in a flimsy circle until the path of light stopped on both Leo and Cole, who clung to the wall, grabbing the cracks in the rocks with their fingers until the tips bled. The sound grew louder and Cole cursed the light that had found them, that had turned directly on them and pointed. The aquarium rocked against AL4, while the other two robots lost control on the uneven ground and toppled into a metallic clutter.

"Pretend you're the rock, pretend you're the rock," Leo said, his voice so choked with fear that Cole pitied him. They could smell *them* now, coming up from the darkness; they could smell what was in their mouths, like the rancid stench of decaying meat.

The robots on the ground stirred and tried to upright themselves when the howls grew louder, the growls longer, and the thumps closer.

Cole shut his eyes and gritted his teeth together until they almost fastened to one another; he could hear them grinding as his jaw squeaked and groaned. He felt something hot against the back of his neck, something sticky. And the smell. The strong smell. He could hear Leo crying beside him, whimpering as he scrambled against the rock.

"Wha' is this? This isn' right. There's only sposed to be one o' ya. Only one," one of them spoke, in a voice that sounded so awful and garbled that Cole's swollen ear began to bleed. The feeling of its breath pelting against the back of his neck made the skin feel like it was peeling away. Cole could feel sharp daggers dig into his side as he was turned away from the rock; he kept his eyes closed, squeezing in the tears. He wanted to vomit. The smell coming from them was even worse than he could have imagined. There was a strong sense of light in his eyes, and he realized one of them must have picked up the flashlight and was shining it directly into his face. "'Tis a convenience you should meet us half way though, child, for the old man said we would have to climb through brick and fire to get to you." It poked Cole in the gut with its claws. Cole felt like his bowels were going to fall out of his shirt.

The guttural voice rung Cole's head until he thought his temples would implode and stretch apart his eardrums.

Leo shook and whimpered a harsh cry that aroused the wolves' attention. He had crept into a crook of rock. A wolf wearing a leather baldric walked to the little man and grunted in his face until tears streamed down his cheeks and dropped onto his chest. It licked a cloven tongue over its teeth, piercing the plush muscle like pins in a slug. It grabbed Leo by the collar and pulled him from the crook in the rock, and lifted him in the air, its claws folding around his neck until he opened his eyes in a terrible choke. Leo looked down at the wolf. It looked at Leo with its yellow eyes. "We have a messenger," it said. Leo sobbed harder.

A wolf carrying a scroll, bound by twine, took Leo by the arm, removing him from the wolf wearing the baldric. "Give this to the man who holds the stone," it said, speaking in horrible English, turning the language into disgusting grunts that crept from between tar-brazened lips. It dropped Leo into a heap on the floor; he stared up and watched them prod at the robots, obviously recognizing them. Cole held himself against the backfill, his eyes still closed.

The wolves spoke in their guttural language, howling and gnashing their teeth. Leo felt like his brain was going to explode; he held the scroll to his chest and could feel the wolves' hearts through the ground. He couldn't move. He watched them take Cole. He watched Cole disappear into the darkness and he felt himself trying to say something, anything, to get the wolves to come back.

There was nothing. The light was gone. The sounds were gone. Cole was gone.

And Leo passed out, still clutching the scroll in his shaking hand.

PART II

THE INLANDS

"Wizard's Blood deems life eternal,
Dodging death's timeless inferno."

CHAPTER 8

THE OLD MAN

1

They had left the trees behind them; a big patch that stretched to the sky where no birds sang. If he strained hard enough he could still hear *them* whinnying, shrieking like dying horses, but soon the wind would carry that noise far away and he'd only be left with his thoughts.

I'm finally dying.

He shook that drudgery away. That thought was like a sting from a wasp, infecting but manageable. He looked out the side of the cart, which was blanketed in furs and lined in beat leather; there was no path to follow, only the overgrown grasses and the shrubbery which maintained the bumpy ride. When he looked to his left, through the fold in cloth, he could see the distant mountains to the north, a range of them over the Northern Waters where rumors spoke of angels, whom lived in utter contempt of the world beneath them, shunning everything with sneers that drew storms from the seas. The mountains were but hazes through the mist of distance, waving like mirages, almost as if the angels had themselves become able to move the masses, to collect the shelves of rock and physically supplant them from beneath the earth and rotate them.

The ride moved on and the trees behind them grew smaller on the horizon. The ground was burned and diseased, littered with bones. Some of them animal, and others human. The man in the cart shuddered.

He remembers explosions.

He remembers the distant screams, echoed by the shafts; he remembers the bright lights of combusting coal.

The old man in the cart looked to his right; behind him he could see the murkiness of the coast, and the Indin Seas beyond. He could imagine the surf crashing on the rocky coast; he remembered eating an ice cream cone with his wife Judith as the sun just cowered beneath the pink clouds, leaving the sand a purple sponge.

That was the Atlantic. That was then. Now you are here, beyond any means of reason. You are somebody different. You have lived far too long. You should have died in the blast. You should have choked on the carbon monoxide like your men, falling in heaps as the dust swirled, as the flames shot into the tunnels.

"I know," he muttered. He thought about the tumor, but shook the image away. "But the King told me how death could be avoided."

He'd been here for a long time, in this place—this *world*. He had come here by accident. He had woken in a world of spinning dusts beyond the mines, beyond the burning coal and gas…and he was born again, born again under the mists of victory and delusion for the King's army believed he'd been a savage Yilak-hunter. They found him in the rubble and praised him. They brought him back to the great city in a parade for all the army had accomplished in the war against the wolves, and he sat at the King's side, sat by his golden throne and listened. And he learned.

He learned about immortality.

The old man in the cart smiled and took another swig of the bottle he had fastened between his knobby knees. "I woke up as a warrior. And they worshipped me." He put the bottle to his lips again and drank. He drank until the bottle was almost empty.

You're senile. You've professed mad belief in folktale by going on this mindless crusade to the old woods to bring back what?—An egg sac? Do you actually believe you'll find what you're looking for in an egg? Do you actually believe this is your destiny?

"Truth isn't simple. Every part of the world is a cog that works towards some dynamic cause. Truth and certainty are only parts of an infinite scheme—who would have believed the other end of an exploding mine would open to another world? The idea seems ludicrous, but we know it's not the liquor. The Traveling Man told me I'd find salvation in the eggs of the old forest, so why shouldn't I believe in such destiny? I felt his magic work through me. I believed him. I need to believe him. I'm dying again." He lowered his head and rubbed his temples. Yes, he was dying again. He should have been dead long ago. He was diagnosed with lung cancer, an inoperable tumor the doctor had claimed was the size of a melon. That was forty six years ago. And here he could feel the tumor growing again, as if it had just disappeared, as if the transaction between worlds had stolen it. But it was back. He coughed blood.

He rubbed the bottle of alcohol. "If I find hope in a seer's prophesy: if I believe in the King's stories of immortality then why shouldn't I look for the Wizard's Blood?"

The old man looked at his withered hands and rubbed his knuckles. He thought about the stories he'd learned. From the King, from passing mouths expressing such delight in gossip. He spoke to himself with absurd clarity, listening intently to his own voice, for it was this concentration that would carry him the rest of the way. It was this concentration and conversation that would carry him. The wolves weren't much for chat. "There is one Wizard left in the world, so tales say. That Wizard's name is Ae-Granum, and he built the Towers in Wolf Country, built them with the mythic stone that man through the mines holds so dearly. The King lives in those Towers now. He wears a vial of blood around his neck, cut from Ae-Granum's throat after he collapsed in exhaustion, the birth of the Towers before him in a tornado of dust and rock. I want that blood." The old man stared out the cart, watching the land unfold. "This world exists beyond reason. I am in the world of storybooks. Of magic." He ran his knuckles along his palm. "I am a long way from home, so yes, I express hope in the fulfillment of destiny."

2

The old man slept. He didn't dream. In the Inlands his dreams were but memories. He remembered his wife, Judith; he remembered how much she hated his venturing into the mines with the expedition crews, helping them install the Timberset to support the roof; helping them unload the waste rock, and helping them fill the wagons with coal, hopping onto the battery-operated tractor as it climbed back up the shaft. She hated it because he didn't need to go down; he didn't need to because he was the boss, but he had always said to her: "You're only as good as the men working for you, and the men working for me are brutes; there are no better men, and I only wish I could be of their caliber."

"That's funny, because they wish the same thing, only they'd like to live your life, not live from paycheck to paycheck. Your job is to sit behind a desk and make sure everything goes to plan; they go down and risk it, because face it Kenneth, they're dispensable. And your health," she would mutter under her breath.

"That's not right, and you know it."

"I only wish you wouldn't go down there. Every time I imagine you in your hard hat, carrying your flashlight, trying to be a brute, to be one of them, I imagine something terrible happening. I don't wish to hear on the news that my husband died in a freak mining accident only because he wanted to fit in with the working class."

The trail got bumpy. The bottle knocked against his thigh, and out of instinct, he grabbed it and clutched it to his chest.

There was a terrible bump and the cart veered.

The old man knocked his head on the edge of the wagon and awoke to find he was staring up at the crude roof, with its weird ring patterns of wood. The cart veered again. It felt like it was going to tip; he had to grab the sides and steady himself. "What's going on out there?" He felt a tinge of drunkenness creep up on him, and he fell back down. Through the spread in the drapery he could see the Northern Mountains, though they were farther than before. The trail had to cut farther south to venture round the Sordid ruins.

There was no answer. He stuck his head outside and was nearly struck by an arrow, which lodged in the side of the cart, piercing through the wall; the shaft nearly stuck all the way into the interior. A sense of relief swept over him, and beyond the shrubbery he saw a group of men, staying low, only the hilts of their swords showing over the dying blades of grass.

Either they were Hunters or farmers of the north, hoping to cut off the wolf trailhand and regain lost land from the general.

"Ambush," the old man screamed, and the oxen made a sharp turn again, almost bringing the wagon on its side. One of the beasts bearing the cart had three arrows in its hind flank, and it tried to pull away from the pack. The wolves unsheathed their blades and sniffed the air.

They walked on their hindquarters around the cart, their muzzles tilted in the air, dripping foam to the ground in puddles. They held weapons in their claws, swords jutting over their fanned shoulders, baldrics bound over their breastplates like diagonal belts. The wolves looked at the old man, eyeing the arrow that had lodged itself into the cart.

"We can smell you. Come where we can see you, for we shall use your skulls as cups to drink your blood," Grak Ulak, chief of the Yilaks, growled; he stood nine feet tall in the shadow of the cart, wearing only a black breastplate with skulls hanging askew by pieces of twine and hair. An arrow flew from the grass and struck him in the upper thigh. The renegades had made the mistake of showing their location. Grak only pulled the arrow from his leg and snapped it in his claws, till the splinters fell like dust to the ground beneath him. He bared his fangs in a predator's snarl.

He pounced. He jumped fifteen feet into the grass and landed on an older fellow too slow to avert the attack. The man's bow cracked beneath him, the snap partnering his wheezy exhalation as he felt the wolf's claws immerse themselves in his chest.

"Protect the egg sac," the old man screamed from within the wagon, and Jarak the Wolf jumped in front of it and held his sword out. The sac had been covered in shrubbery itself, and was lying upon a makeshift sled of branches and leaves, tied behind the cart by thick rope.

"I saw the life leave his eyes. Dare you test me further," Grak said in a guttural voice that brought chills to the men's ears.

A farmer, who had watched for years the acres of his land fall under the shadow of Sordid annexation, gritted his teeth and fisted his homemade spear. He jumped from the grass and kicked Grak as he passed. Grak stabbed him mid-air. The man fell in a screaming fit, clawing at his gut where blood spurted in shots. "Cowards, you kill our women and our children," he screamed, and Ilak the Wolf, who wore a baldric across his chest, put the farmer out of his misery.

"We kill the men too," Ilak said in a low mutter.

Grak growled and got on all fours; there were two farmers left behind the shrubbery. They both jumped out, carrying ancient swords with blades that had dulled and rusted a reddish brown. One took the path towards Fralak the Wolf, who was born but five years ago, and whose hair was still thick, densely covering his brow and muzzle. The wolf removed his own sword and slashed at the farmer, who parried it in the air as he jumped aside. The fellow, who wore a tunic as beige as the grass around him, rolled into the dying blades until he disappeared. Fralak smelt the air and slashed his sword through the clearing, cutting the grass in diagonal chunks. "You cannot hide. What is your name, so I should title my favorite bowl after I scoop your brains out?"

"Me name is Lagen, son of Foris Ajassen o' the Aena guild. For m' people, I should avenge your merciless threat." The stout farmer lashed out from the grass before Fralak and beheaded the wolf in one swift arc, his dull blade slicing through the wolf's throat like fork through hay.

Ilak pounced on Lagen, and drew his claws into the man's chest until his last breath was just a sigh of hatred, and perhaps gratitude that he should join his father in the tiers. The cart had stopped; two of the oxen were dead, big furry heaps on the ground. Grak had killed the last of the farmers, slashing through his tunic with his mighty claws. He gave the decapitated Fralak a look of disgust and unwound the rope holding the dead oxen; he pulled them away from the cart, and tied the rope around the remaining two oxen.

"What shall we do with Fralak?" Ilak asked Grak.

"He is food for the scavengers. Let him rest with his mistake; let him lie next to the one who beat him, for it will teach him an important lesson." Grak snarled. He slapped an ox and the cart lurched forward.

"Was it injured?"

Jarak turned and looked at the old man and tried to smile. Jarak's muzzle lifted slightly, but his teeth just slashed his bottom lip and it began to bleed. "Your egg is fine, old man," he said, in a kinder voice that calmed the old man in the cart.

The two oxen pulled the wagon, and the old man lulled back. He could hear the sled behind the cart screeching against the earth. They had risked much to retrieve the egg.

They would reach the shadow of the Towers by nightfall.

3

"The King once told me things. Secret things," the old man said to himself, as he stared out at the Sordid ruins, mountains of crumbled rocks and precipices stabbing the dead sky like accusing fingers. He often spoke to himself. It was a sign of his madness. "He sat as he always did, in his throne carved of gold, wearing the very stone the wolves seek, the very stone which built the Towers, twiddling it with his fingers, the reflection shining from his massive crown embedded with jewels. He drank then. He looked at me solemnly, and he took from his gown the vial of ichor; he told me the black crude was the blood of a Wizard, the last of the Wizards, for Ichimad had turned himself into a garden where his strange alchemy turned an army of Yilaks into a forest, where the trees speak in guttural moans, as if the hearts of the wolves still beat. He told me his plans; he took me into his quarters and placed in me a certain honor even his nephew, Haspin, hadn't received. He told me his intentions for the Towers, for even though he told his people they were prisons for the surviving Yilaks, he had different plans. Different plans indeed. For if there was truth in what he spoke, the civil wars may have been averted; for if he sent out his great armies on the final hunt for the wolves, the city would have been saved."

And you wouldn't have gone mad, he thought, with an almost ironic tone, *believing the tales of a damned world, fleeing the very gates of the city before the Hunters revolted. You had gone mad in the castle at the tip of Sadaan, beyond the Joon Mountains, plucking away your sanity with the knowledge that people were being killed; you lost your sympathy then, for even during World War II in your old world you found shame and disgust with the treatment of people. And the King had warned you of it then, perhaps as his reasoning to stop his madness, to tell him to use his powers for other reasons, for goodness, to call upon the rocks beneath the wolves, to uncover their hiding places. You would have saved a place of prosperity; he would have laid in his tomb a legend, not at the fault of the fall of the city, and the very monarchy he beheld for so many years.*

The old man scratched his head. He heard the voice inside his mind so clearly. "The king built the Towers for himself—for his plunder. Nothing else. He had gone mad. With power. With greed."

Outside the cart, to the south, the old man could see where the earth flattened, where the path led from the Towers to the city in Samniite. And to the north the fallen mountains hugged the horizon; no plants grew, only rocks and large trees bare of any leaves that had twisted sideways in an effort to cleanse themselves of the poisonous air. The ground underneath was cracked, and the hooves of the oxen trailed a thick plume of red smoke that occasionally got into the wagon and made the old man cough, remembering the smoke inside the mines as his men, his brutes fell and screamed of their clogged throats.

"Jarak, what are those lights in the country?" The old man asked, as he looked down the precipice, a hundred feet below in the shadows of the Towers.

The wolf glared down. "There is a carriage bearing torches about its quarters; there are soldiers. Pay no mind old man, we will worry about it," Jarak said. The air was getting darker as night fell, and the old man could feel his head clearing; all his drink was wearing off, and with it his mind stabled.

"Grak, there are knights bearing the King's Crest," Jarak growled, pointing at the carriage below them.

Grak growled. His red eyes twinned the setting sun, recessed in his gleaming brow. "Sullak, Shivak, see what they'd claim, for if they bear intentions to fight, bring me back the skull of the one who uses the carriage."

The two wolves jumped down the cliff, bouncing from rock to rock as their claws dug deep into the fissures. The wolves beneath howled upon Grak's arrival, and the cart steadily declined the slope of cracked earth, pulling behind it a great egg sac.

4

The old man could only spread the drapery on the cart; he didn't want to put weight onto his knees. The sun had immersed behind the ruins and the torchlight flickered. The carriage before him was shaped like an apple, and had gold lacing and ivory supports like curved tusks; the King's Crest was indeed laid upon it, a simple golden carving of two leaves and a glowing sun, which stretched its rays towards the end of the marking. Men stood around the carriage carrying swords and spears, with quivers on their backs filled with white arrows.

He could hear the ropes being cut behind him, as the egg sac was cut from the cart.

Sullak walked to Grak, who stood holding his sword, snarling at the armed men who only looked down. The wolves surrounded the carriage.

"It's the heir, and he comes seeking answers, not trouble," Sullak said.

"He was stupid to've come here." Grak showed his fangs through his cut lips and hissed at the men; a faint glow came from the carriage, and the horses that pulled it whinnied and shook, trying to break free of their reigns to escape. "If 'tis my will, I shall show him trouble." Grak pulled a young soldier into his grips and licked his ear, leaving old bloodstains on the side of his face. "What have you come for, maggots?" Grak said, and the man in the wolf's arms sobbed, his tears running through the blood on his face.

A large soldier with a moustache stepped forward. "We have come bearing Haspin, heir to the throne of Samniite."

"There is no throne in Samniite," Grak said, and laughed. The wolves howled, and the moon shone like a pearl over the dead sky. "The palace was burned, we saw to it." Grak wrapped his claws around the sobbing man's throat and massaged it lightly.

"There is no need for violence," a voice said from within the carriage, and the door swung open on its golden hinge, showering a white light from within as the candles bounced across the silken interior. A luscious smell of roasted meat and steamed vegetables wafted out, and the wolves salivated, drooling down their speckled muzzles. A man appeared at the white door, an older man of perhaps sixty, wearing a velvet robe that barely contained his enormous stomach, which fell over his pants like a pumpkin on twin twigs. His face was round, and was speckled red itself, as blood capillaries must have broken in his cheeks and around his nose. He wore a small hat that almost brought his skull to a point, and thus accentuated the very expanse of his bulging beltline. He held an apple in his twitching fingers. "We've come to see Auger, once trusted aide of the King and Crest, minister of the city. We heard from trusted messengers that he was seen in the company of wolves. Our visit, sire, is merely to question his intentions, for under sanction of the Crest, treason and conspiracy are crimes punishable by death. Aye, I come only for the city, not to resume our differences but to question his. Am I to believe this man in yer company was once a destroyer of the Yilaks, who in legend ate their hearts as he hid in the shadows of the mountains?"

Grak looked to the cart with the drawn drapery and snarled. He threw the sobbing man to the ground, leaving only a mark on his throat where his claws had wrapped. "Is this true old man, do you believe you have outsmarted us? Was your tactic to have us enter the Leeg Forest and never return?"

The old man cowered against the back of the cart. He had always hated Haspin, ever since he was a late teen in the old kingdom, the meddler, the jealous fool. He had chanced his life to enter the Yilak camps only to stir trouble within, to fabricate the old man's conspiracy. Well he would have none of that; he could feel his ribs closing around his cancerous lungs, the weakness of his heart, the frailty of his limbs. He was but a prisoner in this cart now. "What he speaks is false, Grak, for you've heard the stories about wizards, about their blood and their conception. What have I to gain from your fall? I have but months to live, if that, and if I were trying to bring you down, would I not want to enjoy it myself? Would I not want to be with my people and rebuild the fallen city, and be praised by them as their king? He seeks to rile you. Look at him. He is of the old order, the order you fought to destroy. Haspin there is just a victim of delusions. He knows nothing of me; he knows nothing of the world I came from; he only knows the stories of a fallen city, a dead race. His mission here was suicide, for he was always jealous of my relationship with the King. Always. He wants to see me suffer, for if the city hadn't fallen, and the Hunters hadn't overthrown the monarchy, I think the King would have amended tradition and given me the throne over his fat nephew. He feared that eventuality. Mayhaps it is he that looks to infiltrate the wolves from within—I've just become their excuse for coming."

Grak laughed again, and the howl pierced the sky. He looked at the old man carefully. "I dare them to call us to war. I know you feel safe, olden. I know you've found a supporter in Jarak, but your weakness is yer belief that he will protect you if it comes to that. If what the fat man speaks is true, I warn ya that death will be your last resort. I can see in yer eyes, old man, and I hear you speak to yourself in the cart; you drink the poison to melt the pain, or is it the fear, for you know what I see, what I *sense*. Something is eating your insides. Your time draws short, and I trust your mind wholly lies on your quest for the Wizard's Blood, for a silly legend in the mind of man. We have courted you like you were one of our own; if you seek to betray us your death will be a slow and painful one." Grak turned around and trudged off. "Let them speak," he said to Sullak, who broke his way through the blockade, pushing aside the torchbearers. Sullak grabbed the fat man from the perch of his carriage, and the wolf slung him over his shoulder like a bag of grain. Haspin kicked his legs like an angry child. He dropped his apple, and the wolf tossed him into the cart; it teetered to the side, and when the rope dug into the ox's harness it yelped.

The old man gave Haspin a sneer, and Haspin dusted off the front of his robe, and patted his stomach to make sure that none of his ribs were broken.

5

"M' uncle wouldn't have appreciated this. You tread on dangerous grounds, and when I heard you were seen walking among the wolves, I knew something was brewing. I took a chance coming here, that much is obvious, and if you think I came to lecture you on the soul of me uncle, yer quite wrong. I'm bored Auger. I'm nothing but a governor of the true throne. After the wolves doused the grounds in salt, and set the city on fire I could do nothing but leave with the loyal army of the King's Crest. I found solitude in Gallia, upon the shores of Lake Gallia, aye, where the olden castle and towns exist like a ghost's memory. I've stayed there many years, learning my duty as a ruler, conducting my own governance over the loyal few who've chosen not to abandon the King's ideals—I have become the ruler of Gallia, in my own right, for I have cleaned up the castle, and rid of their dead; we have the town mill working, and we eat fresh bread everyday, and drink fresh water from the coasts of Lake Gallia, where nothing has ever tainted the lakebed—the wolves of the Hopper Mountains fear crossing the lake, for they know our army will crush them. But order can be boring, old man. Ya understand, aye, what wit' sittin' in exile for so long when ya fled the civil war. Mayhaps you miss the darkness. Mayhaps that's why ya've befriended our mortal enemies, but I have to applaud yer sense of adventure, really, because order *is* boring. I left Gallia with a chosen few, and we've searched the world long and hard, for folk willin' to claim allegiance to the growing city, I don't know. My boredom has instituted its own reasoning, it would seem."

Haspin gave the wolves a quick glance outside the cart and shuddered. "Me uncle made a grave mistake building these Towers; he made a grave mistake believing the entire world was his to run. He should have used his advantage to promote victory in war over the enemy, instead o' forcing his own kind to choose sides. War was never supposed to be between man." Haspin exhaled. "It was no surprise the River People turned against us, and formed their bloomin' alliance with the wolves. Oh had he never gone on his power trip, the drunken fool. Pearl of the Ocean could make waves, he used to say with a laugh. But this is a business proposition, in case I might satiate your curioisty. I come to you, old man, not as an enemy but as a friend. A friend dying, you might say, of curiosity. Why are you with them? Why have you sought refuge in the shadow?" He said this with a hint of irony, something Auger didn't quite pick up on.

"You only want to hear what you feel is just."

"I don' understand."

"You feel I'm here silently fighting for the fallen city, or at least that is what you hope. You hope that I am using my friendship with the wolves to drown them in a war with themselves, as if my smarts were capable of doing so. You feel I owe that much to you, to the King, for fleeing as I had when the King went to his tomb, fleeing inevitable loss, fleeing the revolt that would ultimately destroy the city, fleeing, what you called, war between man. Civil war."

Haspin crossed his legs and took an apple out of his robe; it was a perfect red. He took a bite and looked at the old man crossly. "Mayhaps I do, mayhaps I do, aye, but if an army of Hunters couldn't defeat the wolves, then one man hasn't a chance to draw even a drop of blood. 'Tis commonsense old man." Haspin tapped his leg with his fingers and exhaled, popping his lips. "And the egg draggin behind the cart?"

The old man smiled. He really hated Haspin's smug, fat face. He had been fat since adolescence.

"Ya see, I can tell by yer eyes, you understand just what I'm asking. Adventure, yes, the need to experience, to grow outside limits. Now why do you have a giant egg?" His teeth snapped into the apple.

"I'll find out in due time why I have the egg, and if you have any knowledge of the old tales your uncle should have taught you, or at least the damned tutors in seminary, then you should know the answer to your own question. Do *not* plead your ignorance. I have no time for it."

Haspin smiled himself, and took another bite of his apple. "Street lore, ole man, tales passed through the lips of those with no teeth. And you believe, you believe in all your heart that you will find what you're looking for in that egg?"

"I'll see."

"Ridiculous." Haspin laughed. "Yer the gullible *mite* teethless folk ache to trick with their mindless jabber. There are no more wizards, my uncle saw to that."

"Oh there are; they are all around us. They are the essence of nature. I thought you of all people would have known that. You've heard the stories of Ichimad and the forest of Yilaks, I saw the script in the library years ago, and I heard the tale at a seminary lesson. The wizard's heart doesn't beat nor does his blood flow like ours; his skin is purely for appearance, a container for whatever is within, whatever power it is that should give man immortality. The flowers in the Sordids, the flowers blossomed from blood your uncle stole. Imagine them. They are beautiful, and even through all these years, nothing has taken their glory or trampled them. That is the existence of the wizard."

"You are dying, are you not?"

"Is it not obvious?"

"Well, I can see the realization of it in your eyes."

The old man scoffed. "Then you see my intentions."

"Why would you want to live forever in such wasted lands?"

"I wasn't born to just die. I hate death. I hate the control it has over us all." But it wasn't just that, and Auger knew it. He wanted to see everything again, the way it was when he left it…his wife. *Judith*.

Haspin gave Auger an odd look. "And what if the tales are false?"

"What if we could make the world right again? When the banners lined the roads. Would you want that life again?"

Haspin arched his brow, spinning the apple in his palm. "What are you proposin?"

"To gather your armies and search for Ae-Granum."

Haspin leaned forward with a peculiar glint in his eyes. "He is dead. My uncle told me so."

"Your uncle wasn't truthful with you."

"And he was with *you*, ole man, a liar from the mountains who betrayed the very people who took him in?"

"He told me he watched the wizard disappear in the cloud of rock and dust. If hope persists, Ae-Granum sought to preserve himself."

"An' what if m' drunken uncle spoke the truth to me in sobriety, and lied to you in drunkenness?"

"Believe what you must, Haspin. I'm offering your army a chance to restore what was lost. The city, and maybe even the crown—think what the wizard's blood could make you. Could make your men. They stand in the wolves' shadows right now. They tremble in their presence. What world is that if man cannot stand strong against his enemy?"

"The wizard, ya say. An' this is what yer conspiring?"

Auger said nothing.

"And then what? If, by some miracle, I find the wizard still lives, I drop him off like a package an' take from him what may quench m' thirst? Ha."

The old man didn't say anything.

Haspin studied Auger and gave the man a king's grin, stretching his tent-flap cheeks against either ear. "Ah, silence isn't the way ya face your future ruler. You command me like I was but yer servant, like I seek to bow before you an' weep beneath yer touch. You're vain, old man, vain as a maiden in the olden court. And may I ask ya but one question: what do I get from such a proposal, for ya should know very well that royalty does no errands for free."

Auger leaned forward, ignoring his groaning spine and the stretching split of his old muscles. "You get, ole Haspin, what you've always wanted:

heir no more, for he who wears the crown and fills the throne, restores the order of man."

Haspin smiled, for intentions in the matter were never what they appeared to be.

6

The next morning, when the sun came over the Odin Sea in the east, the old man woke up in his cart carrying yet another bottle. He had drunk it all through the night, for down in the Inlands this bottle became his *morphine*. He lay in pain through the night, feeling his bones ache and his heart lazily beat, trying to keep him alive despite the years that had stacked up on his body. Old man Auger was 101 years old.

The old man gathered as much strength as he could muster; he crawled out of the cart, stepping down on the parched ground with legs that felt as useless as noodles. He almost thought his weight would buckle underneath him. Many of the wolves were already awake, picking their teeth with bones. They had eaten a horse. The egg sac glistened in the sun, as dew had collected on the spun silk strands that were as wide as his thighs. It would take a strong blade to pierce through the sac.

Haspin stood behind the old man and startled him. "You shouldn't be surprised if you don't find what you're looking for, old man."

"All I have is hope, I suppose." Auger had gotten down on all fours and sat, looking up at the fat man. Haspin turned and left. Auger sat and looked at the egg; it pulsated in front of him; he could see darkened shapes within. He touched the egg; it was wet, and despite the frailty of the strands holding it together, it felt strong, as if no sword in the world could penetrate it.

Haspin came back with two strong men. "Here is Hasef and Lor, both masters of the blade, for they served under my uncle and fought in the civil war before we fled to Gallia; the few remaining loyalists. Between you and me," Haspin whispered, "they're both ashamed to be in the company of Yilaks without shedding any blood. True bravado of the loyalist."

"They should feel lucky the wolves don't share their sentiments," the old man said.

"Watch your tongue," the man named Lor said, and he and Hasef walked to the egg, carrying their swords in front of them like flags. They wore tunics bearing the King's Crest.

"Be careful," Auger said.

They both plunged their swords into the egg and there was a ripping sound as they forced the blades towards them; strands sprung out and slapped at the ground, bringing up a wave of dust. A strong smell emanated from the egg, as if something was cooking inside. The egg began to split, bursting at the seams like a cake with too much yeast. Small eggs fell out of the sac like beads, and they bounced down the ground. One misshapen lump rolled into the old man's leg; he looked at it, and ran his hand over it, feeling how moist it was, how fragile.

"Step on it, for if it hatches, yer search will have been in vain," Haspin said, and he stepped on the egg himself. There was a thick squelching sound, and then a pop as the yolk and premature innards leaked onto the rocky ground in a ropy mucus.

For this was the spider's egg sac. And the spiders were deadly.

There were more, popping from within the giant sac as it fully opened. Wolves and men alike jumped on each of them; the ground became a sick mess of ooze. Black forms pressed against the inset of the egg's convex, pattering the glistening strands, trying to break the mould—and feet would slam down on the balls, crushing the monsters inside trying to be born.

"There is something here," Hasef said, as he stood over the split sac, wiping his sword down his pants. He wore the face of a man who'd seen something he didn't quite believe. Hasef had fought for the crown since he was merely a pup, and he'd seen much to account for his vigilant demeanor, but this was far too strange to pass off as an oddity of nature. Aye, for he'd seen irregularities before, he had. But not like this.

"What is it?" Auger asked.

"It looks like—like a man."

The old man was ecstatic. He jumped onto his legs and ignored the pain as he ran over. There, inside the sac was the figure of a man blanketed in mucus.

Haspin craned his neck to see, slightly dumbfounded.

The old man reached into the sac and wiped the mucus away from the body. The figure was tucked in the fetal position, both legs curled into its stomach; its skin was pale, and many veins showed through the flesh, like roads on maps he'd buy in the old world. The veins were purple, and some were quite thick. The back of the figure's head was elongated, in the shape of a spider's body, and at its very tip was a small tuft of hair. From the side the old man could see the figure's eyes, which were closed, and its nostrils, which were small slits. Its mouth was closed, but weird gasps escaped the clenched lips, which were the color of flesh that hadn't seen the light of day for hundreds of years. Was this it? Was this real? Was this his destiny, what he was supposed to find—what the Traveling Man professed he would? He wanted so badly to reach in with a blade and just cut its throat. Cut its throat and hope the fortuneteller was right. Cut its throat and drink to the growing tumor in his chest. To age even. Cut its throat and see if he'd found an unborn wizard. "Let me borrow your sword."

Hasef handed the old man his blade, and he took it in his weak hands; he reached the tip of the sword into the sac and prodded the figure's temple. There was a slopping sound as the mucus swirled beneath its body. The anticipation was killing him—the stories he'd heard and learned over the years filled his head. The Wizard's Blood was fertile. It *grew* life. When the King had cut Ae-Granum's throat, the ichor that had spilled over the parched earth had blossomed a tremendous garden of inexpressible colors.

He sliced the blade across the creature's arm; it opened into a red lip, splattering the bottom of the sac, turning the silk into a scarlet flood. There were no flowers—no air of growth—and weakness captured the old man in its grip. He dropped the sword into the sac, and he fell back himself, cursing the bad luck, cursing his hope, cursing everything.

"I see," Haspin said knowingly.

When Hasef bent down to reach for his sword, something clasped his arm. At first he thought his sleeve had snagged on the side of the cut silk, but when the grip grew stronger he understood there was a problem. He looked into the sac and the figure had turned its head and opened its eyes, its deep red eyes. Hasef had seen in those eyes an image that would take him to his death; he saw his father murdered by the wolves, eaten alive as he screamed, and this memory, something he had tried to forget for as long as he had lived, was his final thought. He was pulled into the sac and with one last struggle, he was no more.

The old man, who had fallen back into a puddle of squished spider guts, saw through the egg sac the figure slowly standing, rising from a diminutive hunch. "This is no wizard. Kill it!"

The King's men had unsheathed their swords, and some had taken out their bows. The wolves snarled and sniffed the air, steadying their swords in their claws, for the first time allied momentarily against a common enemy.

When the figure emerged from the egg, it looked upon the men with its terrible red eyes, and these men saw their worst nightmares; they saw their mothers dying, the city falling to ruin. The old man had seen in those red eyes the murky image of an explosion, and he saw his men running, holding their mouths as they teetered to their deaths; he cried and closed his eyes. *I should have died*, he thought. And he saw his wife's face.

Haspin saw the fall of the throne. The burning city.

The slender creature stepped out of the sac, spittle dripping from its lower lip and marking the ground where it fell.

The wolves, aroused by this *thing's* seeming power and manipulation, attacked.

A young Yilak jumped onto the figure and pinned it to the ground, holding its arms.

"You are so young and weak; you do this to prove to the others you are strong. Pathetic. Your mind is clouded. You possess desires to rule, desires to conquer; you have forgotten though, that ineptitude can get *you* conquered." The figure from the egg snapped at the wolf's neck, severing its carotid vein in a vast fountain of blood.

"Bring the cage," Grak howled, and two Yilaks fetched the enormous iron cage, opening the door to let loose the birds they had kept for Auger's meals. Grak held his sword out and pounced before the pale figure, which had watched the young wolf writhe in pain, baring its dripping fangs.

"You want me in that cage, do you? I see your intentions, Grak. I see you want to rule all, and force the blood of man to drown the world; I see you want to decorate your front with the skulls of the remaining Hunters," the figure spoke into Grak's head without moving its mouth.

"What are you?" Grak roared.

"I *was* a father, a husband," it said, rather sadly.

Grak rushed forward while wolves countered from the back. The figure lolled its head, its wound dripping down its side. The wolves had created a cross current, forcing the thin creature to surveil all sides, and Grak cut off its left arm when its head cocked. He clasped the pale figure's head into his claws and drew him toward the cage, feeling the thing's blood spatter his fur.

Grak slammed the iron door shut, and the figure's pale body fell into the iron bars, slipping in bird droppings. It screamed a high shriek.

7

The old man sat with his old withered hands on his knees. Haspin ate a piece of meat, spreading his velvet robe to sit beside Auger. "Folktales are based on presumption, ole man. And folktales live on through belief."

"Perhaps," the old man said, cursing himself for believing the inane ramblings of a traveling seer—God, he had risked his life for the fortuneteller's wisdom; he'd believed everything the old seer had to say, for Auger always just wanted to know what he had to do. He couldn't choose anymore. His choices were draining. His tumor was growing. He wanted somebody else there for him. That's all. And this proved he had run off on the insane whim of a carnival act—somebody he would have slammed the door on in the old world. *Had he not been so* convincing. Auger shuddered.

Haspin watched the old man for a moment, studying the land around him, the wolves.

And Auger watched the mines on the bluff. There were always fallback plans. He was a cutthroat businessman. He knew that. The wolves would leave soon, but they would wait until night.

CHAPTER 9

HERMES FROM THE MINES

1

Leo could feel something tapping his shoulder, and for a second he thought about Chuck the bully—the mayor—and the terrible irritation as Chuck's knuckles drove into his skull.

"Cole!" He screamed when his eyes opened. All was dark but the two incandescent bulbs that were AL4's eyes. From the dim glow Leo could tell the robot had been tapping him, and again he noticed that his back ached, that his throat yelped in pain, and that everything between his temples flared up like a swollen muscle. He had something clenched in his hand, something both smooth and rough.

"Sir, the other two are broken. I assessed them, and both are quite beyond repairs. The flashlight was trampled and left shattered. I am sorry sir."

"The other two, what are you talking about?" Leo asked. It was dark. He tried to find some source of light that he could use to garner back his vision, but—

But there was nothing, only that dim glow emanating from AL4's eye sockets.

"The other two robots, sir."

"Good riddance," Leo said. He sat up, and the darkness attempted to pull him back down. He could see the stream of light from AL4's eyes fall over the robots on the ground, the ones made in Krollup's image, and Leo saw for himself that they were beyond repair. Leo just saw cables leaking from holes where arms should have been, and inches from his legs, Leo saw the glint of a metallic skull; he could have kicked at it if he wanted, but for now the very idea of moving was exhausting.

"AL4, what about the aquarium?"

He could hear the robot whirring, and he watched its eyes shift, almost as if in hesitation—but that was impossible, for robots were without the hindrances (some would say) of emotion.

"I am sorry sir. It was dropped. It also broke."

Leo knew what was digging into his back then; there were shards of glass, shards that had broken from an aquarium air filter he hadn't heard shatter because his ears and eyes were trained on other things.

"What should I do?" He said aloud. He held the bound leather up to his face and looked at the twine; it was scraggly, and from it burst other strings, like fine hairs that caught the light. *We have a messenger.* Leo's head hurt; that terrible voice came from nowhere. A *messenger*, well, that was whether or not he decided to grasp that sense of responsibility. He didn't know if he wanted to face Krollup. Not as the messenger. Not as the ill informer. He didn't want to watch the very volcanoes of hell draw steam in Krollup's eyes.

No, Leo made another decision, one that seemed heartless enough considering he carried the fate of a little boy in his hands, bound by twine, but what proof did he have of that unless he opened and read what was written, *if* there was even anything written on the inside in the first place.

He could leave it; he could place it on the ground and test the air himself, hold his breath as the smell grew sour.

Or he could open the parchment and read it; there was glass everywhere that he could cut the twine with. Leo was afraid of what might be written on the inside—for some reason he knew the wolves had come up the mines specifically for Cole, and for some reason he was sure that if he didn't deliver the scroll to Krollup, Cole might, no, Cole *would* die a horrible death.

"Sir, the ground is making strange 'S' patterns," AL4 said.

Leo looked into the darkness at those two gleaming bulbs, and saw them shake and bounce from side to side; he could feel it now, the ground was rising and falling, and for a second he thought of the ocean, the steady rush of the tide; in that moment AL4's eyes became the moon over the Pacific. He could hear the rodents all around them now, rushing around in the echoes of their own filth as his feet jerked underneath him.

Leo didn't fear werewolves anymore at that moment.

He clenched the scroll to his chest. He would need it soon.

2

Watching the sun rise over the hills, blanketing David's shoulder with a pinkish corona, Edwin Krollup crossed his legs and blew a thick cloud of cigar smoke and poked his nose into it, inhaling it as if it too were the source of his buzz. Why was he up? Why was he up at *this* hour to watch the sun rise over the hills, on a Saturday nonetheless? There was a sense of fear in the question, because he knew why he was up; he knew exactly what the answer was, and in knowing so he had grown afraid.

Beyond those hills there lay a country, and the people in this country relied on famous screw ups to keep their own lives in check; he had done just that for those people, those people who just now were sleeping in their own comfortable beds, thinking not of fears, but of the advent of the weekend. He had undeniably purchased a fake statue for millions of dollars believing it was real, and he had the gall to call himself an art collector; he had the right to believe *they*, the nitwits of the Ministry, would just sell it to him because he could magically move stone?

Yet this didn't steal his sleep; this didn't pull him from bed at four in the morning, astonishing himself at how dark his eyes looked, how deep the wrinkles in his face had formed over the last couple of days. Thinking about the statue in front of him, thinking about the response to his blunder, that was just the icing on the cake; that was just a mistake, and as far as Edwin could tell, people were prone to making mistakes. It was the other thing he didn't want to think about, because this other thing kept growing inside him. There were times in his sleep that he yelped, and he knew this, and there were times when he pulled the blankets around his head and let the sweat devour his brow because he felt protected—but it was still there, forming like the bud of a flower, the thin drop of rain in a cloud that would fall and immerse itself in the spongy earth; it would spread from that form and it would take upon itself the power to immediately scar that one image in his brain.

Last night, he had a nightmare about his father.

Sitting there as the sun rose, he could almost feel the dead grasp of his father's hand touch his shoulder to twist him around. "What did you open up, Innis?" Edwin asked the cigar smoke twirling about the air. "I haven't felt like this since I was a kid," he said in a voice that shook and stuttered, and feebly reminded him of his granddad before he croaked. In a way it calmed him to speak out loud, to hear his own voice; for some reason he didn't feel so alone. "I don't know whether to sue you for malpractice, or have you set me right again, put me under and erase whatever it is you opened up, because I feel like another part of me is aware. I feel like there is a corridor of doors in my head, and each door has been unlocked unwillingly."

He shook his head and grew aware that he was speaking loudly; he didn't want to alert the staff that he was growing mad, that he was, dare he say it, losing his cool. They might tell the media, the media would pounce all over him, and this stupid stone around his neck would lose all validity because magic eluded the touch of a madman. He was sure of it.

He lifted the stone and looked at it carefully.

The phone rang. His personal phone, which he kept lines for in his office, connected to his cellular phone, and in the Great room by the shelf of books to his right (a phone which he had to replace, since the previous phone had been crushed upon learning David was a fake). He bent over and picked it up, smashing the cigar into a crumbled mess of tobacco between the receiver and his palm. He didn't seem to mind.

It was one of his lawyers, Brad the man (though he sounded little more than a boy) had said, but names didn't matter. Apparently the Ministry of Art had filed charges against Edwin Krollup for voicing threats over the telephone, threats that had been recorded and ready to serve as evidence unless he was willing to settle outside of court.

"I never voiced any threats," Edwin said.

"There was never any doubt in my mind sir, it's just that she presented audio evidence over the phone, and she had traced the call to your house. Evidently enough, she was prepared for the backlash of selling you a fake."

"That's it then, counter-sue them for falsifying sales, and deliberately using it as a ploy to degrade me over global news. I will not let the Ministry run me down yet again, Brad." His voice was crisp now, and retained that sense of his former self.

"The only problem is, sir, you didn't openly ask them for the original David."

"Isn't that implied in the transaction?"

"Apparently not sir—it's like a semantic mindgame. She also has physical evidence if you don't comply."

"She, is it? Mrs. Lorenzo, right? I thought so, that jabbering hussy; she's turned this into a self-motivated advertisement for the Ministry, claiming they're apt to selling off art to collectors worthy of spending the cash. If they got a man to buy a fake for fifty million dollars, than why can't they presume another will follow suit? Her claim is ridiculous, Brad, and the next time you call me this early in the morning I will make sure Linutz & Walsh fires you on the spot, and blacklists you from work in this city. In this country, now hear that!"

Edwin hung the phone up, and almost felt revitalized. He patted the broken cigar from his hand into an ashtray and stood up. He was ready for breakfast. But he was also ready to lose the opened part of his mind again, to lock it up and throw away the key.

It was Saturday, and he knew Innis's office was closed, but personal calls always perked the little fiend up, because personal calls vouched for increased hourly pay. No matter the time, Robert Innis was a man apt to work if the dollar was right.

Edwin picked up the phone again.

3

It was nine O'clock by the time he was seated at the dining table, and he could already hear the bacon sizzling in the kitchen. Innis hadn't picked up his phone, even when Edwin called again and let the stupid thing ring fourteen times. He either fled the country for the weekend with another one of his soon to be ex-wives, or he had turned the ringer off on his phone and left it in the breast pocket of his jacket. That was logical and there was no need to get worked up over it but he could sense that extra presence inside himself; it was like standing in pitch darkness knowing somebody (or *something*) was behind you, but knew if you turned around you'd just be facing the same darkness. It became a curse in that way, and he couldn't wait for the stupid shrink to get out his trusty necklace and dangle it from his fidgety fingers as he thought of the bill he'd ring up. Even though he'd deny it out loud, Edwin felt a sudden calmness fall over him as he let go, as he withdrew his restraints and let the pendant take him wherever it was the pendant took folks under the spell—but now he knew, yes he did, and he wasn't going to let Innis pull open doors at his every whim because the mind was a weird place; it was like a maze. There were dead ends meant to stop you. If you went ahead and blew holes in every one of them, there was no telling what you might come face to face with.

Edwin had an eerie vision of a dusty old projection set with reels of film blanketed under cobwebs, but he shook it away; he shook away the entire idea of that extra presence, because there was no need to think of such things. He wasn't going to let that hussy Mrs. Lorenzo bring him down, so why should he let some botched up hypnosis session urge him to believe that he had somehow turned more of his brain on then he felt comfortable with?

He didn't realize it at first, but both Jimmy and Maggie were sitting at the table with him now; they were staring at him. Maggie was smiling, and Jimmy was unsure what approach he should use today, seeing that every other he had tried was just crumpled in those cold eyes and shoved back at him.

"I noticed you weren't in bed, so I thought I'd surprise you with a family breakfast this morning. Cool you down after those bums in Italy...*did what they did.*" She muttered the last few words and looked down at her lap, her beautiful red hair blossoming out of the shrewd ponytail she had thrown it in before leaving the bedroom.

Edwin only smiled. He wasn't going to let anything bring him down now. The fact that he had slept for only two hours needn't apply, because that thought led back to the horrible sensation that he would die a marked man, marked by the suffering of his father as rock closed around him and collapsed his truck into him like a mechanical overcoat. He rubbed his thumb over the necklace and that image washed away; in fact, his fatigue wore down, and the subtle vibration that wrung up his arm shook him awake.

"I have the cook making bacon and Eggs Benedict," Edwin said. "He's even squeezing oranges into a pitcher, through a filter of course, in case you've never had it freshly squeezed before. Where's Cole?"

Maggie looked up excitedly, as if the shock that her husband referred to her son by name was beyond comprehension. He usually called him 'that kid', or 'those kids', 'those boys' when referring to both, but she couldn't remember when he had actually used Cole's first name, as if his courtesy was genuine. *He does when he's angry, when he's got a bone to pick*, she thought. But this was different. This time his eyes seemed to be at peace, as if this whole debacle with the fake David hadn't happened, had been, God willing, all a bad dream. "He wasn't in bed when I woke up Jimmy, so he's probably in the bathroom cleaning himself up."

Or putting on more of mom's makeup, Jimmy thought, remembering the horrible swelling around his brother's jaw, the horrid application of foundation around his eyes that had ran, and revealed beneath the sickly purple bruise which turned his eyeball into a waxy bulb pushed into one dark gaping socket. Jimmy thought of the bruises on Cole's stomach and almost lost his appetite; it was like looking into a congealed bowl of oatmeal and blueberries, he thought, with that same lumpy complexion.

Cole had asked last night whether or not Jimmy remembered their father, and right now Jimmy could actually answer that question, because Edwin, in all of his new found politeness, reminded him so much of their dad that he could have almost mistaken him for the man in the coffin. Cole would be impressed, very impressed, to notice this change right now, to notice his compliance with this little idea of a Saturday morning breakfast (*which wasn't just a breakfast though, cause mom said so herself, this was an intervention, and the one this little meeting centered around hadn't even gotten to the table yet*). Any thoughts of a hidden terrorist behind the fireplace had disappeared, because this Edwin Krollup wasn't that same man; Jimmy felt his need for power evaporate at the moment. His craving for his cigarettes fell dormant—for the time being.

Where was Cole, though? Putting on makeup couldn't take more than twenty minutes, and even if it did, he still would have smelt the bacon from upstairs; he would have heard the fat sizzling, and his stomach would have gargled, no matter the pain to his bruises.

"Mom, I'm going to get Cole. This isn't like him," Jimmy finally said, and he pushed himself away from the table.

4

Jimmy hadn't slept well, that was for sure. He couldn't remember a worse sleep, well, at least not since his dad brought home the bad news, and the months that followed with the divorce and the undeniable knowledge that his father was going to die. But last night he felt something stripped from him, something so powerful that even he, the stepson of Edwin Krollup, the enforcer of Ivy Raurus, felt helpless.

It wasn't just the feeling of exposure, especially against the clawing of helplessness; it became more of a descent that in his sleep turned him into something he had never imagined he could be. He remembered standing at the wedding reception, wearing his tuxedo that felt so irritable around the neck that he wanted to rip the shirt and bow tie to shreds, but didn't because of the look in Krollup's eyes. He remembered how angry he had been, and how hurt Cole had been when their mother decided to wed the man, to completely shield the boys from their dead father. When she had said "I do" amidst the showering flower petals and the distinct rays of light let through the cracks in the pavilion, a part of him, a part he shared with Cole once, vowed he would hate this man bearing his mother's hand for the rest of his life; that he would never forget his real father, the man who taught him baseball and survived a war only so he could return to his family, to the young boys he would help mature over the years. Yet he hadn't only turned against Cole. He had turned against himself; he had displaced that vow and forgotten his father, and placed all the blame and fall of his own life onto the shoulders of his father because the man smoked, and irresponsibly let cigarettes nail his coffin shut.

When Jimmy finally did close his eyes and find that he could drift away into that deep space, a sense of déjà vu ensnared him—he saw Cole rolling on the dirty ground, his vest bunching around his stomach as grass stained his belly; and he heard the jeers of all the kids around him in a vicious circle. He saw Rod Campbell, whom owed him four cigarettes because his single mom was the team nurse for the Blackbirds baseball squad, a team owned by Krollup, and if he felt compelled to keep his smokes for himself, then his mother would find raising a child without the support of a spouse rather difficult if unemployment reared its ugly little head. Sal Carr was in the circle, and he owed Jimmy fifteen bucks and a pack of cigarettes because his pops was an engineer for Krollup. Jimmy saw them all standing in that circle, jeering his brother, and this certain fury came over him, this fury that told him to bust up that circle and break the nose of anybody willing to laugh at the spectacle.

So he went to do as he had planned, he pushed forward into the crowd, but there was something about his movements that seemed strange, that seemed peculiarly off. When he looked at his hands he realized one thing: he wasn't himself. And he realized another thing too; he wasn't walking right because his foot kept connecting something…and when he finally looked, he saw Cole writhing on the ground, and he could hear the boy grunt below him, stifling his tears because he knew they'd do him no good.

"Hit him Ricky, break his nose, send him crying to his mansion!" Carl Figg yelled from behind him, and Jimmy understood; his guilt, his sense of understanding had placed him within the very shoes of the bully, and though he tried to keep from kicking Cole, he found he couldn't. Nothing would obey him; this was a curse. His mind was his to keep, but only to watch the horrors his brother endured.

"What was I doing this entire time?" Jimmy asked in his dream, a supreme echo that shook the head of Ricky, and muffled from his closed lips as he drew the blankets over his chin. But he saw, didn't he? He saw what he was doing. He was standing in the distance with a smoke in his hand, watching his brother get beat up.

He woke up with his mother nudging his shoulder, whispering into his ear. "Wake up, wake up, we're going to do something for Cole this morning."

"What?" Jimmy asked, wiping sleep from the corners of his eyes and wiping the backs of his hands on his sheets.

"For one thing, I want him to tell me the truth. I know he's been using my makeup, and I know why he's had to. I just want him to know that he can come to us; we'll have a family meeting."

Jimmy got up, and noticed that Cole wasn't in bed.

"He's probably in the bathroom, putting on more makeup. Poor soul." Maggie Krollup trembled slightly. She had gone to the school administration about the bullying, and they had assured her they would uncover the problem; there was a sense of relief with this, but obviously their explanation had been off kilter, and she had perhaps wondered if maybe Ivy Raurus wasn't the right school for Cole.

5

The problem with starting, is stopping, Jimmy thought, as he steered directly to his room, and lifted his mattress to remove the tin case with his first initial on the front. He snapped it open, and lying on top of the bunch was the torn cigarette, the smoke with Cole's lip prints on the filter, and the smudge of makeup on the paper. This right here was verifiable proof that he should quit, if not only for the wellbeing of his younger brother of three minutes. He used to look out for the kid; he even got suspended for punching some punk in the nose for starting something with Cole, but now, now he had become the smoking bully himself. He threw the ripped smoke into the trash and covered it under pieces of paper. He put a new cigarette in his mouth and breathed through the filter for a minute, tasting the pungent chemicals through his teeth. He couldn't light it in the house, nor could he open his window, but just tasting the thing, feeling it against his lip seemed to quench whatever anxiety was coming over him.

Not now, put it back you idiot and do what you came up here for. Find your brother and tell him breakfast was made especially for him this morning. Yes, of course, this wasn't about him right now; this was about Cole, his poor brother with the swollen belly and the purple jaw.

Jimmy left his room without looking in the closet. He wouldn't even think about the vents for another few hours, because the route didn't seem plausible. There was a terrorist down there. A madman.

The bathrooms were empty. Even the Master bathroom, which contained the biggest collection of his mother's makeup, was quiet.

He went downstairs when you were sucking on an unlit cigarette.

That was the most obvious case, but when he went downstairs his mother asked him the same question he wanted to ask her: "Where's Cole?"

6

A breakfast that was supposed to be peaceful and calm, became utter panic. When the food was served, Maggie was certain Cole would join them after smelling what was prepared, but then she scolded herself for having such a thought; she was sure the bullies at Ivy Raurus thought the same way, believing they could always entice a boy like Cole with food.

"I'm sure he woke up and looked out the window and decided it was a beautiful morning for a walk," Maggie said, and she tried hard to believe this; she tried hard to believe her son had just recently picked up an exercise regime to shove back into the bullies' faces, but there was this pesky insistence that pleaded she call the police, to cry help into the morning air like a damsel in distress...*like what the papers had called you after your marriage to Edwin: a broken single mother of two finds able support in billions—a damsel in distress weds Edwin Krollup, of Krollup Industries. The Bachelor is finally spoken for ladies.*

Edwin had looked at Maggie, at her red hair, hair he loved so much, and decided he couldn't sit here in this state, when the inside of his head screamed in unison with his frantic wife. He pushed his seat away from the table, leaving a plate of half-eaten Eggs Benedict and three strips of bacon.

"Where are you going?" Maggie asked.

"I have to go make a phone call."

"But what if Cole comes back? I really think we need to talk to him Edwin. We need to assure him that we'll be here for him whenever he needs us."

"The boy went for a walk. Plus, it wouldn't be a tragedy if he actually missed a meal." Edwin left the room and a wife whose jaw fell open at the sudden transition of her husband, when just minutes ago he had referred to his stepson by his legal name. *He has a bone to pick*, she thought, rather suddenly.

7

Edwin stood in his office and looked at his phone; his anger with Mrs. Lorenzo grew inside his head until his skull felt separated. He was trying to calm himself down.

The brat probably left the house; he probably just went to deal with the punks that had given him a black eye, one that he had covered so terribly with makeup the bruise just looked like it was skin tone.

He knocked his knuckles into his other hand, and cupped the palm so the dull thuds seemed to echo. He snapped the gold key off the breastplate, opened the drawer with the other key so he could open the drawer with his cigars. He took a Cuban and lit it, and smoked it for a couple of minutes, listening to those frantic footsteps all about; listening to the joists creak and the vents mutter as every voice in that house called out for a boy that had obviously left.

You're being sued by the Ministry, Eddie, by the same hussy that tried to politely tell you they had put one over on you; that they had sold you a fake for millions of dollars and that the whole world knew. Now what are you going to do about that? Are you going to stand there with that stinky wrap of rancid tobacco, or are you going to pick up that phone and talk to Alfred Linutz himself, get him to uncover the truths here, and tell the man to stuff the little twerp Brad into a cubicle somewhere without access to a phone? You can't let Lorenzo and her precious team of Art Thugs go until the bell rings the end of Round 1, cause then Lorenzo and her thugs will take this news to the press, and the world will find out you've dug yourself deeper.

Edwin picked up the phone and dialed, and waited while the phone in Alfred's office rang, smoking that stinking cigar until his office was just a black haze.

"Mr. Edwin Krollup, I was waiting for your call," Alfred said when he picked up, in his deep raspy voice that had over the years become grainy, for he was never one to keep a modest tone in trial. "You have poor Brad Little cowering under his desk right now, afraid his job just may be in jeopardy."

Edwin muffled a small grunt.

"You should have listened to him Edwin. Our offices have been in shambles since our friends in Italy called. I don't suppose poor Mr. Little got much through in your conversation, did he?"

"No, he did not Alfred, and I care not for this preposterous build up. Tell me what the Ministry has demanded, and tell me your plan to take care of the fiends." Edwin ran his fidgety hand through his dark hair, the cigar peeking out between his knuckles like a smoking horn as he kept his palm curved over his crown.

"You went to Florence to acquire Michelangelo's David, did you not?"

"Yes."

"And you did so without your lawyer to make sure the transaction was *kosher*. This was your first fault, Edwin. Your second came about when you decided to trust the motives of the Ministry, who were able to hide many pieces of art from the sniveling Nazis, and the tyrant art buff himself, Hitler, who claimed he would rebuild Germany like a neo-Rome. How could you not see that they might just pull the same blinds over your eyes, Edwin?"

"Because our negotiations showed just how serious I was, Alfred, and I can claim to you under this very umbrella of the law that I was more powerful than Hitler at that moment."

"So you claim, of course Edwin, but the only fact of the matter is that power shrivels when it's been tricked. You were tricked. This is something you will have to live with of course, but you made a third fault that brewed many feelings with our friends in the Ministry. Feelings I think best left unbrewed, if you know what I'm saying. You called Mrs. Lorenzo of the Ministry, and acknowledging this very chance, she taped the conversation, truly anticipating the very 'liquids' she might just soak from your sponge." Alfred drew a mouthful of phlegm and grunted, sounding like a piece of plastic caught in a turbine. "You threatened her, right?"

"I wouldn't call it a threat. I voiced my *opinion* about her stupidity for selling me a fake, and then proceed to tell everybody in the world at the same time. I thought that incredibly *low*, even coming from the Ministry." Edwin lowered his head; his hand still mashed on his hair with the cigar horn. He frowned and looked at the desk in front of him, littered with books and rocks and pieces of gold and diamonds which he himself had found in the ground, wishing for something pretty to hold in his hand. "You don't suppose I should have let it be, do you Alfred?"

"No, Edwin, what I do think you should have done was call me, or take my calls when I heard about it. I could have handled the problem for you, and sued them first. Charged the Ministry for defamation of character; it isn't hard to dig up dirt on people either. You pay us good money Edwin, and for clients like yourself, we pull no draws; we dispatch the ruthless bunch, if you see where I'm going. We have people to take care of problems like this, but you left it too late, and now we have a bigger problem than we should have. Now we have to figure our way around a law suit that might just drop your jaw."

"What do you mean by that, Alfred?"

"I mean, I talked to Mrs. Lorenzo myself. I heard the tape of your conversation, just to verify if it was doctored or not, but I know your mannerisms Edwin, your quick jump to judgment, and the tape she displayed was anything but falsified evidence. She faxed pictures of what she claimed you did to the Accademia. She does have a case on her hand, and she told me that the Ministry was willing to solve this dilemma under the table, but what remains is your reaction to her asking price—an asking price she feels fair if she's not to go to the press with photos of the damage done to the Accademia, which I don't even want to know about, and the tape of your threats to the Italian people and the art world. If something like this leaked, the European market would turn their backs on you, and obviously the remainder of the people in the free world would follow suit. People like to hear the dirt on rich guys like you Edwin, but they also like to hate them, and when they find a reason to do so, then guys like you get boiled."

"Guys like me, Alfred…guys like me? What am I, Hitler now? You're treating me just like the hussy at the Ministry; you're patronizing me, Alfred, and if you don't tell me now what to do with this law suit, then I'll take my business elsewhere."

Alfred sighed, and Edwin could hear the meaty strings of phlegm pluck in his throat as air passed by. "I know that my thoughts will only anger you Edwin."

"Have you taken their side then?"

"No, I just know what might…no, what *will* happen if you let this material leak; if you let the pictures and the tape of your conversation leak. Your stocks will plummet, Edwin, and there isn't much you can do after that when your name falls into the toilet. When I say this, I say this as a man looking out for your wellbeing—I think you should pay the Ministry what they want."

Edwin smashed his hand into his desk and the cigar splattered into a messy ball. The gold pieces on his desk rattled, and the books shifted and thumped. Give them what they want? Give them what they want…what was this, had the Ministry bought his own lawyers out from under him? That just couldn't happen, no way, because Edwin Krollup was worth billions, and nothing could take that fortune away from him. As long as he held the stone in his hand there was no limit to his power. "You think I should pay the Ministry? Did I just hear you right, Alfred? Did you just turn your back on me?"

"I didn't turn my back on you Edwin, I just don't want to see everything you built fall to tatters because of one wrong choice."

"How much does the Ministry expect me to pay?"

Alfred sighed again, and Edwin knew it was going to be bad. He gripped the edge of the desk and exhaled, waiting for the old man on the other end to mutter the huge figure under his breath.

"How much, Alfred?"

"The Ministry wants 2.5 billion dollars, Edwin."

Edwin's jaw dropped and the phone fell from his hand.

"Edwin? Edwin, are you there?"

There was a moment when the world had gone gray, and when everything inside Edwin Krollup was just one train of numbers, lurching along in a slow tremble that shook his temples and crossed his eyes. Then color swam back, and he realized he had dropped the phone, that he had actually fainted for a moment.

Two and a half billion dollars? That couldn't have been right, because no such thing in the world could cost that much money, even a filthy lawsuit that didn't make much sense to begin with.

"Tell me you're joking Alfred," Edwin finally said under his breath, trying to sound composed.

Alfred didn't say a word.

"For what, to conceal demeaning evidence? Was that her claim, Alfred?"

In a sad voice that seemed stripped of any professionalism, Alfred said, "well yes, that and for the further preservation of art that you threatened. She also felt it was the uneasiness *you* dealt that caused her car accident. Apparently she wants retribution for that incident also. All the stress that's come with everything."

Edwin gritted his teeth together. "And you suggest I pay this…this ridiculous amount?"

"For the business you have established, yes."

"Alfred, you're fired." Edwin crashed the phone back into its cradle and ran his hands right on up through his hair again, until two tufts were pulled into obscured tusks. He could feel his blood pressure rising, and boy did he want to vent the steam; he wanted to explode really. When he grabbed the stone around his neck his eyes deepened and his feet left the ground. Some of his surprised anger disappeared through his vibrating hand, but—

The phone rang immediately after but Edwin left it.

He looked at the wall with the photograph of the mineshaft, the wall that was actually a door. *When a man is angry, he finds a punching bag,* he thought. *No matter what that punching bag's shape may be.*

8

There was something wrong, but Leo knew that, just as he knew he was going to hand the scroll over and sweat out a terrible punishment. The ground was shaking, and he heard the rocks around him groan, as if they were all shifting, as if something big was coming, bigger than wolves.

AL4 had said it felt 'S' waves in the ground, and Leo didn't doubt that for a second. Not because he had programmed such analysis in the robot, but because he could feel his knees giving; he could feel the ground trying to throw him on his back. The shards of glass jingled like bells as they bounced on the rock, and both fallen robots clanged against the backfill as they were thrown to the side. All was dark but those two bulbs, those bulbs that were AL4's eyes, and Leo looked into them, watching the color form lines in the darkness as the ground bounced the robot up and down, from side to side.

"AL4," Leo yelled over the shifting rocks. "I'm going to push you over and sit on top of you."

AL4 rolled forward, jittering as the ground swayed. Leo trudged towards the bulbs, holding his hands out hoping he wouldn't smash into something that had fallen from the roof, which was supported on the sides by posts he had seen earlier in the beam of the flashlight. He could hear the lumber splitting, as if the mines were collapsing, and he wondered if that was happening; perhaps their time was finally up.

But you know that's wrong, because only the ground is moving, and you know very well why the waves are pulling you back up *the mines.*

Leo knocked his fists against AL4's abdomen and there was a thick clunk. "Lay down," Leo screamed. "Fall backwards." He could sense a hesitation in AL4's eyes again, as if the robot was determining whether or not it wanted to be abused this way. The robot finally gave in, and Leo watched the bulbs tilt until the dim light had flashed two discs on the ceiling, where there were glistening drops of water in the fissures, like diamonds in a mouth. There was a loud thud when the robot hit the ground, and Leo climbed on top of it, mounting his feet against its arms. "We're being brought back."

"Yes sir," AL4 responded. The lumber cracked and Leo could smell sulfur, as if the fissures were splitting all the way to the cores of the earth. He felt like he was on a boat in mild currents, listening to a vessel all around him snap in two.

Though Leo couldn't see, he knew when the rock split completely from the ground and formed a wave, knocking into the head of AL4 and pushing the robot like a crude sled into the darkness ahead.

He heard terrible screeches, and when he decided to open his eyes, he saw sparks spraying out against the walls like firecrackers.

9

The room was empty.

For some reason he didn't find this very surprising, because that was just how his day was going. But still. This took him over the top; this took Edwin's blood pressure to the boiling stage, and he thought for sure that he was going to pop. *Pop goes the weasel*, he thought.

"He went up the vents. He saw them, and when he found the chance he decided to go up. He's in one of the bedrooms now, probably the boy's room, if he even got up the slide." Edwin felt like scrambling up himself, whispering Leo's name to warn the old man he was on his trail, but there was something wrong.

His robots were gone too. Yes, that was it. They couldn't have gotten up the slide, no matter what tricks the little guy used. But he could have hid them; he could have used one of them to hoist him up—

Yes, you saw that stupid robot standing with its arms lifted over its head a week ago, yes you did, and when you asked him about it he said—rather slyly cause you fell for it—that he was using crushed bones as grease for its joints. You had come in at just the right time before the little guy could make it into the vent; you had come in too fast for him to tell the robot to switch positions.

He could feel veins in his head throbbing, wanting to let loose. Where could he hide robots? He had three of them, and three hunks of junk weren't easily maneuverable...unless there was a mine in the very room in question.

He trudged fifteen feet down the mine. He reached around him, feeling the cool rock; he could hear rodents, but he didn't happen to touch sleek metal anywhere.

A sudden thought occurred, one he was quite shocked he hadn't had before; it seemed obvious. He remembered Leo asking him why the wolves didn't come up the mines; he wasn't asking specifically out of fear that the things might just venture back up, he was asking out of pure curiosity, testing his chances perhaps. He had told the little man about the 'Black Damp', the possibility of bad air deep in the mine's gut; and hadn't Leo asked him for an aquarium, a glass bowl he said would be of particular use for a robot? Of course he had. This was before they sent the surveillance robot into the mines, he remembered that much. The aquarium wasn't for any robot. Leo must have figured out a way to use its filter. He had asked for the filter *intact*.

Edwin wanted to smack his forehead.

But why did he ask about the 'Black Damp' *after* he received the aquarium?

"Because he wanted to make sure he'd need it. Otherwise it wouldn't matter if I walked in on him inventing a breathing apparatus," Edwin said, rather humorously. He looked into the mouth of the monster, and knew, somewhere down there in the pitch black a little man was wandering with his robots, wearing a glass bowl on his head like a strange astronaut.

Edwin grabbed the rock around his neck, and for a moment he felt the ground underneath his feet shift.

Until he levitated, of course.

10

Leo shuddered as the terrible screeches heightened, as if the back of AL4 had ground itself directly into the rock like a jigsaw. He could hear glass jingling all around him, and at one point in his journey, he felt a shard slice across his hand, as if thrown at him from the side. He didn't know if he was bleeding, but his fingers had swelled up like cigars; he could barely move them.

The sparks didn't give much light, but what he did see dropped his jaw. He was moving by some incredible force below him, that much was obvious, but the speed at which he passed the fissures in the wall was incredible. How he could be sliding up a slant at this velocity seemed unreal. The timberposts set between the ground and the roof split whenever he passed; he couldn't hear it, but he could see the wood cracking and bending.

AL4's bulbs seemed to be getting dimmer, as if the work done on its back was short-circuiting its wires. The robot's arms were lifted from its side so that if Leo were to slide either way, he would be blocked from going over and into the circus of sparks like some cooked chicken. The scene looked oddly enough like a convertible strolling through tunnels on its hubcaps.

Leo tucked the scroll into his waistband, feeling the rancid wind stream by his face and draw tears from his drooping eyelids. Until he saw the light ahead he thought these mines went on forever, that they were a maze and he would continually ride along on this sled until he died of windburn. The gap grew larger; ahead there was this pure light, one his eyes could barely discern without squinting.

Bones scattered before him, thrown against the walls and shattering into puffs of dust; the dog's skull he and Cole had passed earlier (with the rat nesting in its eye socket) had literally crumbled, killing the rat inside instantly as splinters of rock impaled the rodent. There was a collective roar of mice and rats as they tried to scramble up the fissures, into the safety of the darkness, climbing over each other as the wave of stone in the ground tossed their little bodies into the air and against the rock face with a splat. There was a meaty smack as one rat hit Leo's cheek, falling with a dull thud on AL4's abdomen, until rolling onto the ground with crunching hops, sheering through the sparks and burning its fur.

He could feel the ride dying down, the ground underneath settling. The mine groaned and hummed, and the stench of charred metal filled Leo's nose like acrid gunpowder. There was smoke coming from AL4, and both of its bulbs had shattered; there was an insane look on its face, as if it had somehow contorted its linear mouth into a sneer. Leo tumbled forward when the robot finally stopped, hitting his head on AL4's feet, which were also slightly smoking where bunches of rubble had embedded into folds of steel. There was a thick patch of blood on his cheek where the rat had hit, and his right hand was cut near the knuckles.

There were tears streaming down his cheeks. He could barely see. There was just a thick light everywhere, one that had pushed away the darkness. The ground behind AL4 was still swirling, trying to fit itself back in place, the striations of rock shifting and circling until the ground became smooth again. There was a loud snap as timbersets adjusted themselves, straightening in twisted knots as the mine leveled.

Leo looked up. The square of light had focused. It wasn't *that* bright; he didn't know why his head was blaring. He saw his cot to his left, collapsed with its stuffing falling from the mattress; he saw the monitors on the wall, with the cords snaking out of them and winding the ground; he saw both robots the wolves had ripped, with their wires stringing out like party poppers. So they had come up also, flipping along the path of the rock, creating their own sparks as their flailing limbs and wires snapped into rodents and cracked rock with severe whips. The glass from the shattered aquarium was everywhere before him, tinkling the overhead bulbs.

And he saw Edwin Krollup, crouched against the wall under the vents, standing atop the bones of mice.

Leo flopped his back down and felt the light leave him. He needed a moment of darkness back.

11

"Get up Leo," Edwin said in an anemic voice that barely came from his lips. Leo didn't move.

Edwin pushed against the wall, but found he had little strength to do so. The stone took so much from him when he used it. Edwin's anger was replaced with frustration. "Get up Leo, don't make me come over there and do it for you."

Leo moaned.

Edwin wouldn't take this. He was angry, and he meant to tell somebody about it. Now he had his chance, and he wasn't just going to sit against the wall and let Leo get away with it. No way.

Edwin grabbed the stone again, felt it draw something from him as he touched it—so the robot flipped up as a splinter of rock bulged beneath it, throwing Leo into a heap on the ground. Something fell from Leo's pants, something that rolled along the rock and knocked into Edwin's foot. He picked it up and saw that it was paper, a thin scrap of leather rolled tightly and bound by twine. "Hermes has sent me something from the mines I take it, Leo, you scoundrel." Leo gargled and rolled on his side, moaning. Edwin grabbed a piece of rock and rubbed the twine until it frayed and snapped. He unrolled the scroll and a strange smell came from the creases, like liquor almost—like rum.

The leather was beat well; fine markings creased across the skin like vague cracks. It was an odd color too, a light brown with spots of yellow and shades of red. There was writing in black ink, thick ink that ran before it dried. It was written so that the letters were connected, not only by drips, but by waves, as if the hand that writ never left the skin until all was marked upon the hide.

Edwin read it, and then read it again, a noticeable confusion drawing on his face. A noticeable confusion that became understanding.

The letter read:

> *You have something I want, and now I have something you want. Life throws curveballs and it's up to you to swing or wait for the fastball—I presume you're the type to swing away. You seem that way at least, for it was our first meeting that decided I needed something of some worth before you considered a trade, isn't that right? I will make the exchange when you come down the mines yourself, you coward, instead of those pathetic robots.*
>
> *KA*

12

"Who gave this to you?" Edwin said, grabbing Leo by the damp collar, pulling the little man to his knees.

He felt refreshed—*regenerated*—when he read the letter, when he read those initials on the bottom right-hand corner of the scrap. KA—Kenneth

Auger, the man Edwin had been sure dropped dead (*the way he looked when you saw him, the way his skull profoundly sucked his pale skin like cling wrap*), had instead sent this letter up the mines, somehow finding its way into Leo's pants. But how? And what did this heap of dried up bones have that was his? These questions tipped Edwin on his feet, and drove him to grab Leo, to find out who gave him this scrap of leather, turning him into a disfigured Hermes.

And he used a baseball analogy, as if he knew you own a baseball team; that's funny, considering he's been trapped down there for what, nearly fifty years?

Edwin hadn't considered this at first; he was just overcome by curiosity. So feeling his fingers sink into Leo's neck as he lifted him from the ground, and feeling the hot, rancid breath of that dirty mouth became a makeshift vent for Edwin's fury.

Leo only lolled his eyes at Edwin, his head shrinking away from Edwin's glare as his skull rolled on his spine. Edwin grabbed the stone around his neck and Leo was pulled to the wall beside the monitors, his ankles strangled by two strips of rock that had formed little fingers, cutting off the circulation in his legs. He tried to kick, to shift his right leg, then his left, but he couldn't budge them. He had a knowing look in his eyes now, as if he knew this was going to happen, as if he anticipated it. Edwin didn't like that look at all; there was a sense of helplessness in it that made him feel uneasy, despite the fact that he was the root of its origin.

Leo twitched his lips, and gargled, a sound that tried to be speech, but only formed mere strings of dribble.

Edwin held up the scrap of leather so Leo could see it.

"Who gave you this?"

"I'm so sorry," Leo managed to say. He was on the verge of crying.

"Don't you dare cry."

Leo swallowed and his throat was pregnant with the spit lugging down his pipes.

"Who gave you this?"

"There was nothing I could do, you have to believe me sir, there wasn't a thing; it was just too dark, and there were too many of them."

Edwin held the stone again, and beside him a hole formed in the ground, a gaping hole that split through the rock and formed a chasm. It was into this hole that both destroyed robots fell with a sharp clang and bash until the mouth of the gap was closed again, like two drawn lips. AL4 still lay in a heap, smoking from its newly exposed back, uttering screeches when Edwin flipped the robot to bring Leo closer to him.

"WHERE DID YOU GET THIS YOU BLUBBERING IDIOT?"

Leo flinched at the sound of his raised voice. He looked down at the rock cuffs around his ankles. "The wolves, sir."

The wolves? Edwin opened another large gap in front of AL4, and the rock beneath the hulk of metal began to slope, as if dipping the robot towards the chasm as a threat. The robot was beyond repairs. That much was obvious, but to a man like Leo, a man who required some sense of machinery to keep him sane, AL4 was just in the initial stages of renovations.

Leo renewed his helplessness, staring at the stupid robot from his ankle cage on the wall as if it were struggling to keep from falling, as if it were actually screaming to live. Its back was stripped of its metal casing, and its innards were smoking a black cloud that was sucked back down the mines.

"Oh, I'm sorry I took him down with me, sir, I just knew the way he felt, that was all—just don't drop poor AL4 into the pit like that—"

But Leo was cut off.

"Took who down?" Edwin asked, curiously.

Leo gave a look of astonishment. "Wh—who sir?"

Edwin sloped the rock more and AL4 began to slide; its arms, which were held straight out before it was flipped, were crushed and there was a whinnying sound as the metal caught on rocks and broke them from the ground as it slowly moved.

"Cole. Cole…Cole, I took Cole down," Leo repeated, looking at Edwin curiously himself. Didn't he know?

Of course he didn't, you idiot, how would he…how could he?

"Cole," Edwin said aloud. "So that's where the little spy went." His voice was little more than a mutter, but Leo still heard him. How did Auger know Edwin had any relations to kidnap, especially the likes of a little boy? He turned to Leo, half in a daze, and half motivated by his own sense of curiosity. Leo was shocked to see how the man was handling it; he was sure AL4 would have slid down the gap by now. "Tell me Leo, has anybody come up the mines recently, just to have a ganders, perhaps through the fireplace?"

Leo shrugged awkwardly, and AL4's head clipped the edge of the chasm, spewing rubble into the darkness. "No…no sir, not that I've seen. Not that I've heard, and listening to the wolves last night, that sound, well, I can assure you I would have heard something, even in sleep."

"Not if it was a man that had come up. You're supposed to be watching out for these things, you fool," Edwin said, his voice rising again. "This rushes me, but perhaps that's what the old man intends."

"Sir, please, I am so sorry for going down the mines, but I was merely helping your stepson with his problem—"

"Shut up, Leo. Tell me, how many robots do you have?"

"Uhhh…just AL4 sir, that one right there." He pointed to the wrecked robot distended over the hole.

"Not here, Leo, not in these mines, not these elementary designs that do nothing but break. Where do you keep the robots, the robots that *explooooooode?*" He prolonged the last word as if in a mad rage.

Leo shuddered. He didn't want to think of those methods of destruction anymore. Talking to Cole in the mines brought back a sense of his own morality, attempting to displace (if that was possible) both devils that had leased his shoulders for so long. "I have a shed. I don't know if it's still there, sir, but there is a *faux* wall in that shed, one that can be pulled out, not opened, but pulled." Leo swallowed. "I don't know what happened to my place sir, not since I was arrested…and *saved* by you, so please don't hold it against me if the place was bulldozed and buried."

"Your place is fine. I took it upon myself to make sure of it." He smiled. "How many do you have in there?"

Leo knew exactly how many he had in there. One. The last one too, the robot he was supposed to send into City Hall but decided not to at the last moment. Now it was in a shed, gathering cobwebs like some forgotten armor. "One," Leo said in a harsh voice that sounded like a cough.

Edwin nodded his head. That was as he expected.

"What about Cole sir?"

Edwin looked back at the little man. "The man wants a trade."

Leo looked confused. A trade?

"Ever since your last robot went down the mines, I've realized one thing, Leo. I may not need you anymore."

"I can go to my old house with you. I can help you get the robot, I can help build you more…" Leo said fearfully.

Edwin looked at the robot on the ground. "You've lost your touch, little man."

"What are you going to do to me?" Leo asked, looking Edwin directly in the eyes, as if he had gathered enough courage to confront his fears with one stab.

Edwin responded to this look dryly, for he knew exactly what it implied— if Leo were given the chance, he'd take him down in a second's time. He was capable, Edwin was sure, because he was a man bent on aggressions; his inventions were examples of this. He grabbed the stone and the robot called AL4 fully immersed into the chasm until, with one final clang, it disappeared. Leo looked away. He knew this would ultimately happen, but it seemed harder to face its reality: he was left with nothing now, only the rocks and the rodents.

"I'm not going to do anything to you, Leo," Edwin finally said. "But I have one question. Is your robot tricky?"

"It can be," Leo muttered.

"Then maybe there is one last thing you can do for me." He grinned. He threw the scrap of leather into the deep darkness and closed the gap in the ground that AL4 had just fallen into; there was a sharp clap as the rock fit back together as if it had never been separated. "I also have a favor to ask of you, Leo."

"What?"

Edwin gave him a sour look, one that usually meant he was going to hurt him, but he did nothing. "The police will be coming here soon. I'm calling them regarding Cole's unfortunate disappearance. Nobody can know where the mines are, right?"

"You want me to shut up when they come around?"

"You got it. But if you do choose to speak, or garner their attention and draw them over to you, there are punishments." Edwin grabbed the stone and a chasm formed directly under Leo's feet, which were only secured to the wall by rock cuffs. "It's your choice little man, you can help me out one last time, or you can have a conversation with your robots in the darkness of the hills, until the bedrock closes around you like a vise."

Leo stared down into the gaping hole, trying to keep himself from leaning over. "And after I help you?"

"You're free," Edwin said. For some reason Leo didn't believe him. When Krollup left the room the cuffs snapped back into the wall and Leo fell to the ground—a ground he had feared was still open like a cannibal's mouth.

13

"What's wrong with him, anyway?"

There was smoke in the car, and the smell of coffee and turkey sandwiches. The tinted window was rolled down slightly, but not enough to take the stuffy feeling out of the cabin. "You know how Freud used Oedipus Rex as an analogy to explain an infant male's desire to overthrow his father for a, how can I say this, closer relationship with his mother?"

The man in the driver's seat nodded and stuffed half a sandwich down his throat.

"Well, with Krollup here, I have an inkling that he has a severe case of Kronos Complex."

"What's that?" The man in the driver's seat said.

"It's Greek myth. You know Zeus, right? Well, he wasn't always the King, he was, let's say, an impending birth already doomed to a fate inside his father's stomach cavity. His dad was Kronos, and Kronos was the alpha-god before Zeus came around; he was pre-Zeus, let's say. Kronos had this deep-rooted fear, this paranoia what have you, that his children would in time try to steal his throne, to rid of him just as he deposed his own father, Uranus. Uranus was the sky and he mated with Gaia, the earth, and Gaia became impregnated, naturally, but old Uranus wouldn't let her give birth to any of the children. The children imprisoned in her womb hated their father, and were very open about this. Uranus was aware of their threat, and Gaia and her kids formed a conspiracy against him. Kronos castrated Uranus, and ultimately the sky and earth separated." The man grinned widely and took a sip of his coffee. "You grow wary of certain threats after doing something like that, I suppose, but what happens with Kronos is he and Rhea have kids. Conscious of his own hatred for his father, he took simple steps in protecting himself from such a threat. Kronos ate every kid after Rhea delivered them."

The man in the driver's seat shuddered, and gave a sharp grimace.

"It was foolproof, you see, what threat could a child be if you devoured it before it could even produce any feelings whatsoever? The only problem was his over confidence, I suppose, and Rhea initiated her own conspiracy. Obviously enough, the child she saved was Zeus, whom she hid in a cave, bundling a rock inside cloth that took the child's place. Kronos was oblivious of this, the fool, and Zeus grew into a powerful force, and among the steps he took in becoming king of the gods was overthrowing his own father. A tit for a tat I suppose. Krollup and Kronos have much in common."

"You're not going to tell me Krollup eats kids are you?"

The man laughed loudly, the binoculars wrapped around his neck thudding against his heaving chest. "Not that I know of Eddie, not that I know of. Picture it this way. Krollup is Kronos. Uranus is Krollup's father, and Zeus then becomes a condensed version of his two stepsons. It works rather ingeniously on that level. You see, Krollup lives under two fears: one deals directly with claiming fault. He believes it was his fault that his father died in some freak accident with stones. As a result, he fears the hatred he held for his own father became the same relationship he holds with his stepsons; he fears the two of them are out to rid of him because he has embarked on their territory—their mother. I guess Freud has found a way into my theorizing after all." He took another sip of his coffee and wiped his lips.

"I thought psychologists took a decree of confidentiality with their patients," Eddie said.

"If I was an honest psychologist, Eddie, then the two of us wouldn't be sitting here right now, would we?"

Eddie shook his head. "I was only kidding Robert."

"I know." Robert Innis looked through the binoculars at the towering house in the hills. He couldn't see anything, and he knew their being here was useless, was utterly hopeless considering the sun had turned the mansions many windows into white eyes. But he wasn't just here to catch glimpses of Edwin through the window, going about his ritzy day; he was here to find a logical way for Eddie to get inside the house, to get at least an idea where the mines were, which fireplace they were behind.

He was obsessed about those mines, about the prospect of something else existing at the end of them.

And he was obsessed about the necklace. This wasn't just honest curiosity anymore, because when Robert Innis closed his eyes, he thought he could still see that orange hue in his eyelids, that orange hue that was fading volcanoes.

He'll want to get hypnotized again; it doesn't matter how skeptical he feels about the process. He doesn't want to feel at fault for his daddy's death. You can find out a lot when the minds under your spell. And you can hold it again; you can take the stone in your hands and feel that pulse, that deep thud.

He hoped so at least.

His cell phone rang. It had startled him and he dropped the binoculars. "You expecting a call?"

"Office is closed, so it's probably one of my money grubbing ex-wives. Other than clients, those vultures are the only ones with the number to this phone. Court order." Robert patted his chest, where the braying plastic was nestled inside his inner pocket. "Let them sweat the weekend without my new credit cards, the wolves," he said, and he smiled.

One minute later his phone rang again. It rang endlessly, until, after the fourteenth ring (Eddie had counted) it grew silent. They both waited for it to ring again.

"Who do you think wants to get a hold of you so bad?"

Robert pulled his phone out and flipped it open—the screen read two new calls and he checked who made them.

"Oh jeese," he muttered. "The calls both came from Krollup's house."

Eddie looked at the house through the tinted car window; it was dim but the glow of the windows made him squint regardless. "You think he knows we're out here?"

"I don't know, but we should probably get out of here whether he does or not."

Eddie turned the ignition and the muffled sound of the engine leaked in through the dashboard. A country song suddenly came on the radio, and Eddie hummed it out loud as he pulled from the curb and drove his boxy Caprice down the winding road.

CHAPTER 10

Wolf Country

1

The sun had come out hours ago. The sky lit like a candle, and the clouds that lay like strings in the air exploded into red stripes. The Towers threw their shadows across the country in a black hulk, and the Dead Springs, the poisoned waters of the Asrin River, settled like foam on the dusty coast, turning the rock to sponge. The wolves that had descended the slope, dug their claws into the sediments and climbed down to the spring, the smell of rotting fish wafting over the water like a thick mist. They doused their heads into the spring and shook their muzzles, spiking their fur like quills; a white spit clung to their black lips and splattered against the rock; the pink scars around their mouths, some still fresh, dripped water onto their chin until the hair let it fall back into the spring.

This was morning in Wolf Country.

"You see them, like pigs to slop they are." Haspin sat by his carriage, holding an apple in his hand, picked from the orchards west of his castle, on the coast of the lake where the morning mist didn't smell like rotting fish; where Gallia sat untouched by the decay of the Yilaks.

The old man watched them climb down the slope into the spring. He sat on the gold cast steps of Haspin's carriage, sometimes staring at the King's Crest, the sun bound by two leaves—the prophesy that all lands touched by the sun were subject to the King, were subject to his divinity, but that had been wrong. That assumption had been terribly wrong, because the kingdom fell. "It is the stench of the spiders that stirs me," the old man finally said.

Haspin grunted, staring at the dried slime on the ground, formed with the lumpy mucus of egg yolk. "What is it the wolves were howling about last night?"

"The wolves hunted a stray hound," the old man lied. But it wasn't merely a lie; it was protection. Haspin had come to Wolf Country for other reasons, he was sure of it; he saw it in the fat man's eyes. Perhaps there was a war stirring. Nothing in the world motivated the old man more to try and get home—get home alone and alive, without wolves, without this fat man and his army of men who shook when wolves passed closely beside them.

"We are off," Haspin called out fifteen minutes later; the men he left behind as collateral watched in disbelief the carriage disappear around the Towers. They were certain they would never see the carriage again, let alone the green pastures of Gallia where they had grown up.

The old man stared at the bluff, waiting to see if his message had been delivered. *He will come down,* he thought.

2

Haspin sat in his carriage with Lor, his strongest swordsman, loyal guard of the King's Crest. The two were eating chocolates, the rarest delicacy in all of the Inlands, made from the milk of the few cows left in Gallia. Chocolate was the royal treat; the farmers were paid handsomely for it. The cows' milk had gone sour these days, but you couldn't taste the peculiar tang in chocolate. Blueberries were good with cocoa, and so were jib plants, but Haspin had always been partial to peanuts, much like the King before him. There was a golden bowl sitting between the two men, who faced each other over a small table. Inside there were misshapen lumps of fudge the two devoured in whole bites, smudging their lips in a mahogany that surrounded their mouths in drawn moustaches.

"I could smack the old man, finding slumber with the wolves. I trusted him when your uncle was still on the throne…when there still *was* a throne," Lor said through a mouthful of chocolate.

Haspin put the lid back on the bowl, grabbing two more pieces that he greedily tucked inside his stained palm and rolled into brown ropes. "He is a blind fool believing his cause has set us to motion. Haspin, heir to the throne, does not simply go on a hunt to whet another man's whim. Bring him back the wizard—BAH! He is a liar, telling me the wolves caught a Hound when I saw clearly they had hunted a young refugee boy—he is sick, defending the wolves' actions. There is something going on here, aye, something we're not supposed to know. Doesn't matter." Haspin leaned in over the table. "It will all be over soon." Haspin shoved both melted balls of chocolate into his mouth, and he smiled, showing his streaked teeth to Lor.

"We should hope," Lor agreed. "I hate leaving collateral, men we could use in the line," Lor said. He was drinking a strong apple cider.

"That is the problem with strategy, Lor, for we have to make sacrifices." Haspin said this with malicious intent, licking the chocolate from his teeth and sharing a heartless grin.

Lor stared out the window. "I don't trust the Hunters; they send *us* to Wolf Country, while they wait like cowards for our return."

Haspin smiled. "They're useful in the war, Lor. That's all. Trust was always out of the question."

"I don't like this."

"Of course, for yer a strategist of war; we must work on spontaneity. Now we must believe the Hunters seek our same desire—to destroy the wolves. They will cancel each other out, for it would be at the mercy of the city, yes. 'Tis their destiny. And we will find Ae-Granum, Lor. We will because we must; we will drink his blood to the city, and smite our enemies without a pause for breath. We shall restore the one true monarchy of the Inlands."

"Then ya believe what it is the Traveling Man told?"

Haspin nodded.

"Why?"

"Because he has the Third Eye. And I have seen the outcome o' his tellings. He sat at me uncle's side when the throne was filled. He sees all, Lor, an' knows what he must."

"And what does he expect from us in the end?"

Haspin only shook his head. "What all expect in the end, my dear friend. The return of the King."

Lor smiled, and he held his glass of apple cider towards the fat man across from him. Haspin did the same, only his goblet was filled with malt ale, and they knocked both cups together with a hard clunk. They drank.

3

Cole turned in his sleep; he could just imagine how dark it was around him, how empty it was going to be when he opened his eyes. He was certain he had left the flashlight on all night, draining the battery until it blinked out all at once.

Another thing too, he thought. *You came down the vents on a rope, one that snapped when you tried to climb back up. If you wake up and Leo has decided to go on down the mines to wherever it was he was going, then how do you figure*

you'll get back up the vents without Krollup finding you huddled against the rock
wall crushing fragile mouse bones in between your fingers?

He didn't know, and he kicked his leg out, almost nicking his foot along
the dirty ground that was split and cracked and smelt of rotting worms. He
imagined what Krollup would do when he found him; he could see the man's
stony eyes and nothing else, and he realized there would be nowhere to run
but back into the darkness. This thought kind of scared him; it scared him
because he understood at once just where he was. He was in a mine where the
air was beginning to smell sour, and where the light had ceased to exist. What
if he didn't know which way was home? He could wander forever in the wrong
direction, until finally dropping dead with the one hope that the people who
knew he was missing felt guilty for his being so; felt, in some way or other,
bad that they *had* to remember him as a punching bag. This thought wasn't
that bad, not at all; for some reason it gave his purpose meaning.

Cole's head hurt. When he turned on his side he realized this was all too
real, that the pain wasn't just a part of some dream, but had ensnared his
midsection in tight grips. When he turned, he had ground his bruised flesh
into a cracked rib, and then his body had exploded.

When he opened his eyes he wasn't in the mines.

There were lights coming in from the roof, streamers of white like tape,
and Cole had a feeling that this too was a horrible nightmare. It reminded him
of the wedding under the pavilion, and the way that Krollup held his mother's
hand. The lights had been the same then, and Cole wanted to scream, only he
found he had no voice. His throat was dry, and when he moved the pain in
his stomach told him to stop if he wanted to preserve any ounce of strength
he might have left.

4

Last night the moon had been high, reflected like a pallid face in the
mists of the Dead Springs, its many craters like the empty eye sockets
of a corpse. Bones hung from posts, with straw nestled into crooks lit
with fire, and the tents around Wolf Country—made from stretched hide,
stitched with string (and in some places, with the dried intestines of dead
horses) so tight that no wind could stir nor flap excess skin that folded
aside to reveal doors—drew flickering shadows on the bloodied grounds
as if the earth had been winking.

Horses stood before buckets of water brought from the springs, pacing
on their tethers uneasily.

"They won't drink it, it's like vomit to them," a soldier said, as he stroked
the horse's mane with his callused fingers.

"Then hopefully this blasted quest ends before the horses fall, and *we* are left to pull the carriage of the heir," another said. "What do you suppose it is they wait for?"

Both men looked at the Yilaks. "I don't know," the soldier said.

5

That same night Grak Ulak sat inside the tent looking into the birdcage. The figure was inside, crouched against the black iron bars, which were dappled with bird droppings. The figure wore a sling around its left arm, tied roughly and fitted on its stump. The sling was made of linen from the old man's cart, thick white cotton that had stained a deep red, dripping blood onto the bottom of the cage.

There was a leather strap bound around the figure's eyes, cuffing the slits of its nostrils until breaths sounded little more than tired wheezes. *They had to do it*, Grak thought, *they had to close its eyes because they were attacking each other. Ilak attacked Nrak, dropping the birdcage to grab for his sword—*
Something in its eyes showed them hate.

Grak had the sudden urge to reach through the bars and strangle the pallid creature, to pluck its eyeballs out and eat them in a stew, but there was something about this thing that fascinated him.

Grak leaned forward until his muzzle touched the cage. "How did you get inside my head?"

There was a moment when Grak thought the creature would turn away and pull the leather strap from its brow and unleash the fires of its eyes, but it only sat there, blind yet somehow, not blind. Grak knew that for sure. He knew this figure could see every little thing *inside* this tent, and probably outside it too; it just couldn't see *inside* him. It couldn't dig into his deepest secrets and produce that one image that could turn him against the other Yilaks, or even himself.

"Things like you aren't safe in Wolf Country." Grak spoke in a mutter that would have curled the hair on your head had you been sitting there with him.

"I am not in Wolf Country."

"Oh, and where are you then?"

"I am hanging in the forest. I can see below me. The trees here tower towards the sky—Canopy Trees; they are like the oracles of old. They are very beautiful, not like the rock you call home, the disgusting dust that engulfs your throat. It is no wonder you are prone to such anger, for I would share your sentiments had I been brought up in this pit." The figure spoke like a man, in a crisp voice that reminded Grak of Haspin, the fat maggot in the carriage that believed he could carry on the King's Crest when the monarchy had been destroyed.

Grak laughed, which became a shrill howl. "It is anger you speak of, and it is anger you mock, yet you rose from the egg with a vicious appetite, did you not? You showed your fangs and murdered—is this not anger?"

"You *made* me live. You opened the egg and showed me light."

Grak looked at the pale figure—the pale *man*, he could say, for that's what he sounded like—and he licked his many teeth. "You hang in a forest you say. How is this possible, when you sit here in this cage, bleeding like a stuck hog?"

"Do you have a family, Wolf?"

"Family is indifferent to Yilaks. Meaningless. Human maggots put too much emphasis on it, which is why their race is doomed. I became general only after I killed my father, for he was general before me; there is no sense in allegiance, for if I loved my father the way humans loved their own, we would have been a doomed race."

"You murdered your father when he wasn't looking; you took the crown of thorns from him and gouged his red eyes so he wouldn't see you—so he wouldn't feel such shame and betrayal. You never looked directly at him, so don't tell me, Grak, that there was never love for your father. You disliked his authority; there is a difference, which is why you waited till he wasn't ready; he still scared you, such is the way with fathers. You still think about the deep shudder that left his scarred lips when you plunged your sword in between his shoulders. I heard that in your head when I looked at you. I saw many things Grak, things you never knew you knew, and you tell me allegiance is meaningless? Oh how you lie."

Grak wrapped his arms around the cage and shook it until the pale figure slipped down the bars and lined its back with white stripes. "You know nothing."

"I know I'm doomed," the creature said. Grak could imagine pity in its eyes. "You murdered your father, and I hope that image haunts you until death." The hermit pulled its lips back from its sharp teeth. "You brought the egg from the old forest because of silly superstitions. This wasn't for you, but an old man you don't especially like." The hermit smiled.

"Humans follow stupidity."

"And what then of your cowardice, killing your father as his back was turned; was this not stupidity?"

"Your judgment is worthless."

The hermit sprung quickly to the bars in front of Grak, startling the Wolf. "I would have been released had you not stolen the egg from the Queen, had you not opened the sac and let me live the way I am, a part of the spiders, a mutant, *hideous*. Had you left me with the Queen, I would've been put out of my misery before becoming what it is I am. The old man that controls your army—"

"The old man is a fool that has made promises, that has said he could bring us back our stone to seal our revenge on man; there is no control in his favor. He is a puppet," Grak growled.

"But the old man drove you to get the egg; I saw defiance in your mind, Grak, but your defiance was easily subdued."

"What you see is false, hermit. I fought my father fairly for the throne, and no human is worth defiance. You are a godless monster, and Mystic would not cast a glance even if 'twould save your life."

The hermit struck its head on the bar and there was a dull thud; it had attacked purely out of anger, drops of poison coursing down its lip, smoking as they hit the floor of the cage, boiling the bird droppings into a sickly fizz. It ripped the leather band from its head and both its eyes opened like newly sprung fires.

"I can search your head, Grak, no matter if you shut your eyes to me. I can see your past, your present...AND YOUR FUTURE. They will have your head; the bloodline you seek will have your head." The hermit screamed the last words, but no voice was heard, for it was inside Grak's head that the hermit spoke. Its voice was a high whisper that sounded like the wind through the knotted trees of Ichimad Forest.

Grak could feel something prying inside him, something running around with heavy steps, knocking things over, showing him terrible images; showing him his father's hunched back before he had plunged his sword through his father's spine...this image lasted for a minute, but to Grak it felt like hours, days even, and despite the memories shown to him by some unseen force, it was the image of his father that lasted.

"His governance would have let man win the war," Grak growled, and he cut the hermit's right hand from its wrist, which clung to the bar it had been grasping before slowly sliding into the pool of blood below.

There were howls from outside the tent, and horns were sounded.

"You will never find peace, hermit." Grak reached through the bars and picked the leather band from the bottom of the cage. The hermit had slid against the bars, its eyes flickering like the fires outside, as if the redness was dying, as if that magnificent ability within them had expired—but Grak knew this was wrong. He slipped the band over the hermit's eyes, and suddenly felt clearheaded again, hearing only the howls outside, the horns. He took the severed hand from within the cage and threw it into the darkness where it would rot.

"And in blindness you shall live."

6

Grak went outside into the cool night to see what the jubilation was about. The old man had been sitting in his cart, the drapery pulled open to reveal the plush lining, and the empty bottles scattered about the floor, some dripping that stinking poison onto the fur and turning it a light red.

Grak thought about what the hermit had said, how he, a Yilak, was controlled by this puny, knobby little man, who himself was controlled by a disease that was eating him from the inside. He seemed to hear the hermit lingering in his head, like some distant hum—*you went to the Leeg Forest on his orders, a Wolf abiding by a man's rules, how pathetic.*

The old man held a bottle to his lips, one of the many he brought from the castle in Sadaan when he came looking to get into the Towers, groveling at Grak's feet like a child.

"The hermit claimed it could see my future, but that was only to draw me into its trap—to further claim this old man would control my armies, and would lead them astray. Laughable."

"What did you say, Grak?" A Yilak said from beside the general.

Grak clubbed the wolf in the muzzle and sent it sprawling into the side of a tent.

Upon the ridge over Wolf Country, at the base of the ruins and at the exit of the mines, Ilak and Jarak and the other Yilaks descended the slope. Jarak carried a bundle over his shoulder.

"This is delightful indeed," the old man said, and he dropped the bottle and clapped his hands. The Yilaks howled.

Jarak came to the old man; his muzzle foamed with splattered drool; his scars gleamed the firelight like lamps.

"How did you get him so quickly?" The old man asked, patting the young boy in Jarak's enormous arms.

"They were in the mines already, as if they knew we were coming," Jarak said. The young boy's head flopped over the wolf's shoulder.

"Was it a trap?" The old man asked worriedly.

"If it were a trap, you old fool, then the man with the stone wouldn't have let them get this far," Grak said, giving the boy a look over, studying him with his red eyes.

"He was with another, an old man, like you," Jarak said.

Auger wiped his lips until his mouth turned red. "Ah, the man in the cot, the man I've seen sleeping behind the brick stack." The old man shut his eyes and thought for a second. "Long hair on the sides, but none at all on top?"

Jarak's yellow eyes lit. "We left the message with him."

"Good, then we wait," the old man said. "Set him here, next to me, so when he wakes up I can offer an explanation; there is no need scarring a young boy's mind when he isn't a target but a means to an end."

Grak stepped in and pushed Jarak aside; the boy muffled a short cry as his side shifted. He wouldn't let the old man bark orders at the Yilaks, and it infuriated him to believe that Jarak would have set the boy down, responding to such a demand. "Stay your mouth old man, and get back to your bottle." Grak pulled the drapes closed on the cart, and heard the old man fall back. He looked at Jarak.

"Set him next to the demon."

7

On Saturday morning Edwin strolled into the Krollup manor through the backdoor, holding under his arm a draped object that looked rather heavy, judging by the contorted twist of Edwin's upper lip, and the furrow in his sweaty brow. He set the object on the stoop as he opened the door, and warded off any of the staff who felt it was their duty to help him maneuver whatever it was he was holding.

"Get away, this is none of your business," he said, and he waved his arms frantically until the women teetered away, and the men jogged.

Krollup went into his office (locking the door behind him), and pushed the rock arm into the backfill, opening the wall that was actually a door, stepping from plush carpet to slick rock that smelt of oil. He finally set the wrapped object on the ground with a clunk and he looked at Leo.

Leo was sitting on the bed with his face buried in both of his callused palms; there was still blood on his cheek, and Edwin could tell the little man's ankles were both very swollen. His pants folded up slightly on one side, revealing a purple swell that stretched his dirty socks until the seams looked like they were going to burst.

"Is that it?" Leo asked, quite shocked Edwin had gotten it so quickly. It only felt like hours since he had been forced back up the mines. But days might have passed without him knowing, because he had fallen into a stupor. Edwin smiled; there was something horribly gratuitous about it, something Leo didn't quite like. "I drove over to your old place. Lawns been seen to every week. Fence was just painted. It still seems lived in. Such a shame. Such a waste. I went out to the shed, like you said. That was pretty neat how you painted the plywood to look like shelving. You might have tricked the naïve onlooker, or the landscaper looking for shade, but Leo my boy, I noticed right away, as if there was a sign over it."

Leo sighed. There *was* a sign over it. Leo had told him exactly where the robot was hidden—behind a *faux* plywood wall that had to be pulled out.

"I pulled the plywood away and the darkness seeped out like water, and I mean that, it was incredible, as if there was a vacuum in my hand turned on full throttle. And there it sat, under the same blanket you see it in now, covered in dust of course, and the odd cobwebs, but nothing a sleeve can't wipe off. Show me, Leo, get up and show me how it works."

Leo tried to get up, but his ankles resisted, almost scolding up at him. "I can't sir, I think my ankles are broken."

"Hogwash," Edwin said, and he touched the rock hanging from his throat. The mattress tilted up flinging Leo to his feet.

Leo grimaced as the pain sang in his calves; he could feel his knees wobbling, wanting badly to teeter.

Edwin ripped the blanket off the robot and dust exploded in the air. Both men coughed, waving in front of their faces.

"It's incredibly light," Edwin said, "considering what it's made of."

Leo looked at the robot. Even under these dim bulbs it found a way to sparkle. Dust and spider webs had speckled the smooth skull, and there were dried up insects on its shoulders like moles. Leo blew the bugs off, and brushed away the dust and spider webs, wiping his hand down his side after each swipe. He ran his hand down the arch of its dome, feeling the pronunciation of his artistry; his hand left streaks caught by the light, and he wondered if it worked. He wondered if maybe he might be able to fulfill a wish he had been thinking about for some time.

I want to shut the devil up for good, he thought, and he slid his forefinger down the flat spine of the machine, which was opened at either side showing its cable innards. There wasn't a button for this particular robot, because he had designed it acknowledging the simplicity of switching a button on and off. He wanted something spectacularly confusing, something that might explode if you touched the wrong panel. There were buttons of course, each of them in their own specific places (there was one at the nape of the robot's skull, colored bright blue as if imploring human contact—if touched, the robot's head would explode, thus triggering the main bomb in the abdomen, which had the power to blow up a two story building), but none of them were any use in disarming the machine.

Leo looked at the cables in the abdomen, the way they crisscrossed and looped, and the way each of them detailed their own destruction in some way. With a fedora tipped on its head, and a tailored suit fitted around its hulk, Leo wondered if anybody could tell the difference between *real* and *steel*; he wondered if anybody in City Hall had even recognized it as a robot, or if they just passively assumed the 'person' in the hat and suit was shy.

"Does it work?" Edwin asked. He seemed to have the same look in his eye, only it wasn't because this was a work of his artistry. Edwin was baffled by the level of destruction this little thing could...*would* impose, Leo guessed.

"I'll check." Leo smiled, because if this thing did work, the devil on his shoulder was telling him to do one thing: *blow up the house, and take Krollup with you.* He pretended to press buttons (which didn't matter if the robot wasn't activated), but with his right hand he had fidgeted with a red wire that was loose and laid with its frayed end out of the robot like a deformed hair. He fit it roughly into its circuit, and when there was *supposed* to be a beep, and a stir as movement jerked along the robot's limbs, there came only a disconcerting stillness. Dust must have jammed it or something, he didn't know, so he licked his finger and shoved it into the circuit; there was a sharp pinch as he swirled his finger, and when he pulled it out he noticed that he'd popped a blister. He stuck the wire back into the slot, and there was a thin whir but it was abruptly cut off.

"Our trust in technology is rather useless, when magic does the trick," Edwin said under his breath. Leo didn't know if he was supposed to hear that, or to even understand it, so he just kept his mouth zipped. "Can you fix it?"

Leo looked at the robot sternly, tracing the wires, pulling them to see if anything was loose.

"Can you?"

"Of course, sir. This *is* my design." He smiled, but saw the look on Edwin's face and looked down.

Edwin heard a thin knock through the rock; it was on his office door, he was sure of it.

"That's my wife, Leo, and she will greatly desire phoning the police. I know much of desires, Leo. You wanted the robot to work just as much as I did, only your purpose for its functioning differed from mine. You want to blow me to kingdom come, don't you Leo?"

Leo felt faint and the pain flared in his legs again. Even his hand seemed to blow up where the shard of glass had sliced his knuckles.

"You learn things when you get to my level, Leo: trust is for morons. I can't trust you with this robot, which is why I've never allowed the materials for you to build a machine capable of destruction. I don't trust your motivations." He stopped because the knocking on his office door grew louder and faster. It sounded like his wife was trying to break down the door. "I can do one of two things, Leo. I can take this robot away, and thus strip you of any meaning, or I can trust that this favor you promised me is concrete. You won't go trying to blow that thing up prematurely, and I won't break both your ankles and send you down the mines with a wave of rock leaving you for the wolves." Edwin cocked his eyebrow at Leo.

When Edwin left the room two things happened. One of them had become routine, and Leo expected it, but the other threw him off his guard and sent him tumbling forwards. First, the rock arm exploded from the backfill and blocked the door, though right after, and unexpectedly, a sheet of stone lifted from the ground and formed a blanket against the brick stack; the tendrils of smoke that slipped through the sparse grout had disappeared. When the sheet of rock lifted, the ground swayed and felt like ice, and Leo fell without realizing what it was that had happened.

He could have done this long ago, blocking the fireplace entirely, blocking my view of the outside world, and stealing any chance of yelling for help, Leo thought. *But then you wouldn't have felt tempted to do so; your whole existence here has been a test. If the bricks had been covered, then your motivation to believe there was actually a way out would have diminished, and you wouldn't have done any work at all. Having a working world ten feet from where you slept made you believe there was still life out there; that there was still a chance you would get out.*

Leo looked at the sheet of rock for a moment and stuck his fingers into the robot, hoping for the chance to push a button and watch the bright light before both he and Edwin became giant fireballs.

8

Edwin opened his office door in the middle of a frantic knock and his wife fell into his arms.

She was a mess. Edwin noticed the ponytail she'd thrown her hair into had messily tore into strands of greasy red curlicues that tickled at her jaw from either side; there were deep marks on her cheeks where tears had obviously marched their course. She sniffed up and looked at him accusingly.

"Where on earth have you been?"

"I had business to attend to."

"And I suppose you haven't heard then?" She broke into sobs, and Edwin found he had to drape his arm around her shoulder before she could stifle her tears. His shirt turned into dotted fabric, and the spots where her tears had dropped seemed to be spreading; he hated the feel of them on his shoulder. "Nobody has seen him, nobody has heard from him. I called his friends' houses…err, the neighbors down the hill, Jimmy's friends' houses; I've called the school five times, and all I get from them is either the machine or a grumpy caretaker who can barely speak a word of English, but knows easily enough how to yell, 'school's closed'. It has been hell Edwin, and you tell me you've gone to tend to business…I don't even care how much you may dislike my boys at times. I know they're apt to break rules, but this is beyond mere childish pranks, Edwin. My son is missing, and nobody knows where he's gone."

She wrapped her arms around his neck and collapsed into him. Edwin could feel the necklace push into his chest.

Just tell her where he's gone, and tell her he's safe just as long as a trade is made.

Edwin shook that thought away. There was no way he would tell her about the mines. That wouldn't just crush her, that would convince her that her son was gone for good, and Edwin didn't want to do that to his wife, no matter his feelings for those little brats. Cole had obviously been prying in Edwin's secrets, found the door in his closet and decided to investigate; the answer was rather simple, but giving it to this wailing woman was a mistake. He would get back Cole; there were ways of doing that without making a trade. He thought about the picture he had whittled on the General's throne—the carving of the statues entering the mines. Their time drew close. Edwin felt for the necklace to make sure it was still there. This had become a terrible habit, and though he didn't want to openly admit it, proved his obsession.

"I want to call the police." Maggie said, wiping her eyes with the back of her arm, staring at him out of those reddish sockets.

Edwin looked at Maggie and his eyes focused back on her. For a minute he thought he was floating, but that was just the haziness of his vision.

"Don't you have to wait twenty-four hours before calling in a missing person?"

"I don't care. You're a big man Edwin. You have pull. Find a loophole." She swiped her forefinger and middle finger against her thumb in a circular motion—*you have money dear, and I think you know how to use it,* she thought.

9

Maggie found Jimmy crouched against the wall by the window in his room; he had both knees tucked into his stomach and it too looked as though he'd been crying.

Maggie knelt down next to him; her cheeks still damp and her nose still runny. "He's letting off steam, that's all Jimmy. He's left the house to work away whatever it is that's bothering him—problems *with* school, problems *at* school. There's nothing to get worked up about, honey."

She stroked his hair away from his face; there was something in the boy's eyes that alarmed her, something that didn't seem right, as if Jimmy was in a mode of deep contemplation. She didn't think a boy could possess such a look, and this worried her; it reminded her of a madman on the verge of suicide. "What's wrong, Jimmy?"

Jimmy looked away; the sun fell through the window like lines drawn by hand, and each seemed to pierce a hole in his guilt, trying to uncover it, and he *knew* he was going to tell his mother what was bothering him, just as he *knew* Cole ran away because of him.

Before his mother found him in his room, Jimmy had been sitting with his tin box on his lap; he had been opening it and closing it, attempting to resist that horrible urge to grab a cigarette and light it, feel it quench his anxieties like an opened drain in a sink. But—

The lid on the box turned into something else as he lifted and closed it; it became Cole's sweater, rising over the swelling of his stomach, and the smokes were Cole's purple bruises. He didn't know why he saw this; he couldn't even begin to guess what the transformation meant, but he knew he couldn't smoke any of them, not now, because this was *his* fault. As he ran around the house, checking rooms he hadn't even been in before, he realized something about his dream last night—it wasn't just a punishment on his behalf, but it was a subtle warning, almost as if Cole had injected him with his thoughts.

When his mother asked him what was wrong he knew what he wanted to say, but he didn't know how he could. His mother lived in this world where she believed her sons respected Edwin Krollup and the life she chose for them after their father died—that was clear enough. She also believed that the relationship between both brothers was a force within itself, a bind that could never be broken despite the common rivalries between them. She knew he looked after Cole. Jimmy knew all of this, and he knew he would do one thing if he told her the truth about what was bothering him: he would sever that certain appreciation his mother had for him.

Guilt is like that, he thought. *It tears through your defenses because fault is a much more powerful caliber than failure—if you had just arrived late this wouldn't be a problem, but you watched Ricky beat up Cole, you watched and you smoked.*

How could he keep this shame bottled up? How could he look into his mother's eyes and tell her more lies? Tell her that he hadn't seen any of Cole's bullies? Tell her that boys he had brought *into* this house hadn't beat up his brother? He couldn't. Not anymore. If lying had created part of this shroud of guilt, then truth could perhaps remove a part of it—a tit for a tat.

"Mom, I can't remember dad," Jimmy finally said, both ashamed because this was the truth, and because he had chickened out—he could feel his guilt tightening up.

Maggie looked at Jimmy; she stroked his hair and set her hand on his shoulder. "Is that what's gotten you upset?"

Jimmy shook his head. "I dunno, I guess that's part of it."

"He loved you," she said. She meant it of course, but she could have said other things and meant them too. Roger was a good father, but a lousy husband as the saying went, but it wasn't just that—Roger had secrets even his two sons didn't know about, and she knew her boys were angry at her, were angry with the divorce, but they had formed the separation on one fact, a fact they could relate to because of her obvious distaste for it. Roger had smoked, and the boys had realized how wrong this was; they had formed the divorce on that one issue, and she was fine with that because she didn't want Jimmy or Cole to dislike their father; she wanted them to find some happiness in memories. Roger had gone to the war, and he had traveled with his business but every time he had returned much earlier than the boys' had known. Roger was a liar; he didn't come home to them because he had others he could come home to. But that didn't matter because sleaze caught up with sleaze, she liked to say, and finding out he had cancer turned him into the man she fell in love with—the man she had had two beautiful boys with. Yet where was the point in founding your marriage in a man that was clearly dying? She hated the finality in the decision, the way it changed her image of family but—

"He loved you very much, Jimmy. I remember he told me once, and this is when you were very young, that when he was away with the troops, he thought about you and Cole every day. That was his sole meaning in life, and you can't lie when you're facing death—the truth is sort of scared out of you." She smiled. She could see that he was crying again.

"Cole hated it that I couldn't remember him, mom," Jimmy sniffed. "I was...I *am* just so mad at him for dying, for lying to us—and Cole couldn't see that he had blinded us."

"What do you mean?"

"We hated that he smoked, so he told us that he quit, but we found him smoking after he promised us he would never touch them again." Jimmy punched his hand; he was angry. Not just at the thought of his father, but at his own cowardice. He wanted to tell her the truth about Cole, not his father. "Cole doesn't realize he was lied to, and I got so mad at him for being so blind, mom. I got so mad at him because he lives under dad's rules as if dad was perfect. He wasn't...he *isn't*. I always used to think that if he was honest to us about quitting, he may just still be alive."

"You can't burden yourself with such thoughts, Jimmy."

"It's not just that though. Dad was like paper in a way; he was weak, and he started to rip because of cigarettes. When he ripped all the way through he left you with nothing. I remember that much. I'm not too young to understand poverty. I know why you married Mr. Krollup, and I always see him smoking cigars and it just makes me so angry that dad had to be so weak.

Mr. Krollup isn't ripping; he's growing *stronger* if anything. Dad didn't have that power, and I wondered where the point was in making myself believe he did. I used to want to be like dad, mom. I used to want to join the army like he did. I used to want to teach kids like me to play ball, maybe even have my own kids one day, but where would the fulfillment be if I ripped in two so easily, if anything I did could kill me like it did him. I know Mr. Krollup hates me and Cole, and maybe that's why he's so powerful. Maybe caring too much makes you weak."

"He doesn't hate you, Jimmy, and your father wasn't weak. He was a different man than Edwin."

"But I don't want to be different. I like what Mr. Krollup has. He has this sense of power. People are afraid of him, and knowing so must make him feel good. I know how that feels, mom."

Maggie pulled Jimmy against her chest and patted his head. "Different men have different fates, I suppose, but that doesn't mean one is better than the other. Your father smoked, sure, but he also neglected his health. Even when he started feeling sick, he thought it would pass. If it wasn't for you two boys urging him to go see the doctor, he would never have found out about the tumor, and he may have died much earlier, and at a more painful expense."

"I don't think Cole is hiding, mom."

"What do you mean?"

"He loves dad. He doesn't care that he's been lied to, and I just don't understand that. But we're different, and not just in that belief either. He's upset at me because he thinks I replaced dad with Mr. Krollup."

"Don't be silly, Jimmy," Maggie said. She had been staring across the room, at the bunk beds and the open door that looked out into the hall.

"Mom, I lied to you before, about kids at school. Cole is a different boy, I guess he's like dad in that way, because he easily rips; he's weak. But I guess you knew that, because you called the school about the bullying. It hurt me to watch Cole struggle to hide his bruises from you guys, but…I hate myself for this mom—but there's this longing for power in me, like Mr. Krollup I guess, that wants to see others get hurt." Jimmy swallowed and watched the surface of truth corrode that shroud of guilt. "Ricky beat Cole up at school…"

"Ricky, your friend Ricky?"

Jimmy swallowed again. He nodded his head. He was scared his mother might wallop him, or worse, leave the room without looking back. "I watched him do it mom. I watched Ricky beat up Cole, and at that moment I didn't care because I thought it might prove to Cole—"

Jimmy started sobbing. He couldn't finish that thought. He just couldn't.

"—When I saw Cole last night mom, he showed me his stomach…the guys had been hitting his stomach because the principal had lectured them on bullying—so they hit him where the teachers couldn't see the bruises. I let this happen. I was so stupid. So blind." He clapped his hand over his brow and cried into his palm. Maggie heard him say: "he ran away because of me."

A part of Maggie wanted to console her son, and another wanted to get up and leave the room; the latter sense tried not to believe her little boy ran away, but there was this insistent nagging that told her the evidence was there. His own brother had allowed the bullying, had allowed his own friends to do it. No wonder he had hidden his bruises; he was just as ashamed of having them as Jimmy was for letting them be.

"You think he ran away?" She asked bluntly.

Jimmy hid his face in his shirt. "I would've stopped him if I knew," he said.

Maggie stood up, careful not to show her own tears, which were welling on the tip of her lids.

She left her son crying by the window. She left him not out of a terrible urge to spite him, but because she was so ashamed he perceived power in that way, that her own definition of family had changed. Jimmy had let his brother slip and fall, and he hadn't offered his hand to help him up; this pained her to think, and it pained her even more to accept, but she was deeply ashamed of Jimmy—and God forbid, a part of her wished the boys were switched, that Jimmy was the one missing. She wouldn't be able to sleep knowing she had this thought, and she would forever question herself as a mother. When Edwin Krollup would send her to her mother's house for a period of grieving, there would be consolation based on this very belief—that Maggie Krollup had failed both her sons.

10

Cole *almost* fell out of the bundle of cloths he was lying in; there was an urgent insistence to pinch himself, to make sure this was just some terrible dream, something the gases in the mines had produced—but the image wouldn't leave him. He was awake, and the smell of rotting meat was real, and the light in this room—tent?—proved he was no longer in the mines.

He didn't know if he should be scared; he didn't know if he should scream and run around the room throwing his hands in the air in utter panic. His first instinct was to find Leo; a part of him knew Leo would have the answers. Another part of him declared he was alone, and that he had been left to rot finalizing some diabolical revenge Leo had in plan ever since his face was booted in the vents. Although ridiculous, he couldn't deny the chance it bore some truth, because here he was, his eyes adjusting to this light, waiting for some crazy voice to tell him this was all a trick, and that the illusion had masked his own room. Everything had been a dream in such a case—

He felt a cold sweat—he felt everything hit him at once. He reached for the Aspirin that wasn't there.

"No," he muttered, feeling the box of chocolates he had thrown in his pants last night, the box of chocolates he just *had* to bring; the box of chocolates he had found dented at the bottom of his book bag. He pulled them out of his pocket with distaste. "Is that chocolate?" A voice said, and Cole hoped it was Leo, arising from his own deep sleep, awaking to this new light, in this new room. "Oh, it's been ages since I've tasted chocolate. Ages." Cole could hear something sniffing like a dog, and the sound became muted by the rattling of metal, the tinkering of points on a flat surface.

"Leo?" Cole asked the bright air around him, his eyes focused, but still not quite in line, you might say, with the objects and their shadows.

"Not Leo, boy. Chocolate." The voice took a hissing clarity that scared Cole because it didn't sound like any noise a human could make.

Cole held the box of chocolates out in front of him, barely able to read the words on the container. He rattled the box.

"Do you mock me? I smell, but I cannot see."

The lights began to crisscross and Cole understood he was getting better. The mines hadn't totally destroyed his eyesight. He looked around, trying to find the source of the voice, the hiss. He had held the box of chocolates out so the 'voice' could come and get them, but the 'voice' seemed indisposed at the moment, and Cole feared something of his might be useless also, something he hadn't tried to move yet.

He wiggled his toes, moved his legs, twisted his abdomen, bent forward then backward; turned his neck from side to side; blinked both of his eyes. Cole seemed to be in working order.

"Why aren't I in the mines?" Cole asked. He felt as if he were talking to the Wizard of Oz or something, somebody equally terrifying as he was good-natured.

"I'll answer your questions when you feed me some of that chocolate."

"How can I give you chocolate when I can't even see you?"

"How can I trust you're putting chocolate into my mouth when I can't see you? The world is full of questions, lad, and you have to provide some of the answers yourself; that's just the way it works I've found out."

"Give me a moment. I can see the lights above me. I know you're speaking from my right." Cole turned his head to the right. "I can see something. I can still see light, as if the dark was just a bunch of curved bars or something."

"Yes, yes, good, come here then, come here to the bars."

Cole stepped forward, unsure why he was drawn by this voice. Unsure why he was even listening to it, but a strong sense urged him forward and removed a piece of chocolate peanut from the box; it would start melting soon. He could see the dark bars, and he held his hand out to grab one of them.

"I can smell it boy. There are nuts in these ones, aren't there? Where did you get chocolates, for the cattle have passed disease in their milk ever since the fall of the city?—and the plantations have fallen to ruin also. Boy, you're a baggage of surprises aren't you?"

Cole could hear something shift in front of him, and despite the cold feeling it gave him, he still couldn't move. He was stuck to this cool bar as if his palm were welded to it. "Hurry and take the chocolate, I think I'm going to be sick." And he was, because he wasn't in control of himself right now.

There was a shadow between the bars, and he could smell blood. The chocolate was plucked from his fingers by something hot and wet, and Cole pulled his hand out of the bars as quickly as possible, falling backwards when his fingers finally let go of the bar. He heard a crunch as the peanut was bit into, and then he was surprised to hear a gagging noise.

"Ahh, awful, like mud and hair and the rotten stem of a Riccy weed." There was more spitting until chunks of the treat fell to the ground in slops—Cole could hear thin splashes as the crumbled peanut fell to the wet ground. The bars had formed into linear lines against the light now. "Where did you get this garbage?"

"At the store, of course."

"A store you say? So you believe I'm gullible I see, for you took me as a fool, pulling dirt from the ground and placing it into my mouth."

"That is not true. I gave you a *Glossettes* Chocolate Peanut; they're only the best you can buy."

"*Glossettes*? Where is that, a colony in Gallia perhaps, beyond the Hopper Mountains?"

"What? No. Where have *you* been? *Glossettes* are better than *M&Ms*."

"Where have I been? I've been hanging in a cocoon."

"A cocoon?" Cole was stumped, and thought for sure that he was dreaming, had to be, actually. "It doesn't matter. You promised you'd answer me when I gave you chocolate."

"I promised such only after tasting chocolate, not dirt, you conniving boy."

"Look, I 'm holding a box of *Glossettes* Chocolate Peanuts." He rattled them again. "I took one out of this box and you snatched it from me."

"I'm working on blind faith, boy, for I'm blindfolded."

"Then take off the blindfold and I'll show you what you ate, then you can answer my questions."

"I have no hands to remove the blindfold with."

"I'll take off your blindfold, and then you can answer me. Sound fair?"

He could sense a pause, and then there was another sickly shift in front of him, as if a snake had slithered along a countertop. Cole could see the shadow between the bars again, but nothing beyond that. The light behind the bars had become so bright that bad vision or not, anything standing in front of it was just a silhouette.

"I've stuck my head against the bars. Are your eyes still adjusting?"

"Yes," Cole said.

"Then feel for a leather strap; it is quite tight but your favor will be rewarded."

"How do I know?"

"Because my eyes have all the answers."

Cole felt for the bars, took one in his hand and reached for the shadow between them. He touched slick flesh over soft bone. It was like running his hand over a skinned plum, and when he touched the rough edge of the leather, he traced his palm along the band, wiping the slop from his hand. He couldn't find any knots, and realized he could just slip this over the skull like the collar of a shirt; it was just a matter of getting his fingers behind the scrap. The leather was tight, and Cole felt worried he might actually puncture the bone if he dug his knuckles in too roughly. He heard noises around him, coming from outside the room—howls, and he realized these noises had persisted for a long time, but he hadn't consciously noticed them until now.

Your mind's elsewhere Cole, you know that.

He did, and when he strained to hear further, he burrowed his fingers behind the stuffy leather until the tips of them had hooked underneath and were ready to pull. When the band was off and flung to the ground, Cole fell backwards.

"Ahhh, the light, so beautiful, like the patterns of the sun through the brush of the Canopy Trees. Show me the chocolates."

"Answer my questions," Cole responded.

"First the chocolate, for that was the initial demand anyway."

Cole reached into the box and took out another. He felt it snatched from his fingers as if by the mouth of a lion.

"So it has taken my taste also," the voice sighed, and there was real pity in it, pity Cole wanted to sympathize with.

"Why aren't I in the mines where I fell asleep? Where is Leo? And most importantly, who are *you*?"

"Let me look at your eyes, boy."

"Why, I can't see you? You're just this shadow against the light behind the bars."

"You needn't see me, boy, I just need to see you."

11

There was this relief as if burdens had been lifted…as if his weight didn't matter anymore. Cole realized his head had been entered. It was like dying, he supposed, traveling down a tunnel filled with images of his life, some good, and some bad. He felt like his top was being pulled off, like the nails holding down his scalp were prying from his skull in a slow screech, letting the wanderer in to roam freely.

Cole couldn't see the red eyes of the hermit, but they could see *into* him; they could travel through the bone and dodge the electrical messages, the firing synapses, like a tall man watching his head under a doorjamb. The hermit watched kids punch the young boy—this Cole; the hermit saw the hatred in their eyes and realized itself that malice transcended the ages… and even the worlds, because this Cole wasn't of the Inlands. He was from somewhere else, beyond the thrones of Mystic (in fact, the boy seemed to believe in a Jesus Christ, though with questionable confusion); he was born of a world far advanced. The hermit closed its red eyes behind its pallid lids. "I can see no more, for I've found your answers."

"What did you do to me? It felt like something was running around my head showing me old pictures." Cole's vision had started piecing itself together rampantly, and the boy realized he was in a tent of some sort.

"I'm sorry Cole, I won't bother you again," the hermit said, and its voice seemed sad.

"How do you know my name?"

"You can learn much from the mind, for within it lies secrets you yourself are not aware."

"Did you hypnotize me? Is that why I fed you chocolate? It felt like I had lost control of myself."

"You're a confused; you're like the old man I've seen. He has left his mark in two places, and sub-consciously realizes his difference."

"What are you talking about? Where am I?" Cole seemed frantic—no, he *was* frantic. He felt something inside his head and now this mysterious voice that had been luring chocolate from him was speaking in riddles that defied sense.

"You want to believe you're dreaming. I want to tell you such is true, but your desperate need for *Aspirin* (as you have called it), for relief, has proven you're awake in the most literal sense. You fell asleep in the mines as you remember, but something happened before you fell into a stupor."

Cole stumbled back into the bundle of cloths, looking at the flies above him, trying hard not to think about the stench of the skin flung around him in a tent. He shoved the box of chocolates back into his pocket. "The sound of a train," Cole mused to himself. "How do you know all of this? You weren't there with me and Leo."

"Forget it Cole, you want answers and I'm trying to remind you of them. Are all from your world so impatient?" The hermit asked.

Cole turned to his right to try and look at the source of this voice, but only saw the shadow between the bars. He found solace in staring at the manic flies above him, looking for clumps of meat. "I don't understand what you mean by *my world*?"

"You heard the sound of a train, and though I do not know what sound a train makes, I'm sure the comparison drawn relates quite well with the claws of a wolf. Isn't that so?"

Cole shut his eyes. The claws of a wolf? He saw himself in the mines with Leo, the robots behind them in a slow roll—and then that thundering sound, like a train, coming from the gut of the mine. *You have a flashlight, use it*, he thought. So he did, but what did he see?

You're trying to forget; that's what this is all about. Your mind is already so full of worries that to top it off with this would surely push you over the edge.

"Am I trying to forget what I saw?" Cole asked, and he opened his eyes to the streaming lights at the top of the tent, so much like the pavilion at his mother's wedding it was eerie.

"You have burdens Cole, like most, though you're too young to keep so many at the surface. In but a brief moment I saw more nightmares than I could imagine a man on his deathbed would possess. You are in fear that mere strings hold your family together; you have desires to be accepted, but feel utterly hopeless because your appetite is a means of punishment—a target. You're depressed—you see your father, but this man in your head is connected by tubes like a puppet in the old Mercantile Fairs my father once took me to. You mustn't dwell on such thoughts, Cole, for the mind is only capable of floating so much to the surface."

"What are you? I know I'm not in the mines. Maybe Leo brought me to a circus and left me in a tent with a freak mind reader. This could be payback—I *hope* its payback."

"I'm just giving you answers."

"I asked if you knew where I was, not to 'psychoanalyze' me doc. Good for you, you can see into people's heads, but so can Ms Cleo. I can hardly see ten feet in front of me, so for all I know you have my permanent files."

"This Leo fellow told you he was searching for freedom on the other side of the mines. These mines, I take it, are some form of connection, perhaps a line between existences, I do not know, but you have been brought here. For what reason I am unsure, for the wolves do not speak in front of me; they are afraid of what I can do to them."

"Just tell me who you are, and where I am so I can just get outta this tent and call my mom to come pick me up."

"I was once Hayle Parker, son of a miner in north Cassica, but that was a long time ago. That was before the civil war in the city—I took my wife and daughter to the woods and became a Hermit. But now, Cole, now I do not know what I am, for in death there just seems utter confusion."

"I'm talking to somebody dead. Cue the undertaker, funeral starts in five. Come on, this is ridiculous. Isn't this payback enough Leo?" Cole screamed into the tent.

"Quiet Cole. If the wolves hear you they will come."

"I'm sure the other circus freaks keep them tied to poles."

There was a startling yelp from Cole's right that drove his head under the cloths, hoping in one way or the other that he was hidden from whatever had entered the tent.

He heard a clop and a slow drag, as if something were sluggishly coming towards him, something with a peg leg perhaps—something that may have popped the mind reader one over the head to shut him up. He pushed the cloths off his face and realized that he could see clearly. He could see exactly where there was still meat and lard on the skin of the tent, and he could see the little batting wings of the flies as if they were magnified. He slowly turned his head to the right, where the light was brightest.

It's a door, that's why, it's an opened flap—
And a giant black birdcage.

There *was* a black iron birdcage, and there was something inside it, something that could read his mind, and something that had bone softer than his own stomach. For a brief second he could see the mind reader, Hayle the hermit, because something large stood before the door blocking the light, something with broad shoulders that sloped into long gangly arms with bristly hair that grew in awkward clumps; something with pointy ears, drawing long guttural breaths. The hermit was a pale man without any features on his body. His body was pulled against the far bars of the cage, and Cole noticed a red tongue peeking out of his mouth like a snake, one that was barely stained by chocolate. His eyes were blindfolded again, and his neck was stretched by twine that had bound his head to the cross section of the iron bar; the hermit was trying to pull at this twine with one arm that had no hand, and one shoulder that had no arm (and was wrapped in a sheet instead). The hermit's nostrils were mere slits, and his lips cracked; his head was shaped, oddly enough, like the body of a thin spider, and there was a tuft of graying hair at the top that lay in limp strands over its sweaty forehead.

Cole had touched *that*, he had fed *that* chocolate—he wasn't in a circus, he was in a madhouse. The sun streamed back in through the door and he lost the clear image of that writhing hermit. Somebody sat next to him; he could feel the cloths depress and his body sink to the stinking ground, but he couldn't take his eyes away from that cage.

"Your name is Cole I gather, for that is what the blubbering monster called you. Funny, I once dealt mainly with coal; it's incredible how fates intertwine, is it not?"

Cole struggled to get up, to run away. Sitting beside him was an old man...no, an ancient man, who looked like he had maybe just unwound the gauze to show off his mummified body. He had thin strings of hair on his crown that were once a strong white, but seemed faded as if age had denied the rights of color. His skin was drawn into leathery flaps and folds, and his eyes were partially hidden by a collapsed brow. He held a cane in his gnarled hand, one that was made of twisted wood, and his fingernails curled from his fingertips like yellow branches.

"Oh, there's no need to be afraid; in fact I've brought you some food. Dappled crow in willow sauce. 'Tis popular here young man, much like burgers and malts were popular where you're from." He looked up at the lights in the tent, and Cole swore he heard a ripping sound as the old man's flesh moved with his head. He had in his other hand a curved rock that held a small skinned bird, slightly burnt on top with a brown sauce blanketing the tarnished flesh like suntan oil. Cole realized he was hungry, and didn't care who this man was; he grabbed for the stone dish and ripped off a wing and stuck it in his mouth. It was rather sweet, but the meat was tough like jerky, as if the bird had been left on the spit roast far too long. "Good, good, eat up young man, for we need you healthy for the trade." The old man set his cane against his withered knee and held his twisted hand out to Cole.

Cole regarded it with a shudder. Right now he understood his delusions could have been attributed to the very fact that he was starving. He dropped the bird back into the dish, and stared at the old man, and then at his hand. He supposed he should offer his own out of consideration that this fine meal had been brought to him. He took the old man's frail hand into his own, feeling the bones rotate in his grip like a bag of marbles.

The old man leaned in and Cole could smell his breath. The man had been on an obvious bender.

"Nice manners, young man. I see aristocracy hasn't changed with the years. Nice to meet you. My name is Kenneth Auger, and for now, you can consider me and your father business partners." He smiled, portraying a mouthful of brown teeth and gums that had started drooping between them like an orange mould.

Cole screamed, startling the old man.

He only did so because he was reminded of a dream he had had not so long ago. For a second, the cane that leaned against the old man's leg had turned into a pick, and Cole dropped the dish.

12

The next day the old man sat in his cart with a bottle in his frail hand. He was drunk, and the pain today was beyond coping, really. It compelled him to at least crack a new bottle and pin it in between his lips before he had the chance to even test the air of the morning. He sat this way for hours now; listening to the goings on around him, the voices behind the drapery he had left closed.

He had only once returned to the boy Cole, and even then he felt a tad nervous the boy would explode again. That startle yesterday had almost stopped his heart, and he had yet to understand why the boy screamed like that. He knew from the reflections he had seen in water that he was unappealing, but the boy screamed minutes after he had seen the old man— even after he took the old hand into his youthful palm to shake it. Manners were a thing of the past *here*, but he remembered the signs of politeness from his old life, and he knew that despite the custom of those taught morals, fear drew from them a reaction before manners ever could. So if it was his old face, the deep lines of his tough flesh and his drooping eyes, that drew the horrified start from the boy, then his reactions were entirely out of sync with his body language, for he took the old man's hand and took the food he brought in without any question as to whether the bird was edible or not. These weren't signs of a fear based on physicality, the old man insisted—these were fears that had roots in something else.

Legend, he thought. *Such as your desire for the blood of a wizard—based on folklore, but real enough to lead you on this headhunt.*

"Ah preposterous. The boy knows nothing of folklore here, nor would he even understand it if he heard it. Perhaps the alcohol is driving you insane, for your ability to Reason is waning." He grinned. He could just imagine a miniature version of himself perched inside his head scolding every external action and reaction.

The alcohol is but a nuisance to me, a rain-washed image that will only become clear when you come to your senses. And your senses have completely fled you old man, for here you sit, a man that once believed in the manners of which the poor boy holds, a man that believed in moral, and here you sit with the abominable realization that you have taken—have kidnapped this young boy. For what? For the chance you may hold a stone blessed by a wizard—so you may go into those Towers with the able control of your surroundings—so you may find the King's tomb, a tomb you know very well is quite empty. The King may not even be in theTowers anymore, for after he left you heard the townsfolks' gossip before you fled to Sadaan, before the Hunters came from the catacombs to defend the city from the wolves. They spoke of a man walking the countryside, through the farmyards like a ghost; this man was adorned in the jewels of a King. It sounded like more farce, more lore, but you knew the King had left the Towers to roam the lands unguarded, for he wasn't in any harm of the vagabonds and thieves. Who's to say the King stayed in those awful Towers like a prisoner, when he intended so much more from his absence?

"He told me he would return with all the powers of the world—but he would wait; he didn't want to be a mere name, the fool who left the city in shambles. He wanted to redeem himself, I suppose. Perhaps he let the city fall for this very sake. So he could save it."

You're blind to think things will work in your favor. Do you believe Haspin will return with the wizard, if he even finds him? Immortality is a gift anyone would wish to receive. And he hid his intentions from you, just as you hid yours from him.

"He believes his only collateral are the men he left behind. But he spoke of his kingdom in Gallia; he spoke very proudly actually. There are wolves heading there now—I don't think it would be smart for Haspin to deceive me. In fact, we share mutual desires."

Don't you see it old man? You've gone mad. It isn't your neglect for human life that worries me, but your plans with this young boy. You are still alive; you have been given a second life, it seems, and you have chosen to use it for evil. You don't want to be perceived like these wolves.

"I'm not a monster," the old man said. His voice was a long slur.

Perhaps not, but the transition has begun. The answer you truly seek about the boy's reaction comes from your own beliefs, and I'm surprised you haven't yet noticed it, though the drink has taken its toll. In the other world—the world of your wife Judith and Auger Mining, the world where you left your conscience— there are also legends. Think now how people from that world would perceive your disappearance. Perhaps they sent rescue crews into the mines but they didn't find anything because they weren't supposed to, because the connection waned to save the doorway, but who knows?—Their dogs must have died in the mines, or smelt something they didn't entirely trust. Think then what stories folk must have come up with to find answers for your disappearance. Especially kids. I'm sure the mines are considered haunted in the other world, and the man with the stone has built his house on top of them only to do one thing: to conceal the truth that this mine is a chain to another world. This boy heard your name and thought you were a ghost. A phantom.

The old man dropped the bottle. Of course, it was after he introduced himself that the boy screamed.

The drapes were pulled aside abruptly, and the old man almost had another heart attack. Jarak stood in the light like a demon at the end of a tunnel—the old man hated the simile, but felt the dire pull of his age was introducing further the plausibility of this chance in the very near future. He was dying. Quickly.

"Something has left the mines and stands at the bluff."

"What is it?"

"Looks like a man, oddly dressed. He holds something."

The wolves were howling outside, and the old man could even hear the She-wolves in the tents adding their own high pitch.

Jarak carefully lifted the old man and set him on the ground, where his knobby cane leaned against the cart. He slowly walked forwards, ignoring the wolves and the men left behind by Haspin to serve their purpose if he chose not to return; they all looked up at the bluff a few hundred feet before them. There stood a figure at the edge. It was wearing what looked like a long coat and a fedora—*a fedora*, the old man thought. *I haven't seen a fedora since the men at the bank wore them to lunch, all those years ago.*

There was something dangling from the figure's outstretched arm, and it only took a moment for the old man to realize what it was.

"Get the boy," he screamed.

CHAPTER 11

Pamper Duty

1

The police had come to the house expecting nothing more than a casual checkup, finding something the security guards missed or neglected to notice in the first place, which would entail the obvious question: what, then, was the point of security?

Two police officers were sent, and both had something to prove of course, because that was the way with cops, but this little circus job was anything but commendable. "You got to be kidding me," Officer Lela Saxon said, as she set the radio down and looked straight ahead.

Officer Dale Oates only stared out the windshield, holding a coffee in his left hand. He'd noticed how beautiful the trees were turning, how the leaves were beginning to fall into the streets like golden litter—for some reason he loved this time of the year, and even though his intuitive nature was forced to strictly analyze the job at hand, he found police work rather hard to concentrate on when nature transformed on instinct as it did, year after year.

"Dale, for crying out loud, pull your thoughts out of the crapper. We're on pamper duty."

"What?"

"Call from dispatch—apparently there's an urgent mishap at the Krollup place."

Dale clenched the steering wheel—this could only mean one thing. "Did he call with a complaint? Did somebody sell him a fake *Mona Lisa*?"

The two snickered, oblivious to what the urgency implied, but sure that it was just a symptom of the *ritzy blues*—you got that every so often with folks like Edwin Krollup, who wore shoes that cost more than Dale and Lela's salaries combined.

2

"He should build a new venue, that's what it's all about these days in ball. You gotta build the retractable dome, like in Arizona; then fans'll come purely for atmosphere. The purists'll moan of course, but tradition can start to turn ugly. Suppose that's why there's talks they're ripping down Fenway in Boston."

Lela moaned, her thin body masked by her grotesque shirt, which had been a pass-me-down, she thought, and an unkind gesture in a way. "There's no point spending money on the Blackbirds Dale. You gotta understand, when a team blows, there's just no revenue coming in from empty seats. I'm sure Edwin knows that, too. Thing I've never understood about him is why he hasn't shelled out the bucks for a decent lineup—sure Barry Stocks turned down a contract, but Edwin was just being conservative; he's probably scared that if he does spend too much money, and the team still stinks, then he's placed a poor investment." Lela reached for the doorbell.

"I still think you're wrong. I think it's all about the stadium. People wanna go somewhere nice to have a beer. In a way, baseball's secondary to the brewsky—oh, and you gotta have legroom, that's a must, because Krollup Stadium has none. I mean—"

The door opened, slightly squeaking on the hinges. Lela couldn't believe how large the door was, noticing the apparent struggle overcome to bring it to a 90-degree angle

"I am so glad you guys came. I didn't know for sure if my husband gave you all the details, but things have changed since you were first called. My son has run away—he has…"

Maggie Krollup hid her face with her right hand.

"I'm sorry—I just." She cleared her throat; she had obviously been dwelling on this for some time, and at that moment she wasn't just another ritzy woman beckoning to get her nails painted, but a *real* woman lamenting the whereabouts of her son. In a way both officers felt bad for discussing the matter as they did on the drive up. Dale had his own son and couldn't imagine the worry that came with such confusion, such helplessness.

"It's okay Mrs. Krollup," Lela said, stroking the woman's arm. Maggie tried to smile. "In a case like this, worries are just based on mix ups. Your son is probably at a friend's house, and forgot to inform you, but that's the way with kids. You wouldn't believe the amount of calls we get regarding missing children that had just ventured down the street without telling."

"No, no…Jimmy, my other son, he—he told me Cole ran away." She wiped her eyes. Her hair, which was usually so beautiful, looked as though she had set a fuse into her skull and lit it after spraying half her head with hairspray. "There's been rough emotions at school—I knew this, I knew this but I didn't do anything till it was too late."

"Ma'am, is there proof that he ran away? Sometimes the child leaves a letter, explaining his or her frustration. Or the child decides to pack up his or her things, taking clothes and dry goods from the pantry. Have you noticed if he's done either?" Lela asked.

"There was no letter—Jimmy just *told* me." She said the latter under her breath, but both officers still heard her. Another child's confession could be a form of manifested anger, or revenge with a sibling, looking to get his or her brother or sister into hot water.

"Do you know where he might have gone?" Dale asked this time, and his cheeks flustered. Maggie was quite an attractive lady, messy hair or not.

"Yes, does he have any favorite spots he might like to venture out to, maybe just to unload some steam. I used to ride my bike down to the river when I was a kid—especially when my folks were getting a divorce."

"A divorce—yes, he may have gone to my ex-husband's tombstone… Cole's father."

"And where is he buried?" Lela asked, flipping open her notebook.

"It seems much too far for him to walk, though he doesn't seem to mind taking the bus."

Lela cocked her eyebrow. Her patience had simmered down now—why couldn't Mrs. Krollup have realized this before? Why couldn't she have just hopped into her Lexus and driven to the cemetery herself, instead of pulling the police to her house in order to arrange her worries into logical deduction?

"I'm sorry officer. Central Hill Cemetery. I'm sure he's there. He likes to go there every so often. He was so fond of his father." Maggie had stopped crying and smiled.

"That's okay ma'am. We'll scout out this graveyard, and while you wait, please calm down and perhaps check over with his friend's houses. Your son may have popped in after you called the first time."

"Do you need a recent photo of him?" Maggie asked.

Lela shook her head. "No ma'am, we've seen pictures of him."

After the mammoth door was closed and both officers were back in the cruiser, Lela turned to Dale and said: "Doesn't she realize it's *her* tax dollars that are paying for our gas?"

Dale smiled. "Krollup's got accountants I'm sure, that are capable of doing things you only see in the movies—loopholes and stuff not even Uncle Sam's aware of."

"Do you know where Central Hill Cemetery is?"

"Yeah. It's on Central Hill." Dale smiled and pulled out of the driveway and onto the stretch of road winding down the hill like an asphalt coil.

3

They had heard from dispatch that there was a drunken brawl inside, and outside *The Deposit*, a bar that was crawling with low lifes day in, day out—most of which were mining rejects, or had, through the unfortunate turn of the mining industry, gotten 'bad health' as Krollup Industries deemed to call it (a euphemism, if you will, declaring their lungs were rotting through).

Officers' Dale and Lela heard this and grunted; there was obvious impatience in the cruiser, and even as they made two passes through the graveyard, listening attentively to the radio bray its tales of 'real crime', the two saw nothing that resembled a child. In fact, they only saw three people—all of whom were paying their respects to a cracked tombstone.

"This is ridiculous," Dale said. He no longer cared to look at the falling leaves.

"You suppose we should get out and do some footwork?"

"What for? The boy's not here. Krollup just realized she might have missed something when she was clearing her head for his whereabouts. The very idea he might've come here seems farfetched anyway. If a kid is feeling down, do you think he'd really find solace in a graveyard? When I was a kid I wouldn't even dare set foot in one of these places; in fact, sitting here, looking at all these graves like this, is kind of creeping me out."

Lela nodded, looking at the rows of Roman crosses jutting from the ground until they disappeared down the other side of the hill. "You know what, I bet the kid walked in the gates right after we left."

"Probably."

"And you know, he probably saw us and thought there was trouble."

"Amen," Dale attested.

"When a kid thinks there's trouble at his home and he sees a police cruiser, there ain't no way he's coming up along side the car with the clear chance that it may be him the police are looking for." Lela slapped the dashboard with a grunt, as if she was preaching to the choir.

"Amen, sister."

"Now let's get this fish back in the water in time to beat some heads at *The Deposit*."

"I'll turn on the sirens—oh yes, because Lela, importance founds itself in pamper duty, does it not?"

"It sure does."

"And when we get to the Krollup mansion, we're gonna pin the diapers and mean it, right?"

"Oh yeah."

"So why are we hanging with the dead, when we could be reaping the full benefits of pamper duty, because Lela, pamper duty bears importance of a nature beyond homicide, because an unhappy rich family is a sad family with a *whoooole* lotta money."

"Sing it."

Dale flipped on the lights and sped out of the graveyard, spilling tornadoes of leaves from under the car in an eerie formation of oranges that turned into an obscured pumpkin in the air.

The prospect that the two would be on the 6 o'clock news did not enter either of their minds; neither did the potential truth that they *should* have been looking for a ransom note.

4

Maggie trembled when she saw the cruiser pull up on the driveway—the back seat was empty. She had been standing by the window for half an hour, deliberately pulling her hair into clumps that had started falling out.

This wasn't what you expected this morning.

No, it wasn't, and even having that eerie thought brought shivers.

She had called the neighbors again, and she had called Ivy Raurus three more times, only to be blatantly yelled at in German by a grumpy caretaker named Fritz, who had actually lined his brooms according to size in his closet. Her concept of composure was drastically faltering, and she could feel something inside her twist, something like long fingers that dangled behind her eyes; she thought this agitation might just pop her eyeballs right out of her sockets—but it wasn't just that. She had been standing at this window trying hard not to hate Jimmy, clawing at the drapery with her fingernails if those fingers behind her eyes started to push harder, trying to separate herself from this feeling of torture.

"Are you okay, Mrs. Krollup?" A young maid had asked as she dusted the tabletop. She had obvious concern in her voice, considering she was talking to her employer, a woman the house staff secretly loathed—not because she was their boss either, but because she had once *been* one of them, poor, struggling, and now she had climbed that ladder only to reach the top with nowhere to look but down. "She resents us now," they say when they wait for the bus when their shifts are over. "She helps us clean only because she's patronizing us—she is rich, yet she wants to prove our way of life still isn't disabling."

Maggie had looked at the young woman; she looked not as herself, but as a frantic mother with twisted conflicts—she had this desperate need to blame Jimmy, to march right on up to his room and yell at him, let him know that this was all his fault—

But her motherly instincts attempted to drive these torturous thoughts away. She had told herself a million times since she had talked to Jimmy that his definition of power needed honing. Yet she needed to blame somebody. That was just it.

"I'm fine—my son's missing, but I'm fine. Why don't you go clean or something." This wasn't a question; this was a demand, and a firm one at that. The young maid's jaw dropped and her cheeks flushed. She hurried out of the room like a scared deer. She would later tell the other ladies of her encounter, and it would be the final agreement that Maggie Krollup had finally let the power get to her head, like so many of the others.

The cruiser door slammed and Maggie shuddered.

When the doorbell rang she wanted so much just to hide, to conceal herself behind the drapery so the police couldn't give her any bad news. She stood staring at the empty backseat for a moment, searching it frantically, with that strong hope that she might see her son lying down in the back, fast asleep. She turned and walked over the marble floor towards the front door with that stupid statue to its right with its leering head.

She touched both of her temples for a moment and rubbed them. The bell rang again, but she couldn't answer the door in this condition, they were just trying to help; they were doing their job—poorly of course, but at least they showed up. That was more than Edwin could vouch for.

She opened the door and both police officers stood with stern looks on their faces. Maggie knew what that look meant.

"We saw you standing by the window, Mrs. Krollup. Can we assume you had no luck with your son's friends?" The female officer said, going to rub Maggie's arm again, as if rubbing would somehow ward off any worries. Maggie pulled her arm back and looked at the woman in the baggy uniform—even her gun belt seemed saggy, as if her hips were on extra duty just to keep the thing up.

"I saw the backseat of your car empty—can I *assume* you both had no luck?" Maggie blurted out.

Dale cringed, and for a second was reminded of his grade five teacher, the one who used to spank the bad kids with a meter stick—she used to speak the same way, only her eyes seemed to blaze like kindling.

"We're sorry, Mrs. Krollup. We drove through the graveyard countless times and then proceeded to do legwork. We didn't see him. We can assure you we've done everything we can to help."

"Then why don't you have my son with you?" Maggie screamed. Many of the mansion staff poked their heads out of rooms just to see what the commotion was about.

"Mrs. Krollup?" Lela said. Maggie had bowed her head, hiding her tears. Lela rubbed the woman's arm gently and gradually felt some warmth, as if the storm had passed. "I think you should get your husband and we should all sit down and talk about this."

Maggie looked up and patted Lela's hand. "He's busy…you know with work. A man like Edwin Krollup never stops working, and anyway, he just thinks I'm overly worried. Perhaps I am, but just the thought—" She shuddered and then smiled.

"Well that's *overly* nonsense," Lela said. "Get Mr. Krollup, ma'am, and we'll sit and we'll talk. He's as much a part of this as you—both parental figures play vital roles in a child's life. We'd both like to know the reasoning that might drive Cole to run away; this will help us all understand certainties. Remember that feeling you had when you believed Cole was at the graveyard— this will be just the same, only we'll gather more truths."

5

They all sat in chairs except for Edwin, who stood with a furrow in his brow. This had all been nonsensical to him, though he couldn't let them know because that would only garner more questions—sure he knew where the boy was, but what could the police possibly do?

Standing behind Maggie with his arms on the back of her chair was the ticket then. He would stand and nod his head; he wouldn't look obvious of course, but he'd talk when spoken to, and he'd attempt to relieve himself of the need to display his powers in his house. This was the toughest to do, because he felt like the police were nothing but mere parasites that had somehow infiltrated the front gate. Just looking at the two officers made him upset. Maggie had told him the two ordered his presence for this meeting…*ordered* him, as if such were possible, and at that moment, as he sat in his bedroom with his feet up on the table smoking a cigar, he wanted so badly just to crush their police cruiser into a box of shrapnel until the lights shattered and the siren let out one last bleep. "I'm busy," he said, but Maggie was rather insistent, and had started crying—so Edwin felt obligated to stifle her tears. Sure he was in his own personal crisis. He had to think of this trade the letter from Auger spoke of; he had to figure out a way to send the robot down the mines without prematurely blowing the thing up and accidentally cutting off the connection between worlds (if such was possible, he did not know); and he had to try to ignore the feeling in his head that suggested doors were being opened. He had to contend with all of this, yet one missing child—ONE—becomes the grandest issue and he has to be dragged from his thoughts.

"In all honesty I suppose he's just gone for a walk, or has perhaps decided to let off steam somewhere in the courtyard; there are many places to go," Edwin said, slightly smiling at the officers. The two had pads of paper on their laps.

"Your wife has explained to us that she and the staff have turned the house on its top, inside and out, and didn't see a trace of the boy." Dale looked at the tall rich man for a moment, and his eyes were driven away by intimidation.

"Perhaps the boy decided to switch hiding spots as if this is all a game. My wife tends to exaggerate things, officers, and that includes her sense of worry. Your presence here doesn't help that any."

"So you suppose, Mr. Krollup, that Cole is playing a game with his mother, unaware that she is distraught?" Lela shifted in her seat; she showed none of the fear that Dale displayed.

"We were all kids at one time, and the idea of escape was always a bright proposition. Parents tend to smother children. Do you like to be smothered, officer?" Edwin looked at Lela with such intensity she thought her skin was going to vomit sweat.

Lela shifted again. They all sat in a small sitting room off the main hall; there were three statues in the room, and there was a murky sense of age, as if nobody had been in here for years. She had noticed this at once. There were probably rooms in this mansion that nobody had been in yet; it was this possibility she had considered all along, and even for Mrs. Krollup to insist that they had turned the house on its top seemed rather iffy since the dust circulating this room hadn't met an open door for a long time.

"I think that's possible, sir, but children also tend to realize when enough is enough; the idea that his mother is in this condition would drive him into a state of remorse, and this so-called game would have ended hours ago." Maggie smiled and closed her eyes when she felt Edwin's hands tighten behind her head.

"Children also have undeveloped minds, officer, and for you to claim he'd know, by some unknown force that his mother is ailing seems rather fantastic, doesn't it?"

"I suppose."

"Good. Then why don't we all go on our way and when supper is served, I'm sure Cole will reappear as if nothing happened."

"Edwin," Maggie said with defiance.

"No honey, I think it's best these two kind officers leave. I'm sure their being here has alarmed Cole enough."

Lela looked at Maggie and saw the pleading in her eyes. No, the officers weren't going to leave, because this was starting to get fun; this wasn't pamper duty anymore, but almost a test of endurance—who could outlast who, really, and Lela was determined to prove this rich man, this rich art collector who could be easily swindled, that his thoughts on child care were wrong.

"Sir, I'd like to talk to your wife alone for a moment," Lela finally said. She saw the color come back into Maggie's face.

Edwin's eyes turned for a moment, Lela would swear on this. His eyes had been a darkish brown one second, and then the next they turned a dark red. "Very well then," he said, and his eyes were normal again, as if it had never happened, as if the old air in this room played tricks or turned the lights against her. This seemed true because she also could have sworn that the statue standing to Edwin's right *had* been staring to the side with a look of complacency—now it was looking right at *her* with a horrible sneer, its ivory brow upturned into a vent. When Edwin turned to leave she saw the room in its clarity and realized that she had been seeing things; the statue *was* looking to the side, and the old air *was* just a projection of dust in the thin sunlight that had somehow broken through the thick drapery.

When the door closed Lela looked at Maggie knowingly and leaned forward to pat her hands. "Very well then. My mother used to tell me I had to rid the riff raff before any work could get done, and I never second guessed her." She smiled and was worried for a second that Mrs. Krollup would take offense, but Maggie only shrugged with a tight smirk. "Now tell me, Mrs. Krollup, why your other son told you Cole ran away."

Maggie crossed her legs and hoped the officers wouldn't think she was the worst mother in the world—but hoping seemed rather pointless, because Maggie Krollup *knew* she was.

6

"What are they doing?" Edwin asked Maggie, as the officers walked up the grand stairs towards the boys' room. He had a feeling they suspected something; he spoke like a guilty man for some reason, but that one officer, *that* woman, got under his skin so deep that itching seemed impossible.

"They're going to talk to Jimmy," Maggie said. Her eyes were red and her lids were swollen. She had told them the entire conversation as she could remember it, and realized just how painful her son's words had been. She saw in

Lela a look that supported her view in its entirety—that Jimmy had somehow adopted Edwin Krollup's personality and transfused it into a childish role.

"Do you think we can talk to Jimmy, Mrs. Krollup?" Lela had asked. "Or do you think it would frighten him?"

"I think he needs to be frightened," Maggie said, dabbing her eyes with her sleeve. "He needs his mixed thoughts scared from his head." And he did; she thought of his morbid comparison between his dead father and Edwin, a comparison that was solely based on life and death

"Why do you care anyway? It would seem like a blessing that 'the kid' is gone, right?" Maggie shoved past Edwin and walked up the stairs after the police, who strode to the seventh door on the right.

"You're overreacting Maggie. You need to reason this out."

Maggie ignored him.

7

"Some room," Dale said as he pushed a ball on the pool table and watched it roll.

"I can't believe that jerk," Lela said. "With all of that money he thinks he controls the world."

"Yeah, well that's the essence of pamper duty, Lela. We gotta take what he says or it could mean our jobs. At least we can look at his money as the resource that truly built this town—I mean his preparation plant alone employs what? Maybe fifteen hundred people, my dad included."

"No, you see, that's crap. I shouldn't have to sit there and have him look at me like scum. I shoulda snapped my gun out and showed him intimidation."

"And you woulda lost your job; you're always playing fifty/fifty here, Lela. Sure there's reward but there's also punishment. Life wouldn't be so hard if there wasn't." Dale ran his hand along the television screen and looked at his fingertips. Not a spot of dust, as if the room was kept day after day without question. *Krollup has the cleaners in here constantly so he knows what the boys are hiding; the cleaners probably know every little hiding spot in this room. That's why the room where we had that little meeting was so dusty, and this one's cleaner than the President's toilet—because the sitting room doesn't serve any purpose except to seat people; this little dandy's got two boys, two stepsons, and a man like Edwin Krollup's gonna keep tight tabs on them, no matter what.*

"Ah, it just ticks me off. You know how it is Dale. It's cause I'm a woman. I bet he doesn't believe I should be on the force—or, at least he doesn't believe he should be taking me seriously."

"Cut that crap, Lela. He looked at me the same way; it's all about power with guys like Krollup. We're in his house, and we're attempting to command the situation. He doesn't like that."

"I guess. But you gotta admit. I made him furious, especially when I told him to leave the room." Lela smiled proudly.

"Yes you did, but didn't you notice something about him—I don't know what it is now, or maybe it's just that I'm crazy, but I could have sworn his eyes looked like they were on fire."

Lela stopped dead in her tracks. The two had been mindlessly pacing around the room in circles, stopping to rub their hands on the pool table or look out the bay window over the courtyard. "You saw that too?"

"Yeah, I mean it was quick, you know. Real quick, but for a second I thought for sure his head was going to explode, like his eye sockets were pilot lights."

Lela tugged at her belt, which was hanging down her hip in an awkward fashion that tilted her body to one side in an attempt to stop gravity's pull. "And the statue, Dale, did you see the statue beside him? It was staring off to the side like it was thinking or something, but when Krollup turned to leave, when he fully turned I could swear on my life that the statue was looking at me, right at me, and it was frowning."

"It was probably just the lights, Lela, they were weird in that room."

Lela's heart slowed and the excitement, her downright fear seemed to dissolve like a cheap mint. "Yeah, you're probably right."

Dale saw that she was worked up about this; her face was red and she was sweating badly. "I was afraid of him, Lela, that's why I saw his eyes that way. Guys like him have that power of suggestion, even if it is through a stare." He smiled. "I guess he's gotten you pretty worked up too."

"Nah, I'm just tired. Pretty sick of pamper duty too. I'm only sticking around to shove one fact into Krollup's face: that he's wrong about Cole; that Cole *did* run away. I would—"

"Where's Jimmy?" A voice asked from behind them and Lela cringed. She hoped Mrs. Krollup hadn't heard her.

Dale turned around. Maggie was standing at the doorway. Her tears had ceased, but that harrowing look remained, and Dale guessed the woman had aged ten years over the course of a few hours. "He's not in here."

Lela noticed the look on Maggie's face and smiled. "We'll find him, Mrs. Krollup."

They left the room without noticing the rope hanging in the closet.

8

But they didn't find Jimmy.

CHAPTER 12

THE EARTHQUAKE

1

"I would've stopped him if I knew," Jimmy had said before his mother got up.

He watched her leave the room and he knew she was upset; the feeling was undeniable.

She got up and walked away from you Jimmy boy, she walked away without even looking back, and, I swear she had a thought that was as readable as a billboard, just blaring outside her head; she wanted you switched with Cole, she wanted the clear assurance he was safe and you were missing.

This voice was cold, but he agreed because he felt something similar; he knew his mother was ashamed and he knew nothing would ever be the same again. He pulled the tin box out from behind the curtains (he had hid it there when his mother came in the room to talk to him) and snapped it open. A slight stench greeted him, like mints and rotten paper, and he only wished he'd never started smoking, but the temptation of that cool rush down his throat seemed purifying, almost idyllic. He had a lighter and six books of matches; the lighter was in the box with the cigarettes, and the matches were under his mattress. He put a smoke in his mouth (this smoke he had gotten from Tyler Piersen, whose mom was an accountant at Krollup Oil) and lit it; he blew into the vent next to his hand and felt his guilt seem to leave him; that image of him standing at the corner of the school, watching Ricky kick Cole seemed to waft down the duct.

He sat there by the window with the cigarette in his mouth, letting it hang from his lip the way Ricky used to when the two kicked rocks in the playground; he'd talk and let the smoke hang from a scrap of skin and it would wiggle around like a wad of spit, but something about it looked so cool, so adult. He flicked his lighter and watched the flame for a moment.

He sat like this for twenty minutes, with the smoke hanging from his lips and the lit lighter rested between his thumb and forefinger; he seemed lost, his eyes as vacant as the stillness and silence of his room. When the lighter died, Jimmy just tossed it in the can and pulled the matches from under his mattress, sucking his smoke as if the thing might fall from his perched lips at any second. No way, he needed to remain cool.

He sat back and pulled a match out and struck it; the smell was immediate, but he ignored it. When the match burnt down to his fingertip he waved the dying flame out and tossed the frail stick into the trash. The smoke hanging from his lip was nothing but a soggy filter.

There were eighteen matches in the garbage can when he heard the car.

At this point, the cigarette had fallen from his lip and trickled down the vent with a soft thud, but he hadn't noticed; he had been sitting with a blank stare, a few tears finding their way out of his eyelids, plucking matches from the book and lighting them, not watching the flame but waving it out when he felt the heat tickle his fingers.

Turning around was almost mechanical, and although he didn't think this at that point, he knew it, somewhere deep inside him he knew that he was different, that he was forever changed. It wasn't exactly shock that followed either, but almost an acceptance, a peculiar shrug implying he knew just as much.

Outside his window there was a cop car.

2

Jimmy had never been arrested; in fact, he had never been inside a cop car.

Jimmy shoved the books of matches into the tin box and fumbled with the lid as he snapped it shut; he knew that if he didn't hurry they'd get him, and even as he saw them get out of the cruiser, talking over the hood like mechanics, he had the overwhelming sensation that it was far too late to worry anymore.

He ran to the closet thinking: *she left the room without looking back because she was as much ashamed with herself as she was with you. That's what happens when you realize you gotta call the police on your own son.*

3

He saw the rope only because he left the closet door open and the light in his room on.

He didn't understand why the rope was there at first, just dangling from the rack like a stretched coat hanger, but he seemed to realize one thing: Cole *may* have runaway, but he hadn't run far.

Jimmy watched that thin strand of rope swing feebly as the knot shifted on the rack, and he turned to look at the door over the top shelf, the door that stood slightly ajar.

Jimmy could feel his guilt feebly nudge him forward and he realized one thing: he had to get Cole.

"This is your only chance, Jimmy," he said to himself before he slid down the vent, his tin box clanging against the side like an obscured cymbal when he spread his legs to brake.

He felt like a hero.

4

Leo had it, and even if he didn't, there wasn't much left that he could have done. He had the wires fitted, the bulbs tested, the joints loosened, and the frame dusted. He stood there under the flickering light bulbs with his dirty finger under his chin, examining the robot as if it were under the final inspection before being released to the public—*it was an inspection all right*, he thought, *but the only public it would ever meet lived within this house.*

The only way to find out of course was to put that one frayed wire into its place. He did this in an awkward manner, holding the wire in a pinch as he closed one eye and let his greasy tongue lap his chapped lips. He wasn't entirely shocked to hear a long beep, and watch several lights ignite, but it dropped his jaw nonetheless. The robot worked, and Leo, for the first time since he and Cole were in the mines, felt a tinge of relief.

"Just a simple push of this button can take me away for good," he said under his breath, looking at the machine with maniacal eyes, his bushy brows heaving up and down as his baldhead gleamed with sweat. He held his forefinger an inch from the blue button at the base of the robot's skull and felt that old sensation zap him. He was drawn back for a quick moment—back to a place he really wanted to forget, but there was something about the electricity that circulated through him when he worked this way. Leo felt as if there was a shift, as if by some mere accident he was handed all the power in the world, and through his suggestion, could simply maneuver it like an extra limb. He pulled the wire out of the robot and the electricity died inside him.

There was a brief noise, and for a moment he thought Krollup was coming back. He quickly grabbed the wire just in case—if Krollup came back, Leo was going to do one thing. He was going to test his own reflexes before an untrusting Edwin Krollup could get a hold of that thing around his neck to crush Leo's ankles in a stone vise.

But this noise seemed different. Like a long screech really, and he thought there might have been a giant rat running up the mines leaving a trail of white foam behind it, dripping from its hellish mouth as it growled.

There was a thud, and Leo heard a hard grunt; it sounded like something had been firmly planted. Noises were weird in this place though, because they traveled down the mines without circulating first in his little cubbyhole.

"Where's Cole?"

Leo knew that voice. Not because he had an incredible memory or anything, but because the repugnancy behind it had been both nauseating and belittling. He turned around and faced the vent shaft above him, which was clearly hidden beyond the light bulbs hanging from the ceiling like makeshift stars. In the darkness he saw a white orb, glowing like the moon he hadn't seen in a year; he missed these things far more than he realized, and it was his insistence to hurry with the robot that gave him a faint hope to at least see something else before becoming a flame. *He said you're free after you finish the robot though, he's never given such mercy before.*

Of course he was free after he finished the robot. That was a simple tactic used by men like Krollup, whose sole existence revolved around the idea of power, and its many manipulations. *He means to kill you after he's finished with the robot; your purpose has been served, because men like you are expendable—that's your freedom, free as a bird.*

The moon in the darkness was Jimmy's face. Leo didn't have to see the boy's eyes or nose to understand that one fact. The boy had either tripped over his guilt, or had perhaps realized something himself—something Krollup's wife obviously neglected to consider. That Cole might have sought the mines for escape. "She doesn't question them, because she knows not to," Krollup had once said, but Leo didn't believe for a second that Krollup's wife hadn't at least thought about the mines, if not to serve her *own* curious purposes. It would seem weird if she hadn't.

"You drove him away," Leo finally said, looking up past the light bulbs into a darkness that had driven him insane for the past year.

"What do you mean?" Leo could see the boy's feet emerge from the shaft; the boy was quick, because he had leapt from the vent before Leo could answer. Both of his fists were clenched.

"I meant what I said."

"Give him back to me or I'll pummel you, old man," Jimmy said, and Leo knew the boy was being honest; his eyes were on fire, and Leo was immediately reminded of Krollup. He felt compelled to pick a tool up from the ground or something, because he knew this boy meant business, and no matter how decisive his approach, this young boy could still make mincemeat of him.

"I don't have him you imbecile."

Jimmy cocked his eyes. "I have a very worried mother outside these walls—"

"And this is supposed to do what? Force me to sympathize?"

"And she's got cops with her."

Leo looked at the boy, who was advancing on him slowly with his clenched fists and eager eyes. He could flip that wire back into its circuit if he wanted to, turn the robot on with a loud BEEP, really give the kid a scare, but what would that prove really? Cole's brother was showing his sincere concern by confronting *him*, the madman, and that was rather commendable. It really was, because it severed one opinion Leo had of the kid—that he was selfishly inclined to overlook his brother's disappearance.

"I don't have him," Leo finally said, and not because he had given in to this punk's physical suggestions, but because he felt in some way responsible for the exact reason he had stated—he *didn't* have him, and this incredible reality turned him to face the certainty that it was his poor decision to bring a child down the mines with him, believing that his goodwill would somehow look after this kid. He saw those wolves carry poor Cole in the faint light of AL4's eyes, and then he was gone, settling in the dust like a dissolved image, a mirage, he supposed.

Leo bowed his head and looked at the ground, littered with bones and cords and cracks.

Jimmy had noticed something in Leo that guaranteed some truth in this. He had seen rope hanging from the rack in his closet, as if it had snapped when Cole climbed down the vent—but why did that necessarily mean Cole went down the vents in the first place? Sure the door was open, but had the paint dried in the hinges, wasn't there the slight possibility that the hinges were prone to jamming?

Jimmy relaxed his hands. "Did he even come down here?"

Leo looked at the boy. "You genuinely care about this, don't you?"

Jimmy looked as if he had been crying. "He's my brother."

"You hurt him, you know that right?"

Jimmy nodded. "He's talked to you?"

"He showed me things too, Jimmy."

"His stomach."

Leo nodded this time. "How could you have let *them* do that to him?"

Jimmy tapped the box in his pocket and thought about removing a smoke, thought about it but let the feeling pass. "I was blinded."

"That's it? That's all you have to say?"

"I don't have to listen to this, especially from a madman hidden behind our fireplace." He tightened his fists again. "Where is he? I told you, the cops are here."

"And I told you, I *want* to be arrested," Leo blurted, startling the boy. "So come and take me to them Jimmy, do me the pleasure." There was madness in Leo's eyes; they protruded from their sockets and bulged like white grapes from a pasty bulb. He walked towards Jimmy with his hands held out, and Jimmy backed against the wall until the rocks dug into his spine and he was forced to turn his body. "This is how it felt for Cole, I take it, crunched against the wall like a feeble old woman, unable to defend himself. Imagine then what might happen if I clobbered your stomach with a wrench until your gut looked just like Cole's." Leo flapped his gangly hands out and Jimmy cowered against the wall; he saw in Leo's eyes a blank ferocity that cloaked whatever he had taken for sincerity earlier.

"I just want to get that chance back," Jimmy said.

"What chance?"

"I guess that chance to help him again."

"You guess?"

"Yeah, I guess—I *know*—I've had nightmares about it." Jimmy stood up again and looked Leo directly in the eyes. "Don't think you scare me old man, because you don't, and if getting my brother means I have to go through you, so be it." Jimmy did something that surprised even himself—he hit Leo square in the jaw.

Leo stumbled back a few steps and bumped into the robot standing in the middle of the room. He rubbed his chin and looked at the boy. There was pride in the look, as if he had passed some test or something. Jimmy didn't like that look, and he liked it even less that he had hit the madman; his knuckles stung.

"What d-do you say?" Jimmy asked, stumbling over his words.

"I don't have him—in fact, I don't know where he's gone." Leo finally said, still rubbing his chin.

"What do you mean? Where could he have gone?" And then Jimmy realized his mistake. There were many places Cole could have gone if he really wanted to, and most of them, he guessed, were right through the gaping mouth of the mines. Leo saw this sudden understanding himself, and in a moment of clarity, he grabbed the boy.

"Let go of me. If he's hiding, I'll find him."

"No, Jimmy, you mustn't, you can't, not down there, Cole was—"

His voice was broken off by a harsh grunt. Jimmy had cold cocked him again, this time on the ear, and he staggered into the wall and slid down as if his feet were hoisted on wheels.

Jimmy rushed towards the mine, towards the deep black, where noise was but long echoes in a tunnel shaped by explosions.

He ran, and when it got too dark, he had pulled the tin box from his pocket and fiddled with the matches until he had gotten them lit, and then he ran with these.

He had vaguely heard Leo scream something. He wasn't entirely sure what the madman had said—and really didn't care—but the words seemed haunting nonetheless.

"—*taken by the wolves. Not the both of you, not the both of you*—"

5

Jimmy kept screaming Cole's name as he walked down the mine. He held the match out in front of him, watching the small light waver, and it created a circular glow that danced on the rocks at either side.

The ground was incredibly smooth. Where the ground cracked, Jimmy noticed the lumber posts had crumbled and split also, and at one point he saw a rat impaled on a sharp piece of white stone that looked like bone. He had gone in far and hadn't seen a thing; he hadn't heard an answer to his calls, and every step he took further into the mines seemed a step farther away from ever getting back home. He knew this was a morbid thought, but he had used four books of matches already, and had just opened the fifth. When he ran out of matches he could only begin to imagine how the darkness would consume him.

"Cole," he yelled. There was a murky stench, and he could faintly hear rodents chirping; the sounds were coming from within the walls. When he pointed the match anywhere near the rock he didn't see a thing.

When he had pulled the last match from the book, his first real sense of fear gripped him. He held it in his fingers clumsily, rolling it along his fingertips. He pulled out his tin box and plucked out a cigarette, shoving it in his mouth. His teeth were chattering together like snapping bones, but when he felt the filter in his mouth he seemed to calm down.

"Where are you, Cole?" He mumbled to himself. He struck the match and watched the flame flicker. He lit his smoke and when the match died he tossed it on the ground where it disappeared forever in a small fissure.

All he could see was a red dot, which moved wherever he waved his hand; it looked like a line, and when his eyes fully adjusted, he could slightly see a red glare on the rocks.

"He didn't come down here you idiot, that madman was playing with your head. The rope hanging in the closet must have been a decoy or something. Cole is paying you back for what you let *them* do to him, and he knew how much you hated the thought of that madman living behind the fireplace. You fell for it. You wandered into this dark mine without a flashlight; you're out of matches now that you decided to use the last one to light a smoke, and when this smoke is down to the filter, then what? Light another one…then another till you're all outta smokes too? Or do you turn around and walk back in the darkness like a blind dork, holding your hands out in front of you so you don't smash into any rocks? Come on idiot, what's your next plan of attack?" He sat down on the smooth rock and rested his back against the wall. Listening to his own voice was both soothing and frightening; he couldn't see anything, and for a second he believed he *wasn't* actually talking, but was listening to somebody…or some*thing* else that was just beyond his reach in the shadows.

He sat with his knees almost tucked against his chest, holding his cigarette with his lips, smelling the smoke, watching it twirl around in a red glow.

He felt something brush by his leg.

The cigarette dropped from his lips and onto his lap. He saw five sets of glowing eyes, like burning smokes that had fallen from his pocket. He felt sweat run down his brow and drip off his temples; he could hear them now, all of them. They must have come from the walls behind him and then decided to follow him, or at least his light. "Get away," Jimmy said. As much as he hated rodents, he would have taken this prospect over a bundle of hairy spiders. But they didn't leave. He felt them touch him again, rubbing his legs and feet, their slithery tails swaddling his ankles like old fingers. There were nine sets of glowing eyes now, then fourteen—then twenty, until the air smelt of them, their dirty fur and dripping mouths. He kicked his right leg out and a couple of heavy rodents flew into the wall; he even heard the disgusting splat.

"Go, leave, GET OUTTA HERE," he screamed, his voice echoing until his head rang. He wished he had more matches, and he knew his cigarette would die out soon, he just knew it, and he didn't even get to enjoy the smoke. The rodents chirped back at him. One crawled in between his legs and Jimmy singed its muzzle with his cigarette; the rat shrieked and scurried away, whapping him with its tail.

Jimmy stood up. They were all around him now.

He dropped the cigarette on top of them, the faint glow showing him just how many there were; his smoke rolled along their backs, the distinct corona tattooing their fur a crimson neon. He felt for the wall beside him, and while he patted the rock he moved forward slowly, feeling them tickle his ankle, listening to them squeak.

And he ran.

He ran down the mine just as Edwin Krollup had thirty years before him. He turned once to watch the cigarette flicker and die in the darkness.

When the air became sour Jimmy just ran harder. Somehow he knew where to go. He narrowly missed smacking into a stalactite, and even though he heard the cone whiz by his ear, he barely noticed it. His throat hurt.

Cole's not down here, he thought to himself. Other times he yelled that he was lost, or that he wanted his mommy, but nobody heard this, and he knew that.

He was ready to pass out, to drop and let the rats take him, but he saw in the distance a hole in the darkness, a hole his eyes couldn't really focus on. He ran and that hole grew bigger and bigger until he fell through it.

6

He fell, and even though his eyes were closed he could see that terrible brightness through his lids, as if a gigantic blot had been stamped across his eyes. His fingers had plunged into dust, and his throat was raw.

For some strange reason a peculiar thought came into his head: *You're not in Kansas anymore.*

A moment later, before Jimmy could open his eyes and really taste the fresh air, a hand had cupped over his mouth and another had hooked under his arm. He was pulled from the ground, his fingers leaving the dust like roots from a fallen tree. He opened his eyes and noticed somebody leaning over him, somebody with shaggy hair like cropped wires—somebody wearing a mask.

"Be quiet, we musn't disturb the wolves." The voice was a soft whisper, and Jimmy fainted; he fell back and looked into the bright sky before closing his eyes again.

7

"Mr. and Mrs. Krollup, please, have a seat," Detective Saul said, and he motioned the both of them to sit. He was wearing black slacks and a white shirt that had come undone, and his hair was scruffy. He had been at the house for a couple of hours now, not because he felt some insistent need to practice his own pamper duty, but because he relied on impulses, like most cops. He constantly ran his hands through his thinning hair, wishing he could leave this place for a nice meal, or better yet, a smoke, but he knew he'd be here for a while now, a long while because he was sure—he was *certain*—the gardener had the boys. This wasn't just some hunch either, and even though he had an ulcer, and a wife that barely spoke to him, he had an intuitive sense, as if he had shackled the right side of his brain together with the left.

They were in the Master Bedroom, and Saul had shut the doors behind him; there was a mess of people in the house now—mostly cops, but he was sure a few reporters had weaseled their way into the yard, by either following a cop car, or scaling the fence around the other side of the house. He could see the news vans out the bedroom window and wondered how they had found out so quickly.

Saul formed his fingers into a makeshift chapel.

"What have you found, detective?" Maggie asked. "I know you've found something, I can see it in your eyes, so please tell me—tell us."

Saul looked at Edwin. "Mr. Krollup, do you have a fulltime gardener?"

Edwin cocked his eye. "Yeah, why?"

"How many do you have?"

"Just one in the fall. Mario. I usually hire students to help in the summer. He wouldn't like it if you called him a gardener, though. Mario like's the title lawn technician; it seems to me this pretense glamorizes the actual job, but I suppose he feels a certain meaning comes with the title."

"Does he feel unappreciated in any way?"

"What?"

"I mean, has he been known to voice distaste with you as an employer?" Saul ran his hand through his hair again.

"If he had he would have been long gone by now. What's your point, detective?"

"Do you trust him?"

"He's my lawn technician. I trust him with the use of my shed. I trust that he will keep the yard trimmed and the gardens in full bloom; I trust he will sweep the walkways and polish my statues, but why do I have the nagging feeling that this isn't the trust you imply?"

"Because it isn't," Saul said, and he looked at Maggie, who had brushed her hair since the afternoon, and had thrown on a pair of clean jeans.

"Please detective, please don't go through this, I want to know where my sons are," Maggie said.

"Mr. Krollup, was Mario the lawn technician on schedule to work today?"

Edwin shook his head. "These days he comes in four days a week, and I give him the weekends off, especially in the fall, because he doesn't need to tend to the flowers."

"But he could have come anyway, not to work of course, but to visit?"

"He has security clearance."

"Does he have a key to the house?"

Edwin cocked his eye again. "No. He works outside. If I ever caught the man in my house I'd have him thrown out with nothing but the clothes on his back—and that's if he's lucky."

"Are there ways for him to get in, though?"

"There are always ways to do anything, detective."

"Saul, call me Saul, please. Now tell me Mr. Krollup, to change the subject quickly, and I know this may upset you, but do the boys know about the mines?"

"Why does that matter?"

"Because I have two theories, and it seems one of them hangs on a thread while the other is just an impulse. I get those a lot."

"I'm sure the boys know about the mines, but I have long since had them leveled to build this house. I wanted to build my future on this city's history; there's a sense of pride in the notion." Edwin smiled, but it wasn't a real smile; it was almost as fake as the gemstone on Saul's middle finger.

"Yes, I can see that," Saul said, never buying into the rich man's charades; it was all an act, so he nodded like the fool Edwin wanted him to be.

"Detective, please," Maggie pleaded.

"Okay, okay, I'm sorry. I've dragged this through the mud long enough. There's rope missing from your shed."

"So?" Edwin said.

"Your lawn technician is probably one of the only people with access to the shed, correct? Now suppose Mario came in last night and fetched the rope. Perhaps he left something in the back doorjamb to let himself in the house, maybe tape on the bolt, I'm not sure because there were no adhesive traces left, but I'm speculating possibilities."

Maggie muttered something and clapped her hand over her mouth.

"Wait a minute, you are implying my gardener—"

"Lawn technician," Saul corrected.

"—you're implying Mario came into *my* house and took *my* stepson, only to return during the day to take Jimmy, without leaving a ransom note?"

Saul nodded.

"Where's the bloody sense in that?"

Saul shook his head. "The sense, I don't know, but perhaps the man isn't working for the sake of financial compensation, but for something else. How have you treated him during his employment?"

"Fine," Edwin said. He did occasionally yell at the man, but that was because he did stupid things, like trim roses from the garden to take to his girlfriend. "But how would you know to check the shed for missing rope in the first place, I mean, that seems rather coincidental?"

"It does, but Mr. Krollup, Mrs. Krollup, your boys' room has become a crime scene—forensics found rope fibers in the top bunk, and like I said, we work on impulses. Checking the shed was a hunch that may just work out best for all of us."

"Oh my lord, my poor, poor boys," Maggie said and she'd begun crying.

"Now don't worry Mrs. Krollup. Our plan of attack is to go to this lawn technician's house, and if need be, break down the door to bring your boys back—if this, this hunch even pans out. Pray to God it doesn't...pray to God the boys have just taken a long walk or something, but for now we're treating this as a kidnapping."

"A kidnapping?" Edwin said, mostly under his breath, but both Saul and Maggie heard him fine.

Saul nodded. He looked at Maggie, saw the sourness in her expression and scorned himself for being so blunt—his job was based on certainties though, he supposed, and despite the blatancy behind the notion, he realized she was happy the police had a theory...anything to found hope on, really. "I'm sorry."

Maggie tried to smile. Edwin walked over to the detective and pulled him aside. He bent down until his lips were almost touching Saul's ear. "Listen detective, you and I both know you're working on strands here. You're putting together something, anything to prove you've made progress, and I appreciate that for the sake of my wife, but there's far more at stake here, and I'm sure you know all about that too. The media came because somebody here tipped them off. I have a fair idea who that somebody is, but that doesn't matter, because for now the news maggots are working on a hunch." His breath was hot, and Saul could feel the man's hands digging into his arm; there was a weird vibration coming from him too, and had he looked at Edwin's eyes, he would have noticed the man's corneas had turned a dim red. "They aren't to find out about this Saul, you understand me? If news of this gets out...if news of a kidnapping gets out, well, that's extra unneeded publicity if you know what I'm saying—I don't want those maggots hanging around here any longer. I want them to realize nothing's going on, just protocol. I'm holding this on you Saul—if news gets out, if those maggots get anything on me, on this kidnapping, I swear to you, I will spend as much money as I have to to make sure you don't work in this country ever again."

"I understand the circumstances you're under Mr. Krollup, but I don't intend to comply with any of your threats."

"For the sake of my family's honor, get the media off my property."

Saul looked at Edwin with fierce clarity, then finally nodded. He turned to the door when Edwin pulled him back again.

"Oh yeah, and get rid of Lela *Saxon*, the female officer with a bite to her bark."

"Why?"

"I know her type, Saul. She called the news maggots."

8

Maggie looked at her husband after the detective left. "What did you say to him, Edwin?"

Edwin smiled and patted her arm; she hadn't found any comfort in it, and even decided to pull away harshly, as if his touch had become vile to her. "I told him to be careful when he goes to Mario's house. I don't want to put the boys' lives in jeopardy."

She didn't suspect a lie, not at this point, so Maggie just smiled. "Do you think Mario would take the boys? He seemed—he seemed so nice."

"It's assumptions for now Maggie, but it wouldn't hurt to question the man just in case. You heard Saul, he said they found traces of rope in the top bunk—Cole's bed." Edwin walked over to the window and saw, over the fence, *that* female cop standing with the reporters, standing out like a sore thumb in that baggy uniform. He knew she called the reporters because it was something he would do; she was like him, and though he should have been commending that one fact, he felt instead a throbbing anger with her.

A moment later he watched Saul walk down the driveway with his partner, a younger man with a horrible limp. The limping cop walked to an old Buick and Saul walked over to the young lady. After the two talked (Edwin couldn't tell what either was thinking; people kept getting in the way, blocking his view of their faces) Saul got in the driver's seat of the Buick, followed by a handful of cops jumping in their own cruisers. The cars sped off in increments, and Lela was left standing in the middle of the news pool—an angry cop with a worthy story to hype.

9

"He's the type that lets the money go to his head," Saul said to his partner, Ray Lettermen, who had had a hip replacement and walked with a terrible limp—he had been shot pointblank a year ago, and was just now getting used to walking without a cane.

"But Saul, you can't let morons talk to ya like that, no matter money, no matter political status, you hear me? He's telling you how to do your job, and Saul, there's a line, a definite line, and Krollup there crossed it."

Saul ran his hand through his hair again. His mind was unclear—it was actually waving back and forth. "You got a smoke?"

"No. Your skin looks yellow, Saul, you gotta quit killin yourself."

"Doesn't matter," he said, rubbing his lips, "just something to take my mind away I guess."

"Whaddya gonna say to Lela?"

Saul pondered this for a moment. He certainly wasn't going to fire her. She was a good cop, and she was an even better people person; they needed more cops like her, that was for sure. "Gonna tell her to take the rest of the day off. I just don't need Krollup any more aggravated than he already is."

Lettermen laughed, shuffling his step like a toddler just learning to walk. "You know how she's gonna take it, right?"

Saul nodded. He did, he knew exactly how she was going to take it: she was going to go ballistic.

"What about the gardener?" Lettermen asked, still chuckling to himself.

"Lawn technician."

"What did you say?"

"Krollup says the gardener likes to be called a lawn technician. I guess importance is contagious in this house."

Lettermen laughed even harder.

"We're gonna try to question him at his place—very carefully."

"What do you think though Saul?" The two were walking down the driveway towards the steady drone of the news vans.

"I think we're either hunching on a coincidence, or those boys are in trouble."

"You think you may be right about that rope hanging in the closet?" Lettermen looked at Saul like an awestruck kid.

"I don't know. I certainly didn't want to tell the Krollups anything."

"How did you tread around ransom notes?"

"Said there wasn't any."

They walked a moment longer in silence. Lettermen constantly grunted as his flesh pinched in his hip; he dragged his feet behind him in a slow drag.

"You think that rope—that *noose* means he wants to hurt the boys?" Lettermen finally asked.

"I think if Mario the lawn technician took those boys, and left a noose in the closet made from the rope matching the fibers we found in the top bunk, then yes, I think he certainly wants to hurt the boys; it may be his calling card for all we know." The two left the front gate, pushing away microphones that had been shoved in their faces. "Go to the car Ray, I'll talk to Lela."

"Be careful," Lettermen said with a smile.

10

"You called them?" Dale asked Lela, as the two stood amidst the news vans, their uniforms drawing swarms of microphones.

Lela smiled, her pretty face cinching up at the side. Her mother used to tell her she'd get wrinkles early, and this always scared her, but now, now she just felt like smiling.

"When?"

"After you called the station to send back up here. I knew there'd be a story, so I figured I'd hit Krollup where it hurts. Guys like him hate the media, especially since it's been down his back this last week about the David mishap."

Dale smiled, and pushed a microphone out of his face with a grunt. "Look at all of them—Channel 9, PA News...even *Coast to Coast* is here, can you believe that? Word travels fast. Unbelievable."

The two watched cameramen struggle to climb onto the hoods of their vans, trying to get a decent shot over the wall. The house stood on the tip of the hill like a castle. She hated it. Standing there outside the wall made her realize one thing: ever since she could remember, something about that house freaked her out. She had always thought the possibility was under the house—the mines, the haunted mines, but now that she had met Edwin Krollup, and had seen his eyes turn into red orbs, she realized her fear was because of something (*someone*) inside the house.

"You okay?" Dale asked her, and Lela smiled. She had been shuddering as she looked at the house, remembering the awful sneer that statue had given her—*statue*...she couldn't believe she was still dwelling on that. "You sure?"

"Yeah."

"I'm gonna check around, maybe grab a coffee from those guys over there, I figure the reporters are apt to sharing. If not, I'll just flash my gun. You want anything?"

Lela shook her head. If she wanted anything, it was to barge back into that house and look Edwin Krollup squarely in the eyes and say: "I got them all here, all of them, the cameras, the journalists, and they're not gonna leave until—"

Until what? Until he took back whatever it was he had done to her? He hadn't done anything but imply his power transcended respect. Dale figured the same thing.

She felt somebody tap her shoulder and thought for sure it was another snide reporter, but it was Detective Saul. His hair was pushed back, and the sun shone through his wiry crown like an unkempt bush.

"Saul, what's up?" She said with a smile, sure he hadn't noticed her daze.

He had a sorrowing look about him, as if the drink and a divorce had transformed him into a premature senior citizen—but he *hadn't* divorced his wife, she remembered. He had survived threats of it, she was sure, but the actual divorce hadn't come around yet; he was waiting for it, she could tell, but that was none of her business. She just noticed what it had done to him—his eyes were weary and his skin had folded over his brow until the shadow on his nose reached his nostrils and hid his eyes altogether. "I was just talking to Krollup," he said.

"And?"

"And he's got a sour spot."

"Tell me something I don't know."

"I think his wife should leave him."

"Knew that too. So what does a great detective want from a lowly officer?"

Saul turned and looked at the house, certain behind one of those windows Edwin Krollup stood with his hands behind his back watching them as if they were pawns on his chessboard. *Like Prospero*, he thought, *from Shakespeare's* The Tempest.

"Well, he's got a sour spot for *you*," Saul said, turning red. He didn't like offending people, even if he was just the messenger. "He's pretty adamant you called the media here."

Lela blushed herself. "Why does he think that?"

"I just think you should go home for the rest of the day."

"Why?" Lela asked. She was unimpressed, with Saul, with everything really. Why do men feel they have to bend over backwards for other men when power is involved?

Saul rubbed his hands together until the sound of rough skin was going to drive her nuts. "Did he tell you to get me outta here?"

"No," he finally said, but she saw the truth in his eyes. She understood his lie for what it was; he was afraid she might do something stupid that would backfire on *him*, because he had made a spoken agreement with Krollup: to send her home by any means possible. "Why don't you and Dale head back to the Precinct and start filling out preliminary paper work."

He's looking at you the same way Krollup did, as if you're an incapable child, an embarrassment he wants stowed away because he's got company coming over. "Where are you going then?" she asked snidely.

"Gonna follow up my hunch. Cross your fingers I'm wrong," he said as he rushed to his navy blue Buick, which had begun rusting around the seal of the windshield.

"They're crossed."

She watched the cruisers follow the Buick down the winding road, leaving their lights off so they wouldn't alarm the press. She walked over to a young man wearing a tweed sports jacket and tapped him on the shoulder. He had long sideburns that grew in grisly patterns, and there was a pen behind each of his ears.

Lela looked at the house in utter disgust: *so you think you can get rid of me?*

"I think I may have something for the six o'clock news."

"I'm all ears, officer," he said, and he grabbed a pen from behind his ear.

11

On Hillside Road, pulled off on the grassy shoulder like a heap of rusted metal, sat a boxy old Caprice; its engine was still running, and the two men inside watched the house on the hill, and the news vans and police cruisers around it.

"I remember you asked me how you were going to get into the house, did you not?" Robert Innis, Edwin Krollup's corrupt psychologist, sat with his hands on his lap, staring at his cousin Eddie in the passenger's seat.

"I did."

"Well something's going on up there."

"Yes there is. What do you think it is?" Eddie asked stupidly.

"You're going to find out."

Eddie gave a concerned look. "I am?"

"We're going to put your old cop skills to the test, Eddie boy," Robert said, patting his cousin on the shoulder.

12

Robert watched Eddie crouch behind a hedge along the base of the outer wall. The front gate was about thirty yards in front of him, but Robert knew Eddie wouldn't be able to go in that way if he didn't keep his cool; there were too many reporters for one thing, and the guard at the gate wasn't as simple-minded as he might have hoped. The guard gave curious inspections of every vehicle leaving and entering the gate, and Robert could tell by the old man's sternness that sneaking behind a car as it entered the premises wouldn't have worked in a million years—especially for a man like Eddie, whose heart was in the right place, but who was conducted by two left feet and hands as enormous as dinner plates.

Robert had the binoculars planted above his nose; he watched a young female officer talking to a handful of reporters who had been jotting everything down as she spoke. "What's happening around here?" he asked himself, almost eager to pick up his phone to call Edwin, to check up on the man. Robert had left this morning because Edwin had called his cellular phone twice—he had the briefest worry that Edwin spotted him outside his house, watching from the car, but something insisted that he was being paranoid, and acting too prematurely on his emotions. He *is* a psychologist, for crying out loud—he, more than anybody really, should have understood that reactions to paranoia drove a person against his or her will to try to escape by any means possible. And he had done just that. Of course he was being careful, but he understood that under the current circumstances, Edwin Krollup was probably just looking for help.

And that gave Robert hope that he would hypnotize Krollup again. Perhaps that's why he finally came back, after carefully deliberating certainties—he was certain, for one thing, that he desired something about that man's necklace, that he wanted to take it off Edwin and try it on himself. And though he hadn't told Eddie, Robert was more interested in the mines behind the fireplace, than he was in the possibility of a vault. He sat in the car looking at the three stacks jutting from the roof, and he wondered which one of them concealed the mines. Perhaps that was why he insisted Eddie find out which fireplace hid the mines, before he went on his mindless crusade around the house, tapping walls for hidden doors and looking behind massive portraits for enormous steel safes.

Eddie sat behind the hedge watching the police, watching the reporters, watching the gate squeak closed behind a cruiser as it left the house. "Oh you big idiot, you were a cop once, flash your wallet to the guard, he's seen enough badges today not to notice you're only carrying your license and three dollars," Robert said, hiding the binoculars as a cruiser passed, opening a road map on his lap and directing his finger down an invisible route. When the car passed he plunked the binoculars on his face again.

Eddie had stood up and straightened his pants; he was a tall man, not an inch shorter than 6'5, but he had an asinine hunch that drooped his shoulders and sunk his neck into his collarbone. He walked up to the gate, tapping his big fingers on the trunk of a cruiser as he walked; it looked like he was trying to blend in, and Robert cringed. The man was wearing khaki pants that hung above his ankles (either he bought them too short, or had his wife Beth hem them, and Beth wasn't the seamstress you could trust your clothes to) and his wrinkled shirt had tumbled out of the back of his pants, hanging over his belt like a flag over a parapet—he looked anything but professional.

Eddie walked to the gate, nodding to the reporters and cameramen as if he belonged there, as if he were one of them. And then he did it, surprising Robert because he had believed for a moment that Eddie read his mind, that he had somehow sent the message out telepathically or something—Eddie flipped his wallet open for the guard and then shoved it back into his pants. The gate opened, and Robert watched Eddie trudge up the driveway. The guard didn't even give him a second look. "So I was wrong," Robert said, smiling.

13

"Oh Edwin, what do you think happened?" Maggie asked. The two of them were still in their bedroom; they didn't want to leave at the moment. There were too many people in the house, and Maggie felt obliged to stay out of their way, just as she felt she needed her privacy.

Edwin stood at the window, watching the reporters gather around in a big circle. They were all writing, and he knew something was going on down there. "I'm sure everything's fine."

"You keep saying that Edwin, but I can hear your lie," she said. She was sitting on the bed with pillows stacked around her body like a padded jumpsuit. "I *am* the worst mother in the universe."

"No you're not," Edwin responded, clearly focused not on his wife, but on that tangled bunch of reporters outside the gate.

"Yes I am. I practically told Jimmy to get lost—I was just so upset, I didn't care at the moment." She started crying again.

He didn't know how he was going to put up with this any longer. In an hour everything would be different, but now, now her shrieking voice and her worry all bundled up into this little vice that crushed his patience. He too was bound by a seeming pressure that wanted to bring him down from the inside—his was the insistence that he had inadvertently killed his father, but ever since he had been hypnotized, ever since he had traveled back down the mines as a child, he had drawn lucid pictures from his head, pictures flashing behind his eyes as if a projectionist had been planted inside his skull that had somehow transferred his memories into film.

"You were upset—it happens. Have you called your mother?"

"Of course I have, Edwin, and she's like she's always been. She's got your optimism. Every time I think of Mario, I think of this secretive, quiet man who prunes the hedges and mows the courtyard. Maybe he was prone to an outbreak—I mean *didn't* you check his references? He might not even be Mario, he might be—he might be John Wayne Gacey, you never know, and he might have dressed up like a clown to take the boys; it wouldn't surprise me if they found makeup on Cole's bed, makeup—"

"If there was makeup, Maggie, it would have been Cole's, because Cole felt he had to hide his bruises, and must have thought that he hid them well, because it seemed to me that he figured he had us all duped. The boys are fine, okay, they're fine." Edwin turned to look at his wife. Her hair had messily fallen over her face, most of it sticking to her tear soaked cheeks.

"What about the mines?" Maggie asked. This was the first time she had mentioned them since they were first married. Edwin flustered and turned away, looking out the window.

"What about them?" Edwin responded; he could tell she sensed something from him, and he tried his hardest to hide it. He wanted to grab his necklace—he wanted to disappear under ground or something, because he could feel her eyes on his back.

"I know they're somewhere, Edwin, and I know you didn't just level them to build this house. Your secret's safe with me. I don't even care why you built over them in the first place; all I want to know is if it's possible the boys found a way into them or something? Maybe they're both in the mines right now, hurt or something, and we can't hear them because of the thick walls—the bloody thick walls."

Edwin turned around to face her again; he almost felt compelled to tell her the truth, to tell her she was partly right, only Cole wasn't hurt inside the mines, he was beyond them, somewhere else, through a door Kenneth Auger unlocked all those years ago during the mine explosions—and now it was he, Auger, who had the boy all because of this trinket Krollup had around his neck.

But that is no mere trinket you wear; inside that stone exists something beyond all worlds, beyond any definition of power and destruction—what you wear around your neck has the ability to shape worlds, and probably, given the amount of patience it deserves, build worlds too. He didn't know where this thought came from.

"The mines were closed off Maggie. Even if they found a way near them, they'd just be stuck in the walls or something."

"But what about the little door that's been painted over in the closet, above the shelves?" She asked. "The boys have one in their room also."

Edwin knocked his hands together. "Old vents, Maggie—what, did you want me to say they were secret passageways? You're letting your imagination get away from you, and I know this is worry, and I understand your reasoning, but you can't find blame in the construction of this house."

Maggie looked at Edwin skeptically. "I know, I'm sorry."

"It's five o'clock; I think you should call your mother again. I don't want you staying here."

"I'm not leaving my house while my boys are missing," she said defensively.

"Is this constructive though? Is this healthy? Is this what you want Cole and Jimmy to see when they return? To understand their mother gave up hope?"

Maggie shook her head.

She would pack her things and leave, but she would face the earthquake first—after the six o'clock news.

14

By the time Eddie was in the house, he felt slightly more comfortable with the position he was in. He used to be a cop, sure, but his sense of the past didn't enable him, nor did it work against him either; he walked around the house with a funny smirk, trying to blend in with officers in uniform, while he wore short pants and a wrinkled shirt with green stains from the hedges he had cowered behind. Being a former cop helped him understand two things: most of these officers were in the same boat as he—utterly confused—and most of them were too busy trying to make a name for themselves to notice anybody around them. Eddie used this to his advantage as he walked around.

There were three fireplaces in the house, he saw that from the outside, but the main floor was like a maze. It opened up to a grand foyer with a great big staircase and chandelier, with hallways veering off at either side of the stairs like Frost's fork in the road. He had taken the right side, ultimately coming upon a Great room with a fireplace to the right. It was a very large fireplace too—the stack must have been twenty feet wide, and fifteen feet deep; there was a fire inside, flickering off the adjacent wall like orange ghosts. On the ornate mantle there was a clock, and above it, on the jagged stone hung a portrait of Edwin Krollup. Across the room there were baseball pennants tacked on the wood panels, and there were signed footballs and baseball bats in cases; and at the very far end of the room, dappled in sunlight like a god within a shiny aura, stood the statue David, atop a pedestal with intricate carvings and swirls that would have taken an artist years to finish.

He had noticed a couple of cops standing at the statue's base, sipping coffee out of Styrofoam cups; they were both laughing. "It's looking the wrong way, and the idiot shells out fifty big ones on this. He must have been looking at his picture books in the mirror."

"Yeah," the other cop agreed.

Eddie walked over to the fireplace, careful not to look suspicious. He ran his hand down the hard rock, fitting his fingers in uneven places. He looked into the fire; it was dying and the logs it had ignited into slim pieces of charcoal had broken into black slivers and ash. At the back, littered in ash and burning embers, there was a brick wall, and he could tell with the red glow that the grout had chipped away between blocks. He stood this way, ducked over with his head underneath the mantle when both officers noticed him.

"What's he doing? Hey, you, what are ya doing?"

Eddie didn't realize they were talking to him. His focus was on that wall behind the fire. For some reason it didn't seem right, not at all, and he knew he should have gone to look for the vault, but when he strained really hard he could hear something behind there, something like beeps and whirrs, sounds he heard at the arcade when he was a kid.

He felt somebody tug on his shoulder, and Eddie, like the big man that he was, easily slapped the hand away and nonchalantly shoved the cop without looking.

"He's a reporter. I don't recognize him," one of the officers said. The two of them pulled Eddie away from the fireplace.

"Hey, what are you doing?" Eddie said in a menacing voice that wasn't dumb, but didn't sound incredibly bright either.

"What are you doing in here? You a reporter?"

"What does it matter?" Eddie responded.

"Oh it does, it really does," the officer laughed, and then the other joined him in a rude cacophony that sounded like a witch's cackle. "No reporters, cap'n's rule, chief."

"I ain't a reporter."

"You ain't a cop either, chief."

"How you so sure?"

"Cause you're dressed like a wino from the slums. Beat it."

15

When Robert saw Eddie trudging down to the car, he knew for sure the big guy was had. He turned the ignition and reversed off the shoulder, spitting gravel in gray flumes that Eddie would spit out when he chased after the Caprice. Robert knew the cops would be watching, and when they saw this idiot get in the car with him, he knew there would be questions, and he wasn't willing to give up that easily.

He saw Eddie waving at him in the rear view mirror, obscured by the exhaust and the plumes of gravel that devoured him in gulps.

When he turned off Hillside Road, he pulled into the grass. Eddie jumped into the passenger seat; he was sweating and his dark hair clung to his scalp like dead spiders, and his oily skin stuck that wrinkled shirt to his sides and armpits as if his pores secreted adhesive. "What are you doing Robby?" He panted. The inside of the car smelt of him now, this deep musk that clung to the upholstery like hooks.

"You were spotted weren't you?"

Eddie nodded. He looked sorry in a way, but his anger wasn't camouflaged by sweat and fatigue any.

"Then why would you come running back to the car? Why would you point me out too?"

"Because—" He didn't continue. Not because he was out of breath, but because he saw Robert's point.

"Did you at least see anything?"

"I think I found the fireplace hiding the mines."

"Did you?" Robert seemed quite surprised.

"I think so."

"And why are the cops and the press there—did you find that out too?"

"I heard something when I left, on the police radio."

"Oh?"

"Something about a lawn technician being a no show."

"That's it?" Robert asked.

Eddie nodded. The Caprice drove away.

16

Edwin had been driven to it, he could have assured anybody of that one fact. His fury was wholly circumstantial, but as police cruisers and news vans were crushed into pockets of asphalt, any notion of instigation was forgotten. As Edwin floated above the ground watching everybody around him scramble, he realized the deluxe advantages of such power, and asked himself if their scoop had really been worth it.

The six o'clock news had come on like every other day, and when Edwin heard his name mentioned he brushed it off as either some type of local celebrity gossip, or further burrowing into the Italian Art controversy—as most had deemed to call it. He had just gotten off the phone with Saul when the news began, finding out that Mario the lawn technician wasn't at home, but with a nice bribe, the cops could get a rush search warrant from the District Attorney and tear apart the apartment before the man even returned. Edwin agreed, and not because he actually believed it was a possibility that the boys were with his lawn technician, but because it settled his wife. She had been frantic all day. She had pulled much of her hair out, and had begun scratching her face believing it was all her fault Jimmy was missing too.

"You're going to your mother's," he reiterated, and she had responded with a dry sneer.

"I can't leave when my boys are missing. How could you even suggest that?"

"Because I did," he said in a flat tone. His head killed, and it seemed to be getting worse too, as if every unlocked door in his mind had cracked open, giving him a slight peek of what he had hidden over the years.

The news started, and at first Edwin had ignored it; in fact, he didn't understand why he even turned the television on in the first place, other than from a particular habit he had formed after he became famous. Maggie had been packing her suitcase, cursing under her breath and crying out loud until the entire expression became a disgusting symphony—*sniff sniff, damn.*

What surprised Edwin the most was that the first story dealt with him; he had ignored the possibility that the reporters at his gate knew anything because he passed the media off as bloodsucking storytellers—meaning their work was primarily based on controversial fiction. He had initially believed that the pseudo-David story still resonated because of a public insistence that Edwin Krollup clear his faults, and that the crummy Ministry get what they deserve, but this was just wishful thinking. The fact that the first story was about Edwin surprised him, sure, but the strangeness of his reaction came from his own ignorance; he had passed off possibilities of this story leaking because he had threatened a detective, and Edwin was very good at imposing his drastic measures. He never believed that he would watch the news and see his own house instead of that bland mural behind the ugly newscaster's head. This was shock because he noticed himself sitting in his room, watching the news *on* the news, as if the cameras were focused right on him; he waved his arm, and watched himself do the same on television, as if he were seated in front of a delayed mirror.

He saw Maggie packing her suitcase on the television, and when she saw this, when she saw herself on television, all worries of her missing sons turned to vanity, because Maggie rushed off to the nearest mirror and threw her red hair into a tidy ponytail, and smeared red lipstick over her lips and rouge blush over her cheeks until her tear streaks turned into a fashion statement. This was all a surprise...a big surprise, and not just for Edwin either—Maggie found in this sickening display the bloodlust and voyeurism of the media, which itself seemed *against* violence and voyeurism. This was when she realized the hypocrisies of the media, and realized she would rather hide at her mother's house than stick around here, knowing her privacy was being breached—

knowing her anguish was being broadcasted so people around the world could feel sorry for her, but thank God the same thing wasn't happening to them.

"Possibilities of a kidnapping are currently being investigated, and a suspect has been identified, but has not yet been disclosed. So this has been a week of turmoil for Edwin Krollup and his family—after suffering the Italian Art Controversy, watching the Blackbirds suffer a horrible 2002 season only to finish with a 38-124 record, they now have to endure the dismal possibility of a kidnapping. Again, no motive has been disclosed, nor has there been any identification of the suspect, though police have issued a statement that they *do* have leads," a young journalist said, her hair tied up in a bun so tight that her face looked stretched and her brow featureless.

"I can't believe them," Maggie said, "I can't believe they'd put people through this just for ratings."

Edwin didn't answer; his eyes had turned red.

The camera had panned over the house, showing the courtyard through the gate, the walkways and the statues; it had scoured the grounds before the gate, the collection of police cruisers and news vans, all lined in a metallic frenzy, lights blaring against the lens, and Edwin saw her—*her*, that Lela officer who thought she could take control away from him in *his* own house. She was still here, standing among the officers with a coffee in her hand.

Edwin broke his second television in a week, only this time he put his foot through the screen, instead of the remote control.

"Where are you going?" Maggie asked, not at all startled by his reaction.

Edwin ignored her, and a few moments later Maggie would feel the earthquake.

17

When he threw open his front door he hadn't a clue what he going to do, but there was a sense of understanding that leaked into his head from somewhere else—somewhere deep, he supposed, because this urge traveled up his throat and behind his eye sockets like a hot flare.

He took his necklace off and clenched the stone in his hand; he felt a bass that rattled his knuckles, and everything he looked at turned red, trapped behind a translucent scarlet sheet; he wouldn't have known this, but his eyes had become a crimson blotch, his veins connecting into this fused blot that erased his pupils.

At this point he had risen in the air, and underneath his feet the ground trembled; there were 'S' patterns that shook the sub-floor, and in many places the concrete cracked, forming air bubbles in carpet and snapping hardwood.

He looked at all of them, the cameras, the journalists, the news vans and the satellites that had towered from them as if they had been stolen from NASA. Everything that happened next happened fast.

First, the statues in the yard changed. This wasn't something he had suggested himself, but had moved due to the pure will of the stone. The pedestals upon which they stood seemed to split down the middle. The statues had all turned to face the gate. Edwin could tell the reporters noticed something was happening; they didn't know what for sure, but many of them had this clairvoyant assumption, sending them to their vans, packing up their cameras. He heard many of them scream *earthquake*, but the 'S' waves hadn't really exploded yet. Edwin watched rocks shoot out of his yard. Edwin hadn't a clue what was happening, but realized the statues had torn their hands from themselves and hurled them over the wall. Many of them now stood in the growing dusts without arms, staggering on their split pedestals as they tried to kick their legs out.

Then the ground exploded. Edwin wanted this to happen. He watched a police cruiser fold in half as the asphalt underneath formed a mouth that sunk its crooked teeth into the car's tires, popping them like cheap balloons. The car split down the middle, caving the roof in, crashing the lights on top into jagged shards of glass. He heard people screaming, and watched with morbid delight as journalists and police alike ran from the road as the ground belched. A news van was bounced into the air by a tremendous wave that crumbled the road, and then crashed on top of another van, severing the satellite link until it toppled like a technological tree over the gate and pierced the grass like a gigantic battle axe. A pine tree across Hillside Road was supplanted and thrown into a news van, puncturing the side; there was an electrical fire as the circuit boards and computers were torn, and within seconds the van exploded as the gas tank ignited. The sound was an enormous thud, knocking the van into the wall; the mortar cracked and Edwin saw the crude shape of the vehicle on the other side of the fence as the stone pushed inwards.

Officers inside the house heard the explosions and felt the ground sway; they ran for cover under granite tables and between doorjambs. Maggie did the same. She stood with both arms against the doorjambs in the Master bedroom; she saw the pillar of flames from the exploding van through the window.

Edwin fell to the ground after four minutes, and everything stopped as quickly as it had begun. He was paralyzed, lying in a heap by the front door, his skin flapped and haggard, his hair thin and fragile.

He passed out.

18

Lela watched the reporters jabbering in front of the cameras, shelling out her scoop as if it were the story of the century. In a way it could have been, and in a way she had supposed all along that Edwin was hiding something. His insistence for the police to leave his premises was proof of that. But she hadn't told the reporters this assumption, because she was working strictly on social observations. He seemed anxious today, and that had gotten her the most; she had been dwelling on this for awhile now, and she would keep a tight watch on him, no matter if he liked it or not.

"Here's a coffee," Dale said, and he handed her a steaming Styrofoam cup.

"Thanks," she said.

"What you thinking?"

Lela smiled. She was certain she looked like she was in deep thought, standing amongst the pandemonium of headline news and yet she couldn't take her eyes away from the house on the hill. "Not much. I just like the idea that Krollup's in there right now with his feet up, watching this. I can just imagine his face."

"Probably something like this," Dale said, and he scrunched his brow and slackened his jaw.

"Wait," Lela said, "he just came out the front door." She pointed to the front porch, which was cast in stone. The door had indeed opened, and there stood Edwin Krollup.

Though he hadn't been standing at all, he had been... *floating*?

Then she felt it, this slight tremor beneath her, nudging her forward slightly.

"What was that?" Dale asked.

"Look, look at Krollup," she pointed, and Dale had looked, but the entire yard seemed sheathed by a gray veneer. "He was floating, he was floating five feet in the air," she said.

"What?" Dale asked stupidly.

And then they both heard a loud crunch. Lela turned and a cameraman was lying on his back; his video camera had split in two, and embedded in the imported plastic like an arrowhead was a stone fist—she couldn't tell for sure, but it certainly looked like a hand. Its wrist had been broken, and dust fell from cracks in rivulets. Then she heard another crack. She watched as a stone obliterated another camera; they were flying over the wall. "Take cover," she screamed. She watched one young man fly into the front fender of a van after a rock crashed into his chest; his camera broke the fall as he fell forward, and little pieces of plastic littered the ground like tinker toys. "Get into your vehicles, everybody."

Dale ran to the cruiser; a rock missed his face by mere inches, smacking the ground with a bounce and shattering a car window. "Lela, follow me," he screamed, but his voice didn't travel far over the sound of crashing rocks and the rumbling ground. Dale slammed the car door and turned the cruiser on. He drove forward when the 'S' waves exploded.

"Earthquake," he heard people yell outside the car.

Lela ran towards Dale when the cop car in front of her was folded in half by the road—the road grew fingers that punctured the cruiser's tires and pushed both ends together. She stopped as the light casing exploded. Shards of glass shot out, and she covered her face.

"Take cover," she screamed, and then she tripped over somebody, or some*thing*, and she felt the ground try to grab her. The van to her right was thrown thirty feet into the air, as if the ground had formed springs, landing on another van with a loud crunch. The satellite tower fell from the van with a thundering crash and she stood up; she saw Dale; he had flashed the red and blue lights. The air was thick with fog, and she ran towards the cruiser. "Watch out," she screamed at a woman who had been standing by her news van, tripping over the cables that had been thrown from the ground in twisted coils. A tree had been pulled from the dirt until its roots were just dripping silhouettes against the gray smoke. The reporter had jumped aside as the tree toppled into the van. Seconds later there was a shattering explosion that pushed the van into the outer wall; Lela, who could feel the sheer heat, dove behind the cruiser while Dale watched the red plume reach for the sky. She could barely stand on the ground. The road shifted, exposing the tar that seemed to suck her feet.

She opened the door and jumped in, her face covered with dirt; heat blisters coursed around her chapped lips.

"Are you okay?"

She was shaking, and the sound of the explosion still rang in her ears. She nodded. Everything settled after this, and the rocking car leveled; she could see clearly outside the windshield now. The road had cracked down the middle, and most of the vans had flipped over.

"An earthquake, here? That's gotta be the first," he said. His voice shook with mixed excitement. Reporters who still had working cameras were shooting the aftermath; the story had shifted, and Lela wondered if Krollup hadn't wanted this in the beginning.

She got out of the car and ran towards the gate. The guard inside was hunkered forward in his chair; his head was bleeding, but she could tell that he was breathing. To her right the van that had exploded was still smoldering against the wall. Swirls of dust fell around it and caught the flicker of the fire like some illusion. She strained her eyes against this and looked for the front door.

He was floating, you saw that clear as day.

She did. She could hear ambulances behind her, and a fire truck, but none of that mattered. She saw through the gate something that frightened her beyond her wildest dreams. Standing in the courtyard were a number of statues without hands—and many without arms. "What is going on?" She asked herself.

She saw Krollup on the front porch and he was lying very still.

19

"The earthquake is said to have some connection with the mines, and many experts have theorized that the mine explosions of 1956 had triggered a dormant fault line. Of course these are just speculations but further investigations are being made into this matter. Again, there was a 'limited earthquake'—we're calling it—on Hillside Road, that has only affected this small region. There is no evidence of this activity anywhere else in the city, but the possibility of a live fault line has worried city officials. Nobody was killed during the quake, which coincidentally occurred during a massive investigation of a supposed kidnapping at Edwin Krollup's mansion; there were eight official injuries, and an estimated nine million dollars of damage done to the Krollup estate and property..."

"An earthquake," Edwin said to himself. "Brilliant. Magical." He sat alone in the theater with his feet up on the seat in front of him. Except for Leo, nobody else was in the house with him, and he liked it.

According to his watch it was 11:06, and though he deeply wanted to go and see Leo, to check on that robot of his, he knew he wouldn't be able to walk even that far. Getting into the theater was difficult enough, and that had been after standing for hours talking to officials, again and again.

"Your home is not safe at the moment," a man had told him, a man with the Seismic Society, who had come studying the ground with his tech support.

"Your point?" Edwin had responded.

"I think it would be best if you left."

"Do you presume you can kick me out of my house?"

"No Mr. Krollup, I'm just ensuring your safety."

"I promised my wife, who I have sent to stay with her mother, that I would stay here and wait for our two boys, you understand me? If I broke that promise I wouldn't just shatter my wife's trust in me, I would throw my own morals into disarray. My stepsons could have been kidnapped, and if I turned my back on that hellish possibility, then where could I ever find my responsibility as a father? Where?"

"I'm sorry."

"Get off my property before I throw you off it myself."

"You're the boss, Mr. Krollup. But we'll be seeing you," the man said smugly, motioning the others to follow him back to their white vans.

Edwin wondered if the police were still outside, if the firemen and the emergency crews were still working away, towing mangled vehicles and cleaning dissected cameras and unspooled video. He hoped so, he hoped they worked all-night and got everything done. If he woke up in the morning to find them on his property, he'd have the ground swallow them in whole gulps. He wasn't kidding. Tomorrow he wasn't going to be bothered.

He had told the house staff to take the day off—hell, the *week* off—and they willingly obliged as they ran from the property. Maggie would most certainly call, but after the earthquake and the media blitz, she was happy to get away from the house—a diminishing resistance in part caused by some hope that her boys weren't near the house during the quake.

Tomorrow he was going to get fixed, if you could put it that way—he didn't see why not. His mind had opened like a mouth with lockjaw, and he couldn't close it for the life of him.

And tomorrow he was going to send the robot down the mines.

CHAPTER 13

THE ROBOT BOMB

1

His yard was a terrible mess. The road was split in two, and most of the trees had fallen over in jangled heaps. The vans and police cruisers damaged during the earthquake had been towed away, and on this fine Sunday morning Edwin Krollup couldn't see a car anywhere on Hillside Road; in fact, he noticed his premises had been taped off.

"They're scared because they think an earthquake's apt to happen again," he said to himself as he walked into his office. He felt better today. Not great but better. His right hand hurt still and his palm was lined with red scars where he held the stone. But better.

Did he want a cigar right now? The question deserved considerable thought, because he had gone through a terrible night—the only things he seemed to see in his sleep were those terrible images behind open doors. Wolves crawling on all fours, others on their hindquarters with skulls dangling from their breastplates; old Ford trucks bent into shrapnel under tons of rubble; an old man, withered like a gnarled branch, writing on rough leather with weak fingers and a peculiar glee in his eyes. Edwin skipped the cigar, he didn't need one right now—a cigar wouldn't shake the undeniable certainty that his mind was 'out-of-whack'; a cigar wouldn't close the doors Robert Innis had inadvertently opened—*but was it an accident he opened what he did?*

Edwin pushed on the wall that was actually a door, and heard the rock arm slip back into the fill. If he hadn't reacted as quickly as he did, or if he had forgotten to grab the stone around his neck, then he would have been a goner, he would have seen a bright flash before his lights turned out. When Edwin entered the room behind the fireplace he saw Leo hunkered against the robot; his face was firmly planted against its arm, and though Edwin couldn't see Leo's left hand, he knew exactly where it was. Leo had fallen asleep this way, presumably waiting for Edwin to show up; his fingers had pinched the frayed wire, and held it as close as possible to the circuit so that when Edwin did show up, he could just simply snap it in place and close his eyes as he heard his flesh pop and burn. Leo did hear the rock arm pull back, but he hadn't opened his eyes soon enough—the crumble of stone had been, at least to Leo, a part of his dream.

Edwin reacted to this not because he had quick reflexes, but because he knew trust was a matter of the weak-minded; if he had trusted Leo a year ago with this same robot, he wouldn't have been standing here right now. Edwin had already been holding the stone when he walked through the door. It wasn't a matter of luck that pulled Leo away from the robot; Edwin had already brought two straps of rock from the wall before he even realized where Leo was. Both slivers of rock grappled Leo's swollen ankles and dragged him against the far wall next to the monitors, almost tearing the frayed wire from the robot.

"You're crushing my legs," Leo squirmed.

"What did I tell you?" Edwin smiled at Leo as the little man struggled against the wall.

"I—" Leo stammered, shocked and clearly frustrated.

"I take it you're finished, since you believed so adamantly that you found a way to beat me." Edwin rubbed his fingers on the loose red wire, which had been pulled so roughly from the robot that it hung straight out.

"You don't understand," Leo said, "I heard noises all day yesterday, so I stood guard by the robot."

"Ah, so in your service to the robot, you felt compelled to hold this very trip wire, which I'm sure turns on the robot, and at the very sign of trouble you were going to what—stab the wire in and listen to the explosion? Is this even logical Leo? Am I to believe that by guarding the robot, you also imply your insistence to blow *it* up?"

Leo struggled a moment longer with the cuffs around his ankles, realized they weren't going to loosen, then stood straight and looked at Edwin. The side of his face hurt where Jimmy had punched him, but it wasn't that bad. "It sounded like there was a war outside. I heard explosions, I felt the ground shake. I was just protecting myself."

"Ah, protecting yourself. It seems selfishness runs in your blood, Leo. Did you not just lose my stepson for the same reason? You let the wolves take him instead of you, am I right?"

Leo gulped because he knew he'd have to tell Krollup about Jimmy too. "Yes, you're right," he finally said. "But I tried to do you a service in return.

I don't know about your wife, sir, but your other stepson seemed quite eager to retrieve Cole; he came down here too."

"Yes, I supposed just as much. If one of them knew about the mines, so would the other." Edwin glanced down the tunnel. Those little brats—those little *spying* brats. The wolves could have them if they were going to be so sneaky—so *damned* underhanded.

"I tried to stop him," Leo said.

"You did a poor job."

"He's down there now, too."

"So?"

"So…you're sending this robot down the mines to—to explode, right?" Edwin looked at Leo fiercely. "You'll see."

"I don't mean to be presumptuous, but isn't there a chance both Cole and Jimmy might be near the—near the robot when it happens?"

Edwin looked like he hadn't thought of this yet. He turned away for a moment. For some reason he seemed older. Leo didn't know why, but looking at Krollup under the light bulbs seemed to give him inexplicable age; his eyes seemed sunken and his forehead drooped until his brow was a furrow of hair and deep wrinkles. He looked at the robot and ran his hand down the arch of its back. "How does it work?"

"It's operated by remote control, but you didn't bring it with you. It can be set with a timer, but time is very difficult to manipulate."

"I see. So if I set the timer for one hour, there's the possibility that the robot explodes in the mine because it actually takes, let's say, an hour and a half to get all the way through?"

"I suppose."

"So what's my best option?" Edwin asked, still staring at the robot.

"That depends on what you're using the robot for?" This was a question, and Edwin regarded the curiosity with a blunt sneer.

"Let's just say it's a message—no man gives me ultimatums."

"So you intend to send it through the mines. Then what?"

"I'll show you," Edwin said, and he left the room. He returned a few minutes later with a gray trench coat and a black fedora; he had dangling from his wrist another stone, secured by twine rather than thick gold. "Uncanny, isn't it," he said, holding the twine stone up against the gold necklace he wore around his neck. "Found the rock in the yard, shoved an 'I-bolt' in and tied the twine. It'll do." He swung the rock for a moment, and then draped the trench coat over the robot's shoulders. Leo was quickly reminded of the robot he'd sent into City Hall—the robot dressed in men's clothing, and he shuddered. Edwin set the fedora on the robot's skull, and then slowly worked both arms into the jacket's sleeves, never minding the constant rips as loose fabric caught. "Your robot at City Hall was an inspiration," Edwin said. "Nobody could differentiate it from their surroundings; it became one of them, you might say, part of the crowd. There's a vicious sentiment in the notion really; believing this cold, inanimate thing might be mistaken as one of *us*, but our ignorance is truly noted. Little did folk know that in mere seconds they could have all been dead, right?"

Leo nodded. It was no use telling Krollup that the robot he had sent in was a dud.

"Life is like that, I suppose, formed on circumstances budding on the horizon. Some people are lucky, and consequence never truly greets them. Others make poor decisions, and they meet the unfortunate circumstances of their choices. I want Kenneth Auger to acknowledge this one truth."

"Kenneth Auger?" Leo asked, quite shocked.

"If this robot passes as me, Leo, then Auger will realize he made two mistakes: one of which was his belief that I might comply with his ultimatums; the other was his belief that I would actually come down the mines myself, instead of the poor robots he insisted I leave in the mines this time—*your* poor robots. So I ask you again, Leo, what's my best option?"

Leo struggled with this. He didn't know the answer, or, he didn't know the *right* answer. "I guess you could rely on curiosity."

"On curiosity? That's it, that's all you can come up with? You designed this thing for crying out loud."

"I know, it's just, well, it was intended for use with a remote control."

"Now you're implying this is my fault then, because I didn't bring your stupid remote?"

The rocks binding Leo's feet grew tighter, and Leo could hear his bones grinding. Soon he was sure they would shatter. "No, it's my fault, I forgot to mention the remote," Leo grunted through his teeth. "There are several spots on the robot that if merely touched will detonate the bomb. I'm just mentioning this because the wolves seemed so eager to pull my other robots apart." Leo tried to bend down and stick his fingers between the rock and his flesh, but he couldn't reach that far.

Edwin loosened the rock and Leo felt the blood circulate his legs again. He let out a relieved sigh. "Of course," Edwin finally said. "That way, it will only go off if somebody touches it. If it were on the timer, there's no guarantee, but this way, this way there's more than a guarantee, there's a—there's an obligation, a contractual certainty," Edwin said, and he pulled aside the long gray trench coat to fit the red wire into place; there was a loud beep and the robot's eyes lit up a murky yellow where sensors danced across the inset of the dome like scanners. Edwin dangled the fake stone necklace on the robot's arm, and then pushed it into the mine; its wheels (which were so tiny you could barely notice them) rolled over the stony ground beautifully. "Let's hope the noise of the explosion carries."

It would. It would carry throughout two worlds.

2

Jimmy was slung over the bareback of a horse. He was still unconscious, and had been since he left the ruins. The ruins were far behind them now, against the horizon like dark bricks, shattered into mere fragments of what once had been a massive precipice. In a way they were like teeth, the rotten fangs of the decrepit world, but the masked Hunter tried not to think of these things. They were riding northwest, through the badlands. There was a breeze from the Indin Sea, nothing that cooled the flesh, but it still felt refreshing.

The horse was at a steady trollop, and if it weren't for the Hunter holding onto Jimmy's sides, he would have been bucked off.

"Where am I?" The Hunter heard the young boy say; it was a weak voice, rather irritable, yet soothing in its own way.

"Barraca, just past the border of Cordoba," the Hunter replied in a whisper.

"Where?"

"Try not to speak now. We shall speak in time. Your body needs rest."

Jimmy had been slung over the horse so that his face was placed against the steed's firm side; in other words, when he woke up, it was the smells that initially produced curiosity, the distant birdsong and the phantom clopping. He remembered he had gone into the mines, and he had remembered his cigarette rolling along the gnarled backs of rats, but this—this was just ridiculous.

"Stop, PLEASE STOP!" Jimmy screamed. His gut hurt, and his eyes felt as if they were going to fall out of his jostling skull.

The Hunter slapped the side of the horse and it gradually came to a halt. "Hai Jilay," the Hunter said. "Hai Jilay."

Jimmy pushed himself up, finding footholds against the thick flank of the horse, digging his sneakers into the hide as if he were rock climbing. He could feel something coming up; oh yeah, he was sure of it... Jimmy vomited over the side of the horse, decorating the dead grass in runny chunks.

He wiped his lip and coughed. He couldn't catch his breath. He felt a hand rubbing his back. He turned to look into a face concealed under a mask. "Who are you?" Jimmy asked startled, looking both at the Hunter and at the surrounding area.

"Ashton, son of David," the Hunter said, bowing his head until his cropped hair almost touched Jimmy's chin.

"Where am I?"

"The Deadlands—these pastures are where the spread of disease lasted longest...*persisted*...when the mountains came down."

"I see," Jimmy said, and then he pushed Ashton in the chest, and the Hunter nearly toppled over backwards. The boy jumped from the horse, almost landing in his puke, and he took off, ignoring the pain in his sides, the constant aggravation of his uncertainties. He ran in utter panic, hiis tin box slapping his leg with every stride, and he seemed to think the harder he ran, the faster he'd realize that he was still outgunning the rats, that the sour air had somehow placed this delusion around him—as if the rats were showing him hope before they devoured him.

What had he come down for anyway? Oh right, Cole. But Jimmy was sure the rats had already eaten Cole. Cole was a slow runner, and Cole didn't have a lit cigarette to fend the rodents off with—oh the constant jabbering about smokes, about health. Cole was all wrong. Cigarettes had actually prolonged Jimmy's life, for the time being at least.

And then, as unbelievable as it may have sounded, Ashton the Hunter landed five feet in front of Jimmy. He had been running, staring straight forward, waiting for the stupid darkness to return, and that horrifying scuttle as hundreds of feet and red eyes followed behind him—and then he had seen that man in the mask flip over his head and land in front of him, holding his arms out as if to catch him.

"Move outta my way," Jimmy said, and he readied himself for the contact. He held his right arm in front of him, emulating that ridiculous Heisman pose—Ashton wasn't a big man; he was actually quite slender. The hilt of the sword over his shoulder seemed like enough weight to collapse his collarbone. Jimmy didn't necessarily feel threatened by the fact that this man carried a sword. Jimmy ran into Ashton believing he would move through the guy like a hand through cigarette smoke, but he didn't; instead his arm caught in the side of Ashton's shirt like a fist in a jar, and Jimmy was instantly twirled until both legs let out. He spun to the ground and rolled in the grass. His tin box dug into his thigh, and he lay there in the dirt, looking at the sky, waiting, just waiting to feel that sword pierce his heaving chest. But—

He felt a hand tug at him, and then lift him to his feet.

Ashton dusted off Jimmy's front and stared at the boy. Ashton was just as confused and curious as Jimmy, but he was a Hunter, and Hunters rarely showed emotion.

"Just let me go," Jimmy said, and he pushed the Hunter away again. He took his tin box out and opened it, grabbing a cigarette. He stuck it between his lips and remembered he didn't have anything to light it with. "Ah crap," he said under his breath.

"What is that?"

"What do you care?"

Ashton shrugged and cocked his eye. It was hard to tell what the rest of his face was doing under the mask.

"Look chief, you got a light? What am I saying, you're probably not even there. None of this is. I'm dreaming." Jimmy looked around him and patted his chest, as if he might find something around his ribcage.

"There's your light," Ashton said, pointing to the sun beyond the weird blue sky.

"Uh yeah, good one. Look, I need a lighter, matches, FIRE, before I go haywire here, okay chief."

"Fire," Ashton said. He picked up a handful of dead grass and rolled it in his fingers as he unsheathed his sword.

"Whoa, wait there, okay, I'm sorry I pushed you."

Ashton shifted the blade and held the grass outwards. He caught the sun on the sword and concentrated on the grass as he rolled it. A few seconds later the dead grass sprung tendrils of smoke, lighting into thin fingers of fire. "Fire," Ashton said with smug satisfaction.

Jimmy snatched the rolled grass from the Hunter's fingers and lit his smoke. He seemed to calm down. "Okay, this is real enough. You can't fake this feeling," Jimmy said. He cocked his eye at the Hunter. "Ashton, right?"

The Hunter nodded, watching the cigarette and the smoke rise from the burning tip in awkward patterns.

"Where am I?"

"I don't like to retrace my steps. I already answered you."

"Okay, why don't we go this route. I was just in some mines, and now I'm not. What happened?" He sucked on his smoke.

"I got you before the wolves could."

"Good, good, I suppose you want a medal Leatherface. Now tell me, have you seen another kid my age, a little big around the middle?"

"I did."

"You did?"

Ashton nodded.

"Good, then where did he go? The sooner I find him, the sooner I can go home and tell the cops I didn't do anything wrong."

"With the wolves."

"I see, well, I'm just going to walk around you here and go on my way."

Ashton lifted his sword so quickly that Jimmy hadn't taken a step before the blade was pressed against his front. "You're not going anywhere young one, for the wise man desires to see you."

Jimmy took two more puffs of his cigarette and then stomped it out on the ground. "Look Leatherface, I've gotta find my brother, okay? Anyway, I don't know any wise men. My grandpa's are both dead—so is my dad, and my mom always told me to be aware of guys like you, using my relations to sucker me into getting a lift. Tell me, what's the family password? You gotta know it if you think some old wise man seems to want to see me, cause Leatherface, I don't know any old men."

"This brother you seek was carried by the wolves from the ruins into Wolf Country. I watched, because the old man beyond the woods informed me—*instructed* that I must bring to him the person who exits the rocks before the wolves can reach him. This is a battle against time now, so we must hurry. The wolves may be gaining ground already."

"Errrrr—that's the wrong answer, the family password is 'see ya, I'm outta here'." Jimmy slid around the sword draped across his front and walked toward the distant rock shambles.

"We can get your brother."

"I don't need your help," Jimmy said.

"You presume you can face the wolves then, a boy with burning sticks?"

"I'll throw rocks at them. Plus, I'm sure Cole's already eaten plenty of them. When that boy gets hungry, anything in his path is potentially a meal. We *used* to have a family dog." Jimmy snickered, and half expected this Ashton freak to dive bomb over his head again.

"Your brother was nearly dead."

Jimmy stopped and turned around. He looked concerned, but he also seemed skeptical. "You're just saying that."

"In the wars, the wolves played with us, you know; they would gently run their claws down our bodies, and dab their tongues on our necks until we stunk of them. They had their fun, but games end. Wolves are as serious as men, and when they grew bored of playing, they would use their claws to roll our bowels out, and their tongues to lick up the blood. Your brother has a certain purpose with these wolves you know, and for now he is a means of playtime, but when this purpose of his ends, I am sorry to say—"

"What?"

"The wise man in the woods knows they are planning something—something he has feared for a long time. Though it used to be a fear he could push back and forget. I cannot say why, but I assume now that your brother's position has reversed this, and I have seen in clarity the wolves motives for this; they have taken this boy from the tunnels because someone on the other end may miss him, isn't that why you ventured down?"

Jimmy nodded. Ashton had gradually worked his way towards Jimmy until their eyes were level.

"I suggest you be careful on your journey for your brother. I don't think they will let him go that easily. Trust me, you will wish for death when they have you strung up in your own cage next to your brother."

"What are you talking about?" Jimmy sounded skeptical, but Ashton heard genuine fear in the boy's voice, like the wavering smoke from that burning stick.

"Just a warning is all. It is luck you need if you believe you can heroically face Grak Ulak." Ashton turned around and walked back to his horse, which stood sniffing the grass, not daring to eat it.

"Listen, I understand you're trying to scare me because I outsmarted you... you're just grumpy cause a kid didn't fall for your old man bit, Leatherface." Jimmy hesitated for a moment, between walking away and heading back to the horse. Ashton had intended this of course. Jimmy's real motivation wasn't Ashton's semantic babbling, but a terrible feeling that what he spoke may have been the truth.

Then there was an explosion. It came from behind Jimmy; he was facing Ashton, who had mounted his horse, his sword twisting on his back. Ashton heard this, of course, but had ignored it, perhaps using it as further incentive to draw Jimmy back to him, and towards the wise man beyond the woods.

"What was that?" Jimmy yelled.

"The wolves," Ashton said. In fact, he didn't know what that sound was; he did know that it scared him, that it drove him to draw the slope on his chest and hope to Mystic that the world wasn't coming to an end before he could drive his blade into the skull of Grak Ulak.

Jimmy took one look behind him, at the rotten teeth of the world like shadows on the ground; he thought he saw a vague black smoke billowing over the crooked crests, but he was sure he was dreaming; this was all a dream, he thought, but even in dreams you didn't want to feel abandoned.

"Hold on, please, hold on," Jimmy said, as he hurried towards the horse. He had grabbed a handful of rocks from the ground when the Hunter's back was turned, shoving them deep in his pockets. If Leatherface got rough with him, then Jimmy would bash his skull in or something. "You promise we'll get my brother?"

Ashton turned to the boy. "I promise."

3

Cole had been curled against the corner of the pavilion, tucking his knees into his chest; his vision seemed perfect now, and he tried not to look towards the birdcage with that thing in it, *that* mind reader with the ugly strands of hair and the missing hand and arm. Sometimes he would plug his ears when that thing would plead for him to untie its neck; he could hear it gagging, and then it would stop breathing, but he could tell it wasn't dead, he could hear the thing's pallid legs squirming over the iron floor of the cage, pushing through bird crap and dried blood.

This is the end, he thought. No, he *knew*.

He knew this was the end not only because everything around seemed real enough—the smell and the sounds—but because he had touched Kenneth Auger, had felt the old man's loose bones roll along his palm when he shook his hand.

"Cole, please help me, loosen these cords and take this bloody blindfold off. PLEASE COLE!" that thing yelled from the cage, and Cole stuck his fingers into his ears as hard as he could, until he almost heard a gruesome pop.

"Shut up," Cole said under his breath, as he rolled towards the ugly hide strung around him. *Don't worry Cole, they don't want to hurt you, you're a means to an end*, some strange voice of reason said.

"Yeah, the end of the mines," Cole muttered through tears.

This was how time had passed for poor Cole—living to believe the imagination wasn't just a sublet of fantasy, but was real. In his head he believed monsters were a part of another world, a world adults forgot because the advent of responsibility became their true fear—working in a job and paying taxes while starting a family that relied on them. Fears grew from maniacal to economical, and monsters under the bed turned into the IRS with the All Seeing Eye, but Cole realized none of this was true, because the IRS was just a mask. Something adults put over their faces so they wouldn't have to succumb to their childish fears. The IRS was an excuse, almost a hesitation really, an uncertainty that adults used; the IRS was demonized because it put pressure on grown ups' responsibilities, but adults knew, for some reason, that those other *things* hadn't died with their childhood, but grew from roots into something too large to comprehend. The imagination was almost like your peripheral vision in that sense, because Cole knew the world was built on two legs: things we understand, and things we don't, so we tend to shift the latter into a heap disguised with excuses. Cole figured that his being here, surrounded by a caged mind reader and werewolves and dead miners, had been in fact his acceptance to believe that his imagination was real, becoming a version of the world's other leg. He didn't like to believe this; he didn't like to believe this was even a possibility, but he had seen the werewolves, he had touched the old miner, and he had smelt his hand afterwards and recognized the pungent stench—liquor. This was real because both worlds seemed to collide.

Cole was picked up from the ground and he opened his eyes.

"Get up," a dark voice said. He was dragged outside, where the sun was bright, and the land was covered in bones.

4

"This is it, he has decided to make the trade," the old man said, standing by Jarak the Wolf, holding his cane in his arthritic hand as if it were a gearshift. "One can only presume if it was because I produced the baseball analogy—impinging on private grounds."

"The what?" Jarak asked in his deep guttural voice.

"Nothing," Auger said, and he watched the figure on the bluff stand still, the necklace dangling from an outstretched arm like a gift to a lover. He could hear the boy struggling behind him, and he anticipated another throaty wail when the kid caught sight of him again. It had initially worried him that Cole didn't yelp in fear when he saw the Yilaks, but he realized this boy was a product of urban legends, and back on the surface assumptions of the old man's supposed death in the mines were prevalent tales. He could taste the liquor in his breath and he wondered if it had changed any up there on the surface—the Brandy, the Scotch, Rum and Cognac. Maybe his tongue had been slowly dying also, and the drink was becoming tainted to his tastes—he hated to suggest his impending death had any impact on his booze, but he wanted to look for the higher light. If he felt alive again, if he felt old age whither away from him, then he knew for some reason that everything would seem better; it was commonsense really. "I don't trust him entirely," the old man said.

Jarak studied the old man; the wolves howled at the bluff around them.

"Well then, get it you fool," Grak said from behind him. "Your trade was successful, was it not?"

The old man shuddered. "I do not know if I trust this yet." Mrak the Wolf brought Cole next to the old man, and Auger looked down at him for a moment; the boy had been crying, but something about his eyes bred a certain understanding, an acceptance almost. *You were hesitating to believe at first, weren't you boy? You were confused, maybe thought you were dreaming, but now, now everything is real, isn't it?*

"Ah, you are a coward old man, though death should not shock you for you're already at its doorstep." Grak walked beside Cole and the boy cowered. The skulls on Grak's breastplate knocked together like a morbid wind chime. "Tell him to come down here, why don't you? For if he feels he would deceive us, then he has taken his own son's life." Grak picked Cole up in his gangly arm and held a curled claw under the boy's throat. "Tell him to come down old man."

Auger looked at Cole's eyes; he watched them grow horribly aware. "Grak, please, put him down, this isn't about him."

"A man does not tell a Yilak what to do," Grak growled.

Auger realized arguing wouldn't help—not that he could argue with Grak. The old man turned to Jarak, who had seeming consolation in his yellow eyes. "Would you call him down here, for my throat is sore and my voice weak?"

Grak growled again. "If you do so Jarak, believe I will skin you and dress the Black Hounds with your hide. You will not heed man's order."

Jarak looked at the old man with those same apologetic eyes, and licked his muzzle. Jarak wouldn't dare argue with Grak either. Not now. Grak believed the old man could bring the stone back; he believed in this other world of which the old man spoke. It was Grak who had *agreed* to go to the woods for the egg sac. Grak had responded to the old man's order then, but now something changed, something he had seen maybe, in the eyes of the hermit mayhaps. Jarak had seen many terrible things himself in those eyes; he was sure Grak had seen his own plagues. Grak had murdered his father for control of the tribes. Jarak held a bitter grudge against Grak for this, but Grak had grown more powerful than any Yilak; those in his shadow trembled. Jarak grew to understand the wolf's drive; he was bound by the illusion that his purpose was absolute control—the spite in Grak's red eyes, the certainty of his dominance established one thing: it cemented his absolute command over them.

"Do it yourself old man, or there will be no trade to make," Grak said, pushing his claw against Cole's throat.

The old man stumbled forward, feeling the definite age of his bones as his ankles crunched against the hard ground. He wanted another bottle with him, but had nothing; it was all in his wagon. Whatever he had left, that is. "Come down," he said, and he knew his voice was little more than a whisper. He felt more and more nervous as he stepped forwards. "Come down."

Grak laughed behind him. "You expect to find control over us when you cannot speak? The world of man is stupid." The wolves howled, and the old man could hear Cole sob through the high shrieks.

Auger breathed in, feeling his ribcage contract in dry snaps, his diaphragm release the putrid air of a man on his deathbed. *This is all quite sad, isn't it?* Yes, it was. Once he had been a man that could bellow out to his brutes in the mines and they would listen to him, and now he was but a bag of bones that could barely whisper. He looked at the figure on the bluff, that long coat billowing out in streaks, the low drawn fedora (*styles must not have changed much—he's a mixture of Fred Astaire and Humphrey Bogart*), the necklace shifting in the wind, hanging from his outstretched arm, and all of a sudden he didn't want to call him down; he didn't want to even see him. *Because you saw something when the long coat blew to the side, you saw a shine, as if the guy was metal plated or something.* He wouldn't know that it was a robot until it was too late, but there would be this peculiar insistence to accept this as a possibility—the old man just didn't want to believe that this guy with the stone actually felt the significance of its magic was more important than his son. *You specifically told him that if he were to send down a robot—a robot like the others, wiry and dull like monochromatic thermoses on legs— there'd be consequences.* He did, but he hadn't believed the man would actually send down a robot; the threat had been a formality. The old man wasn't about to kill Cole if the figure on the bluff was a robot, because Cole was a means to an end. The boy wouldn't meet *his* end over this. *No.* The old man pushed this possibility aside because he wasn't entirely ready for it.

"BRING THE STONE DOWN HERE!" He finally screamed, and he felt like his stomach was going to drop into the back of his pants. His voice echoed. The figure on the bluff stood still, that coat flapping like a flag.

"Even your own kind doesn't feel threatened by you," Grak said in a deep voice. He still held Cole, but he had removed his claw from the boy's throat.

The old man ignored the wolf. "I suppose we're still on his terms," he said under his breath. "He knows one thing: that if he were to will it, we would all be turned to dust by two colliding boulders. WE HAVE YOUR SON COLE!" Auger screamed, and pointed his long finger at the boy hanging in Grak's arm. Nothing. The figure only stood stupidly with his arm held out and that necklace swinging to either side. "There is something going on."

"What do you mean?" Jarak asked.

"We have his son, but he plays games with us." The old man stood very confused.

"Send the men Haspin the Fat left," Grak snarled. "Obviously we're being tested, are we not? A man consumed by power does not want to feel dominated; your race has bred greedy characters, old man, and this distinction does not only seem limited to the Inlands."

"You think this is a stand off?" The old man asked.

"He would have come down by now if it wasn't."

The old man turned to Jarak. "Please carry me to my wagon."

"If you do Jarak, I will pull your arms from your sockets and choke you with them." Jarak saw the terrible look on Grak's face; his dense brow had cloaked his deep red eyes, pricking his ears against his crown of thorns.

Auger turned around and hobbled to his wagon, holding his hunched back with one hand. He told the men Haspin had left behind to prepare themselves—if this was a stand off, he was sure there could be a war.

"He waits," the old man said, his legs hanging over the edge of the wagon, a bottle stuck between his lips, as he rolled the cork along his fingertips. He was watching the figure on the bluff; the wind had picked up and that jacket was flying every which way.

He was finished his bottle by the time the wagon was hitched to the oxen, and the army had progressed toward the mountain pass. Haspin's men were atop their steeds in front of the wagon; the steady clopping of the hooves exploded films of dust in the air. "Like the Prince of Darkness," the old man said, looking at that distant billowing figure on the bluff.

5

Cole had stayed with Grak. He trudged up the path with the boy slung over the crook of his elbow.

"Stop here," the old man said, his head peeping outside his wagon. "We're not going to give him the advantage; we're not all going to march to the very top only to find ourselves pushed by some wave of rock to our death at the bottom of the edifice." He watched that long coat wave in the wind, and though he didn't have the image then, he would realize that the billowing streams of that jacket had been like black smoke—like the very black smoke that would engulf them in a few minutes.

The wolves had halted and the oxen pulling the wagon rested feebly in the shadow of a boulder.

"SHALL WE MAKE THE TRADE NOW?" The old man yelled. The figure on the bluff stood terrifically still. Auger saw the way some of the wolves looked at him, and he understood their surprise; they believed this was an attack, and in thinking such, believed they were trying to counter the stone from the back, sneaking around the path as if the figure couldn't see them. The old man stuck two twisted fingers into his mouth and whistled. Four men on horses veered and trotted up the pass, their banners flipping out behind the horse like fabric tails. "Haspin, I think your collateral may just serve its purpose," the old man said.

6

When the robot exploded it was surprise more than fear that overcame the old man. The men on horses galloped towards the figure, and the old man realized the peculiarities of the situation. "He's not moving; he's just standing there. IT'S A TRICK!"

But it was too late, not that the men on the horses would have ever known what a robot was. The shadow of the fedora cast a dim glow over the metallic face that tricked Haspin's men into believing they were actually dealing with a person. Edwin had been right after all. Some folk were ignorant of the differences between things, living and non. They had moved towards the robot with the blowing trench coat and the swinging rock; one of the men unsheathed his sword and held it out while the other three jumped from their steeds and moved cautiously forward. They would try to scream something over the loud wind, but nobody would hear them, not even the wolves, who had ears that could pick up a whisper from a mile away.

The robot exploded because the man with the sword felt it was his duty to at least present a formidable threat, and he did so by poking the billowing jacket from behind. He couldn't have known any better of course, and he wouldn't have time to dwell on it, but as he reached out with the blade of his sword a subtle part of him shook his head in instant understanding—there was something entirely wrong with this guy. He didn't turn to face them when they approached, and though the soldier carrying the sword had been young, and hadn't actually used his sword in battle, he knew a peculiar mannerism when he saw one. Even if the old man had realized sooner, had even guessed the robot might explode, there wouldn't have been enough time. When the sword touched the jacket, and pushed it into the hulk of the robot there was this deafening thud as the robot's head exploded, sending the tattered fedora into the sky like a smoldering meteorite. This blast sent all four soldiers back against the rock face and their horses into a frenzy; the sword that had detonated the blast was flung over the bluff.

This triggered the next explosion, the big explosion, the explosion Jimmy heard, which persuaded him to stay with Ashton; the explosion Haspin and Lor heard as they moved toward the Leeg Forest, both confused and curious; and the explosion Leo would hear as the echoes carried into the mines. The robot's abdomen, which was a series of cables, pulsated slightly—nobody saw this of course—and then erupted as plates of steel shot outwards like molten Frisbees. The cables disintegrated, and there was a momentary stench of plastic.

The old man was thrown into the back of his wagon, breaking a bottle with his elbow; he didn't remember doing this, but his ears rang with this high shriek until his brain felt like it might ooze out his ears into a puddle around him. The blast seemed to explode upwards, as a billowing black smoke was sucked into the sky like the tails of the robot's long jacket. Jarak the Wolf watched this, amazed; he had never seen fire act like this before. He had never known fire to act so violently, so *independently*—these thoughts were pure shock though, because Jarak had been knocked backwards, and had rolled halfway down the mountain pass. Ilak the Wolf had started on fire, and Ajak had lost most of his fur, his bare chest so badly burned that his slivers of exposed flesh looked like discolored hair.

Grak had watched the towering flames with a growing awareness of what had actually happened. The hot wind blew by him like a giant's fist, but he only stood with his legs apart, his fur matted to his oily flesh like legions of leaches, listening to the She-wolves howl below him from the tents. He stood with Cole in his arms; Cole with his hands pressed firmly over his ears, also watching the flames, and watching the wolves that had strayed too close. The rock face was decorated with bodies, as if they had been ironed to the stone; there were thick spurts of blood mixed with tarnished black on the boulders.

The old man had rolled toward the front of the wagon, holding his arm close to his chest. "Everybody off the pass. The blast may have woken sleeping stones," he screamed. He looked around him, at the towering walls of rock, searching for clear cracks that had become defined after the explosion, looking for dust where cliffs had split and were ready to spill tons of sediments down its side.

The smoke had been progressively carried away with the wind, and the ground at the edge of the bluff had turned an ashen gray; bits of that long coat had been cemented to the rock and burned into pieces of twine.

The wolves all howled.

Grak dropped Cole on the ground. The old man watched the wolf's figure like a bleak shadow against the grainy smog.

"SHUT UP OLD MAN, FOR YOUR BELIEFS HAVE TRICKED US. HOW ARE WE NOT TO KNOW YOU TOLD THE MAN WITH THE STONE TO SEND DOWN FIRE?" Grak screamed in a tremendous howl. Grak turned and looked at the wagon with his red eyes, and he got down on all fours, the sound of his claws ticking against the stone like cracking bones. He jumped at the wagon and shook it on its wheels; the oxen yelped. "Was this your plan, old man, to bring us to the cliff and watch the lot of us burn in your fires?" Grak licked his muzzle.

The old man had been puzzled enough without this. He didn't know what to say.

"Grak, this isn't about him now, he wouldn't have come with us if he knew," Jarak said from behind the wagon, and Grak shot the wolf an angry glance.

"So you have chosen paths, Jarak. You were always prone to following my father; you reason just like a human. It is your instinct you deny," Grak snarled, and he uttered a deep growl.

"There is no sense finding blame, Grak, for it is in the man with the stone you should place fault," Jarak said.

Grak barked and snapped at Jarak with his scarred muzzle, drops of spittle flying from his lips like marbles. "And it is the man with the stone who will pay," Grak said.

And the wolves charged the mines.

For it was their call to war.

7

The old man had been, at first, too surprised to react. He never believed the man with the stone would send down a robot that would endanger his own son. "You are not loved," he said to the boy, who couldn't hear him, but sat on the ground breathing hard, transfixed by the waning black smoke and the trails of dust left by the wolves as they rushed into the mines. The old man absently rubbed his elbow and chewed on his bottom lip.

"Bring me the boy," he finally said, and Jarak looked at the old man, who had grown madder over time. His eyes were vacant, disbelieving almost. He looked at the Towers; the three columns of rock that split the air like jagged daggers. Somewhere in those turrets lived a King, a King the old man had once served, consumed by his powers; a King who had made for himself a tomb where he could live in the magnificence of his riches eternally, because he drank from the vial of wizard's blood he wore around his throat.

Jarak, who had stayed behind as the wolves dashed—at least he believed—to their death at the hands of the stone, picked up Cole and brought him back to the wagon, setting him in the plush lining gently.

I'm mad, Auger thought, but he ignored the sentiment. Instead he had the oxen turn the wagon around and felt the cart bump as the mountain pass beneath rocked the wheels. The explosion was behind him now.

"Your father made a mistake," he finally said to Cole, who was huddled against the corner.

"My father's dead," Cole said silently.

"What?"

"My father's dead." Cole's face was covered in ash and dust.

"I would believe the same thing if my father had betrayed my captors, instead of rescuing me."

"I don't understand what's going on," Cole said, and he didn't, he just accepted the fact, for now at least, that he was in a fur lined wagon with a man he had believed was once a haunting of the mines.

The old man arched his scruffy eyebrows and pinched his elbow between two gnarled fingers. He looked away when he spoke, because a part of him hadn't gone mad yet, a part of him had actually accepted death. "I feel my heart stopping every day," he said in a soft voice. "Everyday for the last forty-six years I have feared death. I have thought about it."

Cole heard something in that voice, something he realized existed without reason, and he understood he was in real trouble. He had, of course, known this before, as he sat listening to an ugly creature squirm in a large birdcage, and as he was dangled from the gangly arm of a werewolf, but it wasn't until now that he fully considered the danger—because now he sensed it not from the wolves or the thing in the cage, but from an old man sitting across from him. He realized man *was* the monster (a notion Krollup helped to actualize), and instead of dwelling on his fears, as he had incessantly done at school, he reacted.

"There are ways into the Towers, ways you can crawl," the old man had been saying in a low whisper to himself, "but the tomb, I don't know where that is—I don't know if it is even a tomb, or if it is a throne, a room hidden by darkness, beyond the touch of evil shrouding that place—"

Cole dove from the corner of the cart and pushed the old man into the ledge; he did this so quickly that Auger had still been talking to himself as he was nudged into the side of the cart, and had been cut off by a long grunt as he felt his back crack. Cole drew aside the flap in the hide and jumped from the moving wagon, rolling down the pass when he hit the ground. Cole sprang up and started to run back up the path, towards the black smoke.

"GET HIM!" The old man screamed from the wagon; his voice was choked with pain.

Cole sprinted. He didn't look back, he just ran for the top of the path. Even when Jarak the Wolf grabbed him, he still figured he had a chance; he even heard his father's voice again, telling him not to worry, and for that one second he didn't.

The old man breathed furiously. This had been an especially bad day.

And for that there were punishments. And rewards. Always rewards.

CHAPTER 14

Wanderer of the Corridor

1

Edwin could hear the robot wheeling down the mine, the flap of that long coat and the screech as its feet swayed around rocks its sensors picked up.

"Oh I wish I could see what's going to happen," he said in a voice like a child's, filled with morbid anticipation.

Leo had been standing next to him, staring down the mines himself, trying hard not to think about the pain in his ankles and the possibility Cole might get hurt—Jimmy too, but something in Leo suggested the older brother could fend for himself; he rubbed his chin and the side of his face when he thought about this.

"Do you think it will work?"

Leo looked at Edwin with contempt. "Yes sir, I'm sure it will."

"*Sure* doesn't make you seem certain, little man. If I don't hear an explosion, I'm holding you to blame."

"I just don't like to think about Cole and Jimmy getting hurt."

"Oh, so *now* you care about the boys, when you seemed quite happy at first that it wasn't you the wolves snatched. You know Leo, you're like some of the men I deal with downtown—a hypocrite, only I think you're much worse because you put your life in front of a child's." Edwin gave a leer smile. He was evil. His tone and gaze suggested just as much.

Leo just stared down—that wasn't true, he really had no choice. The wolves had knocked him out when they took Cole, and Edwin was just trying to make him feel guilty. He would love to see the wolves do the same to Edwin, but he knew, deep down, that he would never get the chance—things like that rarely happened to men like Edwin Krollup, whose power held them on an elevation above most.

"Shhh," Edwin said after a minute. "Did you hear that?"

"I don't think it would have exploded yet sir."

"No, not an explosion idiot. The doorbell." Edwin turned his head for a moment and held his breath. He walked over to the sheet of rock he had formed over the fireplace stack, touched the stone around his neck and the wall crumbled to the ground as if something inside had imploded. A plume of black smoke that had seeped through the bricks briskly hovered around the room. Leo coughed and Edwin shushed him.

And then Leo could hear it too—a doorbell, a long ring that he had heard many times before. But now it was eerie. The house was too quiet, and Leo realized he and Edwin must have been alone.

"Who could that be?" Edwin said in a furious tone. "I thought I got the message through last night," he said under his breath. He looked at Leo fiercely. "Make sure the robot doesn't explode until I get back."

"How am I going to do that?"

"Just do it," Edwin said, and the rock arm blocked the door when he left the room.

2

When Edwin opened the front door he wore a fake smile that was as transparent as glass; he thought for sure it was going to be Detective Saul on the front step with the alarming news that Mario the lawn technician hadn't taken the boys. It wasn't though. It wasn't a cop, nor was it another one of those pesky fellows from the Seismic Society, who pleaded that he get away from the house so they could test the safety of the grounds. No, standing before him, wearing a black shirt and a blazer with ironed lapels, was Robert Innis, his psychologist.

"Oh Edwin, I am so sorry," he said, and he grabbed Edwin's hand ferociously and pumped it up and down until it felt like his arm was being yanked from its socket. "I saw everything on the news—*everything*. How are you holding up?" He stepped into the house, his loafers squeaking on the cracked marble, still holding Edwin's hand tightly in his own. "I just had to get over here right away; this isn't right, none of this, and I just wanted to walk you through this, just in case you need my guidance, that is."

Edwin pulled his hand away from the doctor's. He wanted to hear the robot explode of course, but this was so unexpected; he wanted to shut some doors inside his head once and for all. He grabbed Robert by the collar and threw him against the wall, cuffing him with his forearm. "Tell me what you did to me."

Robert gasped and struggled for a moment. "I don't understand?" He said in a slight whisper that barely escaped his cinched lips.

Edwin leaned in closer until his nose almost touched Robert's, and he said very slowly, "what...did...you...do...to...me?"

"I'm sorry, I...don't know what you're talking about."

Robert could feel the stone in front of him, could feel some weird vibrations coming from it, and he wanted nothing but to slide it around *his* neck.

Edwin let Robert drop from the wall. "What are you referring to?" Robert asked. He had believed, for a brief moment, that Edwin had really seen him and his cousin watching the house from the boxy Caprice—and had gradually come to believe that he, Robert Innis, was a part of this kidnapping the news had been splashing all over the place.

Edwin stood with his arms crossed, staring out the open front door, over the damage of the earthquake. The front gate hung askew from its hinges, as if one swift nudge from the wind would knock it to the ground with a loud clatter; his yard was split in places, and strewn with broken rock and white dust. His statues were merely fragments now, and he had realized that as he hung suspended, engulfed by the smoke of the breaking pedestals, the statues had nearly come to life on their own, without his even telling them to do so. The stone had commanded them, and they had taken care of business. "I find it rather convenient, Robert, that our hypnosis session was uninhibited by a recording device, don't you?" He didn't turn to look at the psychologist; he only stared outside, where Robert had parked his Mercedes by the broken gate, tearing through police tape to do so.

"I told you, the recorder broke, and ate the tape. I told you that."

"Yes, it's just I find it convenient for you that I have no knowledge of what it is you spoke to me about for nearly forty-five minutes."

"Your father."

"So you say," Edwin said, and he turned to look at Robert. "Tell me something. Why did you really come here?"

Robert looked uncertain for a moment. The question was reasonable, but hadn't he already answered it by claiming his visit was due to worry? "I saw the news. I figured you'd want to talk. This hasn't been a good couple of weeks for you."

"No, it hasn't, it really hasn't," Edwin said, and he laughed. "I just find it coincidental that you show up at my door at about the same time I figured I'd call you for a session. You *were* quite adamant to hypnotize me."

"To help the way I saw fit," Robert said uncertainly.

"I feel different now, you know that."

"How so?"

"I feel like there are things opened to me—things I've forgotten, things I shouldn't be seeing so clearly. I feel like there's a projectionist in my head, do you understand me?"

"A projectionist? That's odd."

"Isn't it. Why did you really come here, Robert?" Edwin walked a slow circle around the psychologist. "Was it because you saw that I had called you yesterday? Was it because you had implanted in my head the very idea that you would be coming around about this time, and that I should feel I need your assistance?" He smiled.

"Are you okay Edwin?"

"May I presume you're carrying a new recorder, one that presumably works, and your little pendant, the one that will aid in the hypnosis?"

Robert grinned. "I always carry them around with me." He patted his suit jacket.

"Then why was the pendant in your desk the day you hypnotized me?"

"Is there a point to this Edwin, or are you just jerking me around? Look, I came to make sure you were all right, okay. I hear on the news—*the news*—that your stepsons have been kidnapped on the same day there's an earthquake at your house, and I wonder why I have to hear this on television when I'm just a phone call away—I mean, I *am* your shrink. Listen Edwin, you can play your blame games for as long as you like, but you can't expect me to play them with you."

"You guys are always so good at reverse psychology—I mean, you did invent it—" Edwin said, but he was abruptly cut short, as he fell forward in a heap on the ground.

Eddie, Robert's cousin, stood over Edwin rubbing his knuckles.

"It's about time. Close the door and help me haul him over to that chair," Robert said, and he pulled the pendant from his pocket and let it dangle from his fingers.

3

"You sure he's not going to know about this?" Eddie asked.

"He'll remember what I want him to remember, Eddie. I can give him false memories if I want to. Now stand behind the chair and hold his arms behind him. I'm going to wake him up. When I do, try to tilt his head so I can dangle the necklace in front of him and put him under the spell." Robert and Eddie had dragged Edwin's body to a chair that had been in the hallway outside the Great room.

Eddie braced his legs against either chair leg, which were solid mahogany, and he hugged his chest against the back of the chair as he draped each arm around Edwin's front with both hands pushed under his chin. "Geez, I gave him a lump," he said. Through a small part in Edwin's hair, Eddie could see blood and a goose egg.

"No matter, I can make him believe that he fell down the stairs like an oaf. Hold him that way. Do you have a good grip?"

Eddie nodded.

Robert looked at Edwin for a moment. Why it had finally come to this he was unsure, but he knew for some reason there would be no other way to hypnotize Edwin without a credible witness over his shoulder the whole time; he knew he opened some doors inside Edwin he shouldn't have, but he had been so bombarded by the information he heard that he simply hadn't cared. Watching the news last night had given him an idea—Robert and Eddie had actually parked off on the shoulder near Hillside Road just to watch the police, the firemen and the tow trucks partially clean the mess of the earthquake, taping off the grounds certain the seismic activity wasn't entirely over. They had watched this, and Robert realized he had been right when he was watching the news—that Edwin was *still* in his house, isolating himself from everybody because he wasn't the type to give in, to claim defeat by either the ferocity of mother nature or the command of other authorities. Instead he stood his ground, and Robert realized he would have to concoct a different plan to get into the man's head again, because the doors he had obviously opened inside Edwin's mind had inevitably led to severe questioning. He had turned to Eddie, who was falling asleep in the passenger seat with his chin stabbing into his breastplate: "I have an idea, Eddie. Tomorrow we're going to knock him out; we're going to hit him on the head hard enough to knock him out, but not so hard that he won't wake up again." "Okay," Eddie had responded stupidly, saliva hanging from his lower lip like white snot.

Robert slapped Edwin on the cheek. "Wake up."

Edwin shifted, grunted, and tried to lift his arm to touch the back of his head, but instead snorted and turned his face and rubbed his nose on Eddie's fingers.

"Ah, come on," Eddie said disgustedly.

"Hold still," Robert said. "Keep his head tilted." He moved the pendant from side to side for a moment, getting it ready; it would have to be quick. Eddie was a big man, and was undoubtedly strong, but Edwin seemed motivated by something else. Even when he, Robert, had been pinned by the front door ten minutes earlier, he had felt something else, some vibration that hadn't been normal at all. "Hold him tight, Eddie, because he's sure to lash out."

Eddie nodded, and Robert slapped Edwin again. This time harder, until his head rocked back. He slightly opened his eyes, letting his jaw hang open in a dumb expression that let drool slide over his lip and collect in a pool where Eddie's hands met Edwin's face. Eddie made a disgusted face, as if to say, "come on, this is it, this is gross, lemme close his mouth or something," but Robert ignored him. Instead he slapped Edwin again.

Edwin jerked awake. He looked around blankly for a minute, saw Robert and lunged forward with a grunt. "What's going on here?"

The chair tilted, and Eddie almost fell forward; his hands unclasped and lost Edwin's jaw.

"Hold him up!"

Edwin kicked out, and the chair rocked on its back legs, knocking Eddie's thighs. Eddie gripped his hands together, choking Edwin, and he felt a thick vibration as his forearm brushed Edwin's neck. "You're making a *biiiiig* mistake," Edwin said.

"I can't hold him no more, it feels like my bones are breaking," Eddie whined, but it really did, something about this man's neck was shaking him so violently that he was certain everything inside him was coming loose.

Edwin looked at Robert and his eyes slowly turned a light red, as if his corneas were filling with cranberry juice. Robert dangled the necklace in front of Edwin's face and swung it back and forth, back and forth, in a fluid motion like a tire-swing on a tree branch. Gradually his eyes faded, and the color drained; Eddie's arms stopped shaking, and there was a loud thud, as if something behind Robert had fallen.

Eddie shouted.

He didn't mean to—it was quick and decisive, but it hadn't been wholly intentional. When he held Edwin his eyes had been closed, so when he opened them he saw what had been standing behind Robert right away. "What is it?" He whimpered.

Robert turned around, and lying on the floor three meters from his feet was a statue; its right leg was pivoted as if ready to lift, and its left had broken when the statue fell down. "Wasn't that beside the front door?" Robert asked as he stepped away from the statue, whose arms had both been held outwards as if ready to strangle anything in its path—the sight was rather discomforting.

Both he and Eddie looked towards the front hall and realized one thing: the pedestal next to the front door was empty.

"I don't wanna to be near that thing," Eddie said, and Robert agreed, so the two dragged the hypnotized Edwin into the Great room, where the fire flickered, and the fake David stood near the end windows like the general he would become.

4

He was standing in a corridor with closed doors. It was odd here, and quiet.

He stepped forward, only he didn't step, he sort of drew himself, pulling along an axis he couldn't see, but figured held him in the air like an invisible clothes line. There were thousands of doors on either side of him; the corridor seemed to go on forever, disappearing into a tiny dot in the distance.

Edwin turned and drew himself towards the door to his left; it was massive, hung on cast iron hinges, with deep lines carved in the wood by dexterous hands. He stuck his hand out and turned the giant knob, which was shaped like a lion's head, its mouth opened baring chrome fangs. Edwin didn't understand why he did this; he didn't understand where he was either, but some part of him reasonably urged that he open the door, insisted that he turn the giant knob and pull it or push it open. He didn't expect it to open, he thought it would stick, but the chrome lion's head turned, and he felt the door come towards him on those iron hinges. There was no sound as the door opened. There were vibrations, but he couldn't really feel them, he sensed them in his temples.

There was nothing on the other side of the door, only this blankness that went on forever, much like the hallway. Edwin wanted to close the door, tried to but couldn't; there was something pulling him forward, something tying his arms to his side, severing his limbs from his brain as he watched that blankness come out to him.

"*Don't listen to a word he says. Keep your doors shut,*" a voice said from the gaping nothingness beyond the opened door.

"Who are you?" Edwin heard himself say, but it was a stupid question really; he already knew who it was—it was his own guardian. Some unconscious pulse that watched everything. What he had come to know as the projectionist.

And then he felt something. His hand prickled for a moment and when he looked down he realized he was holding a key.

"*Lock them before they open—he unlocked so many of them already,*" the voice said.

Edwin turned and the door slammed; there was a deafening sound that shot down the corridor like a ripple in calm water. He plucked the key in the knob and turned it until he heard a faint click. *One down*, he thought, and looked to his side as if to humor himself—*thousands to go*.

He drew himself across the hall and locked the door with a jumbled snap. The door to his right immediately sprang open. He saw through the threshold an image he had seen once before with his own eyes: the old man, Kenneth Auger, standing in the darkness of the mine, holding his gnarled hand out.

Edwin slammed the door shut and locked it.

Another door opened in the distance.

He heard his voice coming through it: "*The mines are behind the fireplace in the Great room—the big fireplace. I put up bricks myself, but stupid Leo digs away the grout with his fingers to see, I guess.*"

Edwin pulled himself forward with that invisible clothesline; he shut the door and locked it, realizing what had been through it, what had been fixed inside the doorjamb like a portrait—Robert's smug face, inching forward with a peculiar giddiness in his eyes Edwin had never noticed before.

Another door opened, and Edwin rushed to close and lock it, each time finding Robert's face on the other side like a phantom with a picklock.

5

Robert looked at Edwin, whose face had fallen forwards, and he pocketed his pendant. A part of him insisted that he reach for the necklace, reach for the rock hanging on the end of the gold, but that was just impatience really. He had all the time in the world.

Robert tilted Edwin's chin with his fingers and stared into the man's dazed eyes; there was no recognition in them, they just sat in his sockets like marbles.

"The vault, ask him about the vault," Eddie said.

"Shut up. Edwin, do you remember our last conversation at all, because I don't feel obligated to tread discovered ground if you don't?"

Edwin opened his mouth stupidly, and sat slack-jawed, drops of saliva falling down his chin and onto Robert's fingers.

"Can you tell me where the mines are?"

Edwin sounded more like a robot when he answered than he had during their first session; he spoke in a rough monotone that became guttural and then subtle, wavering between the two in unsteady patterns. *That knock on the head did him some good*, he thought. "The mines are behind the fireplace in the Great room—the big fireplace. I put up bricks myself, but stupid Leo digs away the grout with his fingers to see, I guess."

"The Great room, yes, I knew it, didn't I tell you Robert? I did." Eddie moronically clapped his hands together in glee.

"Shut up Eddie, you'll confuse him, you'll distract him. Edwin, tell me, who is Leo and why does he scratch at the grout in between the bricks you installed?"

Edwin stared forward for a moment, his mouth still open, his tongue draped over his bottom teeth. "Sorry doc, that doors locked," he said quickly, and Robert could swear he saw a slight grin.

"Eddie, make yourself useful. Put out the fire, get rid of the bricks and check if the mines are really behind there—*sorry doc, that doors locked*, please...hurry Eddie."

Eddie jumped and ran towards the great fireplace, where he stood yesterday with his head under the mantle listening to the weird beeps behind the shoddy wall, imagining an arcade in the adjacent room; he shuddered at the giant portrait hung on the stack, that awful painted grimace on Krollup's face. The fire was dwindling away on splinters of blackened wood, and had become nothing more than thick tendrils of black smoke.

"Sorry doc, that doors locked—are you playing with me Edwin?" Robert ran his hand before Edwin's open eyes and waved it. "Edwin, are you playing with me—have you been playing with me the entire time? Did you kill your father, you murderer, you patricidal maniac?" Robert's tone changed with the last question, which sounded more like an accusation.

Edwin shifted. "I don't know. I sincerely hope not."

"What if I told you that you did, that your existence killed him, that he drunk himself stupid because he felt you were a mistake? What would you say about that?"

"I'd say he was weak..." His voice trailed off until his lips only allowed slight gasps.

Robert stood up. "You're still with me Edwin, you've just got somebody in there with you, I suppose, somebody listening, a mediator perhaps. We should fix that though." He watched Eddie pour an ice bucket of water in the fireplace and listened to the dying fire fizzle; he looked at the fake David at the far end of the room and smiled. He was working with a man incompetent enough to believe that statue had been the real thing—*that*...it was looking the wrong way! "Don't listen to whatever's in your head, *whoever's* in your head, Edwin."

"Why?"

"That's the voice that insisted you murdered your father—that's a bad voice, and we have to flush things like that out of our system."

6

A door opened ahead of him and he rushed to close it, only he hadn't been pulling himself, he was being dragged to *it*—there was something coming out of the opening, something with sharp teeth and slanted eyes that peered over at Edwin and licked its lips. "Good doctor says you killed my pa, and murderers need to be punished, I figure."

What was that thing? It had *his* voice for crying out loud, but it walked with a stagger, and it had teeth that reached over its chapped lips like deranged pearls on a rotten oyster.

"You're tainting us fella—perhaps we wouldn't be so deranged if you hadn't insisted we killed our poor pa, God bless his soul."

It was Robert's creation—Edwin didn't know why he knew this, but it had to be the truth. Robert created this thing due to a request he had given to Edwin's impressionable sub-conscious; he reacted to the door Edwin locked by producing a false prognosis—a creature built by a single lie that he, the Wanderer of the Corridor, persistently presumed Edwin was his father's murderer. It staggered forward, licking its lips, glaring its slanted eyes, which had taken an orange hue and seemed to run out of its lids: "All we gotta do is open this here door and push you through, and you can gimme that key, and all is well. Daddy's death won't be our fault anymore. Trust me; it's doctor's orders."

Edwin fell backwards, his feet slipping through the fog hovering over the ground. He could almost smell that thing, its pus, its rancid breath and the crusts building on its jagged fingernails. He looked down at the key and realized something: everything he was looking at, everything around him was ultimately *his* creation. He closed his eyes and his hand tingled again. When he opened his eyes he wasn't holding a key. He was holding a gun—the key had transformed into this gun, which seemed nicely polished and shone the flickering light. The thing with the sharp teeth stopped.

"Why do you feel you have to do this? Wasn't murdering our dear pa *enough* for you?"

Edwin grinned. Robert would notice this on the outside also, but it was more subtle there; inside the corridor, where the doors would soon flap open again, Edwin's mouth reached from ear to ear in an evil leer. He pointed the gun at the sharp-toothed monster with the runny eyes, and he shot it; there wasn't a sound, only a slight *oomph* as the creature fell back through the open door, leaving a fine mist of blood in the air, like the fog on the ground. Edwin hurried over to the door and turned the gun back into the key, simply by closing his eyes and willing it do so; he locked the door.

7

Edwin coughed. A shot of phlegm spat from his mouth and landed on the ground with a disgusting splat. "That's what I think of your creation doc," Edwin said and then he fell silent. His jaw hung open stupidly and he looked forward in that same dull daze.

Robert smiled. So Edwin did have another in there with him, another that had the capability to at least recognize the good doc's own attempts to rid of it. Robert watched Eddie throw another bucket of water on the dying fire and sat listening to it for a moment.

"This is interesting Edwin, it really is. I haven't come across this before, but I have a feeling that I know what to do." Robert closed Edwin's mouth by pressing his lower jaw upwards, clicking his teeth together when Edwin's mouth closed.

"I'll back pedal," Robert said, and he quickly thought back about their first conversation while Edwin was under his spell—the talk of Hunters and werewolves and Towers. *Hunters and werewolves and Towers, oh my...Hunters and werewolves and Towers, oh my.*

Robert heard loud cracks and looked over Edwin's shoulder to see Eddie smashing the fire poker against the bricks; he was fully submerged inside the fireplace, his body tangled in with the smoke so only his legs stuck out, and the end of the poker when he swung it back.

8

If he didn't hurry he was sure it would explode, and though he had no power over its final destination, Leo had crossed his fingers and silently pleaded that the robot wait until Krollup returned. He just didn't want to have to face any punishment, especially for something that wasn't his fault.

"I hate him," he muttered. "I hate him and I hope he fell dead on his way to the door." It was this unpleasant thought—though pleasant to Leo, you might say—he held onto as he waited, staring into the dark mines, uttering few curses in fear that Krollup might wander in just as he began another rant. He rubbed his cut knuckles with his greasy fingers.

"Why couldn't I have just stayed awake the night? Why couldn't I have been ready when he walked into the room? Why couldn't I have just shoved the wire into the circuit and pressed the button on the robot's neck with a smile on my face?" But Leo had grown to understand that the world was full of questions, and despite his belief that you occasionally had to roll up your sleeves and answer some of them yourself, *these* particular questions had him stumped. *Because it wasn't meant to be,* he thought to himself.

He walked over to the brick stack and peered through the cracks. He couldn't see anything more than a few dying flames and the dark wall across the room. He could hear something, voices, yes, he was sure of it, but other than that the house kept that eerie stillness—the silence that reminded Leo that he was alone with Krollup.

He turned his head to look at the mines when he heard a splash. It was rather clear too, and he closed his eye and inched toward a long crack he had made with his forefinger, a crack that had claimed his fingernail and scarred his tip. There was a big man walking away from the dwindling fire. He could smell the soaked wood and ash. He wanted to scream at the man to come back, to help him, but he realized that if he did, he'd get the both of them in a heap of trouble with Krollup.

Then why is he putting out the fire?

That was a good question. Why would that man be putting out the fire, a fire Krollup insisted stay lit if not only to keep people from peering in and suspecting something's (or some*one's*) hidden behind the fireplace?

He watched the big, dumb looking man walk back towards him; he was carrying a bucket carefully, but water still seemed to spill all over the place. He threw it into the fireplace, and Leo heard one last hiss as the fire died completely, replaced by black smoke, which billowed upwards, seeping into the stack like floss between teeth.

Leo forgot about the mines. He was transfixed with this man. He had dropped the bucket with a clang on the floor, and Leo was certain Krollup would have had his big head for this. But nothing.

"What is going on?" Leo whispered to himself.

The big man stepped right into the smoky fireplace with a large fire poker in his fist; he coughed and waved the space before his nose and mouth. Leo pressed his face against the bricks until it felt like his eye had oozed between the chipped grout. And then there was a loud crash, and Leo's head was jerked back while his body was pushed to the ground. That man was waving the fire poker at the bricks!

Leo scurried along the ground, feeling behind him with his scarred fingers, touching rodent bones and cables and steel shavings and wire clippings, leaving footprints in the dust on the rock, listening to the poker hit the brick, watching grout explode into clouds and fall to the ground like snow.

"Krollup's sent him to kill me," Leo said silently, and scrounged the ground for a weapon; he found a wrench and tucked it into his palm. "Come and get me."

Then he heard the doorbell. And the man left; he could hear his footsteps, the echo of his breaths in the deep fireplace as he exited. Some of the bricks had been pushed inwards, others broken completely, and Leo was sure he could pull some of them out, but he didn't find it particularly smart to go wandering around right now; instead he would wait. He patted the wrench against his palm with a thwack, and hid in the shadows beside the mine.

9

"Did you go into the mines when you were a kid?"

Edwin had dribble hanging off his lower lip, but Robert liked to see him that way—helpless, like a child. "Yes, I was forced in by bullies. I have a feeling you know this doc. What are you getting at?"

"Oh, nothing Edwin, nothing at all. Just curious."

"Curiosity killed the cat."

"But satisfaction brought him back," Robert said with a grin.

"I suppose." Edwin had his own smile laid across his face, a smile Robert wanted to wipe off with the back of his hand. Eddie was coughing in the background.

"And this is why you built over top of the mines right, because you went in them when you were a kid?"

Edwin cocked his eye. "Yup. But I got something there, from a Hunter, you know, before I came back up the mines. I remember I was afraid of my father; he wanted milk and I was supposed to pick some up after school. That doors been closed doc. Locked too."

"I see. Who locked the door Edwin?"

"The Wanderer of the Corridor."

"Interesting. Tell me. These Hunters, what are their relationship with the werewolves, through the mines I mean?" Robert looked at the bulge under Edwin's shirt, where the rock hung from the gold chain.

"There was going to be a war between the two. Sorry doc, doors locked."

"What is a Hunter?"

"I don't know."

"You don't?"

"No, but doesn't matter if I did, that doors locked."

"What about the Towers, Edwin. Tell me about these Towers down there?"

Edwin contorted his face for a moment. "I don't know anything about them; it's hard to get proper information when the path there is guarded by wolves. Doors locked."

"Tell me Edwin, are there many doors still?"

"That's a stupid question."

"Why is that?"

"Because there's a door for every question, and you have a heap of them, don't you?"

"I do, but you shouldn't be aware of this at all, you know that right?"

Edwin nodded.

"Are you lying to me about all of this, Edwin?"

"No."

"Why should I believe you?"

"Because I wear this," Edwin said, and he ran his hand by his neck.

Perfect, Robert thought, he had him where he wanted him, but he wouldn't further pursue that line of thought. If the door was closed there, he would never find out what it was exactly that hung from the gold chain. "Tell me Edwin, why it is you believe you murdered your father?"

"Because I wear this," Edwin reiterated.

"This isn't a random memory, Edwin, you should be able to find the door to this memory and see for yourself the truth; that's the possibility of mesmerizing."

"It seems like a random question though. Breaks the chain of thought."

"Don't let it. I'm ultimately here to help you."

"Then why does my head hurt?"

And the doorbell rang; it was loud and echoed throughout the house with a severe clang that seemingly shook the walls. "Eddie, get the door. Tell whomever it is to get lost. Tell them Edwin's under the weather—tell 'em you're a servant or something," Robert yelled, and Eddie ducked out of the fireplace, dropped the fire poker and dusted himself off as he ran towards the front door, carefully walking by the fallen statue.

10

Edwin rushed to close the doors to each of Robert's questions. He'd slam them shut and lock them. Then, out of the blue, he felt like finding the memory of his father's death—he didn't know why either, but he felt obligated to do so. *"It isn't a random memory,"* seemed to blare throughout the corridor. No, his father's death wasn't a random memory; for some reason, he knew just where he kept it (or *hid* it, rather).

He floated towards a large steel door with a thick tumbler on its front; it had rivets bordering the jamb, reminding him of the vaults at the bank—*that was how you created this door, from the image of the vaults—*

Edwin shoved the key into a hole in the middle of that tumbler, and sparks erupted from within; there was a loud clang and the door slowly swung inwards without a sound. He looked in and wasn't surprised to see his mother lying on the ground, holding her face with her hand.

"I don't want to see this."

"Don't you understand what he's doing, he's diverting you, you must close the door, destroy it if you must, and lock the rest of the doors—please, you must," a voice called out in his head, but Edwin ignored it. He pulled himself closer

to the opening, until he could almost smell his mother, that strong mixture of Irish Springs soap and vanilla.

"I don't want to see this, but I must," Edwin said under his breath.

He watched his younger self run into the room; he saw his sister for a moment, but his younger self had told her to wait in her bedroom, so she went running off, crying, trying to erase that picture of her mother on the ground, her face swollen. Edwin watched himself caress his mother's hair, and reach under her neck to support the back of her head; there were tears dripping from her chin, and blood welling in her right eye, which had been swollen shut. "Mom."

Edwin could read his lips; he could see this at every angle, as if his eyes were planted everywhere in the room—in a way they were; he was the master of recollection. This was his memory, and he had the power to shape it. He could see the part in her hair just as clearly as he could see the bottoms of her feet. He knew what he said next—"He did this to you, that monster...that *monster.*"

Edwin looked away. He really didn't want to see this. Not at all.

11

The doorbell rang again before Eddie opened the door. When he did, he saw a woman standing before him with two large men at either side of her.

"Yeah," Eddie said.

"Yes, we would like to speak to Mr. Edwin Krollup please?" The woman asked with an accent.

Eddie looked at the woman, then at both men. "Didn't you see the mess out there? He's indisposed at the moment."

"Meaning?" The woman asked again, with her snobbish accent.

"He can't come to the door." Eddie went to shut the door when one of the big men at the woman's side shoved his foot in the jamb.

"This is a legal matter, sir, and I highly doubt a man like Edwin Krollup would ignore such a duty," the woman said.

"Come back another time, ma'am." Eddie kicked the man's shiny loafer away from the jamb and slammed the door. Despite its enormous size, he did so easily.

When he turned to walk back to the Great room, the doorbell rang again. He gritted his teeth together, wishing he had just brought that stupid fire poker with him. He opened the door only to meet the barrel of a pistol.

"I strongly suggest you allow Mrs. Lorenzo the decency of accompanying Mr. Krollup with a chat," the man with the gun said, and Eddie bit his lip.

The three of them stepped into the house, and Eddie realized the other man had a briefcase handcuffed to his wrist.

12

Robert touched the gold chain around Edwin's neck. "Tell me, where is the Wanderer now Edwin?"

Edwin smiled but shook the grin away and furrowed his brow. "You're tempting me."

"Why do you say that?"

Edwin shrugged. "My mother's face looked so bad that day. My father did a number on it."

Robert ran his finger down the gold chain until it submerged under the collar of Edwin's shirt. He could hear Eddie at the front door. He slid his finger an inch further. "You're there now, I suppose."

"I didn't want my sister to see what *he* had done to her."

"The perilous job of an older brother, I'm afraid to say." Robert hooked his finger under the chain and pulled it out of Edwin's shirt. The rock slung over Edwin's chest awkwardly and thumped a button with a sharp click. Robert looked at the statue of David at the far end of the room. "Tell me Edwin, what exactly possessed you to buy a fake David and believe it was real, when its head points in the opposite direction?"

"It wasn't always that way."

Robert faintly heard the front door shut behind him. He looked Edwin squarely in the eyes. "Tell me, Edwin, why on earth I saw exploding volcanoes when I touched the stone you wear around your neck?"

Edwin's eyes flashed for a moment, as if he recognized the nature of the question—as if he could actually find something within him to counter the hypnosis and shut and lock every door that existed inside him. But that part of him was busy right now, and Robert knew that—that part of Edwin was watching his younger self tend to his hurt mother. The mind was awkward, full of different routes, and it was the job of the therapist to work as a roadmap; this could be used as an advantage, and Robert exacted this opportunity just as a fortuneteller exploits the gullibility of those so determined to believe anything.

"Probably because it didn't like your touch," Edwin finally said.

"How is that possible?" Robert quickly ran his finger over the ugly little stone and felt an incredible vibration; he saw steam in his eyes, and realized the room had turned red, as if covered by a crimson blanket, leaving the vague contours of statues and book shelves and furniture. When he removed his finger everything returned to normal; the feeling was odd, but wonderful at the same time. *That's what brought you back in the first place*, he thought.

"Anything is possible," Edwin said matter-of-factly.

"What is it?" Robert asked, almost pleadingly. The front doorbell rang again.

"Magic."

"What kind of magic?"

"The kind that turns heads, you might say," Edwin said darkly.

Robert looked at Edwin confusingly, but looked at the statue of David for a moment—*really* looked at it. Its head *was* turned the wrong way, that was obvious, but there was a look on its face, a sneer really, one which would prove uncomfortably disturbing to any onlooker. There were cracks along the base of its neck—long cracks, ones he could see from far away. At first they may have looked like intended markings, ligaments perhaps, but they spread like spider legs. David's head had been rotated—but how?

"What does the stone do, Edwin?" Robert heard muffled voices from the front entry. *Get rid of them, will ya Eddie.*

Edwin had begun to sweat. He was trying to hold the answer back, Robert could see that easily, but his intermediary was diverted for the time being—for *how* much longer became the real question.

"Hurry, tell me."

Edwin gritted his teeth. He reluctantly grabbed the rock from his chest and clenched it for a moment, until the chattering sound of his teeth could shatter glass. "I—I'll sh-sh—show you."

13

"Mom."

Edwin watched himself shake his mother. He wanted to leave, but a much stronger part of him urged that he finally find out what had happened. Had he grabbed that stone around his neck when he wished that his father die, the stone he could see now, clear as day, dangling from his neck from twine, almost touching his mother's chest as he kneeled over her?

"I'm going to call an ambulance, mom." He watched himself run to the phone and dial quickly; he stood for a moment, twiddling the twine around his forefinger, talking furiously into the phone until spittle seemed to connect his lower lip with the speckled receiver.

The necklace around his neck burned, and Edwin looked down, ignoring his younger self on the phone, ignoring his hurt mother on the floor with the swollen jaw. The stone was being touched—how he knew this was another question, but there was this insistent push towards the large vault door at the edge of the scene, beyond the phone line held in his younger hand.

"*What does the rock do, Edwin?—Hurry, tell me.*" He heard this voice like a foghorn throughout the corridor; he noticed the vault door was behind him now, and for the moment he didn't care. The vault door slammed shut with a deafening screech, and the tumbler in the middle sparked to life as it fully turned and snapped.

In front of him, miles down the corridor, Edwin saw that a door had been opened. From this door came a light, and he heard his voice, just as clear as he could feel the burning necklace around his throat: "*I—I'll sh-sh—show you.*"

Edwin realized something he neglected to fathom before—that he might just lose the stone that had made him the man that he is. Horror dawned on his face, a horror that snapped his eyelids open and pushed his eyeballs out, unhinging his jaw as his mouth fell and let his tongue loose like a worm—he hurried to the door, the necklace around his neck growing hotter.

14

Edwin held the stone in his hand.

"Well, show me," Robert said.

Edwin looked at Robert with his vacant eyes; there was little recognition, but there was certainly hesitation. He didn't want to do this; he was unwillingly holding the stone, and Robert realized there was a distant look in those eyes that proved Edwin meant to get him back for this. Robert felt a shudder when he saw the look.

"Watch the statue behind you."

Robert turned and the statue behind him, a granite man with enormous arms and curly hair, turned its head, crushing stone as it did so, until a heap of dust lay at its feet on the pedestal.

"What on God's green earth?"

The statue proceeded to step off the pedestal with a thud, and lifted both its arms. Robert turned and looked at Edwin...and he was floating in the chair. Robert snatched the stone from Edwin's fist. The statue stood still.

"The statue in the front hall, the one that left its stoop—that was you? David's rotated head—that was you also, probably out of anger?"

Edwin nodded. "That doors locked," he finally said, but there was sadness in his voice. Robert grabbed the chain and pulled it over Edwin's head, ruffling his hair.

He dangled the necklace in his fingers and looked at the statue. "How did you move the statue Edwin?"

"It wasn't me, it was the stone. Doors locked."

"The stone," Robert said under his breath, when he felt two huge hands grab him by the shoulders and twist him around, turning him face to face with a giant man in a tailor made suit. "Who are you?"

Eddie looked at Robert worryingly; he was pushed against the wall.

"Ah, and there he is, standing in the bliss of sunlight like a king—a wrongfully appointed king mind you. What on earth happened to his head? It's twisted," Mrs. Lorenzo said, looking at David disapprovingly. "The question isn't who we are, but *who* you are and *what* you are doing?" She looked at Edwin's hunkered figure on the chair, his sullen eyes, his sweaty face.

"I'd answer her if I were you, she isn't exactly in the diplomatic mood, if ya wanna call it that—jetlag, if you will," a big lug said, one whose wrist was cuffed to a suitcase, and whose other hand held a gun.

Robert wriggled the necklace into the sleeve of his shirt, feeling that wonderful vibration. "Who are you, answer me first? I believe this is trespassing."

Mrs. Lorenzo smiled. "I could phone the Italian Embassy or the District Attorney for a warrant just as fast as it took me to force my way in, but I don't consider poor Mr. Krollup's present state legally admissible—look at him, he's dribbling like a baby. It's obvious enough what you've done, and I want you to reverse it. You are his psychotherapist, are you not?"

"And you are?"

"With the Ministry of Art. I've come to settle some issues—I suppose I could do that while he's under hypnosis, but I'd much rather watch him squirm. Brunus, if you will please."

The big man with the gun and briefcase stepped forward and pointed the black pistol directly at Robert's head, until he could stare into its ominous eye. "I'd do as she says friend—she's apt to make some hasty decisions, and I'm sorry to say, I gotta heed her commands; it's ma job to do so." There was an ugly leer in his eyes.

Robert squirmed backwards. He stuck his hand in his pocket, letting the golden chain with the magical stone fall from his sleeve while he picked out his pendant; it was a rather graceful switch, and though he didn't need the pendant to revive Edwin from hypnosis, *they* didn't know that. He didn't want *them* to know about the stone; he was going to fully bring the granite statue over and surprise them, yes he was—if only he could figure out how to work the stone, that is.

"Hurry up, friend. Jetlag doesn't breed patience," Brunus said.

"I'm not your friend," Robert said, and he crawled in front of Edwin. He dangled the pendant for a moment, and then clapped his hands.

Edwin awoke with a sudden realization and anger in his eyes. "Innis you worm!" He leapt up from the chair and reached for what was no longer around his neck. The look in his eye was entirely surprising, as if he had realized his eyes no longer worked just as he picked up a book to read. "YOU WORM!"

"Sit down," Mrs. Lorenzo said.

Brunus shoved Krollup to the chair and shoved his gun against his forehead. "Hutchy, cuff his wrist to the chair," he said to the other lug, who stood with his arms crossed. Hutchy reached into his jacket and brought out a set of sparkling handcuffs. He snapped them around Edwin's left wrist and clasped him to the chair.

Krollup gritted his teeth. "You've made a mistake coming here Lorenzo—the Ministry will pay."

"I don't think so," she said, but Robert saw something he didn't like in Edwin's eyes—certainty.

15

"Imagine my surprise finding out from Alfred Linutz himself that you no longer employ his services. How do you think I felt after hearing that? He had assured me that you would comply with my demands, but upon discovering you fired your lawyer, I had to trudge onto a plane and fly here myself with *my* lawyers to make ends meet." She pointed to both big men, Hutchy (who had a large head and slicked back hair with a golden hoop in his left ear) and Brunus (a man with shoulders as wide as most doorways, and a head like cabbage—awkward and full of bumps).

"Your demands were ridiculous, and I just want you to know that the Ministry will pay."

"I see you still take your anger out on statuary," Mrs. Lorenzo said with a grin, looking at the fake David. "And no Mr. Krollup, the Ministry will not pay, you will. In the amount we all agreed upon, those were the terms, and I don't care that you fired your lawyer, his word stands as a testament to this agreement, for his word binds truth because he spoke in your best interest."

Edwin struggled with the handcuffs.

"Stop that," Brunus said. He emphasized the gun in his hand.

Edwin looked at both Eddie and Robert, who were against the far wall by the fireplace, watching Edwin struggle with the cuffs. He knew Robert had the stone, and wanted him, for the moment at least, to use it, but knew that if he did, he'd never get the stone back again; he'd have no way of doing so either.

"I have with me a suitcase containing two exhibits, or so you'd say in your judiciary courts. Brunus, show him what's inside the case."

Brunus stepped forward, stuck his gun in its holster, a leather strap tucked underneath his armpit, and took from his breast pocket a small sterling key; he unlatched the briefcase and set it in front of Edwin. "You lash out, Krollup, and I'll brain you."

There were photographs in the briefcase, a surveillance video, and a tape recorder. "Much like your house outside," Mrs. Lorenzo said, "only in this case damage is going to cost you a whole lot more." She laughed. The photographs depicted the damaged Accademia, Edwin could tell that much, and he was sure the tape recorder contained vocal evidence of his tele-threat over the fake David; that much was a surety, but believing such artifacts could muster so much money took a brainless idiot, and Edwin wasn't brainless.

"That's all you have, that's all you have against me? And you want two and half billion dollars for that? *That?*" Edwin laughed a maniacal laugh that chilled Robert's bones.

"Oh Edwin, let me just warn you, I don't intend on taking this to court; in fact, I'm not leaving your house until the money's transferred. I'm sure all it's gonna take is a little negotiating."

With that Brunus stepped forward and whacked Edwin across the face with the handle of his pistol.

Robert rubbed the stone in his pocket and felt the vibration.

16

Leo scrambled against the wall. Where was that big man with the poker? Everything seemed too quiet now, as if the world had shut down; it was an awkward feeling, almost pleasant, but distressing also—it compelled him to at least maneuver a couple of those bricks out of the stack. Leo got up and let the wrench dangle loosely from his hand.

And he heard the explosion.

It came from the mines like a punch in the head, and though it wasn't loud, Leo knew what it was immediately. He stopped dead in his tracks and turned towards the mines.

There was an odd rumble, a short waver in the silence, as if the house had shifted, but it ended almost before it began. Before Leo could even register the vital importance of what had just happened, disregarding the impending danger Krollup would inevitably impose when he found out the robot had exploded—before all of this, Leo fell to his knees, letting the wrench crash on top of cables.

"Oh no—Jimmy, Cole," he muttered under his breath.

For the moment, Leo forgot about the big man and the loose bricks; instead he found himself tucked into the fetal position on his collapsed cot, his dirty thumb in his mouth, whispering over and over again: "This is my fault—I made it, I'm a murderer."

And the wolves came up the mines.

CHAPTER 15

QUEEN OF THE LEEG

1

The Leeg Forest stood before the two like a giant wall holding the sky from the earth. The dead grass, yellow and marred by fire, abruptly turned into lush Canopy Trees, large trunks of auburn wood, infested by moss in patches, which stretched to the sky hundreds of feet above only to yield to thick clouds of leaves.

"We're going in there?" Jimmy asked; he was red in the face, and had just stubbed out another of his 'smoking sticks', as Ashton called them.

"You mustn't raise your voice here." Ashton pulled his quiver of arrows from the sack on his horse's side, and slung it over his shoulder.

They stood by a lake, which for as far as Jimmy could tell, was calm and bordered only by long grass. "I shall leave Jilay here, for the woods are no place for a horse," Ashton said. He patted Jilay's side, and the horse galloped to the lakeside and dunked its head in the water. Ashton held what looked like an empty balloon in his hand; it was made of a fine hair, and Jimmy could see stitches in parts, but they were small, and mostly hidden by the fur. "The water of Fog Lake is pure," Ashton said, and he dipped his hand into the water and splashed his face; his short-cropped hair stuck up in black spikes. He set the balloon in the lake and submerged it. When he lifted it from the water the balloon had been filled, shaped like a droplet, and tied off at its thin top.

"Whatever you say, Leatherface," Jimmy said smugly. He patted his pocket, where he had stuck a handful of rocks.

Ashton cocked his exposed eye. "You speak mockingly."

"If you say so."

"I do not understand."

Jimmy laughed, but silenced when he saw the seriousness in Ashton's eye. "Why do you wear that thing over your face?"

Ashton smiled. The side of the mask crinkled, and his exposed eye squinted. "Have you ever been in battle, boy?"

Jimmy shook his head.

"Then you haven't seen its disabilities. There has been a war with the wolves ever since I was born, and I have sworn my father's vengeance to destroy the Yilaks in their country. To understand my face, you'd have to understand loss."

"You lost your father?"

Ashton nodded, watching the horse lap up the calm waters of the lake.

"I lost mine too. My scars." Jimmy held up the tin box with his initial on the front; he opened the case and showed Ashton the cigarettes. "It's funny though. These things killed my dad, and yet here I am, and here *they* are."

"What are they?"

"What are they?" Jimmy asked in a weird tone.

"Things are different through the mines, I presume."

"I guess. They're cigarettes, smokes, though on the other side of the mines, they're called 'cancer sticks'…or 'coffin nails'—I like that one the best."

"Coffin nails," Ashton muttered; he tied the balloon canteen to his belt and looked at the sky. "I've never understood our insistence to do the things we shouldn't be doing. Such is why your father died, I presume; he neglected to imagine the horrible consequences of his actions. Hunters are taught to remember this; 'twas a code in the catacombs before the civil wars, written on the walls by candlelight, or so my father used to tell me. Remember everything is a sequence, and what we do now determines how we survive later in the chain—was a good sentiment, but so many have thrown wisdom to the hounds. I was hidden with my mother in the catacombs during the war, where the wolves couldn't find us, no matter their smell, their sight. I was just a child then, but I remember some things. I remember we were determined our fathers would triumph.

"War started the decay, and I have grown to believe the Hunters' wisdom is as shoddy as the belt I wear—made from twines and leather. My course of action has sought vengeance for my father's death, and I bear the scars of my fighting to do so." Ashton paused. "Your brother is with them, the wolves." He turned to look at Jimmy. "Before this is over, Jimmy, I want you to understand the consequences of your plans, your ideas; you're in utter disbelief, I can see that. The Hunter can read the eyes much as the shaman can read the plants, the roots. You have to believe that anything you plan on doing, whether you desire to escape from me, to travel back east for your brother—you have to understand, Jimmy, that everything you have planned is already being countered. By me, by the course of time, by the elements—you can leave me, but then you would have started your own sequence of decay. By coming with me to the wise man, we both can start to understand the path we're on now. This is the right path, Jimmy, the only path that can save your brother."

Jimmy's head was lowered, and the falling sun shone through his hair like a crown. "How do we know he's still alive then?"

"Because he serves some purpose for them."

"How do you know?"

Ashton gave the boy a stark look. There was truth in his eye—truth and caring, mayhaps. "Because they kill for sport, Jimmy, and your brother survived the night."

Jimmy looked at Ashton, snapped open the tin box and pulled out a cigarette. He twirled it around his fingers for a minute, then stuck it in his mouth. "Tell me, Scarface, why can't I hear the birds here?"

"Because the birds left the forest years ago."

The cigarette dropped from Jimmy's lip and settled between two long pieces of grass. "A spider," Jimmy said in a low mutter.

"Where?" Ashton blurted, reaching behind him for his sword.

"There," Jimmy pointed to the ground, where sitting on top of a nest of dead grass was a black spider with glistening eyes and hairy legs, watching the two uneasily.

Ashton relaxed. "Do not mutter the word spider in front of me like that; it is a careless thing to do."

"I hate spiders," Jimmy said, eyeing the spider with a sneer that just might have been more disgust and fear. "I hate them more than anything…I've never seen one so big; it's like a cat. It's watching us." Jimmy quickly reached around back for one of Ashton's arrows, grabbed a long shaft and held it in his hand like a dagger. He was going to throw it when Ashton stayed Jimmy's hand, holding the boy's wrist firmly.

"You mustn't do that," he said, lightening his grip while grabbing the arrow with his other hand. "You don't want to disturb the Higher Beings." He looked up at the trees, where the leaves waved in the wind, where no birdsong was uttered.

Jimmy watched the spider scuttle off into the forest, listening to those hairy legs patter over dead grass and fallen leaves.

"We must be quick and quiet. They already know we are here."

The two stepped into the forest, their legs disappearing into the murky woods like bodies through a wall.

2

"'Twas a scout," Ashton said in a low whisper, as he ducked his head under a gnarled branch, which had fallen from above and twisted like an old bone in the darkness.

"What?"

"The spider; it was sent to see us." Ashton touched the bark of a tree and looked at his fingers. "This forest has been disturbed, Jimmy, and we'd best not disturb it further."

Jimmy nodded, then patted his pocket again; this insistent feeling of security kept him hopeful. Looking into the woods made him realize one thing: he had to get out. The forest was dark, and only a silent breeze crept through the high branches, riddling the leaves with a sharp moan; there were sharp drops in the ground, where the earth had been cut and shattered, letting large roots stick from the dirt like the long hands of the dead. Jimmy had almost tripped over one of these roots, but Ashton had quickly grabbed him by the arm and steadied him.

"Trees are growing too big," he said. "Soon the ground will ultimately collapse under their weight." He bent down and dug a fistful of dirt from the ground. "It's tired and dying; the darkness has overcome the soil." He blew the dirt from his hand and watched it separate listlessly in the dank air.

Ashton stepped over a pile of rocks and cowered for a moment; he put his finger over his mouth and crawled forward. The leaves above shook with the wind; there was an unsteady feeling in the forest, Jimmy could feel it, as if the air had become electrically charged—*it's like the feeling you get before a storm*, Jimmy thought.

"There is an awkward smell here—something is rotting," Ashton said under his breath. He stood and unsheathed his sword.

The two stepped over dead leaves, the stench around them growing stronger. Before them, in a clutter of leaves and wiry twigs, lay a heap of burnt fur, with patches of red and white that looked like jelly.

"Stay here," Ashton said as he moved forward, clutching his sword in front of him. His unease drew him forward with discretion; he could smell its death, but he could also sense something else, something *alive* about it. This feeling was awkward, because what lay before him in a heap was smoking, and the hair it did have was mostly plastered on by blood and dirt. It was a Yilak, that much was obvious; it was curled neatly in the fetal position, and Ashton had to wonder if it was left here to die, to suffer as its flesh burned. He poked the wolf with his sword and there was a popping sound; its arm deflated and a thick jelly drooped from the wound like a tear, splattering the ground with a thump. Hundreds of little spiders fled from the cut, diving into the mucus coursing through the dirty hair, eating it, poking into the jelly with their pincers.

"Scavengers," he muttered. This Yilak had been young; its teeth were still budding and the hair that hadn't burned looked full and vibrant. Its eyes had already been eaten out, and its tongue, partially decomposed, lay out of the side of its open mouth like a slug working its way from a burrow. "'Tis a stray wolf, for it didn't get far into the wood before falling," Ashton said as he walked back.

"What killed it?" Jimmy asked, watching the little spiders devour the jelly, climbing over top each other.

"The woods I suppose."

Jimmy paused; there was something cryptic about that answer, something he didn't quite like. "Why aren't there birds here?"

"The woods are dead. *Leeg* means long here in the old language, and these woods are old—the birds have fled for freshness. They are like you and me, for we cannot survive the same when we are old. Age is a nuisance."

"You're like a teacher, you know. You expect me to understand what it is you're babbling about."

"You don't understand?" Ashton said, sarcastically.

"I understand these woods are old, but so are the trees by my house, but I wake up to birdsong every morning. Birds probably don't even understand age, they just live by the weather, and it isn't winter here. If it was I might believe the birds flew south, but here, there's nothing, just this odd feeling in the air, as if there's a generator somewhere close. I don't like that feeling, and to tell you the truth, this silence irks me even more."

"Just believe there are better woods to live in." Ashton walked forward, sheathing his sword as he did so.

"Why was there a scout outside the forest? That spider was obviously sent by somebody—some*thing*...but why?"

Ashton exhaled. "You are a curious one."

"I just want to get my brother, but he's the other way, and I want to figure out why it is we're going *this* way, this way through an old forest without birds, but—but a forest that feels the need to send an incredibly large spider to watch us when there's nobody around to even warn?" Jimmy wanted to grab the rocks from his pocket and throw them at Ashton and run the other way, towards Cole, but it didn't feel like the right time.

"Keep your voice down."

"Why?"

"Because we might wake things—animals, mayhaps, deep in their burrows. Our trail is open for now."

"What were you talking about earlier? The Higher Beings?"

"You told me you dislike spiders, correct? Then believe your curiosity is best left unheeded. These woods are old Jimmy. I have been through them many times and the feeling has always been the same—isolation. But beyond the forest exists our answers, and for your brother's sake, you should believe that despite the blatancy of curiosity, some things shouldn't be answered, for our sanity sometimes relies on the things we don't know."

Jimmy groaned. "I can hear fear in your voice."

"Fear is natural—I should know, Jimmy."

They walked forward, leaving behind the messy wolf carcass and the scavengers devouring its insides—they walked towards the unending trees, the twisted roots and the crumbled earth. These woods were old, but Jimmy knew something had kept the birds from nesting in the trees, and he constantly looked upwards, trying to find something, some creature that may have felt threatened by their coming, but he only saw the shuffling leaves, the waning beams of sunlight through the canopies. Ashton would tell Jimmy to stay still while he moved forward, unsheathing his sword as he did so. But he would return soon enough to alleviate any plans of escaping.

"We are going to the coast, you know. Have you ever seen the ocean?"

Jimmy nodded. "Of course I have. I own five boogie boards, and when I'm fifteen, my mom tells me she'll buy me a surfboard. My stepdad owns a resort in Florida; we went there last summer."

"Florida? Sounds exotic," Ashton said.

"I guess, but it gets tedious. My stepfather doesn't like having us around— me and my brother, that is. I guess we're used to it now, but at first we needed a man, you know, a father. When my dad died it got real hard. My mother paid her dues; she deserves the rich life. I do this for her."

"Sacrifice is the motto of the Hunters, written in our blood. We protect the women and the children, the old and the young; it is our duty to fulfill the needs of the people. You're like me Jimmy; your sense of heroism to retrieve your brother, yer duty to your mother, these are great attributes. It's just curious why you'd put those sticks into your mouth. They stink of death, you know."

"Yeah, and thanks for reminding me Scarface, I was getting a little agitated and I *almost* forgot about my smokes." Jimmy took out his tin box and withdrew a cigarette. "A light please."

Ashton pointed at the surrounding darkness. "The sun doesn't come here."

Jimmy frowned and slammed the tin box shut. "Are we safe, I mean right now?"

"Why do you ask?"

"Because I don't think we are." Jimmy stuck the box into his pocket.

A sudden excitement sprang into Ashton's exposed eye and he stuck his forefinger against Jimmy's lips. "Be quiet," he said in a whisper. "We are not alone."

3

"I hear voices," Ashton said. He looked at the trees around him, at the ground, at the dying brush and the fallen leaves. "They are loud; they call attention to themselves, and I'd best be far away when they're heard." He stood still for a moment. "Come this way Jimmy. Steady yourself. I know of a hovel; 'tis a way into the gut, by the creek."

"I don't hear anything," Jimmy said, as he started to jog behind Ashton, pushing aside twigs.

"They are off in the distance now, but our paths should meet, for to the west here the brush grows thicker towards the coast; we are being driven to the east, and so it is to the hovel we should go." He took out his sword and cut a vine in front of him, so that it swung either way and dragged on the ground. "I would like first to see who these voices belong to, before they are silenced for good."

Jimmy didn't like the sound of that at all.

4

The hovel's roof had slanted, and had almost fully caved in on its right side—not quite, but enough for the wood to split. It was made of canopy, and Jimmy had noticed that a couple smaller trees had been chopped, and only their stumps jutted from the ground near a small pond by the foot of the shack. Weeds grew like stalks of bamboo, tickling the underside of windows covered with thin wood which had been cut with holes, so whoever had lived in the dwelling could look out without being obviously noticed.

Jimmy and Ashton had passed another wolf while they ran, but neither paid much attention to it; the Yilak had been draped over a fallen branch, its fur completely burnt off revealing charred flesh which had been mostly eaten by the scavengers.

When Jimmy saw the hovel he realized the complete isolation of this place, and he wondered how his brother was faring. He wanted to see Cole more than anything now—but he was being dragged away, and every step was increasing the distance bewteen them.

"The Mark of Mystic; 'tis the slope," Ashton said when they got to the front door, a sheet of bark that had been sanded. Ashton was pointing to a diagonal line on the grain of wood which had been drawn with tar, obviously with the tip of somebody's finger; it was a line that declined from left to right, and ended with a dip. "It's a charm, for the belief of protection from the Mystic Mountains gave security—no evil can pass this way," Ashton said with a peculiar glint in his eye, one that Jimmy didn't believe.

Ashton pushed the door open. When they both entered, he pushed a table against the door, and slapped the surface with his palm as if testing the sturdiness of the old wood.

"Why did you do that?" Jimmy asked, looking at the table, and then at the concealed windows concernedly.

"The Mark of Mystic has failed before," Ashton said. He shoved the table harder against the door until it sounded like something snapped. "You mustn't dwell on curiosity now Jimmy," Ashton said as he looked around the small hovel. It was a simple rectangle, marked only by two small cots made of twisted branches and leaves, a large stone pit that had probably been an oven, a fire pit made of oblong rocks in the corner, the table that had been wedged against the door, and three chairs, each sanded like the door, but with leaves on their surfaces. On the far wall there was written something, probably with the same tar used on the front door. Jimmy couldn't quite read it in the gloom so he stepped forward.

Written on the wall with a shaky hand:

THEY CAME FROM THE MOUNTAINS

"What does that mean?" Jimmy asked.

Ashton had wandered towards the window on the eastern side of the shack. "It sounds like a warning is all."

"A warning from what?"

Ashton kneeled in front of the window. "From whatever the inhabitant of this hovel felt obligated to draw the slope of Mystic on his door for. Be quiet so I can listen."

5

"They come closer, I can hear them, I can see the darkness ahead waver as if separating," Ashton said, and he focused.

"Why has Haspin met with Hunters? His mind has slipped with the growth of his belly." There was snickering after this comment, but the voices were coming closer. Ashton could hear the leaves above shake in a way the wind could not produce; it sounded like something big had been moving them all aside.

"The same reason he has been associating himself with all our enemies, I suppose. He believes he is a diplomat of the King's Crest." This voice was much deeper.

"Then why is it we're blindly scouring these woods on a Hunter's whim?"

"I don't know."

"I've heard stories of these woods; we're walking in a crypt, and all it is you can muse about are the ill-fated decisions of a man who believes he is still the heir to a throne that has been diminished." Ashton could tell there existed not authority, but aggression in this voice, one that he was certain the other men around him believed to be a force of wisdom.

But what had they said of the Hunter? Together with the King's line? "What?" Ashton said, silently, to himself.

"Why do you suppose an old man would live in these woods?"

Ashton leaned closer to the wall, nearly buckling the studs against his shoulder—what exactly were they searching for?

"He lives beyond them, for the Hunters told Haspin they've seen the dwelling themselves, covered in leaves at the edge of the sand, camouflaged to look like the sand and stones."

"Why does Haspin want the company of an old man anyway?"

"These are just his orders."

"Mayhaps he isn't but a mere man," said another voice, more cautious and unsure.

"And what is that supposed to mean? Don't tell me you believe this old man is otherwise."

"Well, you never know."

"And what of the monsters from the tales, aye?" the wise voice spoke. "Are we to trudge mindlessly through these woods, speaking in our loudest voices only to warn them in advance of our coming? I've heard stories o' the city, the city upon the trees. A city spun of silk, aye, an' yet you mindless drones trudge under its path arguing nonsense you'll never understand."

Ashton thought he could see them now, emerging through the murky distance, their heads shrouded by the mists of the forest.

"A city above the trees?"

"Stay your lips, we've woken them," the wise voice said.

Ashton saw that the men had unsheathed their blades; there were more than fifteen men, walking in tandem; they wore jerkins with the King's Crest impressed upon them. Ashton realized the men were looking up; he could hear the leaves also, louder now, shaking violently.

Ashton quickly removed his bow and an arrow from his quiver; he stuck the arrowhead through a hole cut into the wood, and he directed the tip towards the men. He cinched the bow back and watched; they all stared up, holding their swords out in front of them stupidly.

"There is a shack, there beyond the cut trunks, it is mere paces," one of them yelled, pointing with his sword, and there was a terrible screech, like a horse whinnying, and long whirrs as something large and fast fell from above.

"Then *they* will do it instead," Ashton whispered, and he relaxed the bow when he was bashed in the head and fell forward into the wall.

6

Jimmy was mostly concerned about the table in front of the door. If that posed any problem, he wasn't quite sure how else he could get out; the windows were boarded over, and the collapsed roof was still too high to jump through. It was by chance really that he decided to throw the stones at Ashton's head while he shoved the table away from the door. The table was heavy, probably made from the thick bark of the Canopy Tree, and though it shifted nicely on the floor, Jimmy had been rather uncertain if he could both throw the rocks and push the table at the same time. It was the memory of playing catch with his father and Cole that garnered any chance that he'd hit his target.

Jimmy's reasoning was simple enough: Ashton—*or Scarface, or Leatherface the Hunter, what have you*—was kneeling under the boarded window reaching for his quiver; he muttered something under his breath and pointed the arrowhead through a spy hole, therefore supplying at least one possibility— that his mind was elsewhere now, and if Jimmy decided to throw the rocks and leave through the front door, he wouldn't be expecting a surprise flip five feet in front of him again as he tried to make his escape. But the question remained—how would he pull it off?

And an image popped into his head. He was holding a regulation baseball. Cole stood about thirty feet away to his right, and his father about forty-five feet away to his left, both patting their mitts. This wasn't only catch, but had become, to Jimmy at least, a chance to shine, to admittedly portray one God given talent. Cole had his book smarts, and Jimmy realized twins could be driven by opposite motivations: where one maneuvered strictly by thinking, the other maneuvered by pure action, and Jimmy realized at that moment why he had seen that picture in his head. Because his father had always told him to aim for the middle of the glove, "because pitchers make the best cash son, and they only have to work once every five days. Can you beat that?"

Yes he could, and he would. While Jimmy leaned against the table, he reached into his pocket and grabbed the biggest stone he had shoved in there;

he rubbed his thumb over it for a moment and looked at the back of Ashton's head, his cropped hair poking over his leather mask like grass on the top of a hill—

"*Throw it son, aim for the middle. Pitchers make the best cash—*"

And Jimmy threw the rock; the thwack of the stone connecting with Ashton's skull sounded eerily dull (*it was like when you dropped that watermelon off the bridge in the summer, the same sound, the same thud*). He turned the table over on its side and ran out the front door; he sloshed through the creek and ran towards the cut in the earth, the winding roots rising from the slimy rock like hair from a goblin's head.

And he heard the high whinnying above him. Jimmy stopped and looked up. In the canopies high above the woods there were large shadows blocking the sun; he heard something falling, and falling fast. He started to run forward, the darkness enveloping him, that shrill scream puncturing his temples. He was certain he'd heard men screaming also, intermingled with that whinny. Jimmy turned his head towards the screams, positive he'd find two angry eyes staring back at him, perhaps those of Ashton's, mixed with the running blood from his cut. But—

Instead he heard a loud thud in front of him, and felt the air around him leave the woods; for some reason Jimmy understood why there were no birds in the forest, and he understood this before looking forward. He traced his palm over the few remaining stones in his pocket and slowly turned his head.

What he saw didn't exactly surprise him; he didn't scream because he couldn't. He could have honestly confessed that before the idea of screaming ever surfaced, Jimmy had in fact considered releasing his bladder. It was the scout he had seen outside the forest that had given it away, and yet Jimmy was still quite determined to at least do one thing: Run back to Ashton.

When he did turn he was only confronted by three more, easing their ways towards him. Jimmy was surrounded by spiders—spiders the size of Buicks, their legs stretching beyond their graying bodies at either side like hairy arches.

At last Jimmy found his voice and he screamed.

7

The rock had hit Ashton in the back of the head, but he was lucky enough to have caught the stone off the leather stretched around the nape of his cranium. The sound Jimmy heard, which was more like exploding fruit than it was cracking bone, was the cushioning of the thick hide. He had stumbled against the wall, breaking the arrow he held in half as his body weight stuck the arrowhead against the base of the wall, and the end of the arrow against his collarbone; there was a clear snap, and Ashton hit his forehead feebly against the wall.

The first thing he'd done was drawn another arrow and whisked it into his bow. He stood slowly, expecting to find Jimmy in the grasp of whoever had hit him (the very idea that the boy was behind this had still eluded him). The rock had plunked by his foot. "It is okay," Ashton said, hiding his bow in front of him as his back was turned. If somebody *had* gotten into the shack, whether through the roof, or through the floor, Ashton would have had to consider the possibility that his skills still needed honing, for he could hear voices nearly a league away, but when footsteps were but mere feet from him, his senses deceived him.

Ashton turned quickly, springing the arrow back in the bow, and he held it forward only to face nothing at all. The table was overturned and the front door was swinging lazily in the light breeze. *Of course*, he thought suddenly. Was he so incredibly dimwitted that he immediately toss the boy's reactions out the window without considering Jimmy's tone and curiosity somewhat conspiring? The boy had asked, rather concernedly, why he had pushed the table in front of the door. Jimmy had obviously seen this shack as his only chance to get away, to corner the Hunter and hit him with something he had picked up from the ground—but when Ashton had moved the heavy table in front of the door, Jimmy had watched, for a second at least, his hopes vanish.

Ashton stuck the arrow back in his quiver and secured the bow on his shoulder. He could still hear the whinnying, but there was a worse noise to the east now—an awful silence. And he realized the air smelled different, as if the noxious fumes of the dying ground had surfaced.

Then he heard the boy scream. ashton left the hovel, jumped over the creek with a flip and landed with a bounce that turned into a run, as he rolled under roots and hopped over stones.

8

In a clearing of sagging earth and winding roots, Ashton saw Jimmy. The boy was frozen in place, and by the scratches on his face, Ashton could tell that he had been nervously doing one thing: making sure he was really awake before screaming. ashton was certain of one truth: Jimmy was lucky to still be alive.

The spiders were studying him, were hissing to each other, whinnying in shrieks, the language of the Northern Mountains, for that was where the spiders were originally from. These spiders were male; their abdomens were thin and shone a waxy gleam like lichen on jellystone. The dorsal surface of their thoraxes were long white stripes on top of gray slime, and Ashton could see the sap of the trees dripping from their sternums, falling where their long legs met their slim bodies. He reached around back for an arrow; he could scare them, perhaps drive them away, but kill them? He wouldn't even consider it, for starting a war with the spiders would be his final assurance to Mystic that he was done for. He silently stuck the arrow in his bow and guided its point toward the closest abdomen, pulsating with a gelatinous gleam—

When he was struck on the back!

Something was clinging to his tunic, something heavy. He turned around in circles, holding his breath, holding in his scream, for if he were to startle the spiders, he would be putting Jimmy's life in far more danger. He could feel the heat of the thing's touch on the back of his neck; he reached behind him and found a grimy leg—no two—no four legs, all clutching his tunic, the greasy hair trying to loosen the grip in Ashton's palm. He pulled the spider from his back and whipped it to the ground in front of him; it let out a long screech, its palps nearly rotating as it tried to shift but realized three of its legs were mangled. It was the scout spider, and had it bit him, Asthon realized, their roles would have been reversed.

The scout shrieked until Ashton put his arrow into its belly, more to stop its suffering than the elongated signal. The giant spiders had all turned towards Ashton, their eyes shining whatever light found its way into the woods. The spiders let out one final tumultuous howl; Jimmy covered his ears when he was firmly grabbed in the claw and twisted in the dripping joints of a male spider's front leg. He screamed.

The spiders moved forward, calculating the scout on the ground and the Hunter at the foot of its body.

Ashton saw the fear in Jimmy's eyes, a fear he had tried to hide by muddling Jimmy's curiosity with cryptic explanations; his intention hadn't been to watch the poor boy suffocate in the prickly grasp of the Mountain spiders, or the Higher Beings as folklore had so deemed them. Instead, like he had done so many times before, he had hoped they could sneak under the city above the canopies to meet the wise man. Now everything had been in vain, because they were had, the spiders had descended, and it wouldn't be much longer before the scavengers devoured them from the inside out.

But Ashton wouldn't allow this; he was a descendant of a fierce bloodline, and if he was to go down, then he would prefer legend remember he went down a hero, much like his father before him. Ashton clipped his forefinger in a loop of twine he had distended from either sleeve on his tunic. When his fingernail found the twine, he pulled his finger upwards and the rope tensed, pulling a spring on an arm brace that unlocked and erected three blades, tearing through his tunic and fanning from his forearms like splinters of bone. Ashton lunged forward, kicked the first spider in the eyes before it could react, ran up its thorax and flipped onto the next spider; there was a moment when he thought he'd get bucked off the spider's back, and subsequently slip on the slime that stuck its hair to its abdomen, but the blades protruding from his lower arm cut into the tough skin, and he pulled himself up and jumped towards the spider holding Jimmy in its leg like a flopping fish in a bear's paw. The spider behind Ashton writhed in pain as mucus pumped out of the small wounds like mustard vomit, and burnt the ground as it dripped off the spider's side.

"Jimmy, hold on," Ashton called as he jumped on the spider's leg which strangled the boy. Ashton grabbed onto the leg and clutched with both arms; the other spiders screeched and the leaves above shook with utter torment. Ashton began to slip down the leg; his arrows chattered behind him and his bow slipped down his arm, stopped by the blades cutting through his sleeves.

The spider brought its leg against the ground with a crash. Jimmy screamed. The smell here was horrible, as if the two had drowned in a swamp infested by rotting corpses, but Ashton tried to ignore it; he couldn't very well pull one arm around to block the slits in his mask. Instead Ashton wrapped his left arm around the spider's leg, hooking his hand against the slick hair, and with his other arm he slashed into the spider's tibia with his arm-daggers. The spider roared. Ashton could feel blood pelting his face, dark red blood, which smelt much like overcooked vegetable stew.

The spider's leg loosened around Jimmy, and Ashton hacked again, feeling the warm blood spatter his hair. "Get ready Jimmy, brace your legs," he yelled against the whinnying of the spiders as they circled their prey, scuttling along the fallen leaves, leaving large divots in the ground that would fill with water in the mornings, coaxing the small animals out of their burrows to chance the probability of making it for a drink.

Ashton swiped once more and the spider's leg fell off, leaving a messy stump like a prickly arrow in its side. Both Ashton and Jimmy dropped next to each other, rolling on the uneven ground and knocking into decaying logs.

The spiders' shadow fell over them, and Jimmy rushed to clutch his arms around Ashton. "I'm sorry I hit you, but please, please don't let them touch me again," he said in a low drawl that smelt of tobacco and vomit. Ashton pushed both sets of blades into their locked positions, settling when he heard a slight click in the brace. He drew his sword.

"If war is what you want, then war is what I'll give," he said, and the spiders drew forward.

9

Their shadows grew like budding clouds of darkness, inscribing their malevolence on the ground like poison in a well. The spider with the missing front leg thrashed furiously, kicking at its dismembered tibia and patella with an eagerness that might have fused it back on its writhing body had it been possible. Blood spewed from its stump in waning patterns, collecting in the divots the spiders' claws left in the ground.

Ashton held his sword before him, blood running over his brow, into his mask, over his eye until it looked like an obscured patch. He made no effort to wipe the blood away, and for some reason it made him seem more admirable. The spiders hissed and cowered on their back legs, cinching their abdomens underneath their bodies so that their thoraxes rose in the air and embellished the long streaks of white that showed long veins within. Some spiders had six eyes, others had eight, each of them intent on Ashton and Jimmy, neither swaying nor blinking; their palps twitched and drops of poison fell to the ground, frothing on the fallen leaves with a crisp smoke that curled them into black twigs.

"Your sword is merely the sting of pests," a voice called out over the wind.

"I have slain many with this blade, and it will not fail me now," Ashton said, clenching the sword with both hands, looking at each of the spiders with hesitation—which one would he attack first if it came to that?

"Ohhh, but we can see beyond your words masked one; there is uncertainty, and in effect, your indecision clutters reason."

"Don't egg them on, please," Jimmy said, watching the spider with the missing leg jig around the clearing.

"We can use the little one's fear against you," the spiders spoke. Ashton pushed Jimmy to the ground and told him to grab the log, to grab it and to never let go. "Close your eyes."

And then Ashton heard a golden voice, a voice that had probably once belonged to a beautiful maiden. The spiders surrounding the clearing separated. Their eyes fell away from their prey for the first time. Jimmy even opened his eyes and stared forward, beyond the trees, beyond the gloom of the woods.

There was an incessant rattle as the earth shook, and beyond the Canopy Trees, hidden by an ancient mist, came the harmonious voice: "You have brought trouble in the quiet woods; you have called out to us, have woken us from our deep lament. What is it you've come for?"

Ashton strained to see who it was, who was speaking. He had heard of the angels, but had never actually seen them; they were intangible in that they took the forms of the bodies they entered, and Ashton wondered if maybe this voice was the result of that transaction. The trees trembled, and seemed to open, to swing away towards the clearing like gates beyond a moat.

"Tell her for crying out loud, tell her," Jimmy said.

The spiders relaxed. Even the poor spider whose leg had been chopped off settled, its ugly head pointed toward the quivering trees.

Ashton hesitated. "We look to the coast beyond the woods, for there lives a friend."

"And why not venture over the mountain pass?"

"Time is a commodity we do not have," Ashton said, still straining to see the body attached to the voice.

"You brought a horse, yet you left it at the edge of the woods, so Haran announced—he *was* our detection, our eyes, our scout. If time were against you, then your horse would have been in your traveling party."

"The woods are no place for a horse."

There were loud thuds; the trees quivered and the ground shuddered. Whatever animals still lived in the forest hid in the deepest recesses of the woods. Something was being dragged, as the scrape of dirt and stone created a sharp tone, like bone on clay.

"You murdered him, and for what? For what misdeed did Haran deserve an arrow?" The voice turned dark, and Ashton saw a bloated shadow behind the trees, which became like bars against the silhouette of a giant.

Ashton saw the smaller spider beyond the circle of gleaming monsters, lying on its back with the shaft of an arrow protruding from its belly; it was a simple answer really—either it was him or the spider—but he didn't believe she would understand this.

Jimmy muffled a cry and covered his eyes again. What was once beautiful had turned, like most in these woods, into a despicable force, repugnant to the ear and even more so to the eye. The slithering sound grew louder and Ashton, who had almost dropped his sword in acknowledgement of that voice, gripped his blade tighter and watched the waning light between the trees fill with the slow blob.

"The scout was our eyes on the outside, a spider who lived for hundreds of years feeding off our scraps, dwelling beneath us in the deepest caverns. He kept watch while we slumbered, while our young trained and sucked the life of the mountains. When we were driven from the caves to the woods, Haran was able to notice those spiders tainted with the mountain's disease, the disease which drove us here. The disease that infected our dead. These woods aren't safe. Not for man."

Ashton watched the space between the trees fill in like the gradual bloom of a flower. And then a small light from above showered upon her, and for the first time, Ashton saw the Queen of the spiders.

10

The other spiders crouched to the ground, uttering praise in screeching hisses. What moved toward them, like a bloated slug with spindly legs, watched only Ashton as he stood with his sword; she had twelve eyes, each glinted with a pearly white, bordered by a soft red that matched the fuzz growing on her brow, parting at her fovea like mended weeds in an old forgotten garden. She wore a crown like a ring through the whiskers, made of silk and leaves, and there were large strands of silk flowing from her like the billows of a royal robe. Her swollen abdomen dragged beneath her, pushing the dirt away at either side like waves against the turf. She squeezed through the trees, her inflamed body bulging as the trunks pushed her legs against her side, releasing putrid air through her jaw.

The Queen dwarfed the other spiders, in both size and elegance. She stood nearly fifteen feet high, and her palps were marked with crimson hair that matched her rimmed eyes. There was a mark on her back like a star, and though it glistened, the sheen wasn't because of slime, but was because of some inner radiance, some incandescent glow that within her belly pulsated with her long and steady breaths.

"A Hunter," the Queen said interestingly. "Standing before me in this clearing of the Leeg Forest like a prince among man, though I see in you a hesitation to reveal certain truths. Behind the mask perhaps lies a revelation that could prove even *my* observations an injustice." She lifted her front legs from the ground and rested on her belly, as if the sagging earth had become her throne.

"I know the disease of which you speak. I heeded the farmers at the edge of Lake Aena, near the Northern Mountains, years ago, who with the aid of a friend, Cesar, drove the demons from the animals—the demon who revealed itself as Legion," Ashton said. He remembered the trail by the Odin river where he was met by a young farmer, a chap with Mystic's slope drawn on his forehead with tar, seeking help for his herd had all died from sickness, and had risen from shallow graves to walk again. *Aye, and that's when Cesar the Traveling Man told you about Ae-Granum, opened your eyes to your own quest, to your own destiny—everything happens for a reason. Purpose.*

"You?" The Queen said, and though her eyes didn't move, Ashton could sense them squirming all over his body, studying him. "Yes…Legion, their bodies like the puppets of whatever glows in their bellies." A drop of poison fizzled from her jaw and dropped to the ground with a loud splash, melting a log and bunches of leaves—the drop had been the size of Ashton's bow. "Why then, would a hero of man enter the woods and murder a scout?"

"I was defending myself, for I was protecting my young companion here. So, I could ask you the same thing, for we entered seeking a safe pass."

The spiders around Ashton shifted uneasily and glowered at him with their hateful eyes, dripping poison themselves and clawing at the ground in anticipation of the attack.

"We were just defending ourselves, Hunter. We don't take too kindly to strangers. Why would we allow you to walk below us in our woods, speaking aloud only as bait to lure us from our trees? The wolves had done the same, the putrid Yilaks of the Sordids, who destroyed an old race of spiders a millennia ago, in the war deep in the caverns of the Sordid Mountains—they entered our woods and drove us from the trees; this was merely days ago, when I still carried. I'd been stranded to the ground after birth, so I dragged the egg behind me, covering it with silk and branches and leaves, feeding off the stray animals, sucking the ground dry. The wolves cut the egg sac from me, and took it for themselves; a few of them we caught and slaughtered. Their bodies are strewn about the woods for the scavengers, for the wolves aren't fit to feast upon; they reek of things long decayed."

Ashton thought about the wolves he and Jimmy had seen while walking, the wolves that had been half melted and infested with scavengers. "I've seen it, the egg sac. The wolves brought it back to the Sordids, to Wolf Country, and I saw them, with men bearing the King's Crest, ripping open the sac to release the eggs—"

"You lie," the queen said.

"No, for every egg that rolled out was stomped upon, even burned."

There was a long collective shudder in the clearing as the spiders all heaved. "Then it is true, for I felt within me the deaths of all my children, as if my heart had stopped," the Queen said sadly, but with an opulent integrity that proved her voice angelic. "Why do you tell me this, if not only to torture me?" The Queen sobbed.

"Stop it," Jimmy screamed. He had been standing, shocked by the Queen's size, but drawn by her voice, and the commanding tone in his own voice interested every spider as they turned to look at him. "You're looking to blame us, I can understand that, I really can. I've blamed people my entire life, and when you hold onto blame you burn with hatred. It's just a stupid excuse to find faults. No matter what Ashton says, you'll just argue with him, or disbelieve him because you're looking for some reason to hate him; you thought you found it when he killed that little spider"—he says little now, of course, because the scout seemed of normal size compared to the others—"but then he assures you it was because of protection. Now you're blaming him for telling you that wolves destroyed your egg. Let me tell you, those wolves have my brother too, and if Ashton's right about them, then I can assure you this seems like something they'd do."

"You are brave, young man, but I see in your eyes a confusion that separates you from this world. You are from across the seas mayhaps, and you have inside you an enlightening intelligence, but—"

"I'm not from across any seas. I'm from the other side of the mines, and where I'm from, you'd be inside a toilet bowl right about now, with mangled legs and guts on either side of Kleenex," Jimmy said.

"I see fear in your eyes, yet you confront it," the Queen said. "There are little left of you. Fear usually draws violence, not reason, for the men who wore the King's Crest feared our declension, and even began to spray us with arrows; they only believe in war, so we confronted them on this basis and gave them what they wanted. We slaughtered five men and sent the rest running south, through the trees, through our webbing. But with you two, I'm confused. You claim you search for a friend beyond the woods, a friend *we* have *never* encountered, and I still wonder if mayhaps you aren't scouts yourself, for the wolves, aye, sent to establish our course."

"Because that's stupid and you know it. I can tell by the tone of your voice; it's called irony, because you know that's not why we've come here," Jimmy yelled.

"He's right," Ashton added, "for I've been through these woods many times before, to see my friend, for he was a friend of my father's and has become my friend in turn. I have come through these woods not to stir trouble or awaken you, but to travel unseen—I warned Jimmy here countless times not to disturb the woods, for I feared the consequences. You are a subject of folklore in the lands and it is left to me to speculate your decisions."

"And what is it you want from your friend that desires such hastiness?" The Queen asked.

"My friend is a wizard, and only he can help me destroy the wolves."

"A wizard? Wizards do not exist here anymore."

"He is the Last Wizard, the *Lone* Wizard, driven to the edge of the land and hiding by the old King who slit his throat—I'm sure you've heard the tale, for it is resonant even beyond the Inlands. The royal men you drove from the woods were also looking for him, but they search with blind faith; they know nothing of him. This is a race against time now, which may heavily depend on the fate of this world, among others, it seems."

The Queen glared for a moment. "A wizard," she said again. "Kannef and Jarat." Two spiders approached from the circle in the clearing, both with hairy backs and white stripes like scars in their gray, scaly flesh. "To walk to the coast, Hunter, would take you hours, for the ground is deceiving and the trees grow dense with the sea breeze." She pointed a long leg at the ground. "Use leaves as saddles, for the gel in their hair will hold you. The spiders do not use the ground when traveling." She looked up towards the canopies. "Understand the consequences if no wizard exists on the coast," she said darkly, and Ashton and Jimmy picked up giant leaves that had fallen from above.

11

Jimmy gathered leaves in his arms. "Why are they doing this for us?"

Ashton exhaled slowly. He had sheathed his sword and stuck his bow back into his quiver. "I think, Jimmy, that spiders rely on faith also. The Queen is a spider who has lost her children. I lost my father. I've lived on revenge my entire life, and I think she's beginning to understand my drives."

"What do you mean?" Jimmy whispered, looking hesitatingly at the spiders around the two.

"Perhaps she believes we were sent not only to question the wizard, but to give the spiders hope that their undoings will be avenged."

"Is there really a wizard?"

Ashton nodded. "You're starting to accept things I take it."

"A spider the size of a city bus will do that to you," Jimmy said uneasily.

Ashton, of course, had no idea what a city bus was, but didn't question it; it really wasn't necessary to do so anyway.

"Are you okay riding atop a spider? I knew how feel about them, so I never told you the truth."

"That was smart. I wouldn't have come into the woods if I'd known." Jimmy looked at the spiders, at their slimy backs and the greasy hair that seemed plastered to their gleaming bodies. "I think it'll be okay," he said after he gulped. "I guess after hearing them talk you realize they're not so different than us at all—well, except for their legs. I still hate those dangly legs." Jimmy picked up a big wet leaf and slapped it over his arm. "By the way, thanks for saving my life. And I'm sorry about hitting you." Jimmy touched the back of his head and gave a small grin.

Ashton smiled.

12

The leaves draped over the back of Jarat stuck nicely with the ooze that had greased his hair and matted it to his cardiac sign, like graying rot on some ancient white. Jimmy was apprehensive about getting on the spider; he had touched the thing's wet abdomen, and had at first thought he was going to vomit, but the feeling passed.

"Ride with me, and you can hold me instead," Ashton said, as he climbed aboard Jarat's back. The spider had hunkered down; its legs massive arches on either side towering over the two like cage bars.

Jimmy looked at Jarat, who had turned to face him and watched with his unblinking eyes. Jimmy could sense many years behind that gaze, many adventures. "Hi."

The spider responded with a slight bow, and Jimmy swore, though he would question its actuality the entire ride, that he saw Jarat smiling.

Ashton held his hand out. The back of his head still stung but he ignored it. Pain was the enemy. But enemies could become allies, for here he sat, on the back of a spider, his legs braced around its abdomen, sitting atop wet leaves that were sucked down by a sappy grease—*the world is changing.* Jimmy grabbed the Hunter's hand, dug his foot into the spider's side and climbed up.

"Yesterday I would never've dreamed about doing this," Jimmy said.

Ashton took hold of clumps of hair, and Jimmy wrapped his arms around the Hunter's slender frame.

The spiders ascended the trees, clambering up the thick trunks with ease, bolting through the twigs and branches, exploding through leaves and hopping from web to web, clinging to the silk strands with their claws. Ashton and Jimmy had their legs wrapped around the spider, and when Jarat surfaced above the canopies, both the Hunter and the young boy looked out upon Spider City—pillars of silk like rays of pearl that shone every angle of the sun like glitter; spun webs that had formed houses and bridges, with leaves stuck in wreaths and banners.

Ashton could see everything from here—the mountains to the east, to the south, even the infinite stretching ocean, like foams connecting the firmament to earth.

And the spiders moved northeast, atop the canopies, over the webs and through the pillars of silk, the land under them like something they had forever left behind.

CHAPTER 16

FACE OF DEATH, FACE OF LIFE

1

Auger stood with a bottle in his hands looking at the darkness the bomb had left on the bluff. He was utterly shaken; he felt cheated really, and ultimately felt as if he had been intentionally set up to anger the wolves. This wasn't about them in the end of course, but a very strong part of him insisted he not let this go easily.

You're thinking of sending the poor boy into the Towers—what purpose is there in doing that?

Auger grunted. There were wolves diving into the Dead Springs, and he could hear the loud mutters of the She-wolves inside the tents made for them—he heard them, but never dared to look. Legend had always claimed they were fiercer than the males, and he surely hadn't wanted to look into darker eyes than those of Grak's.

He tipped the bottle to his lips; his elbow still killed, but that wasn't the worst pain. The worst pain was his pesky mind; he had been feeling the collision of his thoughts like feet against the ground, constantly jumping up and down. His shadow spread in front of him and made him look like a giant—a giant with three legs. His cane was propped under his elbow.

He had thrown the boy back into the tent with *that* demon—

"Of course," he said out loud. A couple wolves looked up at him. "I can send the hermit in with the boy." He took another long drink.

2

When the robot had exploded the wolves at the camp readied for war; this was just instinct, though those that were around when it happened hadn't heard such a noise since the wizard collapsed the mountains; the younger wolves remained baffled. The She-wolves howled from the tents.

This was just a reflex. The wolves were bred on the constant threat of war and invasion, and realized it was their duty to fulfill their position in battle. No matter a wolf's age, he could wield a blade or an axe; many of the wolves that reacted to the explosion hadn't been over five years old yet; they had a hindering look of awareness, which was countered by fear. Wolves, despite the beliefs of popular myth, did not want to die; they feared death just as Kenneth Auger fears it, but they, through many years of indoctrination, have learned to disguise the weakness by removing any doubt they have when facing death. When wolves go to war, they do so willingly. They ignore the possibility that they won't return because fear is a human emotion, an emotion like love, which ultimately roots itself like a disease and spreads until becoming incurable—a parasite. The threat of war had, for years, become a way of life; in fact, wolves had begun to believe that by dying in battle, they would only return stronger with the mark of Mystic—this had been a shared belief regarding the strengths of Grak Ulak, whose fearlessness led the wolves to sack the city of the King and overthrow many of the Hunters, the base of the bloodline. When the wolves learned Grak had taken a pack of Yilaks through the mines to face the man with the stone, they insisted upon packing weaponry and joining their General to face whomever it was they'd meet in those cursed caverns. Because Jarak stayed behind and instead tended to the old man, they too, like Grak, shared their distaste with the old wolf, who for almost fifty years was among the highest-ranking Yilaks in Wolf Country.

"What was that noise, that fire?" A wolf howled when the wagon pulled by oxen returned to camp.

Jarak looked at the Yilak with his aged yellow eyes; he pulled back his scarred brow, which was matted with soot and ground rock: "We have been deceived."

The wolves howled again, holding their swords and axes, all stained with grime. "Where is Grak?"

Jarak knew this question would arise. When turmoil seemed imminent, Yilaks looked to their general to establish a set course. Jarak looked down for a moment, realizing his reasoning to stay behind would be scrutinized by the packs, and knew that his insistence to care for the old man would ultimately bring about his downfall. But Jarak, like Grak's father, hadn't been tainted by the notion of war and vengeance; if getting a sword in the back while he turned around was his fate, then he'd take the blade like Grak's father had before him. "They have gone into the mines. To their deaths," Jarak said with a grunt and saw the disapproval in the wolves' eyes.

They howled, and the She-wolves joined, like chortling hyenas. "So we go to war," Azak the Wolf said, who stood in front of the pack, brandishing a long blade stained with peeling blood.

"To go into those mines only invites an opportunity for the man with the stone to crush you," Jarak said.

"So fear stayed you from joining the invasion?" Azak asked.

Jarak grunted and looked at the wolf squarely. "The old man has other plans."

"The old man has brought this on us all," Azak said, and the others howled. "Your care for the old man has proven your emotions Jarak. You reason like a man—perhaps you too are a man dressed in fur." The wolves laughed.

Jarak had pounced on Azak, startling the stalled oxen, spilling dust from their billowing manes. He pinned the wolf on the ground and bared his dripping teeth. "Remember who it is you speak to," Jarak snapped, saliva slinging from his lip like congealed foam, slapping Azak's forehead, blinding one discolored eye. "Until Grak returns, I am in charge of the Sordids, *I aime Rocasza*," he howled in the old language of the mountains, repeating himself in a guttural roar.

And he was, for now at least. Jarak was in charge of Wolf Country, and he knew that until Grak returned from the mines—*if* he did—he would be potentially safe from assassination. *Potentially.*

3

The old man walked over to Jarak. He walked slowly, wobbling with his cane, feeling an obscured pull along his thighs, a resentment in his bones that worriedly plead he stop and rest. The old man could feel something else inside him, something perhaps emphasized by the alcohol. He could feel his stomach clenching, as if ready to purge everything inside his body until he was completely drained; it was a horrible feeling, and when Jarak saw the struggle in the old man, he got up, dropping the blood stained bone in his claws to meet the old man halfway before he collapsed in exhaustion.

Jarak watched the wolves suspiciously, as they all eyed him from the corners of the camp—they had certainly found his weakness, and he knew they would use the old man to draw something from him, perhaps fear, or another of his human emotions. "What is it?" Jarak said, conscious of the yellow and red eyes on his scruffy back.

"I had a feeling for a moment Jarak, a bad feeling, as if everything inside me wanted to come out, wanted to leak out." The old man shuddered.

Jarak realized himself the difference in the old man, the way he looked, the way his eyes had sunken farther back in his wrinkled head; the way his brow was littered with spots and dark moles, chunks of thinning hair that would come loose soon, either because of his rotting skin, or because of the hot sun.

"It is coming soon, I fear, sooner than I had hoped."

"Death," Jarak said.

The old man nodded. "I am afraid to be angry right now. I know I should be. I held that man's boy to him and he gave me an explosion. There is no other option. He's going into the Towers for the wizard's blood round the King's throat."

Jarak looked at the old man oddly.

"He'll go through the southern crawlspace the wolves dug."

"He will not come out alive," Jarak said, uncertain why the old man would want to send the boy into the burrows.

"I don't believe the ghosts will harm a child," the old man said. He seemed to be talking to himself.

You're insane, he thought.

"I AM NOT INSANE!" The old man screamed at himself. Jarak jumped back a step; he had been frightened by a man…a *man*! "I am dying," he said in a lower tone. "I have no other choice."

You do. You can die. You can die and finally see Judith again.

"I don't want to die."

"Are you all right?" Jarak asked.

The old man looked at the wolf. "We'll send the hermit in with the boy," he finally said.

"What will that do?"

"That demon saw into our heads; it saw into *mine*. I could feel it; I could see it. It would have seen my diseases I'm sure, like mouths with sharp teeth in my blood, in my bones. What if the ghosts feel the same way when they look into its eyes?"

Jarak grunted. "They are dead."

"So is the demon," the old man said matter-of-factly.

Jarak spied the wolves watching him and the old man; he wished he could slaughter them all. It was an awkward thought.

4

Cole undid the rope around Hayle the Hermit's throat, momentarily brushing his knuckles against the soft skin. He had contemplated doing so for what seemed like hours, ever since he had returned from the cliff side, but his sense of hesitation drew on the feeling he had gotten when the hermit was inside his head.

"I cannot see inside you when my eyes are covered," the hermit had said reassuringly when Cole returned. Hayle rubbed his throat with the stump on his left arm; it left odd streaks on his pallid skin. The rope had left a deep divot in his neck, like the twisted joints on a balloon animal.

"I want to go home," Cole said, and he felt on the verge of crying again. He had thought he could run away, but he was wrong. Home seemed like a memory, and perhaps it was this nagging nuisance that insisted he talk to the hermit in the birdcage; the same hermit that had hypnotized him earlier, and whom he fed chocolate to only to watch it get spit out. He realized that if he did have an ally here, his best chance was to make it with Hayle; he sensed how the others feared him.

"I do too," the hermit said. "My home does not exist anymore, but for the pictures I see on the inside of this blindfold. I suppose your head was built for such a purpose Cole, to close your eyes to the filth we've had to endure here, only to remember the places you've taken for granted." The hermit smiled, showing its sharp teeth. "I've been having this feeling Cole, ever since hearing the explosion—something is going to happen. Soon. We are sitting in a battleground. I feel war comes on all fronts. I think the explosion was a message; there are tides in the earth that sense everything before it happens—the course of time you might say."

"My home is different," Cole said as if he hadn't been listening, and now he *was* crying. "I had a feeling I was near it when I was on the cliff. I don't know why, but I know I was near it; I could smell my mother, I think."

The hermit shifted forward, pushing himself on his knees. He pulled himself towards the front of the cage. "She misses you I'm sure."

"Yeah," Cole said.

"Perhaps she sends her scent to you as a trail."

"She doesn't know I'm here—wherever here is, exactly." Cole rubbed his eyes and looked at the lights streaming through the top of the tent, like the rays through the pavilion at his mother's wedding.

"Shhh. They come now, I can hear them, a wolf and the old man," the hermit said in a whisper.

5

Jarak left the old man's side for a moment; he was conscious of the wolves' eyes and realized he had to do what was necessary to keep them at bay for the time being. His time serving under Grak had taught him one thing: that survival and respect became driven by the same instinctive desire, and though Jarak would have rather followed Grak's father than suit up in iron chest plates, and wear a helmet that squashed his ears to invade the city of the King, he understood that he'd have to divert paths and portray at least hints of dominance.

Jarak scanned the crowd of wolves, thinking only of Grak and of the way he had stuck his sword into his father's back. He found Azak sitting in the shadows of the Towers, running his claws down his sword; he was seated with his legs splayed out in front of him, his back to a tent. An odd ferocity ranged through Jarak, a mighty feeling he had ignored for much of his life; he supported the wolves' views on vengeance, but seemed relentless to at least try and change the archaic ideals they held regarding warfare.

Azak continued sharpening his claws on the sharp edge of his sword; there was a scuffled sound—he was, ironically, planning his own methods to rid of Jarak and the old man, his intent only to stand out among the rest in front of Grak. Azak had been licking his lips, watching Jarak and the old man talking, obvious conspirators who had driven Grak into the caves—he had this rising anger, like the bubbling water of the Dead Springs, only he honed his patience. "I will be next to the chieftain," he had said under his sour breath, watching his image in his rusty, dirty blade—an image that had been distorted, but resembled most of what made Azak: dirty fur and crooked teeth.

Azak hadn't the time to look up when Jarak jumped on him. The timing was impeccable really, because the shock had led Azak to drop his sword, rather than raise it in defense, as most wolves had learned. He saw in Jarak's eyes something he would envy until his end—he saw a violent madness in them that he had been trying to duplicate himself. They were the vicious eyes of Grak Ulak. Azak let out one last whimper before lessening his struggle; he realized he had waited far too long, and realized part of Grak had rubbed off on old Jarak also. He watched the old wolf lift his dripping throat into the air and then he shut his discolored eyes and opened them no more.

"I am the prince of wolves. *I aime Rocasza*," Jarak howled into the air, flinging Azak's dismembered throat into the side of a tent; it stuck for a moment, and then slowly slid to the ground with a fat thump. Jarak had proved his dominance to the wolves, and when he joined the old man to go to the boy, he realized that fear had overtaken many of them, and instead of watching him enter the tent, they readied themselves for Grak's return.

Jarak hated their optimism.

The old man hadn't noticed anything; his mind, or at least what was left of it, was pinpointed on the possibility that he still had a chance at further life, and that that chance was somewhere in the Towers.

6

When both Jarak and the old man entered the tent, Hayle the Hermit changed so that his almost friendly, elongated face, turned to blindfolded rage; he lunged at the side of the cage with such ferocity that the bars seemed to quiver. Cole closed his eyes.

This startled the old man out of his thoughts, and he only bashed the cage with his cane. Jarak grabbed the hermit, sticking his hairy arms between the bars; he pulled the sickly figure back with a hard thud.

"There is fear in your touch," the hermit said with distaste. "I can taste it." Hayle snapped at Jarak's left arm and missed by mere inches. The sound of his long teeth closing together was like a dozen doors being slammed. Jarak growled and shook the cage.

Cole struggled to move away, ultimately hitting his back against the tent.

The old man moved towards Cole, an awkward look on his face—he was in constant conflicts with his mind, and at the moment, though nobody else could hear it, his mind was yelling at him, yelling at him in a shrieking voice that would wake the dead. Nothing annoyed Kenneth Auger more than the out of place judgments made by the conscience. He was being called INSANE, a MONSTER, neither of which he believed; he was facing something he had feared ever since he was a young boy and understood what death was. The fact that he was standing at the steps of some unknown abyss deeply frightened him. He had always feared death, ever since he had found the tumor, but there is always a fear of the unknown in us all, and though the drink sufficed this path he'd taken, the fact that he was in this world and not his own had at times driven him to the brink where he sought death as an escape. He remembered thinking of jumping out of a window in the castle in northern Sadaan, just beyond the Joon Mountains; he remembered wondering what his last thoughts would be as he was falling closer to the ground. Would he regret doing it? Right now he embraced life, because he saw in death an open chasm that left him falling forever without a destination—at least in suicide he knew he wouldn't be left dangling in midair with suppositions about his life had he not jumped. Suicide would have been *his* control, done on *his* own merits.

Kenneth Auger hated the idea that his mortality wasn't his to control— *but.*

But he could change that. He had heard stories, the ancient folktales of this world, legends that told of giants and fire breathing dragons, magic that could control armies, and languages that could persuade the elements to act upon your every whim; he was a man born on the ideals of a world that scorned the surreal, that attempted to answer the unknown with logical explanations that would tide over the disbelievers. But here he was, now, in a place where his alliance with wolves, faltering as it was, seemed to reverse the ideas of his old self, his old beliefs; he was bound by different convictions, a part of him urging he believe not what he see, but what made sense—and in reality none of this made sense. None of this could have been real.

For some reason, when he stepped out of the mines and into this world, polluted by the exploding rocks of a collapsed mountain, he felt different; he could no longer feel the exhausting grip of the tumor inside his chest, the tiresome worry that made him selfishly question God and His motives. None of that existed anymore.

He seemed born again.

Death scares us all, but there's nothing you can do about it. But there is, there is something you can do to stop death. The King did so; the King stuck a knife into the wizard's throat and drank his blood like your common vampire—and he breathed eternity.

Man wasn't meant to live forever.

But why not embrace the chance? It was all a matter of hesitation, his indifference to common belief and his grasp of legends. *A wizard's blood deems life eternal, dodging death's timeless inferno*, the story read—he remembered the impact that line had on him as he sat in the library with the scroll laid out in front of him, the absolute insistence he had had to believe its every word.

And the Traveling Man told you your destiny.

The fortuneteller had come driven by horse and carriage, wearing an odd hood over his wiry head, his aquiline nose poking from the darkness like a shark's fin. He read Auger's palm, staring deeply into his eyes. "Yer afraid. That's normal, but out and beyond there exist answers even I cannot tell. Yer past is a line, aye, a tunnel darkening with every blink, with every sleep. Yer becoming somebody else, and yer past is being eaten. Death, aye, rows an' rows o' tombstones lining the ground in circles, each line bordering the next like the lid of an eye; 'tis inevitable you should face this consequence," and he raced his thin finger down the old man's hand, reading the wrinkles in his palm, "but ya insist the truth of stories is absolute…a part o' ya does. The other vies to bury you beneath yer wicked beliefs. No matter, I see ya following the path o' suggestion; you believe the tales you've read in the city. Mayhaps ya'll find yer answer in an egg, through the murk of the deep woods, clouded by canopies. Seek the wolves sire, aye, for their help is necessary. They guard yer path, an' would accept a trade to help. I know. A trade for the stone. Bring it back to this world and you will live. Remember the King, sire, for in his actions the eventuality of yer answer exists."

It was a paradox, Auger realized. He would have to chance death to beat death; it was the age-old adage of canceling the other out.

He chanced death by confronting the wolves with his own proposition in exchange for their help—he told the wolves he would give them the man with the stone if they helped him in the Towers, if they helped him retrieve the wizard's blood from the King's neck. But they had laughed and howled at his eagerness to enter such damned grounds—there is no surviving the Towers, they had said. But that was a lie. David the Hunter survived, the old man had responded.

"Only to die in my hands," Grak said, tearing the leg from a roamer with his curved fangs. "That is its curse."

He went to the Leeg remembering the Traveling Man's words, that his answer would be found in the egg sac, where in the stories men had seen humans hatched from the silken interiors like mutated arachnids, drowning in the embryo as the spiders dragged them to the sea, pushing their greasy heads under the surf until their bodies flailed no more. Nobody knew where the wizards came from—if they were born or just made by Mystic as some stories claimed to say. Even here, in a world of such imaginative circumstances, people still had to clarify the truth in every event, and give everything a history, a story. Some said the wizards were born from flowers. Others said they came from spiders. The townfolk told the stories. It was Auger's insistence to believe them.

Auger stood before this little boy, this boy whose father had sent down an exploding robot. *There was nothing in the egg but a pallid hermit*, he thought with disdain, *but the stories say everything happens for a reason. Everything has purpose. That's why you found the hermit, perhaps.*

If the Towers were dangerous, he'd chance this forgotten boy then; he'd send this boy into the tunnels to search for the King, to bring back the vial of wizard's blood worn around his neck. He'd send the mutant in with him, perhaps to counter the gaze of the ghosts, and to ultimately pin the King with the most horrible images, presenting the opportunity to grab the vial and bring it back to the old man. The boy was dispensable. This became a point to the man with the stone, no matter the wolves coming up for him through the mines right now. This boy was chancing death to turn death away from another man; the reasoning seemed admirable, because he had been in the boy's place not so long ago.

"Cole," the old man said in his raspy voice. "I'd like to speak with you."

7

Jarak stood by the cage, constantly checking the door in the tent, as if there still existed a plot against him.

"You're worried. I can feel your anxiety," Hayle the hermit said to the wolf, slightly turning his malformed head. The blindfold was still wrapped around his eyes, cuffing his nostrils; there was a subtle wheeze when he exhaled.

Jarak grunted. "You know nothing."

"What is it exactly you wish to gain from the boy?"

Jarak looked at the hermit and clasped the cage bars; the sound of his claws against the iron a high clink.

"You're stuck in the middle of thoughts—I can feel your hesitation," the hermit said in a very low voice. "You are nervous; you breathe slowly. You do not want to be heard."

Jarak closed his yellow eyes. This hermit had seen inside his head, and what was it the hermit had left brazened in his vision—none other than Azlak Ulak's fallen body with the hilt of a sword protruding from his back. When Grak murdered his father for dominance in Wolf Country it not only led the Yilaks to decay, but demanded they fight with each other. Conservative supporters against Grak's vigilantism waged war against him; there wasn't *just* a civil war in man's city. There was a war within the wolves' very troops that could have decimated the race for good, doing the King's work without bloodying the hands of man. When Jarak looked into the hermit's eyes, he saw himself holding Azlak's fallen body, cradling the wolf in his arms with the understanding he'd have to reform himself in order to survive. Grak had become powerful, too powerful.

"There are bad tidings ahead," Jarak finally said.

"What is your name?"

"What does that matter?" Jarak asked.

"I have a secret for you, wolf, a secret I could have told Grak the other night, but decided against it for I would rather devour my own heart than aid him."

Jarak's ears perked up, and he opened his eyes; they seemed to shine like fog lamps. "What is your secret?"

"I have seen a conspiracy within your country."

"Are the other wolves deciding an attack on me?"

"I would not know, for I do not know who you are. I am blindfolded."

"Jarak. Jarak Roschak."

"Ah, Jarak, he who misses the mountains; he who misses many things." The hermit smiled, showing his sharp teeth. "I saw your own plan, a plan in the making I should say, for you yourself may not know it yet. A wolf against the wolves, a notion I would have thought impossible until meeting you. You remain fighting under Grak by force, not by willingness; you have in you a desire to avenge the old general's death. Your misery is your acceptance of this new rule; you fight for Grak out of an allegiance to the wolves, a decaying allegiance." The hermit licked his pallid lips with his lizard tongue.

"The wolves have become mindless under Grak; they march forwards without foreseeing consequence. Azlak the Great had foreseen the life of battle, and instead decided on maturing our race before marching to war; we were left to rot when the mountains came down. Those left of us, those who survived, were obligated to hide in the fallen caverns, to hide from the King's men as they slaughtered the injured wolves struggling beneath rocks. Azlak was against the idea of wandering aimlessly to a war we were not ready for; our numbers were too low. When we heard of the civil war in the city, we figured man had done it to themselves. Grak murdered his father for the crown, and he taught the wolves a life they were not ready for. Grak taught the young to march to death, and for what?" Jarak spoke in a whisper; his breath was hot.

The hermit nodded. "Man is conniving too."

"What do you mean?"

"The old man looks to deceive you all. I have seen this. He sought the magic stone to both get into the Towers safely, and to retrieve the wizard's blood from within; he has promised he would show you the world he was once from. His memory of this world is hazy; he misses a woman there, but he has never had any intentions of bringing the wolves back with him. He would kill you all before he would taint this other place. I have seen in all your heads a curiosity and lust for this other world, but you will never get there. You were all very slow to believe an old man would help you conquer worlds. Would help you retrieve the stone in your ongoing pillage."

"You lie only to stir trouble," Jarak said.

"Mayhaps I have just waited for the right wolf to tell. Mayhaps with your persuasion, the old man will let the boy go free, and instead take *you* to this world."

Jarak turned and watched the old man and the boy's shadows against the tent; they had wandered around the corner, speaking to each other in muffled voices.

8

"Why are you doing this?" Cole asked.

The old man looked down, and for one awful minute, Cole believed his ancient face had begun to fall apart. His brow was patchy, and there were dark moles around his jowls that seemed terribly swollen and alive—but his flesh was scales, old and folded, and Cole believed he had started to crumble into dust, but it must have been the light. "Come," the old man said, his breath rancid.

He dragged Cole aside, pulling him by the sweater. The tent was a large rectangle, built with partitions that were made of twisted wood beams and tightly strung wool. The birdcage sat near the door to the south, and twenty or so feet to the north was a partition that separated most of the floor space from a vacated area with nothing but bones tossed sparingly on the ground, and hunks of junk metal in the corner (these pieces of metal, some with wiring hanging askew, and others with wheels, made Cole think about Leo). This was a killing field.

The old man looked at the boy knowingly. There were two sides to this man; that much was evident. He was torn between sanity and insanity, like many people, only in this man both were in a constant battle. "How is it up there now?"

"What?"

"On the other side. How has it changed?"

"I don't know what you're talking about."

"Don't play dumb with me, Cole. I've heard you speak to the hermit. You long to go back too. Look at me. I'm over a hundred years old. I came here in 1956, when the mines exploded—when the mountains exploded. Time is strange here, yes, almost not right. But the face I see, the bones I feel, should agree with my age. What year is it back home? How does it look now that I've been gone for so long?"

"Why don't you go look for yourself. You don't need me to tell you," Cole said shyly, and he looked away. He was afraid.

"I would have—*could* have if your father hadn't tricked me."

"My father's dead," Cole said with abrupt certainty.

"He's dead?" The old man moved in closer until his stinking breath and old face loomed mere inches over Cole's. "Then tell me, boy, who the man with the stone is?"

Cole thought for a moment. Stone? What did that mean? And then, of course, he had it, as if his brain had been holding the answer from him. Edwin Krollup had an ugly stone he wore as a necklace, a stone he would caress if he thought nobody was looking. Cole had believed that stone was from one of Krollup's first mines, a memento perhaps. "Edwin Krollup," he finally said.

The old man relaxed a moment. "Edwin Krollup." He pondered the name for a moment. "And this isn't your father?"

Cole shook his head. "I hate him."

"Where is your father then?"

"He's dead. I told you before."

The old man wasn't listening. *There is a reason for everything,* he thought. And the old man had done something dumb at this point; he had trailed off into a cumbersome thought that drifted his head to the side. Cole had seen this as an opportunity. Instead of nodding his head in agreement with this senile mummy, Cole grabbed the twisted cane from the old man's gnarled hand, and bashed him in the side. Not on the head. Cole was prone to guilt. When he kicked Leo in the vent, he was sure he had inadvertently killed him, and this surety drove him to second guess his conscience, assured him he was a murderer; he didn't want that kind of aggravation again.

Cole hit the old man's thigh, driving him against the partition. The wall knocked over and smashed on the ground, with the old man on top of it. Cole had picked up a thick bone, and as the partition collapsed, he had thrown it at the wolf near the cage.

9

Jarak turned away from the cage and saw the shadow of the boy and old man through the partition. There was a rising fury within him; he had trusted the old man, and in the end Auger was only going to betray the wolves. *But the hermit seeks to open your anger, searches for reasons to destroy you from within,* Jarak thought—

And he saw behind the partition, in a matter of seconds, the boy snatch the old man's cane and whack him with it; there was a loud crack and then the partition fell. Jarak growled, but he was knocked in the shoulder by something the boy had thrown. This all happened so quickly that Jarak hadn't the time to fully react, or realize what was going on. His senses were beginning to deceive him.

Cole darted past the cage. This time he wasn't going to fail; he knew the odds were against him, but he also knew that despite the irregularity of this place, something had to have been watching over him.

"Go boy, to your mother," the hermit hissed, and Cole felt compassion for the monster. *I will,* was his last thought before he was thrown against the side of the tent. Cole didn't even make it to the door.

10

Jarak saw that a bone had hit him in the shoulder; it was thrown quite hard.

He watched the boy run past him, and saw belief and hope in his young eyes; it was scary to recognize such things, because Jarak had forgotten both. It wasn't even instinct that grabbed the boy and tossed him against the wall.

Rather, it was displaced fury. Jarak threw the boy and turned directly around to pounce towards the old man, who was struggling on the ground.

Jarak picked him up by the shirt and dangled him loosely in the air. "You lied to me," he spoke in a horrible growl.

The old man was dazed; he didn't break anything, but at his age, he realized, unexpected falls were prone to infectious discomfort. He only moaned.

"You promised us you could bring the stone back to the Inlands." He shook the old man. "The hermit saw deceit inside you. You used us. You used *me.* I turned my back on my duty, on the wolves, to aid you, and in turn you have conspired to destroy us all with the very stone that has already ruined our home. I should tear your heart out; I should slash your throat and let the hermit drink your blood; I should eat your face and let you wander the Barrens and chance the hounds with blood on your shirt."

Cole was unconscious on the floor; he dreamed of course, but not about the wolves. Rather he thought of his mother.

"He wanted to murder you all," the hermit said with a sly sneer behind the wolf.

"Shut up, or you too will face the hounds," Jarak spat.

"It's wrong," the old man muttered; it was a weak voice, and for a moment, Jarak believed he was finally dying.

"Tell me, how is it wrong?"

"I don't see you as one of them," the old man said through a gargling throat.

Jarak dropped him. He fell like a bunch of twigs.

"Then how do you see me?"

The old man, who was sitting on his backside with both legs splayed either way, looked up with blazing eyes. "I see you—I see you differently than I see them. The wolves are like Grak. You're not. What is it worth to fight for them, Jarak?"

The wolf turned and looked at the hermit, who was clutching the bars, his malformed head squeezed uncomfortably between two of them, the blindfold wrinkling in the middle. It wasn't worth anything but allegiance. But what was allegiance to a general who assassinated the true ruler of the Yilaks? "Our race is doomed," he said aloud, not meaning to do so. But it was the truth. There existed in his mind the portentous thought that the wolves would get it in the end, that by some twist of events, the wolves would fall into a trap that would ultimately defeat them. Jarak believed he had met that trap at this very moment, within this old man who had succeeded in infiltrating the Yilaks, but there remained Jarak's allegiance. Did he dash from the tent and alert the wolves that the old man had planned all of their dooms, or did he let himself sever his ties with the doomed race and watch as a spectator their inevitable fall, a fall he had foreseen for many years?

"I fight for them because my father before me did," Jarak said.

"Did your father fight for Grak?" The old man asked weakly, and Jarak knew that if he didn't answer him, the hermit would. He was sure the hermit had seen within him the answer clearly enough.

"My father died in the civil wars defending the old general—the civil wars Grak started when he murdered his father for control of the tribes," Jarak said in a low tone, and at that very moment he knew what he wanted. He knew what he wanted because he finally severed himself from the wolves. Jarak got down on all fours, like his ancestors had before him when they roamed the mountains and hunted the goat without sword, but with claws and teeth. He looked at the old man; it didn't matter if what he spoke wasn't the truth. For the moment, the old man gave Jarak something to believe in.

"Forget sending the boy into the Towers, old man, forget it, and the two of us will ride like man and horse through the mines, through Grak's tomb, for the stone bearer will have destroyed them all, will have crushed the other wolves beneath the sheets of slate. We will barter with him for our safepass. The hermit told me you missed a woman there; we shall meet her, and we both shall be free of the torments of this world." Jarak helped the old man to his feet and felt, for the first time since Azlak Ulak had been general, a sense of euphoria.

"I am dying. I will never make it that far," the old man responded. He was shaking. "In both worlds, I am dying. I need that blood, Jarak. I need it." He looked at Cole, who was squirming on the ground. "*He's* my only chance."

"You mustn't," the hermit blurted. "Let the boy go back to his mother, and I shall go into the Towers for you. I shall finish your damned errands Kenneth Auger, husband of Judith, who used to love sitting by the coast, watching the foam of the tide and listening to the waves as the concerto music played on the pier. Let the boy go."

"Never speak of her," the old man screamed, and the hermit fell backwards. "You know nothing; you are only a disgusting maggot. I'm sending the boy into the Towers because of *you*. You've done this to him because you care for him. You *care* for him. You would never let anything happen to him, would you? Then you have negotiated his safepass—*you* and you alone. You have doomed the boy," he screamed and the hermit squirmed on the cage floor, "because you care for him. Doom, it seems, is your nature."

11

The Towers stood over a thousand feet tall, with three large rock turrets like long daggers sticking out of the earth; they were all connected like the tines of a fork, but the middle spire was the tallest. It pierced the clouds above the world until the top was barely discernable. Long Necks flew from the Barrens to circle the Towers and caw at the sky, perhaps waiting for scraps left behind by the wolves—something the wolves weren't prone to leaving. The Long Necks had better luck scrounging off the Black Hounds in the desolation to the south of the Sordids. Today there were three birds overhead, and they loomed curiously looking down, craning their ugly necks so that their gnarled beaks poked their breasts, probably shredding their tarnished orange feathers, sending them into the wind. The old man stood with Jarak, not watching the birds, but staring at the tunnels in the Tower's base. They weren't big, but they could fit a fair sized wolf if he hunched and crawled, careful not to snag his fur on the fissures above or below. There were eleven tunnels, each in line with the other—

"There is a curse in there," Jarak said. He was still on all fours. "There are probably hundreds of rooms, on level upon level of floors until the clouds can be seen through pores in the rock, and I tell you old man, for I have seen those who returned. There is a spell put on the inside, a spell that stalls you, stays your feet once you exit the tunnels; we disturbed the Towers when we dug into them, but that was Grak's choice. The entrance is a hall carved from stone with pillars and an endless ceiling, and a door long since sealed over the years by the Tower's growing magic. And down the great hall there exists an ancient guardian, for whatever enters the Towers does so with ill intent, and that guardian sees all, and punishes those it encounters."

The old man grunted. "Then how did David the Hunter survive?"

Jarak didn't know. He could only picture David the Hunter's lifeless body in Grak's claws, flailing around with broken bones; he could only sense the astonishment, the sense of defeat as the Hunters realized their leader was gone. He felt the same once. Still did. Azlak was to the wolves what David was to the Hunters—a reason to keep fighting, to hold onto allegiances.

"The King once told me he had the wizard release the souls of dead knights into the Towers to protect his horde until he returned. The wizard made a Great Judge, the King said, one who stood a giant among man, and who found guard before the King's chamber, before the door that had secured the talismans. If there was this all-powerful guardian, then why wasn't David tried before it? It is all happenstance."

Jarak looked around, at the wolves watching him from the corners of their eyes. He knew many of them would gladly rip his throat out, and he knew that waiting here at the base of the Towers was a bad idea. The hermit had warned them of the war before entering the tunnel; he said he felt it through the ground. The explosion spoke those very words to the mutant, and Jarak believed him. Not because the hermit searched his head, but because he felt the same way ever since Grak took the pack of wolves into the mines. He had a feeling Grak would bring a war back to Wolf Country, a war that would destroy everything. The old man promised he would bring the stone back to the Inlands, but Jarak believed it was Grak who would finally fulfill their desire.

"We should go now. You can climb onto my back and we can see for ourselves Grak's dead body among the rocks of the mines. We can go south, north. The world is our path."

"You are afraid of what the mutant said, about war, aren't you? I knew you were different than the other wolves, Jarak, for I've never seen fear in any of them."

"I am afraid if we stay here longer the wolves' suspicion will avail and they will do to us what they have intended since we returned from the bluff after the explosion."

"What's that?" The old man said weakly.

"They will kill us."

The old man realized the wolves were staring at them, turning their heads every so often; they were waiting for something. "If I leave now, I will die anyway, so what does it matter if I wait here for eternal life?"

Jarak growled, wanting to stand up and hack the old man's head off himself, regain the trust of the wolves, but he stayed his fury. "You sent the boy to his death. You will wait here till your death also then."

"Faith, Jarak. Faith isn't all dried up in these lands yet."

12

Cole crawled in the tunnels, breathing hard while trying to ignore the pain. His side hurt where he was flung against the tent, but it cushioned his body; it was the impact with the ground that hurt the most. He had not brought his Aspirin, which was unfortunate, and the chocolates he had in his pocket seemed rather noisy in this dank, closed space. They rattled when he moved his hips. The tunnel was long, but was lit at either end with sunlight (behind him) and an odd lime glow in front of him, a glow he didn't quite understand.

Cole was in front, and could hear the hermit behind him, his knees dragging on the rocky ground as he pulled himself forward with his right wrist and the stump on his missing left arm. The air was weird, and was getting stranger every foot he moved forward. "I'm scared," Cole said in a low whisper.

"I know," Hayle said. "But if this means anything to you, I have a feeling we're safer in here than we are out there. There is an odd tingle in the air, building momentum. Something is happening. I don't know why, but I can feel the spiders in the woods, I can feel them gathering; they are calling to each other, and I can hear their voices; they are planning something."

Cole exhaled loudly. "Tell me a story."

"A story?" Hayle asked.

"I have this terrible feeling, I just can't shake it, you know, like I'm crawling to my death. Like this tunnel is the final path, and that light at the end is—" Cole shuddered. "A week ago I would have never imagined this. A week ago this would have been a nightmare." Cole could feel loose rocks in his palm as he moved forward. "I used to look to my father when I felt this way. For a while I could hear his voice, like he was with me or something, but now, now I can't hear him at all. It's as if he's been scared out of me. I feel—I feel hopeless."

Hayle still wore the blindfold. Jarak would not agree to take it off; the very thought of igniting foul thoughts in an already unstable country was unheard of. There would have been a short war—Jarak against the rest of the wolves. Jarak would have slaughtered a few before ultimately falling.

"Maybe you could tell me a story about yourself. I don't know. Tell me how you can walk inside my head and flip through it like a photo album."

"A photo album?" Hayle asked.

Cole shrugged. "How can you see inside me?"

"There is an old story I used to like when I was young. My father used to tell it to me; he was a miner in Cassica, when business was profitable. He told me of the olden days, when the people lived with the Giants, and when magic was abundant in the world; he told me of the creatures in the old times. There were many. You couldn't walk a step without bumping into a different lot, he'd tell me. He told me of a doomed race once, a race of seers who cursed folk who looked them in the eye. Could charm a room, they could, put a spell over ya and let you disappear in a memory. The Trailodites were dissenters from the throne, or so my pa used to say. God's army sent the lot of em into the sea, but some folk believe there are some of em left in the world, some of em left charming man's eye with illusions." The hermit was silent for a moment.

"I think I met a fellow like them once, an *oldun* called the Traveling Man—he came to my hut in the woods and warned me that I would make a terrible choice. He told me the end was when the mountains emptied. I tossed the information off as rubbish and handed him small change to chase him away from my place. How he found my hovel, that's a mystery; I was hidden beyond the great trees of the Leeg, in the swamp that fills when the tide comes in on the west coast. I was in hiding. The world had gone to flames, and demon's seed had been sowed; I took my wife and daughter from Cassica—the wolves devoured my herd, they did, so we left to the woods, through the mountain pass, and I built us a small house, away from everything. I didn't want to fear the teeth of the world closing on me anymore; I didn't want my family to live with that same fear. But that seer was right. The *Traveling Man* was right. They came from the mountains. The day we heard them we feared the world had come to an end. The sun blotted out overhead and the trees shook as if some mammoth hands had taken their trunks and twisted them.

"This was years ago Cole. My mistake has cursed me."

Cole had stopped and turned around. The end of the tunnel was near. "What happened?"

"The woods were our home; there were beautiful little Wallops in the forest, like rodents with floppy ears. They were delicious and easy to catch. We were foragers; we lived on a land we owned; we were beyond the taxes of our landlords in Cassica, who turned to irredeemable corruption when the city of the King fell; they feared the wolves too, but paid them off nicely if it meant saving their own lives. We became that compensation, the farmers, the peasants—we were force fed as a protection levy, our animals and crops were given as dues, as a tax to the wolves when they felt it necessary. Many fled. Many were caught. We made it to the Leeg because we went north and braved the mountain pass.

"I am years past my death, but I crawl with you on a damned mission; I can taste the poison in my mouth, like rancid fizzling meat. I just wanted to save my family—isolate them. *Free* them. Free, not governed by the sheer chance we may be given as payment to the wolves, just to save the life of a crooked landlord, who in the end was always found brutally slashed in his yard, claws of the wolf across his chest. In that sense I saved my family, but when the spiders came to the woods I feared for my own life before theirs. I chose my life Cole. *My* life."

"What do you mean?" Cole asked.

"My wife and daughter had been picking berries during the day. When we could see the waning sun on the ground, we knew it was the safest to leave. I was inside, still building the hovel, sanding the walls—I even shoved wooden slats over the windows and plucked holes in them so we could spy the shadows; it was all very strategic. The two of them were picking these scrumptious purple berries that grew on reeds in the swamp; they were great when ripe, but then ripeness never really mattered. We ate what we could. The Wallops had begun to disappear. Underground is what I've always supposed, but I'm sure they were scared away from their woods—these were their woods long before they were ours. It's the sound I remember the most. Like a high whisper, but I didn't understand the words I was hearing. The sounds came from above. I know because I ran to the window and looked outside the peepholes. There were growing shadows around my wife and daughter, and I realized I could no longer see the sun, as if it were being blocked by something.

"I was rooted by hesitation. I yelled at my wife to come in, to drop the berries if it meant she'd be faster, but she didn't listen at first. She was telling my daughter Baroone a story. I could tell by the way they were laughing. When the first spider fell from above I dropped my tack. I could have used the tool to drive the spider away but this deep sense of selfishness overcame me—I didn't care about them, my wife and daughter, not at all. That spider was looking at *me*, looking at me with this weird fascination and when my wife noticed it she screamed. I hear that scream in my head every waking second. I shut the door on them. I let the spiders take them instead of me and I turned when they were wrapped and hung in the trees. The spiders left them dangling, kicking in the webbing, to lure me out of the hovel, but I wouldn't move. I made a terrible choice. And for it I have paid." The hermit's voice cracked.

"I'm sorry."

"I used old roofing tar to draw the slash of Mystic on my door; I had this insistent belief that Mystic would still save a selfish soul. I *believed* that seer told me because it was my destiny to survive. To survive as the damned. I don't know. I wrote: *They came from the Mountains* on my wall in a fit of hysteria, for I continually heard their tainted voices in the wind; it was my warning, to save others, ya hear—redemption. They were trying to lure me out. They told me they were Legion. When the spiders collapsed my roof I finally gave up. Starving and frail I ran from my hovel, sloshing through the swamp, where I came upon a clearing; the ground had sagged and I heard the trees shake and groan. I fell and let them take me.

"I hung for ages in a cocoon. I know this because I drifted in and out of life, for it was my curse for what I had let them do to my wife and daughter; I sacrificed them for *my* life. I made the wrong choice, as the fortuneteller had told me—choice blinds us, for it selfishly institutes our lives, but were it not for his palm reading, would I have had that nagging idea in the back of my mind that my future was already cursed?

"One day I was eaten. I no longer hung above the forest. I roasted in poison and somehow awoke inside an egg that was opened here, in Wolf Country, back where I had started, where I had tried to escape, only now I could see things I didn't want to see, for in every eye I could see the pains and horrors of life. I am a Trailodite. I am damned for what I let the spiders do to my family, Cole, and I see in you a chance to redeem myself."

"I'm in hell," Cole said, and he had started to cry. The sense that this was reality had hit him before, but now he realized there was little he could do about it. He was in a carved out tunnel with an undead hermit who could see and make others see the horrors of their lives. He had tried to accept this alternate reality, where wolves could talk and men exploded on bluffs—but he was afraid. He was in this tunnel because he was supposed to find something, but the dreary sense of emptiness around him told him the only thing he would find was death. He was twelve years old and had to chance his mortality. "And nobody knows I'm here." *Krollup might. If you were part of a business transaction, then maybe he just might come and get you.*

This thought was ridiculous because Cole knew the bloody truth of the situation—if he died, it was one less stepson Krollup would have to worry about. He felt the hermit brush his arm.

"I can help you Cole. I can make this easier."

"How?" Cole said through tears. "How can death be easier?"

"Because you know its face."

"I do?"

"Yes."

Cole rubbed his eyes.

"If you help me take this blindfold off, I can bring your father back to you."

Cole hesitated for a moment; he clasped his hands and looked at both ends of the tunnel—the way he came from, and the way he was heading. "I don't understand?"

"If you look into my eyes you'll see one scarring image Cole; you may see your father's death; you may see this stepfather you seem to loathe so much, I don't know, but if you chance it, if you look past it, I can help you bring your father back. I don't know how, but something inside me insists I can."

"You can bring my father back?" It wasn't disbelief in his voice, but desperation.

"Not him, but the part of him you remember; there is still some good left inside me Cole; you have to believe it too if we are going to try this."

Cole nodded. "I believe it," he said, and for once he felt a tug of hope.

13

Cole felt the soft bone of the hermit's head as he pushed his fingers behind the blindfold and pulled upwards. The scrap came off easily. The dim light in the tunnel splashed off the hermit's face but his eyes were shut.

"Are you sure about this, Cole?"

Cole thought about this. "Will it feel like the time you were inside my head?"

"Stronger," the hermit replied honestly.

This scared Cole—the last time the hermit had looked inside him he had felt infested, watching his past unfold like a map. Why was this so hard? It afforded him a chance to see his father again, or at least a part of him—but he sat in this realm of uncertainty that proposed he either slip the blindfold back on, or look into the eyes behind those pallid eyelids and chance a terrible image to find beauty behind it. Cole looked at the end of the tunnel, and he realized all along what he wanted; he wanted comfort. He was afraid and he knew his father would be there if he needed him. That was the answer he knew all along.

"Open your eyes."

Hayle did because he heard the sureness in Cole's voice. He opened his pallid flaps slowly and revealed red eyes that reflected the end of the cave like yellow pupils. But Cole saw none of this. Cole was elsewhere. He was transfixed on the image that had haunted his life.

14

Cole saw his father. That was his scarring image. His father wasn't in a hospital bed hooked up to tubes and monitors, his hair falling out in sickly patterns, his skin sweaty and reflecting the bright bulbs over the bed as if his skull were igniting within. No, instead he saw his father with his back to the wall behind his house; it was cold outside because he could see his father's breath—no, but that's wrong. He had a cigarette tucked in between his fingers, as if he was hiding it after every drag, blowing the smoke towards the ground and looking up at every sound. He *was* hiding, Cole realized, because he had promised his boys he would never touch the things again. His father's death built itself up from this lie, and Cole realized all his hatred, all his sadness emanated from this image, this damned image of his father killing himself. That smoke could have been a gun and it wouldn't have made a difference. He was dead. This was the past, and the past always comes back to haunt us.

Tears fell down Cole's face, dripping off his chin. He watched his father continue to smoke, and he realized the man would be dead within a year.

"Look past this, Cole, look past this. There are places beyond this image that would redeem your father; he is the face of death for you, but he is also the face of life—he drove you to become what you are. This image is just a hamper and you have to believe this if you're going to move forward."

Cole cried. He wiped his face and watched his father smoke and smoke and smoke, until he could imagine what he'd have to look at—a man in a bed like a puppet with saggy skin, saying his last good-byes.

But Cole did look past this image; he looked past this image because he hated remembering his father this way, and Cole began to realize that he could manipulate what he saw, as if the hermit's eyes were screens projecting a picture he had the power to access and change.

"I can see us playing catch," Cole said. "Jimmy's there, and dad looks healthy."

"I know," Hayle said.

"It's as if he never left me," Cole said.

"Remember that image Cole, put everything you have into remembering it. I want you to look at me and think of your father the way he looked playing with you, not the way he looked hiding from you. Those are two different men—one is the face of death and the other is the face of life, that face you find to give you strength. Look at that face Cole, remember it as it was."

Cole did, and something strange happened. Something fascinating. The hermit didn't look pale anymore and his eyes certainly weren't large red orbs reflecting the little lights in the tunnel. His head had changed so that the oblong crown seemed to shrink, and his slit nose turned into a slight bridge with nostrils enveloped by rosy flesh.

"Dad?"

"For now, Cole, for now," the hermit said.

"I don't understand?"

"I don't either, Cole. But it feels right. I know no harm will come to you."

The two of them crawled towards that ugly light at the end of the tunnel.

"Do you think we will find what Kenneth Auger wants?"

"Yes."

Cole smiled. The hermit looked like his father, a father with a strangely shaped head and little hair, but his father nonetheless, and Cole could read the pain that had gone into the transformation; the hermit's cut limbs had begun to bleed again.

The two climbed down from the end of the tunnel and looked out into a vast hall with pillars of stone like twisting serpents. The rock had been formed into arches that extended into darkness, and Cole could tell no ceiling existed above him, but a never-ending space he was sure many had been lost in.

The light in the room was a mystery, for there were no torches, no lanterns. The floor was smooth and many of the walls looked wet, like rocks from a riverbed.

Before the two there was a great hall that followed under the arches of stone. They were not alone—once Cole felt the air on his skin, he knew the two of them had company.

"I suppose we should explore if we're going to get out of here as soon as possible, hey kiddo?"

"Yeah."

And they heard noises from a distance—down the hall, where it was dark, and where it seemed miles separated them from whatever it was hiding in the shadows.

PART III

WAR WITH THE WOLVES

CHAPTER 17

Invasion of the Mines

1

Leo was on the cot when he heard the wolves. They sounded like growling locomotives, and it took little more than a second to realize what that noise belonged to, since he had already heard it once before. Leo flipped the ripped mattress out from under him, and swiftly slid into the broken bed frame, covering his shivering body with the bed.

He was hungry but immediately forgot about food; there were mice on the ground near him, he could smell them and hear them, but he didn't dare move. He could feel the rocks beneath him quivering—so his exploding robot had done one thing. It had brought the wolves back.

They'll smell you, was Leo's last thought before the wolves exited the mine.

They came like a tornado, the sound a rush of air through rusty grates. He pulled the mattress tighter to his head like a rectangular bonnet, and he waited. He waited and he prayed.

He could hear them sniffing the air, a collective wheeze through their dripping nostrils. How many were there? He didn't know, but he could still hear more coming up the mine, their echoes adding to the tumultuous bellow of their growls and snorting noses.

They moved closer to him; Leo could hear their claws tap the stone floor. The mice had scurried to the edge of the wall and whined, trying to climb up in utter panic. Leo wanted to tell them to quiet down, but he already knew the wolves could smell him—his sweat and the oil on his flesh; his dried blood.

The mattress was flung from his head against the wall, sliding down the monitors and settling on its tattered edge at the base of the rock. Leo stared up into the yellow and red eyes of the wolves.

"I know this one," one of the wolves spoke in a low whisper, "for he was to deliver the old man's message to the man with the stone."

"Move away Ilak," another growling voice spoke, shoving several wolves aside. This new wolf stood before Leo, who had to crane his neck to look into its red eyes; it wore a crown of thorns on its head, nestled between its pointy ears; this wolf wore a black breastplate with skulls hanging on twine, each knocking against the other producing a dull chime that sickened Leo.

The huge wolf reached down and picked Leo up by his shirt. Leo's ankles, which were quite swollen and stung with every movement, dangled in the air. It was just his luck—he sent down an exploding robot, and instead of Krollup getting what he deserved, the wolves decided to pick on poor Alvin Leonardo.

The wolf studied Leo with his beady red eyes, countering the little man's gaze with a furrowed scowl, wrinkling his muzzle, baring long fangs that seemed endless in his gaping mouth. "You know of the man with the stone?"

Leo winced, but said nothing.

The wolf lifted Leo higher in the air and shook him; his ankles knocked together and he stifled a scream. "And what of the explosion—did you send such magic to disarm us? *US?*" The wolf exposed his claws, which were long and curved like Arabian scimitars, each stained with gore. Leo wondered if he would feel one of those pointed claws against his throat, and the thought scared him.

"The boys, are the boys hurt?" he blurted.

"The man with the stone, where is he?"

"Grak, there are voices," the wolf called Ilak said, and Leo realized just how many werewolves there were. All he could see from his perch in Grak's grip was a long line of fur and weaponry, leading into the mine.

"What?" Grak said sharply.

"You *must* hear them too, crashes, explosions and voices through this wall."

Grak lowered Leo and turned his attention to the brick stack, which was showing sparse light in waning rays through the chipped grout and broken bricks. "Ilak, go to the country, ready the rest of the wolves." Grak tossed Leo against the mattress, and the poor man slid to the floor with a slight thud. He licked his teeth with an outrageous swipe. "For we go to war."

Ilak retreated through a part in the crowd and pounced into the mine, springing on all fours like a jackrabbit.

Grak turned forward, unsheathing a long sword, the skulls twisting on his front, drops of peeling blood on the slopes of each cranium like post mortem freckles. And he exploded through the brick stack. It was like nothing Leo had ever seen. The wolf sprung forward and whipped his arm outward, pushing the bricks into the fireplace like a bulldozer. There was a long howl, and the wolves attacked.

2

Edwin spat blood from the corner of his mouth; he had been pistol-whipped twice, and the side of his face looked like an inflated purple balloon.

Mrs. Lorenzo sat cross-legged in a chair she had dragged from the far side of the Great room; she sat staring at Edwin with pity in her eyes. She didn't pity him, but pitied the options he insisted she had to follow; she wasn't normally a violent person, but when pushed to the edge a part of her snapped. Things had to go her way, had to go the Ministry's way.

"Whaddya lookin at?" Hutchy said to Robert, who sat beside his cousin Eddie, hunkered against the wall near the fireplace. The thug had a smug leer on his fat face, and he twirled his pistol on his forefinger.

Robert ignored him. Eddie just looked away. Eddie was furious of course, because he knew if he were given the chance, he could disarm that lug and break both of his arms, but for the gun he was left useless against the wall, waiting. Waiting for what, he didn't know.

Robert had the stone in his pocket; his fingers trailed over it and he could feel that vibration, that sense of an overwhelming power, but he didn't know how to manipulate it. Edwin had never told him how to manipulate the stone, but instead insisted the stone had a will of its own. If so, then why hadn't the stone willed itself to ultimately protect him and his cousin?

"Your silence is endearing Mr. Krollup, but I assure you, no matter your legal counterattacks, I will receive my proper dues. I'm sure your former legal assistance informed you of the drastic consequences if you wished not to comply. Your face will be wiped off the earth, you understand me, don't you? And I don't mean death—a far worse fate awaits you if you further pursue this line of negotiations. Your stocks will plummet when global audiences realize your true nature—every celebrity has a dark side, I suppose, but what then would be your excuse?" She leaned forward, uncrossing her legs. When she noticed he wasn't going to respond, she motioned Brunus over.

Brunus walked over with his gun drawn. "I suggest you begin answering her, Krollup. I'll tell you now, my hand never gets tired of drawing blood, and I come from a long line whose trigger fingers are perpetually flexed.

One reason, Krollup, one reason and I'd jump at the chance to splatter your brains." Brunus smiled, flashing a pair of gold molars. Edwin grinned slightly, though it pained him to do so, and Brunus whapped him across the cheek. Edwin's head rocked back.

"Enough of that Brunus, you don't want to kill the fool before we receive our benefits. This should be easy Krollup. It has been rumored you're worth anywhere between thirty and seventy billion dollars—where's the harm in demanding a slight percentage of that for compensation? This will both clear any injustices the Ministry feels, and it will shred evidence we have against you, evidence that could cause unneeded conflict between the Italian and American government. Alfred Linutz was for the proposal. Why are you being so stubborn?" Edwin didn't answer; he was looking away from her. "For crying out loud, answer me you fool. If it takes a few teeth, a few broken bones, that doesn't matter much to us. Really, Krollup, both Brunus and Hutchy would be happy to pain you beyond comprehension."

Edwin wasn't in the mood for this; he had other plans today, and it seemed the quickest route around the Ministry was through Robert and the stone.

He didn't dare mouth Robert's name, nor did he dare speak aloud; instead he caught Robert's eyes and motioned them towards the granite statue that had already partially stepped off its pedestal.

"Are you mocking me?" Mrs. Lorenzo asked, studying Edwin's awkward facial expressions.

"Are you?" Brunus yelled, as he pushed Edwin back into the chair, his breath stinking of pungent meat and cheap mints. Brunus dug the muzzle of his pistol into Edwin's rib cage and twisted it. "Answer her."

Edwin looked at Lorenzo and smiled. "Yes," he said in a confident tone that dropped her jaw.

Edwin was hit again, but that didn't detract from his motivation to gesture to Robert. He looked at Robert then closed his eyes, scrunching his brow as if in deep contemplation—*you have to will it you fool*, he thought, *you have to will movement through the stone, then it will happen. Haven't you begun to understand it yet, hasn't it spoken to you?*

He thought this of course, but he didn't wish it. He was certain when Robert did figure out how to use the stone, he would become addicted and Edwin knew there would be little chance of him retrieving it—unless he was forced to pry it from Robert's dead fingers. If it came to that, he'd do it.

"Why do you insist upon getting hurt?" Lorenzo asked in a concerned voice that wasn't concern at all, but masked contempt.

"Because, my friend, if it takes a little receiving before dealing out the pain, then I can stand to manage a few bruises." Edwin grinned. Robert did too; Eddie was too busy staring into the fireplace. He was certain he heard some strange noises through the crumbling bricks.

"I'm not your friend," Lorenzo smiled herself.

"You'll wish you were before the end," Edwin said smoothly, and he wiped the blood off his face with his free hand.

He noticed Robert had begun to float in the air, and as surprised as Robert was about this, his attention was mainly on the granite statue behind Hutchy, which had enormous arms sculpted into sinewy muscles. When Eddie had seen his cousin levitating, he had tried to pull Robert to the ground, believing this was some act of ancient magic the Ministry of Art practiced.

"Let go," Robert said, with a smile. He felt like he could rule the world. Everything around him spoke with its own voice, the earth, the statues.

Eddie did let go, and Robert floated higher and higher, until his knees could have brushed the mantle over the fireplace.

"Hey, what's goin on here, whaddya doin up there? Get down from there!" Hutchy screamed, roughly grabbing his gun from his forefinger and threatening Robert with it. But Robert wasn't wholly there. Rather, his focus was on the statue behind Hutchy, which walked slowly and with an awkward stop motion; it slammed Hutchy's back with a ferocious swing of its rock arm. There was a loud crack and the gun dropped from the thug's hand as he flew toward the wall and slammed to the ground.

"What's going on?" Brunus screamed, and Mrs. Lorenzo hid behind her chair.

"Well, what are you waiting for Brunus, shoot it!"

Brunus did. He shot the statue, chipping away at the stone; puffs of dust exploded in the air.

Eddie had grabbed Hutchy's gun, fumbled with it a moment, and shot at Brunus. Brunus jumped out of the way, and if it wasn't for Eddie's lousy aim, would have probably sported a few new holes in his face to accompany his mouth and nostrils.

Brunus dove behind Lorenzo's chair, and she shoved him out to finish the battle.

"There is a walking statue out there—I ain't goin. Here, take ma gun n' you do it," Brunus screamed.

"You see, it wasn't some rigged device Mrs. Lorenzo; in fact, this should be my testament to you that *your* statues ruined the Accademia. They were obviously sick of imprisonment. Isn't that why they're attacking you now?" Edwin laughed, and struggled with the chair as he stood up.

"What have you done?" Lorenzo asked.

A few more shots pelted off the floor. Eddie was entirely inside the fireplace, blindly pointing the gun outside and shooting.

Robert floated but was showing signs of physical stress. The stone was draining him.

The statue moved towards Brunus and Lorenzo. Lorenzo shoved Brunus out and the statue went to slowly grab for him, but he ducked, instead shooting messy divots in its granite abdomen. The statue overturned the chair, its movements rigid, and Lorenzo scurried to Edwin.

"Make it stop, please. I'll tear up the photos, burn the negatives, rip the tapes to shreds. This visit never happened. Just make it stop," she pleaded.

"Undo my cuffs," Edwin said sourly.

"Brunus, the keys," Lorenzo screamed.

Brunus, who was in the middle of a shot, aiming at both the fireplace and the statue, turned and looked at Lorenzo. "The keys?"

"For the cuffs, NOW!"

Brunus dove towards Edwin, shot once more at the fireplace, and rolled neatly into a heap at the foot of the chair. He fumbled in his pocket; he had never expected this to happen. When he found the key he handed it to Edwin. Edwin undid the cuffs and threw the chair to the side.

"Make it stop, please," Lorenzo pleaded. "I have children."

"Robert, there's something behind the fireplace, somebody's back there," Eddie yelled. He jumped from the fireplace, his clothes covered in soot. Both he and Brunus had quit shooting at each other; the statue had fallen on its face, breaking an arm off at the elbow, and Robert had fallen back to the ground.

"Oh thank you, thank you," Lorenzo kept repeating.

"Shut up," Edwin said. He ran over to Robert; his fingers were deformed and abnormally twisted, each gripped so tightly around the stone it wouldn't have been awkward to confuse the lump with an odd formation on his palm.

"Give it to me," Edwin said.

Eddie stood over Brunus and kicked him in the stomach; the big thug doubled over and dropped his gun, which Eddie slid away.

"Never," Robert said. "So this is where your fame and fortune came from: a device, magic. You destroyed competition merely through suggestion and this thing willed it be done. Your mines, your oil, all conjured through this." Robert smiled.

Edwin pried one finger off the stone.

"Eddie, don't let him have it!" Robert screamed, and Eddie left Brunus to grab Edwin off his cousin. He did so with one hand. Eddie pushed Edwin to the ground.

"Leave him alone," Eddie said.

And the fireplace exploded outwards.

3

"What is that?" Jarak asked. He and the old man stood by the tunnels into the Tower. The old man ignored Jarak, but he wasn't completely there anymore; instead, he was clinging to some kind of hope that would bring him salvation, magnetized to the tunnels with the assurance Cole would emerge carrying that vial of black ichor—Wizard's Blood.

Jarak had been on all fours staring at the bluff, where he noticed a wolf had exited the mine between the two boulders.

"It has begun," Jarak said.

Ilak, who stood on the bluff, howled at the wolves, tipping his snout to the sky.

The wolves howled in return.

"It isn't safe here old man, we should leave."

"Never," Auger mumbled. He stood propped against his cane; he didn't look away from the base of the Tower.

"There is going to be a war. The mutant was right. The wolves are readying. I sense death comes here today."

The wolves armed themselves with long swords, already stained with blood, hundreds, thousands of them pouring from the caverns at the base of the bluffs, jumping from fissures, the Wolves of the Mountains, wearing chest plates adorned with scalps and bones, axes jutting over their hunched shoulders.

The She-wolves howled from the tents and the ground shivered.

A part of Jarak longed to ready for war himself, but he pictured the old General's head in his arms, dead eyes staring upward—he was against this. Grak was leading the wolves into a crypt.

The wolves charged up the mountain pass.

4

Mrs. Lorenzo screamed. Bricks scattered the floor amidst a reddish dust that caught the sunlight through the windows, drowning the room in a bloody glow.

Edwin was on his back, and when he heard the crash, he rolled over—but he crawled towards Robert, who still clutched the stone, and whose head had turned and watched Grak emerge from the fireplace, ducking his head under the mantle.

"Brunus," Lorenzo screamed, and the thug, whose greasy hair had fallen in his face, rolled over himself, clutching his stomach. "Your gun."

His gun had been kicked to the other side of the room—Grak saw Brunus first, pulling himself along the floor with his fingertips, trying to dig in with his loafers. Grak pounced forward; this was no time for questioning, not now, and Grak knew just as well as anybody that if he showed patience he would allow time for the man with the stone to attack—whichever one he was.

Grak landed behind Brunus, and as he was raising his long arm to bring the sword into Brunus's back, there was a loud clap and he felt the flesh in his left shoulder explode. He turned his head around, dropping his heavy sword beside Brunus, who muffled a slight scream, pulling himself ever closer to the pistol rested against the wall.

Eddie stood with Hutchy's gun in both shaking hands, struggling to keep it straight. In the light Grak noticed a small line of smoke rising from the muzzle, catching the reddish dust in a winding swirl. Eddie saw the fury in those red eyes and realized if he didn't shoot now, if he didn't shoot in between those eyes he was a goner. Even the wolves who stood at the threshold of the fireplace noticed this, and they waited; they waited not because they feared this smoking weapon, but because curiosity stayed their feet, for they were determined to watch their General utterly unleash himself.

Eddie pulled the trigger.

Click.

He was empty.

Grak must have noticed this, and though he had no idea what this contraption did, or how it worked, he saw a resonant hopelessness in Eddie's eyes.

Grak jumped forward and Eddie dove.

"Eddie—" Robert screamed, and he closed his eyes; the granite statue on the ground rose, as if lifted by ropes from above, and steadied at the base of its feet, teetering from one side to the other.

Edwin pulled himself forward, a rage in his eyes that ignored the emptiness he felt without the stone around his neck; he watched Robert levitate, his back horizontal to the floor, clasping the stone in his reddening fingers.

Grak grabbed Eddie's leg and lifted him in the air, holding the big man inverted like a prize fish; he sprung his claws out like daggers, curved at the tips with discolored specks. Grak meant to disembowel Eddie when he was struck in the back.

The granite statue had hit Grak with its remaining arm, shattering at the elbow as it connected with the wolf's spine. Grak howled, dropping Eddie on his head; he rolled over and crawled to the wall.

The wolves jumped through the fireplace, tackling the armless granite statue to the ground, pulling out chunks of rock like grass from spongy earth.

There was an irritable chipping noise, and Mrs. Lorenzo stuck her fingers into her ears with a pop, as she hid underneath a table.

Robert, who floated ten inches in the air, was violently pulled back down by Edwin.

"Give me the stone."

Robert was sweating, and his eyes had sunken in his brow; they seemed small, and though Robert was scared, he knew he had to protect the stone; he couldn't lose it, he had never felt this powerful. "NO!"

Edwin punched Robert in the face and dug his knee into the psychologist's stomach, twisting it.

"It doesn't want you," Edwin said, and he hit Robert again. Edwin pried a couple of Robert's fingers from the rock, breaking them as they snapped back against the man's dirty knuckles.

And Eddie was thrown into them, knocking Edwin off of Robert; he stumbled across the floor. The stone followed. It clambered across the floor, Robert's blood streaked across it. The mark of a man who didn't want to let it go.

Grak, whose back felt broken, stumbled forward; he had picked up Eddie and thrown him, fetching his sword to finish the rest of them off. His mouth was dripping white foam, which splattered to the ground like whipping cream. Grak saw the stone when Edwin did, but only realized what it actually was when he saw Edwin's resilience to retrieve it.

"THE STONE!" Grak howled, and the other wolves, who were still pouring in from the fireplace, perked their ears and stopped. Edwin remembered that voice, and when he saw Grak's face, he remembered it also; they were from his nightmares (*the wolf that tried to smile*, he thought grimly). In fact, this seemed translated directly from his nightmares, the wolves coming up through the mines; he realized at that moment that if he didn't get the stone everything around him would disappear. The wolves would will it so.

Robert also struggled forward, but Eddie had fallen on top of him, pinning him down. He reached out, his voice wavering as he grunted, trying to pull them both forward.

Grak jumped forward and slammed his sword into the ground, piercing the blade through hardwood and concrete; it whined like a guitar strum. Grak's claws ripped the floor when he landed; he hooked a claw into the gold chain and picked it up from the ground, his red eyes glowing with the ignition of realization—here he held the very thing that had destroyed his Country, that had slaughtered his kind. There was an awkward silence in the room, and even though fear would have stayed most, Edwin sprung from the ground and jumped into Grak's side like a linebacker against a wall. Despite the surge of power through Grak's system, his ailing spine crunched, and he twisted around, snapping his jaw.

The wolves advanced. There were seventeen in the Great room now, some who had broken their claws on the granite statue, scratching themselves with agitated reluctance to try and grow them back.

Grak picked Edwin up by his neck and choked him.

And Brunus shot Grak. This time a puff of flesh and hair exploded near his left armpit, and Grak dropped both the stone and Edwin. Grak howled.

Brunus shot again. Not at Grak, but at a wolf jumping towards him—the bullet caught the wolf through his leather breastplate, puncturing his tough skin and kissing his heart. The wolf dropped dead on top of a few remains of the granite statue.

Grak had turned and looked at this man with the gun, feeling the hole in his side, shocked, to say the least, that such a small device could motivate such power. Whatever had hit him, had gone entirely through his body, for he bled in two places, from his back and front—there was a hole the size of his eye through his breastplate, and it spat wads of blood through his hair. Grak had watched Pizak the Yilak fall in the air when that weapon had shot again, a splash of blood spilling from the wolf's back. Grak stuck his claw into the hole in his front and studied the blood on the tip of his talon.

Many of the wolves were hesitant now. Brunus stood up, leaning against the wall, reddish sweat falling down his face; he held his gun out, shooting another wolf that stepped forward to test him.

For the moment Grak had forgotten about the stone; it was his mistake, but curiosity forced him to question this other mystery, and to eat the one who held it in his fidgety hands.

5

Edwin's neck was streaked with blood, some of his own, and some from Grak's claws. His persistence had paid off, for now at least, and though the thought hadn't occurred then, he would later remember a subtle feeling that he wanted to kiss Brunus. If Brunus hadn't shot Grak, everything would have been over. How could he have been so stupid and let Robert get the stone in the first place?

Edwin had fallen from Grak's claws and landed roughly on his side. A part of him knew what came next, and instead of diving for the fallen stone (*he hadn't known the stone had fallen yet*) he closed his eyes and waited for what undoubtedly came next. It was this hesitation, this uncertainty, which led another pair of hands to chance the stone.

Mrs. Lorenzo, who watched everything from beneath a table, had forgone her fear for the moment, realizing that Edwin's control of the statues at the Accademia hadn't been due to some spectacular rigging job, but due to this awkward stone that had fallen to the floor, its chain clinking against the ground. She wanted the stone; she could feel its power pulsing. When she realized the giant wolf's attention was diverted, she confronted her own conflicted emotions and crawled out from under the table.

She wrapped the chain around her finger and pulled the stone toward her—when she finally touched the rock she felt raw, she felt like she could breathe fire. The intensity coursing through her fingers into the rest of her body supposed she clasp the stone in her hand and rid of the wolves once and for all—

She was tackled from the side, and both Lorenzo and Edwin tumbled under the table.

"GET OFF!"

"Give it to me," Edwin said. He pulled at the chain. Mrs. Lorenzo's fingers trembled, but she wouldn't let it go.

"Let me keep it, Edwin, and I'll forget about the lawsuit," she whispered.

"There is no lawsuit," Edwin said, and he finally ripped the stone from her tight grip.

"I told you the Ministry would pay," he said, and Edwin Krollup stood up, holding the stone in his hand once more. He felt like himself again; he didn't feel naked anymore, like an alien, exposed to weakness. He realized now that he could send the wolves back, just as he had done once before, in a wave of rock through the mines.

6

Grak did pull his sword from the concrete, but Edwin had crawled away by this point, tackling Mrs. Lorenzo to get the stone. Grak pulled the sword and ran towards this man who had put a bloody hole in *him*—the General of the Sordid Yilaks!

Brunus was pinned to the wall; he could run to his left, towards the statue of David, and dive through the windows, but he knew the wolves would get him. He knew he only had three bullets left. He had a clip in his holster, but removing it and snapping it into his gun was another story, a story that deserved time, and Brunus didn't have any to give.

His life had been comprised of ill deeds. As he stood watching the wolves, he saw within them a version of himself; he was a wolf also, a hunter, a predator. Now he had become the victim. He stood cornered, his partner's dead body heaped on the other side of the room and here he was forming a conscience; it took an encounter with werewolves to blossom sympathy. Until now, Brunus had been a robot, hired by the Ministry to do foul deeds when foul deeds needed doing.

When he saw Grak rushing toward him with his long sword drawn, he knew he had three bullets, and if he took this one wolf out with them, then he'd have to contend with the others with an empty pistol—unless he could install the fresh clip in a matter of seconds. But he couldn't do that. He was shaking all over.

Grak was seven feet from Brunus when the wolf was thrown aside.

Three statues had advanced, each with dust spraying from their joints as they moved, one leg forward and then the other, crisp rock crushing into fine grains that sprinkled the floor like salt.

Edwin was at the end of the room, floating and watching.

This bought Brunus enough time. He shot all three bullets into the crowd of wolves, slipped the new clip from his holster, discarded the old one, and slammed it in the gun.

Grak stood up and howled. Mrs. Lorenzo screamed behind Edwin.

The wolves confronted the statues.

One statue, a nude woman with fine hair chiseled down her back, grappled with three wolves and pushed them towards the fireplace. One wolf, whose sword had been used in the war with the Hunters all those years ago, slashed through one of the statue's thin arms, sending it to the ground in a crumbling explosion. Five more wolves rushed the statue and tore through its delicately carved head with sharp claws, until the statue was little more than a walking torso.

Brunus had run towards the statue of David, shooting as he ran. He had to conserve his bullets. He was on his last clip.

Grak ignored the statues. He watched Brunus, the man with the gun. Grak wanted to control fire the way these weapons did; he knew these exploding devices would one day revolutionize their wars.

All three statues had fallen.

Edwin brought a wedge of rock through the subfloor of the house, like the tip of an arrow. It broke through the concrete with a sharp snap, crumbling the floor into long splinters of wood. He raised the rock to the ceiling, impaling four wolves, and knocking the others down as the house seemingly sloped.

More wolves spilled in through the fireplace.

7

Grak followed Brunus when the floor exploded. Grak was thrown forward. He turned and watched a shelf of rock pin wolves to the ceiling, leaving their long arms dangling like tainted vines from a treetop.

"The man with the stone, get him," Grak yelled, but it wasn't in the common tongue that he spoke. He spoke in the old language of the Sordid Mountains. Brunus thought his ears were bleeding when he heard it.

Edwin drove the wolves back with another wave of stone, which completely shattered the floor. Pieces of concrete were strewn in the air, smashing into wolves, others putting holes in the ceiling; the room was alit with dust like a window through a glaze of falling snow. Another splinter of rock came from beneath the house and pinned more wolves against the ceiling. Edwin could hear the furniture upstairs sliding around as the second story floor shifted.

"What's goin on?" Brunus yelled in utter confusion. Brunus had cowered against the far corner of the room, covering his face as chips of stone flew at him.

The man's voice snapped Grak out of his daze.

Brunus had just enough time to draw his gun when he saw Grak jumping at him. The wolf was fast, but so was Brunus's trigger finger. Brunus got off two shots before Grak's claws swiped through his suit jacket, ripping it to shreds. Both shots hit the mountain of rock that had grown through the floor.

Brunus shifted to the right and pulled himself along the windows; he smashed the butt of his gun against the pane and almost broke his hand. The thick glass barely cracked. Grak pulled Brunus's arm before he could try to smash the window again, and he tore the gun from the poor man's hand.

Brunus screamed and Grak pushed him through the window, bursting the glass around the man's flailing body. Grak hooked his claw around the trigger and accidentally put two bullets through the ceiling. Yes, he could use this on the man with the stone; there was no way to get close to him, but if he could use this from a distance—

He turned and shot the gun again. The bullet exploded in the far wall, twenty feet from Edwin's head. Lorenzo shrieked as plaster fell around her hands; she pulled herself into a ball under the table, turning it over with a crash so the top formed a wall in front of her. Grak shot again; he had no sense of aim, yet, but he realized the explosions were nearing the man with the stone. He used the holes in the wall as guidelines. Grak moved his arm to the right a few inches. He pulled the trigger again; this time Mrak the wolf got in the way of the shot, and the right side of his head was incinerated.

"MAKASSHA!" Grak howled, a curse in the old language that hadn't been spoken in years.

He shot again. The hole appeared five feet from Edwin. Edwin saw the flash reports from the gun's end, though he couldn't hear the gunshots; he had seen the puffs of plaster swirling around him. The room was, at the moment, filled with the loud clashes of swords against stone, the rumblings of the moving earth beneath them, as rock was conjured through the house, and the terrible whines of wolves as they realized they would fall.

And Edwin used *his* general for the first time.

8

When David stepped off his throne, Grak heard a loud thud. He was thrown against the wall, slamming his back so that the hunch in his sloping shoulders seemed to straighten. The gun fell from his claw and clattered to the ground with a metallic bang.

Grak snarled, picked up the gun and shot at the huge statue. Puffs of marble exploded and David punched forward, putting his hand through the wall, shattering through the exterior stone.

Grak jumped at David and knocked the statue backwards, scratching the sleek stone in shallow divots along his chest. David threw Grak to the ground, smashing bits of rock into the wolf's gunshot wounds. Grak howled and shot at the statue again—when the windows were smashed in.

Shards of glass showered the room like glittering drops of water, sprinkling the ground with the sound of hard rain on rock.

The statues were coming in the house from the courtyard, stepping through the broken panes with legs that cracked when they moved. Grak had had enough. To stop the statues, he'd have to stop the one controlling them; it was a simple system, and it was the General's job to disarm the opposing army. Grak slid under David, springing up behind the statue; he shot twice more, hitting either side of Edwin, exploding the wall into chunks of powder.

David spun Grak into the opposite wall; his body went through the wood paneling, knocking the skulls on his chest against each other until the twine snapped; a few skulls rolled around on the ground.

Grak wasn't going to subject the wolves to this anymore—if this battle was going to persist, he'd lure the statues to Wolf Country, where Ilak was already readying the Yilaks for imminent war.

"RETREAT!" Grak howled. The wolves hurried through the fireplace.

David caught a couple wolves and slammed their heads together; there was a disturbing crack and both monsters were dead before they hit the floor.

The statues halted. Edwin fell to the floor in a heap, his forehead glistened with sweat, draping his thin hair to his face; his cut lips were bleeding and his jaw swelled up where Brunus had hit him. But he didn't feel tired; he felt tired when he didn't have the stone. He felt sick almost. When he realized the stone was no longer around his neck, he felt useless—no, he *was* useless. And *he* hadn't called the statues from the courtyard; they had come by their own accord, as if the stone had developed a will of its own. It was the same way yesterday during the earthquake; the statues had thrown pieces of *themselves* over the wall. Edwin had just conjured the earthquake; the rest was a tributary of his actual commands. The stone was becoming more powerful within itself. There were thirty statues inside his house now that were direct proof of this.

He walked forward, towards the clutter of dead wolves and broken rocks and disabled statues. Robert was still breathing, and the big man draped across the psychologist's legs was breathing also. Both were covered in dust and pebbles. He walked towards David, who stood facing forward, both arms hanging at his side. He had carved into David's throne, his pedestal, the very image he had been planning all along—the invasion of the mines. But it didn't seem just like *his* plan anymore; it seemed like the stone was coaxing him to follow the wolves down the mines also, by bringing an army of statues from the courtyard to aid the battalion.

Out the window he saw a line of statues, all standing still, all waiting for their turn to step through the windows, some without hands, others with broken legs and cracked torsos.

"Is it over?" Mrs. Lorenzo asked; she had peeked out from the over turned table.

Edwin had forgotten about her. The suitcase of evidence had been trampled and covered in rocks, lost forever.

"It's far from over," Edwin said, more to himself than to her. He took one last look at the statues lined up outside, all of the empty pedestals around the courtyard.

"What were those things?"

Edwin ignored her.

"What were those things Krollup? Is Hutchy dead? Is Brunus dead? This is going to start an international incident you know—SPEAK TO ME!"

Edwin left the room.

9

Behind the loading bay Edwin had All Terrain Vehicles, which his staff used to haul carts of shipments to storage. Edwin grabbed the keys for an

ATV off the hook, opened the cargo doors, and wrapped a chain around his shoulder. Edwin drove the ATV through the house, leaving tire tracks on his hundred thousand-dollar floors.

He pulled into the Great room, where Mrs. Lorenzo was leaning over Hutchy, checking his pulse.

"He's dead," she said in a choked voice. "I didn't come here for this. If you had just transferred the money."

"Shut up."

Edwin touched his necklace, rose a few inches, and the bricks in the fireplace exploded outwards scattering the room with more broken stone; the mantle split in two and fell either ways, and his self-portrait flew across the room, only to smash into the tower of rock impaling a handful of wolves. The canvas ripped and the frame shattered. He had turned the fireplace stack into a door, separating the rock like a curtain.

The statues moved through the new door first, and they seemed easier to control the closer they got to the mines, as if there was some drawing force inside them. He drove the quad through the fireplace after David entered, a loop of chain secured to the steering column so that he wouldn't float off the quad.

Leo was in the corner of the room with the mattress pulled over his body. Edwin ripped the mattress off the little man. Leo had been crying. He seemed let down when he realized Edwin was still alive.

"I was certain the wolves would have finished you off," Edwin said, and he took the chain from his shoulder and wrapped one end around David's extended arm.

Leo looked at David with a gaze of admiration, ignoring Edwin's comment; he had always wanted to see the statue, even if it had been changed, walking as if Michelangelo had included in the final product a working marble brain. Leo felt anemic, and though he had left his wrench across the room, he had little desire to retrieve it; instead he pulled his knees into his chest.

"I heard the explosion," Leo said, almost defiantly. He was *supposed* to keep the robot from exploding, that was the command from Krollup. Leo knew Krollup admired the actuality of manipulating the impossible, and he must have figured that if he could control all of these statues, then little Leo could control the timing of his robot's detonation.

"Figured just as much when the wolves blasted through my fireplace. I thought I told you to hold it off till I got back—didn't I?"

"What's going on in here?" Mrs. Lorenzo said, peering through the door in the fireplace.

"GET OUTTA HERE!" Edwin screamed, and Leo winced, struggling to move away. Edwin rose a few inches off the ground, and Leo knew from experience the consequences when Krollup levitated.

"Your threats mean little to me, Mr. Krollup," she said, and she pointed a gun at him, a gun she had lifted from Eddie's unconscious hand, loading a clip she had found in the holster under Hutchy's armpit. She had never used a gun herself, but had seen one used enough times to establish the imperatives—point and pull. "Now, since we've been sidetracked I feel it's necessary to finally finish these negotiations."

She stepped into the entrance of the mines, which smelt of dead mice, oil and smoke—with the added touch of Leo's sweat and blood. "You do know this is self-defense, do you not? Yes. My lawyers were both killed, and who's to know you didn't commit the act, Mr. Krollup? I could put a bullet through your skull right now and consider it heroism."

Leo's ears perked up. He wished she'd do it already; he knew that by prolonging the situation, there was always an inevitable reversal of control. He learned that lesson when he fell asleep against his robot, which he had intended to blow both himself and Edwin to Kingdom Come.

But she had waited far too long; she was all talk, and though Leo would have liked to warn her, he found he had little voice to do so. There was a statue behind her, *walking* like a man. Edwin, who floated in the air, had found a way to blur the boundaries between real and unreal. Mrs. Lorenzo was grappled from behind, one long stone arm reaching across her chest, forcing her to drop the gun before she could get a shot off.

"GET OFF ME!" Lorenzo screamed. She tried to pry the arm off but couldn't. Edwin left her that way.

"Get on the quad Leo."

Leo looked up. "But—but you promised you'd let me free when I sent the robot down for you."

"You didn't fulfill your promise though, did you?" Edwin pointed at the dead wolves, lying in heaps around a mound of rock that had broken through the hardwood. "GET ON THE QUAD!"

Leo slowly stood up. "Why?"

Edwin breathed in frustration, ignoring Mrs. Lorenzo's screams of struggle and protestation behind him. He bent down, picked up the handgun and stuck it in his belt before Leo could get the idea. "Because I need a seatbelt," he finally said.

"A seatbelt?"

"You have to hold me down on the quad because I tend to float when I use the stone. Come on, tell me you've noticed." Edwin smiled, staring at the rock arm over the secret door to his office. "Look at it this way, Leo. When we reach the end of the mines, you're free to do as you like, okay, and everything's forgotten—I'll even give you the quad. I won't hold you for both my missing stepsons, and I won't hold you for the premature exploding robot. Get on." Edwin smiled.

Leo didn't like the look of it. "Where are we going?"

"I have some wolves to contend with," Edwin said with a simple grin, and Leo hopped on the quad.

Edwin had wrapped the end of the chain around the ATV's steering column. "Hold my belt," he said, and they moved forward. David was pulling them.

Leo slid his fingers under Edwin's belt and realized he was only fifteen inches or so from a loaded gun, which hung out the front of Edwin's pants.

"Any funny business, little man, and I *will* kill you," Edwin said, as if he had just read Leo's mind.

They moved fast down the slope of the mines. David's steps were long, but neither Edwin nor Leo could see a thing; it was pitch black.

And the quad moved down the mine, pulled on a chain by the statue of David, surrounded by the trampling feet of close to sixty statues, through the dank reek of the wolves.

Wolf Country would see war today.

CHAPTER 18

THE SANDGLASS

1

Jimmy could see the beach ahead of him, miles of sand stretching in either direction, and cliff sides falling into the sea towards the north where mountains loomed. Jarat the Spider had carried both Ashton and Jimmy towards the edge of the Leeg Woods, bouncing on top of the canopies, springing from branches and climbing up and down old webbing. The spiders moved at a speed no horse could match—and Jimmy realized it felt like he was on a roller coaster.

There were strands of web like suspension cables connected to rocks on the beach, strung tight to the topmost branches of the Canopy Trees at the edge of the forest. Jarat sprang and slid down the webs, followed by Kannef; both spiders landed in the sand, scuttling their long legs against the grain. The pebbles exploded when they landed, and both Jimmy and Ashton had to shield their faces, almost falling off Jarat's back.

Jimmy nearly screamed when he saw the water. There were large waves, water dividing around crests of spindly refuse breaking through the surf. There were spiders in the sea, lying on their backs with their legs splayed towards the air, some broken at the top, others twisted around and dangling at awkward angles. Jimmy realized this must have been a graveyard. It explained why the webs were strung up from the trees—bodies could be rolled down at great speeds so they could drive themselves through the sand into the water.

"Don't stare too long, Jimmy, 'tis rude," Ashton said. "This is a graveyard. Soon the creatures of the sea will take them."

"Many of them were brought here the last few days," Jarat whispered in a piercing shriek, "after the wolves came to steal the egg sac. There are still more strewn about the woods—the wolves surprised us, but that will never happen again."

"There is no house here," Kannef the Spider said accusingly, as he twisted around the beach, looking from side to side.

Ashton jumped off Jarat and walked towards the trees, where along the crumbled earth there was a shelf of rock over the sand, vines and broken branches scattered on its top. "There is, but it is disguised," Ashton said. At first glance, the broken branches and vines looked real enough, shaped to appear as if draped over the small cliff, but as Ashton neared the shelf of rock, the stone seemed to jut outwards, squared near the top where one could notice—barely of course—that a branch was shooting a small line of smoke from its leaves. It was a disguised chimney. The shelf of rock was actually a house.

Jimmy ran to meet Ashton, and the Hunter knocked on a door that to the spiders—and to Jimmy—looked like two vines draped from the spongy moss overhead.

The vines opened and Jimmy looked inside a dim room where standing in front of him was a thin man wearing only a loin cloth, a shrubby gray beard nestled around his face, and the subtle remainder of an old tattoo on his chest—it was the mark of a hand.

"It's about time," the man said, and Ashton stepped into the house.

2

The house was simple, but seemed larger than its exterior suggested— perhaps it had actually been dug into the earth under the roots, but Jimmy was certain the heavy trees would have collapsed the ceiling.

Stacks of parchment concealed the walls, and there were odd shapes of glistening glass scattered around the room. There was a smoking pot hanging over a pit of twigs lit with fire, and Jimmy's stomach grumbled. He hadn't eaten for hours, and whatever was stewing in the pot smelled heavenly.

"I wish you would take that ridiculous thing off your face, Asha. Your father wouldn't have appreciated—" the man with the beard spoke in a raspy voice before he was cut off.

"I am Ashton. Ashton the Hunter. My father would have understood," he said and the old man smiled.

"Of course you are; it's just I'd rather stare into both your beautiful eyes," he said jokingly.

"My face is scarred."

The old man smiled again. "And it should be." When he smiled, Jimmy saw a large slash across his throat beneath his mangy beard, healed into a black scar.

"And who is this young man?" The old man asked, beaming down at Jimmy.

"Jimmy," Ashton said.

"Yes, of course he is. I saw you leave the mines young man. Made such a racket I was sure *they* would have gotten you before Ashton, but Ashton's quick, much like his father. Yes, his father." The old man patted Jimmy's arm. "You look hungry." The old man picked up a bowl and blew out the fire by simply puckering his lips and exhaling. He dipped the bowl in with his bare hand and scooped out some stew; it was still smoking, and Jimmy realized it must have been made with fish. He ate it heartily, ignoring his scalding mouth.

"I brought some water from Fog Lake," Ashton said, grabbing the balloon canteen from his belt.

"Thank you." The old man took a long swig and then wiped his mouth.

"Jimmy, stay here and eat, okay? I have to talk to—" Ashton said when he was interrupted.

"Oh my manners, I am so sorry young Jimmy. I am Ae-Granum, but you can call me Granum. Ae is just a prefix from the old days that means 'from'—language is always changing, and so I figure I should change with it. Or my name at least." He smiled, and Jimmy returned the favor.

"Nice to meet you," Jimmy said, slobbering stew down his chin; it was the best stew he had ever eaten.

Granum and Ashton left Jimmy alone to eat his stew; they both walked through the only door in the house, which led to the back where Jimmy had supposed the roof would collapse if it were built underneath the heavy Canopy Trees.

3

"The wolves have gone into the mines," Granum said. "The stone is still on the other side. Only time will prove whether they retrieve it or not—poor Jimmy, why has he gotten himself into this?"

"His twin brother is with the wolves," Ashton said, taking a drink from the balloon canteen. "The other side seems to breed the virtue of the Hunters also, for Jimmy figures he can single-handedly rescue him."

"You shouldn't be ashamed of what you are," Granum said. "Please take that ridiculous mask off—your father would not have agreed with your refusal of acceptance. Isn't deception against the code of the Hunter?"

"I didn't come here for this—I came here to do as you asked. And you haven't spoken a word about the stone to the boy."

"What would I say that I don't already know? The threat has grown larger if the wolves have finally planned an attack. They've watched those mines for many years, and they've waited just as I've waited. This act was spontaneous, without proper judgment—but sometimes those decisions are the ones that work best in the end. We are pressed for time, Asha. So pressed for time."

ashton just nodded his head.

Granum exhaled deeply. "I must get the stone. When I sent your father to the Towers it was only so he could bring it back to me. I hadn't the foresight to see the consequences—parts of me are waning, bleeding from me like ichor from a wound." Granum looked down at a piece of warped glass on the table; it was thick and resembled a pool of crystal water. On the surface of the glass Ashton could see Wolf Country; he could see the Yilaks readying for war, calling to arms, as they all scurried to their weapon halls inside large tents. They were squeezing into breastplates, shoving helmets over their pointed skulls, their ears poking out the top.

"They look as if they expect a war," Ashton said.

"They do. A wolf left the mines to warn them—they have breached the other side; it is only a matter of time."

"What are they saying?"

Granum dipped his head lower to the glass; he could hear within it, using the vibrations of each moving image. Granum had lived for years using assorted pieces of Sandglass to contact the outside world. "They only howl, but I have suspected ideas of inner-conflict within the packs—many of them have spoken aloud the desire to rid of Jarak, but they have spoken this quietly in the confines of the shadows; they fear Jarak, I suppose. They ready for a war in the mines." Granum touched the glass and the image moved forwards, passed tents and piles of bone, towards the base of the Towers, where Ashton could see the tunnels dug into the foundation—one of which his father had used to steal the stone before he would die. Die by Grak's hand. "But I watch Auger. Curious," Granum said, as the image stopped on an old man, hunched forward on his cane. Next to him stood a wolf on all fours.

"What are they standing there for, when war is coming from the mines?"

"Old man Auger has been acting strangely for a long time. I have watched him for years in his solitude beyond the Joon Mountains; he has become increasingly insane. Some believe him an otherworlder. He has become my puppet ever since the Traveling Man went to his castle—such beliefs we have in destiny. Actions are easy to puppeteer. We both have used him to try and bring the stone back to this world; he is the sole reason the wolves have gone into the mines, you know."

"Then why does he just stand there?"

"They must have sent something into the tunnels—I have glass pieces that access the past in the other room, though. Time can be twisted in Sandglass. Ever since the explosion it seems his agenda has changed."

"The explosion, you saw the explosion in the Sordids? What was it?"

Granum smiled. "I was very afraid at first, for you had already grabbed the boy and were off to see me. I thought the man had come from the mines with the stone, for some*thing* exited, dressed strangely, its face concealed by a hat, holding a stone from a piece of twine. At that moment I believed the Inlands were doomed, for the will of the wolves would have forced the stone into a seed of destruction. As soon as the oddly dressed creature was confronted, it exploded."

"Exploded. I have never heard such a noise before. I heard it from miles away, with the ruins as a wall to block most of the noise."

"Aye, but when I saw the explosion, I realized myself that we are closer to the end, of everything around us, everything in bloom; the decay of the world. We must act soon, or there *will* be a war, a war with fire, a fire beyond the technologies of this world. I know this." Granum lowered his head. "Time runs short; it always comes to war. *Always*. And the sequence is always the same. The end of everything." Granum turned towards Ashton. "If the wolves get the stone before we do I fear—I fear their vengeance. If only the Guardian had stopped me on Logres," Granum had said touching the glass again, and the projection lifted to a much higher height above Wolf Country, and the troops of Yilaks marching up the mountain pass towards the mines. "If only I hadn't gotten the stone."

4

Jimmy finished his stew and grabbed another bowlful; there were bones poking out of the broth, but they didn't deter him from spooning the chunky stew into his mouth as fast as he could. The wizard must have put a spell on the pot or something; there was no way fish could taste this good. Back at home Mr. Krollup employed some of the world's best cooks, and even their seafood cuisine couldn't match this backwoods concoction.

The wizard's house was very dark; there were two windows, and each of them seemed tinted by a lime glow. The windows must have been concealed by leaves. Jimmy finished the stew, debated on whether or not he wanted another helping, then decided on looking around the room instead. There were pieces of scroll everywhere, hanging on hooks, folded and piled in towers. Jimmy picked one up and looked at the writing; it was in weird letters he had never seen before, and there was a picture of a sun rising over two leaves, bordered by golden fleece. It was a beautiful drawing. There must have been hundreds of parchment, and Jimmy wondered what they all said; they must have been important if they inhabited such space in the house of a wizard. He wondered why a wizard hid himself away from everything anyway, disguising his house; it was as if he didn't want to bothered. Or found.

Jimmy wondered how Ashton knew the wizard lived here, how he found this concealed house when at first it looked only like another rock decorated with moss. And he wondered why the wizard was so insistent on taking Ashton's mask off. Jimmy liked his fair share of horror movies, but he wasn't fond of the idea of seeing Ashton's scars; he could just imagine what it would look like if a sword pierced your brow. There must have been flaps of skin hanging everywhere on Ashton's face, like drapery.

Jimmy saw a piece of oddly shaped glass sitting on the floor. At first he had dismissed it, but then he realized there was a picture on it—a *moving* picture. It must have been his imagination, but it was just like a television. An ancient television, sure, but he was seeing it all the same. What was this? He wanted to think strange things; he wanted to guess, to assume the way he figured Cole would if the boy were with him right now. Perhaps he had traveled to some distant past. Perhaps this was the world after dinosaurs, the world before the Bible. He waved his hand down the front of the glass; there was a slight buzz and his hand vibrated.

He saw tents in the glass, and at the top of the picture there was an ugly rock with holes littered across it. He saw moving figures, lots of them, moving toward the bottom of the glass, all of them carrying swords and axes—they were wolves, just like the fallen wolves he had seen in the woods. "What is this?" He had whispered to himself.

And he saw four figures leave the tent to the right—a wolf was leading one of them rather violently, its blindfolded head lashing from left to right; its left arm was missing. Jimmy fell to his knees. There was an old man also, walking slowly and with the aid of a cane, and there was—

Cole. Cole was walking with them; his sweater was dirty and his pants were stained with mud.

"Cole," Jimmy said into the glass. He tapped the glass and it felt like his fingers were burning. He clutched his hand to his chest, wincing. "Cole, look up, look up, it's Jimmy, please." Jimmy grabbed a rolled up scroll and knocked it against the glass. He could smell the burning ink, the pigments in the paper spoiling.

Cole and the other three stood at the foot of the massive rock; they looked miniscule next to it. He watched the old man and the werewolf talk. Cole constantly looked over his shoulder at the caves in the rock; he looked scared. "Don't you do anything to him," Jimmy said angrily, "don't you hurt him." After a moment both Cole and the blindfolded figure climbed into one of the tunnels. The wolf pushed the creature missing its left arm—and then they disappeared. Jimmy put his face as close as he could to the glass, until if it were physically possible, he could cinch his eye into the tunnel with Cole. But the darkness hid them.

Jimmy jumped up; he felt anger overcome him, and all of a sudden he wished he had gotten away from Ashton, charged through the woods without the spiders finding him, so he could have waited for Cole at the caves. Jimmy ran to the back door and ripped it open.

5

"'Tis guilt that has stayed me here," Granum spoke in a mutter. "Oh the legend is a lie, you know. What folks say, what ears hear—the stories were blindly penned by those whose imagination seem to exaggerate all. I never climbed to the top of Piphany Mountain on the island of Logres as so many supposed; I never took a stone from its peak and waited for lightning to strike it, fusing my blood into its fissures, binding the powers of Mystic and the wizards. Legends can be fabricated, and so can people's beliefs." Granum stroked his beard. "Some folk say the stone built the mountains in the south, long ago—the Giants used it hundreds of years ago to build the mountains in Yadiron, bordering the sea from land for the Giants feared seawater; and before then some say the folk of Sussa built the island of Logres as an escape from the ongoing war with the Giants. Who knows? History is lost in this world. The wolves lost much of it when they burned down the city—aye, but the stone has seen all things, and lived all things. And it will live again, for its teeth sink and its music tempts.

"It is a parasite—I felt so many times its hungering teeth in my soul; it leeched onto me, and the more I used it, the more it took from me; 'twas how the King cut my throat. How he took my blood and left me with this scar as a reminder. Oh how Mystic has punished me. But the stone is gone from me, and that has angered me the most; it is alive. It breathed my breaths; it saw with my eyes. I have unleashed it on the world."

Ashton looked at Granum concernedly. "It was the King's evil, his greed that brought the stone back to the Inlands. Did he not trick you into believing you were doing a good deed for the people of the world? Did he not say 'twas for yer own good graces in the will of the folk? Did he not insist you were building a prison for the wolves, and not a castle for his own plunder?"

Granum looked up. "I *am* sorry Asha, it burdens me though to think all of this could have been averted had the Guardian stopped me. And it was my fault sending your father into the Towers to fetch the stone, but I lied to him also—I insisted it was so I could finally destroy the talisman, but all along I heard the stone calling my name; it has a voice, like poison it is, but I heeded it, didn't I? And I sent your father to his doom in return."

Ashton rubbed the old man's shoulders, his wrinkled flesh hanging from bone like cloth from a clothesline. "In the end, Granum, it is your noble wish to destroy the talisman that matters. Mayhaps that is why you have seen this war of fire. It is your sign, and you must overcome guilt to confront it."

And the door banged open, Jimmy standing at the threshold with a scowl and clenched fists.

6

"I saw my brother in the glass. What's the meaning of this? Why can I see *this* in glass?" Jimmy was looking at Granum when he spoke.

This of course had startled both Ashton and the wizard.

"What's wrong, Jimmy?" Ashton asked.

"Are you both in on it? I looked into a sheet of glass and saw my brother with a wolf, an armless *THING*, and an old man. Why would you have glass that showed me this image if you weren't in on it? Was the purpose of bringing me here to keep me from saving my brother? Are you working for the wolves?" Jimmy ran forward, and noticed that both the wizard and Ashton had been looking into a sheet of glass also, and that the two of them were watching the same image he had been. "I see, I see, I guess you didn't expect me to see the same thing on the screen outside. If you're a wizard, wouldn't you have been able to have the smarts to hide glass showing incriminating evidence, especially when the person you're hiding it from is in the same room?" Jimmy reached inside his pocket and grabbed another stone, one he'd picked up outside the Leeg Forest hours ago. He held it up and looked at the Hunter and wizard with a cocked eye. "Tell me what's going on or I smash this," and he nudged his head toward the glass on the table, which portrayed the bird's eye view of the old man and wolf standing outside the tunnels.

"Jimmy, please don't," Granum said, with the full knowledge he could snap his fingers and turn the stone into a serpent, but he had realized already the fear behind the boy's eyes, and didn't want to pursue the same lines and scare the boy further.

"Jimmy, it's Sandglass," Ashton said. "It's a projection from the mountain tops. Mystic's Eye. God's sense."

Jimmy hesitated a moment. "What do you mean? I saw my brother in it. Why did I see Cole in the *GLASS*?" He clenched his fingers around the stone until they turned red. "Tell me or I smash it."

Granum looked at the boy. Jimmy must have looked into a hind-glass, which showed events from minutes up till hours ago—Granum surrounded himself with such pieces of glass; he was a being with only two eyes, and those were only capable of watching one sheet of glass at a time. It was a matter of manipulating time that helped the wizard see all.

Granum exhaled. "Sandglass is the Wizard's Eye Jimmy. During the high tide, much of the coast is drenched with seawater, and during the storms Mystic throws lightning at the ground—with that enormous burst of heat and energy, the seawater and sand turn into glass. But it is the source from which the glass is formed that develops the projections; the eyes of the mountains fall to the earth, some say, and those who can work the glass have the chance to manipulate the perspectives of the world; it isn't easy, nor does it work all the time. 'Tis the wizard's craft. The Sandglass works with patience. What you watched was an image seen from the tops of the Sordid ruins Jimmy, and I'm not in any team with the wolves; rather I have been stuck in my home for reasons beyond explanation and I find it is my duty to watch over the world, if not only to maintain my sanity." Granum smiled. "The Sandglass is the perspective of everything above us, Jimmy, and it would be terrible if you destroyed nature's eye—the consequences would be unheard of, I'm sorry to say."

Jimmy looked at them both. "What are they doing to Cole? Why would they send him into a tunnel?"

"Tunnel?" Granum said, and he looked down at the Sandglass, at the image of the old man and wolf, standing outside the tunnels. "Oh my, they've sent him into the Towers," the wizard said, and he looked at Ashton worriedly.

"You say that like it's a horrible thing—what are they doing to my brother?"

Granum kneeled down and looked at Jimmy. He turned the stone into a flower, and the boy's clenched fingers dropped the stem. "Don't worry about your brother, Jimmy. We will get him, I promise." He patted Jimmy's head.

"Let's go now. HURRY," Jimmys nearly screamed.

"We have an agenda. Asha, take Jimmy outside, I must dress, and I must secure the glass."

"Why?" Ashton asked, grabbing Jimmy's arm.

"Because I must bring it if I am to come with you," the wizard said, closing the door behind the two as he led them out.

Ashton smiled. The wolves had the force of a wizard to contend with now.

7

Jimmy looked at Ashton. "I'm sorry. I've been testy, I know, but when I saw my brother, when I saw him going into that tunnel, I knew this was my fault. If it wasn't for me, he would have never been here in the first place." Jimmy patted the tin box in his pocket and looked at the charred twigs underneath the pot—why hadn't he lit a smoke when he had the chance?

"Regret always leads to suffering Jimmy. You mustn't dwell on faults."

"Written on the walls of the catacombs, right?" Jimmy asked with a smile.

Ashton nodded.

"You know, I had a weird thought a couple of minutes ago, you know, before I looked into the Sandglass, or whatever—I thought that maybe those mines are like a weird time continuum or something. Have you ever thought that? Everything here seems so outdated. What you call Sandglass is called a satellite and television where I'm from. Maybe the Sandglass is an early prototype, you know."

"You never know the will of Mystic," Ashton said, patting Jimmy's shoulder. "That's why life is so interesting. Because the mysterious keeps you guessing."

Jimmy looked around the house one last time—at the pieces of Sandglass, and at the stacks of parchment; out the window concealed by leaves, dressing the room with a lime tint. "Why is he out here? I mean, why is the wizard hiding? He must be if he's protected himself with woods infested by giant spiders, and disguised his house to look like rock."

"He's keeping out of sight—but he watches everything," Ashton said absent-mindedly. He was walking towards a piece of glass leaning against a stack of parchment. Ashton knelt down before the glass and ran his fingers over the dusty floor.

"Are you okay?" Jimmy asked.

Ashton ignored him. He watched in the glass the image of the King's men traveling alongside an apple shaped carriage, moving west along the Odin River in Cassica. The King's men rode alongside Hunters. Why would Hunters be with the King's men? For years they were mortal enemies, opposing forces of the civil wars; it was Ashton's father that decided to rid of the monarchy, and yet here he watched the two companies mingle, moving as quickly as possible towards the Leeg. This was a hindglass, showing events passed mayhaps hours ago, and he wondered where these men were now. He waved his hand over the glass and the image quickly faded into a shot of oxen running in a remote field. He cursed under his breath.

When he felt Jimmy's hand on his shoulder, he touched the boy's knuckles and stood up.

"Are you okay?"

"Yes, I'm fine. Go wait outside. I have to talk to Granum."

Jimmy nodded and moved towards the door. "You promise we're going to get my brother right? We're not going further west, or down south to talk to some other old man—we're going to get him now, right?" ashton nodded.

Jimmy looked back once more and then left, closing the door behind him.

"Yes, we'll get your brother Jimmy, if we survive," Ashton said under his breath. He opened the wizard's door and caught Granum throwing a blanket over the glass.

"You frightened me, Asha."

"Stop calling me that—Asha isn't the name of a Hunter." The Hunter walked to the wizard, who was now wearing a long robe that was tied in the middle by rope.

"Very well then. If it were up to me things would be different though. This feels odd, getting ready for an adventure; it's been so long, Ashton." Granum smiled.

"I thought I was the only one who knew where you lived."

"What are you talking about?"

"In the woods, I heard men speaking of an old man beyond the forest; they didn't make it far. The spiders descended on them, but their information shocked me."

Granum looked at Ashton, and continued covering the glass with a large quilt. "The many times you've come to see me Asha, have you ever once wondered if others had been behind you?"

"Of course, I can tell these things. I have my father's senses."

"Yes, but what if these others are Hunters also, and share your sense, therefore shaping it to dismiss them."

"What are you talking about?"

"You are a curiosity among the Hunters Asha; you claim to them you are the son of David when they know he never had a son, but you fight, you move like he did. You live alone and fight alone, and in the code of the Hunters, your search for vengeance is selfish, for Hunters fight for the common goal, for the plight of the people. This was your father's motto, so how could the supposed son of David the Hunter dismiss such a powerful oath?"

"Women are to be protected, not to do the protecting," Ashton said angrily.

"Your mother agreed with the notion, I suppose," Granum smiled.

Ashton paced for a moment. "They *followed* me through the woods and *watched* me enter your house?"

The wizard nodded, and tucked the quilt around the back of the glass.

"You knew this and you didn't warn me?"

"Warn you of what Asha? I have yet to understand your true motivations. I wonder sometimes if you are really ready to face your impending tasks, your purpose. You say your face is scarred yet 'tis shame that stays that mask on your face; you conceal your identity when you know deception goes against the Hunter's code, and yet you believe you do so for the will of your father. David would have scorned your actions. If I had to warn you of anything, I should have warned you about obsession; *your* obsession for vengeance demeans your father's spirit. Do you believe it is his will for you to avenge his death, all the while forgetting to live your own life?"

"David was disappointed in me. In what I wasn't." Ashton looked down.

"That's ridiculous, Asha."

"Please, I've always hated that name; it reminds me too much of him, of my childhood."

"Though Ashton, this name is just Asha's inversion, is it not?" Granum twitched his nose, which in effect made his beard tremble.

Ashton ignored the wizard, remembering the conversation he'd heard in the woods while he hid in the hovel. "The Hunters told the King's men about you also. Is there a conspiracy? Have the Hunters completely turned their backs on my father and instead turned to the King's Crest?"

"Would you like me to unwrap the glass and see where they are at now, would that help?"

"Just answer the question."

Granum chuckled. "Your father was a proud man, Asha; he too believed it was his right to know all. Do you want to know something—I am a target, for it isn't my magic these men are after. The Hunters and the royals have been driven together by one common goal, and to do so they have decided to work as a team in accomplishing success; it would have been your father's way also, not the route you've taken. Loneliness, isolation. Right now their opinions conflict. Each side believes the other a traitor, but I'm sure in the end everything will work out because the goal remains the same."

"What is that goal?"

"To defeat Grak once and for all."

"They have formed an army? But I saw them in the glass; there were hardly enough of them to contend with the wolves."

"That's where I come in, I'm afraid to say. The King's men were used to breach Wolf Country and establish the Yilak's course, using old man Auger as an excuse to sidestep battle—I have watched this in the glass, Asha, sorry, *Ashton*, and beneath the genius exists treachery. The old man you saw at the tunnels in the Towers, he is dying. He wants what every man lusts—eternal life; he has become, in effect, a blind man following a course led by another. Me. No man can foresee the consequences of immortality, but death presents a threat man wants to overcome; men want to be the master of their domain without the inevitability of their fall. And this old man introduced an option the King's heir had overseen—I have watched their eyes light up at the thought of never ending life, Ashton, and man's war with the wolves has been sidetracked because of a belief that battle will be easier if the consequences of war can be forgotten."

"The old rhyme from the stories, how does it go—*A Wizard's blood deems life eternal, dodging death's timeless inferno*—yes, yes, I remember…there is more, but I have forgotten the lyric. They're searching for you because of this nursery rhyme, this belief?" Ashton looked at the cut behind the wizard's mangy beard, a beard he grew to conceal the wound.

"Aye, but it's not merely a belief; my differences are a mortal's advantage. But the Hunters aren't retrieving me for this reason. The Hunters remain strategic to the war, and if they believe they can infiltrate Wolf Country from within, then battle will be easier. The old man asked Haspin, the King's lone heir, to help him find me, the last Wizard, as a sort of last resort if his other plans fall through—I watched the two of em discuss me as if I were a piece of meat awaiting their lips." He scratched his throat. "The Hunters believe they are bringing me back to Wolf Country as safe access beyond the mountain pass, only to use me as a diversion to attack both from within and without the Sordids. It is war and hope they have on their side, and if they should chance the woods to see for sure who lives in the disguised house, then they believe they should take that chance. How would Auger know if I was or wasn't a wizard if I were brought back to Wolf Country? That becomes the main line of logic. Until I was poked with a blade, until my blood birthed flowers on infertile ground, until I showed some form of my magic, my *species* would remain a mystery, giving enough time to establish battle on all fronts. Diversion."

"What of the King's men? I do not believe they would risk their necks only to use you as a war tactic. I believe they'd tell the Hunters this, yet they would rather drink your blood before you even got to old man Auger, and they would stab the Hunters in the backs, declaring open war on the Hunters and the wolves, believing their immortality would aid their success."

Granum smiled and lifted the glass under his arm; the ends of the quilt came unfastened, and the wizard pointed his finger and the blanket automatically seamed itself together. "Thus creating the inner-conflict within the company of man."

"I have to warn the Hunters."

"I'm sure, Asha, that they will be waiting for us. Fate has woven itself into the actions of this impending war—the King's men search for a wizard, and they have joined forces with the only people that know of his location, because they followed you through the woods out of curiosity.

"In the end, Asha, I believe you will take off your mask for good."

8

Granum left his concealed house carrying the Sandglass in a quilt, which was fastened at the bottom.

"Ah, so 'tis our ride," he said, looking at the spiders. "I spose I should introduce myself, since our meeting has long been postponed—a tragedy considering we have shared the same woods for many years." Granum smiled.

The spiders moved toward the wizard, almost bowing down on their front legs. "A wizard, here in our woods," Kannef said in a high whisper. The spider was looking at the concealed house in disbelief—spiders were equipped with uncanny perception, yet this rock eluded them for as long as they had come to the beach to leave the dead.

"We must go," Ashton said.

Granum shared his infectious smile. He didn't look like a wizard; he wore a grubby robe that must have been hundreds of years old, bound in the middle by a frayed rope that had seen better days; his beard was sparse, and grew in gray patches, and his hair was so incredibly mangy that to Jimmy, the prospect of running a comb through the tangles would prove impossible. But within and without him there seemed a corona of certainty. Perhaps it was his smile. When Granum smiled, those who looked upon him knew at once whom they were dealing with.

"The wolves have gone into the mines," Ashton said, and he hopped onto Jarat's back. He slapped Jarat's side as if the spider were a horse. "Take us to the eastern edge of the woods, we must get to Wolf Country before nightfall."

Granum walked over to Kannef the Spider and bound rope around the spider's belly, slop dropping from beneath its abdomen like rocks to the ground; the sand fizzled. Granum shoved the glass under the rope, pointed his finger and the rope tensed and knotted around the quilt. He tugged at it and made sure it was tight. The wizard swiped his arm over Kannef's back and a comfortable saddle made of cotton formed; he climbed into his perch, struggling at first, like any old man, and after several failed attempts at climbing the spider's side, he floated into the saddle.

"Jimmy," Ashton yelled. "I thought out of all of us you would want to leave the most."

Jimmy seemed to ignore the Hunter's voice. He stood still, staring at the sea, at the white surf stained red and black, bubbling around the jutting bodies of glistening corpses. He suddenly swung upwards and was plopped onto the back of Jarat; Ashton had grabbed Jimmy under the arms, pulling him onto the spider's back.

"Hey, come on, be careful, you could have dislocated my shoulders."

"There is no time for could-haves. Jarat, we must hurry. I would like to reach the wall of the Leeg in an hour."

"That isn't possible," Kannef the Spider responded.

"Why is that?"

"Because the Queen has insisted on meeting the wizard; she wants to know exactly why she let you survive our woods," Kannef said bitterly, and the spider ran up the webbing to the topmost branches of the Canopy Trees.

Arguing wouldn't have helped matters, and Ashton knew that; he would have rather cooperated with the spiders than oppose them, and in the end his decision seemed the most accountable.

Jimmy, Ashton and the wizard headed for Spider City, while in Wolf Country Cole walked in the darkness with a hermit that resembled his dead father, and in the mines Edwin Krollup floated above the seat of an ATV, held down by Leo's hooked fingers, which inched ever closer to the gun propped out of Krollup's belt.

CHAPTER 19

A Victim's Escape II

1

Leo heard the wolves and statues clash. It was pitch black, and Leo, using his left hand, gripped the edge of Edwin's thigh and hooked his right fingers closer to the gun.

Edwin felt dead, but he also felt vibrant with life, as if he were a puppet for some greater force. Leo could tell Krollup was breathing; he moved his left hand closer to the front of Edwin's pants, spinning the floating man an inch with his right hand. Leo had a plan; he knew the end of the mines were near. He couldn't see them yet, but he could feel something, some breeze, some noxious drift of air that smelt of acrid dusts.

Leo could hear swords clashing, and he could hear the guttural voices of those wolves ahead of him. For some reason he was sure he could slightly see David's frame in front of him, pulling the ATV on a chain.

Leo had made sure the keys were still in the ignition before deciding on pulling through with his idea; he'd checked nearly twenty minutes ago, and found, to his luck, the key chain dangling with the ring on the end. He had never felt so certain. Sure he thought he had Krollup outwitted with the robot bomb, but he had fallen asleep. Not now though; it seemed Krollup had fallen asleep this time, but Leo knew he still had to be careful. Leo heard a wolf yell out in the distance:

"RETREAT!"

A sudden glimmer surfaced across his mind. If retreat were possible, then they were close to an exit. He instinctually reached out for the key chain, felt it in his palm and grabbed Edwin's thigh.

And he could tell the light was changing. He could see the flesh overtone of his fingers against Krollup's pants. He wouldn't move him yet, he'd wait and do it in one quick motion; there was little sense caging himself in the mines.

2

"What is that noise?" Cole asked. The light was still awkward in the Towers, emanating from within the walls like lime lanterns.

"I don't know," the hermit said. "It sounds like an avalanche." It did. It sounded like something was falling.

"Do you think there was another explosion?"

"No," the hermit said; he walked with a drag, and his right arm hung by his side, dripping blood from the stump on his wrist; the stump on his left arm did the same.

They had walked down the main hall past different corridors on either side. Each corridor seemed disguised by mist. They weren't alone, but they couldn't go back to the tunnels. Kenneth Auger and the wolf would kill Cole if they didn't finish their duty. He knew that.

The hermit had told Cole that according to popular legend, each room in the Tower was guarded by an ancient spirit the wizard called upon to protect each treasure. What they heard, what they felt behind the shrouds in the corridors were only the ghosts of knights of the King's Crest; they were an illusion, Hayle had said, looking at Cole reassuringly. He wasn't certain if the legends were true, but he found his assurances to Cole self-comforting—that was the significant threat of these Towers; they drove an undead being to seek an alternative to the possible truth.

They walked on toward the darkness that both hoped was the end of the Tower.

"What does the old man want?" Cole asked in a whisper.

"What the King is wearing around his neck, a vial," Hayle said. He felt something inside him wanting to give; it wasn't painful exactly, but it was tiring. He had re-shaped his bones. Somehow he had found in this boy's gaze the power to give him an image Cole would appreciate. This was why fate had intervened, he realized. Perhaps he had waited years in a cocoon, in the Queen's poisonous belly, so he could protect this boy the way he should have protected his wife and daughter.

"It's getting louder," Cole said. "I think its coming from that room over there." Cole pointed to the archway to his left, about fifty feet ahead of him. The rock wall sloped from the ground and wound upward into the darkness; each wall was lit from within. The doorways were perfect curves in the stone.

Whatever was happening in that hallway was strong enough to shake the ground.

Cole fidgeted a moment. The noise was terrifying. For the first time in what seemed like ages, he reached into his pocket for his chocolates; he shook out a couple, rolled them around his palm and shoved them in his mouth.

"It's okay you know, Cole," Hayle said. "Nothing will happen to you. I'm sure of it. That's why I'm here. That's why I changed. There is a reason for everything. Wait here a moment."

"No, you can't go over there. I won't let you." Cole grabbed Hayle's slithery shoulder and nearly lost his grip.

"I think this is the way we have to go, but we're not going this way if it isn't safe."

Cole closed his eyes. He thought he saw something in his head, some vague image; it broke apart before he could firmly grasp it. "No. We should stick to this hall, I know it. I don't know why, but I do. I think that sound's supposed to throw us off, supposed to scare us away. It seems *thin*. If the rooms are guarded, there must be things in this place we're not supposed to see. I've read about things like this, you know. Diversions. Misdirection. We're being drawn to that room but we shouldn't be. We're being tricked."

The hermit smiled, his fangs showing slightly under his rosy lips. "I hope you're right Cole, but don't you want to get out of here as fast as possible?"

Cole looked down and nodded.

"It's always better to be certain. My father used to tell me that; there's no sense wondering what if. If there are two roads, make sure you take both at least once in your life, or you'll die with regrets."

"You sound like Robert Frost," Cole said with the hint of a smile.

The hermit moved slowly towards the hallway.

"Cole come here," the hermit said; he seemed delighted. "You're never going to believe what you're seeing."

Cole didn't think twice. He liked the sound of enthusiasm in the hermit's voice; it really reminded him of his father. He ran over and what he saw dropped his jaw.

The archway led to a large circular room with the same sloped walls and greenish tinge. There was another doorway across the room, but it was the space between both doors Cole and the hermit were fascinated with. Cole hoped this wasn't the way they were supposed to go.

The ground before them was littered with huge boulders, but they all shook violently. Hundreds of rocks fell from the darkness of the ceiling, exploding into the ground. When those stones hit the ground, the rocks that seemed already embedded in the cracked surface shook loose and rose into the air, disappearing in the darkness above.

"Watch this," the hermit said.

Five seconds later the rocks fell with a loud crash, and the other boulders lifted into the air, by some magnetic force in the roof or something. Something strange. Something new.

"It's a cycle. They fall in five-second increments. Look, the trick is to watch where each stone falls. I don't think they change; they're assigned a spot, as if they rise and fall on an invisible axis."

"We're not going in there," Cole said.

"It's a test of patience. The King must have assumed burglars were hasty. Look, over there. Bones. Somebody's tried to get through. Whatever is beyond this room must be very valuable, very powerful."

"I can't go in there. I won't. This isn't the way. My real father wouldn't make me go in there."

Hayle looked at Cole. "You don't have to come, Cole. It wasn't my decision to bring you into this place, you know that right?" Hayle watched the rocks fall again; there were minute spaces in between each that had never been touched by falling stones, but they were far and few between. The hermit realized he only had five seconds to reach each safe point. But he was weak. "The King must be beyond this door, unless he felt necessary the inclusion of further tests."

"Let's just take this main hallway. I think we're being misled, we're being pinpointed maybe. This room draws people, like a surveillance plot, and then, then something comes every now and again to get impostors—I know about security, you have to believe me."

"Cole, our world is different than yours. I have seen in your head the world you belong to, the fears and concerns you have about that world; it is strange. But you must realize, the King wouldn't misuse his resources to draw people into a trap; he wants to lead people into believing they have hope, they have a chance in receiving what he stole from the Inlands, only to watch them get crushed. I will be back shortly, Cole. I know I will."

The hermit turned, watched the stones fall and then moved into the large room, stepping carefully and quickly; he jumped, rather feebly, into a spot on the ground that looked as if it hadn't been touched in a thousand years. He waited and the stones fell, and rose, around him.

Cole couldn't watch. He had a terrible feeling. He thought he was right; he thought this was a drawing room, that the room was a magnet for the forces within these Towers. The King was leading people into believing something valuable was beyond this room. He had tricked Jimmy the same way before. Once Jimmy had wanted Cole's dessert and had threatened to beat him up if he couldn't have it. Cole put his cookies into the drawer next to his bed and stood defiantly in front of a box he put on top of his desk. By standing in front of the box, Jimmy had assumed Cole hid the cookies inside it. When Jimmy opened the box he found two rather large spiders Cole had grabbed from a vent—Jimmy screamed and ran away without punishing Cole, and without getting the cookies. Cole looked up and saw the hermit dancing in between two stones, one which had just fallen, and the other which was rising on its invisible axis.

And he felt something like cold breath on his neck.

Cole turned and looked into the eyeless sockets of a decayed corpse, which stood not on the ground, but in the air, its legs dangling uselessly as if thrown by the wind. When it opened its mouth to reveal dripping teeth, Cole screamed.

"DAD!"

The hermit turned, and the stones fell.

3

Leo decided once and for all that this was the time. He couldn't expect things to happen anymore. The keys were in the ignition and the exit was in sight, an outline of light obstructed by the silhouettes of wolves and statues.

The problem he'd considered was whether or not he took the quad back up the mines. Was that a world he wanted to go back to? Did he want to return to a world where he was perceived as a terrorist, the Robot Bomber, or did he want to find a new niche, perhaps on the other side—the light at the end of the tunnel?

Leo had started unraveling the chain from the steering column, which had been jammed in the front; he pulled with one arm, steadying Krollup's body with the other. He could hear the wolves yelping, the sharp sound of sword against stone. He could feel David's strength through the chain as the statue pulled the vehicle; he left the end of the chain wrapped loosely around the steering column, which was pulled tense with every gigantic step of the statue. He had two things to do, and knew he couldn't screw up either. He had to get the gun that was propped out of Krollup's pants, and he had to hurriedly wrap the chain around Edwin to pull him completely off the quad.

Leo grabbed the gun first. If he had fully taken the chain off the quad and tried to hold it while he reached for the gun, he would have been pulled from the ATV and dragged along the ground. Instead, he twisted Edwin's front to the left, and pulling Krollup along his belt loops, found the gun and tugged at the handle. It was stuck.

He realized that if he pulled it any harder, he would've awakened Edwin's senses. They were nearing the exit. Leo would have to use the statue's momentum as an advantage.

Leo turned the keys in the ignition; there was a slight click and nothing happened. The engine didn't turn over. "No," he mumbled. He tried again, and the headlights flared inside the mine; shadows leapt from the fissures and the wolves shielded their eyes. It worked.

Leo touched the chain, exhaled loudly, and heard Edwin say something in a weak voice: "I warned you."

Leo ignored him, quickly grabbed the chain, threw it around Edwin's waist and grabbed the gun, using the statue's force to pull the buried muzzle from his pants. Edwin was pulled off the quad and dragged along the wall.

"LEO!" Edwin screamed, clutching the stone in his hand. Leo felt a shelf of rock try to tip the quad over and he revved the engine, grabbed the handlebars and accelerated. The ATV sped forward and he almost collided with David. Leo fumbled with the gun, aimed it at Edwin and with a sudden understanding of the reversal of fortunes, pulled the trigger.

Nothing happened. The stupid safety was on, and before he realized how to fix his mistake, the quad had sped past the statue and was nearing the exit. He bowled over a wolf before the beast could swipe out with its axe, lost control when he ran over the creature's legs and barreled toward the ravine at the edge of the bluff.

Leo veered the steering column and the quad literally lifted on its right tires, spinning to the south, spitting loose rock at wolves, pelting gravel off statues. He looked behind him, trying to find Edwin, but the world was covered in fur and stone; alongside the ruins Leo watched statues pin wolves, beating them and throwing them aside like hairy rags. There was a granite bull bucking wolves over the cliff, sending yelping beasts for cover, its horns crumbling into its head; there was no clear path back to the mines, Leo could tell that much.

He had seen something very peculiar, something that had caused him to shade his eyes against the waning sun in a lifeless sky. He saw a wolf dashing through the camp below, amidst the swarm of howling wolves. This wolf ran on all fours and carried a man on its back, swiping at others as it passed; it seemed like the wolf was trying to reach the pass up the cliff side. Leo had stopped to watch this, both in part of its oddity and in hopes of finding either Cole or Jimmy among the shadows, but he realized his mistake right away. He felt a strong wind by his side and noticed a wolf had swung its blade at him, missing merely because a cracked statue had snapped the creature's neck before it could swing again.

A feeling of relief swept over him, and it urged him to go. There was a path southeast, alongside the broken mountain that looked like chipped teeth in the earth. Leo drove this way, over fallen wolves, among the stench of blood. When the mountainous ruins ended he turned southwest, into the cracked Barrens. The sounds of battle were behind him.

He had escaped.

He had escaped with a taste for blood. Had he known the gun wouldn't fire, or had he actually meant to kill the man, his captor?

Leo drove with this unnerving thought, wondering if Edwin had finally fallen, had been dragged to his death or stomped by wolves. He heard gunshots behind him, and he wondered if Edwin had brought another gun.

Leo drove southwest until he disappeared beyond the murk of desolation. He would meet Edwin again; he would meet Cole and Jimmy again, but in the end he'd have to realize his own demons, and understand that technology had always been the root of his problems. Though he had escaped Krollup, he would always be in another's clutches; it was his fate to be victimized, and soon he'd realize just that: he hadn't escaped at all. In fact, soon he'd have to explain the mechanics of an ATV in a world where transportation relied on horse and carriage. Leo would again be forced to aid in destruction.

In the end, as he once told Cole, he'd have to confront his devils.

4

Edwin was pulled off the quad. He slammed against the wall and the chain tightened, scraping the rock with sparks that felt like they were going to ignite his back. For the first time he had become fully aware of what was happening. This time, holding the stone felt different. It seemed like the power had been displaced, and instead of an overwhelming sense of dominance, Edwin felt like a piece of meat strung on somebody else's fork.

"LEO!" He screamed. Edwin forced a sliver of rock from the ground to throw the quad over but the little man accelerated forward. Edwin scrambled against the rock face, trying to squeeze out of the chain.

There was no sense struggling. When he realized the gun was missing from his pants he knew exactly where it went, and he forgot for the moment the reason why he had come down the mines. Edwin closed his eyes and waited; he knew it wouldn't have mattered had he flipped the quad with rock or sent a statue after Leo, because there were enough bullets in that gun to make sure he was a goner. after a long moment he opened his eyes and saw the tail end of the quad outside the mines. He exhaled briefly. "That was your biggest mistake little man; you should have taken me when you had the chance. Now your—" But he couldn't finish the sentence. It wasn't because speaking took too much of the energy the stone had already drained from him, but because David had pulled him into a stalactite at the end of the mine, which hung against the wall of the cavern, knocking him to the ground.

Edwin dropped the stone when he fell, and it tumbled outside the mine with him, beyond his reach.

5

Jarak saw the wolves explode out of the mine. He realized what had happened. They were met full force on the other side, and Grak must have called for a retreat; they were bringing the war back to Wolf Country as the *mutie* hermit had supposed.

"It has begun," Jarak said. "Old man, we must leave now."

Auger stood before the tunnels. "No," he said, in a rickety voice.

Jarak stepped forward. More wolves came from the mines, others turned around and drew their weapons as if to confront the opposition head on. War was close. He listened for a moment. He could hear through the dead air shrill howls of fear, yes fear, but also a feeling of redemption, of revenge. The wolves were beaten on the other side. Grak had taken them on a suicide mission; he had led them into a tomb. He saw Grak exit the mine; he held his long sword in one hand, and something else in the other. The wolves separated for the General. They believed that in dire events a course would be established to manipulate the unfortunate, and that their General would assume that duty.

"MAY-NAKI. MAY-SONEY A JIMEKO!" Grak yelled in the old language, and the wolves raised their weapons into the air and howled. *For revenge, for war and victory.* The army of wolves heeded the words of their General—for revenge, for victory.

"Old man, we mustn't linger any longer, war is upon us. He has brought it back with him."

The old man ignored Jarak. He leaned forward, drawn to the tunnels chipped into the base of the Towers.

"Forget the boy, forget the King. We stand in damned lands."

"NO! We wait to test fate, Jarak. You must understand that. Or do wolves neglect commonsense? We wait for an answer to all of our problems, and you still fear war. When the boy returns, the war will fear us!"

Jarak leaped forward, kicking up dust when his claws penetrated the rocky ground. "You sent the boy to his grave, for he'll never return from a place wolves couldn't survive."

"You have no faith."

"I have commonsense, old man." The wolves, who had gathered into an army at the base of the bluff and up the mountain pass, began howling again. Jarak looked over his shoulder. Something strange had left the mines. There were figures emerging, some of them very tall, others short and wide, but these figures moved oddly, and held themselves with an awkward demeanor; they weren't men, but they looked human from this distance. Their flesh—if it was flesh—seemed black on some, ivory white on others, as if the shadows of man had risen from the ground to walk alongside their creators. They were strong and pushed the wolves in front of them, until many had fallen over the bluff, smashing into readying wolves outside the cavern. Many wolves were impaled on spears; others rolled down the cliff side only to get up with a rough howl.

"We must go now."

The old man struck Jarak with his cane. "You must understand me wolf, I haven't the option to leave. I *know* that mutant was given to me for a specific purpose, or else I wouldn't have gone miles for an egg; I *know* that it has aided the boy. It is my faith that leads me to believe Cole will be back. Faith is *all* I have now."

Jarak, no longer willing to listen to the old man, did what he figured was his only option.

"What are you doing? NO!"

Jarak had wrapped his arm around the old man's waist and thrown him on his back, flexing his shoulder blades to lock the writhing figure between his fanned muscles. The old man dropped his cane on the ground, and he reached out for the tunnel, wiggling his arthritic fingers with the hope that by grabbing air he could find an invisible rope that might pull him back toward the tunnels.

The old man repeatedly smacked Jarak on the back. "You must leave me and go yourself, Jarak. PLEASE, you must."

Jarak ignored the old man, and though he couldn't see him, believed Kenneth Auger was weeping. The wolf, running on all fours with an old man straddling his back, broke through the crowd of wolves. "We must get to the mountain pass."

6

The corpse had snapped forward, and strings of foam fell from its mouth; it wore tattered clothing, which draped towards the ground in strips, and it carried in one writhing hand a dagger that curled like the devil's smile, stained with gore that seemed to move along the wavering blade.

Cole had collapsed backward and stumbled into the wall. He was transfixed by the empty eye sockets, which seemed to lead into farther tunnels of the Tower—Cole didn't know why he thought this, but he believed this thing was an access to floors above, perhaps, beyond the darkness that concealed the ceiling.

Cole had screamed "DAD," and the hermit turned to see the corpse advancing, and the stones fell. There was a loud whoosh sound, and an even louder thud; the doorway was blocked—the stones had fallen in front of the opening.

"Cole, run," Hayle yelled over the wall, but knew the boy couldn't hear him.

The corpse floated above the ground, dangling its twisted legs beneath it like strings from a disheveled kite. Cole reached behind him for the wall and pulled himself to the side when he noticed the others.

There were more ghosts coming from the doorways he and Hayle had already passed. They all floated above the ground, some with torn clothing, others in glistening mail, carrying banners on pikes, banners that showed the golden image of a sun and two leaves in an arch. Some ghosts held swords that grew and shrunk, reflecting the tinted light of the Towers; and others rode on horses that seemed made of greenish muscle, which dripped to the ground like legs, ending on bulbous balls that dragged.

The rocks lifted and Hayle moved forward, pulling himself with the embedded rocks, which had already begun vibrating as if trying to break free from the ground. Cole was right, this room had drawn the guardians; it was a trap. The bones he had seen randomly tossed throughout the room hadn't been because the trespassers were impatient enough not to notice the pattern of the falling stones, but because the ghosts had advanced on them while they dodged the rocks, diverting their attention from the first test. "Cole, RUN!" The stones fell.

Cole did hear the hermit, but realized his legs were stuck; he couldn't move them. The eyeless corpse swiped its dagger out and the blade seemed to grow teeth, snapping at the air as if it were alive and hungry. Cole believed it was both.

"I can't," he said. "I can't run. I can't move."

The other ghosts moved forward, disappeared, then reappeared closer. These ghosts had eyes, Cole saw, but had no eyelids with which to blink; they wore helmets over their scarred heads that flapped with a metallic sound that eerily growled and whispered throughout the archways. The horses snarled, revealing toothless gums that had decayed.

The stones lifted along their invisible axis. Hayle had five seconds to move forward before the stones fell from above. He was weak. He couldn't exactly feel pain, but knew something was wrong. He could tell that he was losing blood; he could tell that it had something to do with his transformed image.

Hayle reached the doorway.

"DAD!"

The stones fell.

Hayle screamed.

The ghosts turned their rickety heads and saw the hermit. Hayle had been pinned underneath a rock, and he was struggling to pull himself out. A rock had fallen on his leg. The ghosts disappeared, only to apparate five feet before the doorway, the smell of earth and flesh clinging to them.

Hayle's eyes turned a deep red. He saw many images. Wolves tearing through doors and murdering families; fires pulverizing the streets; mothers holding dead sons, and sons holding dying mothers. He could see the ghost's fears; he could protect Cole.

The ghosts writhed in utter torment; they were knights of the Old Order, from many years ago—the men that fought in the civil wars, others of an older bloodline. They formed among them a thousand year old alliance to the King's Crest, and found that even beyond death they were bound to the Throne. Though Cole couldn't hear it, the ghosts had all screamed to be let loose; the hermit could hear their pleas very clearly, for they pleaded in his head with voices that were shrieks.

The eyeless corpse grabbed Cole's arm in a grip that felt like cold lips sucking—it raised its dagger, which had very evidently grown teeth and begun snapping. The corpse lowered its head so that Cole could look into its sockets. There was a moment when Cole believed he would enter into them, and crawl to the center of the ghost's head to spend an eternity in darkness.

"DAD!" Cole screamed.

The corpse astonishingly drew back, as if shocked by Cole's loud voice. It snarled, and its teeth dripped onto its wriggling tongue like strings of oil, seemingly closing its mouth like a grate.

"That one has no eyes, I cannot stall it," Hayle said weakly. The rock lifted and the hermit had pulled himself forward; his right leg was shattered. "It doesn't see, it listens, it smells. RUN!"

The corpse had swiped its dagger and Cole ducked; the blade touched off the wall and Cole could have sworn he heard the weapon curse.

"RUN!"

Cole did. He ran away from the clutter of writhing ghosts, from the eyeless corpse, from Hayle, who he was sure he would never see again. Cole ran until his sides hurt, but he couldn't stop; he could feel the air behind him closing in. The corpse was close; it was like a vacuum. Cole didn't feel like he was getting anywhere fast. The Tower was playing with him, showing him hope and then blinding the end of the hall in darkness and smoke.

Cole wanted to quit. He wanted to fall to his knees and let whatever was behind him have its way, but—

But beyond the murk, beyond the dimness and haze shrouded through the many archways, Cole was sure he saw a door, a large door set inside the rock like the trunk of a tree on a mountainside.

Cole ran towards the door with a new hope.

7

David pulled Edwin roughly along the ground; Krollup tugged on the chain but it was too tense.

He turned his head. The stone was outside the mine, still on the gold chain, puffs of dust clouding it. He realized something, something that shocked him. The statues were still moving on their own accord. He watched his granite bull buck two wolves over the side of the cliff.

He reached out along the ground, trying to snag a rock or a loose root jutting from the ground, but he found nothing. David punched a wolf that had struck him with its sword, and the wolf flew over the bluff, yelping as it descended. *The bluff*! Krollup thought, he would go over if he didn't get out of this bind. He tried to get his thumbs underneath the chain—when the chain was cut. The links exploded. A wolf had cut through the manacle after missing David—the blade had been stuck in the ground, and David had turned to pick the wolf up and tossed it over the side of the cliff. Edwin slowly got to his feet and was knocked back down by another wolf, which had backed into him while averting a blow from a short male statue wearing a toga. Edwin rolled along the ground, the chain following him; he grabbed for a jutting stone but missed it, instead grabbing a fistful of pebbles.

Edwin's legs went over the side of the cliff first, followed by the rest of his body. Had he gotten the chain off his waist he would have surely died, but the same rock Edwin had unfortunately missed grabbing a moment ago, had instead snagged the loose end of his bind. Edwin had clenched his teeth and closed his eyes awaiting the fall and realized after a minute that he had dodged death two times within a span of ten minutes—Leo had forgotten to take the gun off safety before pulling the trigger, and now a chain held him suspended over a hundred foot drop grounded by hordes of wolves.

Edwin rotated his body, and felt, as he grabbed the chain with both hands, a part of him die. He could barely find a grip, and when he did it just felt like his hands were tearing. What was happening to him? Whenever he lost the stone for only a minute his body seemed to go berserk. He slowly pulled himself upward an inch when a wolf was thrown over his head, brushing him lightly; the chain shifted and Edwin felt something give. He had to get back up the bluff and grab the stone before the wolves realized just what it was laying on the ground.

He pulled on the chain and it shifted again, roughly lowering him. The chain was coming loose! Edwin realized what he had to do. He looked up at the edge of the bluff; it couldn't have been more than five feet from the top of his head. Edwin dug his hands underneath the chain, which was digging into his flesh like teeth, and tried to pry the links, tried to squeeze out of the loop—when the chain was pulled upwards.

Edwin sprang over the side of the bluff and landed splayed on the ground, so that his chin smashed into the dirt. David had pulled the chain; it had clipped to the bottom of the statue's foot and as it walked forward, the chain went with it. Edwin slid out of the loop. The stone was still lying on the ground, and Edwin dove forward, ducking a wolf's blow, and dodging the swipe of stray claws. He landed beside the stone and when he reached out for the chain, the stone leapt away from him, as if it had sprung hind legs.

Edwin jumped to his left at the leaping stone when he heard a gunshot, and saw the ground beside him explode in puffs of reddish dust.

Edwin turned and ran at the stone; his legs jumbled and he fell forward. The stone bounced away. Edwin spit out a mouthful of dirt—

And a wolf picked up the stone by its chain. Edwin froze.

The wolf looked at the stone for a moment, studying the golden chain from which it hung—in a minute everything would change, but Edwin, who lay face down in the dirt with streaks of blood and dust lining his face, watched in horror this wolf carry his stone in its grubby claws. For that one moment Edwin readied for what he believed was his final moment; he had survived a near fall and a shoddy gunshot, but he didn't believe luck traveled in threes.

David and Grak fought behind him but that didn't matter—time had frozen before him. Time had been formed on the twisting gold chain looped loosely around a wolf's claw, and time, it seemed, had been reshaped. and the wolf was thrown backwards.

Edwin's worry seemed to divert his attention. Amidst believing the war was over, the gold chain he had put into the stone himself disintegrated; it started like firecrackers, exploding around the wolf's claw, and dripping to the ground like molten beer. The wolf, shocked, had started on fire, and then was thrown backwards into the mountainside. The stone remained in the air, floating as if it still hung on the chain around the wolf's claw. This had startled Edwin; he had never seen the stone do this before, and that came from a man who'd owned it for thirty years. Rocks had started spewing from the ground directly beneath the stone, pelting statues and wolves alike; it was as if something were coming from the ground, as if something were driving itself upwards, and Edwin, who had shielded his face, watched two thin limbs emerge from the ground and connect themselves to the stone.

And then the stone itself began to crack. Edwin felt weak. He realized a part of him went into its ability to do such a thing; he didn't know why he had this thought, but it felt true. The stone grew two spindly arms like blossomed stems, and the stone, which now stood five feet tall, caused the world to shake.

Edwin, who was still lying on his stomach, thought he was going to vomit when he felt the 'S' waves. Rocks began shooting from the wall of the mountain, knocking into wolves and statues alike, sending each over the side of the cliff or rolling down the mountain pass, knocking others down as they slid to the bottom.

Edwin realized after all these years, that the stone he had worn around his neck and used to make him the man that he is, had itself been alive also.

It was a leech, he understood. And now he knew why the statues were brought in from the courtyard. The stone was urging Edwin to go down the mines. The stone finally wanted to come home.

8

The door was wood, set inside a chiseled arch that rose thirty feet and was bordered by an odd pattern in the rock. There were lines laid in the stone, waving against each other in curves as if mocking the movements of serpents. Cole ran forward, breathing heavily, wanting more than anything to stop, to lay down and pant; he hadn't looked back once but knew for some strange reason that if he did he wouldn't like what he'd see.

The hallway seemed to thin as the door neared. It became like an inverted 'v', and it seemed, to Cole at least, like he was running uphill, as if the floor had sloped slightly. The chocolates in his pant's pocket rattled but he ignored them; instead he offered his attention to the exertion of his getaway. He realized the more he thought about sweat, the more he actually perspired. His short hair flattened against his head, and streams of sweat dripped down his brow, stinging his eye and washing streaks of eroded dirt from his face.

As soon as he got to that door he was certain he could shut the eyeless corpse out. Maybe the ghosts were only allowed in the hallway, which was why they used the room of falling stones—so people wouldn't attempt to get to this door.

But what if this door has its own guardian?

He hadn't thought about that. Perhaps he wasn't running away from the eyeless corpse as much he was being led to another monster—perhaps this had been the plan all along. Maybe this whole place was just a hunting ground and he had become the prey, tricked for the moment into believing he had a chance.

Cole turned around for the first time as he ran and saw the eyeless corpse merely three feet from him, brandishing the dagger splattered with gore and its own mouthful of teeth.

There was an awkward motivation within him to dive; he didn't know why, but would in a few seconds when he turned forward again. Cole had begun slowing down. Not because he wanted to, but because he had to. He had run the equivalent of two football fields, a distance he could barely walk without a break. Cole turned, and because he was young and had the heightened reflexes of his youth—not to discount the factor that he could vaguely see everything happening in his mind—he was able to dive into a roll on the ground without second guessing himself.

He had gotten closer to the door then he had at first thought, and when he did turn his head he saw not the door in front of him, but a shadow against the rock, and against that shadow the swift arch of a glistening blade. Cole fell forward and rolled sideways, feeling the dense air separate above him as the blade slashed through it. Cole saw, remarkably enough, the eyeless corpse's head fly from its shoulders and bounce along the ground, disappearing through the far wall—the eyeless corpse had been floating where he, Cole, had just been standing!—had he not dove forward *his* head would have been rolling along the ground in a sickly pattern. Cole felt obligated to run his hand over his throat.

The eyeless corpse, which was headless now, fell backwards and through the ground, as if through a square of water. The shadow turned toward Cole, and he saw for the first time what it was that actually stood over him, a husking frame against the tinted light of the Tower's invisible lanterns.

The door was laid within a deep recess in the rock wall, about ten feet by Cole's estimations, and beyond the chiseled fissure there sat on blocks a tall throne with armrests made of bone and stone, and an arched back that must have extended twenty feet from the ground, with twisted spires that had impaled a few poor souls—there were bones nestled in cluttered heaps at either side of the throne, and some, Cole had realized, still hung from both spires as if rotting tendons had somehow snagged on rock. What stood over Cole had two beady eyes amidst its cloaked head, and shoulders that fanned ten feet across, coming to steel curves at their ends. It was nearly as tall as the throne, and it stood with a hunch that caused its arms to fall forward; it carried swords in both dark hands—which were covered in black gauntlets with decorative bones inlaid against the knuckles.

"I am the Judge—those who enter the Tower come before my throne."

The voice was booming, but not quite a voice. Cole didn't understand the noise he was hearing; it was like a strange engine. Cole stood slowly, breathing hard.

The Judge lifted both swords so that they lay against its shoulders. "My army stands frozen so the Tower says, for you came in with two, yet arrive alone. Your companion has hatched his own devilry on my knight's of the Old Order. What is it you seek?"

Cole had been wondering long and hard what he should say to this thing if the chance arose, and when it did he still felt entirely clueless. His first thoughts reminded him that the blade which beheaded the eyeless corpse had originally been intended for him, and that if he did choose to speak, something in his voice may just spark another violent impulse. "The King," Cole finally said, unsure why he decided on saying anything at all. He flinched when the Judge moved.

"NO," it said. "Nobody is to see the King, for the King lies in eternal slumber from the nuisances of the world." The swords lowered from its shoulders, and there was a distinct clang as both rested on the ground. The Judge sat in its throne and stared down at Cole. Cole looked at the bones cluttered at the throne's base and stepped backwards.

"Come to be judged," it said in its booming voice that wasn't a voice but an automated rumble.

9

The stone now stood on two legs which had sprouted from the ground, legs made of jagged stone. Two arms had grown from within the stone, and hung spindly to the ground like vines. They were more like tentacles

Edwin froze…the stone looked like an awkward insect now, with long legs and a tiny abdomen, and the longer it stood still, the harder the ground shook. Many wolves were frozen also, watching this odd little stone's serpentile arms dangle gently and caress the ground.

The statues still moved.

The rock upon which Edwin lay seemed to breathe, seemed to welcome the stone's presence. "What are you?" Edwin asked under his breath. There was no answer, but—

But the stone stepped forward and raised both spindly arms, wrapping them around the necks of two wolves. The wolves stabbed at the arms desperately until their blows grew weaker. Edwin watched something leak out of their eyes; he didn't know what exactly, but realized a part of them had changed. Their fur turned colors.

It had been a coarse brown, and then their fur turned a sickening gray, and most of it started falling out. The ground began to shake more violently.

The stone dropped both wolves on the ground, and they writhed for a moment before falling still; they both had lost most of their fur, and looked skeletal, as if their flesh had been sucked to bone.

Edwin looked at his own hands and realized something. They too had become frailer. He had noticed this when he hung suspended over the cliff side. When he tried to grab the chain, both palms ached until he decided to let go. The stone had taken from him also, just as it took from the wolves, but Edwin supposed he had started its creation again; he had given the stone whatever it needed to begin its metamorphosis.

The ruins behind the stone exploded outwards, sending debris into wolves that knocked them over the mountain pass. Boulders lifted from the ground and crashed on top of statues and wolves alike, rolling down the path in oblong revolutions that crushed anything in its course.

The stone had grown a foot or two; its legs had become thicker, and its abdomen had swelled. It wrapped its stringy limbs around another two wolves, tossing them aside when their fur had turned and ultimately fallen out. The ground screamed now. Whatever this thing was had the attention of its surroundings.

10

Jarak halted when the rocks from above exploded outwards and fell into the camp like scattered bombs. Wolves separated, trampling over each other in attempts to dodge the falling debris.

"WATCH OUT!" Ninak the wolf called, and a boulder smashed into a tent, crumbling the wooden supports into dust; the strung hide fell inwards and buried into the ground underneath the weight of the rock and rubble. For a single moment one could hear the faint whimper of the She-wolf inside the tent, but silenced as soon as the snapping wood took precedence.

"What is going on?" The old man asked weakly.

Jarak jumped forward and slid beneath a slab of earth that had dislodged. "I think the man with the stone has finally come."

"Oh, good. We should go ask him for it." The old man stifled a short laugh. "We are done for good wolf."

Jarak grunted, his voice drowned out mostly by the sounds outside the slab of rock. "This is where Grak has failed the wolves. It is their end. You and I though, old man, you and I aren't a part of this." The wolf pounced from beneath the shelter of the shelf and ran towards the pass. He noticed many wolves had retreated into the caverns, unknowing of course, that if the man with the stone desired, he could close the caverns and fill the spaces with crushing rock; the wolves were fleeing into hungry mouths.

Jarak looked forward in time to notice the rolling boulder coming from above; its momentum had gathered quickly, crushing wolves in its path. Jarak turned toward the rock face and let the boulder pass; it settled on top of a pile of corpses with a loud snap.

The old General wouldn't have allowed this. It never would have come to this.

11

Cole didn't like the idea of being judged. He didn't like the idea of being here, and he missed his mother more every minute because of it. He had been bullied for so long that the custom seemed to span into two worlds now. He thought he had found escape with Leo, a reason to mount everybody's guilt exponentially, and inexorably urge that they—the bullies, Jimmy—come to terms with their own deviance, but instead he was taken (he didn't remember much from the mines, but he did remember waking up inside the tent, waking up a victim again). He was at the wolves' disposal; he was sent into the tunnels for this very reason, and now he stood before the throne of the Great Judge posed with the immense threat that his head wasn't safe.

He watched both swords resting feebly against either armrest of the gigantic throne; the Judge's hands had both been laid on its knees and it hunkered forward, sitting perfectly still, but waiting, waiting for this boy to come forward to plead his case, a case the Judge would ultimately settle by raising those blades. Cole knew how it went because things like this only existed in the movies—well they *used* to. Not until he realized there was a world built on the powers of the imagination.

Cole did what he felt was necessary. He had run towards the door because the door had seemed like the only option at the time. And he knew this was the end. This was the right place. There weren't any tricks here.

"Come to me," the Judge said in its rumbled voice and Cole did otherwise. Cole dove towards the door set inside the recess of rock, and he shouldered the wood hoping that it would crack open just enough for him to slide through.

It didn't.

Both swords clashed against the rock at either side of the door and sparks exploded. Cole rolled out and both blades swiped over top his head; the air seemed to fill with hot iron.

The Judge's beady eyes estimated Cole, estimated the young boy's prowess, much as a knight might observe an opponent; it raised both swords and held them together in front of its black chest, which swirled like smog, forming for brief moments the glare of an iron breastplate, only to swirl into the opaque image of a tornado.

Cole ran towards the door again, and his foot snagged on a crack in the ground. What happened next became the weirdest thing Cole had ever seen in his life. Firstly, the fact that he fell owed much to his chances of survival, for as he teetered over, feeling the ground leave him, the Judge had unleashed yet another blow of his cutlass. This time, though, the Judge's sword had cut into the thick wood of the door, causing a bottom fraction to crumble and create a hatchway. Cole wouldn't notice this until later. Secondly, when Cole fell, he fell at such an angle that caused his pants to rip, catching on the many snags littering the ground like teeth. The seam split, and Cole's pocket flapped open, vomiting out his trusty box of chocolate covered peanuts, which erupted from the opened pack like pearls from a snapped necklace, scattering the ground with dark spots. And what happened last surprised Cole the most. Since he had fallen, he had anticipated a mighty blow to the back; he had even waited a moment just to ease his passing, but his concentration had been broken by a voice. Not his own, but the *great* Judge's, which didn't sound so great anymore.

"Chocolate?"

Cole rolled over on his back, saw the box two feet from his thigh and the assortment of chocolates on the ground around the open flap.

There was a loud sniffing noise. "Chocolate? All these years and the King has never given us chocolate."

Cole smiled. He remembered Hayle's delight when he sensed that Cole had chocolate on him. Chocolate must have been a popular delicacy here, in the world of imagination.

But your chocolate tasted like dirt to Hayle, he thought, and his body went numb. He quickly got to his knees and pulled himself forward. What if the Judge ate the chocolate, and realizing the morsels tasted like dung, intended to seek revenge on the boy who'd fed it the treat?

Cole scurried toward the door and saw for the first time the broken fragments of wood on the ground.

"How long has it been since you've eaten chocolate, Affel?"

"Many years now—in life 'twas. I can remember feeling the candy melt on my tongue, much like wax to a flame."

Cole heard two distinct voices now, which sounded more like men than the automated rumblings of the Judge. Both swords dropped with a sharp clang, and as Cole reached the recess in the rock where the door was laid, he turned. The great Judge had disappeared. In its place kneeled four men, all wearing iron plate armor and black gauntlets; each man had reached before him for a piece of chocolate and grabbed nothing but air. Their fingers traveled entirely through the candy; they were ghosts trying desperately to interact with the physical world, but couldn't.

"They are under some spell."

"Aye, we should put our mouths directly over them—our hands have been useless for so long it doesn't surprise me now that they should act up."

Each ghost rested his head against the ground and opened their mouths, revealing blackened teeth and rotting gums. They each inched forward until a piece of chocolate had nestled inside their mouths—

But they had moved too far forward, it seemed, for the chocolate appeared on the other side of their craniums, as if the chocolate covered peanut had speared its way through each man's head.

"'Tis a spell, for I tasted nothing. Perhaps these treats are faulty. There are many more scattered along the ground." The ghosts stood and moved forward, finding another spot to kneel.

Cole didn't understand. Where did the Judge go?

That is the Judge, he thought suddenly. Of course it was. The Judge had been formed by these men, had been put together like crude pieces of Lego; their armor was what he had seen when the smoke in its middle had settled.

But why could it break the door with its sword when it's having such trouble just eating chocolate?

Because it wasn't meant to eat chocolate, he realized, holding a crumbled piece of door in his clenched fist. It was made to serve whatever lived behind this door; the Judge was ultimately comprised of four knights, bound by some paranormal cohesion, and it wasn't supposed to separate. But Cole had found its weakness. Through the Judge's initiative to protect this door, Cole had firmly established there still existed desires in the dead, and these desires entailed the satisfaction of consuming dessert. The temptations of the flesh.

Cole turned and crawled through the broken door, while behind him four knights foraged the ground trying to shovel peanuts into their endless mouths.

CHAPTER 20

ALLIANCE IN SPIDER CITY

1

"What was that?" Jimmy asked, both pointing and holding onto Ashton's back for dear life. The spiders were on top of the trees, springing from the branches and landing on webs that had been strung like netting over drops to the ground below.

Jimmy had seen it first because he was looking down through the webs, watching the ground pass underneath, the rivers like miniscule tracks of fog in a netherworld. Beneath the canopies there were lower branches that strung out from the trees awkwardly, bound together in some cases by strands of silk that had been spun from tree to tree. Jimmy had seen two large figures pass below them that were mere shadows against the backdrop, moving quicker than both Jarat and Kannef.

Ashton turned and looked at Jimmy.

"Something passed below us—BELOW US," Jimmy said loudly, over the passing wind.

"It was probably nothing."

"No, it was *something*."

Ashton turned forward and prodded Jarat's back. "Did the Queen send reinforcements behind us to make sure we returned to Spider City?"

The spider uttered a long screech that could be picked up perfectly in the wind. "No, the Queen believes both Kannef and I are capable enough to return." There was a hint of annoyance in its shriek, if that was at all possible.

"I didn't mean to offend you," Ashton said, leaning forward. "Jimmy said he saw something move underneath us."

Jarat stopped. The stall was so quick that Ashton could barely hold onto the spider's side while his body jerked forward. Had he let go he would have been slung over the spider's head and fallen to a nasty death. Jimmy would have followed suit, since his hands were firmly clasped to Ashton's side.

Kannef stopped fifty feet ahead after realizing Jarat had halted. There was a high pitch strung over the air, a whistle that could manageably disturb both dogs and humans equally. Both Ashton and Jimmy clasped their ears. Granum sat back in his comfortable seat as if he hadn't noticed.

The spiders were speaking to each other.

"What is it?" Ashton asked, breathing heavily.

"We are being tracked," Jarat said. Kannef began walking towards Jarat, testing each branch, when between both spiders the leaves rustled and seemed sucked in for a moment. Then the leaves exploded upwards like shrapnel, settling in the air like large flakes of green snow.

Ashton removed his bow and arrow and nocked the weapon before Jimmy could blink. Standing between both Jarat and Kannef like snarling dogs, were two spiders that had been tinted black, and whose eyes had seemed, in the light above the trees at least, like white-rimmed blood clots.

"It is Legion," Jarat called out, and the black spiders leapt from the trees. Both spiders jumped either way, separating the shower of leaves in the air. Jarat reversed and Ashton shot the underside of the spider's belly, which was decorated with dripping fur and a yellow diamond that seemed like a window, as if something were inside the spider's cavity peering out, something with human eyes and fingers that tapped the thin membrane. The arrow stuck into the abdomen and black goo poured from the wound, staining the treetops. The spider fell forwards, skidding along the leaves and stopping on its side. There was a stiff crack and the branches snapped; the spider fell below, bounced from the web strand like a ball, curled its legs and fell to the ground with a muffled thud.

The other spider had jumped towards Kannef, unaware of course who this spider held on its back. Granum watched with keen interest from his perch. To him the incident seemed in slow motion. The spider sprang from the branches, and then hung in the air.

Granum looked at Ashton questionably. "Why is it when I freeze the target you stop and stare, but when the object is moving towards you, you find it within yourself to shoot the bloody thing to the ground? Shoot the spider!"

Ashton removed another arrow and shot the spider, watching in its eyes the realization of its doom. The spider fell on its back, uttered one last screech and curled its legs towards the sky.

"And there you have it," Granum said, crawling out of his comfortable perch atop Kannef. "My, my, I have seen many times in the Sandglass the ferocity of Legion, but I had yet to see up close their reasoning for such madness." He walked towards the fallen spider, ran his hand through his beard and snapped his fingers. The spider's legs stretched away from its belly, snapping like twigs from their joints, and falling to the ground hundreds of feet below. "Let me take a close look here," he said, bending over the spider's belly, which rose four feet from the ground in a sickening hump. "Asha, come here will you, I would like you to see this. You of all people will understand what it is that's going on in here." He tapped the belly and pulled his finger away quickly. "Nasty feeling, that was."

Ashton, who had shouldered his bow, carefully hopped over to the wizard, testing the branch with each step.

"Look inside the diamond."

Ashton did, and he saw what he had seen inside the other spider; there was something human looking out from the pattern, a slight yellow tinge to its face as it looked from the wizard to the Hunter. "What is it?"

Granum smiled. "You haven't figured it out yet? Wasn't it you that began digging up the coffins of the dead in Cassica's farmlands, only to tie them closed with the strongest rope? Why would you have done that?"

Ashton looked at the wizard. "Fallen Angels," he finally said. "Parasites of the mountains. This is a virus, trapped within the spider? I have never seen one with a face—I have only seen the face of its body, its host."

Granum pointed to Ashton's sword.

"No, I can't release it."

"Oh, you're not releasing it. The spider that fell will only become food for the scavengers—the Fallen Angel will be carried with them until it clasps to a bigger, more reliable source. This way the wind will have its effect; it doesn't want to come out. It is worried. Mayhaps it is young, and has only begun realizing the niceties of living away from those blasted mountains. Either way, back to the mountains it shall go."

Ashton unsheathed his sword, hesitated for a moment and stuck it into the spider's belly; there was a sickening pop, and a ghastly air seemed released from the spider's innards. The diamond split down the middle with a quick rip and the face disappeared. The spider quickly turned to dust, sifting through the leaves like sand through an hourglass.

"I have found," Granum said, "that when one is in an incredible hurry, he is always sidetracked by the most disturbing company." He smiled and clambered onto Kannef's back, who had watched in shock two Legion spiders fall to their doom by the hands of man.

They would reach Spider City in fifteen minutes, watching over the horizon a city like diamonds develop against the skyline.

2

There were bridges everywhere, made of leaves and web, spanning across treetops, billows of silk flowing from the branch railings. Each bridge arched slightly, and sparkled as if dew had been painted along each strand. There were buildings that reminded Jimmy of his city, web skyscrapers that rose fifty feet into the air, decorated with ivy, and there were rows of barracks, made with wood supports and tightly strung web. They were following a path which went directly through the center of the city. On either side spiders stopped and watched the strangers, some glowering, others bowing slightly.

In front of them, across the bridges over gaps in the path, stood a billowing silk turret that looked like a can of soda. It made Jimmy thirsty just looking at it. The spiders slowed as they neared the silken silo, decorated with arrangements of moss and ivy, shaped to look like wreaths. At the base of the spire there was a separation in the webbing, which had pulled strands to either side like drapes. Standing in front of this opening were four spiders, each curled so that the hunch of their backs stood erect.

"She wishes to see the old one," the spider in the front said, and all four moved aside.

Granum only smiled and sort of waved his hand at Jimmy and Ashton.

Jimmy saw a great hall before him when the spiders moved aside, a hall with drapes of webbing that blew freely in the wind. At the end of the hall he saw a great seat with silk distended from the top of the spire like white crusted waterfalls, and sitting within it, like a bloated slug, was the Queen. Each of her legs looked curled inwards, and her head seemed bowed.

Jimmy couldn't see anything more because the spiders obstructed the opening, arching their backs again.

"Why does she need to see Granum?" Jimmy asked Ashton.

"Because these are her woods, Jimmy, and we entered without knocking on the door; it's really a matter of courtesy more than anything else."

"It's more than that," Jarat chimed in, obviously eavesdropping. "She has for days readied an army; that's why we were so quick to attack when we found the King's men in the bush. We are gearing for war."

3

"What's taking them so long?" Jimmy asked. The Queen's guards blocked the door so effectively that even when Jimmy knelt down to try and look under their swollen bellies, the spiders in the back just crouched.

"There's no need to get frantic," Ashton said absently. He had begun noticing things around him—just beyond the bridges to the south, which flapped awkwardly in the wind, there stood a cluttered group of male spiders, standing perfectly still and staring straight ahead. There was an irritating chitter in the air, one that became, to Ashton at least, like the sound of a saw driving slowly through thick bark. *It's the spiders,* he thought. *They're waiting for something, they're gearing for something, but war is far away now; it is fought in Wolf Country, not in the Leeg.*

The Queen had been talking to Granum for what seemed like hours. Jimmy felt like he was waiting in line at the stupid government offices his mother dragged him and Cole to before she married Krollup. "If you boys wanna eat you're gonna have to be patient," she'd say, as she paced from foot to foot. But this time Jimmy wasn't worried about eating; in fact, just thinking of his mother made him want to get Cole that much more.

Below them, strung from the branches in the canopies, Ashton had noticed cocoons hanging, bunched together like bee nests on white twine. He wondered if any of the King's men were writhing around in the web sacs, pushing at the gelatinous interior with hopes of dropping to a respectable death on the ground below.

"What are they talking about Jarat?" Jimmy asked, kicking aside a few dead leaves that had fallen from the side of the Queen's spire.

Jarat looked approvingly at the growing mass of spider bodies on the other side of the bridges, chittering to each other over the loud winds of the stratosphere. "It's an old battle cry," Jarat said, more to Ashton then to Jimmy. The spider had noticed Ashton was watching the group precariously.

"Where is your war?" Ashton asked. He thought he knew, of course, but was bewildered why the troops would seemingly meditate above the canopies rather than attack the enemy.

Jimmy sat down angrily. His question had been ignored; he had meant, what were the Queen and Granum talking about.

"Many would like to believe we're taking a stand against Legion, you know. The spiders we passed in the city are just like you. They live above the treetops waiting for the soldiers to bring food from below; they live a life away from the problems of the world. The cocoons beneath us will ripen until they are ready for feasting, but we chance theft, always, for Legion lurks in the shadows. You saw them, black they are, like the night, moving shadows; there are many of them, more then we used to believe, and most of them are the dead, come back to life because of the mountain parasites. We were followed into the woods; there is no safe haven in the Inlands. That is why we take the dead to the sea. Because the water makes sure they are stolen from the coast. We used to leave the dead on the forest floor, but many returned to the city, hungry, angry, violent. I have seen my own friends, my siblings die, and I have watched them come back from their grave; they look at me as if they do not know me. It is a sickening thing, this Legion, and we wish it were gone."

"You war is with Legion?" Ashton asked, thinking their enemy was something entirely different.

"Many of us hope so. The Queen is quiet about such doings. We are left to speculate. We don't want to be driven from the woods like we were from the mountains."

"Fallen Angels," Ashton muttered. "They look like us. In a way we are the enemies, death is our opponent. Mayhaps with the—"Ashton stopped himself from getting carried away; he'd rather not tell the spiders of the stone. The stone itself had the power to become an axis of war, to drive every force against the other until the world was in battle. But wasn't it possible—if he were to get the stone, to bring it back to this world—to just bring the Northern Mountains down like the Sordids had been many years before?

"Mayhaps with the what, Hunter?" Jarat asked, but Ashton just shook his head.

"Legion has done hell to the farmers and miners in Cassica; it would just be nice to rid once and for all the parasites of the mountains."

And with that, the spider guards separated from the door and the wizard walked out, holding the Sandglass.

4

"It's about time," Jimmy said as he jumped up. "Let's go."

Granum walked by Jimmy without sparing the boy a glance. Granum had an apprehensive look about him, and to Ashton, it was very unbecoming and unsettling. For something would have had to've gone terribly wrong for Granum to show such defeat, and Ashton didn't want to think of such possibilities. Perhaps the Queen hadn't believed he was a wizard, and felt obligated to obliterate all three of them because of such reservations. They were brought here for that reason, weren't they? The Queen wanted good evidence as to why she was letting them pass through her woods unscathed. But the look in Granum's aged eyes suggested otherwise.

Granum pulled Ashton's arm roughly. "We need to speak."

"What is it?"

Granum shuddered and his eyes seemed to sink farther into his old head. His beard, though mangy to begin with, seemed more sparse and decrepit now. He pulled Ashton to a bridge overlooking the treetops to the south.

"We have to go now, please, come on. We've wasted enough time already," Jimmy screamed, arousing many spiders' attention.

"Jimmy, go back to Jarat and wait, and do *not* create a spectacle of yourself," Granum said angrily, shooting the boy a furious glance.

When Granum and Ashton reached the bridge, the wizard set the Sandglass carefully on the railing.

"What is it Granum? I don't like the look of you. I haven't seen you so worried."

Granum said nothing and pointed to the Sandglass. Ashton looked down and saw Wolf Country again, but the land seemed marred, seemed overturned; he noticed boulders had flattened tents strewn about the area. The air had a sickening whorl to it, as if the wind had decided to manifest in circular patterns that resembled a darkish brown, porous vomit. Ashton saw through the smog an unsettling sight. The wolves stood howling at the sky, holding their weapons above their head as if in victory. And standing on all sides of the wolves were statues, some full tilt, others smashed to pieces. Ashton noticed a dark statue that resembled an ox, for some reason, lying on its side, its bulging chest cracked so that its head seemed separated from its torso.

The wolves had begun attacking these statues, pushing them over the cliff, tearing their arms from their bodies and piling them on the mountain pass.

"What's going on?"

"The stone is back," Granum said, but his voice seemed on the verge of insanity.

"Why are there statues in Wolf Country?"

"Because of him," Granum said, pointing under a shelf of rock that seemed indistinguishable among the anarchy. Ashton saw clearly, though, what the wizard was pointing at. Underneath a lip in the rock cowered a man covered from head to foot in dust, hidden by rubble. "He brought them from his world using the stone. He created an army of statues."

Ashton realized this man's army must have worked for a short time. Around the base of the cliff, and alongside the mountain pass there were bodies of wolves thrown in cluttered heaps.

"Where is the stone?" Ashton asked.

Granum looked at the Sandglass, and then back at Ashton. "The Guardian took it."

"What?"

"The Queen was curious if I really was a wizard, but heard before hand, I suppose, of our encounter with the Legion spiders, and heard how I had frozen my attacker in the air. She didn't merely ask if I was a wizard as much as she begged me for guidance. She had asked if I knew that her egg sac was stolen by the wolves, and I told her I had seen much of what happened in the Sandglass, and she looked at me as if I had offended her, for she questioned why I hadn't come to the spiders' aid if I had seen everything happening. I told her what happened to her egg sac in Wolf Country, how each egg was destroyed, and how the wolves found the mutant, the *humanoid* within. She seemed disgusted with the notion; the spiders blame Legion for such atrocities. When I spoke of the wolves I noticed a hatred stirring in her many eyes, a certain machination of her thoughts.

"I showed her the Sandglass, and saw to my dismay, that the war had already started, and cursed our unfortunate ability to become sidetracked. I knew our coming to Spider City drastically went against time, but knew, eventually, what it was the spiders wanted to ask of me, of *us*. I saw it in Kannef's eyes when I first sat upon him; the Queen has been driven by hatred and vengeance, much like you Ashton, and when she chanced upon you in the woods her desire for vengeance increased with the actuality of what happened to her egg sac. The Queen is the only spider capable of breeding in Spider City; did you know that Ashton? The race of spiders depends on the Queen, and she seeks reprisal for the destruction of her brood."

"I knew it, she wants a war with the wolves," Ashton said, still watching the wolves dismantle statues in the Sandglass.

"I showed her the Sandglass, and she watched the statues and the wolves battle, each of her eyes so intent I believed they would explode. She asked what it was the wolves were fighting, and I told her that much didn't matter, for they were a means of beginning the war. But I saw the stone, Asha, lying on the pass, covered in dust with a gold chain secured to its top. I believed for the moment that if we hurried I could still get it, I could still retrieve it, but I realized what was happening." Granum looked down for a moment. "The stone is a prison, Asha, aye, a prison for a being from the old wars. The wars of long ago, what you might hear on the tongue of storytellers. The stone is a parasite, a sponge, and you feel your core start to shrink when you touch it. The stone is but a shell. But it has cracked, Asha, and for the first time in hundreds of years the one within has decided to show its true form. The man under the shelf of rock isn't merely hiding, but is, I suppose, recuperating, for I saw the stone wrap its tentacles around the hulking necks of wolves and suck from them their merciless vitality, until they were merely tossed aside like bags of bone."

"What is the stone Granum? What is it really?"

"I haven't the time to explain now, Asha, but realize that in history there were those content with the way the world ran, and others who decided to delve into the deepest caverns to discover every secret—interest in the unknown, Asha, leads to unpredictable findings."

Ashton realized for the first time that the mines had been closed off. There were piles of rubble blocking the entrance. "What happened to the stone, Granum, why are the mines caved in?"

Granum looked at the Sandglass discontentedly. "The Guardian knew where to find the stone; perhaps he could feel it, but all this time, all these years, the Guardian has been waiting on the Towers. Waiting just like me. For the stone's return."

Obsession.

"I'm beginning to understand what Jimmy was saying about riddles. You're speaking as if I was there to watch with you Granum. Tell me what happened."

"The head had broken from the stone; the shell had fully broken, and its body, its *real* body was emerging. I knew the wolves were doomed, but couldn't fathom what it would do next; it had years of living to make up for, years it had lived through somebody else, I suppose, but a confined existence leads you to stretch your legs, if you'll pardon the expression. But the Guardian came from the Towers and took the stone, took it and went west, towards the isle Logres, Asha, and I just don't have the strength to go back there. But I *have* to. Now. The stone has gone back to Logres and I must retrieve it."

"What about Jimmy's brother—what about the wolves? Are you going to let them win?"

Granum shook his head and looked down. "You don't understand. I have foreseen the apocalypse. Mystic has showed me that much. The end, Asha, will be wrought with fire. I am plagued by these dreams, these visions, and if we're heading to the final wars, my dear, I need the stone to counter the enemy. For the enemy will come in droves. I've seen it."

Ashton looked at Jimmy, who was watching them intently, still taken aback by Granum's furious tone. "What about the boy? What about his brother? I will surely let neither die, and yet I have to contend with *this* army. Every wolf in the Sordids has taken up arms, Granum, and for a moment I believed we had hope, for I thought we had the company of a wizard."

Granum grinned, but it was pushed and very thin. "You have much more company then you think," he finally said, and he looked at the army of spiders, chittering to each other in a deep meditation.

5

Jimmy and Ashton left Spider City ten minutes later on the back of Jarat, followed closely by Granum and Kannef; behind them stood the Queen on her roost like a waving mother, watching her many children off to play. The trees shook as the army of spiders moved eastward.

Spider City was behind them now.

6

The stone had begun cracking. Rocks exploded from the ground and crashed at the bottom of the edifice; it seemed like the ground was turning over, as if the vibrations were supplanting the underside of the rock.

Edwin shielded his head from falling debris, and slowly crawled towards the edge of the rock face, still watching the stone crack, standing on crooked legs that had blossomed from the ground. He couldn't find the strength needed to stand upright. Something was terribly wrong, that much was obvious.

The top of the stone cracked. There was a splitting noise. The stone's spindly arms had fallen to its side and seemed to shrivel; they looked like roots now, like the roots you'd find dangling from an aging uprooted plant. The arms finally crumbled and fell to the ground with a thick clump. Edwin pulled himself into a small alcove in the rock face, which burrowed into a small nesting area that looked into the caverns below.

I bet those arms were temporary. I bet whatever's in that stone wants to come out and play, and I bet whatever it is, it'll be uglier than sin. The stone bulged. Something prodded from the top of the broken stone, something with stringy hair that poked from crevices and stuck straight out, curling and dipping to the shaking ground.

And Edwin heard for the first time the voice of the stone.

It was a low utterance, yet the voice sounded strangely human. Not quite, but *similar*. After the words were spoken, two huge craters erupted from behind the stone, lifting into the air and settling on the ground below.

More hair spilled from the top of the stone, which continued to bulge, slightly cracking, and oddly enough, pulsating.

And then Edwin saw the old man riding on the back of a wolf.

Minutes later the mines would cave in.

7

Jarak saw the stone while he ran forward, standing on two weird rock legs that seemed fused to the ground; it looked oddly like an insect with a tiny abdomen. Two spindly arms lay at its side, and as Jarak neared the stone, both arms began to whither and fall off.

The rocks behind the stone exploded outwards, and the image in front of the wolf became a thick haze. Jarak pulled closer to the rock wall, scrambling through wolves, who themselves were struggling with statues that had grown ever stronger.

Jarak pounced on the chest of a statue, knocking it to the ground, and ran over the jumbled marble towards the mines, which were cloaked in smog.

"We are almost there," Jarak said to the old man, who was clutching Jarak's side, staring longingly at the Towers. Jarak realized the statues were on his side; they had become enough of a diversion to sneak through the pass basically undetected, leaving the mines an open route for escape.

When Jarak reached the opening of the mine something happened he hadn't anticipated. There was a sense of hope he hadn't felt for years—since Azlak Ulak had fallen to be precise—but he knew for some reason (though he tried to deny the possibility) that obstacles were endless when you had faith in your own salvation. He had lived for years under the ruling shadows of the Ulak family, and he had paid his allegiances to the wolves, his people, but he realized that in determining to turn his back on that innate oath, he would have to face the General before abdicating his position by the chieftain's side. It was a terrible thought, but when he first heard the gunshot, he understood exactly what was happening: Jarak had gotten too wound up in hope, a human emotion, and he had let it suffocate him.

When Jarak was shot, his first thought was to get to the mines no matter what. He had heard the gun clap and then felt an explosion in his right arm, but he could handle that; he dipped slightly, and felt the old man slide down his shoulders. He could manage.

"What was that?" Auger asked, lying on his stomach. His ignorance of his old world had seemingly led him to forget the simple sound of a gunshot.

Jarak jumped towards the mine and was shot again, this time through the neck, and this time the pain was incredible. His yellow eyes flashed a certain understanding, and instead of trying to move forward, his front legs gave out, collapsing to the ground with a loud thud. Kenneth Auger flew from Jarak's sloped shoulders and landed in a roll inside the mine; he felt his hip snap, and when he knocked into the wall, he felt his left elbow pop out of place. He screamed.

Jarak was lying on his stomach, blood spurting from his muzzle and staining the rock.

The old man turned to look at the wolf and saw Grak step on Jarak's back. Grak was carrying a handgun.

8

Grak reached down and flipped Jarak over. The wolf looked up lazily, lolling his yellow eyes back and forth. Thick spurts of blood spewed from his neck whenever he breathed.

"You are like my father," Grak said. "You instinct like man, and you rally behind human emotion, believing your kinship with that diseased puke will lead you to the world on the other side. It is not much, Jarak, though it contains weaponry beyond our mere axe and sword. You and I could have ruled side by side, carrying this thing of fire, but you chose to ally with the enemy."

Jarak gargled blood until a bubble formed between his teeth; it popped and splattered the fur around his eyes. "Your father was the only true General of the Yilaks, traitor," Jarak said in a low grunt that sounded phlegmy. He had wanted to say that for many years now, but not under these circumstances.

Grak howled, stepped firmly on Jarak's arm and stuck his claws against the wolf's throat. "Why do you fight for a dying man?" He asked with an almost unbelieving teeter to his voice. Jarak didn't answer.

Grak looked into the mines now, and found the old man cloaked in darkness, thrown in a heap against the rock face, clutching his side.

"Run old man," Jarak said weakly. The old man couldn't hear the wolf over the noises of battle. "RUN!"

This time the old man did hear, but his prospects weren't good. "I can't, I think I broke my hip, it's twisted around." Why had he come up here?

Grak had pointed the gun at the old man. "You are much closer to death's door then you know old man. I suppose you know what it is I hold," the general said, wavering slightly as Jarak tried to move both arms pinned underneath Grak's feet.

And then the statue of David, the old man had seen it with his own eyes, surprised Grak from the back and grabbed the wolf by the arm, flinging him to the side. Grak fired off another shot, but it exploded on the ground near Jarak's left arm.

"Jarak, get up, we're almost there. Jarak," the old man shouted, dealing with the incredible pain and effort it took to remain conscious.

Another blood bubble popped in Jarak's mouth, but the wolf said nothing. The old man tried to move forward but screamed; it felt like something had exploded inside him, something that decided to grow teeth and bite. His flesh felt loose around his hip, and he wondered how truly bad it was. He had been right though; he would die if he chanced the mines. He wondered if the boy had gotten the wizard's blood. It was this kind of thinking, this kind of speculation that led a teetering mind towards insanity. Kenneth Auger was on the verge, and had been for many years now. Perhaps it was the fact that he had exited a world he was accustomed to, only to have to assimilate in a world that, as Cole put it, seemed built on the powers of imagination. The possibility seemed insane, so it was only a matter of time before he went mad; it was inevitable really.

Kenneth Auger watched the Inlands through a haze, and even as he felt sleep overtake him, he watched Jarak's poor body get flattened by tons of rock that had fallen from the roof. Much of the debris rolled toward him, but none actually touched him. Only the darkness touched him, he supposed, but that wasn't so bad. It felt like sleep really. Sleep seemed good. Kenneth Auger, whose hip had rotated under his flesh like a tongue rolling under a lip, closed his eyes.

He wouldn't wake up until he saw the flashlights.

9

When the mines collapsed, Edwin had been fully tucked into the alcove in the rock, almost dangling above fissures that led to the dark caverns below. Edwin could hear the wolves inside howling, some in pain, others in fury.

He had seen Auger pass on the back of a wolf, but he had ignored the sight. On any other day the sight would have led him to double take, but there was something else that held his attention, and even when he heard gunshots to his left, they couldn't pull him from his current fixation either.

The stone's growing hair, he thought, watching the top of the rock crumble away, spewing pebbles into the air; there were long strings of hair poking out, all of which seemed to sway in the air—but Edwin didn't so much believe they were waving in the breeze as much as he believed they were *pulling* at some unseen axis in the air. *Something's trying to get out,* he thought, rather eerily.

The rock had been growing. Edwin had realized this himself. The stone he wore around his neck could easily fit in his hand, but this stone, standing on two rock legs, had grown five times larger than his fist. But it wasn't stopping. It looked as if it were beating, pushing in and out like a heart, and every time its pulse pumped outward cracks formed, and the stone grew more.

"What are you?" Edwin asked. He wasn't intending an answer of course, but realized he was going to get one.

The stone exploded.

It was quick, like a gunshot really, and when the thin plume of dust settled, Edwin saw something hanging in the air, tucked tightly in the fetal position. Its hair had been strung out, still pulling at whatever its ends had grabbed in the empty air. Both rock limbs that had formed in the ground had both toppled forward and lay useless in rivulets of wolf blood.

What hung in the air had arms and legs, Edwin could easily tell that much, but they weren't like his own. They hung limp and Edwin could see dangling fingers, with chipped nails sprouting from each end.

It must have been scratching at the inside of the stone, Edwin thought. *But how could it have fit inside?*

He pulled himself forward to try and get a better look. The figure, hanging distended in the air and tucked in an uncomfortable ball, had turned its malformed head, its hair falling to its side. Dust billowed from its hair as it settled. It stretched its torso, *if* that was a torso, and its legs reached for the ground. They were incredibly skinny, this thing's legs, and its knees looked like doorknobs sticking awkwardly from gray flesh. That was the first thing Edwin seemed to notice. This thing was gray; its flesh hadn't been exposed to any light for years, and it had begun rotting.

The second thing Edwin noticed was that this figure's body had been stretched like elastic; it was as thin at its torso as it was at its legs. It was a straight line, ending abruptly at a long head with a mane of stringy hair. And there were folds in its limbs—lips of flesh that hung in sags where skin bunched against bone. It stood naked, but hair grew in places and curled to others, forming a vest of fuzz, but its eyes, Edwin noticed, hadn't opened.

Perhaps they were sensitive. He didn't know why he had this thought, but decided because its flesh was so gray, that its eyes must have also been blocked from the sun. If it were to open its eyes too quickly, Edwin realized, it would probably go blind. It hadn't escaped the stone to go blind, had it?

Edwin felt compelled to go meet this thing. It didn't look evil. It looked fragile, standing amidst ruins with frail limbs and rotten flesh—he felt sympathy for it. He felt sorry for this poor soul.

"Are you okay?" he said. Edwin's voice was weak, but he knew this thing could hear him; he knew, too, that this thing *recognized* his voice. He had for years given it vitality through holding the stone. He was, in a way, this thing's salvation, for he had ultimately brought it back home.

The skinny figure lolled its head toward the alcove and opened its eyes.

Its eyelids were like scaly gray patches, and when they peeled open, Edwin could hear flesh rip. Its eyes were like his own, and Edwin found in them an answer to all of his questions.

This thing was hungry; it had been trapped, and it was worried. It was worried, Edwin understood, because something was looking for it. Something like a guard.

"A prison," Edwin said to himself.

The skinny thing from the stone had walked towards Edwin, and two wolves flanked the figure from either side.

"NOOOO!" Edwin screamed. He reached out. But he heard something both terrible and wonderful. The thing spoke, its gray lips forming words that sounded wretched and grating, evaporating his sense of decency. There were elements in that garbled tongue that reminded him of the patterns in stone, the ragged lines and fissures, the way the pick sounded against coal, or the way dynamite sounded against limestone. It was the voice of every noise rock could make.

Both wolves had disappeared, and it would only take a second for Edwin to realize what happened to them, because Edwin too had used the same tactic before to intimidate Leo. This figure had given the mountain pass mouths, which swallowed in whole gulps a number of statues and wolves, closing the gaps when the bodies were gone. Edwin saw, about thirty feet from his alcove, a few wolf legs sticking from the ground, closed completely within rock.

A minute later the mines would collapse.

Edwin was certain he was meant to go with this thing; he was certain he had come down to break this thing from its prison. He still felt weak, but he tried to move. He could slowly pull himself forward, but when he went to get up, his knees buckled, knocking his chin against the ground.

The sound he heard next was the loudest of them all. It was like an earthquake. Edwin turned to look at the Towers and saw rocks falling from the left spire, rolling along its slope like sleds. There was a cloud of dust that exploded from the ground, and he saw the rocks standing up!

But they weren't rocks, were they? Against the base of the Towers, it looked as if a man had stood, a man with crooked shoulders; this odd man stepped forward, crushing a tent in his path.

The giant was moving fast. When Edwin blinked he realized what *it* was before him, but *it* was no man; its silhouette had been deceiving. It looked like a man, of course, had he been dipped in molten rock and left to dry. Its eyes were caked over with ash, and moved very slowly, tufts of smoke billowing from each socket. It had pulled itself up the edifice with hands as black as coal; the ground had cracked underneath its massive weight, and when Edwin blinked again, he realized the giant had the thing from the stone in its grip.

A second later it had stepped over the rock wall, crushing it with its step.

And the mines collapsed.

Rock spilled from the fallen edifice and rolled everywhere.

Edwin would wake up almost forty minutes later, a nice sized rock lying by his head, and a bump matching its girth underneath his dirty hair. And when he would wake up, he would see something entirely different.

10

They were at the edge of the Leeg now. The tree line stopped abruptly, reminding Ashton of an edifice at Wolf Country. Granum had halted the spiders, whistling loudly; the noise was shrill, and seemed dense in the thin air.

"They're down there," Granum said to Ashton.

"The Hunters?"

"Yes." Granum looked over the dark sky.

"I assume there will be a struggle," Ashton said, reaching over his shoulder to massage the hilt of his sword.

"The struggle isn't with your people, Asha. Your war is with the wolves."

"What's going on, let's go," Jimmy called out.

"He's right Granum," Ashton said, "what do you suppose we do? Do we confront the King's men, the Hunters, or do we travel around them?"

"You have much at stake if you choose to do the latter, Asha."

"What do you mean?"

Granum shuddered slightly. "You left your horse at the lake."

"Jilay," Ashton said absently.

11

The Leeg Forest was a wall of trees against the field, a fence that from a distance looked like clouded pegs shoved into the earth by giants thousands of years ago. Ashton and Jimmy rode upon Jarat the Spider's back, sitting atop wet canopy leaves they had grabbed from the treetops. Granum sat in his perch on Kannef's back; the Sandglass was secured underneath the spider's belly, wrapped in a quilt.

"We shall go first, we do not want to alert them," Granum said. He had been specifically looking behind Jarat, where the trees bent under the mass weight of the Queen's ensemble. There was an awkward chittering, and Jarat and Kannef descended the trees, sliding down the bark with legs that found holds in moss and cracks.

Jimmy felt like he was on a rollercoaster with an incredible drop; his stomach seemed to rise into his throat and threaten him with the prospect of vomiting his guts. He wanted more than anything to raise both arms in the air and scream, but knew that if he did, he'd tumble over Ashton to a messy death on the forest floor.

They hit the ground with a terrible lurch, and the spiders skidded to a halt, smashing into fallen branches, crumbling them into fat splinters that exploded in the dark air.

"We must exit slowly," Granum said, "for the men beyond these trees wait not for spiders."

Jimmy could see the sparse light of the fields beyond the trees, which seemed like tangled brush at the edge of the forest.

"I hate that word 'slowly', I thought we were in a rush," Jimmy mumbled.

"Our safety is of great importance also," Jarat said.

"I mustn't startle them. I believe Jilay is a hostage at this point—if they have seen my horse outside the forest, they must believe I entered. That is why the King's men trampled through the brush. How could I have been so stupid? I left Jilay as a beckoning."

"You knew not that you were being followed," Granum said.

Ashton sighed, looking at the waning beams of light through the forest wall. "We must go." The leaves above them had begun falling from the treetops in hordes. Jimmy looked up and only saw darkness.

Every space in the canopies had been filled in.

12

The wall of the Leeg seemed like an impenetrable defense. The trunks of the Canopy's were like the thick pillars of the old palace in the city. It was between these that Jarat exited, emerging into the light like a monster from the forest's womb. Kannef followed.

Ashton, Jimmy and Granum shielded their eyes from the sun, which sank deeper in the western sky.

There was a quick plunk sound, and Ashton realized an arrow had been shot at them; it stuck into a nearby tree with a sturdy thud, and when his vision adjusted he saw a carriage against the horizon, a carriage that looked oddly shaped like an apple.

He quickly pulled his own bow, nocking an arrow in the weapon.

"Stay your bow," somebody called, somebody with a deafening voice. There were many bodies against the horizon, and Ashton realized that it was hopeless; he stuck his bow and arrow back into his quiver, and searched for his horse.

Another arrow shot, but this time it plunked off the ground three feet in front of Jarat, ricocheting into the spider's side. "Don't shoot!" Ashton called in a voice that, Jimmy thought at least, sounded broken.

"Why are you on top of those *things*?" somebody called out. Ashton knew the voice belonged to a member of the royals; the voice was rushed and wavered—whoever spoke was obviously disheartened by the sight of two spiders.

"Just move forward," Granum said. "We have to clear this up quickly; there is no point dwelling on a question and answer basis. They must know our business is elsewhere, and that patience is not a commodity we have to give."

"But they seek you; when they see clearly that an old man has been brought back, you know the next arrow is meant for you."

"There's nothing we can do about that now."

"There is an army of them," Ashton resigned.

Granum chuckled; it was his intention to lighten the situation. "You forget, Asha, what we left in the forest."

Jimmy saw the group of men, most on horses, cluttered on the horizon and he gulped. This wasn't what he had anticipated; it seemed the distance between him and his brother had just gotten larger.

They moved forward, and Ashton searched frantically for Jilay.

13

The groups of men were divided, the Hunters standing to the left of the apple-shaped carriage, and the men bearing the King's Crest to the right.

"Where is Jilay?" Ashton said as Jarat moved towards the gang of men.

"A Hunter wouldn't have left his horse in such an obvious place," a Hunter said, a Hunter sitting atop a horse with a bow secured around his shoulder, wearing a gray tunic with a black belt probably made from the flank of an ox.

Ashton jumped down from Jarat. His bow was accessible, but it was his sword he would reach for; he didn't believe the Hunters wanted any problems, but was sure, as he had already told Granum, that the King's men were thirsty for wizard's blood. Ashton watched them from the corner of his eye, and they too shared his curious gaze, though most looked at the spiders uncomfortably.

"Take off your mask," another Hunter said.

Ashton ignored him. He found Jilay tethered around the thick neck of another stallion, the ropes dangling from Shavin the Hunter's hand.

When Granum approached and dismounted the carriage door opened. A fat man stood at the threshold holding an apple in his plump hand. "Ah, so our visitors have finally come." He said so eyeing the spiders cautiously. He walked down the first step, took a bite from his apple, and Ashton saw another man had been inside the carriage also; this second man stood hunched he was so tall, and when he left the carriage door he almost fully crouched forward. He had a moustache that curled over either side of his lips, and he held a sword in his hand, a large sword that had writing on its hilt.

When the fat man saw Granum a small twitch formed on his rosy lips. He dropped his apple, and as if this were a sign, the giant man holding the sword rushed forward.

"What are you doing, Lor?" the fat man asked in a whiny voice.

Lor readied his sword and when he jumped from the carriage steps, the point of his blade nearly three feet from Granum's throat, an arrow whizzed by his head, planting itself in the carriage.

"What are you doing?" Shavin the Hunter asked, reaching for another arrow.

"Shut up Hunter, if you know what's good for you."

"We were to retrieve the old man," Shavin said, "that was the plan, and yet you wish to draw blood. What is wrong with you?"

"Do not presume anything is wrong with me Hunter, you filth, you scum." Lor rushed towards the Hunters this time, and each man riding horseback armed his bow and pointed it directly at the big man's skull.

"Lor, stand down," the fat man said.

"Oh Haspin, it is no use teaming with this filth; if I hadn't tried to draw blood, did you believe they wouldn't? This has all been a sham, you know, and it was a matter of time before either side tested the other."

"Do not speak to me with that tone, Lor. Yer still a commander of *my* army." Haspin stepped forward and slapped Lor across the face, turning to smile at Granum.

Lor turned red and looked at the Hunters for a long second, debating on whether his position at the heir's side was worth such humiliation. He was certain he'd fought many of these men in the civil wars, and just looking at them, *knowing* he was temporarily on their team made him feel sick to his stomach. Shavin and the other Hunters held their bows aimed at Lor.

"There is no need for such exacerbated actions," Haspin said. "We are all civilized, are we not? We are all men of good blood, and why shouldn't men of good blood proceed together, rather than separated as enemies?" Haspin looked at Granum, and then at Ashton; he smiled at both, curling his lips so that his fat cheeks looked more like tent flaps. There were chunks of apple in between his rotten teeth. "Where are you three off to, on the backs of spiders nonetheless?" Haspin said, winking at Jimmy. Jimmy didn't return the favor.

Ashton, who had taken out his own sword, looked at Haspin skeptically. There was something behind this fat man's eyes, something he was sure

Granum had noticed also. "We go east," Ashton said. He said so in a voice that sounded strained. Shavin looked at Ashton awkwardly. "I have come to retrieve my horse."

"Your horse? Ah, right, the horse we found by the lakeside." Haspin looked toward Fog Lake; the water seemed murky now, reflecting the pink clouds in the sky. "You know what it is you ride, isn't that so masked one?"

"Yes."

"My men were slaughtered by your transportation. I sent them into the forest for an investigation, and only half of them returned."

"You shouldn't have sent them armed into our woods," Kannef said, and Haspin looked at the spider disgustedly. Lor wiped his lip and spat at the ground; he would have liked to take the head off that sniveling creature.

"Is that reason enough to kill? Over territory…you'd think that seemed rather backward."

"Is there a point to this?" Granum asked, and Jimmy said 'yeah' behind him reassuringly.

Haspin stepped forward. "We were led to believe, old man, that someone strange lived beyond these woods, and we were sent to retrieve him." Haspin clicked his tongue against the roof of his mouth. "You see, these are pressing times in the Inlands."

"We know," Granum said.

Haspin smiled slightly; he saw behind Granum's mangy beard a large scar he was quite positive his uncle had inflicted. "Where is it you head since you've found your horse?"

Ashton stepped forward, still carrying his sword. "What business do you have in our destination?"

"Mayhaps you can call us roadblocks, and we demand a fee for yer passing." Haspin looked at Ashton contemptibly and returned his curious gaze towards Granum. "Tell us then, where it is ya came from?"

"From the woods, obviously," Jimmy said impatiently from Jarat's back.

"Stay your tongue boy," Lor yelled out.

Jimmy grinned at the big man, with a look of defiance. And that look would stick, for Lor had a memory for such insolence.

"Enough," Haspin said. "That's enough hostility for one day, we are curious is all. Why were you in the woods, then?"

"We are friends of the spiders, as you can see," Ashton said. "We must go though."

"East, you go east, towards the Sordids. Those are damned lands, and very unsafe. You shouldn't go that way." Haspin put his hands in the pockets of his robe.

"Where do you suggest we go then?" Ashton asked.

Haspin had ignored the question though, and as he had reached into his pockets, he had advanced towards Granum. Ashton had anticipated this. Haspin pulled a dagger from his robe and jumped towards Granum; Lor followed suit. Had this been the plan all along? To stall the big man, try to make amends, and then use this trust to further pursue bloodshed. Ashton knew these men had waited outside the woods to question him about the old man from the forest; they hadn't expected, though, that the old man would arrive with him, on spider backs nonetheless. This had all been very unexpected, and he had seen unrequited lust in the fat man's eyes. Ashton blocked Lor from getting closer to Granum, and before he could turn to divert the fat man's attack, Granum instead decided to freeze poor Haspin as he leapt from the ground.

"What is happening to me?" Haspin asked worriedly, his mouth barely moving as his jaw seemed snapped shut. His feet hung three feet above the ground, and the royalist men staggered backwards, their horses rearing. Lor dropped his sword.

"He *is* the wizard!" Haspin tried to scream from his clenched lips. "Get him!"

Lor shoved Ashton, and he flew against a horse, staggering to the ground. Lor bent to pick up his sword and felt a blade against the back of his neck. A Hunter had reprimanded him.

The King's men drew their arrows, and the Hunter's followed suit; both parties aimed at each other, calling back and forth to sheath their weapons.

"Trust me Hunter, when you remove your blade I will turn to meet you with my own," Lor said with a grunt.

An arrow singed over Granum's head and struck the apple-shaped carriage.

Lor used this diversion turning to flick the Hunter's sword from his neck, while grabbing his own from the ground; he pulled the Hunter from his horse and held the sword against the flailing man's throat. "I told you." Lor smiled. "Put your weapons down, all of you. Let Haspin out of your spell or I will cut this man's neck." Lor looked at Granum and licked his upper lip; his moustache trembled.

Granum scrunched his eyebrows. "You mean to prove your will is steel, but you no less mean to cut that man's neck than I mean to cut your lord from my spell. I can see it in your eyes."

Lor pressed his blade against the Hunter's throat, backing into the carriage so nobody could counter him from the back. The Hunter stood with a straight face.

"Is that so?" Lor smiled; he found the wizard's words startling. He had killed many men before, and had meant each act.

Jimmy, who had bent forward, sticking his face into a mat of spider hair, peered out discreetly, gel sticking his chin to Jarat's cardiac sign like strings of lime jelly. He felt the spider quiver beneath him. "What are we gonna do?" Jimmy asked.

Jarat said nothing, but instead released a high pitched shriek that to Haspin and the others sounded like a whinnying horse. The horses actually responded by veering back and toppling forward with their front hooves.

"What are you doing, stop it—shoot them, shoot them all!" Lor screamed; he was strangling the Hunter with his forearm.

Before anybody could release an arrow, the trees that made up the wall of the Leeg rustled violently.

The Queen's ensemble descended from the Canopies, some using web to glide, others jumping from trunk to trunk; there were hundreds of them, spiders marching from the forest like thunder through the sky. There was an awkward chittering, heard over the distinct rumbling in the ground, the explosion of legs against earth.

Lor's jaw dropped.

"Mercy Mystic," Shavin the Hunter said, drawing a slope down his front; his men rotated their aim, and watched the spiders descend. "'Tis an army," he said under his breath.

"I know what it is you want from me, Haspin," Granum said to the fat man hanging in the air, a dagger clasped in his frozen fist, "but your uncle was the last to leave a scar on my flesh." He snapped his fingers and Haspin fell to the ground; he let the dagger roll from his grip.

Haspin looked *past* Granum, and watched the army of spiders form a line against the forest wall.

"You are going to war," Haspin said absently, still peering at the spiders.

"We wish to *finish* a war once and for all," Granum said.

"Where is your war, sire?" Shavin the Hunter asked, still looking at the spiders.

"Like you, good Hunter, our war is with the wolves."

"Let us go then, we shall surprise them," Shavin said.

"We cannot surprise them," Granum said.

"Why not?"

"Because war has already come to Wolf Country."

"Impossible," Shavin said, accompanied by a hearty grumble from his men. "Haspin was just there, and if there was going to be battle, 'twould have been us in the middle of it."

"I'll show you," Granum said, and he turned to grab the Sandglass.

14

The Sandglass was laid on the ground, and Granum swiped his hand over the image so that it swirled; he mumbled something under his breath and suddenly Shavin could see Wolf Country on the glass's surface—like magic. The battle was over, but it was obvious that it had occurred; there were bodies strung throughout the grounds, and crumbled statues littered the pass like fragments of sculpted mountain.

"What happened?" Shavin asked.

Granum didn't answer; instead he waved his hand over the glass again and the image transferred. There was a quick blur as colors faded into others creating a clear picture of a lake, reflections of the mountains painting the surface like a lucid canvas.

Haspin had been standing beside Granum, his dagger tucked into the sleeve of his robe. But he dropped the weapon when he saw the image in the glass.

"What is that? Why do you have a picture of Gallia?"

Spotted along the coast were shacks and trails, farms and orchards, and at the peak of a small hill a mile from the lake there was a modest castle.

Granum didn't answer, and pointed at the glass so that the image shifted again; it seemed to follow a path north, through fields and forests where horses grazed and birds nested, and trampling the grounds nearly a days travel from Gallia were a pack of wolves.

"Wolves. They are dressed in Sordid garb." Haspin crouched. "They are heading towards Gallia." He fell to his knees and watched this image. "Is this real?" He trembled. He knew the answer before he even asked.

"You left a few men at Wolf Country, and you believed they were the *only* collateral old man Auger needed to believe you'd ever return?" Granum looked at Haspin. "After you left, a troop of wolves were sent to Gallia. He outwitted you, my lord."

Haspin wiped his lip. Everything was going as he had wished it would. Haspin slowly stood, straightened his robes, took one last look at the army of spiders and turned towards his carriage. "Fasten me to the horses," he said curtly. "We go to Gallia; we go to defeat these rogue wolves."

Lor gave the Hunters one last look and snarled. "We will meet again, scum." He clambered into the carriage and the King's men rode southeast.

"We must let them think otherwise," Haspin said to Lor, tossing an apple from hand to hand. "Let them believe we ride to Gallia to fend a few wolves." Haspin smiled. "Everything is happening exactly as he said it would. The path to the Towers will be open at last."

Lor, who was drinking a pint of ale, watched the Hunters fall into the distance. "The Traveling Man is wise."

Haspin nodded. "Soon the armies of the throne will be united, Lor. Soon the city will be rebuilt."

15

Ashton walked beside Jarat, holding his horse's reigns in his hand.

"He promised he'd get Cole, Ashton, he promised," Jimmy said, trying to hide his tears.

Ashton nodded. The wizard had motioned him over as he secured the Sandglass beneath Kannef. "I must go," he'd said, and Ashton realized there was no arguing with him. He saw himself that the mines had collapsed; there were two boys from a different world in the Inlands, and both were homesick. And home was so far away from them now.

The wizard rode south on Kannef's back, leaving a melancholic longing sketched across the Hunters' faces. "Where has he gone?" A Hunter had asked, and Ashton only kicked at the ground—"He has other business to attend to."

"I'll get Cole," Ashton finally said. "Granum will get you back home."

"What do you mean?"

"I mean he'll get you home."

Jimmy looked down—just thinking about home made him depressed. Was it only yesterday that he had been in his own room, contemplating whether or not he should tell his mother everything he knew about Cole's behavior? He remembered the police, the real reason why he had gone down the vents; he wanted to be a hero because guilt had finally caught up with him. Jimmy looked east; there were tiny crowns of rock jutting from the horizon. They were going there.

"Was that just a spell in the glass, a spell to drive Haspin the Fat away?" Shavin asked when he rode next to Ashton.

Ashton shook his head. "They looked to slaughter you as well as the wolves."

Shavin nodded and inhaled the brisk air. "We figured just as much. We were on guard though. Trust was never an option."

"It never is," Ashton said with a hint of annoyance in his soft voice.

"Hai Zom, hai." Shavin's horse reared and stopped, stomping at the ground impatiently. "What is that supposed to mean?"

"You have been following me through the woods. The wizard told me. Trust has left the Hunters."

Shavin smiled. Truth was a nuisance, the smile suggested. "The Hunters are a community," he finally said. "When you approached to fight with us, Ashton, you asked of the impossible—our numbers were too low to attack the wolves in their country."

"Or was it your cowardice was too high?" Ashton said smugly.

"I didn't want to lead my men into a meaningless slaughter; we would have been butchered. What were we to think when you approached claiming you were David the Hunter's son?"

Ashton looked at Shavin with his exposed eye. "You were sposed to believe me, believe that not all had been lost when David fell."

"Ashton, David never had a son. I knew him well—he was like my brother," Shavin said, and Ashton looked away. "Why don't you take off your mask?"

"I am scarred. I've lived in places you men have nightmares about. I've camped in the ruins only to wake up to the wolves howling—I lived where you ignored."

"No, we're not insane; it was never ignorance." Shavin itched his face, looking towards the Sordid ruins. "You are a mystery to us, you know. The Hunters believe you are insane. I admire your persistence, but I feel the others are right. If we're to believe you are really of David's lineage, then can you blame our insistence to find out the truth?"

"What has spying on me led to—what truths have you come to?"

"Take off your mask."

"I told you, I'm scarred."

"We all have scars. Look here, and here," Shavin said, pointing to a slash on his chin where no facial hair would grow, and to a divot in his collarbone. "To be a Hunter is to bear scars."

"We must go; it is getting dark. We have many miles to cover." Ashton slapped Jilay's side and the horse trotted forward. Shavin grabbed Ashton's arm.

"David had a daughter."

Ashton scoffed at the comment. "I heard she died. You didn't do your duty to protect the women, for isn't that all they're worth? A Hunter's protection." Ashton turned away. The army of spiders trampled forward. "Shavin, you fight your war, I'll fight mine," Ashton said, and Shavin looked away just as he had done the day Ashton suggested they invade Wolf Country, all those years ago. It wasn't exactly a sign of disrespect, but a showing of separation—the Hunters weren't the community they had once been; there were secrets within the order, and Shavin knew it. David the Hunter's daughter hadn't died, he knew she hadn't, because David's wife, Mary, had told him so. Isabella had moved on, but Shavin didn't completely believe that either; he gave Ashton one last look and turned to his men.

"Very well," Shavin said. Shavin controlled a group of fifty Hunters, some of whom survived the last war with the wolves, others of a new breed, young men of the world, virgins of the sword. "It is time, men, to do our fathers justice, to do David justice, to do the people of the Inlands justice; we have for years waited for this, and tonight, tonight we fulfill the destiny of our order." He called out in a loud yell that sounded more like a throaty yelp, and the Hunter's responded with their own collective rendition. Many knew they marched towards their tombs, but they believed goodwill was on their side, for they had allied with the likes of a wizard and an army of spiders, and for the first time in hundreds of years, an interspecies coalition had formed against one common enemy.

"Hold my hair tight, Jimmy," Jarat said. "We are anxious to meet the wolves head on tonight."

CHAPTER 21

THE MADNESS OF A LONELY KING

1

Cole crawled into a large room, barely scraping through the small hatch in the door without snagging his sweater. This room was different than the rest in the Tower; there was still an awkward glow, but there were waning spots of glimmering light from outside, as if the rock had been chipped away to reveal deep fissures. The room was a large oval, just like the chamber of falling stones, only this room had a different feel to it. There weren't giant boulders in the middle of the floor waiting to rise on some unseen axis, but across the room there was a table pushed against the wall. Hanging from an arm of rock over the table, like a beam support across a ceiling, was rope; it dangled to the tabletop and simply rested on the table's surface. The rope had been tied into a noose.

Cole walked forward. There was something to his right, something glowing a light blue—it was a box, he realized, a box that shot blue rays from between its boards. Further to his right he saw a throne; it was built with solid gold, and its seat was a padded purple cushion. There were chests at the throne's base filled with gold medallions and purple jewels.

Why would anyone want to brave the Judge—a guardian he had single-handedly defeated—(well, with the help of the Glossettes company, he supposed, but they didn't exactly exist here, did they?)—to get into this room? He knew this had to be the King's chamber—the throne was the big give away—but Cole supposed this mission had been pointless. The table hadn't contained any food scraps, and there wasn't any sign of *life*; he did spot bones littering the ground, but for all Cole knew, they could have been the King's broken remains, withering in the gloom of this wretched place, waiting for the proper burial the great Judge had refused. Cole walked towards the glowing box. He was sure that if anything in this room demanded retrieving, it was whatever cast the eerie glow inside the chest.

The top of the box swung open easily, and when the lid slammed against the backside of the box, Cole unmistakably heard the ocean.

There was a bead rested in the box, a bead rimmed by a white border made of bone; the bead was a light blue, but it constantly changed, turning from dark to light, and Cole was certain he had seen the odd outline of something inside, something struggling against the bead's inner cavity.

Cole reached into the box when he was grabbed from behind.

And his mouth was clasped shut before he could utter a scream.

The eyeless corpse! Cole thought; it had come through the door behind him after it found its head!

2

Edwin woke up with a startle. His head hurt, and when he opened his eyes he felt dust run into his sockets. It was dark. There was some light, flickering light, and there was a pallid glow in the air. His body was covered with small pebbles, and when he moved they rolled down his shirt, into his pants, his pockets; it was aggravating.

Edwin pushed himself up and hit his head. Where was he? He was in an incredibly small pocket in the rock, an alcove that had almost been fully camouflaged by broken rock. Edwin could hear the wolves. There were deep cracks in the alcove, cracks that must have led to their caverns.

The stone, Edwin thought suddenly. *Where had it gone*? This thought had come after he felt around his neck, noticing at once that the chain was missing. He remembered, strangely enough, that the stone had been floating along the pass, and that it had broken—and he remembered the strange creature that had dropped from its inside, plopping to the ground on spindly legs that wanted to buckle under its weight. And the giant—

The giant had come from the top of the Towers, rolling down the slope in a heap of rubble—and it had stood at the Tower's base, walking over in giant strides, taking the thin creature into its grasp...and then it had gone. He wanted to help the poor thing from the stone, he remembered that much. There was a moment when he realized it was he that had broken the creature from its prison, and he knew for some strange reason that the creature wanted to thank him.

The rubble, he thought suddenly. Where had it come from? If it had been there when he crawled toward the alcove, he would have been blocked from hiding. "The giant," he said aloud, feeling the top of his head where a chunk of rock had hit his scalp and knocked him out.

Edwin pushed the rubble out of the way; he carefully checked the mountain pass for wolves, but they were all on the grounds now. Edwin saw his statues in the early glow of the moon, piled in awry clutters scattered down the pass, heads and twisted arms and torsos, all cracked and broken, all defeated. He knew now, at least, that the statues had fallen dormant when the creature from the stone was taken.

What Edwin saw next drove him to an unexpected insanity.

The mines were gone. The boulders had collapsed, lining the pass with debris. There was a heap of fragmented rock, which exploded under the heavy foot of the giant as it stepped over the ruins; the rocks had slid down the face, and the boulders had split and broke into pieces. Edwin saw, although slightly marred by darkness, a large footprint embedded in the stone pass, cracking the surface into webs towards the rock wall.

Edwin ran to the blocked mines. He tried to move some of the rubble, wrapping his weak arms around crumbled granite and shelfrock that wouldn't budge an inch. It was no use. He needed the stone.

Your obsession, your wants will drive you mad—

This thought was in a voice that didn't sound like him at all. He had heard this voice before: every time he used the stone, every time he dwelled on its power. For years he was being warned by a conscience he had ignored.

"Oh what do you know?" He said in a furious tone, settling his back against rock, trying to lift with his legs. "I'm stuck here, and if I'm stuck here, then those two boys are too."

The nagging voice in his head shut up at once. For now, Edwin stood before the blocked mines, not scratching his head or trying to budge rock, but staring slack jawed at the Tower's outline against the dark sky.

It had always been about the Towers, hadn't it? Curiosity had always been the counter-force against reason, against logic, which supposed he should have destroyed the path between worlds years ago. None of this would have happened had he listened to intuition. But he wanted to see what else was inside those Towers. If the stone had come from those Towers, then perhaps there was something more powerful inside waiting to be found. *Yes, and the stone told you so*, he thought.

With his remaining strength, Edwin gathered himself from the side of the crumbled sandstone, and limped slowly to the rock face. The wolves he could see were on the ground, some carrying torches, others dismantling standing statues, but most pulling ropes. There were ropes wrapped around boulders that had fallen on tents, and wolves were trying to pull the stones off. Edwin could see the snapped posts, the crumpled canvas, or leather—whatever had been inside the tents when the stones had fallen, hadn't the chance to survive such a devastating attack.

Edwin was covered in dust and seemed camouflaged by the rock in the moon's glow. He clutched to the side of the rock face and walked down the pass. He saw the statue of David's head amidst a pile of fallen statues.

He hadn't thought, yet, that his only choice now that the mines had collapsed was to find Cole and Jimmy—it seemed altruism had lain in slumber with his wilted conscience for as many years as he had worn the stone around his neck. As far as he was concerned, the boys were slaughtered, were strung over the wolves' camp like trophies.

For years it was this kind of poison that tainted his mind—whether it was wholly because of the stone or not seems debatable, but Edwin had searched long and hard for the truth. He had been driven to live shrouded by guilt and hesitation since he was young, and soon enough he would find the truth; he won't be expecting it, but Edwin, who feels weaker with every step down the mountain pass, will stumble into the truth. He *will* watch his father die.

This will be his last and only memory.

3

Cole had done what he couldn't pull himself to do with Leo behind the fireplace—oh, those days seemed so far behind now, as if time had doubled over on itself. The hand clasped roughly over his face felt like leather, and he knew, judging by the flapping skin on the eyeless corpse, that the ragged flesh would probably feel like a cheap suitcase, but he could feel something through the touch, something he believed the eyeless ghost wouldn't, by nature, be able to do. He could feel the thing behind him breathing. Cole realized his only way out of the situation was to open his mouth as much as he could and try to find a flap of skin to bite down on.

He cinched his lips, tasted the rotten flesh, the salt, the dirt; he could taste the age of the hand too. This hand was old. The flesh wasn't exactly loose, but seemed formed into bone, and what Cole felt run over his lips was a hardened worm. Cole bit down. There was a loud crunch, and the thing behind him fell backwards and screamed, though the voice which bellowed out seemed little more than a slight whimper.

Cole thought he would run; he thought he would run to the door, but what he saw when he turned surprised him. Crouched on the ground, panting, wasn't a powerful ghost, nor was it a piece of the Judge's "puzzle"; rather, bent in pain on the dusty floor cowered an old man. He caressed his finger, looking up sporadically with drooping eyes in a face shaped like a skull, despite the long, sparse white beard that ended in dirty splits at his chest. The old man wore a crown on his head, but it was far too big; it kept slipping over his ears until, with his other hand, he pushed the golden crown over top tufts of thinning hair.

The old man wore a filthy purple robe. The man's shoulders hunched as if the weight of the thick material was snapping his bones.

"What are ya doing in here, boy?" the old man finally asked, still crouched on the ground, tending to his finger. Cole noticed how long the man's fingernails were; they ended in long blackened curls, as if they had been dipped in tar.

Cole didn't know what to say. He figured this was the man, the *King*, he and Hayle were sent in to the Towers to fetch, but he forgot what it was he was supposed to grab.

"Answer me. It's been years since I've heard anything spare the low howls outside, the clatter of swords beyond my door." The old man stood up. His robe billowed out around him, and his crown slipped down his skull, flattening his dirty hair.

Cole saw what he had done to the man's finger; he had left a large bite mark around his knuckle.

"Awfully quiet, boy," the old man said. "As if ye've forgotten something." He walked towards the box with the bead inside and snapped the lid shut. "Spying eyes." He smiled, baring brown teeth and cut gums. "Mustn't take the Pearl of the Ocean boy; mustn't disturb it. *It* wants out; it wants to escape the hold, but I won't give it the initiative. It wants to drown me, it does…I heard it tell me so. It wants me to live miserably for all time beneath water, rather than in this room, where no matter how many times I hang myself, my breaths never cease, my neck never snaps. Immortality, boy, is like a monster you cannot escape—a monster that at first seems beautiful, a lovely companion, but as it grows older with you, it takes a far meaner shape." The old man had sat down on the box; he was looking at the far wall, at the table and the noose.

"Are you okay?" Cole finally asked. He didn't know why, but he figured it was the best thing to say. The old man's eyes were distant, but most of all, they were sad. They were very sad.

"None of us are okay. In one way or another, boy, we are all mad. You are mad for testing the Towers, believing you could survive. I am mad for believing immortality would make me more powerful than any King in the history of any world; I am mad for collecting these talismans," he patted the box, "which would like nothing more than to suck everything from me and break from their cages."

"What are you talking about?" Cole asked.

"Oh yes, what indeed. It's cold in here, isn't it? Aren't you cold, boy?"

Cole shook his head as the old man stood up and twirled around in front of the box.

"I find the cold invigorating. I have believed so for years, boy, and you'll feel the same soon. Your flesh becomes more receptive with age, I believe. Ye've ruined my door, ya know?"

Cole looked back at the huge wooden door, with its crumbled corner.

"Mayhaps the draft is coming from the door then, wouldn't you think?" The crown on the old man's head slid over his ears and he lifted it again. "I'm not allowed near the door, isn't that funny?"

"Why not?" Cole asked, certain this old man was mad. His eyes weren't merely sad, they were *crazy*. He didn't like standing here anymore; he wished he could find this vial now—what had Hayle said about the vial, anyway? He couldn't remember.

"Oh stupid boy, he'd never let me out. He doesn't believe I'm the King anymore. He used to. I haven't seen myself, spare the distorted reflection in gold or a wavering image in water, but he told me I was an impostor, I was too old and decrepit to be King. I mustn't leave, I mustn't chance it. I don't want them to take me to the roof of the Tower and leave me in the darkness. Why else, boy, would I try to hang myself? Don' be an ignorant fool."

"The Judge won't let you out?"

The old man shook his head.

"But you're the King, it told me it was *protecting* you from the nuisances of the world."

"Used to protect. Now it guards. Things change boy, like appearances. You'd think a wizard's creation would have the sense to understand aging, wouldn't you? Oh, but I've pondered such questions for a long time…for a very long time."

"A wizard's creation?"

"You ask so many questions." The old man, the King, looked towards the door. "I'm sure this was his idea all along though, pay back for cutting his throat, I suppose. Aye. He knew I would age, and he put a spell on my guardians to only recognize the man I had once been. Man wasn't made to live this long. I was tricked. He knew one day I would become a prisoner in my own Tower, to my own throne—mayhaps he knew my true intentions. Oh well. Blast his blood, boy, blast his blood," the old man opened his robe and pulled out a phial strung from a necklace. There was a crude black liquid stained along its sides, and at its base there was a lumpy buildup of the same blackened goo. "I should have brought literature with me, something to read. I do not think I remember how to read. Oh well, eh boy, oh well."

"Whose blood are you talking about?" Cole asked, shyly.

"Huh, chile?"

"You were talking about blood, and I wanted to know whose blood you were talking about."

"Ah, Ae-Granum's blood."

"Are you a—a vampire?" Cole asked. It was a brave question, and he'd surprised himself by asking it.

The King smiled again. "Ye would think so." He shook the phial. "I had many plans with this blood you know, boy. Long ago I was a great King. I realized my time was coming up—I would soon become just another portrait on the palace walls, another name in the great literature of the Inlands. I had done nothing spectacular. My father had taken an army to the Arike Mountains and set fire to the caverns. Killed hundreds of wolves, wolves he believed were readying an attack on the city. A heroic deed. People like to hear tales about wolves; we become vicious animals when it comes to stories of death, haven't you noticed, boy?"

"I guess."

"You guess?" The King stood up on the table and picked up the rope. "Death is a fascinating thing. What is it? Is it your final affirmation to Mystic that you are ready to chance the mighty throne?"

"I think its God's way of making everybody left alive miserable."

"Death strikes you hard." The King slipped the noose around his neck. "Why would ya think such?"

"Never mind."

The King tied the rope firmly around the rock.

"What are you doing?" Cole asked.

"Death is fascinating because it's inevitable. Man must face it at one time or another. This scares people. Because they've grown so accustomed to life—" The King jumped off the table and hung in the air from the noose, gagging.

Cole ran over and grabbed the King's legs.

The King laughed through gags. He kicked his legs out and found the table behind him. He pulled the noose over his head when he stood on the table; there was a dark red mark on his neck. "I hung for five days once; I know because I can see the sun through the fissures. I counted each sunrise. Sometimes you wait for death and it doesn't come."

"How can't you die?" Cole asked shocked, looking at the noose.

He offered a smile. "There are more than just this," the King said, looking at the box with the blue bead. "And I wanted all of them. Every talisman hidden behind its own guardian. There are four of them. Yes. Four. And they're waiting to get out, speaking through those who hold them. Talismans of the four elements. Ya'll see, boy, just how true my words o' warning are."

The King hobbled over to the box, lifted the lid and pulled out the bead. It looked heavy, but the King held the bead easily. He closed his eyes, and for a quick moment Cole thought the old man had finally bit the dust, had grabbed onto the bead and lost whatever it was that kept him alive.

It's the phial, Cole, that's what Kenneth Auger wants.

But then Cole felt something under his feet; the rock floor began filling with water, as if it had become a porous sponge built atop a swamp.

"It makes you weak," the King said. When he set the bead down, the water disappeared back into the rock.

"What was that?" Cole asked in disbelief. *Water doesn't just appear and disappear, especially through solid rock.*

"Pearl of the Ocean. Controls water. Such power, boy, is beyond words— killed many giants you know, in the old wars. How could I not want to retrieve all four talismans? How could I not send my armies out amongst the world to find them? I *tricked* the wizard into getting me the stone—but he always wanted redemption in man's halls after setting down his sword in the old war. A lowly wizard, he was. I found the pearl in Sangeon. The River People were using it to control the pirates, aye, to control the imports." He slowly scratched his face, then grabbed the phial, twisting the cork from its top. "Even with immortal life, boy, you feel the stress of the talisman's temptation." He stuck his fingernail into the phial, swished it around for a moment, then lifted it out. There was a glob of black lacquered on his nail, and he sucked it from his finger. "Ah, revitalizing. You can only ingest so much, boy, without feeling eternity run unbound throughout your head in a temper tantrum."

The black goo inside the phial, that's what's keeping him alive, Cole thought. He had to get the phial—if he was to get home and see his mom, see Jimmy, he knew he had to get that phial.

"I had the stone once too, but it was taken from me," the King said absently.

"Why did you come here? I mean, you're immortal, couldn't you have looked for these other elements?" Cole asked, looking at the phial longingly; he had to keep the King busy with thought.

"I wanted my people to think I was dead, dumb boy, for 'twas the foresight of my seer, Cesar. My *prophecy.* Yes, good ole Cesar, had the Third Eye he did—I wonder what ever happened to him." The King exhaled, lost in thought. "I was to return when the city needed me, when all had failed and civilization as we know had toppled. I would return with the power to control the elements, a power so strong I'd need immortality if I were to believe it possible. I would return and set things right—put the Hunters in their rightful graves. Give the farmers rain. But I got old. Too old, and now I'm a prisoner—aye, but we've been through this. Why are you confusing an old man? I wish you'd go away now."

Cole stepped forward. He had looked back at the door; it was a quick run, and he hoped the Judge was still dismantled.

"You're still here? What is it with you pests? Has the Judge sent you in to hassle me? Leave me. You and your stupid questions have tired me."

Cole sprang forward and grabbed the phial and ripped it from the King's neck. Cole turned and ran for the door.

"Boy! What have ye done?" Cole heard the King scream behind him. His voice wavered; it was very weak. "I need that—PLEASE, it has slowed my aging. PLEASE! BOY!"

Cole dove headfirst and slid under the door.

4

Cole ran.

The great Judge, who wasn't so great anymore, had still been crouched, trying to pick up chocolates that either plucked right through grasping hands, or slid through the backs of heads. He could hear the King's voice behind him, pleading; the vial felt warm in his hand, and for a moment he felt like chucking it against the wall. If everything he had been through was for this, was *because* of this, then he felt he had the right to discard it, to explode the glass and watch the black goo splotch the rock walls like tar.

And then Cole heard it. Water. Water behind him.

The King had taken the pearl from the box. Cole turned on his motors and ran faster, feeling the stitch in his side, feeling the vial knock his chest. He quickly looked back and saw that the hallway behind him, which was arched towards the endless ceiling, had filled with water. This water seemed perched back against the wall as if it was ready to pounce—Cole had never seen water do this before. The water bubbled against the wall, frothing at the edge, rippling at the center where Cole was sure it would explode first. And then the water pushed outwards, as if the vertical sheet had curved, forming a distinct dome in its center. The water shot a dripping limb from the pulsating dome that grabbed the ground and pulled the rest of the bubbling liquid. The water splashed loudly and rocketed against the walls, pulling itself forward, drenching the corridor, breaking loose rock from the walls.

Cole would have to hurry. He couldn't outrun water, but he could use one of the doorways littered randomly on either side of the hallway. There was one ahead of him, about forty yards to his left—the wall sloped outwards and he could tell there was a recess in the rock.

He could hear the water but he ignored it.

He was twenty yards from the doorway.

Fifteen.

The water was closer, like a shark; he could feel the brisk mist against the back of his neck.

Ten yards. The stitch in his side became a throb. Cole was exhausted, and before he could dwell on this certainty, his foot snagged a loose rock and he toppled forward, landing on his side with a loud crunch. Cole closed his eyes, listening to the water come closer, the sound of a hundred waves crashing in unison; the sound of snapping jaws.

And then it was silent.

Cole opened his eyes. The water was gone.

Cole stood up, dusted his front, stretched his back and started walking again. *What happened?* he thought—and then he remembered how the water had disappeared in the King's lair, how it had just sucked into the ground. The King had dropped the pearl.

Cole walked in the direction of the tunnels he and Hayle had crawled through.

He walked looking for the hermit.

Cole would meet someone else first though.

And so too would Hayle.

CHAPTER 22

WAR WITH THE WOLVES

1

There was a space between the Sordid ruins and the Towers, a valley where boulders became rubble, and where the ground was cloaked in shadow; the valley stretched two hundred yards, but easily masked outsiders behind randomly strewn fragments of rock. There had been countless attacks by rebel farmers in the past, invasions which had been crushed. Grak had enforced a strict policy which deemed the northern way never be left unguarded. Ashton knew this; he had seen the set up. Wolves occupied the valley, and countered from the back. Ashton had seen a small group taken down this way; they had entered Wolf Country carrying only pitch forks and pikes. Ashton watched these men fall. He could do nothing but watch. He is a rogue Hunter. He is a stray. He is alone.

The northern way was on a ground that sloped into the wolves' camp. The elevation could be useful. The light from the torches in the camp provided an eerie wave which illuminated from between the strewn rock; it was like a beckoning, for the fields and desert north of the Sordids was only dark wasteland. Ashton had seen this light, pulling him toward the valley with its terrifying magnetism.

"We must be slow," Ashton called from his perch on Jilay, who settled on the hard ground, shaking his heavy mane. "There are scouts." Ashton pulled out an arrow and felt the tip on his fingers.

The spiders formed a line in the darkness; the moon branded the tops of their abdomens, giving them a corona that assumed, to Ashton at least, an image of spirituality. It was a soothing notion. The Hunters halted and Shavin rode beside Ashton. He understood the friction between the two, but

Shavin also realized Ashton's advantage. The masked Hunter had watched these barbaric wolves for years, had studied them. This had become Ashton's rule of thumb, and Shavin would have to abide by this inevitability.

Ashton turned, his exposed eye glinting the moonlight. "How did you plan on attacking them?"

"We were going to use the wizard—"

"I mean before that. Granum told me you sent Haspin into the country, mayhaps as a scout. What was your plan of attack before you realized you could use the wizard as an advantage, as a diversion?"

Shavin looked towards the rocks, like black teeth outlined in bright enamel. "With what little men we had, we figured...*I* figured we'd have to surround their camp and use the elevation. We'd have to snipe them from a distance before resorting to combat."

"What had Haspin told you about the grounds?"

"In the morning the wolves bathed in the springs. It seemed the best time to attack."

Ashton sighed. "Did he mention the wolves go to the springs in increments? Everything in Wolf Country is presupposed, Shavin. Grak is a good General, is a great leader. When there are a hundred wolves in the springs, there are two hundred in the rocks above the grounds, watching. I have seen them. I have hid in the crook of rock, one meter from the clawed feet of a wretched wolf; I rubbed bird droppings over my body so it wouldn't smell me. I want Grak's head, Shavin, but his head has always been well guarded. The reason Haspin's men got into Wolf Country was because Grak had been away from the camp. Before wolves decide on outcomes, they ask Grak for directions. Haspin was lucky to have left alive."

"What should we do then? It seems we have marched to slaughter," Shavin said, "but time has led us to this outcome, Ashton. Many have died this way before us. I am not afraid of death; I am afraid of a decadent world for my children, and their children."

"We have the dark as cover. There are wolves guarding the northern way. Our best chance is to kill the scouts without allowing them time to alarm the other wolves. We have but one chance at doing this; we cannot merely harm them, we have to slaughter them quickly."

"And then?"

Ashton sighed again. The spiders were quietly chittering, and he realized they were getting impatient. To them, this attack was supposed to be quick; there wasn't supposed to be strategy. "We have to drive the wolves into the caverns at the base of the bluff. Many were killed in their war with the statues, but there are still more of them than there are of us. We cannot let them break our perimeter attack. If they get the chance to counter us from the back, then we'll be facing war on two fronts. Jarat," Ashton whispered to the spider at his side, "what can you see?"

"There is a wolf perched on the rock; it is crouched and carries an axe; its eyes glow."

"There is a wolf behind it, I believe. They would not leave a wolf alone; they use the cover of the rock. Mayhaps this wolf isn't alive—mayhaps it's a tactic. Yes. Jarat, is this wolf breathing? How does it hold its head? Does it blink?"

There was a moment of silence. Jimmy was tossing uncomfortably on the back of Jarat; he was breathing heavily.

"It doesn't blink. I cannot tell if it is breathing."

"You see. A diversion. Wolves use them as well. Probably a casualty of war. We shoot the dead wolf and they verify our positions—no, we must leave that wolf—but, but we can use it; we *must* draw the scouts from the rocks."

Shavin pulled his bow and arrow out. "That is our job. Hunters are stealth. The spiders will counter the wolves from the eastern edge of the Towers." He turned his head and spoke to the other Hunters. They all pulled their bows in unison; the sound was a quick snap and wisp, like a branch breaking and a quick swish through air.

The spiders began moving in a long arch to the north; they were merely shadows leaving a plume of dust.

"Jarat, you stay here. Keep Jimmy safe."

"No, I have to get Cole, Ashton, I have to."

"Jimmy, we will—we *have* to make sure everything is safe and clear before you can come."

"What? But you told me..." There was a sign of hope in the boy's voice, a sign of hope he was sure would get crushed.

"Jimmy, there is an oppressive stronghold in the Inlands—"

"I can't believe this, you promised me—"

"Keep your voice down Jimmy."

"Fine, go then. GO," Jimmy said in a louder call.

"You'll stay here?"

Jimmy patted the top of Jarat. "Yeah." He said this with uncertainty.

Ashton nodded. "I *will* be back. With Cole. I promise." Ashton turned and Jilay trotted towards the Hunters.

"We must draw the scouts out," Ashton said.

2

Jimmy watched Ashton ride toward the dark ruins. He tapped the giant spider. "Jarat, we have to go there. I know where Cole is. I can get him. I *have* to get him."

"But Ashton told us to stay."

Jimmy jumped off Jarat's back. He began walking towards the Sordid ruins.

"Jimmy, you can't just go there alone. You heard Ashton. The wolves are prepared for us."

"I don't care," Jimmy said. He started jogging. "I know those guys won't get my brother. I could tell from Ashton's voice. They'll just leave the both of us stranded out here, and you never know, by morning some other monsters will come out of their desert burrows to feed on us. If I'm gonna take a chance, then I'll take one finding my brother."

"Hold on," Jarat the Spider said.

"What now?"

"Get on my back, we'll follow the spiders arch and meet them on the eastern edge of Wolf Country."

3

The wolf was hunched forward on the ledge, its head propped on its chest plate. Ashton could see the wolf's eyes glowing a pale white. Jarat was right; it wasn't blinking.

"The shadows play tricks," Ashton said as he climbed off his horse. "The wolf's axe will replay any light off the rocks, the shadows will dance and create a movement the other wolves hope we'll try and shoot. It is all very strategic." Ashton bent down and rubbed his hand along the dusty ground. He stopped when he found a fistful of shrubbery. He pulled the lifeless plants from the cracked ground. He found more and began piling them; the plants felt like old snakeskin in his hand, falling apart at the slightest touch.

Ashton removed an arrow from his quiver, looked at it a moment and then broke it in half.

"What are you doing?" Kerr the Hunter asked, mortified the masked stray would destroy a weapon but fifty yards from the enemy.

Ashton, sensing the hostility in Kerr's voice, smiled; he realized just how out of touch these "next-of-line-Hunters" were. The bloodline really was in regeneration. David would have known; he would have come up with the idea. Ashton began rubbing both ends of the snapped arrow together over the shrubbery; it was dry enough, he hoped, for even the slightest spark to catch.

"Fire," Shavin said. He must have realized the overall plan. "Hurry, gather around the shrubbery, there's no need alerting the wolves of our presence."

Hunters had jumped from their horses and gathered around Ashton. Some shielded their arms over the shrubbery.

"Shavin," Ashton said over his shoulder. "I want you to set up a team of six sharp-shooters. Send two farther east, toward the valley. Send another two to the base of the broken boulder, and send the last around back; I want them to counter stragglers. There are wolves who will flee back through the rock to warn Grak. I want them armed and ready to shoot exactly on my command; the two at the base of the rock, you will stifle the fire after I start it."

Shavin nodded and sent his team of six—Mino and Zak ran towards the valley; Kerr and Viakin ran to the base of the rocks; and Asron and Sid took towards the southern edge of the ruins, where there was a crude path cut into the backside of the rock. Mino and Zak held their bows and cinched arrows in the weapons, watching the vague outline of the hunched wolf with the glaring white eyes.

"What do you suppose the masked one will do?" Mino asked, breathing heavily; he was afraid because he had heard the stories of the wolves, of the past. Tonight, he realized, he too would be involved in the shaping of humanity. Whether or not he survived was his concern.

"Hopefully give us light," Zak said, "for I cannot see anything in the shadows."

Ashton saw a spark, and the shrubbery began smoking. He just had to keep rubbing the arrows; his palms were sweating, but something inside drove him, motivated him—he was the source from which revenge blossomed. He was sweating, and his pulse was racing—he was anxious. He had waited a long time to finally face Grak again, to face the wolves with the Hunters as his father had done before him.

The shrubs finally caught, and there were dry snaps as the twigs exploded; the waft of smoke devoured Ashton's face, pulling him from his thoughts. He quickly grabbed another arrow and lit its end in the fire. Ashton stood up, removing the bow from his quiver as he stamped out the fire on the ground.

"Move," he said to the gathered Hunters. "Shavin, this is my command."

Ashton shot the fire arrow into the wolf hunched on the rock-ledge; the alcove lit up a fierce orange glow and the shadows disappeared into the rock. Two wolves jumped from the fissures, necklaces of bone rattling on their chests, and before they could howl, Mino and Zak put arrows through their skulls. One wolf toppled forward and slid down the rock, falling nastily to the ground twenty feet below, and the other leaned into the burning wolf on the ledge.

Ashton ran forward, taking out another arrow.

Another wolf came from the alcove, and turned to run through the backside of the rock, just as Ashton had assumed. Asron had been on the path, and shot the wolf through the eye.

"Put out the fire," Ashton said. "It is an alarm as much as any howl."

Kerr, who had been climbing the steep rock face, lost his hold on a lip jutting from the wall and fell. Viakin took to the path cut into the rock. "We must put out the fire," he hurriedly said to Asron and Sid.

Ashton ran toward Kerr and used his shoulders as a lift; the Hunter had been bent forward, and Ashton leapt off his back onto the rock wall. He grabbed onto a lip of rock and climbed up the ledge, meeting Asron, Sid and Viakin at the two burning bodies.

"We must push them over the side," Ashton said, conscious the light must have been seen over the rocks. All three Hunters sat down and kicked out; they had to push from the top and try to disentangle the two wolves. Both wolves teetered for a moment.

"Kick again," Ashton said. He could feel the flames ripping his legs.

They lunged out again, and the wolves toppled over the ledge. The side of the rock face ignited a reddish glow that showed creatures with burning eyes in the darkness of each fissure.

Ashton breathed out heavily. "For now," he said slowly, "we use the darkness as cover. If there are any more wolves in the ruins, we counter them from the back; we must preserve our arrows. We fight this war from a distance; there is no need countering an enemy face to face—our numbers are low, but if we present a threat from the front, the spiders can surprise the wolves from the back; it is our duty to divert attention until our quivers empty."

Shavin walked beside Ashton and smiled. "You surely have much of your father in you," he said.

"But I will not die in this war," Ashton said.

The Hunters clambered over the ruins until the torch light of Wolf Country flickered into view.

4

The wolves had bound ropes around boulders and were trying to pull the massive rocks off fallen tents. Ashton wondered what had happened. He realized much of the ruins had collapsed onto the mountain pass below.

"What are they doing?" Somebody asked from the shadows.

Ashton knew what they were doing, and he hoped none of the rocks would shift an inch. The wolves were trying to save their mothers; their race depended entirely on the existence of the bloated women, who after years and years of pregnancy, developed the lazy insistence to lie on their backs and grow bellies that engulfed their entire bodies. He had seen one once. The She-wolf had left the tent, teetering on tiny legs that could barely hold her huge body; she was massive, much like the Queen spider, only her sense of duty seemed established when she had seen the sun—she squelched in absolute hate and retreated back into the tent, where she would remain impregnated. The She-wolves were used to the darkness of the mountains, but these ruins were unsafe; the wolves were forced to build a camp on the grounds that would become Wolf Country, at the foot of the Towers. The wolves were forced to build large tents over the women; the women were forced to give birth. It was Grak's cycle, his motivation of leadership, his continuance of a disgusting species.

Watching them struggle to get the boulders off the tents proved one thing to Ashton: that Grak was afraid, and perhaps for the first time in his wretched life, he realized he must take caution if the wolves were to survive.

"They are weary," Ashton said. He couldn't see the spiders beyond the Towers, but he knew they must be there, waiting. Their patience, he noticed, existed only because they wanted to win this war; their alliance rested on a balance of initiatives. The spiders were sure the Hunters would begin this war; they also knew that by forcing the wolves to confront battle at the foot of the ruins, their attack from the back would force the wolves into the caverns.

There were broken statues littering the grounds, reflecting torchlight like forgotten remnants.

Ashton stood atop his stoop on the crest of rock and unsheathed his bow and arrow. "There are hundreds of them down there," he said, twisting the arrow in his hand. "There aren't enough arrows to slaughter them all. We must shoot the front line. I want them to know they are being attacked from the ruins." The Hunters stood and took out their own arrows; they all stood on a low peak of the ruins, which sloped toward a cleft which further led to the mountain pass, shaped like a bowl over Wolf Country. "Mercy Mystic," Ashton said. "For our fathers; for the Inlands—for the blood of the Hunters."

Ashton heard down the line the Hunters mutter, "Mercy Mystic," many in voices that wavered. He understood his command was all that kept this group together. Each man stood with his own demons, his own fears; each man stood with his own realization that the reality of war had finally evolved, and that they were involved; the future ultimately rested on their decisions. One Hunter felt vomit surge into his mouth. He swallowed it, never allowing the bile to pass his throat again; another Hunter remembered how his father had died with an arrow through his chest, and felt, for a slight second, the same burn through his tunic, a familiar burn that must have been his father warning him. He would let a single tear fall down his cheek when he released his first arrow. Many remained calm. Shavin had fought with David in the last war; he knew and understood fear. He knew the power of the wolves.

Many remained calm because they desired revenge. ashton licked the hide strung over his face, tasted the salty grain, tasted his breath, and he let fly the first arrow; it flew with a high ark and landed in the chest of a wolf two hundred and fifty yards away, toppling the bleeding beast into another wolf, who turned and saw the arrow sticking from the breastplate. This wolf let out a tremendous howl.

"ATTACK! AZEENI MOROJA!"

"We must move closer," Ashton said, pulling out another arrow. He climbed down a couple steps, slipping on loose rubble. The Hunters followed.

The collective howl from the grounds rose and the torchlight wavered as if in unison.

Ashton shot another arrow; this time he hit a wolf pulling rope through the side of its skull, causing it to topple forward. The rope loosened, and the other wolf pulling the boulder ultimately snapped the rope as it binded on the other side of the stone.

And fire shot into the air like streaming tales of flapping orange and yellow. The mountain pass exploded with flickering light. The wolves were shooting fire-arrows at the ruins; they were looking for the invaders masked by shadow. Ashton pulled another arrow and shot a wolf through the eye, splitting its skull as splinters of wood exploded from its bushy scalp.

Shavin flipped down the sloped ruins, avoiding a fire-arrow, which wedged deeply into a fissure, igniting a nest in the darkness which shriveled as the flames consumed it. Shavin shot a wolf lighting its arrow in a torch, but his precision had been off; his aim had sent the arrow into the wolf's leg, but the wolf panicked, stupidly shifting its torso and knocking the torch forward. The torch knocked into another wolf with a bow, setting its fur on fire, and this wolf ran forward howling in utter pain, collapsing into the side of a tent, which too burst in flames—there was a frantic struggle below as wolves were sent to douse out the tent and preserve the shrieking She-wolf inside. Hunters shot the wolves sent to the springs for water.

"Bless you Mystic," Shavin said, when he realized his mistake had been ratified.

Kerr the Hunter, who had six arrows left in his quiver, rolled down the slope of the ruins, landing uncomfortably on the mountain pass. He pulled two arrows and crossed them in his bow; he shot in a high arch, and the arrow pointing downwards punctured a wolf's chest, while the other arrow shot in an ark that landed in the top of a wolf's cranium, splitting its helmet in two.

The wolves rushed the mountain pass.

"Hurry, they come," Ashton yelled, "hit the front line and cause a blockade. Knock them back down the slope."

The Hunters turned their aim from the ground to the foot of the pass. Wolves drove up the pass, those in front carrying curved shields made of iron.

"Shoot in an arch."

Kerr shot two more arrows, both hitting wolves in the middle of the trampling herd. and there was a terrible exploding sound from the herd. Ashton realized it sounded similar to the explosion heard over the ruins while he and Jimmy traveled to the Leeg. It was awkward because the sharp clap could be heard over battle. Ashton had never heard such a sound in war.

"KERR!" Shavin yelled. He rushed to the Hunter who was lying on the pass, a pool of blood forming under his body. Shavin rested his hand under Kerr's head and looked into his eyes. "What is it, there is no arrow?"

Kerr muttered and blood spewed from his mouth.

Ashton shot into the oncoming troops and met Shavin. "What is this?"

"There is no arrow...what could have done this?" Kerr went limp in Shavin's arms.

Ashton bent forward. He touched the wound on Kerr's front. "It is hot. Like his blood is boiling." Ashton looked towards the oncoming wolves. "Come. We have a score to settle."

Both Hunters turned to meet the wolves.

And the spiders attacked from the north.

5

Edwin Krollup had been off the pass when the Hunters attacked. He had crept along the base of the rock wall down the sloped path, listening to the wolves, feeling inside him the urge to sit, to lay face down and let life slip away, but there was also an odd magnetism he felt with the Towers. Each moment he felt his motivation slip, there seemed a pull from the rock formations, and he picked up his dragging feet and stepped forward with a renewed exuberance.

In the moonlight Edwin looked like a phantom, a moving stone shaped like a man, but colored in the pallid strokes of the moon's glow; he was hidden, and though he hadn't thought so at the moment, the realization that being covered in dust saved his life.

He existed in a different way now, that much was obvious. Ever since the stone fell from his grip, it seemed something else escaped also, something not as broad as his sanity, but something that contained within itself the capacity to reason—the Edwin Krollup masked by dust and darkness wasn't the same Edwin Krollup that forced the wolves down the mines. The Edwin Krollup walking in utter delirium (but finding through some sheer will power and magnetism a safe path to the Towers) was a man stripped of thirty years. The stone had been his personality, and now he had a part of him taken away. He saw in the spindly creature from the stone a chance for his own saving grace; his chance to rescue his severed personality, but reality had exacted its toll, and perhaps Krollup now realized the harsh impositions of reality. He had been, for so long, blinded by greed and power—but had this all been because of the stone?

The stone had stolen much from him. Edwin realized this when he first touched it, when he was lost in the mines as a child and wished he could find his way home only to be inexplicably transported to the boarded mouth of the mine. He had let the stone take hold of him, but there was still a part in him, a part which issued some constraint. Edwin Krollup's restraint, though, had a tougher time scratching the surface; rather than allowing himself to ultimately collapse under the harsh scrutiny of his conscience, Edwin permitted a sense of guilt to send him to a psychologist. Edwin's father died. His truck was found under a pile of rubble; the man was drunk, but Edwin still felt sorrow, pity, and found a strong sense of responsibility bound to the stone around his neck. Perhaps something inside him had been calling out, something that realized his insides were gradually draining—without the stone to keep him physically strong, Edwin would have realized just what the thing inside the stone had taken from him.

"I couldn't have killed my father," he said weakly, struggling to move forward. "I would have known better. Wouldn't I?" He didn't know. He didn't know anything anymore.

Edwin clutched his side. His breathing had slowed, and he found it harder to swallow air. "Why am I thinking of this, why am I having these thoughts? Shut up."

You touched the necklace, you wished your father would die, and you wished his death was by your hands—you murderer.

"No," he said, silently, calculating the distance from the Towers, listening to the sharp sound of whizzing arrows, falling wolves. "Why are you saying this? Leave me alone!"

You've locked me out for far too long Edwin—the doors in your corridor may fit your key, but I've found a way to slip through the keyhole. What will you do now that you've lost that precious stone? What will you dream? How will you confront your fears? You are a new man; you are born again, a different ghost in the same pitiful machine.

Edwin clasped his hands over his ears; he felt like screaming.

And he saw them.

They moved in a gigantic pack, like herding bulls, trampling the ground with their many legs. Had he not stopped to close his ears, to try and stifle the painstaking voice in his head, he would have been pulverized; he stood merely ten feet from the closest parading spider, feeling the brisk breeze pass, the stench of hundreds of years, of toxic rot, of putrid breath, and the low chittering that would find, in time, the ability to penetrate his nightmares.

"Oh good lord," he said slack-jawed. He couldn't remember ever saying anything remotely religious before, but he found in the moment an insistent belief in anything, anything with the power to stop all this, to stomp on every one of the giant beasts before any of them touched him. He turned and watched. He watched the wolves find, to their surprise, that their excursion to the Leeg hadn't been entirely forgotten.

The spiders clashed with the wolves in such a fashion that to Edwin, at least, reminded him of those old movies that tried to portray men fighting radiated mutants. He saw spiders jumping over others to land on wolves who stuck their swords through the falling spiders' bellies, releasing a stream of yellow chunks that ultimately left the wolves a pile of bones under the spiders' carcasses.

The chittering grew louder.

"Forward," the wolves called out in wavering voices.

Edwin turned and moved toward the Towers; his stomach was churning. The smell grew exponentially worse.

He would reach the tunnels minutes later, sweating, apprehensive about entering, but certain it was better inside than out.

6

Jarat rushed towards the eastern edge of the Towers, following the spiders' divots in the dried ground; their markings led an arch into north Wolf Country, and Jarat scurried as fast as he could. His legs looked like obscured wheels, traveling back and forth, and Jimmy found he could barely hold on. His hair stuck straight back, and when Jarat did finally stop, Jimmy realized his fingers were numb from holding on so tightly to greasy clumps of the spider's mane.

The Queen's ensemble waited at the base of the Towers, dwarfed by the massive edifice, a line of hunched backs which steadily rose and glowed a fine outline of the moon.

"What are they waiting for?" Jimmy asked, listening intently to the subtle chittering, which was more like a vibration than an actual sound. Like the hum of a generator.

"There is no plan," Jarat said, "but they know when the time is right; they know the Hunters will begin the war."

Jimmy patted Jarat's back comfortingly, brushing his palm over sticky gel which hours ago would have proven disgusting, but became to Jimmy an overwhelming sense of familiarity. "Are you upset you have to babysit me?"

"We are all assigned our duties, Jimmy. We all play our parts."

Jimmy smiled; it was a good answer. He had felt guilty ever since the Queen's ensemble had convened next to the Towers; he sensed in Jarat a subtle hostility that suggested the spider would rather fight along side his kind than keep stead of a child.

Jimmy craned his neck, trying to see more than just flickering light and shadows. "What do you think will happen?"

Before Jarat could speak. Before Jimmy was able to even blink, the spiders rushed forward; it was awkward really. At first Jimmy believed this part of the world had been collectively sucked into a giant vacuum—the spiders exploded into a mad dash that seemingly brought the air with them. Jimmy felt like he was struggling for breath, but that had just been surprise—that had been utter shock. The spiders jumped forward, some leaping over others, until the sight became partially hidden by the dexterous hands of night, which chose what one could see, and what one couldn't.

Jarat inched forward.

"You can go with them. I know you guys probably have honor and all, just like humans. I'll be okay."

Jarat shook his head. "No it's not that, I saw a man, a man that looked like a ghost."

"I can't see any man," Jimmy said, looking either way.

"Oh, he is there, I assure you, crouched among the shadows; he is paranoid. He has gone to the tunnels in the rock."

"The tunnels," Jimmy said, remembering the image he had seen in the Sandglass. Cole was forced into tunnels, into tunnels carved into a base of rock that looked exactly like the edifice before them. "Go to the tunnels, that's where my brother is." Jimmy felt certain he would find Cole now; he had made it this far. He had survived the darkness of the mines; he had survived the Leeg woods, and now he was going to chance, *no*, to pursue heroism amidst a war.

The base of the Tower was very wide, and sloped oddly into the ground, but didn't seem connected in any way to the parched earth; rather, it seemed to have been placed on top of the ground like a hat. The tunnels lined the bottom of the base like random freckles on a person's leathery neck.

"Can you still see the man, the ghost?" Jimmy asked.

"No."

"Did he go into a tunnel?"

"I don't know."

"You have to know...that ghost was leading us here...was trying to bring us to the tunnels because it knew *I* knew Cole was forced into them. Don't you understand, that ghost must have been like a guide or something...some kind of magnet—" There was a hint of annoyance in Jimmy's voice—not annoyance with Jarat, but with himself, because he believed in the slight chance that somebody above, God, or perhaps his mother (he hoped) sent the image of a man to lead him to his brother.

"It wasn't a ghost," Jarat finally said. "We are in treacherous grounds Jimmy, and it is my duty to protect you. We must leave to safer grounds."

"What? No, you can't just turn around. I have to get my brother—I came to this stupid place to get my brother, and I saw him myself in the wizard's glass, I saw him crawl into one of these tunnels."

"Yes, but which one?"

Jimmy stopped. He hadn't realized just how many tunnels there were, how many fissures there were in the rock that resembled tunnels; he didn't want to be forced to pick and choose. He was certain whatever he'd find inside those tunnels was sure to surprise him, despite his blossoming familiarity with the existence of the Inlands. He was sure that each tunnel led to a corresponding location, holding its own peculiar obstacles, and that he had only a small chance of guessing which one Cole crawled through. He tried to remember the Sandglass—the way they walked from the tent in a slow trot to the Tower—the way he felt when he saw Cole, and how he realized it was his intentions that drove *his* brother to this place—the way the old man stared into the tunnels with a sense of longing. The old man!

"What is that, on the ground over there?" Jimmy asked.

Jarat, whose eyes were accustomed to seeing in the dark, found a stick lying at the base of a tunnel. "Nothing but a branch."

"A cane! The old man was carrying a cane—that's the tunnel."

7

"Shoot into the ruins," Ufrak the wolf yelled out over the howls. The wolf had removed a gnarled bow and lit an arrow on fire, shooting it atop the bluff so that the rock exploded in flickering reds.

The She-wolves yelped from the tents. Arrows whizzed into the wolf packs from the crumbled mountains; the wolves were exhausted.

"We fight phantoms of the night," Exrak the wolf said, holding to a rope listlessly as he blankly watched the starry night throw arrows at the herds. And Exrak, whose hearing had always been exceptional, like most wolves, felt a slight burn on his shoulder. But he couldn't fully blame his hearing for the mistake—these were testing times, and the wolves realized that, and during testing times, one's emotions can be easily swayed. Exrak wasn't fond of excuses, nor was he apt to using them, but blame his hearing he did. He felt his shoulder burn, right through the leather straps distended from his breastplate, and the wolf turned to meet many eyes. He wouldn't have time to question his hearing, but he could seemingly use his senility (as he called it) to excuse his mistake due to poor hearing; he was an old wolf, had seen the mountains crumble all those years ago, but to think he would die this way seemed preposterous.

His shoulder burned because a drop of poison had fizzled entirely through his shoulder pad, and before he could lament, or even consider fighting, he felt his entire head immerse into a moist pool, where gel seemed to slide through his own fur, melting his flesh as he moved along.

"SPIDERS!" The wolves howled.

And the spiders pounced from the darkness.

The wolves had two fronts to defend.

The spiders hadn't fought in many wars; in fact, their kind had always been fond of segregation, where they existed harmoniously amongst themselves. Spider City, built atop hundreds of feet of trees, was a testament to this bordered existence. To fight in war, the spiders supposed, was an act they'd participate in if these borders were ever disrupted. The wolves disturbed their sanctity when they entered the Leeg to steal the egg sac—war had been pending ever since, but the spiders knew the wolves were a formidable opponent; it wasn't a matter of cowardice, but a matter of preservation that stayed the spiders in the Leeg instead of following the enemy out of the woods. The Queen, like Grak, insisted the meaning of a powerful species came from its duration in the world. The spiders had survived the world of giants, and they too would, the Queen had said, survive the world of wolves. It was the initiative of a wizard that finally drove the Queen to a certain understanding—that by speculating outcomes, one is only surveying fifty percent of chance. Speculating war would only prove the others victory over you—to go to war, to defend your kind, would prove to the wolves, prove *and* show, the mighty existence of a kind whose mark on the world wasn't merely coincidence; the spiders were as much a part of the gears beneath the world as men, as wolves—but by purely speculating outcomes one was already claiming defeat.

The Queen had nodded in understanding.

The Queen's army lusted blood, and they drove to Wolf Country thirsty.

When Exfrak slipped down the moist gullet of Inna the Spider, the wolves realized at this point the spiders' mark on the world.

"Switch fronts," Lervak the wolf called, and he turned, carrying his large axe in claws that trembled. There were hundreds of spiders advancing from the darkness. A spider had jumped from the middle of the swarming pack, its legs perched at its side—Lervak drove his axe into the spider's belly and felt its tremendous weight fall on him, knocking his wiry frame to the ground where he would literally melt, stewing in the spider's innards.

The spiders and wolves collided.

Spiders wrapped themselves around wolves as they mercilessly drove their swords upwards.

8

Ashton and Shavin both turned to meet the oncoming wolves trampling up the pass.

Ashton unsheathed his sword. "I have dreamt this on many nights," he said under his breath.

"How does it turn out?" Shavin asked, removing his own sword; his hands were trembling, but he was still composed. Like Ashton, he was conducted by feelings of vengeance.

"I succeed where my father didn't."

And Ashton jumped forward; he rolled on the ground and swiped his sword through three wolves' ankles, wolves who had slammed their own swords into the ground behind Ashton. They fell forward in a bloody heap and Ashton turned, springing from the ground like a cat and sliding his blade through each of their necks, cuffing the blade on bone; he retreated to the ruins where he would use the darkness.

Shavin, whose agility had been deteriorating with age, found his attack less acrobatic, but he countered the wolves with equal delight, and with equal outcome. He stood and waited, watching Ashton rush forward, moving in ways he hadn't seen in many years—David had moved that way, he thought, but he found he couldn't ponder on the past. Shavin drove his sword into the midsection of a wolf, parried another wolf's blow and took its head off with one swipe.

"HUNTERS!" the wolves howled, and the wolves below answered. They realized this was a preconceived battle, and understood their own mistake, advancing up the pass when the spiders attacked from the north. "VILE HUNTERS!"

Asron shot three wolves with arrows, used sliding rubble to surf down the slope and unsheathed his curved blade, using his momentum to drive his sword into a line of wolves waiting for him, their glowing eyes hungry. "It is our time, wolves," he said.

Ashton jumped from a piece of crumbled sandstone, and flipped over a wolf, feeling the air separate beneath him as a sword passed. He landed behind a wolf far too slow to turn, and he stabbed it in the back, kicking it over as he pulled his sword from the wolf's spine. Ashton met Shavin, whose sword was stained a grimy black, dripping with gore. "There are too many of them," Shavin said, breathing deeply, wiping sweat from his dirty brow.

"I can see hesitation in their eyes though," Ashton said, breathing deeply. "They realize their mistake, sending an army up the pass when the real threat is below. Watch them; they jump down the bluff to counter the spiders. It is our time, Shavin. Our time!"

"They jump down the bluff, Ashton, because they are being told to; it is command I hear in the howls. Grak is on the pass with us."

Ashton smiled, his mask wrinkling. "Then we must silence their decision-maker." Ashton rushed forward, uttering a high pitched scream. He removed an arrow from his quiver and jumped, carrying his sword in one hand, and a polished arrow in the other. Shavin watched Ashton drive the arrow through the skull of one wolf as his sword sliced the head off another.

"David never had a son," Shavin muttered under his breath, watching in astonishment the agility of Ashton, of this masked Hunter. Telling himself reminded him...no, it *validated* the truth, for Shavin had fought with David. David would have told him he had a son. Secrets were against the Code of the Hunter. Deception was against the code. David wouldn't have ignored the codes. He had written most of them.

David had a daughter.

9

When the She-wolves emerged from the tents it looked like the spiders had at least driven the wolves towards the caverns; it would have proven quite an easy battle from that point because the wolves would have been pinned, but the spiders had left their own backs unguarded. There were tents scattered about Wolf Country; these tents harnessed the sunlight, and bathed the women in darkness; they were nurseries, where young wolves fed until they were fit to enter the world of war. These tents were ignored by the spiders.

It was a high-uttered screech that seemed the most alarming; it laid the first doubts to the spiders' line of attack. Just as they had proven war on both fronts for the wolves, it seemed the wolves had countered with the same threat. The spiders hesitated between two options: either they continued with the planned attack and drive the wolves into the caverns, or they separated and forced two battles on the ground, allowing the wolves a chance to drive forward, and ultimately join with the She-wolves.

The spiders generally looked to the Queen for command, but they found their decisions were now left to a collective source; it was agreed upon, in a high chittering that swirled in the dense air of war, that the spiders would split and meet their new opponents. The spiders turned and saw, to their dismay, that the wolves behind them were twice the size of the wolves squirming to find entrance in caverns to regroup.

A She-wolf, who stood on two hind legs that seemed pushed into the ground under her tremendous weight, picked a spider up in claws that curled two feet from her deformed fingers, and crushed its abdomen into a bag spewing ropy mucus to the ground in clumps.

The spiders would attack the She-wolves with reservations they had previously denied—this war would not be won easily.

10

Sid the Hunter jabbed his sword at a wolf's gut but missed, and Krak the Wolf used the opportunity to finally end the match, grabbing the Hunter in his claw and tossing him against the jagged stone like a sack of grain.

The Hunters were all falling in the same fashion—they were exhausted, and saw in the swarming packs of wolves a tireless machine that would proceed until each of them were broken and scattered among the ground.

"Force them to the grounds, to the spiders," Asron yelled, who himself had been injured. He had been driven to combat a wolf brandishing an axe, and before he could sever the monster's head, he felt the tip of the axe slash through his tunic and puncture his right arm; he clutched his arm to his side, barely clinging to his sword. The Hunters heard the She-wolves howl.

"This war will end soon; we will all meet our father's again, for their failure is ours," one Hunter spoke, holding his side where an arrow jutted from between his ribs.

"Mercy Mystic," another said, drawing the slope down his front. A moment later he would fall with a sword in his chest; he would fall still finishing the slope of Mystic with his finger.

11

It was dark. Fire flickered nearby, sending shadows against an outcrop of rock. Ashton used the shadows to draw the wolves; he knew that by instinct the Yilaks were able to see at night, but like humans, their vision had been so influenced by the light of day torches became a staple of Wolf Country when the sun set. He used the shadow not for cover, but to create another self, a growth from his limbs that moved along the slopes of stone like a dark phantom—the shadows of the flickering flames drew the wolves much as the fire had been used on the ledge at the northern valley; it provoked an attack that could verify positions. In the darkness Ashton judged by sound. By reflections.

He heard the sharp clang of metal against rock, the flap of hair as the night breeze tousled fur; the sound of joints creaking, teeth snapping. Sounds became the enemy, the target, and Ashton, who had his father's senses, used his better judgment to establish which sounds came from the wolves, and which sounds didn't. The Hunters had been fighting all around him. The spiders fought on the ground. Every noise had been intermingled. Ashton had learned to drown some noises out while emphasizing others; he did this by imagining. He saw in his head three Hunters to his right fighting; he listened closely for their footsteps.

Ashton held his sword against his chest, felt the cool blade touch his skin. He made sure neither the fire nor the moon could find any reflection on his blade; this was how he saw his targets—the wolves held their swords against the black sky, leaving a glistening sparkle along their edges which shone like diamonds. The moon had become, to Ashton at least, an ally.

This war wouldn't, *couldn't* be won easily, Ashton knew this, but he also understood the world's grievances; this war had to be fought. For years the Inlands had decayed. The wolves had stolen mankind's settlement. Ashton knew the war had been pending. Tonight, as he stood against the rock face, he realized it was his time, the Hunters time, to take back what had been lost.

He saw in the shadows that familiar sheen, the glisten on the edge of the sword; he heard fur flapping in the wind; he heard the guttural growl that for so many years had ground him with a longing to finally silence it. There were three wolves, he could tell that much. One was carrying a sword and an axe, an axe that was dripping blood. He heard the splat against the hard ground.

Ashton jumped out from his cover against the rock face. He didn't utter a single noise. He jumped with his sword forward like a spear, catching the first wolf in the side, piercing his leather chest plate with a long rip and crack as the Yilak's ribs shattered. The wolf howled, Ashton pulled his sword from its flesh and quickly cut its head off, silencing the shriek as its mouth had been permanently shut.

Ashton stabbed the wolf carrying the axe, and kicked its body into the third wolf causing a chain reaction that would send both Yilaks into a violent roll down the mountain slope—both wolves repeatedly toppling over the rogue axe until neither were whole when they hit the ground.

"The horses," Ashton called out, grabbing his bow. "Call the horses to the northern valley; we must drive the herd to the ground. We won't last much longer hand to hand." Quicker than the blink of an eye, Ashton grabbed an arrow from his quiver and nocked it in his bow.

Shavin whistled. It was a tired whistle, but it was loud, and it had a peculiar vibrato which seemingly carried throughout the ruins. He hoped it would reach the other side of the ruined edifice; he hoped the horses would hear it.

"For the line of the Hunters. And for the blood of your fathers. It is death or victory. Never loss. Never retreat," Ashton called out. It was an old idiom, one he had heard his father shout at boys when fatigue set. When Ashton spoke these words, hope rekindled in the eyes of the Hunters. Ian the Hunter, who had been struggling to stand up, looked at the moon for a moment, clutching his stomach to stop the blood from gushing onto his belt—he saw in the moon an image that urged he stand and fight till his last ounce of strength drained from his already weakening body. This war wasn't about him; it wasn't even about the Hunters. This war was about progression, was about the future. This war was about change. And when Ian stood up on two shaky legs that wanted to send him back to the ground, he felt not pain but happiness. Because of him, of the Hunters, the world was going to be safe again.

Ashton felt a kind of warmth cover his body. His father had been a great man, a great leader. "But you took him from me," Ashton said, looking at the wolves, the slight glare of their eyes reflecting the moonlight. Ashton ran his forefinger down the shaft of his arrow, plucked his bow—he felt an insatiable urge growing inside him to finally end this. He was no longer hiding in the ruins, hiding in the shadows spreading bird droppings over his body to cover the scent of man; he was no longer pulling stray wolves aside to slaughter them, hoping he might face Grak again. Tonight he was leading his father's men in battle. Tonight the war would end.

Ashton emerged from the shadows, carrying his bow firmly planted against his right shoulder.

And he heard a sharp explosion.

Ashton dropped his bow and fell to the ground.

12

It felt like somebody had crushed the bones in his left arm, and when he fell on top of his bow, feeling the sanded wood snap under his weight, he realized how disgusting the wound smelt. Like a rotten *roamer*, some might say, but Ashton thought it was different—not of this world, actually.

It wasn't exactly painful, but it was different. It burned. What had happened? The sound was like a sharp clap. Ashton felt his arm. His blood certainly felt warm, like it had on Kerr. He tried to rotate his shoulder. He could, but it hurt.

And he smelt rancid meat. He knew right away what was happening, and even though he grabbed his sword, it wasn't quick enough. Something roughly grabbed his arm and pulled him to his feet with ease. His wound exploded, and Ashton bit his lip. "Drop your sword." A guttural whisper in his ear, muttered with the common lisp of a wolf with torn lips.

Ashton muttered to himself; he had never expected to die this way, in the clutches of a wolf. His shoulder had been torn open, but his other arm was good, and it held a sword.

He did drop the sword, but caught the hilt as the blade spiraled downward; he caught the hilt and rotated his wrist so that the blade pivoted upwards and caught the wolf's inner thigh. The wolf uttered a terrified screech and Ashton jumped away, pulling the sword with him, feeling blood splatter his arm—when there was another explosion. The wolf standing in front of Ashton fell forward.

Grak stood on the pass behind the wolf's body, and in the dim light of the moon accompanied only by flickering fire arrows in the crevasses, Ashton could see in the Yilak's claws a shiny object with smoke billowing from its end.

"This one is mine," Grak said with horrible sincerity.

Ashton felt a terrible urge to let go, to drive forwards without any worry of consequence.

"I met your father under the same circumstances. He believed he could lead an army of men into my land and survive. You brought spiders, but your mistake was believing they might make a difference. Our wives, our mothers ate spiders in the mountains years ago." Grak stepped forward, crunching the ground, his skulls rattling on his chest. "You want to know why I didn't kill you when we first met, masked one? Because I realized it would come to this. I would rather slaughter you in front of your pitiful army of Hunters, than hold your dead body like a trophy before those who want to see you dead."

Ashton gritted his teeth. They had met once before, but Ashton had been younger then, stupider; he had been a youngun solely driven by revenge, without belief in consequence. Life had been revenge. He had attacked Grak on a path five miles from Wolf Country, killing the wolves surrounding the General. The wolves had just been in Cassica, had just disemboweled a landholder who wouldn't oblige with their wishes. Ashton had watched the entire event unfold; he had watched the poor farmer cower against his doorjamb as the wolves forced their way in; he had watched as the farmer ushered his wife and children into a trapdoor; he had watched the farmer cry with the realization that his stubbornness, his strong will meant his life. Ashton had watched the wolves slaughter this poor man, because this poor man, who held some basic powers in the community council, wouldn't support the Yilaks' annexation of the northern territories. Ashton waited. He followed the wolves, some on all fours, others on their hind legs. He watched them take a horse from an enclosed field, and strip its meat from its bones. Ashton had been, then at least, naïve enough to believe that if he slaughtered Grak he could bring his father back. He hid in the bushes and shot the surrounding wolves with arrows, finding, coincidentally, that he had emptied his quiver before he could kill Grak. He jumped from the bushes, his exposed eye glinting a remarkable hate—"*I am David the Hunter's son. I am the line of the Hunter!*" He rushed forward, his sword drawn.

And they fought. Briefly.

For the battle was never finished. It had rained on them, sheets of glaze between the two that masked one from the other. They had become invisible. And neither shed blood. Ashton was forced to flee into the brush, swinging blindly against the torrent, finding cover beneath a tree and watching the world split in half when lightning struck. ashton was beginning to realize something—

You wouldn't have won then, Ashton thought to himself. *You wouldn't have won because you fought Grak believing only in vengeance—now the war is only part of change. Grak is the axis around which this morbid world rotates. Your father died trying to do the same thing; he tried to save the Inlands.* ashton spun the hilt of his sword, rotating his blade.

"This isn't about my father," Ashton said, and Grak scowled, hiding his left eye under a mass of brow. "This isn't about me or you; this is much bigger than the both of us."

"I couldn't have said it any better Hunter. This *is* bigger than us. There are other worlds out there—I have been to one, Hunter, and I have seen the advantages." Grak lifted the shiny object and pointed it at Ashton.

There was another explosion, and the end of the object flashed. Ashton flew backwards, landing on the ground with a muffled thump. His sword danced away from him, cutting divots in the ground as it bounced away. He didn't understand what happened, but his right leg burned.

Grak stood over Ashton, and before the Hunter could reach around back for an arrow, he was ruthlessly tugged to his feet, where he teetered under his weight, feeling an awkward pull in his thigh—he thought of what Granum had said, how fire would be controlled to create weapons, to create...what had the word been? Gunns, that was it. Grak held a gunn in his hand. There was a much bigger picture here. The mines weren't merely a connection between two worlds, but a sequence of evolution, a parasite—the mines had brought this exploding weapon into the Inlands. Granum had been right. War would be fought with fire, rather than sword and arrow. The end *would* be fire.

Ashton could feel his heart beating in his thigh; he could feel warm blood soaking his leg, filling his boot. He could feel Grak's moist snout touching his ear, wiping mucus along the side of his face. "You led the Hunters to their final defeat, son of David," Grak said. "HUNTERS! THE WAR IS DONE. THE WAR IS OVER. YOU HAVE ALL MARCHED TO YOUR DEATHS, FOR HERE I HOLD YOUR SAVIOR IN MY GRIPS, WITH THE VERY WEAPON THAT WILL REVOLUTIONIZE WAR!"

The Hunters saw Ashton in Grak's claws. It was useless. It was finally time to admit defeat.

The spiders were fighting a losing battle on the ground, facing two fronts, attacking She-wolves in droves only to be forced off by Yilaks.

The war halted at the sound of Grak's commanding voice. The country silenced. The world stopped.

Ashton thought about his father, about how he—the greatest warrior who had ever lived—felt when he realized he was defeated. "You will only make me a martyr, like you did my father," Ashton whispered. "I will become a legend, and Hunters in the future will scream my name in this war."

Ashton felt something cold prod his temple; he had at first believed it was Grak's claw, then realized it must have been the gunn. There was something startlingly terrifying about having it pressed against his face.

"Please, Grak Ulak, we are at your mercy. Our numbers have dwindled," Shavin said, stepping forward, carrying his sword flat on his palms, staining his flesh with gore. "If we lay down our swords, there is no need for more bloodshed."

No, don't do that, Ashton thought. He could feel Grak behind him, but he knew the wolf was contemplating something. The wolves would allow the idea of surrender to resonate, but as soon as the Hunters set down their blades, the wolves would finally end the war for good; the bloodline would be lost, drenching Wolf Country only to dry and crust as days passed. The Hunters would be forgotten.

And Ashton thought about Jimmy and his brother. The mines had collapsed, but Grak got what he wanted from the temporary connection between worlds; he was introduced to this magnificent little weapon, this weapon that exploded and contained within it a limitless power. His thigh hurt, and his shoulder hurt, but it was the inevitability of what came next that hurt the most—Ashton couldn't speak. His voice seemed closed shut, and the more he bled, the more he felt like slithering to the ground. Ashton was admitting defeat.

He was admitting defeat, and he couldn't even warn Shavin.

"You surrender, Hunter?" Grak asked, cocking his red eye at Shavin, who kneeled down, placing his sword on the ground.

The spiders chittered from the grounds below; there was a sense of anticipation building up. Everybody realized something was going to happen, but they didn't know what.

Ashton watched Shavin kneel down; he watched the Hunter, who had fought with his father, place his sword before him and stand, and he felt the coldness leave his temple.

Grak pulled the gunn away.

Ashton found the loop of twine in his palm, and he tried to pull it with the tip of his finger. His body didn't seem to want to obey. *Come on*, he thought, watching Shavin closely, feeling, or sensing Grak's arm raise by his head, holding that gunn, aiming it. There was a reason for everything, Ashton thought. *You built the spring on your armbands because a part of you must have known you would really need them.* His sword was on the ground ten feet ahead of him, collecting dust. He did need them, but if he couldn't pull the loop in his sleeve, he was sure Shavin would die. Ashton clenched his fists, and straightened his fingers along his palm, feeling the ridge, the slope of his thumb—he found the loop but he couldn't hook it. Come on…

Good…

Daggers shot from Ashton's sleeves and he swiped up with his left arm; there was a thick crunch, and Grak howled. Grak's hand and the gunn both fell to the ground with a meaty plop. Ashton reached back with his right arm and dug the blades into Grak's chest plate, shattering a skull in the process.

Grak howled again, and with his good arm, pushed the Hunter away from him. Ashton flew backwards, landing on his back. Dust ground into his bleeding thigh.

And the battle resumed.

Shavin picked up his sword. The spiders scurried after the wolves.

Ashton stood up.

Grak had been hunched forward, his shoulders sloped, the outline of his bramble crown a wiry frame in the dim glow of the moon. The stump where his hand had been spewed blood in globs, but Grak ignored it. He bent forward and picked the gunn up from the ground.

Ashton picked up his sword.

"My father called me his *Asha*. It was my nickname when I was a child. My father never called me by name, always *Asha*. I have lived for years, fighting for years, behind a mask, behind a lie. I believed I was my father's mistake, for in the code of the Hunter women are to be protected. David wanted a son. How could David the Hunter conceive a daughter? How could the Hunter's bloodline live through the veins of a woman? I have vowed to kill you, Grak, but I did so under the reasoning that I was a man, that I was *Ashton*—I neglected my true roots. The Hunter's bloodline travels through my bloodstream—I *am* a Hunter." Ashton reached up and tore the mask off *her* face. Her face was unlined spare a few wrinkles on her forehead, which was parched with dirt and sweat. Her eye, which had been covered, seemed to accentuate the beauty in the eye which had been exposed; together they had formed a beautiful symmetry. Her cropped hair sprung up where the mask lifted (hair she had cut with her sword, hair she had cut to look like a man, a rugged man) and her lips seemed plump, rosy. When Shavin saw Ashton's face, he would see David's eyes, but he would see David's wife in her lips, those full lips. "I am going to kill you Grak. I am going to end this now. Not as Ashton, but as Isabella, daughter of David the Hunter." She twirled the sword in her hand.

Grak laughed.

The Hunters had gathered around, astonished. They knew a lie existed behind that mask, but besides Shavin (who had the sinking suspicion), none realized this masked Hunter had any real ties with *the* David the Hunter; they all believed it was some delusion, it was some morbid type of validation to prove his...*her* mark on the world.Isabella rushed forward, still twirling her blade. Grak pointed the gunn and pulled the trigger with his hooked claw.

Nothing happened. Only a dry click.

Grak tried again and again, a sense of worry forming in his red eyes, awakening like some long lost memory. Isabella flipped through the air. She brought her sword down on Grak's shoulder, severing his tendons with a sharp snap; the gunn fell to the ground with a distinct clang. Grak swiped out with his claws, his arm swinging in the air awkwardly; it caught Isabella's shoulder, and she was flung backward. She landed in a roll, knocking into a piece of broken statue that saved her from sliding down the slope to the grounds. Her thigh and shoulder screamed in agony as dust filled the wounds.

Shavin grabbed her arm and helped her up. "I don't see any scars," he said, looking at her face. There was a slight grin perched on his lips.

Isabella pulled her arm away. "Get the horses," she said, stepping feebly forward. "Drive the wolves to the ground."

Granum told you you would take that ridiculous mask off, didn't he? Today is just full of his prophecies come true—

Isabella lunged forward, ignoring the flaring pain in her thigh and in her shoulder. Grak jumped away, and clasped to the rock face, his claws breaking into the stone like fingers in mud.

"You want to know how I killed your father?" Grak asked, a peculiar glee in his garbled voice. "I broke his spine. He was but a fish in my paw—and yer nothing but a woman parading in a man's war." Grak jumped from his perch on the wall and landed in front of Isabella. His snarling lip revealed glistening teeth. "His body felt boneless; it was very flexible." Grak sprung forward so quickly that Isabella had very little chance to sidestep. Grak wrapped his claws around Isabella's throat and lifted her in the air; she dropped her sword at Grak's feet. "I shook him back and forth until I heard his back snap—he pleaded I let him go. He renounced the Hunters, the code; he was as much a coward as your friend who laid his sword on the ground in surrender. You have to realize, daughter of David, that if your father couldn't defeat the wolves, what chance did you believe a woman had?"

Isabella gasped for air, clutching at Grak's strong claws. They wouldn't budge from her throat.

"The wolves' mark on this world is permanent. You should have realized this after I slaughtered your father, you pitiful girl." He squeezed harder, Isabella's face turning purple.

"There is a light, to the north," somebody screamed, and Grak turned.

Oh father, I tried, Isabella thought, feeling her life slip away from her, feeling weakness overcome her. She had never thought she would give in. Death seemed to tempt her; it was an escape. Her father must have felt the same way, clutched in the claws of Grak Ulak; he must have pleaded death take him before his head popped.

Now dear. Now. It is your fate. Isabella heard her father's voice in her head. *Yes, aye, yar, indeed.* Fate. Purpose. Isabella had revealed her true self not because she realized deception had bound her soul, but because she believed she would triumph as her father's daughter, not as the son he never had. She gritted her teeth. She lifted her arm, the weight of the daggers protruding from her ripped sleeve trying to drag her limb down. That wouldn't happen, not now. This was for her father.

She dropped her arm on top of Grak's hairy wrist. The daggers peeled at his flesh and his claws opened as he looked over in disbelief. Isabella fell to the ground in a crouch, her throat lined with claws deeply ingrained in her flesh. She felt the ground, digging through dirt for the hilt of her sword... hurry...hurry...

She found it!

"I am Isabella, daughter of David the Hunter. I *am* a Hunter, for I **AM** the the bloodline—"

Grak stood nearly nine feet tall, but when Isabella drove her sword upward in an arch, she caught the wolf's throat despite their difference in height. Her blade tore a flap from Grak's neck, and when he fell forward clutching his front, she finished the job. She put her sword through the arch of his spine, and for a split second she thought she had screwed up, she thought that Grak was going to turn around, his head peeling from his body, hanging askew on a string of skin, and he was going to slash her throat. But Grak fell forward.

When he hit the ground his head twisted around baring his dying red eyes in a frozen glaze, and his bramble crown tumbled from his head, rolling on the dusty ground like an ancient tumbleweed looking for its burial.

Grak, the General of the Sordid Yilaks, was finally defeated.

Isabella looked towards the light at the northern valley; she almost had to shield her eyes.

"The wizard has returned," somebody yelled.

Isabella collapsed next to Grak's body. She fell facing the gunn lying on the ground. She reached out and tucked the weapon in her palm, feeling the cool steel against her flesh, her sweat tingling; it was so light. How could a world's destruction be contained in such a tiny instrument?

Isabella thought of the stone and understood.

It wasn't the weapon, but the one who held it.

She clutched the gunn against her chest and closed her eyes.

13

Granum stood at the northern valley, emanating a white glow from within—the Wizard's Lantern—holding the reigns of the Hunter's horses in hooked fists, like black lines protruding from the center of the sun.

The wizard had returned.

CHAPTER 23

COLE AND THE WIZARD'S BLOOD

1

Jimmy crawled through the tunnel as quickly as possible. He heard noises but he wasn't certain if they came from behind him, as part of the battle, or if they came from the darkness ahead. He watched the end of the tunnel grow clearer, highlighted by an odd lime tint. For some reason Jimmy didn't feel safe anymore; at first he'd been overcome with the satisfaction of heroism, believing he had found his brother, but now, as he crawled toward the opening, he realized just how awkward life had become.

"I'm in a different time," he said to himself in disbelief. The idea had arisen before, of course, but now its clarity seemed to shove more and more proof into his face; this Tower wasn't on the Earth he knew, and if it was, no person he'd ever heard about had been inside.

When he got to the end of the tunnel he climbed out and onto the ground, which seemed sloped, leading toward a gigantic hallway with walls that disappeared in a murky darkness. The tint he'd seen in the tunnel emanated from the walls. He could see two tunnels behind him: the one he had come through, and an opening about fifty feet to its right; this opening had a much greater fall to the ground.

Jimmy didn't know if he should call out Cole's name or not; the thought had crossed his mind as he crawled through the tunnel, but now that he stood in this incredible room, he thought it might seem peculiar to hear his own voice the way he had in the mines. He was certain his voice would echo, and he was certain there'd be a response from the darkness; he had just traveled on the back of a giant spider—he wasn't going to put the idea of peculiarity past this place.

"Cole," he said in a soft voice. "You in here?"

No, he's not, so just turn around, get back in that tunnel and run back to Jarat.

He couldn't do that though; he thought about his mother, the way she looked when she walked out of his room, the way she must have been hurting inside when she realized she had to call the cops. This wasn't about him. No, it was about reclaiming something—he reached into his pocket and pulled out his tin box. He took out a smoke and put it in his mouth, sucking on the filter for a moment. It relaxed him. He needed to be relaxed.

"Cole," he said, this time louder.

Nothing. Only the eerie silence, the slight muffle of battle from the tunnels.

Jimmy took the cigarette from his mouth and held it between his fore and middle fingers; he wished he had a light. If he could just have one drag, he knew he'd calm down—but it wasn't just nerves. In fact, it felt like his insides were turning over.

"It's just nerves," he said to himself. "There's nothing in here, cept for Cole. COLE!" He screamed this time, walking forward, feeling his heart through his arms but persuading himself he had left the trouble outside; he was safer in here.

2

Cole had been, for the moment at least, looking for Hayle. He had peeked into every doorway, finding in some cases that the King had used puzzles in most rooms. He had seen in one chamber a single door laid in the rock across the room with an iron lock in its middle, and a key hanging from the never ending ceiling off a thin piece of twine. Cole didn't know if the key worked, because he realized this room, like the chamber of falling stones, had probably been another surveillance point. If the key were successfully reached, Cole was certain the missing weight on the twine might warn the ghosts, which would hurry over to welcome guests before they had the chance to use the key in the lock.

Cole had put the vial around his neck, and tucked the phial underneath his sweater. It felt weird against his flesh. But powerful.

Wizard's blood, he thought—*gives the power of immortality, but who would want such power? The King certainly regrets it...* And Cole heard his name. It seemed distant, but an overwhelming sense of home washed over him.

Cole ran. He didn't care that the King might grab the Pearl of the Ocean and try to drown him again; he only cared about finding the source of that voice.

3

Jimmy called out once more. He had crumpled the cigarette in his hand and dropped the ball of shredded paper to the ground, spilling much of the tobacco. When he had finally reached the corridor, where the walls narrowed and emerged from the darkness at either side he could have sworn he heard footsteps. Something was coming towards him, and he cursed himself for calling out so loud. Why was he so stupid? He knew something bad would happen if he called attention to himself—but no, despite his wracked nerves, he still had to scream into the unknown.

When he heard the pattering steps he had at first decided to turn and run, to dart for the tunnels, climb aboard Jarat and find slumber away from the war, away from this place. But something held him back. He didn't know what exactly, but his feet seemed tacked to the ground.

His heart hammered against his chest.

The footsteps grew closer. His wheezing breaths felt sticky in his throat. He felt like vomiting but remained as calm as possible. Inside, his heart, his blood, everything about him was racing in dire pandemonium. He felt like the cage around a herd of trampling bulls.

"Cole," he felt his lips purse, heard his voice tremble. He didn't expect himself to speak, but when he saw the body emerge from the misty distance, running with both arms clutching either side, he realized just whose footsteps he'd been hearing.

"COLE!"

Jimmy ran forward.

4

Both boys jumped into each other's arms, Cole just as surprised as Jimmy.

"Jimmy, Jimmy is that you, is that really you?" Cole screamed, holding his brother out of shock, holding him tight, feeling Jimmy's body against his own—there was a moment when he believed the Towers were throwing an illusion at him, but this seemed too real, didn't it?

Jimmy held Cole tight. He wrapped his arms around the boy's shoulders. He hadn't thought of illusions; rather, he remembered the image he had seen in the wizard's glass, the image of Cole entering the tunnel, the way he, Jimmy, warned whoever stood outside the edifice that if his brother was harmed he would seek revenge. In a way he prodded along his brother's body looking for wounds; it was instinct really, a feeling that surfaced before the notion of heroism ever had a chance.

"Jimmy, Jimmy," Cole muttered, holding his brother just as tight. "It can't be you, it just can't be." Cole believed this, no matter how tight he held him.

"Cole, come on, we have to go. We have to get out of here." Jimmy released his arms and stood back. He stared at his twin brother for a moment; every memory surfaced like a twinkle, its own miniscule shine. He saw in Cole the perfect image of his father, the way he believed his father would have looked when he returned from the war.

"Wait, no. Why are you here?" Cole studied Jimmy. He cocked his eye, remembering the chamber of falling stones, the temporary diversion—had the Tower possessed that kind of power? Could the Tower manipulate his thoughts and create this articulate manifestation of his brother?

"Cole?"

Cole stepped back, clutching the phial beneath his sweater. "Why? — How?"

"Because I talked to mom and I realized how big of a jerk I was—how I ignored the things that really mattered. I wanted to be like Krollup, Cole, and that sort of idea...of—of power reshapes your mind. I realized you ran away because of me."

"But how did you find me?"

"I hid in the closet and saw the rope. I figured you went down the vents, but the Robot Bomber told me you went down the mines; he tried to stop me from going after you, but I wouldn't let him—I *couldn't* let him. I ran from the rats in darkness. All I really remember is darkness, but when I woke up I was on horseback."

"Horseback?"

"I was with a Hunter, going to see a wizard; we met the spiders Cole, and right now as we speak, outside those tunnels, there's a war going on. We need to get back home."

"Jimmy, you're not making sense. Stay away from me." Cole ran past Jimmy, brushing his shoulder, almost pushing him over.

"Cole, come on, where're you going?"

Cole had run a fair share, and although he'd like to believe this new exercise had proven exponentially on his endurance, he of course had to compete against a born athlete. Jimmy turned on his heels and grabbed Cole's sweater.

Cole fell forwards and grabbed his temples; he started rubbing them, muttering to himself. "You're not there, you're just a picture from my head, you're just a picture from my head."

"COLE. STAND UP FOR CRYING OUT LOUD! I'm here to take you home."

"If you're really Jimmy prove it to me."

"How?" Jimmy asked, astonished.

"What did dad look like?"

Jimmy stopped breathing. He had fumbled over this thought before. He couldn't find the perfect image of his father; he just wanted to remember him the way he had left, a clutter of bones nestled in pallid flesh—but what had his father looked like? He hated his dad. He hated his selfishness, the way he could lie to two boys—the way he smoked behind his and Cole's backs. He didn't want to remember his father, but he realized Cole was delirious. Whatever Cole had gone through with the wolves had certainly proven alarming.

"He looked like you Cole," Jimmy finally said. "He was taller, of course, but he had your eyes. He had longer hair because he didn't insist on keeping his short like you do yours. He had broad shoulders, but then he got skinny. He kept getting thinner, and we always thought he had gone on some unnecessary diet, but that wasn't true. He was dying. Cole, our father is dead."

Cole fell back on his rear. He started crying, but he covered his face. "Why are we here, Jimmy? *What* is here?"

Jimmy knelt down and rubbed his brother's shoulder. "We're in the Inlands, Cole. Another world. The past."

"What?"

"You know how you like those movies...umm, like *Back to the Future*? Remember how Marty goes back in time in that snazzy car? Well, I think the mines are that car, Cole. Everybody travels by horse. People use Sandglass instead of televisions, swords instead of guns; spiders are bigger than people..."

"And wolves can talk, and hermits can take different shapes," Cole continued. "I don't think the mines are some kind of time traveler Jimmy, I think, somehow, we've managed to enter a world built strictly on the grounds of imagination. It feels like I'm reading a book. That's what this is—like a story or something. Almost make believe." Cole stood up.

"Whatever it is, we have to go. It isn't safe here."

"Not yet," Cole said. "We have to find Hayle."

"Who's Hayle?"

"For now, Jimmy, he's our dad. He saved my life."

"COLE! LOOK OUT!" Jimmy had spoken fast, and his words were jumbled but Cole caught the gist. Cole, who had begun standing up, fell forward again, feeling the air over top slice, the slight wisp of something passing over his head.

Jimmy pulled Cole, sliding him along the ground, ripping his already torn pants, and Cole jumped to his feet. He quickly turned to see a ghost, carrying its head in the crook of its arm, both sockets missing eyes. It carried a dagger with snapping teeth and it swiped out again.

Jimmy and Cole ran back towards the tunnels.

"What was that?"

Cole shuddered. "There are more of them," he said in a wavering voice.

5

The two of them ran as fast as they could, and when Cole fell behind, Jimmy slowed down to grab his brother by the arm.

"Come on."

Jimmy couldn't really see anything behind them. Each step they took forward seemed to cover the path behind them in darkness.

Cole stopped, pulling his stretched sleeve away from Jimmy. "We can't just leave him here. He saved my life."

"Who?"

"Hayle."

"We can't stop, Cole, that thing was right behind us, I saw it. Everything we've passed is dark; the lights are turning out after every step. Something wants us gone."

Cole walked to his right. "I know he's here. Look." Cole pointed to the ground. There were dark smears, a red trail that led on a curve further right.

Before Jimmy could question Cole about the trail of blood, or even ask whom this Hayle was (though he had the sneaking suspicion it must have been that armless thing he watched enter the tunnel with his brother), Cole had taken off along the glistening crimson path.

"Cole, where are you going?" Jimmy chased after his brother, and tried to get in front of him, tried to stop him. When he passed Cole, he tried to cut him off; he tried to grab his arm and drag him back towards the tunnels but he tripped.

He had collided with something—and not a rock either, but something soft. His pant leg felt wet. He rolled along the ground for a moment, trying to collect himself.

"Hayle, are you all right?" Cole asked. The hermit no longer looked like his father. His skull seemed to be dripping, and the stumps where both his arm and hand had once been were starting to bubble; his red eyes lost their luster, the corneas running out of their sockets. His leg was mangled and lay useless before him.

"They retreated after you ran, Cole. I watched them float into the darkness; they wanted to bring me, I could feel them, but they no longer wanted to watch their own misery. They are trapped here; they are the souls of the Tower's body." Hayle forced a smile, showing sharp teeth that didn't seem threatening anymore.

"Hayle," Cole said, "what have they done to you?"

Jimmy stood up and looked at the creature.

"Jimmy," Cole screamed, "don't look into his eyes."

Cole hadn't been fast enough though; he had forgotten.

Jimmy had quickly glanced into Hayle's eyes before the hermit turned its malformed head.

"Are you okay?" Cole asked.

Jimmy exhaled. "I saw Ricky beating you up, Cole. I watched Ricky striking you...and I did nothing to stop him. What just happened to me?"

"I am sorry boy," Hayle said, his back turned. "It is my curse to remind you of such. Ah," he screamed, "my head aches, like splinters have broken in the bridge of my nose. The spiders are here, I can feel them."

"We're going now Hayle, come on, grab my shoulder," Cole said, ignoring the hermit's delirium.

"Did you get what we came for?" Hayle asked painfully.

Cole nodded. He touched the phial through his sweater.

"There is somebody else in here with us," Hayle said. He moved his arm, pointing his bloody stump towards the tunnels. "He knows both of you, for I saw inside his head."

"Who?" Cole asked.

But he felt something touch his shoulder.

"RUN!" Jimmy yelled, grabbing Cole.

"Hayle," Cole screamed.

"Run, both of you."

Cole saw the ghosts had descended from the ceiling, falling from the darkness, bringing the black with them like kite tails, billowing jackets. Corpses on horses, galloping from the distance, their chain mail clinking against gushing muscle that had been dripping to the floor.

Cole had seen Hayle's eyes start glowing, and the group of them, the ghosts and the hermit, seemed pulled together by some force, some force seemingly compelled to unite them.

Cole watched Hayle lift in the air, his crushed leg hanging beneath him like a useless flap of skin. Hayle was pulling into them—and the ghosts were trying to drop him, a counterbalance of paranormal emotions. Hayle would waver above the ground, dipping occasionally, but he would pull himself up; he was using an unseen rope distended from the corpses' clutter. He was forcing them away from the boys.

And the eyeless corpse, its head still cocked awkwardly in the crook of its arm, swirled from the darkness like smoke, forming into the crude image of a rotting man. Cole knew Hayle's magic would have little impact on this ghost, for it had no eyes to see its curse; it was up to him and Jimmy, and whoever else was in the Towers with them.

"Hurry," Jimmy called, "it's getting closer."

Cole's side hurt; he had a terrible cramp. He was tired, and every joint in his body seemed relaxed by a numbing sensation; his limbs finally quit on him.

"Cole." Jimmy stopped. "What are you doing?"

Cole had stopped and turned to face the eyeless corpse, which hung above the ground and swirled from side to side, holding its head like a pet. The ghost was trying to smile, baring darkened teeth covered in scum. Cole didn't know what he was doing, but he realized he could do something—or at least try.

The corpse was getting closer, its snapping dagger biting at the air, its mouth revealing teeth that had somehow sharpened. Cole understood the Judge had done this thing a favor; it had cut off the ghost's head so that it could use it as a weapon. The corpse had stuck two gnarled fingers into its empty eye sockets and lifted its head from the crook of its arm like a bowling bowl.

"COLE!" Jimmy yelled.

But Cole didn't listen to his brother; he stood and watched the corpse wind its ripped arm back and release, letting go of the head, its biting mouth revealing teeth that had turned into razor blades. The head flew at Cole, the wind whistling through its eye sockets.

Cole's first thought had been to duck—but he felt some awkward kind of power around his neck, some peculiar pang that erupted along his collarbone.

The wizard's blood!

Cole reached into his collar. He pulled out the phial and held it in front of him.

The head stopped six inches from Cole's nose, its mouth frozen in a gaping yawn, showing an array of pointed teeth with bits of lip hanging from divots. Cole stepped forward with the phial and pressed the tube against the corpse's head; there was a burning sound, and when Cole pulled the blood away, he noticed he had left a slight mark on the ghost's forehead, a mark in the exact shape of the vial.

The head pulled back into the crook of the ghost's arm, and it disappeared, turning into a swirling smoke that blended into the darkness.

"What was that Cole? How did you do that?" Jimmy asked.

"Not now. We have to go." Cole turned and ran.

In a minute the two would run into Edwin Krollup.

6

He was lying about forty yards from a tunnel, cut into the rock about six feet above the ground. He was lying on his stomach, and it sounded like he was crying. Cole had run forward, but Jimmy stopped him, pulling his arm.

"Hold on. You don't know. I'm not playing around, not since I've seen what's in here."

Cole turned and looked at Jimmy; he didn't feel aggression in his brother's grip, but rather a light pull that assumed he, Jimmy, was generally looking after him—Cole didn't think he needed a bodyguard, not after he saw what the wizard's blood was able to do.

"Let's go that way—to that tunnel." Jimmy pointed to his left, but Cole didn't want to just leave this man stranded, especially inside these Towers. He knew for certain the ghosts would return.

"Come on Cole, we have to get to Jarat, he'll make sure we're safe. He said so, it's his duty to protect me—*us*."

"Wait," Cole said, ignoring his brother. The man on the ground was pushing himself up on his fists, feebly, grunting as his arms straightened.

"Oh my God," Jimmy said, "it's Krollup."

The two didn't know what to think at this point; they were certain their stepfather—a man who banned them from the dinner table for even the slightest noise, and whose very shadow scared the living daylights out of the both of them—hated them with the utmost sincerity.

"What is he doing here?" Cole asked, his jaw hanging open stupidly in shock.

"You don't suppose he came here to get us?"

Cole smiled. "I think that *had* been the plan. That's why I'm here. He never showed up though."

"What do you mean, plan?"

Cole looked at his brother. "You don't think I came to this place under my own free will. The wolves took me from the mines. I don't remember much, but Hayle saw it in my head. It was planned, all of it. These things down here, they know who Krollup is."

"His stupid name extends over time—"

"And worlds," Cole cut in.

Krollup fell forward on his face. Cole ran and grabbed his stepfather under the arms.

"A little help."

Jimmy ran over and helped Cole.

When Edwin looked up at the boys, his eyes were rolled to the whites. He was drooling.

"We have to get him to the tunnel. We'll hoist him onto the lip."

"What's the point in even saving the jerk?" Jimmy asked.

"What if he did come to get us?" Cole said. It was a stupid question; he knew Krollup had come under his own twisted agenda. "We have to pretend that's an option."

The two dragged Edwin when he screamed.

"I did it, I killed my father. Roll roll go the rocks...yes, it was me. He's dead, dead, dead. I'm a murderer...I saw everything in its eyes...like windows...I am damned damned damned—" He fell silent abruptly and went stiff in the boys' hands. His head lolled forward.

"Is he dead?"

Cole checked Krollup's pulse. "His heart's beating a mile a minute."

"What's wrong with him?"

"Didn't you hear? I think he looked in Hayle's eyes."

Jimmy paused. "What exactly is Hayle, Cole? I saw things I didn't want to remember when I looked at that thing—"

"That *thing* saved both our lives. Anyway, we have time for explanations later. Let's get Krollup outside."

"It's not any safer out there than it is in here," Jimmy said.

Cole pulled Krollup by the armpit. "But the only way back home is out there."

"Do you know the way?"

Cole smiled. "Yes. I've already been there."

The two pushed Krollup into the tunnel with a hard shove; the man slid easily over the slick surface, only catching on loose snags which broke under his weight. Cole and Jimmy would each grab a shoulder and pull the man through the tunnel.

And they each believed they would be home soon; it was the insistence that all bad things came to an end—something they had been taught all their lives—which pushed this belief on them. Which, nevertheless, blinded them.

The mines had collapsed. Neither knew, of course, but the two crawled believing their meeting in the Tower had been fate.

Maybe it was.

A part of Cole, a part he tried to ignore his entire life, seemed awakened by this thing hanging from his neck, this thing with the power to exile ghosts, with the power to end death.

Put some in your mouth. Everything will change then—remember those pills from your dream, **Invisi-fat***? This blood, this ichor is even better. What did the King say?—you feel eternity run unbound inside your head. Yes, that would be nice.*

Cole felt the phial under his sweater, stuck to the sweat on his chest.

Jimmy has his cigarettes, he thought. *It wasn't wrong to be dependent.*

"What was that stuff you pushed against the ghost's forehead?"

Cole looked at his brother. He had been lost in his thought. "I don't know. Something Hayle gave me. Said it was a good luck charm."

"I guess it was a repellant too."

The two continued pulling their stepfather, pulling him towards the gritty sound of war.

CHAPTER 24

LELA SAXON

1

She waited until she was off duty. She knew the land had been blocked off, and she knew about the potential earthquake scares, but she had had an insistent curiosity about Edwin Krollup ever since she had seen his eyes turn red. She had seen it as clear as day.

It had been, at first, a reason to combat sexism, discrimination, because she was a woman on the force. A damn good cop too. She had seen in Edwin Krollup's eyes an objection to her badge, an objection to her power of suggestion, and something about this persuaded she get back at him. She had done so by tipping the media—but realized in the course of events, that her move angered Edwin beyond comprehension.

But was it coincidence, she thought? Had the earthquake been natural, or was it a form of summoned providence to end the journalistic tirades outside Krollup's estate? She had clearly seen there were statues standing in the courtyard without hands, hands that were flung over the outer wall.

And she had seen Edwin Krollup floating. She knew she saw him in the air. If he hadn't been on the front step after the quake, she wouldn't have been so persistent; she would have believed she was prone to delusions.

She drove to the Krollup estate in her gray sedan, which badly needed new brakes and shocks. She wore a blue blazer over jeans. She had her holster hanging beneath her armpit. She always carried her gun. Lela Saxon chewed gum slowly, snapping it with her teeth and blowing bubbles, which she popped with her tongue.

She was glad she wasn't back at the precinct. Everything was chaotic back there because they knew an explosive pamper duty case was apt to crack global coverage in the press; the police had her to blame on that one, but Saul had made a wrong call. Forensics had traced rope fibers from the bed and closet to traces found in the courtyard shed, forcing Saul to deductively suspect the gardener's motives. He had obtained a warrant, searched Mario the Lawn Technician's apartment only to find shag carpets, cheap linoleum with Kool-Aid stains and a bureau with pictures of Mario's lovely mother—a woman who had apparently just passed away. Mario had come home fifteen minutes after the police entered his apartment; he was detained for questioning.

The police had called Krollup.

Krollup hadn't answered. There was a general fear around the force, one that kept the police at a comfortable distance from Hillside Road—nobody wanted to test the unstable grounds. The clean up crew, she heard, had worked at such breakneck speed last night that most of the damage had been hauled away in a mere three hours. But Lela didn't believe there was an earthquake. She was born in California, and she had been in many quakes. She learned in school at an early age the correct symptoms and reactions to a quake. Yesterday wasn't an earthquake, she believed, but a reaction to something else, something different. The Seismic Society hadn't disclosed their findings to the public, which she assumed meant either of two things: they didn't understand what it was they stumbled on, or that there was indeed an active fault line located inside the hill, and they didn't want to alarm people prematurely.

Yesterday, that quake was controlled. She didn't know why she had this thought.

Lela pulled into the Hillside Road turn off; there were barricades set up on the road, with a warning written in red letters: NO TRESPASSING. Lela stopped the car, spitting her wad of gum out. She swung the barricade off the road.

When she got back in her car something inside urged that she turn around, that she put the barricade back and drive home to take a nice hot bath. To become a cop she believed she had to neglect this insistent pestering, which reminded her all too well that she was a female, and that a female should be feminine. This, then, reminded her of her mother, a woman who had been against her admission into the Academy; a woman who believed Lela should wear an apron and look after a man. But Lela wasn't interested in that life. She liked to feel cuffs in her hands, the butt of a gun against the inset of her finger.

She hit the gas pedal and sped up Hillside Road.

2

There had been tape strung up on the road leading to the house, but it had been pulled off. The clean up crew had gotten most of the dangerous, combustible materials out of the way. The vehicles, which had been crushed by pockets of asphalt, had been towed away. All that remained were the few trees that had toppled.

But there were two cars parked in front of the gate, which hung awkwardly on broken hinges. One of the cars was a rental. The other was an expensive Mercedes Benz; she wasn't at all surprised to see an eighty thousand-dollar car on Krollup's lot, but due to the current circumstances, she was surprised to find anybody on the premises at all.

"Damn," she said to herself, hitting her steering wheel with her fist. She believed she would be alone. She had at first believed Seismic Society returned. She couldn't see anybody investigating the yard, but that didn't mean anything. She parked her sedan next to the Mercedes, turned it off, and stepped out. It was cool outside. Winter was coming. She could feel it. Her joints would sometimes ache; she hoped she wasn't developing arthritis, but knew it was inevitable. Both her parents were prisoners, were forced to suffer when it rained, were forced to rub Ben Gay over their knuckles, looking at their gnarled fingers, fingers which had once been straight and youthful. Time, Lela realized, had a way of escaping you.

She walked through the broken gate. The wall was partially destroyed, and much of the lawn was torn where, she remembered, a satellite tower had teetered from its post atop a van, collapsing over the outer wall with a ferocious slam. And then she noticed something different.

There were no statues in the yard.

Their pedestals remained, casting shadows along the dying grass, over the juniper bushes, but the statues were gone. Lela bent down. She touched the grass at the base of a white pedestal, small arches carved in its side. The grass was flattened. She stood up, still staring at the grass. It looked like a footprint, though awkward, as if the foot had been blocky, had been encased inside a brick or something.

These footprints led away from the pedestals and onto the path—and back onto the grass, where dozens more joined them.

"What is this?" Lela said. Her mouth felt dry.

She followed the prints around the side of the house.

Three statues stood outside a broken window. Two of them were missing their hands, and one of them looked like it was stepping inside the house. She stepped in closer. There were shards of glass in the grass catching the midday sun. She picked up a long sliver of glass and held it in front of her face; there was blood splattered along the end.

"I got you Krollup," she said softly, and she saw something in the bushes at the base of the windows that caught her eye. It was a hand. There were long scratch marks in the dirt. Lela rushed around the statues to find a large man lying awkwardly in the hedges, wearing a tailor made suit with pieces of glass sticking from it like transparent quills.

"Oh my God," she said, flipping open her blazer to unholster her Glock.

She searched frantically along her belt line and jacket pockets for her radio, or her cellular phone, but she must have forgotten them in her car. She couldn't just wander back there now; she couldn't make herself a target in the middle of the courtyard. She inched along the wall towards the front of the house, holding her gun steady in front of her. She listened carefully for noises.

She heard nothing, spare the odd birdsong in the trees around the house.

When she got to the front door she had fully expected the knob to stick, but it turned, and she muscled the large door open. She peeked inside the house. The front entry was decorated in marble, leading to the Grand Staircase; there were two hallways to follow from the foyer. Either she could take the corridor to her right, or to the left. She studied the room. She looked for shadows, for movement.

Wasn't there a statue beside the door? she thought, turning to find another empty pedestal. That didn't matter. She could feel her heart.

And she heard a noise to her right.

Lela made sure her sneakers didn't leave an annoying squeak when her heels lifted off the ground; she walked slowly towards the corridor to the right of the staircase.

3

There was a statue lying in the middle of the hall; it was broken, but it reminded Lela to glance back at the empty pedestal beside the front door. When she looked back she caught her reflection in the foyer mirror, and had to relax her finger; she almost put a bullet through the glass.

She steadied herself. There was an odd silence in the house, and she realized the corridor was masked by a tinted glow. Reddish dust swirled in spots of sunlight like steam. Lela Saxon, who frequented shooting ranges often—had since she was a young girl, much against her mother's wishes—

smelt strong wafts of cordite in the air, as if the reddish glow in the light had been gun powder.

When she walked forward she felt a minor slope in the floor. There were two more hallways that led to rooms on either side of her. Holding her gun out in front of her, she quickly checked both doorways.

There was another noise. It was sharp, like something snapping, and it didn't take long for her to notice the broken hardwood leading to the room ahead of her. The hardwood had broken into sharp splinters which stabbed upwards, as if a tree had grown so large its roots had begun reaching out of the ground.

She was frantic; she had never been thrust into a situation like this. She had broken up barroom brawls, but it had never gotten to the point where she had to draw her gun; her gun had always been a measure of power, of intimidation, but now she stood holding it in a shaking hand. She had flashing images of Edwin Krollup's eyes turning red, the way he seemed to float on his front step before the earthquake. She knew something wasn't right about him, and it seemed her curiosity had led her towards some truth.

She wished Dale was with her, but realized the danger she was in. He had a family, a new child; she didn't want to drag him into this. All of a sudden she wished she hadn't come. She wished she had just left when Saul told her to; she wished she hadn't tipped off the press. Maybe the earthquake was her fault. She had seen movies where people could will certain things to happen—what was it called...*telekinesis*, she remembered, and perhaps it wasn't too farfetched to believe Edwin Krollup was a minority example of this case. Maybe he had the psychological power to cause certain things to happen, and when he had seen the story on television, it had triggered his insanity. She gulped. If that was the case, her gun wasn't going to prove useful.

Dale would tell her that she was over-exaggerating, and that her imagination was wholly caused by Krollup's ability to manipulate power; it was all an illusion really. The house, the cars, the industry—they were all there to support his self-important duty, that being, the exponential absorption of power. Edwin Krollup was merely a manifestation of every man's desire: to rule. She would have to accept that, or she was heading for a major disappointment in the real world. Maybe it was this truth that infuriated her the most. That was mainly why she had informed the press. Because Lela realized he was more powerful than she was.

But that doesn't explain the dead body outside Lela, the statues, or even the strong scent of cordite; you came out of curiosity, but perhaps it was fate that dragged you past the broken gate. This is your time.

That was true. This was her time. She clenched her gun and stepped forward, through the smoke, the reddish dust.

The room was huge, she could tell that much. But she could barely see across the entire thing. The sun had caught the dust and magnified its particles, masking the room under a red veneer. The floor had been sloped, and much of the rubble, mostly subfloor, broken hardwood and chunks of concrete, had piled at the base of the wall. The middle of the room had completely split, and pillars of rock had exploded from the ground—but that wasn't what drove Lela to scream. She found something else on the floor. At first she believed they were rolled up rugs, rugs made from authentic bear hide perhaps, but the way they had been placed, and the way their limbs splayed proved to Lela the awful truth. These weren't bears littering the floor, and, to Lela's astonishment, pinned to the cracked ceiling between daggers of rock and plaster—these were something else, something she hadn't seen before.

And one of them moved. It was a simple gesture in a way, but its burly arm twitched.

Lela couldn't hold it anymore. She screamed.

But she had done something that surprised her. She pulled the trigger and shot the beast on the floor, the beast with the twitching arm. The thing's hide exploded near its shoulder.

"What's going on?" She screamed, holding the gun as tightly as she could. The sweat on her palm dripped to the floor. There was another stiff crack, and Lela realized a portion of the ceiling was caving in. Puffs of plaster exploded, and with a long creak, the paneled wall split in half. There were three men lying against the wall.

She squinted her eyes, trying to see if Krollup was with any of them; she couldn't tell.

There was another snap, as the load-bearing wall started to crumble.

Not now, she thought. She ran forward, trying to avoid the beasts on the ground, the rubble, the broken statues which were torn apart. One man was lying on his side, his jacket flipped open revealing an empty holster. This alarmed Lela. The man was dead though, and she could tell by his twisted midsection that his spine must have been broken.

The other two, one lying on top of the other, had pulses. Lela dragged the lighter one aside, pushing the larger man off of him; she was sweating by the time she returned for the bigger man, who was breathing in harsh gasps.

The paneling on the wall split. The gaping hole in the wall, with a split mantle hanging on either side, began to crumble. Lela grabbed the big man under the arm and maneuvered him away from the wall, pulling as hard as she could. A section of the wall fell where the man had been lying.

"What is happening?" Lela said under her breath. She saw, to her dismay, a woman clutched inside a statue's arms, her head lolled to the side. Lela ran towards the statue, which stood outside the hole in the wall.

"Ma'am, wake up, wake up. What did this to you? What's going on?" Lela checked the woman's pulse; she was fine, it seemed, but she didn't respond to Lela's voice. A chunk of plaster fell on Lela's shoulder. She wrenched on the statue's arm, trying to pull it away from the woman's body, but it wouldn't budge. A beam above Lela snapped, and dust rained on the ground. Lela smashed the butt of her gun on the statue.

"Come on," she said, frantically, feeling a vibration wring up her arm. She ran around the statue, trying to push it over; it teetered on its feet, but remained relatively balanced.

Another beam snapped, and she could hear the furniture on the floor above shifting, as the room must have sloped. Lela realized the only way to get this woman out of the statue's tight grip was to dislocate her shoulders by pulling them over her head and slipping her downward. If it meant her survival, she was sure the tactic might work, but it was a matter of time. Lela grabbed the woman's tense arms and tugged them up, watching the ceiling closely. When both the woman's arms were over her head, Lela stopped. She couldn't do this. She couldn't pop the joints out of the sockets, at least without vomiting.

She bit her lip and reached for the woman's right arm when a portion of the ceiling caved in. Lela dove through the hole in the wall, landing on her side uncomfortably. A cloud of plaster fell from above, followed by the heavy wisp of a couch, which knocked the back of the statue as it landed with a crash on the broken hardwood. The statue teetered for a moment, and then fell forward.

Lela closed her eyes, listening to the crumble as the statue's weight most definitely crushed the poor woman in its grasp. But—

That hadn't happened. Instead, by true virtue of luck, the statue had fallen at an angle that locked the woman in a cage between its stony fists and the ground. When the statue hit the ground, its left arm broke at its shoulder, collapsing from its body like the leg of a feeble insect. This disrupted the balance of weight on either side, causing the statue to roll to its right, landing on its back with a crunch that allowed the unconscious woman to easily roll off the statue's chest and onto the ground with a soft thud.

Lela stood up. The air had been shrouded in a white dust, and she saw that much of the ceiling had swung downwards like an inverted door, allowing furniture to land on the first floor.

Where was she, exactly?

The room was made of rock, and there were television monitors on the wall, most of the screens shattered—noises seemed to echo her heavy breathing.

Lela Saxon turned around.

There was a dark hole in the room, one that seemed endless. Before Lela would think of leaving to grab her radio, she would step forward and look inside the hole, immersing her head into the darkness where the distant sounds of water dropping and adjusting timbersets welcomed her.

Lela Saxon had found the mines.

TO BE CONTINUED...
The Inlands Trilogy II
Chain of the Worlds

Printed in the United Kingdom
by Lightning Source UK Ltd.
109782UKS00001B/157-159